EVIL IN A MASK

The latest of the Roger Brook stories, continuing his story through the years 1807–1809. Napoleon is at the height of his powers. By now he is the complete autocrat, his lust for power driving him to wage needless wars that are bleeding France white.

Roger Brook, still the most valuable and resourceful of secret agents, moves amongst the centres of power of Europe and beyond: Talleyrand, Metternich, the Shah of Persia, men whose decisions mark the fate of nations.

But, interwoven with the historical pattern, runs the thread of Roger's passionate involvement with the lovely Lisala de Pombal—a woman as licentious as she is beautiful. A woman who plays her part in leading him from one desperate situation to another.

BY DENNIS WHEATLEY

NOVELS

The Launching of Roger Brook
The Shadow of Tyburn Tree
The Rising Storm
The Man Who Killed the King
The Dark Secret of Josephine
The Rape of Venice
The Sultan's Daughter
The Wanton Princess
Evil in a Mask

The Scarlet Impostor
Faked Passports
The Black Baroness
V for Vengeance
Come Into My Parlour
Traitors' Gate
They Used Dark Forces

The Prisoner in the Mask
The Second Seal
Vendetta in Spain
Three Inquisitive People
The Forbidden Territory
The Devil Rides Out
The Golden Spaniard
Strange Conflict
Codeword—Golden Fleece
Dangerous Inheritance

The Quest of Julian Day
The Sword of Fate
Bill for the Use of a Body

Black August
Contraband
The Island Where Time Stands
    Still
The White Witch of the South
    Seas

To the Devil—a Daughter
The Satanist

The Eunuch of Stamboul
The Secret War
The Fabulous Valley
Sixty Days to Live
Such Power is Dangerous
Uncharted Seas
The Man Who Missed the War
The Haunting of Toby Jugg
Star of Ill-Omen
They Found Atlantis
The Ka of Gifford Hillary
Curtain of Fear
Mayhem in Greece
Unholy Crusade

SHORT STORIES

Mediterranean Nights   Gunmen, Gallants and Ghosts

HISTORICAL

A Private Life of Charles II (*Illustrated by Frank C. Pape*)
Red Eagle (*The Story of the Russian Revolution*)

AUTOBIOGRAPHICAL

Stranger than Fiction (*War Papers for the Joint Planning Staff*)
Saturdays with Bricks

IN PREPARATION

The Ravishing of Lady Mary Ware (*another Roger Brook story*)
The Devil and all his Works (*Illustrated in colour*)

Dennis Wheatley

Evil in a Mask

ARROW BOOKS

ARROW BOOKS LTD
178–202 Great Portland Street, London W1

AN IMPRINT OF THE  HUTCHINSON GROUP

London Melbourne Sydney
Auckland Johannesburg Cape Town
and agencies throughout the world

✳

First published by
Hutchinson & Co (*Publishers*) Ltd 1969
Arrow edition 1971

*Made and printed in Great Britain
by The Anchor Press Ltd,
Tiptree, Essex*

ISBN 0 09 004640 4

For
Wing-Commander Anthony Wellington,
DSO, DFC, to whom I owe my knowledge
of Brazil in that country's early days; and
to his dear wife, with most grateful thanks
for their many hospitalities during my
visits to Rio.

D.W.

Contents

I

The Field of Eylau

Roger Brook had been lucky, very lucky.

On this night he was in his late thirties and, from the age of nineteen, he had spent at least half the intervening years on the Continent, acting as a secret agent for Britain's great Prime Minister, William Pitt the Younger. Yet only once had he been caught out, and then by a friend who shared his views on the future of Europe, so had refrained from having him shot as a spy. He had passed unscathed through the hell of the French Revolution, been present at the siege of Acre, at the Battles of the Nile and Jena and numerous other bloody conflicts. Yet only once, at Marengo, had he been wounded.

But now, at last, his luck had run out.

Meeting Roger in a salon or ballroom, the sight of him would have made most women's hearts beat a little faster. He was just over six feet tall, with broad shoulders and slim hips. His brown hair swept back in a wave from his high forehead. Below it a straight, aggressive nose stood out between a pair of bright blue eyes. From years of living dangerously his mouth had become thin and a little hard, but the slight furrows on either side of it were evidence of his tendency to frequent laughter. His strong chin and jaw showed great determination; his long-fingered hands were beautifully modelled; and his calves, when displayed in silk stockings, gave his tall figure the last touch of elegance.

Even on that February morning of 1807 as he sat his fine charger, booted and spurred, his long, fur-lined cloak wrapped tightly round him against the bitter cold, a woman's eye would have singled him out from among the score or more of gallant figures that formed a group a little in the rear of the Emperor

9

Napoleon. But his state was very different now, and he had little hope of living through the night.

Fifteen months earlier, two great turning points had occurred in the war that Britain and France had been waging—with only one short interval of uneasy peace in 1803—for the past fourteen years. In October 1805, Nelson's victory at Trafalgar had, at last, freed England from the threat of invasion. But in the same month Napoleon had dealt a shattering blow at the Third Coalition which Pitt, with dogged determination, had built up against him. At Ulm the Emperor had smashed the main Austrian army; and, in November, entered Vienna in triumph. A month later, at Austerlitz, he had inflicted another terrible defeat on both the Austrians and their Russian allies. Utterly crushed, the Austrians had sued for peace. By the Treaty of Pressburg he gave it to them. But it cost the Emperor Francis nearly three million subjects and one-sixth of his revenue. This loss of sovereignty over numerous territories led, in the following August, to Francis' resigning the greater Imperial dignity and becoming only Emperor of Austria. Thus ended the Holy Roman Empire after an existence of over one thousand years.

Meanwhile Napoleon, anxious to keep Prussia quiet while he dealt with Russia, entered into negotiations with King Frederick William III. As French troops were occupying the British territory of Hanover, the Emperor was able to offer it as a bribe; and the shifty, weak-willed King agreed to accept it as the price of an alliance signed at Schönbrunn.

But neither party was being honest with the other. Napoleon was secretly putting out peace feelers to the British Government, which included an offer to return Hanover to Britain, while Frederick William was in secret negotiation with the Czar Alexander to double-cross the French. When the Emperor and the King became aware of each other's treachery, both realised that war between them was inevitable. In September the King, gambling on the traditional invincibility of the Prussian Army, had sent Napoleon an ultimatum. It proved a futile gesture, since the dynamic Emperor was already on the march, and he advanced with such speed that by mid-October the two armies clashed.

Prussia had for so long sat timidly on the fence that her army had lost all resemblance to the magnificent war machine created by Frederick the Great; whereas that of France was inspired by an unbroken succession of victories, and was superbly led. At Jena, by a swift concentration of the corps of Lannes, Soult, Augereau, Ney and the Guard, Napoleon overwhelmed one-half of Frederick William's army. At Auerstädt, Davoust, although outnumbered by two to one, destroyed the other.

Relentlessly pursued by Murat's cavalry, the surviving Prussians retreated to the east. At Erfurt sixteen thousand of them surrendered to him. Fortress after fortress fell, and on the 25th of the month, Davoust captured Berlin.

It was in November, while in the Prussian capital, that the Emperor had initiated his new policy designed to bring Britain to her knees. Known as the Continental System, it decreed that every port under the control of France and her Allies should be closed to British shipping. At that date England was the only country that had undergone the Industrial Revolution. It was through her trade that she earned the great wealth which enabled her to subsidise the armies of her Allies on the Continent. So Napoleon hoped that by depriving her of her European markets he would not only render her incapable of supplying such subsidies in future, but also bring about her financial ruin.

Meanwhile, his armies were pressing on into Prussian Poland and, on December 19th, he established his headquarters in Warsaw. Soon after Jena, Frederick William had tentatively asked for peace terms, but Napoleon refused to negotiate unless his enemy would retire behind the Vistula, cede to him the whole of Western Prussia and become his ally in the war against Russia.

It was not until Christmas that the French went into winter quarters, and the respite the Emperor gave his troops was all too short. His restless mind had conceived a new plan for getting the better of the Czar. Until Poland had been eliminated as a sovereign State in the latter half of the last century, by the three partitions of her territories between Russia, Prussia and Austria, she had been a great Power; and her people were noted for their bravery. He would incite them to rebel against their Russian master, by offering to re-create an independent Poland under his protection. But Frederick William was getting together another army in East Prussia; and, if it were allowed to join up with the Russians, the French might be outnumbered; so Napoleon decided that he must move fast.

Even so, it was the Russians, being acclimatised to fighting in ice and snow, who moved first. The Czar's principal Commander, General Bagration, made a daring move westwards, in the hope of saving Danzig from the French. By ill luck he ran into Bernadotte's corps. Immediately Napoleon was informed of this, he directed his main army northward with the object of driving the Russians into the sea. Through a captured despatch, Bagration learned of the Emperor's intention. Swiftly he retreated towards Königsberg, but at Eylau he turned on his pursuers, and there ensued the bloodiest battle that had been fought in the past hundred years.

It was upon the field of Eylau, on the night of February 8th, that Roger lay stricken and despairing of his life.

The campaign had been the most ghastly that the *Grande Armée* had ever endured. Not yet recovered from its serious wastage at the battles of Jena and Auerstädt, and its exertions during scores of mêlées while pursuing the Prussians, it was short of every sort of supply. The terrain over which it had been advancing was a vast, sparsely-populated area of plains deep in snow, and frozen lakes. At times there had been sudden, partial thaws, so that the land became a sea of mud in which the men's boots were frequently sucked off and could be retrieved only with difficulty. The cold was excruciating and the rations meagre to semi-starvation point. The officers no longer attempted to prevent looting and atrocities. The soldiers, desperate for food and warmth, had treated the wretched peasants in every village they came upon with the utmost ferocity, seizing their food, torturing them to reveal hidden stores, pulling down their hovels to make camp-fires, then leaving them to die.

On the night of the 7th, after confused fighting, the Russians had been driven from the little town of Eylau and retired to a strong position formed by an irregular line of hills.

Dawn filtered through dark, heavily-laden clouds. The artillery on both sides opened fire as the French columns began to advance. Davoust's men pushed back the Russian left and Napoleon ordered Augereau's corps to attack the enemy centre. Battling against driving snow, his leading troops succeeded in seizing a slight eminence that could give the French a valuable advantage. But the Muscovites were strong in cannon. From their iron mouths there poured discharge after discharge of grapeshot, ploughing wide lanes of dead and dying through Augerau's infantry, until his corps was nearly annihilated. As it fell back, a horde of Cossacks came charging down on the survivors, completing its destruction. Davoust's corps fared little better, having been forced to retreat under the massed fire of the Russian batteries.

By midday the battle had degenerated into wild confusion. There were scores of small bodies of troops locked in bloody hand-to-hand conflict with, here and there, gallant but futile cavalry charges. Napoleon, now worried, but determined to be victorious, then launched eighty squadrons of cavalry against the Russian centre. With fanatical bravery, the Cuirassiers charged the Muscovite infantry, hacked a way through them and, reaching the enemy's cannon, began to sabre the gunners. But Bagration had not yet used his reserves. The fire from his second line of infantry halted the French horsemen. Only moments later, fresh *sotnias* of Cossacks were launched against them, and they were driven back in disorder.

Meanwhile a body of four thousand Russian Grenadiers had emerged from the tangled conflict and, with a fanaticism equalling that of the French, fought its way through their lines straight into the village of Eylau.

The Emperor and his staff were standing there, watching the battle from a cemetery that stood on high land. Berthier, his Chief of Staff, fearing that they would all be killed or captured, ordered up the horses. But Napoleon calmly stood his ground, while giving the signal for his grand reserve, the Imperial Guard, to go into action.

All day these veterans of a hundred fights had sullenly remained idle. Now, fresh and vigorous, the finest troops in the *Grande Armée*, they rushed to the attack, fell upon the Russian Grenadiers and massacred them.

As dusk drew on, the outcome of the battle still remained uncertain. The best hope for the French lay with Davoust. His troops had succeeded in clinging on to a village they had seized that morning. From it he threatened the enemy's flank; a determined drive against it could have brought victory. But it was not to be. At the urging of Scharnhorst, the Prussian General Lestocq with a division of eight thousand men, had made a forced march from Königsberg. They arrived just in time to check the attack that Davoust was about to make.

When the battle opened, Ney's corps had been many miles distant from the main army. At the sound of the guns he, too, had made a forced march in that direction. Only his coming up in time could save Davoust's near-exhausted men from destruction by the newly-arrived Prussians.

The forces engaged had been approximately equal: some seventy-five thousand men on either side. Nightfall brought only semi-darkness, owing to the snow. Over a great area it had been churned up or trampled flat by batteries changing position, charging cavalry and struggling infantry. In innumerable places it was stained with the blood of horses and men. Here and there the white carpet was broken by dark, tangled heaps of corpses several feet high. Others were scattered in pairs or singly where they had been shot or struck down. Fifty thousand men lay there in the snow; dead, dying or seriously disabled. Roger was one of them.

During that day he and his fellow *aides-de-camp* had galloped many miles carrying scrawled messages from the Emperor to corps and divisional commanders. Several of them had not returned, others were bleeding from wounds received while carrying out their missions. Roger had remained unscathed until the terrible battle was almost over. Night was falling when a galloper arrived from Davoust to report the Marshal's desperate situation. During the day Ney had sent several messages to say that he was on his way. The arrival of his corps was the only remaining hope of saving Davoust. Napoleon cast a swift glance at the now much smaller group of officers behind him. Unless his messenger made a great detour, he would have to pass a wood still held by the Russians, and time was precious. His eye fell on Roger. As he was personally known to every senior Commander in the *Grande Armée*, in his case a written message was superfluous. Raising a hand, the Emperor shouted at him in the harsh Italian-accented French habitual to him:

'Breuc! To Ney! Tell him that I am counting on him. That without him the battle may yet be lost.'

Instantly Roger set spurs to his horse. He was no coward and was accounted one of the best swordsmen in France. He had fought numerous duels and was prepared to face any man in single combat with sword or pistol. But he loathed battles; for during them, without a chance to defend oneself, one might at any moment be killed or maimed by a shot from a musket or by a cannon ball. Nevertheless chance, and at times deliberate fraud, resulting from his activities as a secret agent, had made him the hero of many exploits, with the result that he was known throughout the Army as *'le brave Breuc'*. Napoleon undoubtedly believed him to be entirely fearless and that, he knew, was why he had been chosen for this dangerous mission. Much as he would have liked to take the detour behind the village of Eylau, he had no choice but to charge down the hill and across the front of the position still held by the Russians.

Crouching low over his mount he had followed a zigzag course, at times swerving to avoid wrecked guns and limbers, at others jumping his mare over heaps of dead and wounded. As he came level with the wood, his heart beat faster. Hating every moment, he urged his charger forward at racing speed. Along the edge of the wood muskets began to flash, bullets whistled overhead. One jerked his befeathered hat from his head. Sweating with fear, he pressed on. Suddenly the mare lurched. Knowing the animal to have been hit, he made to throw himself from the saddle. But he was a moment too late. Shot through the heart, she fell, bringing him down with one leg pinned beneath her belly. He felt an excruciating pain in his ankle and knew that it had been broken by the stirrup iron, caught between the weight of the mare and the ice-hard earth.

For a few minutes he had lain still, then endeavoured to free himself. Had his ankle not been broken, he might have succeeded in dragging his leg from beneath the mare's belly. But his pulling on it resulted in such agony that he fainted.

When he came to, the Russian fusillade aimed at him had ceased and he could hear only distant, sporadic firing. Again he attempted to wriggle his leg from under the dead mare, but with each effort stabs of pain streaked up to his heart, making him, in spite of the appalling cold, break out into a sweat. At length he was forced to resign himself to the fact that, without help, he must remain there a prisoner.

Whether Ney had arrived in time to save Davoust he had no idea; nor who had proved the victors in this most bloody battle. As far as he could judge, it had been a draw, so any claim to victory could be made only by the side that did not withdraw to a stronger position during the night. At least it seemed that in the Russians Napoleon had at last found his match, for they were most tenacious fighters. As he had himself said of them. 'It is not enough to kill a Russian. You must then push him over before he will lie down.'

But Roger was no longer concerned with the issue of the war. It was not his quarrel, and he was now silently cursing himself for his folly in taking part in it. After Trafalgar, he could perfectly well have remained at home in England and settled down as a country gentleman. Although he was generous by nature, he had inherited his Scottish mother's prudence about money; so he had saved a great part of his earnings and these, together with the money left him by his father, the Admiral, amounted to a respectable fortune. It was not even the call of duty that had caused him to go abroad again, but simply restlessness and discontent.

As he lay there in the snow, his head, in the fur hood of his cloak, muffled against the biting cold, he thought back on the events that had driven him to his decision. Georgina, he admitted, could not really be blamed; yet it was a whim of that beautiful, self-willed, tempestuous lady that had led to his again having himself smuggled across to France.

He had been married twice and had had many mistresses; but Georgina, the now widowed Countess of St. Ermins, had been his first love and remained the great love of his life. To her indignation he often twitted her with having seduced him when they were in their teens; but that had been on a long-past afternoon just before he had run away from home to escape having to become a Midshipman. Four years had elapsed before he had returned from the Continent. By then she was married, but had taken him as her lover. In the years that followed, he had spent many long spells abroad, but always on his return they renewed their passionate attachment. There had even been a night when both of them had decided to marry again then, with wicked delight, had slept together. After both of them had been widowed for the second time, whenever he had returned from one of his missions, he had begged her to marry him. But she contended that it was not in his nature to settle down definitely and that, even if he did, their being together as man and wife for any considerable time must inevitably take the edge off the wondrous joy they had in each other when, for only a month or two, they were reunited after a long interval.

At length he had accepted that; so, on their return to England after Trafalgar, he had not again pressed her. But he had expected to be a frequent warmly-welcomed visitor at her lovely home, Stillwaters, near Ripley, where they had so often known great happiness together.

Alas for his expectations. The unpredictable and impetuous Georgina had suddenly become serious. Just as at one time she had declared herself to be utterly weary of balls, routs and a score of beaux constantly begging her to sleep with them—and, overnight, had metamorphosed herself into a model wife interested only in country pursuits—so now she announced that everyone owed a debt to the Navy that had saved England from the horrors of invasion, and that she intended to pay hers.

Her plan was to buy a big house near Portsmouth and convert it into a convalescent home to accommodate from fifty to a hundred seamen. She would engage a doctor and a staff of nurses and herself become the matron. Under her supervision relays of these poor, wounded heroes should be nursed back to health and strength and taught some trade that would later enable them to earn a wage in civil life sufficient to support them.

Roger had heartily applauded her idea, for in those days Britain's treatment of men invalided from the Services on account of serious wounds was a scandal that cried to heaven. No sooner were they able to walk on crutches or, still half-blind, able to make their way about, than they were put out of the hospitals near-penniless, to fend for themselves. Thousands of them now roamed the streets of the cities, begging their bread.

Georgina's great wealth enabled her without delay to carry out her project. Roger helped her find a suitable mansion, assisted in furnishing it suitably and engaging staff. By February, the first inmates were installed and Georgina, relinquishing the fortune in jewels, unadorned by which she was normally never to be seen abroad, and exchanging her gay furbelows for more sober attire, had entered enthusiastically on her new role as ministering angel.

So far, so good. But, as far as Roger was concerned, not for long. Gone were the happy days at Stillwaters when Georgina had entertained big house parties and Roger had delighted in conversing with her other guests: statesmen, ambassadors, painters and playwrights; the dinners for fifty with dancing or gambling afterwards until the small hours. Gone, too, were those halcyon midweeks that they had spent alone, dallying in her great bed until nearly midday, and later picnicking in a boat on the lovely lake.

At the convalescent home, life was earnest; the state of its inmates depressing. In vain Roger had endeavoured to reconcile himself to the role of comforter and adviser as he listened patiently to the stories of the stricken seamen. And Georgina had thrown herself into her part so determinedly that often when night came she was too tired to make love.

To break the monotony of his wearisome round Roger had made several trips to London. But they, too, proved unsatisfactory. He was a member of White's, but he had lived for so long abroad that he had few friends. More and more he had begun to long for the companionship of those gay paladins with whom he had shared many dangers in Italy, Egypt and across the Rhine.

In England he was a nobody: just the son of the late Admiral Sir Christopher Brook. In France he was 'le brave Breuc', and A.D.C. to the Emperor, an intimate friend of the Empress Josephine and of all the members of the Bonaparte family. He was one of the very few Colonels to whom, for personal services, Napoleon had given the second rank in his new order of chivalry. Roger ranked as a Commander of the Legion of Honour, and, as a Knight in the new Napoleonic aristocracy, again ranked as *le Chevalier de Breuc*.

By May, acute boredom with Georgina's Home and a London that offered no advancement to him had decided him to return to France.

In 1800 Roger, sent by Talleyrand as Plenipotentiary Extraordinary to England with an offer of peace, had quarrelled bitterly with his master, Pitt, for refusing it. Thenceforth, he had no longer been employed by the British Government, although he had undertaken certain missions for the Prime Minister and aided Britain's cause whenever possible.

In May 1806 he would have at least gone to Pitt and enquired if there was any special information about the plans of Britain's enemy that he might secure for him. But in January of that year, broken-hearted by the news of Austerlitz and the collapse of the Third Coalition, the great and courageous man who, for over twenty years had been the mainstay of resistance to the terrorists of the French Revolution becoming dominant over all Europe, had died.

His regime had been succeeded by a so-called 'Ministry of All the Talents'—a coalition led by Charles Fox. The great

Whig was one of Georgina's friends, so Roger had often met him at Stillwaters, and found it difficult to resist his personal charm. But the fact remained that Fox had shown ardent sympathy with the French Revolution, and actively advocated England, too, becoming a Republic. For many years he had consistently thwarted and endeavoured to sabotage Pitt's plans for the defeat of Napoleon and, during the brief Peace of 1803, had received and lionised in France. Such treachery Roger could not forgive, and nothing would have induced him to serve under such a master.

In consequence, with no brief, but believing that he could do neither good nor harm to Britain in Napoleon's Continental wars, Roger had reported back for duty, to be warmly received by the Emperor and his many friends in France.

Yet now, a prisoner beneath his horse, the cold steadily creeping upon him, he realised how stupid he had been to risk death in one of Napoleon's battles, instead of settling for a safe, if humdrum, life in England.

His chances of survival were very slender. It was just possible that French stretcher-bearers might come upon him; but they were comparatively few and the casualties in the battle ran to many thousands. There was an equally slender chance that he might be picked up by the Russians; yet it was more probable than either that the vultures of the battlefield would find and kill him.

All armies in those days were dogged by swarms of camp-followers: women who made a precarious living as whores to the troops, and men who, after every engagement, went out by night to rob the wounded of all they possessed, and even stripped them of their clothes. The still greater likelihood was that he would remain lying there in the snow until he slowly froze to death.

He seemed to have been hunched beside his mare for many hours, yet it was only a little after midnight when, muffled by the fur hood over his head, he caught the sound of voices. Pushing away one side of the hood, he heard a gruff voice say in French:

20

'Here's another. From his fine mount and fur-edged cloak he must be an officer, so he should yield good pickings.'

In the money belt that he always wore about him Roger had over one hundred louis in gold. To offer it in exchange for his life he knew would be useless. These human vultures would only laugh, kill him and take the money from his dead body. Squirming over, he pulled a pistol from the upper holster of his horse.

As he moved, he heard the voice exclaim, 'Quick, Jean! This one is still alive. Bash him over the head with your iron bar and send him to join the others we have done well from.'

His heart beating madly in his chest, Roger turned over. Above him there loomed two tall figures, made grotesquely bulky by furs they had stolen from several dead men on the battlefield. Raising his pistol, he levelled it at the nearer. Offering up a prayer that the powder had not become damp, he pulled the trigger. There came a flash and a loud report that shattered the silence of the night. The man at whom he had aimed gave a choking gasp, sagged at the knees and fell dead in the snow.

With a furious curse, the other flung himself upon Roger. The pistol was single-barrelled, so he could not fire it again. In spite of his imprisoned leg, he still had the full use of his muscular arms and torso; so he grappled desperately with his attacker, pulling him down upon him.

The man was strong and ruthless. Seizing Roger by the throat, he endeavoured to strangle him. In such a situation Roger would normally have kneed him in the groin, but he was in no position to do so. Gasping for breath, he used his hands. Stiffening his fingers, he thrust them violently at his would-be murderer's face. One finger pierced his antagonist's left eye. With a howl of pain, he released his hold on Roger's neck and jerked himself up. Knowing that his life hung in the balance, Roger seized his momentary advantage. His hands fastened on the man's throat. There ensued a ghastly struggle. Thrashing at Roger's face with clenched fists, the human vulture strove to free himself. As in a nightmare, Roger knew that his eyes had been blacked, his mouth smashed so that his lips were swelling, and he could taste the salt blood running down from his nose. But, ignoring the pain, he hung on.

Gradually, the blows he was receiving grew weaker, then ceased. In the dim light reflected from the snow, he could see his attacker's face becoming contused and blackened. His eyes bulged from his head, his tongue jutted out from between his uneven teeth. After what seemed an age, he collapsed, strangled, across Roger's body.

Groaning and exhausted, Roger feebly pushed his victim from him. Panting from his exertions, he lay there, still a prisoner of the horse that pinned down his leg. By a miracle he had fought off this brutal attempt to murder him. Temporarily the violent struggle had warmed him up, but it was as yet early in the night and, with the increasing cold, he had little hope of surviving until morning.

2

The Bill is Presented

One benefit at least that Roger derived from having been attacked by these human vultures was that both were clad in thick furs which they had evidently looted earlier from other casualties on the battlefield. Handicapped though he was by his trapped foot, he managed to wriggle a big, coarse, bearskin coat off the man he had strangled. The one he had shot lay beyond his reach, but he was able to use the bearskin as extra cover for his body and free leg which, until his desperate fight for life, had gradually been becoming numb with cold.

After a while his thoughts turned again to Georgina. It was, no doubt, the gipsy blood she had inherited from her mother which enabled her to foretell the future with some accuracy, and form with Roger a strange psychic link which, for his part, he attributed to their complete understanding of each other's mind and mutual life-long devotion. There had been occasions when he had been in acute danger and she many hundred miles away, yet he had clearly heard her voice warning him and telling him how to save himself; and once, when she was nearly drowning in the Caribbean he, in Paris, had fainted and fallen from his horse, later to learn that his spirit had gone to her and imbued her with the strength to swim ashore.

He wondered now if she was aware of his present desperate plight and would, in some way, aid him. But he did not see how she could, as he had left no means untried to free himself; and no warning of the approach of human vultures was necessary as long as he could remain awake.

From Georgina his mind drifted to another lovely woman: the Countess Marie Walewska, Napoleon's latest mistress.

When Napoleon married Josephine, he had loved her most desperately, whereas she was indifferent to him, and only persuaded to the match by her ex-lover, the then all-powerful Director, Barras. So indifferent to him was she that she had been flagrantly unfaithful to him with a handsome army contractor named Hippolyte Charles, during Napoleon's absence on the Italian campaign. Her husband found out, but was still so much under her spell that he forgave her. No sooner had he set sail for Egypt than Josephine began openly to indulge in further amours. His family loathed her; so, on his return, provided him with chapter and verse about her infidelities, hoping that he would get rid of her. Having, while in Egypt, had a hectic affair with a most charming young woman known as *La Bellelotte,* he was inclined to do so; but Josephine's children by her first marriage, Eugene and Hortense Beauharnais, whom Napoleon loved as though they were his own children, interceded with tears for their mother so effectively that she was again forgiven.

But thenceforth Napoleon did not scruple to take any woman he desired, and Josephine's tragedy was that, all too late, her indifference to him had turned to love. At intervals, between dozens of the beauties from the Opéra and the Comédie Française spending a night or two in his bed, there had been more lengthy affairs with Grassini, the Italian singer; Mlle Georges, the Nell Gwyn of his seraglio, who truly loved him for himself and kept him in fits of laughter; a gold-digging tragedienne named Thérèse Bourgoin; the autocratic and inveterate gambler Madame de Vaudey who was one of Josephine's ladies-in-waiting; then Madame Duchâtel, a ravishing blonde with cornflower-blue eyes, who was another of Josephine's ladies.

By then, the knowledge of Napoleon's infidelities had been causing Josephine to have bouts of weeping and, half-mad with jealousy, she invaded the room where her husband and la Duchâtel were disporting themselves. Furiously declaring that he was not as other men, and above petty marital conventions, he had driven Josephine from the room.

Yet he continued to regard her with great affection. He still frequently slept with her and, when he was worried, it was she who read him to sleep. During the Prussian campaign he had missed her dreadfully and frequently wrote to her in the warmest terms, urging her, for his sake, to face the rigours of the northern winter and join him.

But soon after his arrival in Warsaw the tune of his letters to Josephine had altered; the gist of them being that the climate would prove too severe for her, so she must remain in Paris.

The reason for this sudden change of heart was known to all who were in frequent attendance on him. On January 1st, when on his way to Warsaw, his coach had been surrounded by an excited crowd, cheering this legendary paladin who, rumour said, was about to restore Poland to her ancient glory. At an inn at which the coach had pulled up, two ladies had begged Duroc, Napoleon's A.D.C.-in-Chief and Marshal of his Camps and Palaces, to permit them to pay homage to the hero. Duroc had courteously agreed, and one of the ladies was the flaxen-haired, blue-eyed, eighteen-year-old Countess Walewska.

Napoleon, much taken with her, instantly recognised her again when she appeared at a grand ball given in his honour a few nights after he had established himself in the ancient Palace of the Polish Kings. But, from shyness, the young girl had asked to be excused when he invited her to dance. No doubt this had made him more eager to pursue her, which for some days he did, with growing annoyance at her ignoring his letters and refusing him a rendezvous.

The fact was that Marie Walewska was, although married to a seventy-year-old nobleman, chaste, of a retiring disposition and deeply religious. The thought of taking a lover was abhorrent to her and, although normally Napoleon never took 'No' for an answer, in this case help had to be called in.

Prince Poniatowski, the head of the movement for Polish liberation, pointed out to her how valuable she could be to her country's cause by becoming the all-powerful Emperor's mistress. Moved to tears as she was by this appeal to her known patriotism, she still refused to succumb.

The affair became the talk of the town; men and women,

friends and relations all joined in to badger poor little Marie into giving way for the good of the cause. Driven half out of her wits, she at last agreed to allow Duroc to escort her to Napoleon's apartments. Duroc, who was one of Roger's closest friends, told him afterwards that, although the couple had been closeted together for three hours, Marie had been in tears the whole time and left the room as chaste as she had entered it.

Utterly exasperated, Napoleon played his last card and sent his brilliant Foreign Minister, Talleyrand, to talk to her. That elegant aristocrat, a bishop under the *ancient régime*. a Liberal leader during the first Revolution, an exile during the Terror, after Napoleon one of the two most powerful men in France for the past eight years, and not long since created by his master Prince de Benevento, was not only as subtle as a serpent in negotiating treaties, but also a past-master in the art of seducing women. Where all others had failed, he had persuaded Marie that the gods had blessed her above all other women by enabling her to serve her country and, at the same time, endowing her with the love of the most powerful man on earth.

Napoleon was invariably kind and courteous to women, and extravagantly generous to his mistresses. His gentleness and charm soon won Marie's heart. Their happy association lasted for many years. She was one of the few women that he ever truly loved and, in due course, she gave him a son.

Charles Maurice de Talleyrand Périgord, a grandson of the Princess de Chalais, debarred from succeeding his father as Marquis because an ill-cared-for broken ankle, causing him to be lame for life, had disqualified him for the Army, had played a key role in Roger's life.

At the age of nineteen, Roger had been knocked out and carried unconscious into Talleyrand's house. During his subsequent ravings, Talleyrand had learned that his guest was not, as he purported to be, a Frenchman born in Strasbourg who, on his mother's death, had been brought up by her sister in England; but was in fact the son of Lady Marie Brook and a British Admiral. He had kept Roger's secret and, for many years, believed that, as was quite common in those days, Roger

26

was a foreigner who had decided to make his career in another country and was completely loyal to it.

At last Talleyrand had found out that Roger was still loyal to the country of his birth and that, ever since 1789, owing to the high connections he had made in France, he had acted as a master spy for Britain's Prime Minister. But on two counts Talleyrand had refrained from having him arrested. Firstly, it was Roger who during the Terror had procured for him the papers that had enabled him to escape from France. Secondly, from the very beginning of his diplomatic career, Talleyrand's secret aim had been to bring Britain and France together; his conviction being that there could be no lasting peace in Europe until her two most powerful nations permanently buried the hatchet.

Talleyrand was unique among his contemporaries: an aristocrat by birth and breeding, he still dressed in silks and went to receptions with his hair powdered, yet he had succeeded in dominating the horde of strong-willed, self-made men who had emerged from the Revolution. Cynical, venal, immoral, he pursued his unruffled way through court and camp, although he detested having to follow Napoleon on his campaigns—on the way to Warsaw his coach had become stuck for a whole night in the snow. When in Paris he lived in the utmost luxury and, to meet his colossal expenditure, he exacted huge bribes from the foreign ambassadors; but only to listen to their desires, not necessarily to further them, and that had been customary with Ministers of Foreign Affairs in every country in Europe for centuries. That he was immoral he would never have denied; the lovely women with whom, at one time or another, he had been to bed were legion. But he was a man of great vision, whose steadfast ambition was to bring lasting peace and prosperity to France.

Most men holding such views and serving a master to whom war was the breath of life, would long since have thrown in their hands. But not Talleyrand. Again and again, calm, imperturbable, even showing apparent willingness, he had bowed before the storm and negotiated treaties made against his advice; yet always with the hope that if he remained at his post a time would come when he could stabilise the position of France within her own natural frontiers and bring the other nations of Europe to look on her as a friend.

As early as October 1805 Talleyrand had sent from Strasbourg a well-reasoned paper to the Emperor. His argument was that the destruction of the Holy Roman Empire could do only harm to Europe. By remaining strong it could act both as a counterpoise to Prussia, and keep the barbarous hordes of Russia in check. After Napoleon had entered Vienna in triumph, Talleyrand had adhered to his policy, begging the Emperor to let the defeated Austrians off lightly and enter into an alliance with them; thus evading the danger that Hungary might break away and go over to the Czar.

Talleyrand's despatch had reached the Emperor just after Austerlitz, in which battle he had administered the *coup de grâce* to Austria and also routed a Russian army. Elated by his double victory he had brushed aside the wise counsel of his Foreign Minister and imposed a brutally harsh fine on the Emperor Francis, taking from him his Venetian and Dalmatian territories, and other big areas of land, to reward the German Princes who had sent contingents of troops to fight beside the French.

That summer he had arbitrarily united sixteen of these Princes to form under his suzerainty the Confederation of the Rhine. Talleyrand had obediently brought them into line, while looking down his slightly retroussé nose. He, and his Austrian opposite number, Prince Metternich, knew well enough that such a hastily-assembled kettle of normally antagonistic fish could prove no substitute for a strong Austrian Empire.

In that summer, too, Talleyrand had again endeavoured to bring about a peace with Britain. Charles Fox had all his life been so strong a Francophile that his then being in power favoured it; but negotiations had broken down over the future of Sicily.

The age had opened when Napoleon was to play ducks and drakes with the ancient thrones of Europe. He had recently made his elder brother, Joseph, King of Naples; his youngest brother, Louis, King of Holland; and his brother-in-law, Joachim Murat, Grand Duke of Berg. But Joseph was as yet in possession of only the land half of the Kingdom of the Two Sicilies. The Bourbon King Ferdinand had fled from Naples to the great island and, protected by the British Fleet, still held it. Such was Napoleon's loathing for Ferdinand's Queen, Caroline—the intriguing elder sister of the ill-fated Marie Antoinette—that he was determined to conquer the island at the first opportunity, and laid claim to it as part of Joseph's Kingdom. Pledged to continue to defend the Bourbons, in honour bound Britain could not agree to abandon them. Then, in September, the grossly obese Fox had followed his life-long opponent, Pitt, to the grave.

There had followed the whirlwind Prussian campaign. After the defeats of Jena and Austerlitz, Frederick William had asked for terms. Again Talleyrand had urged the Emperor to show mercy to the defeated and bind them to him by an alliance. Napoleon would not hear of it. An alliance, yes; but not until Prussia had forfeited half her territories. In vain Talleyrand had pointed out that, with both Austria and Prussia broken, there would be no major Power left to help resist the Muscovite hordes overrunning Central Europe and invading France herself. But Napoleon, by then the arbiter of Europe from the tip of Italy to the Baltic, and from the Carpathian mountains to the North Sea, had become so overwhelmingly confident in his own power to deal with any and every situation that he had refused to listen. The Prussians had sullenly withdrawn to the north, and were still giving the Czar such help as they could.

It had begun to snow again: large, heavy, silent flakes. As Roger drew his furs more closely round him, he wondered how it would all end. The French had taken a terrible hammering that day at Eylau, but no one could dispute Napoleon's genius as a General. Roger would have bet a year's pay that, before the year was out, by one of his fantastically swift concentrations the Emperor would catch the Russians napping and inflict a terrible defeat upon them. But what then?

Britain alone would remain in arms defying the might of

the Continent's overlord. But she was in a worse way than she had been at any time since the beginning of the struggle. The so-called 'Ministry of All the Talents' consisted almost entirely of weak, incompetent men who lacked a firm policy, and spent their time quarrelling amongst themselves.

If Napoleon's Continental System proved a really serious threat to Britain's trade, industrial interests might force the present futile gang to agree a humiliating peace. Again, should Napoleon succeed in defeating the Russians, he would have no enemy left but England; and would march the *Grande Armée* back to Boulogne. For the time being Trafalgar had rendered invasion out of the question; but, with every dockyard in Europe at his disposal, the Emperor could, in a year or two, build a fleet strong enough to challenge again the British Navy. The great Nelson was dead. Would his successor succeed in defeating a French Armada; or, awful thought, would Lasalle's Hussars and Oudinot's Grenadiers yet ravage and burn the peaceful farmsteads of Kent and Sussex?

As the falling snow formed a blanket over Roger's hunched body, he knew that the issue was, for him, academic; but he tried to cheer himself by looking on the brighter side.

There was another possibility. During this past year the Emperor had succumbed to *folie de grandeur*. He had absolute confidence in his 'star' and considered himself a superman whose decisions could never be wrong. Hence his abrupt dismissal of Talleyrand's far-sighted policies. But it is said that 'pride goeth before a fall'. It was not only the rulers and the armies of Austria and Prussia that had been humbled by defeat. The peoples of those countries, countless thousands of whom had casually been made citizens of foreign states, resented most bitterly the fate that Napoleon had brought upon them.

At least there was a chance that they might be seized with a patriotic fervour and rise in their wrath against this oppressor. Between '92 and '96 it had been the *people* of France who had not only overthrown the Monarchy, but defied and defeated the trained armies of Austria, Prussia, Piedmont and Spain. If Napoleon had his back turned—for example being occupied with the invasion of England—might not the Germans and Austrians combine to massacre the French garrisons left in their cities, and regain their freedom?

The fanaticism that had imbued the early armies of the Republic with the courage to achieve their amazing victories turned Roger's thoughts to France as it was now, under the benign but iron hand of the Emperor. In '99, when he had become First Consul, the country had been in a state of anarchy. There was no justice in the land. Every Municipality was a law unto itself, flagrantly robbing such citizens of any means who had not escaped abroad, yet neglecting the roads in its district until they became almost impassable. The country had swarmed with bands of deserters who pillaged and murdered at will. In the cities the Churches had been turned into gaming hells and brothels, half the houses had become rat-infested tenements, and the streets were half-choked with the accumulated filth of years.

Within a year, in one great spate of inexhaustible energy, overriding every obstacle, the First Consul had cleaned the country up. The venal Municipalities had been replaced by Prefects, answerable only to him. The roads were repaired, the diligences again ran on time, the inns were made habitable and their staffs were no longer surly and offensive. The cities were cleansed, thousands of new schools opened, justice restored and the finances put in order. That one man could have achieved so much in so short a time was miraculous and, as an administrator, Napoleon had Roger's whole-hearted admiration. But a price had had to be paid for his services. The French people had lost their hard-won liberty. By a series of swift, crafty changes in the Constitution, Bonaparte had made himself a dictator whose will no man could question. Yet, because he had brought order out of chaos and again given them security, they had accepted this new bondage without a murmur.

As Roger recalled those days of hectic endeavour to retrieve France from the appalling state of disorder into which she had fallen during the ten years of the Revolution and Directory, the image of another personality entered his mind.

31

This was Joseph Fouché. Equally, perhaps, with Talleyrand, after Napoleon, he had for many years been the most powerful man in France. He was, too, the only other who knew Roger to be in fact the son of an English Admiral.

Fouché was the antithesis of Talleyrand. He had started life as a lay teacher of the Oratorian Order, become a close friend of Robespierre and was the Deputy for Nantes in the Revolutionary Convention. In '93 he had emerged as one of the most ruthless of the Terrorists. As Commissioner in Nevers he had looted the Cathedral and sent scores of bourgeoisie to the guillotine. In Lyons he had put down a Liberal revolt, had trenches dug outside the city, then had the captured rebels —men, women and children—lined up in front of them and mowed down with cannon firing grapeshot.

During the reaction that took place under the Directory, he had been lucky to escape with his life and, while in exile forty leagues from Paris, managed to sustain himself by breeding pigs. Somehow he had become an army contractor, made a small fortune, then suddenly emerged again as Chief of Police.

From Roger's first year in France right up to the autumn of '99, a bitter enmity had existed between him and Fouché. Each owed the other a long-harboured grudge and, on numerous occasions, they had pitted their wits against each other, with death as the forfeit. But at the time of *Brumaire,* when Napoleon had made his bid for power, their interests having become common they had buried the hatchet.

Roger had brought the aristocratic Talleyrand and the rabble-rouser Fouché secretly together, because he knew that both believed Bonaparte to be the 'man with the sword' who could cleanse the Augean Stable that France had become. Talleyrand had stage-managed the *coup d'état* out at St. Cloud while Fouché had closed the gates of Paris, thus preventing interference by troops still loyal to the Convention and the Revolution.

Confirmed in his office as Chief of Police by Bonaparte, Fouché had then worked wonders. His spy system was all-embracing, his files contained particulars of every important Frenchman in the country, and out of it. He worked eighteen hours a day and maintained a large staff of highly efficient subordinates. He was aware of every incipient conspiracy and every love affair that mattered. Although himself a Jacobin, he ruthlessly suppressed all his old colleagues who were anti-Bonaparte. He controlled a vast army of agents and his powers had increased to a point where his word became law from one end of France to the other. Meanwhile, he had amassed a vast fortune.

By the autumn of 1802 he had become so powerful that even Napoleon became afraid of him, so dismissed him and split his Ministry into two. But by the summer of 1804, the Emperor had reluctantly come to realise that, when he was away on his campaigns, Fouché was the only man capable of preventing trouble in France, so he had been reinstated as Minister of Police, and given special powers to deal with any emergency.

He was a tall, pale cadaverous man whose features resembled those of a living corpse. Habitually he never looked anyone straight in the face. His eyes were like those of a dead fish and, as he suffered from a perpetual cold, his nose was always running. Unlike Talleyrand, he was careless in his dress and his waistcoat was often stained with snuff. Unlike Talleyrand, too, no pretty woman ever graced his bed. He was completely faithful to a dreary wife who was as ill-favoured as himself. In 1804, when creating a new aristocracy to support his throne, Napoleon had made Fouché the Duc d'Otranto.

Although Talleyrand and Fouché had combined to bring General Bonaparte to power as First Consul, their outlooks on life were as different as oil from water, and they loathed each other. But Roger, while having a deep affection for the former, also admired the latter for his extraordinary efficiency, and for a long time past had been on the best of terms with them both.

As the steadily-falling snow formed a thick layer over Roger's furs, his limbs gradually became numb. He felt a great desire to fall asleep, but knew that if he did that would be the end. He would never wake up. Vaguely he realised that he could not have been granted a less painful death. Even so, his instinct was to keep life in his body for as long as possible. From time to time he rubbed his face and ears hard,

33

flailed his arms out and in, beating his chest, and kicked about with his free leg. But gradually his movements became more infrequent, and his mind wandered from one disconnected episode to another:

His divine Georgina in bed with him, bidding him nibble her ears, which she adored; himself angrily telling Pitt who, in 1799, had refused the peace terms offered by Bonaparte, to keep the money due to him and instead give it to the charity for soldiers and sailors wounded in the war; the evening when, on an island in the lagoon of Venice, he had singlehanded defended Napoleon from a gang of conspirators come there to assassinate him; the Emperor's sister, the beautiful Princess Pauline, standing naked in his Paris lodging while she implored him to risk her brother's wrath by demanding her hand in marriage; his horror and fury on that dark night in India when he had come upon Clarissa dying of exposure as a result of a Satanic ceremony performed by the fiendish Malderini; the sunshine and flowers of the Caribbean, which he had so loved while married to his second wife, Amanda, and had, for a while, been Governor of Martinique, Georgina again, happily playing with her son, Charles, and his own daughter, Susan, who shared the nursery of the little Earl. Then for a moment he was again a little boy himself, feeding a saucer of milk to a hedgehog in the garden of his home at Lymington. The pictures faded from his mind, and he slept.

He was awakened by being roughly shaken and gave a cry. A voice said something in a strange tongue. Roger had a flair for languages. He had learned to speak Russian from his first wife, that beautiful tiger-cat Natalia Andreovna, whom Catherine the Great had forced him into marrying; and, during the past two months, he had picked up a little Polish. This was neither, but seemed like a bastard form of German. He sensed that the man had said:

'Here's one who is still alive.'

Three other men crowded round him. Between them they dragged the dead mare off his leg, then hauled him to his feet and ran their hands over his limbs, evidently to find out if he

34

was wounded. As they released him, his weight came on his injured foot. It gave under him and, with a gasp of pain, he fell across the horse.

All his rescuers were muffled up to the eyes in furs. One towered above the others and must have been at least six foot five. Stooping, he thrust a flask into Roger's mouth and poured vodka down his throat. The fiery spirit made him choke, but his heart began to hammer wildly, restoring his circulation.

Straightening up, the giant spoke to the others in clear but heavily accented German, 'His ankle is broken. But he'll be all right. Get him to the wagon.'

Looking round, Roger realised that it had stopped snowing; but instead of the battlefield being dotted with the dark forms of fallen men and horses, it was now, as far as he could see in the dim light, an endless sheet of white. It was only as he was half carried, half dragged forward that mounds here and there showed the places where Frenchmen and Russians had breathed their last.

On the edge of the wood there stood a covered wagon. With callous indifference for his broken ankle, the men lifted and bundled him into it. Inside, it was pitch dark, but the sound of movement told him that he was not its only occupant. After a moment, a gruff voice said in French: 'Welcome to our *bive, camarade*. You're the third of us they've picked up. What's your rank and regiment?'

Cautious from long experience of dangerous situations, Roger did not immediately reply. Then he decided that nothing was to be gained by concealing his identity and that revealing it might even secure him better treatment; so he answered:

'Colonel de Breuc, *aide-de-camp* to the Emperor.'

'*Ventre du diable!*' exclaimed the other in an awed voice. 'Not *le brave Breuc?*'

Roger managed a half-hearted laugh. 'That's what they call me. Who are you?'

'Sergeant Jules Fournier, Sixth Battalion Imperial Guard.'

'I'm glad to have an old soldier with me. Who is our companion?'

Another, younger voice came feebly out of the darkness, speaking French but with a German accent. 'I'm Hans Hoffman, Colonel, a Private in the 2nd Nassau Regiment of Foot.'

In the next few minutes Roger learned that the Sergeant had a shattered knee-cap and the Private a bullet wound in the thigh. Both were in considerable pain, but thought themselves lucky to have been saved from freezing to death. Roger did, too, and greatly as he disliked the idea of having become a prisoner of war, felt that he had been fortunate to be picked up by Prussians rather than Russians.

A few minutes later a fourth body was bundled into the wagon. He turned out to be a French Corporal of Chasseurs. In one of Murat's charges, he had had the big toe of his right foot shot away and been thrown from his horse. He, too, was in considerable pain, and had no sooner settled himself than he began to mutter an unending flow of curses on his ill-fortune. His name, they learned, was François Vitu and he came from Marseilles.

Two of the bear-like figures who had rescued them clambered into the back of the wagon, then it set off. The journey seemed interminable and every jolt of the unwieldy vehicle caused the wounded men to give groans of pain.

At last the pale light of dawn enabled them vaguely to see one another and, half an hour later, the wagon came to a halt. The four prisoners were unceremoniously pulled out of it and promptly collapsed in the snow.

Looking round they saw that they were in a clearing of the forest, at one end of which there reared up a small, grim-looking castle. From both sides of it there ran out tall, thatched barns and stables. Roger was a little surprised not to find himself in the usual type of prisoner-of-war camp, but he supposed that the castle had been taken over for that purpose.

Pulled and pushed, the wounded men were dragged not to the castle, but to one of the barns. In the centre of its earth floor there was a circular depression in which large, red-hot stones were glowing. At either end of the barn, cattle were stalled. Above one end there was a loft stacked with bales of hay.

At an order from the giant leader, one of his men threw an

36

armful of branches on the glowing stones, and the new wood swiftly flared up. Grateful for the warmth it gave out, the four wounded men huddled round it.

Two women then appeared. One was a big, coarse-featured blonde, with huge, jutting breasts; the other a wrinkled harridan. With them they brought basins of water and a supply of coarse bandages. Between them they washed and bound up the wounds of Roger and his companions. The giant's men then carried them one after the other up to the loft, broke open some bales of sweet-smelling hay, and laid them on couches of it.

Roger was greatly puzzled. During the terrible battle, many others of Napoleon's troops must have been captured; but there were none here. And when, on entering the barn, the tall leader of their rescuers and his men had thrown open their voluminous furs, beneath them they wore no sort of uniform. Still wondering vaguely and with some apprehension about what the future held for him, he fell asleep.

He, and those with him, did not wake until late in the afternoon. They were aroused by the big man and the fair woman with the huge breasts coming up the ladder to the loft.

The man no longer wore furs, and was dressed in a kaftan. He was broad-shouldered as well as tall. His head was crowned by an unruly mop of flaxen hair, and he had a smooth, aggressive chin. Looking down on them, he gave a laugh, slapped the woman on the backside and said in his heavy German:

'I am Baron Herman von Znamensk, and this is my wife Freda. She will look to your wounds, so that in time you will be able men again. That may take a few weeks; but no matter. By then either your army will be deep in the heart of Russia, or the Czar will have driven it back in confusion. Either way, it will be too distant for there to be any chance of your being rescued by one of its columns.'

For a moment he paused, then, his steel-blue eyes flashing hatred, he snarled, 'You French swine and your self-styled Emperor have torn my country apart. Without cause or justification you have descended like a swarm of locusts to devour

37

our means of livelihood. Every head of cattle, every quintal of wheat has been stolen by you from my outlying farms. But the four of you shall pay me for that. Henceforth you are my serfs, and shall labour for the rest of your lives, under the whip of my overseer, making good the damage that your upstart Emperor has done me and mine.'

3

An Appalling Future

It was a sentence too terrible to contemplate. To have become
a prisoner of war, however unfortunate, was one thing; to have
become the chattel of this blond giant for an indefinite period
quite another.

For a moment Roger remained silent. To show angry resentment would, he knew, prove futile; so, in a quiet voice he
began:

'Herr Baron, I appreciate your feelings at the losses you
have suffered during this campaign; but there is a better way
to recoup them than by detaining us here to labour on your
land. I am an officer, and ...'

'You were,' sneered the woman. 'But now you are no better than any other man and, when your ankle is mended, you
shall plough and hoe for us.'

'*Gnädige Frau*.' Roger forced a smile. 'I am not only an
officer. I am an *aide-de-camp*, and the personal friend of the
Emperor. I pray you, send word to him that I am here. I have
no doubt at all that he will ransom me, and the three men
you have taken prisoner with me, for a much greater sum than
you could make from ten years of our labour.'

The Baron gave a harsh laugh. 'Send a message to your
bloody-minded, war-mongering Emperor? And what then?
A squadron of Hussars would arrive here overnight, rape
the women, drive off the cattle, hang me and burn the castle
to the ground. Is it likely? No, my fine cock sparrow, you are
staying here and when your ankle is mended we'll measure
out the amount of turnip soup you are given each night in
proportion to the sweat you have exuded during the day.'

Obviously for the moment there was no more to be said.

While the Baron looked on, Freda of the wobbling breasts redressed their wounds. As she finished with the last of them, one of the Baron's men came up the ladder with a big basin of the vegetable soup. When he had ladled it out into tin pannikins, all four of the prisoners ate of it ravenously despite its indifferent flavour.

Looking on at them, the Baron smacked his man cheerfully on the back and said with a smile, 'This is Kutzie, my overseer. You will obey him as you would myself, or it will be the worse for you.'

Kutzie was a small, thickset man. He had an oafish grin which displayed a gap in his front teeth where two of them had been knocked out in a brawl. In his belt he carried a knout with a long leather thong. Drawing it, he playfully flicked each of the prisoners in turn. Roger felt the sting of the lash on his calf and could hardly suppress a cry. The Sergeant took it stoically. Young Hans Hoffman let out a groan, Corporal Vitu responded with a spate of curses.

The Baron and Baroness laughed heartily; then, accompanied by Kutzie, they descended the ladder and made their way back to the castle.

German was Hoffman's native tongue and, during the campaign, Fournier and Vitu had picked up enough of it to have got the gist of what the Baron had said. When their captors had disappeared, the Sergeant rumbled, 'May all the devils in hell take them. What are we to do, Colonel?'

'Plan a way to escape,' replied Roger grimly.

'It's all very well for Your High and Mightiness to say that,' sneered Vitu. 'Hopelessly lamed by our wounds as we are, how can we?'

'Shut your trap!' bellowed the Sergeant. 'Or when we get back, I'll crime you for disrespect to an officer.'

Temporarily Roger ignored the Corporal's insolence and said, 'We shall have to be patient; wait until our wounds are healed. Meanwhile our best policy will be to give these people no trouble and allow them to believe that we are resigned to our fate. It is getting dark again, and the more sleep we get, the sooner we'll recover. We'll talk things over in the morning.'

With no more said, but mostly gloomy thoughts, they wriggled down into the hay and made themselves as comfortable as they could for the night.

They all woke early. For the first time Roger took careful stock of his companions, and asked them about themselves.

Sergeant Fournier was a typical old soldier, with one ear shot away and a thick, drooping moustache. As a ragged *sans culotte* he had been with Kellermann at Valmay, that most extraordinary turning point in history, where the French, merely by standing fast and firing their cannon, had broken the Austrian attack, caused consternation in their aged commander and led him to abandon the attempt to invade France. Fournier had then served under Lannes in the glorious campaign in Italy in '96, been transferred to the Army of the Rhine, distinguished himself in General Moreau's great victory at Hohenlinden, later been promoted to the Consular—now the Imperial—Guard and had since been present at all Napoleon's battles. He was forty-two, but his lined face made him look much older. He had been wounded seven times and been decorated with the *Légion d'Honneur*. He was a Revolutionary of the old school, yet regarded the Emperor as his God, and his own Commander of the Imperial Guard, young Marshal Bessieres, with admiring awe. Roger knew that in him at least he had one man he could rely on.

Hans Hoffman was a nonentity. He was one of the many thousands of teenagers from the Rhineland whom Napoleon had forced the minor sovereigns, who had perforce become his allies, to conscript and send to aid him in his campaign. Secretly Hoffman loathed the French and, given the opportunity, would have deserted; but lacked the courage.

Corporal Vitu was a very different type. The son of a lawyer who had been prominent in the early days of the Revolution, he was a well-educated man in his late twenties; married and with one son. Even so, he had not been able to escape the call-up by which, now ahead of schedule, the Emperor was compelled to recruit fresh levies to make good the losses of

41

his armies. Vitu had a thin, bitter mouth and a long nose. He was fluent, knowledgeable and aggressive; and Roger soon sized him up as a born trouble-maker.

When they talked over their situation, Vitu said, 'I'll take a chance and attempt to escape when the time is ripe. But I'll not return to the Army.'

'You will,' Fournier declared hotly. 'It's your duty, and I'll see to it that you do it.'

'Duty be damned,' the Corporal declared. 'If it were to defend France, I'd fight again, as you did at Jemappes and Wattignies. But here, in this outlandish place, why the hell should I?'

'Them Prussians would be across the Rhine again if we hadn't given them a licking at Jena; and the Russians with them. Only a fool would rather wait till he had to fight battles in his own country, instead of in the enemy's.'

'Nonsense! Neither of them would have attacked us. What had they to gain by going to war? Nothing! Not since '99 has France been in the least danger. We have been the victims of Bonaparte's crazy ambitions ever since. He's dragged us from our homes to march, starve and fight all over Europe, solely for his own glory, and I've had enough of it.'

Roger knew that the Corporal was expressing the views of a great part of the rank and file of the Army; but, as a senior officer, he could not let such remarks pass, so he said, 'That's quite enough, Corporal. Prussia and Russia are both monarchies. They would impose a King on us again if they could. If we are to retain our liberties, they have got to be defeated.'

'Liberties!' sneered Vitu. 'You must have been asleep for the past ten years, Colonel. The days of "Liberty, Equality and Fraternity" are as far behind us as the Dark Ages. Every law the Convention made has been annulled or altered, and the new Constitution of the Year XII, that Bonaparte gave us soon after he crowned himself in Notre Dame, has turned us into a race of slaves. As for Equality, if the men who won it for us in '93 could see things as they are now, they'd turn in their graves. The people's representative has made himself an Emperor and his brothers Kings. His hangers-on are grand dignitaries, Princes, Dukes and the like. They doll themselves up in gold braid, jewels and feathers, eat off the fat of the land, and get themselves fortunes by looting every country they invade; while we poor devils are paid only a few francs a day and driven to risk our lives so that they can further enrich themselves.'

'You've got something there,' the Sergeant acknowledged. 'Nevertheless, I'm for the Emperor body and soul. He knows what's best for France, and never lets his men down.'

'All the same,' young Hoffman put in, 'I don't think it's fair that he should force men from other countries to fight his battles. Where I come from we had no quarrel with anyone; neither had the Dutch, the Italians and the Bavarians, yet there are thousands of us here who have been marching and fighting for years, when we might have been working happily in our farms or vineyards, with a good wife and bringing up a family.'

'Yes, that's hard luck,' Roger agreed. 'But remember, France has liberated you from the old feudal system by which all but your nobility were virtually chattels of your hereditary Princes. France has paid dearly for that in the loss, for over fifteen years, of a great part of her young manpower. To make good these losses, the Emperor has no alternative but to draw upon his allies.'

'That was fair enough in the old days,' Vitu argued. 'Then we needed every man we could get to fight in Italy and on the Moselle. But that is so no longer. What has the Rhineland or the Netherlands to gain by helping to conquer Poland? And what a campaign it's been! Staggering about in the mud, our uniforms worn to tatters, losing our way in blizzards. It's all very well for you, Colonel, and the rest of the gilded staff. You billet yourselves in the best houses in the towns, keep for yourselves the pick of every convoy of food and wine that comes up from the rear, attend splendid balls, then play chase me round the bed-posts with all the prettiest women. But meantime we have to act like fiends to the wretched peasants to get enough food to stop our bellies from rumbling and sleep in barns so cold that it is not unusual to find that by morning some of our comrades have frozen to death.'

Roger knew all this to be true, but he also knew that his best hope of escape lay in having his three companions willingly accept his leadership; so he tactfully agreed that the Army had recently had a terribly hard time, although he maintained that was no fault of the Emperor's, but due to the exceptionally bleak and sparsely-populated country over which they were fighting.

During the days that followed, the unlovely Baroness Freda came regularly to dress their wounds, and Kutzie twice a day with a big bowl of stew, in which there were pieces of meat that, from its sweetish flavour, Roger guessed to be horse-flesh. As the intense cold would have prevented the dead animals from putrefying, he had little doubt that the peasants for miles round, and the survivors of whichever army had kept the field, were gorging themselves upon it.

On their third day in the loft, it was found that young Hoffman's thigh wound had become gangrenous. No surgeon being available, nothing could be done about it. For some hours he babbled deliriously in German and, on the fourth day, died.

For most of the time while their wounds were healing, they talked of the campaigns in which they had fought, and the Marshals under whom they had served. All of them admired Lannes, Ney and Augereau, who invariably led their troops into battle in full uniform, their chests blazing with stars and decorations.

Lannes was unquestionably the finest assault leader of the Army. He had been wounded a dozen times, yet, given a fortress to capture, waving his sword he was still the first man up a scaling ladder on to the enemy ramparts.

The red-headed Ney was not only the most capable tactician, but had no ambition other than to win glory and, to achieve it, he led every major attack in person.

Augereau, the tall, unscrupulous *gamin* raised from the gutter by the Revolution, and a duellist whom no man any longer dared challenge, was a law unto himself, and led a corps that

44

adored him. He and Lannes were still dyed-in-the-wood Revolutionists. Their language was foul, they took scant pains to cenceal their disapproval of Bonaparte's having made himself as Emperor; yet, as leaders of troops, they were too valuable for him to dispense with.

About the tall Gascon, Bernadotte, who refused to comply with the new fashion and still wore his dark hair long, opinion was divided. He was the only senior General who had refused to support Bonaparte at the time of the *coup d'état*. And, from the days of the Italian campaign they had heartily disliked each other. In the present campaign he had several times been tardy in bringing his corps into action; but he was unquestionably a very able soldier, and he was greatly beloved by both his officers and men for the care he took of them.

For Davoust neither Fournier nor Vitu had a good word to say. He was a cold, hard man, and the harshest disciplinarian in the Army. His one pleasure, when opportunity offered, was waltzing; for the rest of the time he employed himself hanging suspected spies and dealing out brutal punishments to anyone, particularly senior officers, who had in any way contravened his regulations.

For a short period Roger had suffered at Davoust's hands; so had personal cause to dislike him. Even so, he respected and admired this most unpopular of the Marshals. However competent and fanatically brave the others might be, Roger had come to the conclusion that the only advantage they had over the Austrian and Prussian Generals they had defeated was their youth and vigour. Davoust had proved an exception. Not only was he utterly loyal to the Emperor, but he had made an exhaustive study of Napoleon's new methods of waging war, absorbed and applied them.

The Emperor, ever jealous of his subordinates' triumphs, had, in his despatch to Paris, written off Auerstädt as merely a flanking operation during the battle of Jena. But Roger knew the facts. Although completely isolated, Davoust, by brilliant handling of his corps, had defeated one half of the Prussian Army. And he had since further demonstrated his great abilities as an administrator and a soldier.

45

About the flamboyant Murat, Fournier and Vitu agreed. The uniforms that the recently created Grand Duke of Berg designed for himself might be *outré* in the extreme but, smothered in gold braid and with tall plumes waving from his head, he never hesitated to lead his hordes of horsemen against either massed infantry or concentrated batteries of cannon. He had been wounded on several occasions, but never seriously enough not to press home charges that had led many times to Napoleon's victories.

Roger knew him to be an empty-headed, conceited fool, whose only asset was fearless courage; and that politically he would have been a nobody had he not married Napoleon's clever and intensely ambitious sister, Caroline.

Vitu's idol was Masséna. Perhaps the Corporal was a little influenced by the fact that the Marshal also came from the South of France; for Masséna was a native of Nice. But there was no contesting the fact that he was one of the greatest soldiers of the Napoleonic age. In '99, while Bonaparte was still absent in Egypt, Masséna had held the bastion of Switzerland against great odds, defeated France's enemies and saved her from invasion. Then, in 1800, with Soult and Sourier as his lieutenants, besieged in Genoa, with a half-starved garrison, a hostile population, and harassed by a British fleet, he had hung on for many weeks; thus detaining outside the city a strong Austrian army and enabling Napoleon to win the decisive victory of Marengo.

Masséna was still in Italy. The Emperor had made his own stepson, Eugene de Beauharnais, Viceroy. But it was the Marshal who dominated the north, demanding of the cities great sums to maintain his troops, a big percentage of which went into his own pockets. Meanwhile, by charm and lavish presents of stolen jewels, he persuaded a constant succession of lovely Italian women to share his bed.

In central Italy, Marshal Macdonald dominated what had previously been the States of the Church. Down in the South, the foolish King Ferdinand and his forever intriguing Queen Caroline had most rashly welcomed to Naples an Anglo-Russian force of twenty thousand men, thereby breaking the convention by which the French had agreed to withdraw their troops.

Napoleon, himself the most perfidious of men, had screamed with rage at, for once, being treated with his own medicine, and had despatched the able Gouvien St. Cyr to drive the Bourbons from their throne; which he had promptly done, forcing them to take refuge in Sicily.

By that time Bonaparte had decided that to wear a crown himself was not enough to impress the ancient dynasties of the Hapsburgs and the Romanoffs, or even the more recent dynasties of Hohenzollerns and the Anglo-German Guelphs. So he pushed his elder, clever, kindly, unambitious lawyer brother, Joseph, into becoming King of Naples.

How envious the French troops campaigning in frozen Poland, with its ice-covered lakes, poverty-stricken villages and awful blizzards, felt of their comrades quaffing the wine and enjoying the sunshine of Italy can well be imagined; but, wherever the Emperor's determination to become the Master of Europe caused him to go, they had no option but to accompany him. Roger and his two companions might bemoan their fate, but it had been forced upon them. At least they were lucky not to be dead and, as their wounds gradually healed, their hopes rose that they would find a way to outwit and escape from the flaxen-haired giant, Baron Znamensk, who held them prisoner.

The Baroness Freda knew little about surgery, but had enough knowledge to keep their wounds clean and bind up the Sergeant's shattered knee-cap and Roger's ankle in rough splints.

In consequence, after a fortnight they were able to hobble about. The base of Vitu's big toe had healed over, although it still pained him; and all three of them had an awkward limp. But Znamensk thought them sufficiently recovered to be made use of, so they were set to work sawing logs on the ground floor of the barn.

Kutzie stood by and, whenever their efforts flagged, derived obvious pleasure from using his knout to give one or other of them a swift cut across the shoulders. Fournier and

Vitu cursed and reviled him. Roger accepted his chastisement in silence. He was not vindictive by nature; but, as he sweated over the saw, he promised himself that, sooner or later, he would provide Kutzie with a most unpleasant death.

But how to bring that about, and the death of the Baron and his other henchmen was no small problem. Handicapped as they were by their wounds, to get clear away from the castle would be next to impossible as long as Znamensk and his men were able to set off in pursuit.

Night and day Roger wrestled with the question until he came to the conclusion that there was no hope at all of himself and his two lame companions overcoming the half-dozen Germans; but, that, if the Baron could be trapped, there was a fair chance that the others, being no more than brainless oafs, might be cozened or bullied into submission.

At last, early in March, an idea for setting a trap came to him. The saws they used for cutting the trunks of medium-sized pine and larch trees into logs could, in the hands of a fully able man, have become dangerous weapons; but not when wielded by partially-recovered invalids with dragging feet so, when work was over for the day, the saws were hung up on pegs in the wall on the ground floor of the barn.

Crippled as they were, they could not have got far without being overtaken, so no guard was placed over them at night; there was, therefore, nothing to prevent them from fetching the saws up to their loft. Roger's plan was that they should cut through a section of the floor of the loft, so that it formed a trap door secured in such a way that, when a strong catch was released, it would open downwards.

With such limited tools, the job was far from easy. Moreover, to prevent the discovery of this *oubliette*, the cuts had to be dirtied over both above and below, and the trigger arrangement which would release the trap, together with a stout cord running from it beneath the floor, had to be skilfully camouflaged.

It took them several hours during each of three nights to complete the task, and when they had, Roger was far from confident that his plan would work. He was counting on the

48

fact that the Baron took a particular delight in gloating over his captives and making insulting remarks about their country. Every few days, when they were having their midday or evening meal, Znamensk would come up the ladder to the loft and stand there for ten minutes or so, taunting them with the fact that they would never see their homes again, and sniggering while he made such sneers as that, French women being notoriously a race of whores, they could be certain those dear to them would by now be having a high old time with a succession of lovers.

The trap had been cut in the place where the Baron usually stood while, grinning from ear to ear, and occasionally nodding his great mop of straight, flaxen hair, he delivered these provocative monologues. But the question was, what would happen when Roger pulled the cord that would cause the square of floor to drop?

Owing to the situation of the beams, they had been able to make it only two foot six wide and Znamensk was a big as well as a tall man. As he had no paunch, the odds were that he would not jam in the hole; but how seriously would he be injured by his fall on to the hard floor of the barn? Although it was a twelve-foot drop, it was too much to hope that he would break his neck, as it seemed certain that he would hit the floor feet first. But he might break a leg or, with luck, be temporarily sufficiently disabled for his captives, hurrying down from the loft, to get the better of him before his shouts brought help.

The day after they had completed the trap, the prisoners waited with almost unbearable suspense for Znamensk to come up and taunt them. But they were disappointed. Again the following day he did not appear while they were eating their midday stew, and they began to fear that he must have tired of baiting them. At last evening came and, with beating hearts, they heard his heavy tread coming up the ladder. Yet, even then, it seemed that some spirit malevolent to them must have warned him of his danger. Instead of taking his usual stance, feet spread wide and hands on hips, alternately grinning and scowling at them, he paced restlessly up and down, muttering

49

only a few words now and then. It was evident that he had something on his mind and, after a few minutes, he disclosed it.

'Listen, you French dogs,' he snarled in his guttural German. 'If you hear horsemen riding up to the castle and the sound of many voices, don't imagine they are those of your own people and start shouting to be rescued. There are Cossacks in the neighbourhood, and that's who they will be. If they found you here, they'd take you off to a prison camp. But I'm not having that. You're going to work for me. Work till you drop. So I'm sending Kutzie along with a shot-gun. He'll spend the night up here. If the Cossacks do chance to turn up, the first one of you to holler will get a stomach full of lead.'

As he ceased speaking, he came to a halt squarely on the trap. Roger jerked hard on the end of the hidden cord he was holding, and the square of flooring went down with a swish.

The Baron's mouth opened wide, his eyes bulged and his mass of light, fair hair seemed to lift from his scalp as he shot downwards. But, by throwing wide his arms, he just succeeded in saving himself from disappearing through the hole.

The three prisoners had taken the precaution of secretly arming themselves with short lengths of roughly cut branches that would serve as clubs. Knowing that it was now or never, they simultaneously threw themselves upon Znamensk. The Sergeant got in the first blow, Roger the second. Either would have stunned most men, but the Teuton's skull seemed to be made of iron, and was protected by his thick thatch of hair. He only let out a yell, blinked and then, to save himself from a third blow aimed at him by Vitu, he abruptly ceased supporting himself by his elbows on the floorboards, and dropped from sight.

'After him!' shouted Roger and, followed by the others, he shinned down the ladder.

They found the Baron half kneeling on the ground. He was striving to get up, but had evidently broken a leg. Bellowing with rage and pain, his pale blue eyes glaring hatred, he pulled a big hunting knife from the belt of his kaftan. Clearly he was far from finished and any of them who went near enough to knock him out could not escape an upward thrust from the knife which would inflict a very ugly wound.

It was Corporal Vitu who produced the answer. Grabbing up a twelve-foot larch sapling, he used it as a spear and rushed upon the crouching Znamensk. The jagged point of the larch caught him in the throat. Choking, the blood gushing from his neck, he went over backwards. Fournier lurched in and bashed again and again with his club at their victim's skull, until he lay still.

At a limping run, Roger reached the door of the barn and peered cautiously out, fearful that the Baron's shouts would bring Kutzie or one of the other men on the scene. But no one was in sight.

'What now, Colonel?' gasped the Sergeant, still panting from his exertions.

'When Znamensk fails to return to the castle, someone will come to find out what has delayed him,' Roger replied quickly. 'Whoever it is, we ambush him and knock him out. The odds are it will be either Kutzie or the woman. By now the others will have settled down to their supper, then they'll go to sleep. With luck they won't learn till morning what has been going on. But Kutzie will come here for certain. He has been ordered by the Baron to spend the night here, keeping us in order with a gun.'

Semi-darkness had fallen and, listening tensely, they stood veiled by the heavy shadows, two on one side of the barn door and one on the other. The time of waiting seemed interminable, and all of them knew that there was still a big chance that their desperate gamble would not come off. Kutzie might bring one or two of the other men with him for companionship, and they could not hope to take more than one man completely by surprise. All the Baron's men carried knives and would not hesitate to use them. Three lame men armed only with cudgels stood little chance of winning out in a brawl of that kind. And, if they were overcome, they knew the price they would have to pay. For having killed her husband, it was certain that the lumpy Baroness would have them put to death, and the odds were that it would be a very painful one.

It seemed to them a good hour, but not more than fifteen minutes could have elapsed, when they caught the sound of approaching footsteps and whistling. They then knew for certain that it was Kutzie who was coming towards the barn, because his missing teeth gave his whistling a peculiar note. But was he alone? Everything depended on that. And they dared not peer out, for fear that he would glimpse whoever did, and realise that they had come down from the loft, intending to waylay him.

A beam of light flickered over the earth outside the barn. Next moment, all unsuspecting, Kutzie entered. Under his right arm he carried a shot-gun, from his left hand dangled a lantern. He had no chance even to cry out. The Sergeant's cudgel descended on his head from one side and the Corporal's from the other. Although he was wearing a fur cap, the blows felled him. His knees buckled, he dropped his gun and the lantern and fell to the earth, out cold.

'What'll we do with the swine?' asked the Sergeant. 'I've rarely come across so great a bastard. It would be a sin just to kill him where he lies. I've a dozen weals still smarting from that knout of his. I vote we let him come to, then thrash him to death.'

'I'm with you,' agreed Vitu. 'But, better still, let's put his feet on the red-hot stones of the fire until he passes out, then pitch him in and let him burn to death.'

'No,' Roger answered sharply. 'If we did either, his cries would bring his comrades running. Anyhow, we have no time to waste. Though I agree that the brute deserves to die.'

'I have it!' Vitu exclaimed. 'We'll gag him, strip him, tie his ankles and his hands behind his back, then throw him to the pigs.'

Fournier laughed. 'That's a grand idea. Pigs like human flesh. I know of a child who fell into a sty and they made a meal off the poor brat before anyone realised that he was missing.' Without more ado, the two N.C.O.s began to tear the unconscious Kutzie's garments off him.

Roger was in half a mind to intervene; but he knew that

his two companions would resent any mercy being shown to this Prussian brute who had delighted in flogging all three of them, and he decided that being bitten by pigs until one died from loss of blood would be a less painful death than being left to roast slowly; so he let the N.C.O.s have their way.

Kutzie, naked, gagged and unable even to murmur, was carried out from the barn and pitched on to a huddle of grunting pigs. It was one of the most callous things that Roger had ever seen done; but he knew that his own prospects of survival lay in the Sergeant's and Corporal's willing acceptance of his orders, and that, had he even been the Angel Gabriel, he could not have prevented them from making certain that the brutal Kutzie endured a prolonged and horrible death. As it was, with happy laughter, they showed their delight in this method of paying off old scores, and were obviously prepared to accept Roger's future orders without argument.

Having disposed of the Baron and Kutzie, they again spent a few minutes listening tensely. On the opposite side of the courtyard from their barn, but somewhat nearer the castle, there stood a building in which they knew that the serfs had their quarters. From it there now came faintly the sounds of sad, but melodious singing.

With a nod of satisfaction, Roger led the way to another barn, where he knew the horses to be stabled. In it there were seven animals. Selecting three, he had them given a good feed of oats then, with their muzzles bound to prevent them from neighing, he had them harnessed to a *troika* which had been dragged from a nearby coach house.

He had no idea where the French army was but, taking the stars for a guide, he intended to head south-west, feeling confident that, if they could avoid running into enemy patrols, by moving in that direction they would, sooner or later, come upon their compatriots.

Having wrenched off the bells that would have jingled from the inverted U-shaped arch over the neck of the central horse of the *troika*, they piled into the carriage. Roger took the reins and they set off.

A three-quarter moon had come up and its light reflected

from the snow made the scene almost as bright as day. As the *troika* emerged at a fast trot from the trees surrounding the castle, in the far distance Roger saw a black patch moving rapidly across the white, frozen waste. Almost immediately he realised that it was a body of horsemen and they were coming towards him. With sudden consternation, it flashed upon him that they must be the Cossacks whom the Baron had feared might pay the castle a visit. At the same moment, Fournier cried:

'Them's Cossacks! You can tell by their little horses.'

Hauling hard on the near rein, Roger nearly turned the *troika* over, in his frantic haste to slew it round and make off in another direction before they came face to face with the Russians. He could only hope that, against the background of the dark trees, the *trioka* would not have been noticed. Urging his three horses into a gallop, he took a course parallel to the edge of the wood.

For a few moments all seemed well. Then, just behind him, Vitu cried, '*Mort Dieu!* They've seen us. They've changed direction too.'

Roger threw a quick glance over his shoulder. From a trot, the Cossacks had spurred their mounts into a canter. There were about twenty of them and a tall officer some ten paces in front of the others was calling on the *troika* to halt.

For a moment Roger thought of pulling up and running off into the wood; but, lame as he and his companions were, they would be overtaken in no time—that is, if the Russians bothered to come after them. If they did not, without food or shelter and unable to walk either fast or for any great distance, the fugitives would freeze to death.

Realising that there was no escape, Roger lay back on the reins and brought his team to a standstill. With fury in his heart he watched, as the Cossacks, crouching low over their little steeds and giving vent to wild cries of elation, came charging up to the *troika*. With superb horsemanship they brought their shaggy, steaming ponies to an instant halt.

Leaning forward in his saddle, the officer asked Roger in

Russian, 'Who are you? Why did you attempt to avoid us? Where are you off to?'

Roger's Russian was good enough for him to reply. 'To Vilna, may it please you, Sir.'

Stained and bedraggled as the uniforms were that he and his companions were wearing, they were still easily recognisable as French.

Slapping his thigh, the officer gave a hearty laugh. 'What? On the way to your enemy's headquarters? Is it likely that I'd believe that? You are Frenchmen, and my prisoners.'

4

A Desperate Gamble

It was futile to argue. Even if Roger could have passed himself off as a Lett or Ukranian who had taken a French uniform from a corpse, he could not possibly explain away his
companions.

As he gave a resigned shrug, the officer said, 'We were
making for Baron Znamensk's castle, since it seemed as good
a place as any in this neighbourhood to pass the night. Turn
your *troika* and accompany us.'

Roger did as he was bade; but, as the little cavalcade headed
for the entrance to the clearing he was suddenly struck by a
thought that, during the emergency of the past ten minutes,
had not crossed his mind. It so appalled him that for a moment the blood drained from his face.

To have been cheated of his hopes of freedom at the
eleventh hour and taken prisoner by the Russians was ill fortune enough. But a return to the castle must inevitably lead
to the discovery of the Baron's body, and nobody would
have any doubts about who had murdered him. Freda of the
huge bottom and breasts would be screaming for vengeance
and Roger could see no reason whatever why the tall Cossack
officer should not grant it to her by having Fournier, Vitu
and himself promptly shot.

Ten minutes later, when they arrived within sight of the
castle, Roger saw that his worst fears looked like being realised. Several of the barred ground floor windows of the squat
ugly building were lit up and men with lanterns were moving
about near the big barn.

As the cavalcade came to a halt in front of it Freda, her
huge breasts wobbling and her long, fair hair streaming be-

hind her, came running up to the Cossack officer, pouring out a spate of German. Following her came two men, bearing a rough stretcher, upon which reposed the dead body of the Baron. Pointing at it, then at Roger and his companions, she denounced them as her husband's murderers and demanded that they should be handed over to her for treatment suited to the heinous crime they had committed.

The greater part of this was lost upon the Russian, because he could not understand German; but the dead body and Freda's tirade against the three Frenchmen whom he had caught escaping left him in no doubt as to what had happened.

In this situation, where their guilt was so damningly obvious, Roger had only one slender advantage. At least he could speak fairly fluent Russian, and so could communicate freely with the arbiter of their fate. When the Baroness had at last to pause for breath, he said calmly to the officer:

'Of course we killed this pig of a Prussian. And I make no pleas that we did so in self-defence. We deliberately trapped and slew him. Had you been in our situation, you would have done the same. Never have I met a monster who better deserved to die.'

The Russian gave him a puzzled look. 'So you admit to this murder? I suppose you realise that, unless you can produce some quite extraordinary justification for your deed, I shall have you hanged?'

'Officers,' Roger declared quietly, 'are not hanged, but shot.'

'True,' nodded the other. 'And, although your epaulettes and gold braid appear to have been torn from your uniform, by your manner and speech I should have realised that you are not a common soldier. But rank does not convey licence to murder. I am the Hetman Sergius Dutoff. Who are you?'

Roger made a low bow to hide the sudden glint of hope that had sparked in his eye on learning that he had to deal, not with an ordinary, country-bred Lieutenant of Cossacks, but a Hetman—an aristocrat with whom he might have acquaintances in common. For that might just sway the balance in saving him from a firing squad. As he lifted his head, he said proudly, 'I am *Colonel le Chevalier de Breuc*, a Commander of the Legion of Honour, and an *aide-de-camp* to the Emperor Napoleon.'

'Indeed!' the Hetman exclaimed. 'Then you are a prisoner of considerable importance. Even so, this matter of Baron Znamensk's murder cannot be ignored.'

'I did not expect it to be.' Roger shrugged. 'With your permission I suggest that we go into the castle and there discuss it over a bottle of wine.'

'By St. Nicholas!' the Russian laughed. 'You are a cool customer. But your idea is sound. I could do with something to warm me up.'

The Baroness and her serfs had not understood one word of this conversation. Again she began to scream at Roger and pointed to her husband's dead body. Roger swung upon her and said sharply, 'Be silent, woman! This Russian lord demands food and wine for himself and his men. Afterwards he intends to investigate the way in which your husband met his death. And that will probably result in having me and my companions shot.'

Mollified by this, the Baroness led the way into the castle, and gave the requisite orders to her servants. Fournier and Vitu, both looking extremely worried, were detained by the Cossacks in the lofty, sparsely-furnished central hall that had for decoration on its tall walls, only a few moth-eaten stag, boar and lynx heads. The Hetman and Roger followed the Baroness into a dining room that led off it. The furniture was hideous pitchpine and the place stank of past meals, mingled with the urine of dogs.

An uncouth servitor brought a flagon of Franconian Steinwein. Then, with the Baroness as an onlooker, the two men settled down to talk. The Russian made it clear that he intended to mete out summary justice should Roger fail to convince him that he had had good grounds for taking the law into his own hands. Roger had never been more acutely aware that his life hung on his ready wits and tongue; and, that should he fail to convince the Hetman that he had executed rather than murdered Znamensk, he, Fournier and Vitu would be dead before morning.

To begin with, Roger deliberately delayed the actual in-quiry for as long as he could, by asking Dutoff when he had last seen Prince Peter Ivanovitch Bagration, the German-born Commander-in-Chief of the Russian Army. Dutoff knew the General well; so, it emerged to his surprise, did Roger. He then enquired after other friends he had made during his last stay in St. Petersburg: Count Alexander Vorontzoff, the brother of the Russian Ambassador in London; Captain Musiavoff of the Semenourki Regiment of the Imperial Guard; the ex-Prime Minister Count Pahlen, in whose country house he had stayed for a month; and even the Czar Alexander himself, to whom he had been presented.

Dutoff could not fail to be impressed by learning that this haggard, down-at-heel Frenchman was *persona grata* with so many people of the first importance in his own country; and Roger then went on to describe the awful treatment that he and his companions had received at Znamensk's hands. But the Baroness, who had been sullenly watching with in-creasing anger as she saw the sympathy with which the Het-man was listening to Roger, suddenly broke in on their conversation with a spate of vitriolic German. Since she could not make herself understood in words, she pointed at Roger and significantly drew her finger across her throat.

The Russian nodded at her reassuringly, brushed up his fine moustache and said, 'Colonel, all you have been saying leaves me in no doubt that you have lived in St. Petersburg, enjoyed the friendship of many powerful nobles there, that you are both a member of the aristocracy and a very gallant soldier. Moreover, you have my deepest sympathy for the brutal ill usage to which you have been subjected. But the fact remains that only a few hours ago you and your fellow prison-ers trapped the owner of this castle and inflicted on him a most painful death. For such a crime, much as I may regret it personally, I see no alternative but to have you and the other two shot.'

Roger sighed and spread out his hands in a typically French gesture. 'Should you decide that to be your duty, I'll not com-plain. But I pray you, consider the circumstances. Firstly, are you prepared to avow that as a private individual the Baron had any legal right to hold me, Sergeant Fournier and Corporal Vitu prisoner?'

Dutoff shook his head. 'No, none whatever. He should have turned the three of you over to the nearest Prussian or Russian military headquarters.'

'Good. And you will also agree that we had the right to escape if we could?'

'Every prisoner of war who has not given his parole has that right; but not to commit murder as a means of regaining his freedom.'

'But the circumstances were exceptional,' Roger argued. 'This monster and his men picked us up on the battlefield the night following that ghastly conflict at Eylau. He did not go there as a patriotic Prussian, seeking to secure as many French prisoners as he could for his country before they were found and rescued by their own countrymen. He went to collect men whose wounds would not incapacitate them permanently, with the intention of detaining them here all their lives as serfs to work on his land.'

Frowning, the Hetman sat back, took another swig of wine, then said angrily, 'Such conduct is inexcusable. Clearly the Baron disgraced his order as a noble. But these Teutonic Knights are far more barbarous then we Russians are said to be.'

For a moment he was silent, then he added, 'All the same, Colonel, murder is murder. Your attempt to escape was fully justified; but not the snaring and killing of this man in cold blood. Whatever cause you had to hate and fear him, nothing can excuse your having taken his life. Although I can understand little of what the Baroness here says in her outbursts, it is obvious that she is demanding justice, and it is my duty to see that she receives it. Would you prefer to be granted a respite until dawn or have me order my Sergeant to get this unpleasant business over now?'

Roger had played his best cards; his social standing with highly-placed friends in St. Petersburg, his having been made a prisoner unlawfully, his descriptions of the floggings to which he had been subjected, as fair reasons for using violence against a man who had decreed life-long slavery for him. But all to no avail.

Now, he had one card only left up his sleeve and it was a most dangerous one. But, having been condemned to death, he felt that no worse could befall should he play it and it failed. Their glasses of wine being empty, he turned to the glowering Baroness and said, in German. 'The Russian intends to have me shot, but first I have something to say to him, so tell your man to open another bottle of wine.'

Staggered by his impertinence and apparent indifference to his fate, she spoke to her man, who uncorked a second flagon and refilled their glasses. Turning to the Hetman, Roger said:

'Before you have me shot, I would like you to know what led up to our killing the Baron. He had a bailiff named Kutzie —a rough diamond but not a bad fellow. Although they searched us after they picked us up on the battlefield, I had some fifty Napoleons in gold in my money belt, and I managed to hide it from them. When our wounds were sufficiently healed, we began to consider plans for an escape. As the three of us were lame, we knew that we could not get far without being overtaken, unless we had horses. With my gold I succeeded in bribing Kutzie to come to us after dark this evening, and help us to get away in the *troika*.'

For a moment Roger paused, then he went on. 'Somehow the Baron found out. You would hardly credit what he did to the unfortunate Kutzie. But come with me and I'll show you.'

Standing up, Roger led the way out. His heart was now beating violently, because he had not the least idea what had happened to Kutzie since he had been thrown naked into the pigsty; so he was taking a most desperate gamble.

Kutzie might have come to, broken free of his bonds and escaped, to be lurking somewhere in the shadows awaiting a chance to be avenged on the Frenchmen who had condemned him to such a ghastly death. Should the pigs have ignored him, he would still be there, alive and kicking; and, as soon as the gag was removed he would, somehow, succeed in conveying to the Hetman the truth about what had happened.

Should either prove the case, Roger had little doubt that he and his two fellow prisoners would shortly be blindfolded, put up against a brick wall and executed by a firing squad.

Despite the intense cold, as he led the way across the forecourt sweat broke out on his forehead. Although Dutoff had obviously taken a liking to him personally, he was clearly an officer who put duty before other considerations. With a certainty upon which he would have wagered every penny he possessed, Roger accepted it that, if Kutzie were still alive, he, Fournier and Vitu were as good as dead.

From the sty there came a grunting, for which Roger thanked all his gods. That indicated at least that the pigs were awake, so Kutzie was unlikely to be lying among them unmolested. But was he still alive, and capable of blurting out the truth about how he came to be there? That was the all-important question.

Raising a lantern that he had brought from the house, Roger leaned in awful anxiety over the low wall of the sty. To his immense relief, he saw that Kutzie was far past uttering any sound. He was already almost unrecognisable: his body torn and bleeding as the swine, grunting round him, gorged themselves upon his flesh.

The Baroness, who had accompanied them, gave a scream, covered her eyes with her hands for a moment; then, lowering them, glared at Roger and cried, 'So this is more of your abominable night's work. You reveal it only because you are already condemned and evidently take pride in your ruthlessness.'

He shook his head, and replied in German, '*Nein, Gnädige Frau Baronin*. This is your husband's doing. I bribed Kutzie to help us to escape, but the Baron found out, and this is the way he chose to punish his unfortunate servant.'

'It is a lie!' she screamed. 'Kutzie would never have betrayed his master.'

In sick disgust at the horrible sight, Dutoff had turned away. Ignoring the Baroness, Roger said to him, 'Well, Hetman, what do you say now? Were we not justified in putting an end to that monster, after he had jeered at us about having ruined our plan to escape and told us of the awful vengeance he had taken on his wretched henchman?'

The Russian nodded. 'You have made your case, Colonel. It would not have been in human nature, given the chance, to have refrained from according the brute his just deserts. The three of you will, of course, remain my prisoners; but I will write a report in which I'll say that, knowing we were likely to come here and deprive him of you, his hatred of the French was such that he decided to kill you; but you killed him in self-defence.'

Overwhelmingly relieved, Roger expressed his thanks. Sensing that she was to be deprived of her revenge, the Baroness again broke into violent denunciation; but Roger's paramount advantage was that she could not understand what he said to Dutoff and the Russian could not understand what he said to her. So he silenced her by telling her that the Hetman intended to send his prisoners next day to headquarters, where they would be tried by a military tribunal, and had little hope of escaping a death sentence.

Then, changing over to Russian, he told Dutoff what he had said, and added, 'All the same, she is so filled with venom that, should I and the others sleep tonight in the castle, I think she is quite capable of endeavouring to make certain of our deaths by getting her people together and attempting to murder us. So, if you are agreeable, I'd prefer that we occupied our old quarters in the loft of the barn, and you set a guard on us; although, of course, I'll give you our parole that we will not try to escape.'

To this the Hetman agreed; so, twenty minutes later, Roger was rejoined by Sergeant Fournier and Corporal Vitu. For the past hour or more they had believed that there was no chance of their escaping the worst, and they could have hardly been less scared had they shared with Roger the awful gamble he had taken in leading Dutoff out to the pigsty. When he told them how he had fathered Kutzie's death on to the Baron and they had no more to fear than being taken to a prisoner-of-war camp, the old Sergeant impulsively embraced Roger and kissed him on both cheeks; while Corporal Vitu gave way to tears of relief.

The following morning, Dutoff commandeered the best horse in the stable in order that Roger could ride with him. The Baroness was furious, but he shrugged aside her protests and insisted on her accepting a scrawled requisition order, on which he had included the *troika* for the other two prisoners to ride in.

On leaving the castle, the *sotnia* of Cossacks did not head south, in the direction from which they had come, but took a track through the forest that led north. After they had proceeded for a mile or so, the forest ended and they entered the sprawling township of Znamensk, from which the Baron had taken his inherited title. It was a poor place, consisting of not more than a hundred one-storey wooden houses. The few people they saw there looked half-starved, and were clad in tattered furs or sheepskins. From the doorways of their dark hovels, with sullen, resentful stares they watched the Cossacks pass through the main street that led down to the river Pregel. For the greater part of the year a large, wooden ferry attached to a stout rope was used to cross it; but the river was still frozen so hard that there was no danger of the ice cracking under the weight of a body of mounted men.

On the far side of the river they turned east along a road that followed its course and led, as Dutoff told Roger, to Insterburg. As the two officers rode along at the head of the small cavalcade, they conversed in the most friendly fashion, exchanging accounts of the engagements in which they had fought, and gossip about mutual acquaintances in St. Petersburg.

Roger had last been there in 1801, but he had also spent some while in the Russian capital in the summer of 1788, when Catherine the Great was still on the throne. Dutoff, being several years younger than Roger, had never known that bold, beautiful, cultured, licentious woman, and was fascinated to hear Roger's description of the marvellous fêtes, luxury, licence and gaiety of her Court; for he had known only the grim, gloomy one of her son, the mad Czar Paul I, and the sedate, respectable one of his present sovereign, Alexander I.

Alternately trotting and walking their horses it took them a little over three hours to cover the twenty-odd miles between Znamensk and the much larger town of Insterburg, and they arrived a little before midday.

Halting at the prisoner-of-war camp for 'other ranks', that consisted of a group of hutments on the edge of the town, Dutoff handed over Fournier and Vitu to the officer on duty. Before parting with his companions in misfortune, Roger took down the names and addresses of their nearest relatives and promised that if he could find means to do so he would send the news that they were still alive, after sustaining only minor injuries.

When he rejoined Dutoff, the Hetman said, 'Colonel, to my great regret, I cannot avoid taking you to the mansion in which officer prisoners of war are confined. But I see no reason why I should do so as yet. At least I can first offer you luncheon in my Mess.'

'You are most kind,' Roger replied, 'and I accept with pleasure.'

They then rode on to one of the better houses in the town, handed their horses over to orderlies and went in through a spacious hall to a lobby in which Roger was at least able to have a wash and attempt to comb out his tangled hair. Dutoff then took him along to a room in which a score or so of Cossack officers were drinking and chatting.

Roger's ablutions had done little to improve his appearance. On the morning of Eylau he had been wearing a brilliant uniform, but Znamensk had ripped from it all the gold lace and his A.D.C.'s scarf. One of his field boots had been cut off, so that his broken ankle could be bandaged up, and in its place he had been given only a felt sabot. The Baron had also robbed him of his fur cloak, and that morning nothing better could be found for him to travel in than a tattered bearskin. Working and sleeping for five weeks in his coat and breeches had further added to their dirty and dilapidated state and, having had no opportunity or means to shave since the battle, he now sported an inch-long beard.

It was little wonder that the officers could not hide their surprise at Dutoff's having brought such a bedraggled and unsightly guest into their Mess. But no sooner had the Hetman introduced him and given a brief version of his misfortunes than they became most friendly.

His gift for readily getting on well with people swiftly enabled Roger to gain the sympathy of his hosts and acceptance of him as an unusual personality. The fact that he was an *aide-de-camp* of the fabulous Corsican brigand who had made Catherine, and of another night when he and the giant Grand to make them regard him with awe. Most of these Cossack officers came from the distant Steppes and had never visited St. Petersburg. Over luncheon Roger enthralled them with an account of how, when he was scarcely out of his teens,[1] he had one night been bidden to dine *tête-à-tête* with the great Catherine, and of another night when he and the giant Grand Admiral, Alexis Orloff, one of Catherine's many lovers, had got drunk together.

After Eylau, both armies were so weakened that there was no prospect of either taking the offensive for some time; so the Cossacks were acting only as a cavalry screen and made occasional forays to secure supplies. In consequence, they sat over lunch until past five o'clock, and the party broke up only as dusk was approaching.

Roger had been generously plied with a variety of liquors but, having in mind one very important matter that he hoped to arrange before passing out of Dutoff's custody, he had managed to keep sober. As they left the table, he drew the Russian aside, and said:

'Hetman, I have a request to make. You will agree, I am sure, that no soldier wishes to remain a prisoner of war for longer than he is compelled to. I am in the happy position of having known the Emperor Napoleon ever since he won his first laurels as a down-at-heels Artillery officer at the siege of Toulon. If he is informed that I am not dead, but a pris-

[1] *Shadow of Tyburn Tree*

66

oner, I am confident that he will arrange for my exchange with an officer of equivalent rank. Will you be good enough to inform General Bagration that I am here at Insterburg, and request him to send that information to French headquarters under the next flag of truce?'

'Indeed I will,' Dutoff replied, 'and most willingly. I sincerely hope that an exchange for you will be arranged.'

Going out into the courtyard, he called for their horses. Having mounted, they rode three-quarters of a mile to a mansion on the far side of the town. It was surrounded by a garden and orchard enclosed by a wall, outside which sentries were lazily patrolling. At the main gate there was a lodge which had been converted into a reception office. There Dutoff handed over his prisoner, full particulars of whom were taken down; then they bade one another a friendly farewell.

Greatly curious to see what his new accommodation would be like, Roger, escorted by a Lieutenant who spoke a little French, crossed the garden and entered the big house. In the inner hall a dozen depressed-looking officers were either drowsing on old sofas, talking without animation or playing cards. They favoured Roger with only an idle glance as the Lieutenant took him straight upstairs and threw open the door of a bedroom furnished with only the bare necessities. Then he said:

'Monsieur, you are fortunate, as at the moment we have not many officer prisoners. In consequence, as you are a Colonel, you have been allotted a room to yourself. One of the soldier-servants will bring you things for your toilette and perhaps be able to find you some better clothes. The evening meal will be served in about an hour. When you feel like it come downstairs and make yourself known to the others.'

As Roger had no luggage to unpack, he sat down on the edge of the bed and, thinking things over, decided that, had the room not been so cold, it seemed that he would not have much to complain about.

Some ten minutes later, the soldier-servant arrived, bringing with him soap, a razor and a very small towel. Having deposited them on a wooden table, he conveyed by signs that the wash-room was at the end of the corridor.

To his surprise Roger thanked him in Russian and raised the question of his securing for him some extra blankets and a pair of comfortable boots.

The man responded pleasantly. He thought he could find a bearskin rug to go on the bed and tomorrow would go to the hospital. Now and then French officers who had been badly wounded when captured, died there, then their clothes were at the disposal of others who might need them.

Alone once more, Roger regarded himself in a small mirror that, with the exception of a crucifix, was the only thing on the bare walls. He was shocked by his reflection. Due to malnutrition his cheeks had fallen in; his hair, despite the combing he had given it before lunch, looked like a bird's nest, and the lower part of his face was covered with an inch-long stubble of brown hair.

Picking up the shaving things, he was about to go to the wash-room and remove his beard. But, on second thoughts, he decided against it. There had been times when he had worn a beard and, given certain circumstances, to have one now might stand him in good stead. At such times he had posed under a second alias that he used on a few occasions.

He happened to have, on his mother's side, a cousin of nearly the same age as himself, who later became the Earl of Kildonan. His mother's people had been Jacobites and had been furious when she ran away to marry his father, the Admiral, a staunch supporter of the Hanoverian line. They had disowned her and, after Prince Charles Edward's abortive attempt to regain the throne for his father in 1745, they had gone into exile, attending the Court of the Stuart Pretender in Rome. In consequence, Roger's cousin being so remote from France and England, Roger had now and then used his identity.

Having done his best to tidy his hair, he went downstairs. Again the depressed-looking scattering of officers in the big, echoing hall took scant notice of him, apart from a few of them nodding a greeting; as they imagined him to be of no particular interest and just another unfortunate condemned to share their dreary existence. But one young man stood up, smiled and said:

'Monsieur, there are few grounds for welcoming you here, but at least it is pleasant to see a new face in our unhappy company. I am Captain Pierre d'Esperbes of the Hussars of Conflans, at your service.'

Roger returned his smile. 'Indeed, then you must be a brave fellow, since you hold that rank under such a dashing commander as Brigadier Gerard. I am happy to make your acquaintance. My name is Breuc, and I have the honour to be a member of His Imperial Majesty's personal staff.'

There was a sudden tension perceptible among the other officers. Those who were napping sat up. The four at the card table ceased playing and one of them exclaimed, 'Not *"le brave Breuc"*, the hero of a hundred exploits and the man who saved the Emperor from assassination when we were in Venice?'

'I am called that, although quite unworthy of the soubriquet,' Roger replied modestly. 'I am sure that I have done nothing that any of you might not have done had you been in my place at the time.'

They all came to their feet and crowded round him, plying him with questions. 'How long have you been a prisoner?' 'How did you come to be captured?' 'Your limp implies that you were wounded in the leg; have you just come from the hospital?' 'Have you any news of how the campaign is going?' 'How comes it that your uniform has been so stripped of all signs of your rank so that we took you for a junior officer of little account?'

For the next twenty minutes, Roger gave his new companions an account of what had befallen him. Then they were summoned to their evening meal. In a long, dimly-lit room they partook of it. The food was plentiful, but uninteresting. There was no wine which, being a life-long accompaniment of every meal, these Frenchmen bitterly resented; but each of them was provided with a good ration of vodka.

During the meal and after, when they had adjourned to

the hall, Roger was plied with questions about the Emperor. In the now huge French Army, very few junior officers had ever been spoken to by him or met any member of the Bonaparte family; and they were eager to hear what the great man and his horde of relatives were really like.

Roger spoke with great admiration of his master as an administrator as well as a general. Then when he came to the family, he was careful that his criticisms should not sound too malicious.

Napoleon's mother, Letizia, he said, was a woman of immense determination, but narrow mind. Left a widow, she had overcome every sort of difficulty to bring her large family up to be honest and God-fearing. A typical Corsican, she had once remarked that, if faced with a vendetta, she could count on two hundred kinsmen to take up their weapons on her behalf. Her native language was an Italian patois, and she could still talk French only with difficulty. She had flatly refused to play any part in Napoleon's self-aggrandisement so, perforce, he had had to content himself with styling her simply as 'Madame Mère'. When her other children were in trouble, she always took the side of the weakest. She strongly disapproved of the splendour with which Napoleon, as Emperor, now surrounded himself; could not be convinced that his incredible rise to power would be lasting and hoarded the greater part of the huge income he insisted on giving her, so that, in the event of disaster overwhelming him and the Kings, Princes and Princesses into which he had made her other children, she would have enough money to support them all. She was religious, austere and, on occasion, could even browbeat her greatest son into giving way to her wishes.

The only person from whom Madame Mère would take advice was her half-brother, Joseph Fesch, a little abbé who, during Napoleon's first glorious campaign in Italy, had temporarily abandoned the Church to become an army contractor, and made a small fortune out of selling his 'nephew' equipment of dubious quality. He had then returned to his religious duties and, when Napoleon had made his Concordat with the Pope, included in the deal had been the elevation of

'Uncle' Fesch to Cardinal Archbishop of Lyons. Still able and avaricious where money was concerned, he now owned vast properties and was extremely rich.

Joseph, the eldest of Letizia's sons, had been trained as a lawyer, and was a very able man. Fat, good-natured and honest, he gave Napoleon less trouble than his younger brothers. But he was no diplomat, a worse soldier and a poor administrator. The Emperor had, a few months earlier, actually had to push him into becoming King of Naples, as he would have much preferred a quiet life without responsibilities.

Lucien, a tall, awkward fellow with gangling limbs, was the *enfant terrible* of the family. From his teens, he had been a red-hot Revolutionary; even changing his name to Brutus. A Deputy of the Convention, chance had elevated him to be its President during the month of the *coup d'état* and he had made a major contribution to Napoleon's becoming First Consul. But he had done everything possible to obstruct his brother's ambitious measures to make himself a dictator. Although he declared himself to be a true representative of the people, he had not scrupled, as Minister of the Interior, to divert millions of francs from the Treasury into his own pocket, and to use his power to advance the fortunes of a score of ambitious men as the price of their wives becoming temporarily his mistresses; for he was a born lecher. At length, glutted with enough gold to make him independent of his brother for life, he had quarrelled violently with him, and had taken himself off as a private citizen to Italy. Roger declared roundly that he despised and loathed him.

Napoleon, when a poor student at the *École de la Guerre,* had sent for his brother, Louis, to Paris to share his cheap lodging, and had, himself, educated the boy. For years the Emperor had been under the delusion that Louis had the makings of a military genius. But Louis detested soldiering, and proved a great disappointment. Josephine, in the hope of getting a foot into the camp of her husband's family, who loathed her, had pushed her daughter, Hortense de Beauharnais, into marrying Louis. As they disliked each other intensely, the marriage

71

was far from being a success. Louis had become a neurotic, jealous, hypochondriac. Adamantly determined on the aggrandisement of his family, Napoleon had made him King of Holland; but he was disliked by all who came in contact with him and, with gross ingratitude, did everything he could to cause trouble for his illustrious brother.

Jerome, the youngest son, had proved equally troublesome. He had been put into the Navy. In 1803, during a courtesy visit by his ship to the United States, he had gone ashore at Baltimore, and there had been so fêted as the brother of the already legendary First Consul, General Bonaparte, that he had stayed on without leave, fallen in love with a Miss Elizabeth Paterson, the daughter of a merchant, and married her. Napoleon, having already conceived the ambition of marrying off his brothers and sisters to Princesses and Princes, was furious. In vain he had endeavoured to persuade the Pope to annul the marriage; then, not to be thwarted, when he became Emperor, he had dissolved it by an Imperial decree. Greatly disgruntled, Jerome had returned to France and, in the previous autumn, had sullenly obeyed his all-powerful brother's order to marry the Princess Catherine of Württemberg.

Napoleon had, too, been unlucky in the matter of an alliance for his eldest sister, Eliza. In 1797, while he was in Italy, behind his back his mother had married her off to a Corsican landowner named Bacciocchi, a moron of a fellow who had taken sixteen years to rise from Second Lieutenant to Captain in the Army. Realising that no possible use could be made of him, Napoleon had given Bacciocchi a profitable administrative sinecure in Corsica, and sent them back there. Dumpy and plain, although physically less highly sexed than others of her family, Eliza's mind seized avidly upon everything to do with eroticism. A born blue-stocking, her great ambition was to become a famous patroness of the arts and letters. Having badgered Napoleon to allow her to return to Paris, she had started a salon. It failed to attract any but second-rate men of talent, and she made herself a laughing stock by designing an absurd uniform to be worn by all the members of a literary society she had formed. In due course, as Emperor and King of Italy Napoleon, much as he disliked her, had given her the Principalities of Piombino and Lucca; but she ruled them with such ability that he later said of her that she was his best Minister.

About Pauline, by far the loveliest of the sisters, and considered to be the most beautiful woman in Paris, Roger was somewhat reticent, refraining from disclosing that her beauty was equalled only by her lechery. In her teens, Napoleon had approved her marriage to General Leclerc, because he was an aristocrat. But Leclerc had died of yellow fever in Dominica. She had then become Roger's mistress but, during his enforced absence from Paris, married again, this time Prince Borghese—not because she loved him, but so that she might wear his fabulous family emeralds, and on account of his vast wealth. Borghese had proved a poor bed companion but, even had he not been, that could not have prevented pretty Pauline from enjoying her favourite pastime with a score of handsome young men, both before and after her second marriage. Napoleon had given her the Principality of Guestalla in her own right, but she was fated to derive little pleasure from it, as she loathed having to give up the magnificent palace in Paris on which she had spent a fortune in decorating with admirable taste; and she had since become the victim of chronic ill health.

The youngest sister, Caroline, had, apart from Napoleon, a better brain than any other Bonaparte. She also shared his ruthlessness and inordinate ambition, but not his generosity and loyalty to friends. When very young she had fallen in love with the flamboyant Murat, doggedly resisted all Napoleon's efforts to persuade her to accept other suitors that would have better served his own plans and, on leaving school, married the great cavalry leader.

On becoming Emperor, Napoleon had created Joseph's wife, Julie, and Louis' wife, Hortense, Imperial Highness; but he had not bestowed that rank on his three sisters. At a family celebration dinner at which he had announced these honours, Pauline was absent in Italy. The other two had been hardly able to contain their rage at his neglect of them, so had gone to the Tuileries next day. All the Bonapartes had extremely violent tempers and habitually threw the most appalling scenes whenever they suffered a disappointment. The two women had screamed abuse at their brother until he had agreed to make them, and Pauline, also Imperial Highnesses.

During 1806, the Emperor had entirely remade the map of Germany; first welding numerous small Principalities into the Confederation of the Rhine. He had then deprived various states of portions of their territories, to create the Grand Duchy of Berg-Cleves, and made the Murats its sovereigns. Caroline had since been busily dissipating its revenues but, her ambitions still unsatisfied, had packed her stupid, gallant husband off to Poland, in the hope that the Emperor would make him king of that country.

There remained the Emperor's stepson, Eugene de Beauharnais. Napoleon had always had a great fondness for him and, while still a boy, had taken him on his campaigns as an A.D.C. Eugene, although not brilliant, was honest, capable and devoted to his stepfather. In 1805, Napoleon had made him Viceroy of Italy and, in the following year, formed another valuable alliance by marrying him off to the Princess Augusta of Bavaria.

Most of this was already known to Roger's audience, but they delighted in his personal descriptions of the Bonaparte family, their idiosyncrasies and the way in which they had battened upon their illustrious brother; costing the nation hundred of millions of francs, spent mostly in vulgar ostentation with the vain idea that they could impress the ancient sovereign families of Europe and be regarded by them as real royalties.

An elderly Major remarked, 'The "Little Corporal" has done so much to restore the greatness of France, that one can't grudge him the pleasure of showering benefits on his relations; but what does stick in my gills is the licence he allows his Marshals.'

'They, too, have some claim on France,' Roger replied,

'for many of them have made notable contributions to the Emperor's victories.'

'True enough. Ney at Ulm, Davoust at Auerstädt, and in the early days Augereau at Castiglione and Lannes at Arcola. But so, for that matter, have we all. Yet the Marshals are given vast provinces to loot at will. Out of our wars they are making great fortunes, but not a fraction of it ever reaches us. We have to soldier on for nothing but our pay; and that is often in arrears.'

'I wouldn't object to that so much,' said a youngish Captain of Dragoons, 'if only the fighting would come to an end, and we could get home.'

At that there was a chorus of assent, and Roger knew that it now voiced a feeling general in the Army. Some of the older men had been campaigning in, or garrisoning, distant lands for ten years or more. Only by luck had their regiments now and then been brought back to France, thus enabling them to get leave to spend a short spell with their families.

Roger sympathised, but felt that in his position he was called on at least to make a show of upholding morale; so he said, 'It's hard on you gentlemen, I know. But the Emperor dare not make peace until he has smashed the Prussians and Russians for good and all. If he did, within a year or two we'd find ourselves back with the colours, having to prevent our enemies from invading France, instead of fighting them in their own country.'

'And what if we did?' retorted a Lieutenant of Engineers. 'France's natural frontier is the Rhine, and we could hold it without difficulty. If fight one must, at least let it be there where, between battles, we'd have the benefit of comfortable billets, ample food, good wine and women for the asking. Whereas, in this God-forsaken country, we are frozen, starved and hardly better off then the lice-ridden peasants who inhabit it.'

'Things will be better in the spring, and that's not far off now,' Roger said, in an endeavour to cheer them up. 'When the campaign reopens, it needs only one more victory by the

Emperor and the enemy will be forced to make terms which will include all prisoners of war regaining their freedom.'

'And what then?' put in the Captain of Dragoons. 'That would be all very well for you, Colonel. You and the rest of the gilded staff would go riding gaily back to Paris with the Emperor. But most of us would be left here to garrison the cities and fortresses we've taken.'

The elderly Major took him up. 'That's it, and "gilded staff" is right. In the old days they had all risen from the ranks, and were tough, courageous men who cheerfully shared hardships with the rest of us. But since Bonaparte put a crown on his head in Notre-Dame, he's changed all that. He's welcomed back the *émigrés* and surrounded himself with young popinjays: *ci-devant* nobles, who are better at making a play for pretty women in ballrooms than risking their skins on a battlefield.'

Roger frowned, sat forward and asked sharply, 'Are you implying . . . ?'

'No, no!' the Major interrupted him quickly. 'I meant no offence to you, Colonel. All the Army knows the exploits of *le brave Breuc*. And gentle birth is no crime. But old soldiers of the Republic, like myself, take it ill to receive their orders from ex-aristos who were living in idleness in England or Coblenz while we were fighting on the Rhine, in Italy and Egypt.'

With a shrug, Roger let the matter pass, for he knew that there was much in what the Major had said. From those earlier campaigns many thousands of France's best fighting men had never returned and, although the Army still had a leaven of them as junior officers and N.C.O.s, its ranks were now composed mainly of young and often unwilling conscripts; while Napoleon's policy of marrying the new France with the old had led to his giving staff appointments to considerable numbers of inexperienced youths of noble families, many of whom lacked the daring and *élan* of the men with whom he had earlier surrounded himself. In numbers the Army was greater then it had ever been; but its quality had sadly deteriorated.

76

Next morning, the Russian soldier-servant produced for Roger a pair of field boots a little too large for him, but comfortable enough, and the tunic and busby of a Hussar officer who had recently died in the local hospital. Somewhat more presentable in this false plumage, he spent the next six days with his gloomy companions, alternately taking exercise in the walled garden, drowsing in an armchair with broken springs and talking with them about past campaigns. Meanwhile, with the best patience he could muster, he waited for some indication that the Hetman Dutoff had carried out his promise to request General Bagration to arrange for his exchange.

On the seventh day his hopes were realised. The officer in charge of the prisoners informed him that an order had come for his transfer to Tilsit, where the Commander-in-Chief had his headquarters. That midday he said good-bye to his fellow prisoners, without disclosing the reason for his transfer then, with an infantry subaltern as escort, he set off in a well-equipped sleigh for the headquarters of the Russian Army.

Tilsit was on the Niemen and some thirty-odd miles from Insterburg, so it proved a long, cold drive across the still frozen plains, ameliorated only by the fact that Roger had been provided with furs and that the young officer responsible for him had taken the precaution to bring half a dozen large *brodchen* stuffed with caviare, a similar number of *apfel-strudel* with rich, flaky pastry, and a bottle of captured French cognac.

By evening they reached the larger city and, somewhat to Roger's disquiet, instead of being taken to the Palace occupied by General Bagration, he was checked in at another, larger prisoner-of-war camp.

This camp consisted of several score of hutments. In it there were confined a thousand or more French soldiers and, fenced off in a separate enclosure, quarters that housed some seventy officers. Among the latter were three with whom Roger was acquainted. They welcomed him gladly as a comrade in misfortune, but were as depressed as those he had left behind at Insterburg. They were, in fact, even more gloomy about their prospects, as they had learned the results of the battle of Eylau.

For the first time the Emperor had there met his match in the Russians. That bloody battle had proved no victory for the French, although Napoleon had claimed it as one. But he had been enabled to do so only owing to the fact that he had retained the ground he held, whereas the more cautious Bagration, against the advice of his Generals, had withdrawn during the night. Actually, the appalling slaughter had resulted only in a draw.

Again, for fear of causing his companions unhappy envy, Roger did not disclose his hopes of shortly ending his captivity by being exchanged. But he now felt confident that on the next day he would be sent for to the General's headquarters and, anyway, informed that negotiations with regard to him were in progress.

He was disappointed in that and several days followed, during which he had to listen to the complaints of his fellow prisoners at having had to participate in this ghastly campaign, in which blizzards and lack of decent food, near-mutinous conscripts and shortage of equipment had proved a far greater tax on their morale than having to engage the enemy. Nostalgically, they longed to be back in their native France, or in the sunshine of Italy, or even in Egypt—two thousand miles from their own country and cut off from it by the British Fleet—but there at least Bonaparte's untiring activities had converted Cairo into a semblance of Paris on the Nile.

Roger had been in Tilsit for four days when the Camp Commandant assembled the officer prisoners and addressed them:

'Messieurs,' he said. 'The spring will shortly be upon us. Already the ice shows signs of breaking up. Your Emperor is not given to letting the grass grow beneath his feet; so we must anticipate that soon he will reopen the campaign. Naturally, my Imperial master has good hopes of defeating him. But the fortunes of war can never be foretold. General Prince Bagration has therefore decided that it would be wise to send all the prisoners in this camp—officers and men—into central Russia. We shall do our best to ensure that you do not suffer undue hardship, but we have no transport to spare so you will be marched to your new destination in easy stages. Please prepare yourselves to start tomorrow.'

His announcement was received in unhappy silence. Everyone present knew that to protest was useless. After a moment, Roger stepped forward and said in Russian, 'Sir, may I have a word with you in private?'

Nodding, the Commandant beckoned him outside and asked, 'Now, what have you to say?'

Swiftly, Roger told him that at the request of Hetman Dutoff, General Bagration was arranging an exchange for him; then asked him to see the General and secure a permit for him to remain in Tilsit until the exchange had been arranged.

The Commandant shook his head. 'I regret, Colonel, but I cannot oblige you. I have been told nothing about this proposed exchange; and today General Bagration is away, inspecting troops far to the south of Tilsit. My orders are explicit. I can make no exceptions and tomorrow, when your fellow prisoners begin their march to the north, you must march with them.'

5

Fickle Fortune

Roger stared at the Commandant aghast. That an officer in his position should know nothing about such matters as exchanges of prisoners being arranged at headquarters was not surprising. But this order for the removal of the prisoners when General Bagration happened to be absent from Tilsit, making it impossible to get in touch with him, was a most evil stroke of fortune.

It meant that Roger's hopes of shortly regaining his freedom were completely shattered. Communications in Russia were so poor that, except between the larger cities, letters often took months to reach their destination, and the odds were that the prisoners were being sent to some place deep in the country. Having been brought from Insterburg to Tilsit seemed a certain indication that Dutoff had carried out his promise to request the General to communicate with French headquarters on Roger's behalf, and his transfer ordered in anticipation that an exchange would be agreed. But such matters could not be arranged overnight and it might be some days yet before a reply came through.

One of Napoleon's virtues was his loyalty to old friends. In fact, he was so generous in that way that he had frequently declined to punish officers who had served with him in his early campaigns, even when Fouché's secret police had produced irrefutable evidence that they were conspiring against him. At worst, he had sent them off to some distant command, as a precaution against their creating trouble for him in Paris. In consequence, Roger had no doubt whatever that, when the Emperor learned that he was alive, he would at once take steps to ensure that '*le brave Breuc*' did not languish for a day longer than could be helped as a prisoner of the Russians.

But General Bagration had many other things to think about besides the exchange of prisoners; and, when he was told that Roger was no longer in Tilsit, he might quite possibly forget to do anything about him. Napoleon, too, had other things to think about and, once the spring campaign opened, he would be so fully occupied that it might be months before the thought of Roger again entered his mind. Even if Bagration did send an order for Roger's return, how long was it going to take to reach a prison camp in the depths of Russia?

These devastating imponderables having chased one another through his agitated mind, it suddenly occurred to him that, although General Bagration was absent from Tilsit, some member of his staff might know about the proposed exchange and intervene on his behalf. Promptly, he begged the Commandant to visit the headquarters and make enquiries. The Commandant, a pleasant, elderly man, at once agreed to do so.

That afternoon the officers' quarters became a scene of gloomy activity. They were all issued with haversacks, flasks of vodka, and stout boots and warmer clothes for those who needed them. While they packed their few belongings, they commiserated with one another upon this harsh blow of fate. Had they been allowed to remain at Tilsit and the Emperor achieved the defeat of the Russians, as they had all been praying that he would, that would have assured their speedy release; but if they were then hundreds of miles away in the Ukraine or perhaps up in Esthonia, their situation would be very different.

The French had no means of knowing if any of them were still alive or had died on the field of Eylau; so, should the Emperor achieve a decisive victory, it would not be possible for him to require their individual release. Therefore, should the Czar have thoughts of renewing the war when he had had time to gather a new army together, he might decide, in order to weaken his enemy, to release only a limited number of the prisoners he had taken and, unless those now at Tilsit were among the lucky ones, that could mean indefinite captivity for them.

Roger spent agonising hours waiting to hear from the Commandant. If headquarters were already negotiating for his exchange, he could count himself as good as free; but if they were not, he feared that within the week he might be dead. The Commandant had said that the march would be made in easy stages and measures taken to see that the prisoners suffered no undue hardship. That was all very well, but since winter set in, Roger had frequently seen French troops on the march, and the grim evidence of their passing—a trail like a paper chase but, instead of paper, the bodies of men not fully recovered from recent wounds, or youngsters of poor physique weakened by semi-starvation who, exhausted, had dropped out. As there was no transport available to pick them up, they had been left to die in the gently-falling snow.

The Commandant had seemed a decent old fellow; but the officer in charge of the contingent of prisoners might prove a very different type. Roger's vivid imagination conjured up visions of Cossacks using their knouts to drive flagging stragglers on to the last gasp until they dropped. The officers might escape such brutal treatment, but his ill-mended broken ankle had left him lame and still pained him if he put his full weight on it. He greatly doubted if he could manage to walk more than three miles without collapsing. And what then? The Russians had no cause to love the French, and a Frenchman abandoned here and there along the road, to die, would not cause them the loss of one wink of sleep.

He knew, too, the sort of country they would have to march through; for he had traversed it once in the opposite derection; not actually through Tilsit, but from St. Petersburg by way of Paskov, Dvinsk, Vilna, Grodno, Warsaw and Breslau right down to Dresden—eight hundred miles of plains as flat as an ocean until one reached the Saxon capital. He had then been travelling day and night at the utmost speed that a private coach and relays of the best horses available could carry him; and, after a further five hundred miles to Paris, he had arrived half-dead from exhaustion. But at least he had been sheltered from the weather by the coach, and able to keep himself warm under a pile of furs; whereas plodding along those interminable roads, he and his companions would be exposed to icy winds and driving blizzards.

At last dusk fell; but still he waited in vain for the Commandant either to return or send for him. As usual, at eight o'clock, an N.C.O. came to lock them in for the night. In desperation, Roger asked to be taken to the Commandant's office, but the man told him that the Commandant always slept out at his own *datcha* a mile or more away, so would not be available until the next morning.

During the years, Roger had been in many tight corners and had spent many anxious nights, but he could not recall one in which he had not at least managed to doze for an hour or two. Strive as he might to make his mind a blank, he could not sleep a wink. To fall asleep from gradually creeping cold was said to be one of the easiest deaths, and it was not fear of that which kept him tossing and turning. It was intense resentment at the injustice of his having escaped such a fate on the field of Eylau, and the still worse one of being shot at Znamensk, only now, when all had seemed set fair for him, to be condemned by his lameness as one of the many who must inevitably fall by the wayside on the terrible march to the north.

When morning came, the bugle call roused the prisoners at the usual hour. Having freshened themselves up as well as they could and been given a hot meal, they got their things together expecting shortly to be ordered out to the parade ground; but they were kept uneasily hanging about until past ten o'clock.

At length the order came, and they lined up outside, to answer the daily roll call. The Commandant than appeared and walked straight towards Roger. More haggard than ever from his sleepless night, Roger took a pace forward and saluted, then held his breath, hope surging up in him that at this eleventh hour he was to be reprieved. Brushing up his fine moustache, the elderly officer said:

'I thought there was a chance that by this morning General

Bagration might have returned from his tour of inspection, so I did not go to his headquarters until half an hour ago. I am sorry to tell you that he is not yet back, and the principal officers of his staff went with him. So no one knows anything of this proposed exchange you told me about; and I have no alternative but to send you north with the others.'

With an effort Roger rallied himself from this final dashing of his hopes, to thank the Commandant for the trouble he had taken; then fell back in line with his companions.

Led and flanked by a mounted guard of Cossacks, the long column of prisoners left by the main gate of the cantonment, the seventy-odd officers leading. Marching erect and in step to demonstrate their good discipline, they were taken through the principal street of the city, watched by a curious crowd. As they approached the central square, they realised why their departure had been delayed until mid-morning. A cluster of officers in brilliant uniforms were sitting their horses there, to watch them pass. Evidently the General commanding in Bagration's absence had decided to inspect them at that hour.

As the head of the column came level with the group of mounted officers, a command rang out, 'Eyes right.' Roger automatically obeyed the order. Suddenly his lacklustre glance became alive with astonishment. Two yards in front of the main group, sitting a fine bay horse, was a man who looked to be about thirty, wearing a plain uniform with a single star on his chest. It was the Czar Alexander.

For a moment Roger was completely nonplussed. He had been presented to the Czar in 1801. But that was six years ago. Could a monarch be expected to remember one of the many hundred people whom he had received at his Court? Was it even possible to get to and speak to him without being killed by one of the Cossacks riding alongside the column? But death lay waiting on the frozen road to the north.

As one of the senior prisoners, Roger was in the leading rank of the march past. The eyes of both his companions and the Cossacks were turned away from him, as they rigidly carried out the salute. Thrusting aside the officer next to him, he dived under the neck of the nearest Cossack's mount and hurled himself across the dozen yards that separated him from the Czar.

Aware that the Russian sovereigns were accustomed to a god-like veneration from their people, he seized the Czar's boot with both hands and kissed its toe. Stooping to do so saved his life. The nearest Cossack had swerved his pony and stabbed downwards with his lance. Instead of driving right through Roger's body, it only grazed the skin of his left shoulder. Before the Cossack could drag it free for another stroke, Roger yelled:

'Imperial Majesty, hear me I beg! I was among those who cried "Alexander Pavlovich, live for ever" on the morning of March 12th, 1801. I was a friend of Count Pahlen and came to your Court with diplomatic credentials. Lame as I am, the march to the north is certain to bring about my death. I entreat you to have mercy on me.'

Raising his hand in a swift gesture, the Czar checked the Cossack, who was about to drive his lance through Roger's back. Looking down at him, he said, 'Your face is vaguely familiar to me, but not with that beard. Who are you?'

The question put Roger in a quandary he had had no time even to consider when he had been seized by the impulse to risk his life on the chance of saving it. After only a moment's hesitation he replied, 'May it please Your Imperial Majesty. I have enjoyed the confidence of both Monsieur de Talleyrand and the late Mr. Pitt. Be so gracious as to afford me a brief private audience, and I vow that you will find me capable of rendering you more valuable service than could another battalion of Grenadiers.'

Alexander gave a chilly smile. 'Then I'll give you a chance to see if you can make good your boast.' Turning in his saddle, he signed to one of his *aides-de-camp* and added, 'Take this gentleman to the Palace. See to it that he is provided with the means to make himself presentable and given decent clothes, then guard him until you receive my further orders.'

The commotion caused by Roger's having broken ranks had brought the column to only a momentary halt. As he now saw it marching on, pity for his recent companions was mingled with elation that his daring bid to save himself had succeeded. The fact that when he had last seen the Czar it had been as Mr. Roger Brook, the secretly-accredited plenipotentiary of Britain's Prime Minister, and for some time past he had been a prisoner of the Russians as Colonel le Chevalier de Breuc, was going to require some far from easy explaining. But at least he no longer had to fear being left to freeze to death in the snow. With a considerably more buoyant limp, he accompanied the A.D.C., into whose charge he had been given, the short distance to the Palace.

There he enjoyed the luxury of a bath, a valet attended to the slight wound in his shoulder, deloused his hair and dressed it in accordance with the prevailing fashion; then he was given a shirt and cravat of good quality, stockings, a pair of buckled shoes and a suit of blue cloth which was almost as good as new. Where these clothes came from he did not enquire, but as he was much of a height with the Czar, he thought they were probably some of the Sovereign's cast-offs, as it was quite usual for royalties to travel with upwards of two hundred suits and, having been intimate with the lovely Pauline, now Princess Borghese, he knew her to have owned the best part of a thousand pairs of shoes.

Late in the afternoon, having fared ill for many weeks he did full justice to an excellent dinner in a private apartment, with the A.D.C. whose name was Count Anton Chernicheff, a handsome young man of no great brain, but pleasant manners. Over the meal they discussed the campaign and other matters of mutual interest. That night, although decidedly worried that in his desperate urge to gain the protection of the Czar he had impulsively promised services that he might not be able to perform, for the first time since he had left Warsaw he was able to relax and sleep in a comfortable bed. Before he dropped off, he thanked all his gods that he was not lying in straw on the hard floor of a barn or in the stinking hut of some wretched peasant, which must be the lot of his recent companions on their march into Russia.

But soon after dawn he woke and his mind became a prey

to renewed anxieties. When he had been known to the Czar in St. Petersburg, it had been as an English gentleman. Normally it was against the principles of gentlemen to act as spies. Even if lack of money, or a fervent patriotism so strong as to override convention had induced him to become a secret agent, would it be considered plausible that he had, within a few years, established himself so convincingly with the French that he had been appointed one of Napoleon's *aides-de-camp*, and so achieved a position in which he would be entrusted with many of the Emperor's secret intentions?

Eventually he decided that his best hope lay in telling the truth and shaming the devil—or at least keeping near enough to the truth to make his story credible. But a further eighteen hours elapsed before he was called on to face this interview on which his future, and possibly his life, depended.

He had spent a pleasant day beside a roaring porcelain stove, alternately chatting with Chernicheff and browsing through some Russian and German news-sheets that the A.D.C. had brought him; then, at ten o'clock, gone to bed. Two hours later, Chernicheff roused him, to say that his Imperial master was at that moment supping and, when he had finished, required Roger to present himself.

Recalling that it was a curious custom of the Russians frequently to transact business in the middle of the night, Roger hastily dressed, then accompanied the A.D.C. through a series of passages to a small, empty library. They waited there for some twenty minutes, then the Czar walked in.

Alexander was a good-looking man, with fairish, curly hair, side-whiskers, a straight nose and well-modelled mouth. He was again wearing a plain uniform, but a four-inch-deep gold embroidered collar came at the sides right up to his ears and beneath it, rather like a bandage, a thick silk scarf supported his chin.

Apart from Napoleon, Alexander possessed a more interesting and original character than any other monarch of his day. He had been brought up at the liberal Court of his grandmother, the great Catherine, and as a tutor she had given him a Swiss named Laharpe. From him Alexander had im-

bibed the fundamental principle of the French Revolution—
that all men had rights—and, had not the united opposition
of his nobles been too strong for him to overcome, he would,
on ascending the throne, have freed from bondage the millions of serfs who constituted the greater part of his subjects.

Catherine had so hated and despised her son Paul that she
had decided to make the youthful Alexander her heir; but
had died before signing the new will she had had drawn up.
She had, however, secured for him as a wife, the charming
Princess Maria Luisa of Baden, and the young couple had
fallen in love at first sight, with the result that their Court
was the most respectable in Europe.

Paul, previously an eccentric who, during his mother's reign,
took pleasure only in drilling and harshly disciplining a bri-
gade of troops allotted to him to keep him out of mischief,
after coming to the throne had developed increasing signs of
madness. Seized with uncontrollable rages, without the least
justification he exiled scores of his nobles to Siberia; and,
becoming obsessed with the idea that his assassination was
being plotted, he was considering doing away with his principal
Ministers and even his wife and son, although both the latter
were completely loyal to him. But his Ministers were not;
and their fears for themselves had led to his murder.

Considering those eight years of Paul's reign, during which
his heir had been under constant apprehension that he might
be thrown into a dungeon from which he would never emerge,
it was remarkable that Alexander should not at length have
mounted the throne a suspicious and vengeful tyrant. On the
contrary, he had remained a man with high ideals and while,
for some time, he had retained his father's Ministers, he had
gathered about him a group of friends: Victor Kochubey,
Nicolai Novasiltsov, Paul Strogonov and Adam Czartoryski,
who were eager to introduce sweeping reforms for the better-
ment of the lot of the Russian people. Yet, despite his leanings towards democracy, Alexander continued to think of
himself as an autocrat whose opinion was final and not to be
contested.

With a brief nod, he acknowledged the deep bows made

88

by Chernicheff and Roger, then dismissed the A.D.C. Sitting down behind a beautiful Louis Quinze desk, he studied Roger for a full minute before speaking.

Roger stood at attention. He thought it probable that anyone being so regarded by an autocratic sovereign would be expected to have his eyes cast down. But he had always found that boldness paid; so he kept his eyes fixed on those of the Czar, while assuming an expression which he hoped would be taken for fascinated admiration.

At length, Alexander said stonily, 'I have had particulars regarding you looked into. It appears that you are a Colonel, a Commander of the *Légion d'Honneur,* and a member of the Emperor Napoleon's personal staff. Now that you have shaved off your beard, I recognise you without doubt as an Englishman who was in St. Petersburg in the spring of 1801, and involved in my father's death. Such a contrast in personalities is beyond all reason. Explain it if you can.'

Roger knew that Alexander had had no hand in his father's assassination, had wept when he had been told of it and, only reluctantly, been dissuaded from having the assassins executed; so the first fence he had to clear was having been one of them.

'Sire,' he said earnestly. 'You will recall that Your Imperial Majesty's father had, out of hatred for your illustrious grandmother, reversed all her policies. Whereas she had been about to join the Powers of the First Coalition to assist in destroying the murderous gang of terrorists who were then all-powerful in France, the Czar Paul had entered into a pact with them. This was so serious a menace to British interests that I was sent by Prime Minister Pitt to encourage the Czar's Ministers, and others who feared to be deprived of their positions and fortunes, to take action against him. Not, I swear, to assassinate him, but to force him to abdicate or, at least, make you Regent—as we, in England, had made our Prince of Wales, when our own King, George III, became afflicted with madness. It is true that I was among the half hundred other conspirators who met at Count Pahlen's mansion on that fateful night; that I later entered the Palace with General Bennigsen and the Zuboff brothers; but neither the General nor I had any hand in your father's murder. It took place in complete darkness, unknown to us, after Your Imperial Majesty's father had refused to sign the deed of abdication.'

Alexander nodded. 'That I accept, as I did in the case of General Bennigsen. But it does not explain why you, accredited only a few years ago as the secret emissary of Britain's Prime Minister, should now emerge as a member of the Emperor Napoleon's staff.'

With a shrug, Roger spread out his hands and replied, 'May it please Your Imperial Majesty, I have been the plaything of unusual circumstances. I am, in fact, an Englishman, the son of Admiral Sir Christopher Brook, but my mother's sister had married a gentleman of Strasbourg and they had a son of about my age. In my teens I became bewitched by the new ideals of "Liberty, Equality and Fraternity", which had at that time brought about the first, liberal, revolution in France. I ran away from home to my aunt in Strasbourg and, with her family, learned to speak fluent French. I longed to be in Paris and do what little I could to help bring about the original objects of the revolution. It so happened that my cousin was killed in an accident, and by then Britain was at war with France; so I went to the capital as a Frenchman, changed my name to Breuc and assumed his identity.'

As Roger paused, the Czar nodded. 'This is most interesting. Continue.'

Roger bowed. 'I lived there through the Terror, and realised that the revolution had become a murderous anarchy. Disillusioned and disgusted by what I had seen, I returned to England. My father sent me to the Prime Minister, so that I could give him an eyewitness account of what was happening in Paris. Mr. Pitt then proposed to me that I should return as his agent and keep him informed about events in France.'

The Czar's brows knitted. Sitting back, he asked with severe disapproval, 'Do you mean that you, a gentleman, agreed to become a spy?'

'Sire,' Roger shrugged. 'I admit it. I was persuaded that it was the most valuable service I could render my country. And I am not ashamed of the part I have played during these past sixteen years. I had the good fortune to become acquainted with General Bonaparte when he was an unknown Artillery officer at the siege of Toulon. I have since executed many missions either in my real identity as Roger Brook, or as the *ci-devant* Chevalier de Breuc, which have enabled Britain to thwart Napoleon's designs. Not least the part I played in helping to bring about your succession, which resulted in Russia breaking with France and becoming the ally of England. That from time to time I must betray the Emperor, who counts me his friend and has through the years bestowed rank and honour upon me, is often against my inclination, since in many ways I have a great admiration for him. But my duty to my country comes first, and I can only ask your Imperial Majesty's understanding of the strange fate that brings me before you as a French prisoner who has in fact served Britain for many years as a secret agent.'

Alexander's stern features relaxed into a slow smile, as he said, 'Mr. Brook, while your ethics remain highly questionable, I cannot withhold my admiration from a man who must on many occasions have risked his life to provide his country with valuable information. Are you, or rather were you in communication with the British Government before you became a prisoner?'

Roger shook his head. 'No, Sire, Mr. Pitt being dead I had no inclination to serve his inept successors. I returned to the Continent only because I became bored with leading an idle life in England and, having for so long been a man of some note in the French Army with more friends in it than I had in my own country, I decided to rejoin the Emperor's staff. Trafalgar made Britain safe from invasion, so she now stands on the side line of this great conflict. I have never had any love for the Prussians, so had no objection to serving against them, simply for the enjoyment I derive from being actively employed. But, should Britain again be menaced, I would, of course, do anything I could to aid her cause.'

After a moment the Czar said, 'Mr. Brook, it seems to me that you have failed to face up to realities. I am England's ally. Should my armies be defeated, which St. Nicholas forfend, Bonaparte will enjoy a clear field to inflict grievous harm upon your country. Although he may no longer be in a position to invade England, he has always had ambitions to become another Alexander the Great in the East. He might well direct his legions against Turkey and Persia, then throw the British out of India and so deprive your country of one of her great sources of wealth. Are you, as you implied the day before yesterday when you broke ranks and cast yourself at my feet, willing to serve me as you served Mr. Pitt, by giving me your help to defeat the French?'

Again Roger bowed. 'I take your Imperial Majesty's point, and, if you will arrange to have me exchanged for a Russian officer of equivalent rank, I will do my utmost to be of service to you.'

'Good,' the Czar nodded. 'Then tomorrow we will talk again.' Picking up a silver hand-bell from his desk, he rang it. Chernicheff, who had been waiting outside, came in and escorted Roger back to the rooms that had been assigned to him. By then it was getting on for one o'clock in the morning. Well satisfied with the way things had gone, Roger got out of his clothes and tumbled into bed.

The following day was Sunday and, after attending service in the big, onion-domed Orthodox Cathedral, the Czar again sent for Roger. This time Alexander had with him Prince Adam Czartoryski and a secretary sitting at a small table, ready to take notes. Prince Adam, although a Pole, was the Czar's principal Minister and closest friend. He had travelled widely, twice made prolonged visits to England, and spoke English fluently.

Alexander was no fool and had evidently decided to make certain that Roger really was an Englishman and not an English-speaking Frenchman who, in fact, was devoted to Napoleon; so the interview opened by Czartoryski's asking him a series of questions about London's leading hostesses and clubs.

Somewhat amused, Roger, as a member of White's, was readily able to convince the Prince that he was well known in London society, and it soon transpired that they had numerous acquaintances in common, including Roger's closest friend,

Lord Edward Fitz-Deveril, known to his intimates as 'Droopy Ned'.

Fully satisfied, Alexander invited him to sit down and join them in a glass of wine, then began to question him about the French Army. Roger said that, to the best of his belief, it had numbered some seventy-five thousand men, only about half of whom were French; but the day-long conflict at Eylau had been so fierce that he thought it possible that dead, wounded and prisoners might well have reduced its effectives by a third or more.

At that the Czar smiled. 'We, too, suffered very heavily, but my domains are greater than those of France, Austria and Prussia put together. It takes many weeks for contingents mobilised in distant parts to reach the battle-front; but they are arriving daily. Moreover, I am shortly about to leave for Memel to confer with the King of Prussia, and I have good hopes that between us we will be able to put into the field an army considerably superior to that of the French.'

Roger shook his head. 'I would not count on it, Sire. Bonaparte's greatest assets are his organising ability and the speed with which he carries out his intentions. You may be certain that, within twelve hours of his having been checked at Eylau, his Chief of Staff was sending scores of couriers to every country now under French control—Poland, Hanover, the Confederation of the Rhine, Holland, Piedmont, Venetia, Dalmatia and Italy, as well as France—demanding the immediate despatch of reinforcements. It would not surprise me if he had not doubled his numbers by the time you engage him in another pitched battle.'

'Perhaps,' remarked Czartoryski. 'But most of his troops will be newly-conscripted, and of poor quality. From the conduct of certain regiments at Eylau and the prisoners we took there, it became evident to us that the *Grande Armée* is no longer the formidable force it was at Ulm and Austerlitz.'

'True, Prince,' Roger agreed. 'The foreign elements naturally resent having to go to war for the aggrandisement of France, and the French no longer display the *élan* that they did, except when under the eye of the Emperor or there is easy loot to be had. Most of them long to be done with campaigning, and return to their homes. That applies even to many of the Marshals. They would be only too glad to cease having to risk their lives and, instead, spend their remaining years enjoying their wealth and honours.'

The Czar took a pinch of snuff. 'They must be a most unusual body of men, and one cannot know too much about the personalities of enemy Generals. Tell me what you know of them.'

Roger smiled. 'The only thing they have in common, Sire, is their comparative youth, combined with long experience of war. Of those on the active list, if one excepts Berthier, the Emperor's Chief of Staff, and the dull Moncey, who is Chief of the Gendarmerie, their average age is a little over forty. They are a self-opinionated, quarrelsome lot and so bitterly jealous of one another that no lesser man than Napoleon could keep them in order. Masséna is probably the most skilful of them; but when they were created Marshals in 1804 and a friend congratulated him, he exclaimed in disgust, "I see nothing to be pleased about—just one of fourteen." '

'I thought he created eighteen,' interjected the Prince.

'There are, but four of them—Kellermann, Lefèbvre, Perignon and Sérurier—are only honorary Marshals, given the rank for their services in the Revolutionary wars. The Emperor's policy, as you may know, has been to overcome the antagonism of the most influential Jacobins who resented his making himself a monarch, by elevating them, too. Lannes, Augereau, Jourdan and Bernadotte were all red-hot Republicans, but have since come to heel. The last, although his worst enemy, he made Prince of Ponte Corvo, whereas most of the others he made only Dukes.'

'Whom would you say was the bravest of them?' asked the Czar.

'Ney, Lannes and Murat must share that honour, Sire. As a cavalry leader, Murat is incomparable. He leads every major charge himself, in uniforms he has designed, smothered in gold and jewels, and wearing a busby from which sprout white ostrich feathers a foot high.'

94

'And the most able?'

'Masséna, Soult, Mortier and Davoust. When they were created, all the others sneered at Davoust's being included among them; but he has since more than justified it. At Auerstädt, without aid or direction from the Emperor, he won a great victory over an army more than twice the size of his corps, and since, so I have been told, he saved the French from defeat at Eylau. Perhaps I should include Berthier: not as a General, but in his own highly-specialised work. That big head of his is a living card index. He could tell you at any moment where every unit in the Army is, and how long it would take to move it from one place to another. As a Chief of Staff, he is incomparable.'

'You have not mentioned Bessières or Brune.'

'Bessières' promotion was also resented by the others, Sire, on account of his youth. But, as Commander of the Imperial Guard, with no disrespect to your own Household troops, he has made his corps probably the most formidable fighting force in Europe. As for Brune, he is a nonentity, and received his baton only because he defeated the English when they sent an expeditionary force to Holland, shortly before Napoleon got back from Egypt. But any bonehead could have outgeneralled a man as stupid as our Duke of York.'

'What of those who were passed over?' enquired the Prince. 'From what I have heard, Marmont, Macdonald, Suchet, Victor and Junot seem to have proved just as able as several of the others.'

Roger laughed. 'The rage they displayed for weeks had to be seen to be believed. Mortier was made virtual Viceroy in Dalmatia, and why he did not get his baton I cannot think. Macdonald, Suchet and Victor also deserved theirs for their fine performances in Italy. But Junot, no. Napoleon realised that he would be hopeless as a corps commander; but he never forgets his old friends, and Junot practically kept him years ago when he had very little money, so he consoled him by making him Military Governor of Paris.'

They talked on for another hour about Napoleon's military campaigns and his ability as an administrator. At length, the Czar said, 'Upstart though he may be, I cannot but admire the man for the way in which he has restored France from a state of anarchy to good order, and in his new code of law he has embodied many benefits that I should like to grant to my own people. For obvious reasons, Mr. Brook, I must continue to treat you as a prisoner; but as soon as I can, I will arrange an exhange for you, and I have good hopes that in the months to come you will find means to convey to me information about Napoleon's intentions, that will prove of value.'

'That will not be easy, Sire,' Roger said thoughtfully. 'Can you suggest any means by which I might do so?'

It was Adam Czartoryski who replied. 'You may have been misled by what you have seen of the Polish people. My nation is divided. One half believes the vague promises of Bonaparte that, given their aid to defeat Russia, he will restore Poland's independence. The other half, which includes most of our noble families and intelligentsia, puts no faith in the half-promises of this self-made Emperor, who is known many times to have broken his word. They prefer to place their trust in His Imperial Majesty, who has assured them that, under the protection of Russia, he will grant Poland independent government. It should not be difficult for you to make the acquaintance of a number of Polish officers at present serving with the French; sound them out about their political views and, when you find one or more who are in arms against Russia only with reluctance, persuade them to desert at the first opportunity and bring with them any useful information you may have for us.'

Roger believed that he owed his life to the fact that, except on very few occasions when he had seen no alternative, he had never divulged to anyone that he was a secret agent; so he at once decided against adopting the Prince's suggestion. Nevertheless, he replied:

'That is certainly an idea worth exploring. But should favourable circumstances arise in which I can, without undue risk of being killed, allow myself to be captured again, that is what I will do; for I could then give you a far more complete picture of the situation of the French than I could convey through any messenger.'

The interview being over, Alexander extended his hand for Roger to kiss, and he bowed himself out from the Imperial presence, to be again escorted by the waiting Chernicheff back to his quarters.

A fortnight went by, during which time he had three more long talks with Prince Adam about the state of the French Army; but, except for these, he idled his time away reading French books, of which a great number were available in the Palace library.

It was on the morning of the last day in March, that Chernicheff greeted him with a cheerful smile and said, 'Your exchange has been arranged. I have orders to escort you to a village on the Alle, a few miles above Allenstein, and there the exchange will take place.'

This meant a journey of some one hundred and ten miles, but the thaw had set in so, instead of a sleigh, they were able to go in a well-upholstered travelling coach, accompanied by outriders who acted as servants, and with a stock of provisions that were cooked for them whenever they decided to halt and have a meal. In most places the snow was melting fast and pouring away in thick, muddy streams to swell rivers and lakes; in others the remains of great drifts of it still formed solid ice mounds several feet in height, over which the coach had to be manhandled; so it was four days before they reached Allenstein, where they spent the night.

Early on the morning of the fifth, Roger said good-bye to Chernicheff and, at some peril, was ferried across the rushing river Alle, under a flag of truce. Waiting on the far bank was a Russian Colonel, who greeted him warmly. Shaking hands, they congratulated each other on their restoration to freedom; then the Russian boarded the ferry to rejoin his countrymen.

The French officer who received Roger told him that, after remaining in the neighbourhood of Eylau for a week, to establish his claim to victory, the Emperor had withdrawn beyond the river Passarge and the upper Alle, where the Army had since remained in winter quarters. Thorn, right back on the Vistula, had become the main base of the Army, but its headquarters were at Osterode, only some twenty miles away.

Furnished with a mount and an escort of four Hussars, Roger set out for Osterode, to learn, when he reached the town, that the Emperor was actually some distance away at the Castle of Finckenstein. On arriving there, he found it very different from Znamensk, which had not been much more than an old fortified manor house. Finckenstein was a vast, grim, battlemented pile, large enough to house several hundred people, and the central courtyard was crowded with mounted officers, and orderlies constantly coming and going.

On enquiring for the Duc de Friuli, Roger was glad to learn that his old friend was there. In the days before the Empire, the Duc had been simply Colonel Duron, Chief A.D.C. to Bonaparte. Then, when the Court had been formed, he had been made Grand Marshal of the Palace or, when on a campaign, *Maréchal de Camp*; but Napoleon had several times sent him on missions as an Ambassador—a use to which he not infrequently put the more intelligent of his military staff.

Michel Duroc received Roger with open arms, listened with sympathy to his account of his misfortunes during the past two months, then brought him up to date with the situation of the French Army.

Eylau had proved an even greater disaster than Roger had supposed. Augereau's corps, losing direction in the blizzard and infiladed by the Russian guns, had been so torn to pieces that it had had to be disbanded and its survivors drafted to other units. Napoleon habitually understated the French casualties in the bulletins that he issued after every major battle. On this occasion he had stated them to be one thousand nine hundred killed and five thousand seven hundred wounded; but the fact was that the effectives had been reduced by nearly thirty thousand men, and the forty-five thousand remaining were in dire straits.

Meat was almost unprocurable and they were barely existing on a meagre ration of biscuits and root crops. Their uniforms were in rags, scores of them froze to death every night and, the front being fluid, they lived in constant fear of raids by the fierce Cossacks, since their own cavalry was incapable of protecting them, because their horses had been so weakened by semi-starvation that they could no longer be spurred into a gallop.

Amazed, Roger exclaimed, 'But it is totally unlike the Emperor to allow his army to fall into such a parlous state. Has he done nothing in these past two months to rectify matters?'

Duroc shrugged. 'After Eylau, he sent a plenitpotentiary to Frederick William of Prussia, offering to restore a part of his territories and forgo his earlier demand that Prussia should become his ally against Russia. But the Czar succeeded in browbeating that miserable, irresolute monarch into refusing our overtures.

'Berthier or, as I suppose we should now call him, *Maréchal le Prince de Neuchâtel*, has since been working like a demon, calling up reserves from Poland, Bavaria, Saxony, the Rhine and has even blackmailed the Spaniards into sending a corps to retain Hanover for us, so that its French garrison can be brought up here. A new levy of eighty thousand men, or rather boys, has been ordered in France. It is the third within the past year and made eighteen months before these youngsters were due to be called up. Mortier, I mean the Duke of Treviso —I shall never get used to these new names—was recalled from keeping watch on the Swedish Army that is occupying Stralsund. A week ago, it took the offensive; so he is now marching his corps back to check its advance. Meanwhile Austria is again becoming restless and, should she join our enemies, could cut our communications with France.'

'What a picture,' said Roger, making a gloomy face. 'And what of England? I take it she has not been altogether idle during this propitious time to make a telling thrust at her implacable enemy?'

Duroc laughed. 'On the contrary, for the first time in years she has ceased to show her aggressive spirit. Our intelligence informed us that it was proposed to send an expeditionary force to support the Swedes in Stralsund. But she could muster no more than twelve thousand men, so thought it beneath her dignity to make such an insignificant contribution to the war against us on the Continent. It is said that the Czar is disgusted with her as an ally who will neither send him military aid, nor even a substantial subsidy to help pay his own troops. All England's present ineffectual Government have so far done this year is to send a fleet that forced the Dardanelles in February and appeared off Constantinople. Its object was to coerce the Sultan Selim into giving way in his dispute with Russia, so that the Czar would be in a position to withdraw many of his divisions from the Danube for use as reinforcements against us up here; and to dismiss our Ambassador, General Sebastiani. But Sebastiani has Selim so effectually under his thumb and the people of Constantinople were so enraged by the insolent demands of the English that, in a single day, they dragged a thousand cannon up to the Bosphorus, did the enemy fleet much damage and forced it to retire with ignominy.'

With a frown, Roger changed the subject. 'All you tell me of the situation here seems quite extraordinary. Berthier's ability to bring up reinforcements by roads on which they will not converge and become congested is known to us all. But what of the Emperor? Has he not used that great brain of his to devise some policy that would cause dissension among our enemies, so that they no longer have a concerted strategy and we could defeat them piecemeal?'

'*Mon ami*, it is quite a time since you have been with us at headquarters. Believe it or not, Napoleon has ceased to be interested in waging war. With him here he has the Countess Maria Walewska. Admittedly, she is a charming young creature: dignified, modest, unambitious. Having now been repudiated by her old husband, she has accepted our master wholeheartedly, and he has become a changed man. The years have dropped from him, and his is like a youth in his teens; positively besotted by her. For weeks past they have been enjoying a honeymoon. For days at a time he never emerges from their suite, and refuses all pleas to discuss business. For ten days or more I have had here missions from both the Grand Turk and the Great Sophy. Only once has he consented to receive these Turkish and Persian emissaries. Yet both could prove invaluable allies in harassing the Czar. Naturally, they have become resentful and contumacious; but there is nothing I can do about it.'

Roger expressed his sympathy, while inwardly much pleased that it looked as though, at last, England's arch-enemy was losing his grip and might, in a few weeks' time, be so thoroughly defeated by the Russians and Prussians that his gimcrack Empire would fall to pieces and Europe be restored to its pre-revolutionary state.

Having asked Duroc to request an audience with the Emperor for him as soon as possible, they adjourned to the senior officers' Mess. There Roger was greeted with delight by many of his old comrades; but several of them were missing, and he learned to his distress that they had died at Eylau.

For three days Roger waited without receiving any summons from his master, and he became more and more impatient at the delay, because he had long been cherishing a means of getting out of Poland as soon as his exchange had been effected.

For a long time past, he had owned a small château near St. Maxime, in the South of France and, on the excuse of a weak chest, aggravated by a bullet through his lung at Marengo, he had usually obtained long leave to winter there; which gave him an opportunity to slip over to England and report very fully to Mr. Pitt all that was going on in France.

But this year he had been caught out. After returning to France in the previous May, he had thoroughly enjoyed his summer in Paris, and it was not his custom to apply for winter leave until December; so he had naturally accompanied the Emperor when, in September, he had left Paris to open his campaign against Prussia. After the double victory of Jena-Auerstädt, he had welcomed—being a born lover of travel and never having been to either Berlin or Warsaw—the chance of spending a few weeks in both those cities; so, when December had come, as he was no longer in the service of the British Government and, anyway, had nothing to report that could be of help to his now moribund country, instead of asking for leave he had lingered on at the Emperor's headquarters. Napoleon's taking the field again in January, much earlier than anyone had expected, had put Roger in an awkward position. To have applied then to spend the remainder of the winter months in the sunshine of the South of France would be regarded as an act of cowardice by many of his comrades, who were unaware of his skilfully-established disability. In consequence, he had participated in the campaign which had ended for him at Eylau.

However, as the thaw had only just set in and several weeks of cold, foul weather were still to be expected, he had made up his mind that, immediately he saw Napoleon, he would ask for two months' leave, in order to escape the miserable conditions that must continue to afflict the Army for some time to come. Instead, he would travel from Poland as swiftly as he could to the shores of the Mediterranean, where no one even thought of war, except to celebrate the Emperor's victories with splendid dinners and lashings of champagne. There, as a rich and distinguished officer, he would lead a life of leisure, spiced with gay parties, in the company of elegant men, and pretty women who were not over-scrupulous about their morals.

No scruples about failing to serve Alexander troubled him. His code had always been 'all's fair in love and war', and he had considered himself fully justified in misleading the Czar in order to obtain his freedom.

On the morning of his fourth day at Finckenstein, he was walking along a corridor when he suddenly saw the Emperor approaching.

Napoleon's face lit up, and he exclaimed, *'Ah! mon brave Breuc!* I feared you dead. When they told me you had fallen prisoner to these devilish Russians and could be exchanged, I was truly delighted. And at this juncture you are more than welcome here. The Turks and the Persians have both sent missions to me. This has led to my conceiving a plan by which I can stab that young fool Alexander in the back. So I am sending General Gardane on a mission, first to the Great Turk, then to the Shah. It will consist of a number of officers. But I need one personally attached to me, who will privately keep me informed how well or ill the mission is progressing.'

Suddenly, Napoleon lifted a hand, seized the lobe of Roger's left ear and tweaked it. 'You, Breuc, with your knowledge of the East, are the very man for this. Procure for yourself everything you may require, at my expense, and be prepared to set off for Constantinople.'

6

The Greatest Statesman of his Age

Roger made a grimace of pain, for the way in which Napoleon tweaked people's ears, although always a gesture of approbation, was far from gentle.

At the same moment he took in the disastrous effect that this idea of the Emperor's could have on his own plans. No carefree, lazy days in the sunshine of the Riviera; no bathing in the warm sea from a sandy beach; no pleasant expeditions into Nice and St. Tropez, where he might make the acquaintance of some charming lady who would become his mistress and add rapture to his days and nights. Instead, an interminable journey over bad roads, staying overnight at pestiferous inns, down through the semi-barbarous Balkans to countries in which all desirable women were kept under guard in harems, and the food would probably prove disgusting. Somehow or other, he must dissuade the Emperor from sending him on this mission, which threatened to ruin the daydreams with which he had been entertaining himself for the past few weeks.

As soon as he had recovered, he said, 'Sire, I have been extraordinarily lucky in that, with the chest trouble by which you know I am afflicted, I escaped pneumonia and death while a prisoner of the Russians; but I suffered severely at their hands, as you can see from my gaunt appearance. I was about to ask you for two months' leave, so that I might recuperate in the South of France.'

Napoleon shrugged. 'But, my dear Breuc, this mission on which I am about to send you will serve that purpose equally well. You will recall that, in the winter of '99, at your own suggestion, instead of going to your château at St. Maxime you went as my confidential representative to the Caribbean, to report on the validity of the excuses made by my miserable Admirals for their lack of success against the English. This mission to Turkey and Persia is of a similar nature. It will take you from the cold and mists of this ghastly country to warm lands where there is the sunshine you need.'

Actually, it had been for Roger's own personal, urgent reasons that, at that time, he had agreed to go out to the West Indies. But he could not admit that; so, hastily, he ventured on another tack. 'Sire, I fear that I should be of little use as a member of such a party. I have never been to Turkey or Persia, and speak the language of neither country.'

Impatiently, the Emperor waved aside his objection. 'That is of no importance. Well-qualified interpreters will be at your disposal, and ample funds to bribe those who act between Gardane and the Pasha and such people, to inform you of their conversations; so that you can report to me whether our mission is really making progress or if the despatches I receive are designed to keep me in a good temper.'

Roger did not at all like this proposal that he should act as a spy on his brother officers. His report on the efficiency of the French Navy in the West Indies had been quite a different matter and one in which, by misleading Napoleon, he had been able to aid his own country. But, knowing his master's lack of scruples, he made no protest about his own. Instead, he said:

'I greatly doubt whether I would prove a sound judge of such negotiations; for I know nothing of the politics of these countries or the manner in which their leading men are accustomed to transact business.'

Napoleon immediately overrode these objections. 'You will be passing through Warsaw. Talleyrand is there, and he will be able to tell you all about the aspirations of the Turks and Persians. As for their statesmen's manner of doing business, the East is the East and you are better acquainted with the ways of Orientals than any other man on my personal staff.'

Again Roger was caught out. He owed his appointment as an *aide-de-camp* to the fact that he had travelled exten-sively in India and home by way of the Red Sea and Egypt. Napoleon had always been fascinated by the East, and it had so happened that after his first triumphant campaign in Italy, Roger, having just returned from India, had again been brought to his notice. Bonaparte, already visualising himself as Sultan of the Nile and another Alexander the Great, had spent several evenings listening enthralled to Roger's accounts of his journey. Then, realising that he had many valuable qualities, the General had made him a permanent member of his staff.

In desperation, Roger declared, 'Sire, you cannot lump all the countries of the East together as though they were inhabited by one people. In India alone, there are more different races, languages and religions than there are in Europe; and none of them has the faintest resemblance to the Persians, or the Turks.'

The Emperor's face suddenly assumed a cunning look. 'In that no doubt you are right. But that this mission should cause these countries to stir up trouble for the Czar is but one half of my intent. Gardane's instructions are, while in Persia, to explore ways by which, after I have defeated Russia, in alliance with the Shah, we could most rapidly make a descent on India. And who, Breuc, knowing India so well, is better qualified to advise and assist him in such a reconnaissance?'

For Roger to point out that, although he was one of the comparatively few Europeans who had crossed the sub-continent from Calcutta to Bombay, he had no knowledge of one in a hundred of the cities and rivers in that vast territory was, he knew, futile. The Emperor assumed him to be as much an authority on it as a man who had ridden from San Sebastian to Gibraltar would be on Spain. And when Napoleon had formed an opinion on a matter, there was no altering it.

Maintaining his usual deferential and cheerful expression when in his master's presence, but inwardly seething with rage, Roger realised that unless something quite unforeseen occurred, his hopes of luxuriating in the sunshine of the South of France had evaporated into moonshine, and that within a few days he would be on his way to Constantinople.

Nothing unforeseen did occur. On the contrary, the next morning Roger was sent for by Berthier. Like Murat, the Marshal had a passion for gorgeous uniforms, which he designed himself; but, unlike the handsome cavalryman, the ugly little Chief of Staff, with a head much too big for his body, succeeded only in making himself conspicuously grotesque. After congratulating Roger on having regained his freedom, he said:

'His Majesty tells me that he has ordered you to join General Gardane's mission which is proceeding to the East. He wishes me to inform you of the situation there and what we hope to achieve. The English have been attempting to detach the Turks from their alliance with us. So far they have failed, but the Sultan is having difficulties with his own people, so it is highly desirable that we should strengthen his position and attach him more firmly to us. This we intend to try to do by furnishing him with supplies of modern weapons and, in due course, sending French troops to his support. But Turkey alone is not powerful enough to make serious trouble for the Russians in that theatre, so the arrival here of a mission from the Shah has inspired the Emperor with the idea of bringing about a triple alliance consisting of France, Turkey and Persia.

'Since the Persians are well disposed towards us and the Russians are their hereditary enemies, there is a good prospect that they would welcome the idea of joining the Turks and depriving the Czar of considerable territories adjacent to their countries while he is fully occupied by us up here in the north.'

'To put it another way,' Roger said, 'the intention of our master is to create so much trouble for the Czar in the south that he will be compelled to despatch forces there that will seriously weaken his army opposed to us.'

Berthier nodded his massive head. 'That is the intention; and, since the Persians have a considerable army of troops who have the reputation of stout fighters, it should succeed.'

'I pray you may prove right. But, as they are only just emerging from the era of using bows and arrows, I foresee a few regiments of well-disciplined Russian Grenadiers making short work of attacks by such rabble.'

'I disagree. If any horsemen in the world are the equal of the Cossacks, it is the Persians. Moreover, it is the intention of the Emperor not only to send large consignments of arms to the Sultan, but also to the Shah; and with them officers qualified to instruct the Generals of those Oriental sovereigns in the most modern methods of waging war.'

With a slightly cynical smile, Roger remarked, 'I am happy to learn that our master's new preoccupation has not altogether robbed him of the ability to enhance the probable success of his brilliant conceptions by supporting them with practical measures.'

Having no sense of humour, Berthier frowned. 'His Majesty has laboured indefatigably on behalf of France; so no man is better entitled to a few weeks of relaxation. We come now to the question of India.'

'Yes. The Emperor mentioned to me his designs upon that country.'

'So he told me; but without specifying particulars. The Persians have waged war against the northern states of India for even longer than they have against the Russians. Once we have settled with the Czar, it is His Majesty's intention to use them to facilitate our chasing the English out of India.

'Gardane's officers are to reconnoitre the routes to Delhi from Egypt, Syria and Persia, also the ports on the Red Sea and the Persian Gulf, with a view to expeditions being despatched both by land and sea. The Shah is to be persuaded to form a Corps of twelve thousand picked men, armed with French weapons, who will attack the Russians in Georgia; the bait being held out to him is the permanent annexation of that country. This Corps, later supported by twenty thousand French troops, will form the army for our advance to the East; and it is thought possible that the Mahratta Princes might be induced to join us. If so, we shall have forces of sufficient strength to overcome not only the British, but every other Maharajah who is sufficiently ill-advised to oppose us.'

This grandiose conception made it clear to Roger that, however much of Napoleon's time might be going to dalliance with the little Polish Countess, he still found enough to evolve plans calculated to take his enemies by surprise and fill them with the greatest apprehension.

After a moment Berthier went on. 'General Gardane is a very able man, and well suited to head such a mission; but His Majesty is of the opinion that you will prove of great assistance to him.'

'In that he is entirely mistaken,' Roger said earnestly, 'and I beg you, Marshal, to disabuse his mind of this idea. It is true that I once travelled across India; but of Persia and Turkey I know nothing.'

'Oh come, *mon Colonel*! How can you possibly say that? Both the Emperor and I are blessed with good memories. I recall that, while you were in Cairo, he had you arrested because you had broken into a Pasha's harem, and made off with a lovely houri who turned out to be no less than a daughter of the late Sultan. Afterwards fortune favoured you and you came to know her—er—intimately.'

'True,' Roger admitted. 'But the Princess Zanthé's mother was a French lady, born in Martinique, and Zanthé herself was married when very young to the Sultan's Viceroy of Egypt. While in Constantinople, she had never been allowed outside the seraglio, so from her I learned nothing about the Turkish people—let alone the Sultan's relations with other countries. She was, of course, a cousin of the present Sultan, Selim III, but no more than one of the countless relatives that result from the polygamy practised by these Oriental monarchs.'

Berthier shrugged and spread wide his square-fingered hands with their knobbly knuckles. 'It is clear to me, Breuc, that you are averse to accompanying General Gardane to the East. But it has been decreed by the Emperor that you should; so that is the end of the matter. As frequently as possible, you will send confidential reports to me upon how matters are progressing. Now, you must forgive me if I terminate our interview, as I have a thousand things requiring my attention.'

His last hope of escaping this new assignment gone, Roger

left the busy little Chief of Staff, and sought out General Gardane, whom he had met on several occasions, but knew only slightly.

The General had already been informed that Roger was to accompany him and, although he naturally had no idea that this additional member of his mission had been charged to make confidential reports on his activities, he talked to him freely and as an equal, knowing Roger to be a member of the Emperor's personal staff. Over several glasses of hay-scented vodka, they chatted for an hour on the situation in the East, and Roger was favourably impressed. Gardane was some years older than himself and, while he had not travelled so widely, appeared to be well informed about conditions in the countries at the eastern end of the Mediterranean. He was, moreover, forceful but well-mannered and urbane, which confirmed Roger's view that Napoleon's practice of frequently sending his more intelligent Generals as Ambassadors—where military matters were concerned—instead of professional diplomats, was a sound one.

To Roger's surprise and chagrin, as they were taking leave of one another, the General said, 'You are aware, of course, that we shall be setting out first thing tomorrow morning?'

It was the final blow to Roger's hopes that he might yet think of a way to wriggle out of this unwelcome business. He could only bow and reply, '*Mon Général,* I look forward to accompanying you.'

Hurrying to the office of the Quartermaster General, he requisitioned everything he could think of that might make his long journey more endurable. In the afternoon, he paid Berthier another visit and secured from him an order on the Paymaster's department. There he drew two hundred Napoleons in gold, which he stowed away in a money belt, and a draft on the French bankers in Constantinople for a further thousand.

That night, unhappy but now resigned, he went early to bed, wondering what this new twist of fate held in store for him.

It was the 12th April when General Gardane's party left

Finckenstein. It consisted of no fewer than fifty persons: the senior officers were Roger, Colonel Couthon of the Engineers, a lanky, gloomy man; Colonel Ladue of the Artillery, a spry fellow with an impish sense of humour; Lieutenant-Colonel Rideau, a bewhiskered veteran of the Egyptian campaign and Lieutenant-Colonel Montdallion who, a few years earlier, had accompanied General Sebastiani on an exploratory mission in 1802, sent with the object of raising trouble for the British in Algiers, Egypt, Syria and the Ionian Isles. There were a dozen junior officers; the rest were cooks, grooms, servants and interpreters detached from the Turkish and Persian Missions, the greater part of which, after again being received by Napoleon, were to travel in easy stages back to their own countries.

Two days later, Gardane's mission reached Warsaw, where they were to stay a night and supplement the meagre supply of provisions that was all they had been allowed to take with them from Finckenstein. Excusing himself to Gardane, Roger made straight for the ancient Palace which had for centuries housed the Kings of Poland and in which, after the Emperor had left it, Talleyrand had become the master.

After only a short delay, Roger was most warmly received by the ex-Bishop, now His Serene Highness the Prince de Benevento. Immaculate in black silk, lace ruffles and cravat, a square, gold quizzing glass dangling from his neck, and leaning on a jewelled malacca cane, this most potent survivor of the *ancien régime*, now just over fifty-three years of age, limped forward smiling, and said:

'*Cher ami*. The news that you had survived Eylau reached me only two days ago. I was more delighted than I can say. But I see with concern that you, too, now have a limp.'

Roger returned his smile. 'If only I can acquire the habit of making it as elegant as that of Your Highness, I'll not complain. I suffered much hardship while I was a prisoner; but that I am still alive and again free is the great thing. How fares it with yourself?'

'By no means happily. I still rejoice in technically holding the office of His Imperial Majesty's Minister for Foreign

III

Affairs; but in fact I am become no more than his chief sutler for the Army. Not a week passes but he replies to my recommendations about the foreign policies we should pursue. "I give not a damn for diplomacy. Send me bread, meat, anything you can lay your hands on for my troops, and fodder for the horses." '

With a laugh, Roger replied, 'Surely that suits you well? Such contracts should serve greatly in adding to your already considerable fortune.'

Talleyrand sighed. 'Alas, no. Unlike our friend, Fouché, it goes against my principles to acquire money by selling goods of poor quality to our own army. To support my modest tastes, I have had to make do by accepting now and then a pittance from one or other of our allies to further their interests—if, that is, their interests coincide with those of France.'

Roger glanced round, taking in his old friend's conception of 'modest tastes'. The room was a lofty, sixty-foot-long salon, with blue walls, gilded panels and a beautifully-painted ceiling, from which hung two large, crystal chandeliers. The carpet was Aubusson, the chairs covered in the finest petit-point. On a huge buhl desk stood a pair of solid gold, six-branched candelabra and, open near one of them, an oval velvet-lined case in which sparkled a fine diamond necklace —doubtless intended as a gift for some lovely Polish lady who had recently become the fastidious statesman's latest mistress. He was, admittedly, living at the moment in commandeered 'lodgings', but the room was typical of the luxury with which he habitually surrounded himself, and it was well known that the bribes he had extracted from foreign Ambassadors during the past ten years had run into several hundred million francs.

Tinkling a silver hand-bell, Talleyrand went on. 'You will, I trust, do me the pleasure of dining with me and sleeping here tonight. Then you can tell me all that has befallen you, and in what way I can be of service to you. No doubt you will recall my extreme dislike of work; but, alas, I still have some letters that I needs must glance through before they are despatched. My secretaries are reasonably competent at writing them for me, but there are times when they do not catch my exact shade of meaning. Meanwhile, I will have you conducted to an apartment, and wine sent up to refresh you after your journey.'

As Roger expressed his thanks, a servant appeared and took him up to a handsomely-furnished suite. There he luxuriated for a while in an enormous marble bath, drank a couple of glasses of champagne and cheerfully demolished a plate of Strasbourg *pâté* sandwiches.

At dinner he sat down with some twenty-five other people, several of whom he knew. Having for so long had to make do on spartan fare, he did full justice to an epicurean meal and a succession of fine wines, topped off with some Imperial Tokay his host had recently received as a present from the Emperor of Austria. After they left the table, Talleyrand devoted no more than half an hour to his other guests, then politely excused himself, and, leaning on Roger's arm, led him away to a small library.

Talleyrand had not arrived in Berlin or Warsaw before Roger had left those cities, so it was a long time since they had met, and they had much to talk about. Roger gave a brief account of his misadventures after Eylau, then said:

'I should be grateful to know whether you think this mission that I have so reluctantly been compelled to accompany is likely to prove successful.'

'How well are you informed on Turkish and Persian affairs?' Talleyrand enquired.

'About Persia I know nothing; about Turkey a limited amount. You may perhaps recall my telling you that, while in Egypt and Syria, I had an affair with a Turkish Princess named Zanthé. From her I learned that extraordinary changes had taken place at the Sultan's Court during her childhood. Her mother was Aimée Dubucq de Rivery, a young French lady born in Martinique, and a cousin of the Empress Josephine.'

Talleyrand nodded. 'I have often heard the story of the strange prophecy made to these two young women by a soothsayer, that they would both become Queens. After being edu-

cated in France, when returning to Martinique, Aimée was
captured by Barbary pirates, was she not, then sent by the
Bey of Algiers to his master, the Sultan Abdul Hamid I as a
present?'

'Yes, and fate decreed her arrival at a very opportune
moment. Abdul Hamid's heir was Selim, the son of Circassian Kadin who, at that time, was Sultan Validé—the mistress of all the women of the harem. One of Abdul Hamid's
wives, an evil woman, was endeavouring to persuade the
Sultan to have Selim murdered, so that her own son, Mustapha, should succeed. The Circassian selected Aimée and
trained her to win Abdul Hamid's affections, which she did;
and she succeeded in protecting Selim, so that he did succeed
and is the present Sultan.'

Again Talleyrand nodded. 'Aimée not only became Abdul
Hamid's principal wife, but has ever since enjoyed Selim's
devotion. Mahmoud, Aimée's son, is the present Heir Apparent. It has long been the custom for Sultans to keep their heirs
prisoner in special apartments from fear that they might con-
spire to supplant them. But Selim's trust in Aimée is such
that he has allowed her boy full freedom and acts as a father
to him. Moreover, she has persuaded Selim to introduce many
reforms, carries on a regular correspondence with her cousin
Josephine, and was responsible for bringing about the alliance
between Turkey and France. That was sadly shattered when
Napoleon invaded Egypt in '98, and deprived Turkey of one
of her richest provinces; then at Aboukir totally destroyed
the Turkish army sent against him. But in 1801 we restored
Egypt to the Turks, so our alliance with them was renewed.
Owing to this amazing woman, during the past twenty years
the Sultan's Court has become strongly impregnated with
French culture.'

Roger shrugged. 'I see, Prince, that you are as well informed
regarding the Turkish royal family as myself. But I am completely ignorant about the situation and aspirations of the
Turkish nation. For such enlightenment as you can give me,
I should be truly grateful.'

Sitting back, Talleyrand replied, 'The key to Turkey's

policy has for long been, and must continue to be, her relations with Russia. For many years the Russians have cast covetous eyes on the Sultan's dominions in the Balkans, with a view to gaining access to the Mediterranean. Since Catherine the Great's time their hope of acquiring the Sultan's European territories has increased, because the Turkish Empire is by no means the great power that it once was and, under Abdul Hamid, it suffered a still further decline.

'As you are aware, owing to the practice of polygamy, by which every Sultan begets many sons, it became the horrible but usual practice of each Sultana to endeavour to have the sons of her co-wives put to death, in order to ensure the succession of one of her own sons. In escaping death, Abdul Hamid was fortunate, but the fathers, too, feared that one of their sons might have them assassinated in order to succeed. So this unfortunate Prince was kept prisoner by his predecessor, Mustapha III, in a gilded cage for forty-three years.'

'*Mon Dieu*, how awful!' Roger exclaimed.

'A far from pleasant experience,' Talleyrand concurred. 'And, you will appreciate, not one calculated to produce a knowledgeable and strong ruler. In consequence, during the sixteens years of his reign, he lost control of a great part of his dominions. The Mamelukes defied his Viceroy in Egypt and virtually became the rulers of that country. Up on the Danube his tributary Princes, the Hospidars of Wallachia and Moldovia, refused to obey his *firmens* and the Serbians also proved extremely troublesome.

'That was the situation when Selim III ascended the throne. Owing to the protection and unbringing of your—er—charming friend's mother, he suffered none of his predecessor's disabilities. On the contrary, he had imbibed Western ideas of a Sovereign's duty to his people, and set out to introduce many reforms that would have benefited their lot.

'But one must remember the vastness of his Empire. It stretches from Morocco to the Red Sea, from southern Arabia to the Danube, and includes the whole of the Balkans. Only a Roman Emperor with the wisdom of a Marcus Aurelius or the iron will of a Hadrian could control pro-Consuls appointed by him to rule great territories so far distant from his capital.

'It is, therefore, not surprising that Selim's attempts at reform have been constantly thwarted by the Pashas who are virtually subject Kings in his more remote dominions. Naturally, they are averse to any reduction in their power. He was faced with a rebellion by the Wahhabis in the Nejd, which he had great difficulty in putting down. The Serbians are demanding independence, and one of their patriot leaders named Kara George has made himself master of Belgrade. Further north, the Hospidars of Wallachia and Moldavia have treacherously sought Russian aid to defy him.

'Last, but not least of his troubles are the Janissaries. As you must know, they are a picked corps numbering many thousands; mostly Circassians, taken from their mothers at birth and reared with the sole object of making them an admirably trained and absolutely loyal private army, prepared at any time to sacrifice their lives for their Sultan.

'Time was when they were a much smaller body and served only as Household troops. But Abdul Hamid sent large detachments of them to strengthen his armies in distant provinces. During the past few years, a number of these professional warriors have gone over to the Pashas who defy Selim's authority. Even his own Praetorian Guard in Constantinople has become disaffected, because they are averse to the reforms he would like to introduce.

'He has made a shrewd move to counter that by creating a new corps, known as the Nizam-i-jedad. They are mainly Turks who are said to be dovoted to him; but every year he strengthens this new corps by transferring a number of picked Janissaries into it, giving them special privileges. Whether he is wise in that, I have my doubts.

'To maintain himself he must have either the support of England or France. England is now Russia's ally, and the Russians are aiding his rebel Pashas on the Danube; so recently he has become more than ever pro-French. Aimée still has great influence with him, and lately she has had the able support of General Sebastiani, who arrived in Constantinople as our Ambassador last August. You may recall that, in 1803,

Bonaparte sent him to make a reconnaissance of Algeria, Egypt, Syria and the Ionian Isles, and his report proved most valuable. He is an excellent man: charming, shrewd and audacious. In him you will find a very valuable collaborator. Incidentally, he married the charming Fanny de Coigny, whose father you may recall in the old days at Versailles as a close friend of Queen Marie Antoinette.'

Roger nodded, and the statesman went on. 'From all that I have said, you will realise that General Gardane's mission will prove no easy one. The Sultan Selim has his hands full enough maintaining order in his own dominions, and I greatly doubt if he will be able to raise sufficient troops to launch an offensive against the Muscovites that would cause the Czar serious concern.'

'And what of Persia?' Roger enquired.

'For the Persians I have a great admiration,' Talleyrand replied. 'They were one of the first races in the world to become civilised, and centuries later they were the only nation that succeeded in defeating the Roman legions.' Giving a sudden smile, he added, 'Except your mother's people, the Scots. But I have been told that was mainly due to there being such a profusion of thistles in the country that they proved a serious affliction on the legionaries' bare legs—and, anyhow, there was nothing further north that made the country worth conquering.'

Roger laughed. 'The Scots had bare legs, too, so it must be that they were hardier. But Persia has suffered many defeats since Roman times.'

'True. She was, of course, overrun in the seventh century by the great wave of Arab conquest that established the Mohammedan religion throughout all North Africa and the Near East; and again in the twelfth century by the Mongol hordes. But she never lost her identity. Even her religion differs as much from the more generally accepted Islamic creed as Protestantism does from Catholicism; and, in certain areas, the ancient cult of Zoroaster continues to flourish after two thousand years.

'Through the ages Persia's contribution to the arts and

sciences has been immense. While Athens was still only a city state, Cyrus and Darius lived in palaces that rivalled those of Babylon. While we in Europe were passing through the Dark Ages, the Islamic nations produced doctors, philosophers and astronomers of the first rank. Avicenna, the greatest of them all, was a Persian. Their poets, Firdusi, Sa'adi and Hafiz wrote the most beautiful of all the works that have come out of the East, and their countrymen held them in greater esteem then than they did their victorious generals. At the time of the Italian Renaissance, Persia, too, had a Renaissance; although neither had any connection with the other. Their paintings on ivory, and designs for rugs and tiles during that period have never been surpassed; the mosques and palaces they built were miracles of skill and good taste. They were great gardeners and to them we owe the development of many of our most beautiful flowers. Believe me, I count you lucky to be going to this land of silks and roses.'

'You certainly console me considerably for having to make this long and wearisome journey,' Roger remarked. 'But you have been speaking of the past. What of the present? Have they continued to progress, and do you think it likely that they will welcome a French delegation?'

'To the best of my belief, life in Persia has altered little from the days of Shah Abbas the Great. He reigned some two hundred years ago. It was he who was responsible for the regeneration of Persia by his eager patronage of the many talented men of his own generation, and he was the first ruler to open his country to Europeans. Not long after the Portuguese rounded the Cape of Good Hope, they formed a fortified settlement on the island of Hormerz in the Persian Gulf. With their more modern ships and weapons, they were able to terrorise the Persians, raid their ports and they treated the people most brutally. Naturally, the Shah regarded them with bitter enmity. Then a hundred years later, when Abbas the Great was on the throne, the English appeared on the scene and drove the Portuguese out.

'Abbas showed his gratitude by giving them trading facilities, to the great benefit of both nations. The French arrived later and it was largely to the establishment by the Capuchin Fathers of a monastery in Isfahan that we owe our influence. The present situation is favourable to us. You will recall that, in 1800, Napoleon had secured the goodwill of the Czar Paul. Between them they concerted a plan to invade India by way of Persia, and asked the assistance of the still-reigning Shah, Fath Ali. The English got to hear of the project, and sent as an agent from India a Captain John Malcolm. He was an able man and persuaded the Shah to oppose the project. But it fell through altogether on account of the Czar Paul's assassination, and his young successor, Alexander, turning against France. Very stupidly, the English then withdrew Malcolm and have since had no representative at the Shah's Court. It follows that, as one of Fath Ali's dearest ambitions is to recover Georgia from the Russians and as Gardane will meet with no outside opposition, there is a very good chance that the Shah will now agree to become France's ally.'

'I am indeed grateful to Your Highness for this valuable exposition,' said Roger. 'I've learned more in the past hour than I could from the dozen books I had planned to buy and read on my journey.'

For a moment they were silent, then Talleyrand asked, 'Since you returned to the Emperor's service last May, have you continued to be in communication with the British Government?'

Roger shook his head. 'Nay. As you well know, were there any way in which I could profitably serve my country, I would. But ruled as it now is by a collection of cowardly fools, no project has been ventured upon that could be aided by advance information.'

'True. The expeditions they sent both to Egypt and against the Turk were a futile waste of effort. But I see you are not up to date with events. Last month the so-called "Ministry of All the Talents" was dismissed by King George because they made yet another attempt to force through the Catholic Emancipation Act. The Duke of Portland is now Prime Minister, and has Canning as his Foreign Secretary.'

'Indeed! You give me then new hope. Canning was one of

Mr. Pitt's protégés, and I am fairly well acquainted with him. He is an able and forceful man, so we may expect Britain to adopt more vigorous policies.'

'I agree. Mayhap another descent on Holland, or, to better purpose, an expedition to aid the Swedes in Stralsund. Could they succeed in defeating Mortier, they would be in a position to outflank the Emperor in the north. Moreover, Hanover, Hesse-Cassel and Western Prussia might rise behind him and cut off his communications with France.'

Roger raised his eyebrows. 'You think then that the Germans are already contemplating an attempt to throw off the French yoke, should a suitable opportunity offer?'

'I do. And should they do so, Napoleon will have only himself to blame. I implored him to be lenient with these people and thus make them friends of France. But he would not listen to me. By imposing such harsh terms, he has caused a bitterness in their minds that is now making them think only of revenge. The same applies to Austria. After Ulm, or even Austerlitz, he could have granted terms that would have made Austria his ally against Russia. But, like the Corsican bandit that he is, he insisted in robbing her of the Tyrol and her Venetian and Swabian territories. The result is that the Court of Vienna is now sitting sullenly on the sidelines. I am certain that Count Stadion, who replaced Cobentzel last year as the Emperor Francis' principal Minister, favours resuming the war while we are so fully committed against Russia. Francis is held in check only by the counsel of the Archduke Charles who, although he is their best General, urges restraint until the Army has recovered from its losses in the last campaign; and a bribe I have offered is that, should Napoleon, as he promised, restore independence to the Poles, we will not deprive Austria of her Polish lands.'

'Think you he really intends to re-create Poland as a Kingdom?'

' 'Tis possible. Murat is hoping for it as a promotion from being Grand Duke of Berg-Cleves. Louis, too, although the most vain, stupid and ineffectual of all the Bonaparte brothers, would prefer it to being King of Holland, so has arrived on the scene with a hundred suits of clothes to stake his claim. But the Poles here are rapidly becoming disillusioned about the goodwill of the Emperor towards them. Believing him to be their saviour, they welcomed him with open arms, but now they are coming to the conclusion that he has only been making use of them.'

'Then, on all counts, in spite of Napoleon's many victories, the future does not look too bright for him.'

Talleyrand took snuff, flicked the fallen grains of it from his satin lapels with a lace handkerchief, then replied. 'Far from it. To my mind, he has reached the pinnacle of his power and glory—and his usefulness to France. You know my personal history better than most men. Born a noble, I was one of the leaders of the Liberal Revolution in '89 that sought to deprive that kindly but stupid man Louis XVI of absolute power, and secure for the upper and middle classes a voice in the affairs of the nation—in short, a similar form of democratic government to that which has made England so rich and powerful.

'The extremists got the better of us, and brought about the Terror. It was to you, *cher ami*, that I owed my escape from France and my life. Hated and despised by the majority of my fellow exiles for having helped to initiate the original Revolution, I could only wait abroad for the Terror to burn itself out. As soon as it was safe to do so I returned to France, and still hoping for better times put my services at the disposal of that despicable junta of self-seekers who ruled for six years as the Directory.

'When Bonaparte returned from Egypt, I realised that he was a man who could rescue France and bring order out of chaos. Both you and I helped him to attain power, and our hopes were realised—even to his agreeing to offer peace to England. And peace, peace, lasting peace, is what all Europe needs so desperately. Above all, as we have always agreed, an honest *entente* between our two countries is the only certain means of ensuring peace and prosperity throughout the whole world. That Pitt, Grenville and your King proved suspicious, intractable and rejected Bonaparte's overture is our great tragedy.

'But I did not despair. As First Consul Bonaparte leaned upon me, giving countless hours to absorbing what I could teach him about diplomacy of which, as a soldier, he knew virtually nothing. Again and again I prevented him from acting rashly where France's foreign relations were concerned. Yet, as time went on, he tended more and more to disregard my advice. During the past few years, there have been innumerable occasions when I have ignored his outbursts of temper and allowed him to abuse me in the language of a guttersnipe. This I have supported for one reason only. Because I believed that, as long as I retained my post as Foreign Minister, I could, better than any other, direct his policies for the good of France.

'All my efforts and the humiliations I have suffered have proved to no avail. His fantastic success has turned his head. Any sound judgment that he ever had has been eroded by his insane ambition to become the master of the world. For the welfare of France he now cares nothing. By his senseless campaigns he is bleeding her white. The flower of our youth for two generations has died upon his battlefields, as the price of his personal glory.

'I intend to continue to pay him lip service; so that, should the opportunity arise, I shall still be in a position to have a say in the future of France. My knowledge of your past activities places your life in my hands. But, even were that not so, I count on you so close a friend with views so entirely in accordance with my own, that I will tell you this. From now on, I mean to work in secret for Napoleon's downfall, because I am first and last a Frenchman and only by destroying this madman's power can France be saved from annihilation.'

7

Once more a Secret Agent

Next day, when Roger left Warsaw with General Gardane's calvalcade, he had plenty to think about. Talleyrand's view, that no lasting peace could exist in Europe unless France and Britain came to an agreement satisfactory to both, had long been known to him. That was one thing; but the Minister's announcement that, from passive resistance to Napoleon's policies, he was not going to take such action as he could to bring about his downfall, was quite another. With such a powerful personality as Talleyrand, it might result in extraordinary developments.

At the moment, however, Roger was much more concerned with a problem of his own. Not only was it over eighteen months since he had sent any secret information to the British Government, but after Mr. Pitt's death he would have been most averse to doing so, because for it to have been accepted as genuine he would have had to identify himself as its sender. That could have proved highly dangerous, since he had for so long been one of Pitt's most devoted adherents, whereas the men in the 'Ministry of All the Talents' had been his most vicious enemies. In consequence, to entrust the secret of his double life to any of them was a risk Roger would have taken only if he had considered the news he had to send of great importance to his country.

But now that Ministry had fallen, and George Canning was at the Foreign Office, the situation was altogether different. He knew about Roger's past services, they had met on numerous occasions and more than once discussed the progress of the war over the dinner table in Pitt's house out at Wimbledon.

Napoleon's project for forming an alliance with the Turks

and Persians to harass the Russians in the south-east could have no directly damaging effect on Britain; but any move that hampered Russia was harmful to the Allied cause and, if Canning was informed of the Emperor's intention, he might possibly be able to exert sufficient pressure on the Sultan and the Shah to keep one, if not both of them, neutral. Therefore, Roger had decided overnight that, somehow, he must get this news to London.

But the problem was, how? Before leaving Finckenstein, the route Gardane's mission was to take had been settled. France being at war with Russia, it could not go by the shortest way: Warsaw, Lvov, Odessa and thence across the Black Sea. So, from Warsaw, they would go south through Cracow to Budapest, thence by water down the Danube to Constanza, and there take ship for Constantinople.

The question was, where could he make contact with someone who could be relied on to convey a message safely to England? Poland was under French control, Saxony had sided with Prussia in the recent war but caved in and been granted reasonable terms by Napoleon; thus becoming one of his allies. The Austrian Empire was now neutral, but Budapest, as the capital of Hungary, was subsidiary to Vienna; so no diplomats were stationed there. Further east offered no opportunities and, when he reached Constantinople, even if a British diplomat was accredited to the Sultan, it would take many weeks to get a message sent by him all the way to London.

After some thought, Roger decided that the only possibility lay in Vienna. Before the break-up of the Third Coalition Britain and Austria had been allies. Although the Austrians had been defeated by the French and the Emperor Francis driven from his capital, since peace between them had been restored he, and the diplomats accredited to his Court, would have returned there. There seemed then a good chance that, if Roger could get to Vienna, his problem would be solved.

But Vienna was some one hundred and forty miles from Budapest, and Roger knew that Gardane had already sent a galloper ahead to arrange that craft should be procured and made ready to take the mission down the Danube; so the odds were that it would not remain in the Hungarian capital more than a couple of days at most.

That night they put up at the only inn in a small, dreary town. The senior officers shared the few rooms, while their juniors occupied adjacent houses and their servants the barns and stabling. Having brought their food and cooks with them, they ate a passable meal. Afterwards Roger said to Gardane:

'*Mon Général*, I am a great lover of travel and have visited most European capitals, but not Budapest. So I should like to spend at least four or five days there. The pace at which your mission can proceed is naturally limited to that of the pack animals, which carry our supplies. I am sure, therefore, that you will have no objection to my setting off ahead of you tomorrow. Then I'll be certain of getting my few days in Budapest.'

Although Roger had been formally attached to Gardane's mission, he had no duties to perform, and the fact that he was a member of Napoleon's personal staff placed him in a privileged position. The General was much too sensible a man to antagonise one of the Emperor's people by refusing a quite reasonable request. So he replied with a smile:

'By all means, Breuc. I only wish I were able to leave the party myself and spend four or five nights in Budapest smacking the bottoms of a few pretty Hungarian girls.'

That first day from Warsaw they had covered a little under forty miles, so Roger reckoned it would take the cavalcade at least another week to reach Budapest; whereas he had often ridden over a hundred miles in a day, so he should be able to do the journey easily in three. This left him a margin of four days, which would be ample for him to accomplish the journey between the Hungarian and Austrian capitals and be back in the former before Gardane reached it.

He had himself called at four o'clock the following morning, left his soldier servant to bring on his baggage and, travelling as light as possible, set off for Cracow, arriving there that evening. The best hostelry in the big town was reasonably comfortable and he enjoyed a good supper. The long ride had taken a lot out of his charger, so he left it with the head ostler, to be collected when the French mission arrived there, and arranged to complete his joureny by Post.

The next night he had to spend at a miserable inn, but he reached Budapest at midday on the 19th. Deciding that he could well afford a badly-needed rest, he went straight to bed and slept for five hours. After waking and dressing, he then made his preparations for the following day.

While at Finckenstein he had procured from the Quarter-master a uniform—one of the many that had belonged to officers who had died from their wounds. It was by no means as elegant as the one he had been wearing on the morning of Eylau, but fairly new, fitted him reasonably well, and was suitable enough. But it was out of the question for him to pay a visit to a British diplomat dressed as a French officer. So, producing some of the gold from his money-belt, he arranged with the landlord of the Turk's Head, where he had put up, to get for him second-hand civilian clothes of good quality.

By the time he had made a leisurely supper off fresh-water *ecrevisse*, broiled with fennel, a *Gulyás* of veal and goose livers washed down with a bottle of potent red wine that rejoiced in the name of 'Bulls' Blood of Badescony', the landlord was able to produce numerous articles of clothing for his inspection. He chose a pair of fawn riding breeches, a plum-coloured coat with brass buttons—not because he liked it, but because it fitted him best—a saffron waistcoat sprigged with flowers, a grey cloak and a grey, truncated-steeple hat; then asked to be called at three o'clock, and was in bed and asleep again before ten.

Much refreshed by his two five-hour sleeps, long before dawn, riding Post again, he was on his way to Vienna. On this journey it would be his longest day yet, for the Austrian capital lay a hundred and forty miles to the west. At ten o'clock he spent an hour having breakfast at one of the posting houses where he changed horses. At four in the afternoon he dined at another, and afterwards dozed for a while in an armchair. On the last stage he was very saddle-sore and weary, but kept himself going by occasional pulls at a flask of *Baratsch*—a potent dry Hungarian spirit made from a distillation of apricots—and he entered Vienna shortly after eight o'clock in the evening.

Sliding from his horse in the yard of the Double Eagle, he threw the reins to an ostler, waited only for the man to unstrap and hand to him the small valise he had brought with him, then limped into the commodious inn. Too tired to bother about food, he ordered a quart of *Glüwein* and had himself shown straight up to a bedroom. The hot-spiced brew arrived soon after he had pulled off his clothes and flopped into bed. When he had drunk only half of it, he snuffed his candle and, within a few minutes, was sound asleep.

Next morning he awoke stiff and sore, but had no necessity to hurry out; so he had a hip-bath and a dozen cans of hot water brought up to his room. The warmth of the bath relaxed his muscles and, after lingering there for a quarter of an hour, he felt in much better condition to face the day ahead of him. He also felt ravenously hungry and ate a hearty breakfast. Then he asked for writing materials, and sat down to write a letter to Mr. Canning.

Having congratulated the Minister upon his recent appointment, he went on to express his confidence that, with him at the Foreign Office, Britain would pursue a more vigorous policy than had been the case under the late, supine Government.

He then reported on the poor state to which the *Grande Armée* had been reduced since Eylau, and gave concise particulars about Gardane's mission, its object and probable consequences should it prove successful.

Instead of signing the letter, he wrote as a last paragraph: *This comes from he who was accompanying you back to London after dining out at Wimbledon on the night that one of the wheels of your coach came off, and on your being thrown violently sideways, you badly bruised your cheek.*

He felt certain that Canning could not have forgotten the episode; but no one else into whose hands the letter happened to fall could possibly know that Canning's companion that night, after dining with Mr. Pitt, had been Roger Brook.

Having sanded and sealed his letter, he asked the way to the Hofberg and went out into the town.

The capital of a great empire, Vienna had long rivalled Paris as the finest city in Europe; so Roger was not surprised at the sight of its many fine buildings, the handsome equipages with liveried coachmen and footmen, and throng of well-clad people in the streets. Making his way to the Hofberg, he asked one of the porters there to direct him to the Ministry of Foreign Affairs. As he had thought probable, it was housed in one of the wings of the vast Palace. After crossing two courtyards, he located it and enquired from a clerk at a desk in a lofty vestibule the whereabouts of the British Embassy. Learning that it was no great distance away, on the far side of the Maria Thérèsa Platz, he decided to walk; and, on his way, enjoyed the sight of the fine gardens surrounded by a number of other imposing buildings.

On arriving at the Embassy, he learned that no British Ambassador was at present accredited to the Court of Vienna, but that for the past ten months, a Mr. Robert Adair had been *en poste* there as Minister Plenipotentiary. Giving his name as John Hickson, Roger said that he was a British subject, and would be grateful if the Minister would grant him a very brief interview on a very urgent matter.

After a wait of some ten minutes, Roger was piloted by a portly major-domo up a flight of broad, marble stairs and into a lofty, square room with much gilt decoration. Behind a large desk a middle-aged man with bushy side-whiskers was sitting. As Roger entered, he stood up. They exchanged bows, then he asked:

'What can I do for you, Mr. Hickson?'

Roger produced his letter and replied, 'I have only a simple request to make, Sir; that you will despatch this missive by safe hand at the earliest possible opportunity to Mr. Canning.'

Mr. Adair raised a pair of thick, arched eyebrows and said, 'It is not usual practice for us to transmit private correspondence; but as your letter is to the Minister of Foreign Affairs . . . May I enquire if you are aquainted with him?'

'No, Sir,' Roger lied glibly. 'But its contents will, I am sure, be of considerable interest to him.'

The Minister waved Roger to a chair. 'Perhaps you would be good enough to tell me why you think so.'

As Roger sat down, he smiled and said, 'I did not wish to take your valuable time and bore you, Sir, with particulars about myself. But, since you wish, this is my situation. I am the head of one of the concerns that have their quarters in a large compound termed "The English Factory" in St. Petersburg. Our principal trade is in furs, and one of our best markets is Budapest. Recently I had occasion to go thither. I am fluent in several languages, so while travelling through the area occupied by the French Army, I passed myself off as a German. One evening, while dining at an inn in East Prussia, there were three French officers, obviously of high rank, dining at an adjacent table. As I had been talking to the waiter in German, they must have assumed that I was unacquainted with their language, so they talked quite freely. They were discussing a plan of the Emperor Napoleon's which could cause considerable harm to the Allied cause. So I thought it my duty to send word of it to our Foreign Secretary.'

'Indeed!' Mr. Adair's interest had visibly increased. 'But is there any reason why you should not disclose it to me?'

'None, Sir. But as it concerns the Near East, there is naught that you can do to thwart this project here in Vienna, so I thought it more practical to send the information direct to Mr. Canning.'

The Minister remained thoughtful for a moment, then he said:

'Since you take that view, I will not press you. But it is evident, Mr. Hickson, that you are a superior person, capable of forming judgments on international affairs—and very conscious of your duty to your country. I should like to talk further with you, so I should be happy if you would remain to luncheon.'

Roger stood up, laid his letter on the desk, smiled and bowed. 'I am honoured by your invitation, Sir, and would be delighted to accept it. Yet I must reluctantly decline, because

I have come a hundred and forty miles out of my way in order to get this letter sent to London; and, for business reasons, I must return as speedily as possible to Budapest. I plan to set out this afternoon.'

They parted cordially, and Roger felt there was a good possibility of his having achieved his object. No one would ever know that Mr. Roger Brook, or Colonel le Chevalier de Breuc, had visited Vienna. He had been averse to disclosing the contents of his letter to Mr. Adair, in case, through him or his staff, it got out prematurely that the English were aware of Napoleon's schemes regarding Turkey and Persia. Even should Adair have the letter steamed open, or it fall into wrong hands on its way to London, at least he had protected himself from becoming known as its author.

On leaving the Embassy he spent an hour and a half wandering round the older part of the city, paid an all-too-brief visit to the magnificent *Stefans Kirk,* then went into the shop of a goldsmith in the *Kohlmarkt.*

While on his way from Warsaw he had spent a considerable amount of time debating with himself how he should proceed when he reached Constantinople. Having sent his letter to Canning, he had small hopes of doing anything further to thwart Napoleon's plans; but he was anxious to have a source of information about how negotiations were proceeding, independent of what Gardane might tell him and, if possible, learn what view the Turks really took of the General's proposals. This could differ considerably from that Gardane might optimistically assume, owing to the traditional duplicity of Orientals.

Given luck, Roger thought he might achieve direct communication with the Sultan's advisers; but, as an opening move, he would have to produce a handsome present. So, at the goldsmith's, he bought a pair of not very tall, but charmingly-designed gold candlesticks.

Soon after midday he lunched at the Double Eagle and, reluctant as he was to leave Vienna without seeing more of that fine city, immediately afterwards paid his reckoning and started on his return journey. By evening he reached Pressburg, where he had had a meal and dozed for a while the previous afternoon; dined and slept there. That left him only a hundred miles to cover the next day. On the evening of the 22nd, he was back in Budapest.

After a good night's sleep, he retrieved the uniform he had left with the landlord of the Turk's Head; then, with the financial circumspection he had inherited from his Scottish mother, he settled his bill by making over to the man the civilian clothes that had been procured for him.

His next move was to transfer himself to another hostelry, the Brave Magyar, in order to decrease the chance that any member of Gardane's mission should learn that he had procured civilian clothes and been absent for three days from Budapest.

The first time he had arrived, he had gone straight to bed, and had not even left the hotel until four o'clock the following morning, so he had seen little of the city. With the best part of a day at his disposal, he now took the opportunity to be driven round it. As he was already aware, it was in fact two cities: on the right bank of the three-hundred-yard-wide Danube, Buda; and the left bank, Pest.

In the latter he found little to interest him, as it was a flat, mainly commercial area, with a population containing a high percentage of German Jews, by whose industries the Hungarian State was largely supported; since well-born Magyars considered it beneath their dignity to engage in trade. But the right bank sloped steeply upward, and was crowned by scores of palatial mansions: the town houses of the Hungarian Magnates. Low, rounded arches on the street side gave entrance to their courtyards, and it was evident that the windows in the main frontages all had lovely views over the swiftly-flowing river.

The rounded arches recalled to Roger that, in ancient times, the Danube had been the frontier of the Roman Empire, and Ofen, as the Buda hill had then been called, an important bastion garrisoned by a Roman legion against the barbarous Scythians. Thus, as in the case of France and England, unlike the German lands, Hungary had benefited from the legacy left by that great ancient civilisation.

Rising high above the maze of narrow, cobbled streets that gave entrance to the many mansions, stood out on one side the Royal Palace, built by the Empress Maria Thérèsa in the middle of the past century; and on the other the two-hundred-and-fifty-foot-high steeple of the thirteenth-century Matthias Church. Further on in that direction, Roger came to the Fisher bastion and there left his carriage to look down on the splendid panorama that it offered. Below him on the far bank, like a mottled carpet, spread the innumerable roofs of Pest, to the left the Danube broadened out and divided to encircle the *Margareten Insel*—a lovely well-wooded island—that his German driver told him was a private estate of one of the Austrian Archdukes.

That night Roger went to bed well content. He had not only successfully completed his self-imposed mission, but had seen enough of Budapest to cause Gardane to believe that he had spent several days there.

His calculations about the progress of the mission proved near the mark, as it reached Budapest in mid-morning on the following day. The arrival of such a numerous cavalcade of French troops could not go unremarked. Having asked to be informed of it, Roger learned that it had taken up its quarters at the *Jägerhorn*: one of the biggest hostelries in Pest; so he at once drove there and reported to the General.

Over a gargantuan meal of traditional Hungarian dishes: corn on the cob; a succulent fish from Lake Balaton; chicken cooked in paprika; roast goose breasts and a great *pâté* of goose livers, Roger regaled Gardane and the other officers with an account of the delights to be enjoyed in the city. They listened with envy and a certain sourness that they were to spend only one night there; for Gardane had already learned from the French agent, to whom his advance courier had been sent, that fully-provisioned boats were waiting to transport the mission down the Danube. As an unnecessary delay might have been reported to the Emperor and brought down his wrath, the General had no option but to decree that they must all go aboard the following morning.

After the privations they had suffered in Poland and their

dreary eight-day journey from Warsaw, they naturally spent a riotous night; so it was a sorry crew of bleary-eyed, mumbling men who reluctantly assembled on the wharf.

Three commodious barges had been provided: two in which the officers and their servants were to travel, and the third for their grooms and horses. Below decks, in the barges for the personnel, there were small cabins for the seniors, bunks for the others and accommodation for messing and sitting about during bad weather. The barges were fitted with masts and sails, and in their forepart horses were stabled, to be put ashore and tow them whenever the wind dropped.

With these aids, they made good progress as, instead of having to stop for the night at inns, they slept aboard while the barges continued steadily downriver. The only halts they made were for an hour or so at small towns, to buy chickens, geese, eggs and fresh vegetables. In consequence, they averaged well over eighty miles a day and, on May 1st, arrived at the small town of Cernavada. From there it was no more than twenty-five miles to the considerable port of Constanza, on the Black Sea; whereas at that point the Danube curved north for a hundred miles up to Galeti, on the border of Moldavia, and only then turned east, to meander for yet another hundred miles through lakes and marshes until at last, by several mouths, the great river emptied itself into the sea.

That night they slept in a big caravanserai and, for the first time, savoured fully the sights and smells of the East; as, although they were still in Europe, Rumania was a Turkish province. Next day, they rode to Constanza and, the weather being fine, enjoyed the change after being cooped up for a week on a barge, with nothing to do but lounge about on deck, or play cards. But, soon after they reached the port, they met with the first setback on their journey. Their Turkish interpreter informed the General that, on enquiry, he had learned that no ship large enough to carry them and their horses would be available to charter for some days.

Cursing their luck that this hold-up should have occurred in a dirty, dreary little seaport, composed mainly of ramshackle, wooden buildings, instead of in gay and beautiful Budapest, they did their best to while away the time.

On their second evening there the local Pasha, who ruled the place from an ancient, half-ruined castle, entertained them; but the party proved a dull affair. He could speak only Turkish, and few of Gardane's officers knew more than some sentences in that language which those of them who had served under Napoleon on his Egyptian campaign had picked up at the time.

Roger was the exception, as he had become fairly fluent in it during the months that the beautiful Zanthé had been his mistress; but he remained as mum as the others, having decided that it might later prove a useful card up his sleeve to understand remarks made in Turkish while he was believed to be ignorant of it. In consequence, the sole conversation consisted of their interpreter passing on to Gardane what the Pasha said, and *vice versa*.

The food served was strange to the French: some dishes were so highly spiced that it brought tears to their eyes, and they found eating it while sitting cross-legged on low divans very uncomfortable. Most disappointing of all, no dancing girls were produced, only a small band that played weird, discordant music. As early as they decently could, after many compliments exchanged through their interpreter, they bowed themselves out, and returned to the caravanserai.

Gardane had been labouring under the illusion that the officers he was to leave in Turkey to instruct the Turks in the use of modern weapons had been picked because they were capable of at least making themselves understood in Turkish. Much annoyed by the revelation they they would prove next to useless, he decreed that henceforth they must spend several hours each day receiving instruction in the language from the interpreter. Roger, although not obliged to, sat in on these sessions, as it was seven years since he had parted from Zanthé, and he had forgotten much of the Turkish he had learned from her. To all appearances he proved a poor pupil, but listening in greatly refreshed his memory.

The only enjoyment the members of the mission derived

from their stay in Constanza was the lovely sunshine; but that was more than offset by the irritation inflicted on them by lice and bedbugs. Much to their relief, on their fourth day in the port, a good-sized vessel had been chartered to take them on to Constantinople.

On the 5th May they went aboard and set sail. Roger hated travelling by sea as, in rough weather, he was always seasick, and the quarters below deck were cramped and uncomfortable. Luckily for him, the weather continued clement, although now and then the winds were unfavourable so it took nine days for the ship to cross the south-western bight of the Black Sea. But during the voyage the lessons in Turkish were continued; so by the time they entered the Bosphorus his knowledge of the language had returned to such a degree that he felt confident that he would have no difficulty at all in conversing easily in it.

All agreed on the beauty of the scene as the ship ploughed her way down the narrow waters that, between high hills, separate Europe from Asia. Then, on the afternoon of May 14th, when she entered the Golden Horn and berthed at Pera, they gazed with awe at the splendid spectacle presented by Seraglio Point on the opposite side.

Beyond a high wall on the shore of the promontory there sloped up terraced gardens and groups of tall cypresses to the scores of pavilions that formed the Palace of the Sultan. Above them and further inland, the domes of great mosques and towering minarets stood out against the azure sky.

For those of them possessed of imagination, it was fascinating to think that there, across the narrow strip of water, lay Stamboul, the site two thousand years before of a Greek colony, then, after the fall of Rome, the fabled Byzantium, for a thousand years the capital of the Eastern Roman Empire and for the past four hundred the seat of power from which its Turkish conquerors still ruled an Empire that was in extent twenty times the size of any European Kingdom.

Immediately the ship docked, Gardane sent two of his officers ashore with the interpreter to the French Embassy. They returned with the Ambassador, General Sebastiani. He was then thirty-five, a man of splendid physique, extraordinarily handsome and known throughout the Army for his unfailing charm and good humour. To the amazement of Roger, Gardane and several other members of the mission who were acquainted with him, he appeared to have aged ten years. His face was furrowed, his eyes lacked lustre and he approached them with a dejected stoop.

It occurred to Roger that the Ambassador must have caught the plague, with which from time to time Constantinople was afflicted, and was only now recovering; but Sebastiani's first words explained his sad condition. To Gardane he said:

'General, I am in a poor state to welcome you and these gentlemen. A few weeks ago, my beloved wife, Fanny, gave birth to a child. Soon after she fell victim to a deadly fever, and I lost her. This bereavement has stricken me utterly. I am a changed man and no longer fit for anything. My only wish is to return as soon as possible to France and be left alone with my grief. I have remained here awaiting your arrival only so that I might present you to the Sultan.'

After they had expressed their deep sympathy, he led them ashore and had them carried in palanquins up the steep hill to the Embassy. Spacious as it was, formerly having been a Pasha's palace, it was not large enough to accommodate them all; but, having been warned by fast courier of the mission's coming, Sebastiani had rented two houses nearby for the junior officers. Gardane, Roger, Couthon, Ladue, Rideau and the Ambassador's old travelling companion Montdallion, were to be his personal guests. After partaking of refreshments and being given ample time to settle into their new quarters, the officers staying in the Embassy went down to dine with the Ambassador. He had obviously made an effort to pull himself together and, over the meal, gave them particulars of the situation in Constantinople. Looking at Gardane, he said:

'About the possibilities of your success in Persia I can give no opinion; but here everything favours your aims.

'Very fortunately for us, the English blundered badly last winter by forcing the Dardanelles and threatening Constantinople. The Turks were outraged and, urged on by me, dragged every cannon they could lay their hands on to the waterfront, in order to bombard the English Fleet. Finding themselves outgunned, the Fleet beat an ignominious retreat. The British Ambassador, the Hon. Charles Arbuthnot, having been informed that he was *persona non grata*, received his passports and departed to join the Fleet off Tenedos. Since then there has been no representative here of the Court of St. James, so you need fear no opposition.'

Roger had anticipated that this would probably be the case. It confirmed his assumption that he could secure no help or advice, and must act entirely on his own initiative.

Meanwhile, Sebastiani was going on. 'Contrary to the belief of most people, the Sultan is by no means all-powerful. Selim III was exceptionally fortunate in that, unlike his predecessors for many years past, he was not kept a prisoner for the whole of his young manhood. In consequence, he has a much greater knowledge of statecraft and international relationships than would otherwise have been the case.

'Even so, he is hedged about by the age-old traditions that must be observed by a Sultan if he wishes to retain his throne. To start with, he dare not offend the Janissaries. As you no doubt know, they were originally a corps formed from Circassians taken when very young from their mothers and reared as professional soldiers to form the Sultan's bodyguard. But, with the passing of time, they have become an army a hundred thousand strong. Formidable bodies of them have been sent to support the rule of Turkish Pashas in rebellious provinces, but at least ten thousand of them are retained here to garrison the Seraglio, and many of them now are Turks who refuse to obey the old ordinances forbidding Janissaries to take wives or drink alcohol.

'When the Sultan issues a *firman* to which they object, they carry their soup kettles out from their quarters and beat furiously upon them. It is one of the most sinister and frightening noises I have ever heard; and, unless the Sultan retracts his order, he risks death at their hands.'

Sebastiani paused for a moment to take a mouthful of wine. 'But it is not only the Janissaries to whom the Sultans in the past hundred years have become subservient. Their policy has been controlled very largely by the will of a woman. Do not mistake me, I do not mean that they become enslaved by the charms of a favourite wife or concubine. Naturally, they are influenced in minor domestic matters, such as the allocation of the best apartments, the bestowal of jewels and so on by a *Kadin* or one of the hundreds of odalisques who may have captured their affections; but while a Sultan can have as many women as he chooses to share his bed, he can have only one mother.

'A Sultan's mother is known as the Sultan Validé. To have attained this unique status against fanatical competition, it is obvious that such women must be exceptionally strong-willed and intelligent. In consequence, once her son has ascended the throne, her power is almost unlimited. In consultation with the Kizler Aga—the Chief of the Black Eunuchs, who is known by us as *Son Altesse Noire*—they rule the harem absolutely. Nothing can be done without the Sultan Validé's consent. Moreover, her power extends far beyond the Seraglio. She is regarded with veneration as the protectress of all the veiled women in the Turkish Empire. No war is entered upon without her consent. Every matter of international relationship is submitted to her, and no Sultan yet has dared openly to reject his mother's counsel.'

Sitting back, Sebastiani gave a sad smile, and added, 'Messieurs, in this we are favoured by the gods. The present Sultan Validé was born Aimée Dubucq de Rivery, a French woman and a cousin of our Empress. For many years she has served the cause of France devotedly. She is the mother of Prince Mahmoud, who, it is certain, will succeed; and on the death of the Sultan's mother, in 1805, she was raised by Selim to the Veiled Crown.

'Brief as my time has been as Ambassador—only a matter of ten months—my . . . my beloved Fanny won her affection and became her constant companion. Alas, you are now bereft of my wife's help, and such as I could give you. Even so, you may count upon it that the Sultan Validé will welcome you warmly and do her utmost to aid you in your mission.'

About the restricted power of Sultans and the organisation of the Seraglio Roger already knew, owing to his long affair with Zanthé. The one thing he had been anxious to learn was whether Aimée was still alive and now the reigning Sultan Validé. Upon that his decidedly nebulous plans had been based; so he was much relieved to hear that no harm had befallen her.

He was amused to think how amazed the assembled company would have been had he revealed to them how his own life had been changed by Bonaparte's decision clandestinely to abandon his army in Egypt in '99. With the greatest secrecy he had made his plans and, without informing any but a few of his personal staff, had them accompany him aboard a frigate overnight. Zanthé, believing herself abandoned, had later married Achilles Sarodopulous, the son of an immensely wealthy banker, who lived in Alexandria. Otherwise Roger might have claimed the Sultan Validé as his mother-in-law.

Sebastiani went on to say that he had that afternoon sent a request to the Grand Vizier to present the Mission to the Sultan; but he thought it unlikely that they would be granted an audience for some days. In the meantime, although they were free to go out into the city, they must not do so unaccompanied. It was customary for European merchants in Constantinople to go about in Oriental dress, as anyone wearing Western clothes, being a rare sight, always attracted attention and crowds formed round them, which could prove most embarrassing. He was, therefore, attaching to each officer a Turkish Janissary, as they could be hired for such a purpose. These Janissaries would act as guides and, by a few sharp words, ensure the unimpeded progress of their charges.

Next morning, the Janissary allotted to Roger reported to him. All Turks retained a tuft of hair on the tops of their heads, otherwise the majority of them allowed only their beards to grow; but the Janissaries were forbidden to have beards. Instead, they had very long moustaches which, in some cases, drooped down to their chests. Roger's man was clad in a long, blue cloth coat, an undercoat with hanging sleeves and a big turban, through which was thrust a twelve-inch-long soup spoon—that being an ancient custom of the regiment. Above it sprouted a plume of bird-of-paradise feathers. From his girdle there hung a scimitar, a dagger and a small hatchet. His boots were black, which Roger later learned showed him to be of the lowest rank, the higher one wearing yellow and the highest red. To the casual glance he appeared a colourful and fierce figure; but Roger noted that his eyes were mild and that he was far from young. He announced himself with a deep salaam as Achmet Zuhayr and declared that 'Allah willing—blessed be his name and that of his Prophet'—he would protect Roger from all thieves, pickpockets, casters of evil spells and diseased women.

Regarding it as unlikely that if he spoke with ease to Achmet the surprisingly sudden improvement in his Turkish would get back to any member of the mission, Roger thanked him, talked to him for a while about the city, then said he would like to be shown round Pera.

During the long journey down from Finckenstein, as *le brave Breuc* was one of the legendary figures of the *Grande Armée,* his friendship had been eagerly sought, particularly by the younger members of the mission, and he had spent many pleasant evenings with them, talking of the Emperor's early campaigns. In consequence, he had feared that he might have considerable difficulty in freeing himself from their company when the mission arrived in Constantinople; but, fortunately, they were in the rented houses and none of the senior officers staying in the Embassy was about when Roger and Achmet came downstairs.

For an hour they strolled through the maze of steep, twisting streets. Roger duly admired the famous White Tower, built centuries earlier by the Genoese, the view across the Golden Horn to Stamboul, and that across the Bosphorus to the Asiatic side; then he told Achmet that he wished to buy Balkan clothes, possibly to wear now and then while in Constantinople and, in any case, to take back to France as a souvenir of his visit. Achmet replied that the best value in all things was to be found in the Grand Bazaar.

The Golden Horn was spanned by a long row of *caiques*

lashed together and overlaid with a road of boards, a section in the centre being easily detached so that, from time to time, it could be moved to allow the passage of water traffic. As Roger crossed this bridge of boats, he was interested to see that, while the Pera shore was almost hidden by a forest of masts rising from scores of closely-packed ships, showing the enormous trade carried on by Constantinople with other ports in the Mediterranean, only a few heavily-gilded barges were moored on the Stamboul side. They were, Achmet told him, the Sultan's pleasure boats, in which at times he took some of his ladies of the harem on trips to his other palaces further up the Bosphorus, across in Scutari, or down to the islands beyond the point, in the Marmora. On the shore there were two large pavilions. Beyond them stood the tall, crenellated wall that enclosed the Sultan's huge private domain. Above it could be seen many acres of gardens sloping up to the massed buildings forming the Topkapi Palace.

Having crossed the Galata bridge, they passed the splendid Fatima Mosque and the Tomb of Suliman the Magnificent, then entered a warren of narrow ways crowded with dark-robed, veiled women, street vendors and men selling bread rings on sticks, until they reached the Grand Bazaar.

It consisted of a covered area in which, according to Achmet, there were over a thousand shops. The walkways were criss-cross parallels, with no signs to differentiate one from another, and Achmet confessed that even he might well get lost in them. Every conceivable item of Eastern food, clothes, furniture, apparel and *objets d'art* could be brought there: perfumes, spices, jewels, weapons, cooking utensils and imported goods from China, Persia, India, Africa and Europe.

Their first call was on a money-changer. Roger had transferred a handful of gold Napoleons from his money belt to his breeches pocket. Casually he put them on the counter. Achmet did the bargaining and, after ten minutes of mingled persuasion and abuse, secured what Roger thought was probably a fairly reasonable rate of exchange. They then proceeded to do their shopping. First they bought a large, cylindrical woven basket to contain their purchases; then, item by item, packed into it a complete outfit of rich clothes such as were worn by Balkan noblemen and wealthy merchants.

When they got back to Roger's room at the Embassy, he put his hand in his pocket, smiled at Achmet and suddenly cried, 'Catch.' As he spoke he threw Achmet a gold coin and added, 'That is your pay for today.'

Achmet caught the coin, looked at it and gasped with stupefaction. It was more than he could have earned in a month. Almost tongue-tied with gratitude, he stammered his thanks and protested his eternal devotion to such a generous master.

With a gesture Roger silenced him and said in a quiet, firm voice, 'I have things to do in this city, which do not concern His Excellency the Ambassador or any of the officers with whom I arrived here. Serve me faithfully and say no word to your fellow Janissaries of where I go and you shall receive another gold piece every day. But I give you warning. I have powerful friends inside the Seraglio. Should it come to my ears that you have spoken of my doings, those friends of mine will see to it that your tongue is torn out.'

Having paused to let his words sink in, Roger went on. 'Now, take this basket containing the apparel I have bought. Go over again to Stamboul and rent for me there a room in the dwelling of a discreet man, where I can change into Balkan costume without his talking of the matter to his neighbours. Here,' he added, producing two more gold coins and handing them to Achmet, 'is money that you are to give him as an advance payment for the accommodation and his discretion.'

Salaaming, Achmet took the coins, picked up the basket and, with further expressions of his willingness to do as he was bid, bowed himself out of the room.

From midday on, it had become very hot, so Roger stripped to his underclothes, lay down on his bed and, for a couple of hours, enjoyed a siesta. Late in the afternoon the welcome breeze from the north-west, which is a feature of Constantinople's climate, began to blow, making the city much cooler. Getting up, Roger dressed and went down to see the secretary who acted as the Embassy's treasurer. His trip to Vienna, buying the pair of gold candlesticks and his purchases that morning had nearly run him out of ready money; so he presented his draft and drew in Turkish gold the equivalent of two hundred Napoleons.

Next morning, Achmet reported that he had secured for Roger a room over the shop of a tailor, who made uniforms for the Janissaries, was an old friend and could be relied on not to talk.

However, as it happened, that day, May 16th, was a Friday, and Roger felt that the Mahommedan Sabbath was not at all a suitable day to undertake the project he had in mind. So, joining a number of his fellow officers, he went with them on an expedition up the Bosphorus.

On the Saturday morning, soon after he had breakfasted, he set off with Achmet and again crossed the Golden Horn. Arriving at the tailor's shop, he had a brief talk with the man, implying that he was engaged in a clandestine love affair.

He then produced from what Ahmet, with popping eyes, now assumed to be his inexhaustible supply of gold, three more pieces, which the tailor gratefully accepted, promising on the Koran to say no word about his new tenant's activities.

In the room upstairs, with Achmet's help, Roger changed into the Eastern clothes; then, telling Achmet to await his return, he went out.

Unremarked by the crowds of turbaned men and veiled women, he made his way up to the gate in the high wall that gives entrance to the Topkapi Palace. In its great First Court, the public were admitted, although only high officials were allowed to ride and a rule of silence was enforced by the presence of numerous halberdiers. Crossing the Court, Roger came to a second gate, called the Ortakapi. This was guarded by some fifty Janissaries, one of whom, wearing yellow boots, came forward and asked Roger's business.

'I am,' Roger replied, 'a Greek merchant, and my principle trade is with Venice. When I was there some weeks ago, I chanced to become acquainted with a French officer of high rank. He was on his way to Constantinople with a gift from the Emperor of the French to—Allah preserve her and blessed be his name and that of his Prophet—our beloved Sultan Validé. The poor man was stricken of a fever which carried him off; but before he died, knowing that I was returning here, he asked me to act for him and deliver the present to Her Imperial Majesty.'

It was a plausible story and, after a moment's consideration, the Janissary said, 'It is by no means easy to obtain an audience with the Sultan Validé.'

Roger smiled. 'I appreciate that.' Then he slipped two gold coins into the man's hand, and added, 'But I promised to deliver this present personally, and I am sure Her Imperial Majesty would be happy to receive it. Please see what you can do for me.'

The Janissary shrugged, led Roger into a small room on the left, under the arch of the gate, and said, 'Wait here.'

It was over an hour before the Janissary returned. With him he brought a hugely fat, sullen-faced man with many chins, dressed in rich fur robes and wearing a two-foot-high conical hat. Roger guessed him to be the Kapi Aga, Chief of the White Eunuchs who, many years earlier, had been degraded from charge of the harem to that of the Selámlek—those parts of the palace in which men were allowed—and who performed the functions of porters, teachers to the pages and other duties, according to their degree. To this high official Roger made a low obeisance and repeated his story.

The eunuch eyed Roger coldly, made a negative motion with his head which caused the fat flesh below his chin to wobble, and replied, 'Her Sublimity the Veiled Crown does not receive persons of your sort. Give me the present from the French Sultana of whom you speak and I will lay it at the feet of Her Imperial Majesty.'

Roger salaamed again and said earnestly, '*Effendi*, I swore an oath on the Koran to this dying Frenchman that I would personally deliver the present to Our Lady Protectress of all Veiled Women. I pray you, grant me a word alone.'

With a swift gesture, the Kapi Aga dismissed the Janissary. When he had left the room, Roger produced a string purse that he had ready. It held twenty-five gold pieces. Handing it to the monstrous creature facing him, he said, 'Your Excellency must support many charities. Permit me to offer this humble contribution.'

The small, pursed-up mouth in the great, flabby mask of fat crumpled into the semblance of a smile. Tossing the heavy purse gently in his beringed hand, he said, 'Such contributions from rich merchants are welcome. Be here tomorrow at the same time. Bring with you two purses of gold of the same weight. I promise nothing. But the black swine who now order all things beyond the Gate of Felicity are greedy and must be won over to grant your application. The blessing of Allah—blessed be his name and that of his Prophet—be upon you.'

In the room over the tailor's shop Roger changed back into uniform, then returned with Achmet to the French Embassy. To penetrate the Seraglio was costing him a lot of money, but he had anticipated that it would, and he was not unsatisfied with the progress he had so far made.

Next day, he again presented himself at the First Gate, this time carrying a handsome, round-lidded casket he had had Ahmet buy for him, containing the gold candlesticks. Pressing another couple of gold pieces into the Janissary's hand, he asked him to inform the Kapi Aga of his presence. A quarter of an hour later, the Chief of the White Eunuchs came into the waiting room. After salutations had been exchanged, Roger handed over the two purses of gold. The Kapi Aga pocketed one, but returned the other, saying. 'That you will give to the tall, black eunuch at the Gate of Felicity. I have arranged matters, and he will escort you to the apartments of Her Sublimity, the Wearer of the Veiled Crown.'

Beckoning Roger to follow, the white eunuch waddled out of the room and led the way into the Second Court: a great, open space divided by a central avenue of cypresses, on either side of which were beds of several thousand roses in bloom.

As Roger followed, it suddenly struck him that he might be behaving with incredible foolhardiness. He could perfectly well have remained at the French Embassy and passed his time innocently sightseeing. But, being the man he was, he had been tempted into seeking this audience with the Sultan Validé.

By talking with her, he hoped to achieve one of two things. He could imply that the Emperor would have no great difficulty in defeating the Czar unaided; therefore, in view of the unrest in Turkey's European provinces, she would be wise to keep her garrisons there at full strength rather than reduce them to send more troops against the Russians. Thus he could help the Allied cause. On the other hand if, owing to her devotion to France, she was set upon providing troops, he could later increase his standing with Napoleon by leading him to believe that Gardane's mission would have failed had not he, Roger, held private conversations with the Sultana.

But now it struck him that he was taking a considerable risk. To carry any weight with her he must declare himself to be *Colonel de Chevalier de Breuc*, a member of Napoleon's personal staff, and pretend that he had been commissioned by the Empress Josephine to bring her a present.

It was just possible that she had learned from her daughter, Zanthé, what had befallen her in Cairo. Roger had saved her from being raped by a dozen drunken soldiers, then sold by them for a few francs a time to scores of their comrades. But the fact remained that, having rescued her, and knowing her to be married, he had ravished her himself, although ignorant of the fact that she was still a virgin. If the Sultan Validé knew only the latter part of that story and realised that it was Roger who had deflowered her daughter, she might even order him to be castrated.

8

The Veiled Crown

As Roger followed the Kapi Aga across the Second Court, he barely glanced to his left at the row of ten huge kitchens, each with a tall chimney, or at the stables and Hall of the Dewan, surmounted by a short, square tower and steeple, on his right. His mind was occupied by very uneasy thoughts and, as the eunuch walked with a slow waddle, there was ample time for Roger to contemplate the highly dangerous situation in which he had landed himself.

He had last seen Zanthé and her husband at the first reception Napoleon had given in the Tuileries after being elected First Consul. That they were then in Paris was due to Achilles Sarodopulous' having been sent by his father to open a branch of the family bank in the French capital. In view of his past relations with Zanthé, Roger had thought it only fair to Achilles who, while he was in Egypt had proved a good friend to him, to refrain from seeking them out on his subsequent visits to Paris—much as he would have liked to see Zanthé's little son of whom he knew himself to be the father; but, as far as he was aware, they were still in Paris.

If so, it was most unlikely that Zanthé had made the long journey to Constantinople to see her mother and told her all that had befallen her in Egypt. There was, too, the fact that having renounced Islam and become a Christian of the Orthodox Greek Church, in order to marry Achilles, Zanthé had raised another bar between herself and her family.

But there remained the possibility that mother and daughter continued to correspond. If so, Zanthé might have given her mother an account of the months she had spent in Egypt and Syria. Roger endeavoured to still his uneasiness by the thought that, if she had, she would not have revealed in a letter the fact that she had been the mistress of a French officer. But of that he could not be certain, and this doubt now became uppermost in his mind.

He was not given to panicking, but for a moment he felt that, in seeking an audience with the Sultan Valide, he had taken an absurd risk to achieve what, at best, could prove only a gain of no great importance. But it was now too late to turn back; so he continued to follow the ponderous footsteps of the Chief of the White Eunuchs and, by a great effort of will, forced himself to recall instead all he had heard from Zanthé and, more recently, Achmet about the Seraglio.

It was not, as most people believed, simply a rambling palace consisting of many buildings in which the Sultan maintained several hundred women for his pleasure. On the contrary, it housed twenty thousand people, two-thirds of whom were troops, and over a thousand cooks. The *Harēmlik*, as it was properly called, was a comparatively small part of it.

By far the greater number of buildings formed the *Selámlik*, which was occupied by the guards, eunuchs, ministers and other functionaries, artists, artisans, dwarfs and jugglers. It contained a big military school, over a dozen mosques, ten kitchens, two hospitals, many Turkish baths, several swimming pools, store-rooms, sports fields, a library in which were a quarter of a million manuscripts, prisons, treasuries, stabling for three thousand horses and a score of workshops in which hundreds of men were constantly employed as goldsmiths, weavers, engravers, tile-makers, swordsmiths, upholsterers, potters, carpenters, and in a dozen other crafts.

All these people in the *Selámlik* worked under the supervision of the White Eunuchs, while the Black Eunuchs were entrusted with the guardianship of the women's quarters.

The great majority of the women lived in a big building, having three floors, and a wide, central corridor overlooked from balconies on the two upper floors. Each odalisque had a chamber to herself; so in that, it was not unlikely a nunnery, except that instead of austere cells, the rooms were luxuriously furnished. The *Kadins* and temporary favourites had separate suites, with even richer furnishings, and all enjoyed the use of spacious gardens, the many pavilions in them, numerous baths, ball-courts and the terraces from which there was a lovely view over the Sea of Marmora.

Roger brought his mind back with a jerk from these deliberate musings on all he had heard of the Topkapi Palace, for they had reached the Gate of Felicity, which gave entrance to the Third Court. This was guarded by both White and Black Eunuchs, and the Kapi Aga said in his high-pitched voice to a huge Negro, 'This is the Greek merchant of whom I spoke to you yesterday.' Then, without a glance at Roger, he waddled away.

The Negro was richly dressed in an ermine pelisse, jewelled ear-rings dangled from the lobes of his ears and there were several valuable rings on his big fingers. It was obvious to Roger that he was a person of importance and, in fact, he proved to be *Son Altesse Noire,* the Kizler Aga, Chief of the Black Eunuchs. Making low obeisance, Roger contrived to drop the silk net purse containing the twenty-five gold pieces. Quickly he picked it up and handed it to the Negro, as though it was he who had dropped it. Two rows of pearly white teeth appeared between the black man's red lips as he smiled with amusement at this subtle way of giving him his bribe. 'All is arranged,' he said in a little, reedy voice. 'Come with me.'

Passing through the Gate of Felicity, they entered the Third Court. Facing the gate and only a few yards from it there was a magnificent pavilion, in the centre of which, raised on legs, there stood an eight-foot-long and four-feet-deep gold divan, flashing with precious stones. Casually waving a hand towards it, the eunuch said, 'The throne upon which the Commander of the Faithful, Allah's Shadow on Earth, gives audience to distinguished visitors. It was made from eighty thousand gold ducats captured from the Venetians. He has another studded with twenty-five thousand pearls.'

Turning left, they walked some way across the court, then entered a maze of narrow passages. On coming to one that was broader than the others, the big Negro, who evidently took pleasure in showing his domain to those privileged to enter it, said, 'This is the Golden Road. Along it, faint from exaltation, are carried such odalisques as our Imperial master has deigned to cast his handkerchief to, signifying that he desires them to be brought to his bed.'

Through an archway on the far side of the Golden Road, they came to a spacious courtyard, lined with orange, apricot and pomegranate trees growing in large tubs. Crossing it to a low doorway, the eunuch told Roger to wait there, then went in.

Two minutes later he emerged, and bowed. 'Her Sublimity the Veiled Crown, consents to receive you.' Roger returned the bow and, his heart beating a little faster, walked through the low porch.

Beyond it there was a small hall then, behind a heavy curtain that the eunuch held aside, a big room, the sight of which caused Roger to catch his breath in amazement. It was no Eastern reception room with divans round the walls, silk Persian mats of fine design, and small, ebony tables inlaid with ivory. He might have stepped back twenty years in time, to find himself again in one of the smaller salons at Versailles.

The furniture was Louis XVI, the carpet Aubusson, the satinwood cabinets filled with Meissen and Sèvres porcelain, while on the walls hung charming paintings by Bouchard Fragonard and Vigé le Brun.

At the far end of the room there were two women, and there could be no mistaking the one who had created this oasis of a bygone France in the heart of an Eastern harem. She was, Roger knew, forty-three years old, but did not look it. The veil she wore looped from ear to ear was so diaphanous that through it Roger could discern her lower features: a rosebud mouth above a firm chin. Her face was a little on the plump side, her blue eyes enormous, and golden hair on which she wore a little, round pillbox hat, swept back from her fine forehead. Here and there, among her golden tresses, sparkled diamonds, dangling from almost invisible tiny gold chains. It was no cause for wonder that, on entering the harem, instead of being given the name of Jasmine, Sweet-breath, Pearl of the

Dawn or some such soubriquet, she had become known simply as *Naksh*—the Beautiful One.

She was seated in an elbow chair with, across her knees, a canvas of *petit-point*, on which she had been working. Beside her, on a low stool sat a younger, dark-haired woman, more heavily veiled but, judging from her fine eyes and flawless skin, also beautiful.

Bowing low with every step, Roger advanced towards the First Lady of the Turkish world, then laid the casket at her feet and remained kneeling there. To his surprise and sudden perturbation, she spoke to him in Greek.

Not understanding Greek, he was temporarily dumbfounded. But, swiftly recovering himself, he came to his feet, forced a smile and said in French:

'Your Imperial Majesty has forced me to a confession that I was about to make. I am no Greek merchant who agreed to deliver this present to you on behalf of a French officer who died in Venice. I am that officer *Colonel le Chevalier de Breuc*.'

With a sudden frown, her eyes holding his, she asked, 'Why this fiction, Monsieur, and why are you in Eastern dress?'

'May it please Your Majesty, I have accompanied the mission headed by General Gardane, sent by the Emperor Napoleon to His Imperial Majesty the Sultan. But I am only attached to it. I come to you as the personal representative of your illustrious cousin, the Empress Josephine. My colleagues are unaware of that and, had I come to the Seraglio in uniform, it is certain they would have learned of it. That would have been difficult to explain. Hence the disguise.'

Still unsmiling, she replied, 'You are then, *Monsieur le Chevalier*, as I had been led to suppose, a man of resource.'

Roger's heart missed a beat. Again he forced a smile and said, 'As a member of the Emperor's personal staff, I have had the good fortune to achieve some notoriety in the *Grande Armée*, and it seems that Your Majesty has heard talk of that.'

Instead of replying, she turned to the girl beside her and said, 'Fatima, I wish to speak to this gentleman alone.'

Putting aside her work, the girl made a low obeisance and slipped out through a door at the side of the room.

Turning back to Roger, the golden-haired Venus said in a level voice, 'Yes, *Monsieur de Breuc*, I have certainly heard of you. Moreover, those blue eyes and long lashes of yours tell me what I have long suspected. No Greek banker could have given them to his child. You are the father of my grandson. Can you deny it?'

The second she mentioned his blue eyes, Roger's swift brain had leaped to it that the cat was out of the bag. Obviously Zanthé had informed her mother of how a French officer had carried her off in Cairo, and had named him as her seducer. By coming to the Seraglio, he had voluntarily and idiotically put his head into a hornet's nest. Within a few minutes now he might be handed over to the eunuchs to be strangled with a bow-string.

Knowing himself cornered and escape impossible, he took a wild gamble. It could come off only if *Naksh*—the Beautiful One—reacted as a woman. If she maintained the aloofness proper to her station as the First Lady of a mighty Empire, he would be utterly lost. Drawing himself up to his full height, he said, 'Sublimity, my life is in your hands. For the joy the Princess Zanthé gave me I will go to my death willingly. I have only one regret. That it was her and not you that I had in my bed both in Cairo and in Acre. For you are even more beautiful than your daughter.'

He saw her cheeks flush beneath the diaphanous veil. Her big eyes narrowed and she snapped, 'Monsieur! To think of me in such a situation is sacrilege. For what you have just said, a fitting punishment is that I should have your flesh torn from your body, piece by piece, with red-hot pincers.'

Inwardly Roger quailed. Yet, with the courage of desperation, he managed to sneer, 'A decision one might expect from a blood-lusting Turk, but not from a French lady of aristocratic birth.'

She gave a slight shrug and replied, 'It is true that the Turks are a cruel and bloodthirsty people. But there is a saying, "When in Rome . . ." You will know the rest. You are now in Constantinople. By Turkish standards, you have addressed me as though I were a woman in a brothel. It so happens that

I am not only an Empress, but for over twenty years I have been a Turk.'

Standing up, she put out a hand, grasped a silken rope ending in a large tassel, and gave it a swift jerk. A bell clanged hollowly somewhere in the distance.

Situated as he was, in the depths of this vast palace, with its hundreds of rooms, mazes of corridors and thousands of guards, Roger knew that there was not the faintest possibility of fighting his way out. He had not even a sword with which to kill a few eunuchs before they killed him, as no visitor was allowed to enter the Palace armed. By seizing the back of the nearest chair, he could use its legs to fend off an attack; but for no more than a few moments, as the legs were thin and would snap off at the first heavy impact.

Yet, if he were doomed to die, there was one thing he could do which might bring him a quick death and escape from torture. Taking one step forward, he seized the Sultan Validé in his arms.

It was possible that the eunuchs might succeed in dragging him, while still alive, away from her; but he was very strong and meant to cling to her as a drowning man would to a floating spar. All the odds were, he thought, that, horrified at the sight of such sacrilege, they would lose their heads, think only of freeing their mistress and frantically stab him in the back.

As he clasped Aimée to him, she gave a gasp of amazement, then cried, 'Are you mad? Let me go!'

Death might be round the corner, but he was enjoying himself now. Smiling down into her lovely face, he said, 'No, *Naksh*. Holding you in my arms while I die will give me a foretaste of heaven. And, when your eunuchs stab at me, I mean to swing round; so we may even die together.'

At that moment they both caught the sound of the outer door being closed, then footsteps crossing the small hall. Aimée had been striving to free herself. Suddenly her struggles ceased. She went quite rigid and, in a voice that was perfectly controlled, but sharp and commanding, she cried loudly:

'Yussif! Bring champagne. At once! Immediately!'

The footfalls halted and receded. Aimée gave a great sigh

and, for a moment, let her head fall forward to rest on Roger's shoulder. Then, looking up at him, she breathed, 'What an escape! Had Yussif glimpsed you embracing me, even I, with all my power, could not have saved your life. To start with, they would have put a cord round your testicles and hung you by it from a beam; then bastinadoed you daily until your wretched body gave up the ghost.'

'But . . .' stammered Roger, 'but you were going to have me killed in any case.'

'You imbecile!' she retorted. 'Is it likely that I, a French-woman, would have a French officer sent to me by my cousin Josephine harmed? But life is dull here, and it was an opportunity for a little amusement. When I pulled that bell-rope it was to order champagne. Then, when it arrived, we would have laughed together.'

Roger made a wry grimace. 'A dangerous form of amuse-ment, Madame. It might have resulted in the death of both of us.'

She nodded. 'I realise that now. I should have before. Zanthé told me that you were the very devil of a man. And, indeed you are! But for God's sake, let me go now. If Yussif finds us like this when he brings the wine, all I could wish you would be a speedy death.'

As Roger released her and again assumed a most respectful attitude, he said, 'I appreciate that while you would have re-ceived the Empress Josephine's envoy most kindly, you can hardly be surprised that when it became apparent to me that you realised I was the man who had dragged Zanthé into my bed in Cairo, I had good cause to fear that you meant to exact vengeance on me.'

Aimée suddenly threw back her golden head and laughed. 'On the contrary, both she and I have much to thank you for. She came on a visit to me here eighteen months ago, and con-fided to me all that had passed between you. Some man had to be the first to lie with her, and that it happened to be *le brave Breuc* rather than her old husband, the Pasha, who cared only for boys, was her good fortune. Think, too, of the ghastly fate that would have befallen her had you not rescued her from that gang of ruffians who waylaid her.'

Happily now, Roger smiled and was about to reply; but, at that moment the eunuch, Yussif, brought in an ice bucket in which reposed a bottle of champagne, and poured the wine; salaaming many times he retreated backwards and closed the door behind him.

'I hope you like champagne,' Aimée remarked. 'I have a passion for it. It was I who introduced the wine to the Sultan's Court, and both the Sultan, Selim, and my son, Mahmoud, who is now twenty-two, delight in it.'

'I, too,' Roger declared, raising his glass to her before he drank, 'but in England . . .' He paused suddenly, covered his *faux pas* and, with a smile went on. 'My mother was an Englishwoman who married a French citizen of Strasbourg, so I am bi-lingual. Several times I have carried out secret missions in England for the Emperor. As I was about to say, in England the real thing is expensive and difficult to come by. They have a law that no wine may be taken into the country in any vessel containing less than a gallon. It is aimed at preventing people smuggling in single bottles. But in cask— even a small one—champagne is no more than a very mildly effervescent wine. The English can obtain champagne as we know it only when smuggled in; so it is extremely costly.'

She nodded. 'Poor people. But they have all sorts of silly customs that deprive them of half the joy of life.' Glancing at the casket at her feet, she added, 'Show me now, please, the present that my dear cousing has sent me.'

Kneeling down, Roger produced the gold candlesticks[1] and, with little cries of pleasure, Aimeé examined their delicate filigree work. Then she asked after Josephine and her two children by her first husband, the Vicomte de Beauharnais.

Roger was able to report that Eugene continued to be devoted to his stepfather, the Emperor, and, although still very young for such responsibility, was proving an excellent Viceroy for Napoleon as King of Italy. About Eugene's sister, Hortense, he could not give such good tidings. Against her

[1] The two candlesticks may be seen today by visitors to the Topkapi Palace, Istanbul.

will and that of her husband, Louis, one of Napoleon's younger brothers, they had been forced to marry and become King and Queen of Holland. Hortense was a sensible young woman and, despite her loveless marriage, putting a good face on matters, so had become very popular with her subjects. Louis, on the other hand, had turned out to be a vain and stupid neurotic. He was wasting Holland's resources by fabulous extravagance, opposed his great brother's wishes with childish petulance and, as a King, could hardly have been a greater failure.

Of Josephine, Roger spoke guardedly. 'She is greatly beloved. As a born aristocrat with traditions, tact and charm, she has made an invaluable contribution to the establishment in Paris of a new royal Court, of a splendour far surpassing that of Versailles in Louis XVI's day. Kings, Princes, Grand Dukes and nobles of aristocratic lineage come reluctantly, driven by their countries' necessity, to seek the goodwill of the middle-class Corsican usurper who now dominates Europe. They have arrived expecting among themselves cynically to mock the pretensions of this *parvenu* Emperor. They have gone away impressed with his swift, clear-seeing mentality and delighted by the gracious reception of them by his Empress.

'Yet,' Roger went on, 'one trouble remains. Napoleon desperately desires an heir. He has now been married to Josephine for eleven years. Despite the fact that she had two children by her first marriage, she has failed to give him one.'

Aimée's blue eyes held Roger's intently as she asked, 'Do they still sleep together?'

He nodded. 'At times, yes. For years past the Emperor has had a succession of mistresses; but he retains a strong affection for his wife. There are occasions when his campaigns necessitate his leaving her for many months, as is the case at present; but when they are living at the Tuileries, or St. Cloud, on most nights he goes to her room.'

'Then, unless he is impotent, it is a scurvy trick of fate that my poor cousin should fail to become *enceinte*. But tell me of this present campaign and the object of General Gardane's mission to the Sultan.'

Roger related the salient facts of the defeat of Prussia, the battles of Jena and Auerstädt, then he said, 'The Muscovites are proving more stubborn enemies than any that the Emperor has so far encountered. His object in sending General Gardane on this mission is to persuade Turkey and Persia to attack the Czar vigorously in the south, and so draw off Russian forces that would otherwise be employed against him in the north.'

With an unhappy look, Aimée replied, 'Turkey is already honouring her alliance with France by waging war against the Russians in Moldavia, and naturally we should like to assist Napoleon further. But it would be difficult to strengthen our army there with sufficient reinforcements to carry out a successful offensive.'

'Why so, Madame?' Roger enquired; although, from what Talleyrand had told him, he already guessed what her answer would probably be.

It came swiftly and with pent-up bitterness. 'Because our worst enemies are within our own gates. Unlike his predecessors for many generations, the Sultan Selim was not kept in a gilded cage and denied all knowledge of the world until he succeeded his uncle. On the contrary, he received a liberal education. For that, I am proud to say, I was mainly responsible. We are much of an age and, for many years, have been to each other as brother and sister. My son, the Prince Mahmoud, too, instead of being regarded by him as a possible conspirator who might plan his assassination in order to seize his throne, enjoys complete liberty and is beloved by him. Both have imbibed from me the vision of a new and happier Turkey. In this age Turkey can no longer afford to remain isolated. Her only hope of survival lies in gaining the friendship and respect of the great nations in the West. To achieve that, she must accept the civilisation of the West, and abolish the barbarous customs that for centuries have disgraced her in the eyes of Christian Europe. Believing me right in this, the Sultan Selim has introduced many reforms. But reforms always arouse opposition in reactionaries; and we are cursed with many such.'

Roger nodded gravely. 'Indeed, Madame, it is common knowledge that certain powerful Pashas in the Balkan lands have repudiated His Imperial Majesty's authority and that the rebel leader Kara George has provoked a rebellion in Servia that is proving difficult to suppress.'

'Since you are aware of that, you will appreciate that it could prove disastrous for us to denude our provinces further of troops that remain loyal to us, in order to despatch them against the Russians.' For a moment Aimée paused, then went on: 'Fortunately, the Pasha of Rustchuk, a Bulgarian named Baraiktar, and our greatest General, is entirely to be relied upon. I feel confident that, given a little time, he will restore our situation up on the Danube. I have, too, the full backing of *Son Altesse Noire* and of the Grand Mufti, Vely-Zadé. But for you fully to understand our position I must confide in you that the Sultan, although a man of enlightened mind and charming disposition, has not the strength of character needed to dominate the situation here. And it is here in Constantinople that our real danger lies.'

'You fear a conspiracy in the Seraglio to assassinate him?' Roger asked with swift concern.

She refilled their glasses, drank a little of the wine and said thoughtfully, 'I have no evidence that one is actually brewing; but it has long been a menace, my fear of which has much increased in recent times. I owe my position to the protection of a clever and most lovable woman, a Circassian *Kadin* who was the mother of my late husband and thus became the Sultan Validé. She died in October 1805. As Selim's mother was already dead, he gave me the status of Sultan Validé; although I am not so in fact and shall never be until my son, Mahmoud, succeeds to the throne. To the succession he has a rival, Prince Mustapha, the son of another of the Sultan Abdul Hamid's *Kadins*. She is an evil woman and has twice attempted to have my son poisoned. But on both occasions my devotion to the Blessed Virgin caused Her to intervene and save his life.'

Roger looked up in surprise. 'Can it be, Madame, that you have remained a Christian?'

Her big, blue eyes widened. 'But of course, Monsieur. Naturally, many endeavours were made to persuade me to become a Muslim, but nothing would ever induce me to abandon the true Faith.'

More than ever Roger admired the extraordinary strength of will that animated this frail, beautiful woman as, shaking back her long golden hair, sparkling with diamonds, she went on.

'The increased danger to our lives from a palace conspiracy now lies in the discontent of the Janissaries. For many reigns past, here in the Seraglio, their power has exceeded that of the Sultans. Selim has endeavoured to break it by forming a new corps of Turkish-born soldiers called the Nizam-i-jedad. Not unnaturally, the Janissaries, who are mostly Circassians, became jealous of this new bodyguard. To placate them Selim, against my advice, embodied a considerable number of the younger Janissaries into the Nizam-i-jedad; and that, I believe, has resulted in undermining their loyalty to him. The evil *Kadin* of whom I spoke, although her son is technically a prisoner, has much influence with these malcontent, reactionary troops. It needs only a spark to set off a revolt that would lead to a blood bath, place Prince Mustapha on the throne and secure for his mother her lifelong ambition to become Sultan Validé.'

After a moment, Roger said, 'Madame, I pray you accept my devotion. If there is any way in which I can serve you, or assist in your protection, you have only to command me.'

She gave him a sad smile. 'Alas, there is naught you could do to aid me should my fears be realised. But, now that my dear friend Fanny de Sebastiani is dead and her handsome husband so grieved by her loss that he is abandoning us, it will be a great comfort to me to have here a brave French gentleman to whom I can talk unreservedly. I pray you, *Monsieur le Chevalier*, to come often to see me. I will give orders that any of these greedy eunuchs who demand a bribe to announce your presence, shall be bastinadoed every week for a month.'

Crossing the room to the door through which Fatima had

159

disappeared, Aimée recalled the girl, then jerked the bell rope. Roger reassumed his most deferential manner and began to take his leave. Yussif, the eunuch who had brought the champagne, arrived and escorted him from the 'Presence' back to the Gate of Felicity.

As he passed through it, Roger happened to look to his left, and his glance fell upon a sight that, his mind being so fully occupied, he had not noticed on entering the gate. It was a pile of human skulls: some with the flesh still on them and being devoured by a swarm of big bluebottles. Inwardly he shuddered at this evidence of the barbarities that the courageous Aimée was striving to abolish. Having caught his expression of disgust, Yussif grinned at him and said in Turkish:

'Those are the heads of the men that the Janissaries believe to have been traitors to them. They are placed there as a warning to others.'

'I find it difficult to believe that His Imperial Majesty the Sultan approves of this,' Roger remarked.

The eunuch shrugged. 'That is not for me to judge, *Effendi*. But those of us who are the loyal servants of Her Sublimity the Sultan Validé never know the day when we may find ourselves hung by the neck from the great elm in the First Court.' With a bow, he added, 'May Allah the Merciful, the Compassionate, have you in his keeping, *Effendi*.' Then he handed Roger over to one of the White Eunuchs who saw him out of the Palace.

In the room over the tailor's shop Roger changed back into uniform, then recrossed the Golden Horn with Achmet. Thinking matters over, he was well content with the situation of Turkey as Aimée had disclosed it to him. Had matters been otherwise and the Turks likely to accede to Napoleon's request that they should launch an offensive across the Danube, he had intended himself to reveal what Talleyrand had told him of the Sultan's waning authority in the Balkans and, posing as the confidential messenger of Josephine, tell Aimée that the Emperor was fully capable of defeating the Czar without Turkish help; so the Sultan would be most ill advised to jeopardise further his own position by sending another army against the Russians. But it had proved unnecessary to do that. Whatever promises the Sultan might make to General Gardane, it was clear that he could not carry them out.

As Aimée corresponded with Josephine, it was quite on the cards that she would mention Roger's visit; so he was much relieved that he would not later have to explain away having given her advice contrary to French interests. She would, no doubt, send her thanks for the candlesticks, but that did not worry him. In due course he would tell Josephine that he had made the gift in her name, believing that his having done so would please her. And he felt certain that it would.

About Aimée's own position he was considerably worried; but, in spite of her invitation, he did not wish to give her the impression that he was taking advantage of her friendliness, so he decided against paying her another visit until the Monday. That morning, having changed again in the room over the tailor's shop into the costume of a Greek merchant, he made his way to the Palace. This time he was received very differently. The Kapi Aga was brought at once to the waiting room in the great gate, and enquired solicitously as to Roger's health. A messenger was despatched to the Kizler Aga and, after a brief wait, the visitor was conducted across the court to the Gate of Felicity. There Yussif met him with smiles and bows, then took him through the maze of corridors to the Sultan Validé's apartments.

With her on this occasion, besides the slim, doe-eyed Fatima, were two men. The elder had a long, thin nose, heavily-lidded eyes, a thin moustache and a very full, black beard. He was dressed simply, in a loose silk robe, but above his lofty forehead rose a large white turban, in the centre of which flashed a huge diamond. The younger had a heavier moustache, but a less full beard, and arched black eyebrows above eyes that were as large and lustrous as Aimée's, although dark brown. Instantly, Roger realised that he was in the presence of the Sultan and Aimée's son Prince Mahmoud.

As he went down on his knees, Aimée curtsied to the Sultan and said in French, 'Permit me, Sire, to present to you a brave French officer, the friend and confidant of my cousin the Empress Josephine: *Colonel le Chevalier de Breuc*.'

Roger's hands were clasped, with his head bowed over them. To his ears there came the voice of Selim, speaking in heavily-accented and bad but understandable French. 'Welcome to our Court, Monsieur. Rise and be seated. Here in this blessed haven from pomp, anxiety and toil, provided by our beloved *Naksh*, we do not stand on ceremony.'

Coming to his feet Roger smiled, bowed and said, 'Your gracious Majesty honours me beyond my deserts.'

Then Aimée waved a hand towards the younger man: 'My son, Prince Mahmoud.'

Again Roger bowed. Smiling at him, the young Prince picked up a bottle of champagne, poured a glass, handed it to him, and said in fluent French almost entirely free of accent, 'One of the many joys my mother has brought us. Because one believes in God, one does not have to deny oneself the blessings he has bestowed on man.'

Roger was surprised at the paleness of the faces of the two Turks, particularly that of the Sultan which, against his black beard, was actually pallid. But, after a moment he recalled having been told that customs forbade any Turkish Prince from ever taking a wife of Turkish blood. All the young girls bought or kidnapped to become inmates of the harem came from distant parts of the Empire with, occasionally, an Italian or Spaniard who, like Aimée, had been captured by Corsairs. The great majority of the odalisques from whom the Sultans chose their four wives were, on account of their outstanding beauty, fair-skinned Circassians. As a result, after many generations, the Osmanli Princes were in fact Turks only by upbringing.

For over an hour they talked freely and, at times, gaily; the lovely young Fatima often joining in as though she were one of the family. Roger gave a lively description of the splendid Court Napoleon had created since he had made himself an Emperor, and of the Kings, Princes and Grand Dukes who attended it to fawn upon him. He told them about the latest fashions in Paris, and gave an account of Napoleon's triumphant Prussian campaign. But he refrained from telling them of his narrow escape from death at Eylau, and that for two months he had been a prisoner, leading them to suppose that it was during that time Josephine had heard that he was to accompany General Gardane's mission to Constantinople and sent him the candlesticks to take, as a token of her enduring affection for her cousin.

At the mention of Gardane, the Sultan said, 'I intend to receive him on Wednesday. Tomorrow we make an expedition up the Bosphorus to Rumeli Hisar. You must come with us. Now I have to attend to business.'

As he stood up, Roger gave thanks for the honour done him and bowed profoundly. Aimée extended her hand for him to kiss and said, 'Be here at nine o'clock, Monsieur; and, of course, in the same costume. I have already explained to His Majesty the reason for your wearing Balkan dress.'

Prince Mahmoud then smiled at him and asked, 'Would it interest you to see my work?'

'Indeed it would, Your Highness,' Roger replied, although he was distinctly puzzled by this invitation. As they followed the Sultan from the room, the young man enlightened him.

'Perhaps, Monsieur, you are not aware of it, but by tradition every Osmanli Prince has to learn a trade. I chose that of a professional writer, and derive much pleasure from calligraphy.'

After crossing several courts, they reached the Prince's quarters, and he led Roger into a spacious, well-lit studio. It contained not only specimens of beautiful writing on vellum, but also a number of drawing boards several square feet in size, upon which verses from the Koran had been inscribed. With charming modesty, the Prince explained that the quality of his work had become so esteemed that he was now commissioned to create these designs which would later be carved in stone by other craftsmen, then gilded to decorate new mosques.

While Roger was admiring these works of art, coffee and sweet cakes were brought; then, when they had partaken of these refreshments, the Prince courteously saw his guest out through the Gate of Felicity.

When Roger returned the following morning, he was led by the Kapi Aga through another maze of passages, then down through a garden gay with flowers, but shaded by many tall cypresses, to the great wall and a gate in it that gave on to the shore of the Golden Horn. Outside the wall stood two large, lofty pavilions from which there was a splendid view across the water of the shipping moored at the wharfs of Pera and the tiers of buildings rising steeply beyond the ship masts. Further along, towards Seraglio Point, were the boat-houses and, at the end of a jetty in front of one of them, lay a great, gilded barge. It was already manned by two score oarsmen.

Roger had made certain of arriving in good time, so a quarter of an hour elapsed while he stood on the foreshore. Then he heard a babble of laughing, girlish voices and turned to see that a bevy of veiled odalisques, escorted by black eunuchs, had emerged from the gate. Eyeing him with interest and chattering among themselves, the girls remained standing near him for a few minutes. Aimée—more heavily veiled than when Roger had seen her in her own apartments—accompanied by Fatima and Yussif, was the next to arrive on the scene. The chattering ceased, everyone made obeisance then, having greeted Roger most affably, Aimée led the way on board.

The stern of the caique was shaded by a great, silk canopy edged with gold braid and pearls. On a raised platform centrally beneath it stood a broad divan with many cushions. Grouped about it were a number of stools and on these the ladies settled themselves. To the stools there was one exception—a low-backed, comfortable, padded chair on the right of the divan. Aimée sat down in it and signed to Roger to take the stool nearest her.

He had hardly done so when the Sultan appeared, escorted by two huge Nubian guards. Today he was again clad in easy garments suitable to the summer weather, but he wore a jewelled belt from which hung a scimitar, the hilt and sheath of which were worth a king's ransom, and his turban was ablaze with precious gems.

His manner was now aloof and dignified. As he took his

seat on the broad divan, he did not even acknowledge the deep obeisance made by everyone present. At a sharp command from him the barge was cast off and the forty rowers sank their oars into the water. With long strokes in perfect rhythm, the boat sped along, rounded the curve of Pera and turned up the Bosphorus.

Now that they were too distant from the shore for their faces to be seen distinctly, Selim relaxed a little and said to Aimée, 'Your ladies may talk if they wish,' then greeted Roger kindly. Again the babble of girlish voices broke out, and one of the girls began to strum on a guitar.

When they had progressed another half-mile Roger asked Aimée about Rumeli Hisar, to which they were going, as he had never heard of it.

'It is an ancient castle,' she replied. 'There are two of them: one on either side of the Bosphorus where it is at its narrowest. Rumeli Hisar is the one in Europe and Anadolu Hisar in Asia. They were built to defend Constantinople from an attack by sea from the north. Although there is little danger of that in these days, garrisons are maintained in both. From time to time we make an expedition to one or the other, simply for the outing; and the views from the battlements are truly beautiful.'

When they were opposite the castle, Roger saw that it was a formidable fortress surrounded by a wall that ran down on both sides of it to the water.

Preparations had been made for the reception of the Imperial party. The Commander of the garrison, Evliyá Pasha, welcomed his sovereign with humble submission but evident pleasure. Scores of slaves then bore them all in litters up the steep hillside. Having admired the view from the battlements, they descended to the central courtyard. Awnings had been erected to shade it from the now blazing sun, and about it were set numerous divans with low tables.

Refreshments were then served; but no champagne today. Although Aimée had seduced the Osmanli Princes into sharing her enjoyment of her favourite wine, they still did not dare ignore the prohibition of the Koran in public. Instead, there were refreshing sherbets and Hydromel—a honey-water, unfermented mead. With these were offered golden dishes of small, spiced buns, sweet cakes, rahat-lakoum, and a great variety of nuts and nougats. These proved to be the strange hors d'œuvres to a gargantuan meal: whole sturgeons on huge platters, lobsters first boiled in their shells, roast ducks coated with honey, peacock pies decorated with the heads and feathers of the birds, great dishes of venison crowned with antlers, pilaus, kebabs and ragouts; followed by a dozen different puddings, each a masterpiece of the chef's artistry in the use of icing, spun sugar and crystallised fruit.

When at last the feast was over, the Sultan withdrew to enjoy a siesta inside the castle, while the rest of them remained to chat idly or doze on the divans, through the heat of the afternoon. On Selim's reappearance, everyone livened up. A dozen of the veiled odalisques swayed gracefully in an intricate dance, then others performed solo or in groups on instruments they had brought.

Roger looked on with mingled boredom and interest. The music meant nothing to him, but he found it intriguing to watch the women. Except for Aimée and Fatima, every one of them was straining her talent to the utmost, and by sinuous movements endeavouring to attract Selim's attention, in the hope that he might throw her the coveted handkerchief as the sign that he would summon her to his bed that night.

But the Sultan remained impassive, and Roger had the instinctive feeling that all this apparently light-hearted gaiety was forced. A secret fear seemed to lurk beneath the laughter and a foreboding of dark days to come. His belief that trouble was brewing and that they were all aware of it was strengthened when, long before sundown, Selim abruptly ended the party and ordered a return to the barge.

Silently they were borne in the litters down the hill and re-embarked. Almost in silence they were rowed back to the shore of Seraglio Point. As they landed, faint but menacing, they caught the sound of heavy spoons being beaten on the bottoms of kettles—that century-old indication that the Janissaries had become mutinous.

9

Crisis in the Seraglio

As the sound coming from the massed buildings up on the hill reached their ears, everyone who had been on the Imperial pleasure party immediately fell silent. In the stillness of the late afternoon, the sinister drumming came to them louder and more threatening. Into Roger's mind there flashed a picture of thousands of long-moustached, angry, armed men seated cross-legged: row upon row in the great Second Courtyard, beating rhythmically on their soup kettles with the long spoons that they habitually wore thrust through their turbans.

Aimée was standing beside him. In a swift whisper he said to her, 'You must return with me to the French Embassy. You will be safe there.'

She shook her head. 'No. My place is here. But it is as well that we returned early. As long as they keep drumming, they will harm no one. And this has often happened before. They will make some new demand. Selim will either have to accede to it or take strong measures to curb their insolence.'

Having rendered thanks to the Sultan for his day's entertainment, Roger made his adieux to Aimée and Fatima; then, as they went through the gate in the great wall up to the Seraglio, he was escorted by a eunuch along the shore until he could turn inland outside the wall, walk up to the tailor's and change back into uniform.

That night he could hardly sleep for worrying about what might be taking place in the Seraglio, but in the morning there came no news of trouble there, so General Gardane and his companions all donned their smartest uniforms and rode across the Galata Bridge. The sight of this cavalcade of foreign officers on horseback caused considerable excitement, and an ever-increasing crowd pushed and shoved on either side of them as they rode up through the narrow streets towards the Palace.

When they reached the open space adjacent to the great mosque of Aya Sophia, Roger was relieved to see that preparations had been made for their reception, as that implied the state of things inside the Palace to be normal. A regiment of cavalry, with gleaming scimitars, was drawn up. Beyond them, on either side of the First Gate stood triple ranks of Albanian infantry armed with tall pikes with double axe heads. As the French approached, their arrival was announced by a fanfare from a score of trumpets. From the gate there emerged a gorgeously-clad Turk, wearing an enormous feather-ed head-dress. Behind him rode his orderly, holding aloft a wrought-iron standard from which dangled three tufts of horsehair, signifying the officer's high rank. Salutes were ex-changed and the 'three tail' Bashaw, with Ambassador Seba-stiani on one side of him and General Gardane on the other, accompanied them through the First Courtyard between the massed ranks of hundreds of Janissaries, wearing helmets from which bird-of-paradise plumes curved down almost to their waists.

According to custom, at the Second Gate they all dis-mounted. White eunuchs lumbered forward to act as horse-holders until their return; then, holding themselves very erect, they marched solemnly across the Second Court, in which were massed line after line of Selim's newly-created bodyguard, the Nizam-i-jedad.

As they approached the Gate of Felicity, Roger saw that the pile of skulls to the left of it had been increased by a dozen or so newly-severed bloody heads. Those, he had little doubt, were the heads of loyal retainers whom Selim had had to sacrifice to the Janissaries in order to keep them from open revolt. He was sorry for the Sultan, who seemed to be a pleas-ant, kindly man; but mentally condemned his weakness. About Aimée he was worried, because in her he had recog-nised a kindred spirit, and greatly admired her courage and intelligence as well as her beauty. He would have given much to be in a position to protect her from the danger that so clearly loomed over the present Imperial family; but saw no way in which he might possibly do so.

Beyond the Gate of Felicity they could see into the pavilion where there stood the wide, golden throne with its lustrous bands of flashing gems; but it was unoccupied. The sun was blazing down from a cloudless sky. Already the Frenchmen, in their tight-fitting uniforms, were sweating profusely. Five minutes passed, ten. They continued to stand rigidly to attention. The strain was terrible. Rivulets of perspiration were running down their faces, and General Gardane was praying that none of his officers would disgrace him by fainting.

Roger was praying that this delay in the proceedings was due only to the Oriental habit of seeking to impress visitors by keeping them waiting; and not that, after all, Selim was dead or a prisoner, this show having been put on to conceal it and that shortly they would be informed that he had been taken suddenly ill, so could not receive them.

Two minutes later, he was relieved of his fears. There came another blast of trumpets, then a herald cried in a loud voice:

'Behold and tremble. Here cometh the Caliph of Islam; the Commander of the Faithful; the Padishah of Padishahs; the Lord of the Barbary States; the Shadow of Allah upon Earth.'

With stately step, Selim emerged from between pearl-embroidered curtains at the back of the throne room. In spite of the heat, from his shoulders there hung to the ground an enormous ermine stole. His scimitar sheath and its hilt, his belt, breast and hands positively blazed with jewels. From an enormous diamond in the centre of his turban there rose a gently-waving aigrette. It was the largest jewel that Roger had ever seen. He had been told its history. It was known as the Spoon Diamond, because two children had found it on the seashore and had given it to a spoon-seller in exchange for two wooden spoons. The spoon-seller had sold it to a jeweller for a single piece of gold. The jeweller had had it cut and sold it to the then reigning Sultan for a fortune.

The Sultan Selim was followed by a small, elderly, wizened man, wearing a dark robe and a flat turban the size of a small cartwheel—obviously the Grand Vizier. After him came a huge Negro in a tall, conical hat, whom Roger knew to be *Son Altesse Noire*.

Selim took his place, cross-legged on the wide divan; the other two sat down on low stools on either side of him. Meanwhile everyone else present had gone down on their knees, the Turks touching the ground with their foreheads.

The herald shouted, 'The Descendant of the Prophet— blessed be his name—permits that you raise your eyes.' Everyone looked up, but remained kneeling. The 'three tail' Bashaw who had been kneeling between Sebastiani and Gardane, took each of them by an arm, raised them to their feet and, as if supporting them lest they faint at the tremendous honour done them, led them forward through the Gate of Felicity to the step up to the throne.

Again all three of them knelt. Selim, without a trace of animation on his features, extended the first finger of his right hand, upon which blazed an emerald the size of a pigeon's egg, to Gardane. The General kissed it and said in Turkish:

'Most gracious Majesty of divine descent, I humbly crave to present to you a letter from my illustrious master, and your faithful ally, the Emperor of the French.'

Unsmiling, Selim made no reply as Gardane proffered the gem-studded casket containing Napoleon's letter. Then, after a moment, with a gesture that almost conveyed contempt, Selim waved his heavily beringed hand in the direction of the Grand Vizier, and said, 'My Minister will give consideration to this matter, and inform me upon it.'

As Gardane handed the casket to the Grand Vizier, Selim uncrossed his legs, came to his feet and, raising his hand, said in a loud voice: 'May Allah, the Merciful, the Compassionate —blessed be his name and that of his Prophet—have you all in His holy keeping.' Then, without another glance at anyone, his black-bearded head held high, he strode out through the curtains at the back of the pavilion, followed by his Grand Vizier and the Kizler Agar.

The troops came to their feet. Orders were shouted by their officers, and they presented arms as the French mission marched back through the Second Court, remounted their horses outside it, then at the First Gate took leave of the 'three tail' Bashaw. Limp and gasping from the heat, they recrossed the bridge of boats and, half an hour later, lay on their beds endeavouring to recover from the ordeal to which the audience with the Sultan had subjected them.

That night, at dinner in the Embassy, Sebastiani said to Gardane: 'General, I have remained on here only because I felt it my duty to accompany you on your presentation to the Sultan. I am positively haunted by the thought that my beloved Fanny's death was due to my having brought her to this city of dirt and disease. In my wretched state I can no longer be of any assistance to you here, and I have learned that a ship is leaving for the Piraeus tomorrow; so I am sailing in her. I have made the necessary arrangements for my staff to carry on all diplomatic duties. It remains only for me to wish you success in your mission.'

When they had condoled with him, he went on, 'You must not be discouraged by the coldness of the Sultan's reception. The aloofness he displayed is no more than tradition leads his people to expect from him. In private he is a very pleasant man, and he is highly intelligent. But you must not expect to receive any reply to the Emperor's letter for some days. The probability is that one day next week you will be sent for to discuss it with his Ministers. Even then, no decision will be given. You may have to wait another week or more before you are again summoned to receive a formal answer.'

During that afternoon Gardane had received a missive from Ibraham Pasha, the 'three tail' General who had conducted them into the presence that morning. It was an invitation for them to cross the Bosphorus with him next day and dine at his villa in the hills above Scutari.

As Roger had received no summons from Aimée, he was glad of this opportunity to spend a day in the company of his brother officers; for he feared that if he went off on his own too often Gardane might begin to wonder what he was up to.

Ibraham Pasha was a fat, jolly man. He spoke French fairly fluently and brought with him two other officers, both of whom had visited Paris in pre-Revolution days. The party crossed the Straits in a large barge and on the Asiatic side found grooms and horses waiting for them. They then rode through the town and, for about five miles, up a winding track that took them to the flat, grassy top of a mountain. From it there was a splendid view of the Turkish capital. The sun glinted on the domes and minarets of the many mosques in both Stamboul and Pera; and the blue waters below were dotted with the scores of vessels large and small sailing under a light wind along the three channels formed by the Bosphorus and the Golden Horn.

Having rested there for a while, they rode down to the Pasha's villa, which proved to be a small palace with a lovely garden. Like the majority of highly-placed or wealthy Turks, he observed the Koran's prohibition against alcohol only in public; so the excellent meal he had provided for them was made doubly agreeable by a plentiful supply of very palatable Greek wine. In the cool of the evening, they returned to Pera, having had a thoroughly enjoyable time.

The next day being the Mohammedan Sabbath, Roger did not go to the Palace, but on the Saturday afternoon he again presented himself. Aimée received him with obvious pleasure and he spent over two hours with her and the gazelle-like Fatima, who also asked him many questions about the countries in which he had travelled. With some amusement, he noticed that she could not keep her eyes off him, so he had obviously made a conquest. But charming as she was, and twenty years younger than Aimée, to his mind she was just a pretty girl and could not hold a candle to the radiant, golden beauty of her mistress.

As he was taking his leave, Aimée told him that next day the Sultan intended to visit Kizel, an island in the Sea of Marmora, just outside the entrance to the Bosphorus, and invited him to accompany them; so he was able to look forward to another day in the company of this extraordinary and fascinating woman.

Since the death of his wife the unhappy Sebastiani had refused all invitations and invited no-one to the Embassy; but on Gardane's arrival he had felt it his duty to arrange a reception. So that night, in spite of the fact that the Ambassador had already left, the big salons of the Embassy were lit with hundreds of candles and an entertainment given for some two hundred guests. All the other foreign Ambassadors in Constantinople, with the senior members of their staffs, were present, and scores of important Turkish functionaries. Many of the latter were eager to return hospitality, so Gardane and his officers were assured of a pleasant time during the remainder of their stay in Constantinople. But Roger, wishing to keep himself free, politely declined such invitations as he was given, on the plea that he suffered from an intermittent fever and feared that for the next week or so a bout of it that he felt coming on would prevent him from keeping any engagements.

On the Sunday morning, again dressed as a Greek merchant, he accompanied the Imperial party to Kizel. The day followed the pattern of that when they had gone up the Bosphorus to Rumeli Hisar, except that, instead of the entertainment being held in a grim old castle, they enjoyed the May sunshine on a broad terrace in front of a small palace.

While they were on their way back, Selim told Roger that on the following day his Grand Vizier would receive the French mission, to discuss the Emperor Napoleon's letter; but Roger was concerned to see that the Sultan seemed more gloomy and ill at ease than ever. And when they landed on the shore below the Seraglio, the reason for his depression was made plain. Again his temporary absence from the Palace had provided an opportunity for the Janissaries to hold meetings and discuss their pretended grievances. For the second time there came to Roger's ears that sinister sound of kettle-beating.

After another anxious night, he accompanied Gardane and two other senior officers of the mission across the Golden Horn. They were received as before by Ibraham Pasha, with ceremony, but the number of troops paraded was considerably less. The Pasha conducted them into the Second Court, but instead of proceeding to the Gate of Felicity, he turned half left, heading for a large building above which, squat and square, rose the only steeple of the Palace. It was, Roger knew, the Hall of the Dewan. Before entering it he cast a glance over his shoulder and saw that there were several new bloody severed heads on the pile of skulls.

Inside the Hall of the Dewan, they were courteously greeted by the wizened-faced Grand Vizier, and several other Ministers. Then everyone present took places cross-legged on the cushioned divans with which the room was furnished. Before each place there stood a hookah with, attached to it, a long tube with an ivory mouthpiece, by which the smoke could be drawn through a glass vase filled with rose water. Roger at once took up his mouthpiece and drew in a breath of fragrant smoke; his compatriots followed his example and the Turks, too, began smoking.

While compliments were exchanged, thick, sweet coffee was served in small cups inserted in gold holders. When the white eunuchs who acted as waiters had withdrawn, the business in hand was gradually approached. High up on one side of the room there was a grille that jutted out slightly, screening a small balcony. Behind it, from time to time, slight movements could be seen and Roger had learned that, concealed in this indoor gazebo, the Sultan listened to all debates of importance held by his chief Ministers.

It was, therefore, no surprise to him that, after nearly three hours of beating about the bush, the Grand Vizier said that he and his colleagues must consult further in private—his real meaning being that he must ask the wishes of his master.

Next day Roger again went to the Palace in disguise. This time he was kept waiting for nearly an hour before Aimée received him; but when she did she explained that she had been detained because she had been in consultation with Selim's *Kadins* about certain new regulations governing the conduct of the ordinary women of the harem.

Their talk happened to turn to French literature, upon which she took him through to another room which was a library. He was amazed to see that it contained hundreds of beautifully-bound volumes imported by her from France. Among them were many works on botany, natural history and philosophy, including those of the Encyclopædists. He had realised that she was well read, but not that she was so learned.

Like her boudoir, the *décor* of the room was *Louis Seize*, but with one exception. In the middle of one wall there was a huge, brick, open fireplace. Seeing him look at it, she said:

'Alas, they would not allow me to do away with that hideous chimney. This building is very old, and they said that if they attempted to take it out the roof covering the whole of my apartments would fall in.'

A little later he asked her about the state of the Janissaries and she replied, 'They are a constant anxiety to us. Every time now that Selim leaves the Palace for any length of time they become mutinous and, although Ibraham Pasha is a good, honest man, he has not the strength of will to control them. Selim, too, lacks the ruthlessness to reduce them to obedience once and for all. Occasionally he has a few of them thrown into prison, but generally appeases them with concessions. Prince Mustapha and his mother are, of course, prisoners in the fine pavilion that we term "the cage"; but I haven't a doubt that they are in secret communication with the Janissaries' leaders and inciting them to make trouble for us. In previous reigns that evil woman and her son would long since have been strangled. But Selim is too kind-hearted. Perhaps my influence on him is to blame for that. Yet, as long as they live, our own lives will not be safe.'

It was Fatima who suggested that her mistress should invite Roger to a small, private supper party she was giving on the coming Thursday. After a moment's hesitation, Aimée said:

'Yes. Why not? At times General Sebastiani used to join us, and His Majesty thinks well of *M. le Chevalier*. So, too, does my son, and it will make a pleasant change for us to have a visitor in our family circle.' She then told Roger to come to the Palace at eight o'clock.

Roger spent Wednesday with three of his brother officers and their Turkish attendants, exploring parts of the city they had not so far seen. As infidels, they were naturally debarred from entering any of the magnificent mosques; but they strolled round the great oblong stadium where, in Byzantine times, the chariot races had been held; descended underground to see the vast, many-columned cistern that Constantine the Great had constructed to supply his people with water during the times of siege, and roamed for an hour or two along the inside of the miles-long battlemented wall.

On the Thursday evening, when Roger was conducted through the Second Court of the Palace, he saw by the lingering twilight that many of the Janissaries were sitting about in little groups, quietly smoking their narghiles or talking earnestly in low tones; but none of them took any notice of him.

In Aimée's apartment he found Selim, Mahmoud and Fatima. They were already drinking the champagne of which they were so fond and, when he had made his salaams, Fatima poured him a glass. The Sultan then began to speak of the Dewan that had been held the previous Thursday and told Roger frankly that he was still undecided what course to take. Russia was Turkey's hereditary enemy and, moreover, he would have liked to give his ally, the Emperor Napoleon, such help as he could. But to find troops for an offensive while several of his own provinces were in rebellion presented a difficult problem.

'Sire,' Roger replied. 'I am a loyal servant of the Emperor, but since you have honoured me with your friendship, I cannot forbear to quote the old saying, "A wise man puts out the fire in his own house before he goes to assist his neighbour in putting out the fire in his." '

Aimée nodded her golden head. 'That is sound advice. But we are not here to talk statecraft. Let us put such matters out of our minds for a while and enjoy ourselves. Tell His Majesty, as you told me the other day, how, when you were a young man in St. Petersburg and that old *rouée,* Catherine the Great, took a fancy to you, you succeeded in avoiding going to bed with her.'

Roger told the story and they laughed a lot. Encouraged by them, he told others of tight corners out of which he had managed to wriggle. About nine o'clock, Yussif appeared and announced that, if it pleased His Majesty, dinner could be served. Then they adjourned to another room. As was the case throughout the whole of Aimée's apartments, there were no divans here, but a fine, satinwood table set with Sèvres china, lace mats from Malines, and Venetian glass. The chairs were of tulip wood, and their seats flower designs in *petit point* worked, as she told Roger, by herself.

The meal, too, showed no trace of Turkish influence and it was clear that Aimée's personal chef was well versed in the French cookery books for which she had sent. As Roger drank with each course in turn Montrâchet Chambertin and a rich Sauterne, he thought how blessed this Oriental potentate was to be able to retire from his burdensome duties of State to these utterly different surroundings, created by a French lady of superb beauty and indomitable will.

A richly-crusted soufflé was about to be served when sounds of commotion came from the next room. A moment later the door burst open and *Son Altesse Noire* came staggering in to them. His face was grey, his eyes bulging. Without ceremony he cried:

'Majesty! We are lost! The Janissaries are in revolt. They have freed Prince Mustapha and his mother from the cage. Even now they are proclaiming the Prince as Sultan. They will be here at any moment. This means death to us all.'

Everyone at the table sprang to their feet. The eunuch who had been about to hand round the soufflé dropped it and fled. Selim remained outwardly calm, but his voice was hoarse as he said:

'I will go out and call this rabble to order.'

'No!' Aimée cried, seizing his arm. 'No. They would hack you to pieces.'

Prince Mahmoud's fine eyes had lost their mild look.

Thrusting out his bearded chin, he shouted, 'A scimitar. Find me a scimitar so that I may die fighting.'

'No weapons will help us,' said Roger sharply. 'While we still have the chance, we must escape. Come! Which way do we go?'

The Chief of the Black Eunuchs shook his head. 'There is no way, Monsieur. All three courts are swarming with Janissaries. A handful of loyal men are holding the passage that leads to the Sultan Validé's courtyard. But very soon they must be overcome.'

Aimée clasped her hands, lifted her eyes to heaven and exclaimed, 'Holy Virgin, protect us.'

Selim shrugged. 'Prayer is now useless, dear *Naksh*. As it is written in the Koran, "the fate of every man is bound about his brow". We are trapped, and it is our fate that we should die here.'

10

The Hovering Hand of Death

It was the 29th May. Ever since the 20th, the day on which
they had gone on the expedition to Rumeli Hisar and returned to hear the Janissaries beating on their kettles, the
fear that really serious trouble was brewing in the Seraglio
had never been far from Roger's mind.

During the sixteen days that the French mission had been
in Constantinople, he had spent by far the greater part of his
time either with a few of his brother officers or, accompanied
only by Achmet, wandering about the city. As a secret agent
of long standing, it had become second nature to him to acquire all the information he could about how the people in
whichever country he was in regarded their government. His
Turkish having become fluent, he had been able to chat with
men of all conditions, and by inference rather than definite
expressions of opinion, he had become convinced of two
things. The Sultan was unpopular with only the rich, who
stood to lose by his reforms, but people of every class united
in lamenting his weakness in dealing with the Janissaries.

They had become entirely lawless and terrorised the city.
In full daylight they held up and demanded money from
people in the streets; bands of them raided and pillaged shops;
they abducted and raped women; they even broke into harems.
Yet no action was taken against them. It followed that if their
revolt succeeded, Constantinople would become the scene of
wholesale massacre and looting.

Faced with this immediate and unexpected crisis, it flashed
into Roger's mind that if only he could get away he might yet
save the situation. Once out of the Palace it would not be
difficult to reach the French Embassy. Gardane was an in-

telligent and resolute man. The staffs of the other Embassies could be counted on to help. Urgent messages could be sent to the barracks of other troops who were jealous of the Janissaries' privileges, and to the Mullahs who, from their minarets, would rouse the people. Their smouldering hatred would burst into flame. In their tens of thousands they would attack the Palace, overwhelm the lawless brigands from whom they had suffered for so long and, perhaps, even save Aimée, the Sultan and her son.

But how to get away? Instantly a possibility came to him. Thrusting *Son Altesse Noire* aside, he ran from the room into Aimée's library. The others followed, to find him crouched in the wide hearth, looking up the big chimney. Few of the buildings in the Seraglio were more than one storey in height. Fifteen feet above him he could see stars in the clear heaven. Swinging round, he cried:

'I'm going up! I'll get away across the roofs and bring help.'

'May the Prophet bless you!' exclaimed Prince Mahmoud. 'But we must come, too, or we'll be murdered long before you can return to us.'

'You're right,' Roger replied. 'But we'll need a rope to haul the women up. Where can we find one?' Hastily he glanced round, but could see nothing suitable.

Next moment the Prince muttered, 'Use this,' and began rapidly unwinding his turban. Roger realised, in the minute or more it took to do this that, sweet-natured and artistic though Mahmoud might be, he was a far more resolute man than Selim, who was standing silent, paler than ever and with drooping shoulders.

Grabbing the end of the long, thick swathe of muslin, Roger tied it to his belt. As the other end came free, the Black Eunuch seized it and was about to knot it round the Sultan's waist.

'Stop!' snapped Roger. Then, forgetting himself in the excitement of the moment, he added, 'In England there is an unwritten law, "Women and children first".' Snatching the turban from the eunuch, he lashed it swiftly under Aimée's arms above her breasts.

Already they could hear the sound of clashing scimitars and screams of wounded men, coming from the Sultan Validé's courtyard, so none of them noticed the *faux pas* Roger had made by implying admiration for the English.

Diving into the chimney, he braced his back, feet and elbows against the soot-blackened walls. To wriggle his way up was far harder than he had expected. Although the chimney was only fifteen feet in height, by the time he was half-way up he feared he would never reach the top; but it gradually narrowed, lessening the strain on his shoulders and ankles. Thrusting up his hands, he managed to grasp the rim of the opening overhead. One final heave, and his head was clear of the chimney rim. For a moment he hung there, panting, then scrambled out on to the roof.

Up there, the sound of shots, wild war-cries and fighting came much more clearly to him. The whole vast Topkapi Palace, usually so unnaturally silent, was in a state of pandemonium. Swiftly he turned, shouted down the chimney and began to haul upon the turban rope. Aimée had lost no time in following him into the wide hearth below, but as he took the strain, his heart suddenly misgave him.

She was not a tall woman and had retained the beautifully-moulded, girlish figure that had been one of her many attractions, so he would have guessed her weight to be not more than eight stone; but she seemed to weigh half a ton. Now he cursed himself for his impetuosity. He should have had Prince Mahmoud or the big Negro climb up after him, then the two of them could, without great difficulty, have hauled the others up.

But it was too late to think of that now. Any moment Yussif and the other loyal eunuchs who were defending the doorway giving on to the Court might be overcome and the murderous Janissaries burst into the library below.

Roger heaved on the thick, muslin rope. It lifted Aimée a foot or so. He heaved again and gained another foot. But the rope was cutting into his hands so painfully that he could have screamed. He now knew that he would never be able to pull her up the whole fifteen feet this way. But, whatever happened to the others, somehow he had got to get Aimée out.

After a moment's agonising thought, he let the rope slide back until her feet again took her own weight. Turning his back to the chimney he drew the slack rope over his right shoulder, then twisted it round both his wrists. Clasping his hands together in front of him, he took the strain again and, head down, threw his whole weight forward. The rope cut fiercely into his shoulder and only by swiftly clutching at his belt was he able to keep his wrists from flying up into his face.

With the sweat streaming from him, he fought his way forward step by step across the roof. At the very moment he felt he could endure the strain no longer, there came a cry behind him, and the fierce pressure of the rope on his shoulder eased a little. He held his position for another half-minute, then the rope went slack. Turning, he saw with a gasp of triumph that Aimée was out on the roof.

By the time he staggered to her, she had undone her end of the rope and was lowering it. Pushing past her, he shouted down the chimney. 'Prince Mahmoud next. And he must climb as . . . as I did. Use the rope only . . . only as a help. I . . . I haven't the strength left to pull Fatima up.'

A minute later the rope became taut, but only for a moment. As it eased, Roger took in the slack; Aimée too, grasped it, and each time Mahmoud levered himself a foot higher, they pulled on it to assist him in his climb. Once the strong young Prince was up on the roof, the three of them were not hard put to it to hoist Fatima. Hauling up Selim needed greater effort, although there were four of them on the rope; but the Kizler Aga's ascent called for no effort. Like Mahmoud, he worked his way up himself.

For all of them it had been a terrible experience; for those who came last the dread that they might yet be caught and murdered, for Aimeé the fear that, although she had reached temporary safety, her son and dear friend Selim might not; for Roger the awful thought that he might have to abandon

Aimée with whom he had not allowed himself to fall in love, but might so easily have done had she been a woman of lesser station. His hands and wrists were lacerated, his right shoulder felt as though it had been seared by a red-hot iron. But he knew that, as yet, there could be no letting up. They were still almost in the centre of the vast Palace, now in the hands of thousands of ruthless enemies. Unless they could escape unseen from it, they would die that night.

Fortunately, there was no moon, but the starlight was bright enough for them to see one another and their surroundings. As they stood there in a little group, they took in for the first time their changed appearance. They had sat down to supper clean and elegantly clad. They now looked like so many scarecrows: their hair and turbans dishevelled, their fine garments torn and begrimed, their hands and faces black with soot.

Roger looked anxiously about him. In every direction there were scores of small domes crowning individual rooms. The squat, square turret above the Hall of the Dewan, the three-storey block that housed the ladies of the harem, and the tall chimneys of the ten kitchens were the only structures that stood out prominently against the skyline.

'Our best hope is a boat,' he said sharply. 'Which is the least dangerous way to the shore?'

'Through my mother's private garden,' Mahmoud replied promptly. 'But we will have to get down to it. Then at the bottom of the slope there is the wall.'

Abruptly Roger said, 'Be pleased to lead the way, Prince. But we had best crawl, lest some of those devils spot us up here on the roof and suspect who we are.'

Getting down on their hands and knees, they made their way between the cupolas over Aimeé's apartments for about sixty yards, till they came to the edge of the roof on that side of the Palace. There Roger produced the muslin rope which he had brought with him. One by one they were lowered on to a terrace. Mahmoud insisted on going last, so had to tie one end of the rope to a chimney pot, which meant abandoning the rope. But that could not be helped.

As they crossed the garden, the night air still held the scent of the hundreds of hyacinths planted there. Aimée began to cry at the thought that she would never see it again. In that little soot-begrimed party, there was no longer a Padishah of Padishahs, a Sultan Validé, white man or black. They were just a group of human beings endeavouring to save their lives. Without hesitation Roger put his arm about her shoulders and strove to comfort her.

Where the garden ended there was a low wall. They scrambled over it and made their way down the slope through an orchard and large, well-tended patches of vegetables. At the bottom of the hill they came face to face with the high crenellated wall. To attempt to go out through the gate that led to the summer pavilions and the boat-houses was far too great a risk, for the guards there would be Janissaries. Even if, owing to the rebellion, they had left their posts it was certain that before leaving they would have locked the gate.

'What now?' asked Mahmoud in an unhappy voice. 'I see no way in which we can possibly scale the wall. So we are trapped here. Our only chance is to hide until morning, then hope that in some way Allah will succour us.'

'No, Prince,' Roger replied. 'My good friend Marshal Lannes, and General Oudinot with his Grenadiers, have scaled taller walls than this, and without scaling ladders. Your turban has served us well, but we have others: mine, that of *Son Altesse Noire* and, if need be, His Imperial Majesty's.'

As he spoke he began to unwind his own turban; the Kizler Aga followed suit. Knotting them together, Roger made at one end a large loop, then weighted the ellipse of the loop with stones as large as cricket balls. Standing well back from the wall, he threw the loop up. The stones clanked on the battlements, but the rope fell back. Again and again he tried to lodge the loop over one of the crenellations, without success, until his arm ached with throwing. The big Negro took over. At his third attempt the loop caught. They pulled upon the rope and it held firmly.

Having got his breath back, the muscles of his arms hurting terribly from the strain he had put upon them, Roger climbed the rope and managed to bestride the battlements. With comparative ease the Kizler Aga swarmed up to sit beside him. Prince Mahmoud went up next. They then drew up the rope and let it down on the far side of the wall. Mahmoud lowered himself by it and stood ready to receive the others. In turn, Aimée, Fatima and Selim were pulled up, then lowered to the Prince. Roger and the Black Eunuch followed. Crossing the wall had taken them three-quarters of an hour, but they were now outside the precincts of the Palace. No-one had seen them and the shore was deserted.

Keeping close under the shadow of the wall, they crept along it, fearful that at any moment one of the guards who normally kept watch by the pavilions on the shore would suddenly appear and challenge them.

When they reached the boat-houses they found them, too, deserted. At the piers in front of them several boats lay bobing gently in the tide. Roger chose one with three thwarts, as the most suitable for the party, because he felt sure that Mahmoud, who was proving a man after his own heart, would be willing to row, and the Kizler Aga could be counted on.

Aimée, Fatima and Selim settled themselves in the stern, the latter taking the single oar protruding from it by which the boat could be steered. He had not spoken since they had emerged from the chimney; but now he asked miserably, 'Whither shall we go?'

'Across to Pera,' Roger replied. 'The safest place for Your Majesty to seek sanctuary is in the French Embassy.'

'I do not agree,' said the Prince. 'It has no defences and only a handful of officers who could resist an attack upon it. Immediately it became known that we are there, the Janissaries will come over and demand our heads.'

'Where then?' asked Roger.

'To Rumeli Hisar. It is commanded by a Pasha known to be loyal to us, and garrisoned by reliable troops. There we shall be in a position to make terms.'

Roger hesitated for a moment. 'I had in mind that if we could get to the French Embassy General Gardane would at once take steps to rouse the mobs of the city against the Janissaries. They are so hated that thousands of people would take up arms to destroy them.'

Mahmoud shrugged. 'Perhaps. But I doubt it. The Janissaries are well armed and well disciplined. The odds are that they would cut to ribbons any ill-directed mob sent against them. At Rumeli our heads will at least remain on our shoulders for another few days.'

'So be it, Prince,' Roger replied. 'You are a better judge than I of this terrible situation. But Rumeli Hisar is a far cry up the Bosphorus, and in our present state I doubt if we'll come to it before morning.'

So it proved. Fortunately, *Son Altesse Noire* and Prince Mahmoud were both strong men, as Roger's hands had been so lacerated during his first attempts to haul Aimée up the chimney that, although he stuck it out, he could do little more than dip his oars in time with the others.

When they came up to Rumeli Hisar, first light was breaking and they were all almost dropping with fatigue. As they pulled in to the shore, a sleepy sentry roused himself to challenge them. 'Go fetch Evilyá Pasha at once,' shouted Mahmoud.

The sentry stared at the boatload of people, soot-begrimed, tattered and, except for Selim, bareheaded. Standing up, the Prince added, 'Tell the Pasha that His Imperial Majesty requires his presence urgently.'

Suddenly the sentry caught sight of the splendid turban, bedecked with jewels and surmounted by an aigrette, worn by the figure slumped in the stern of the boat. His eyes started from his head and his mouth gaped open. Without another word he turned and ran up the steep slope.

Ten minutes later Evilyá Pasha came swiftly padding down it in slippers and a hastily-donned robe. Briefly the Prince told him what had occurred. Salaaming profoundly to the Sultan, the Pasha expressed his distress and unshaken loyalty. Then the officers to whom he had sent to be roused with orders to follow him down, helped the refugees from the boat and up to the castle.

There the Pasha's chief wife welcomed Aimée and Fatima

and took them to rooms that had been hastily prepared for them in the harem. Before they left the men, Aimée turned to Roger and said:

'*Monsieur le Chevalier*, it is to you we owe our lives; a debt we shall never be able to repay.'

Selim then took from round his neck a ribbon from which depended a magnificent star and crescent jewel which he wore on all occasions. Passing the ribbon over Roger's head, he said with tears in his eyes:

'My good friend, you are well named "*le brave Breuc*". While I am still Sultan it is my happiness to decorate you with the highest honour that it is within the power of the ruler of the Turkish Empire to bestow.'

Somehow Roger managed to stammer his thanks; but the pain in his hands and shoulder were agonising, and he was utterly exhausted. Later, his memory of what happened after that was only a vague knowledge that several people had undressed him, put soothing ointment on his wounds, bandaged them and got him between the cool sheets on a comfortable divan.

It was not until late in the afternoon that he awoke. Seated cross-legged on the floor opposite him he saw a Turkish man-servant. As their eyes met, the man smiled, got up and left the room. Ten minutes later, he returned with coffee, rolls shaped like small quoits, sweet cakes and a large dish of fruit. After his exertions of the previous night, Roger felt hungry and would have welcomed an English breakfast, with a choice of half a dozen hot dishes, and York ham to follow, washed down with good Bordeaux; but he made do as well as he could on the rolls, spread with roseleaf jam, and fruit.

When he had done, the servant held out for him a robe of Turkish towelling, then took him along to the Hamam. To him this was no new experience, as he had frequently availed himself of the Turkish baths when in Egypt. More than once he had felt ashamed by the fact that, as a whole, Orientals kept themselves cleaner than Europeans, the majority of whom had a bath only two or three times a year—and even most of the upper classes only once a week—whereas in Cairo and

Constantinople the public baths were used daily by the greater part of the population. This difference in custom had even led, right up to the preceding reign, to high-caste Turks finding Europeans so smelly that they had insisted on all Ambassadors being steam-bathed in the Seraglio before they were presented to the Sultan.

After sitting in the hot room for half an hour, while the perspiration trickled off him, Roger took a dip in the pool, then he was shaved and submitted to a massage that miraculously restored the vigour to his still-tired muscles. Back in his room, he found that fresh clothes of fine texture had been laid out for him, and that a doctor was waiting there to treat his wounds. They were only superficial and the salve applied early that morning had already done wonders.

When he had dressed, he was taken down to a small, arcaded court. A fountain was playing in the centre and seated on divans, smoking hookahs, were the Prince, the Kizler Aga and the Pasha.

Having greeted him warmly and thanked him again for all he had done the previous night, Mahmoud told him that the news was not good, but no worse than was to be expected. All the loyal men in the Nizam-i-jedad had been murdered, and many of the eunuchs. Bands of Janissaries were now roaming the city, seeking out and killing, wherever they found them, the higher officials who were known to have favoured the reforms introduced by Selim. Every shop was shut and every house barred. Many of them were being broken into, but large numbers of the wealthier class had had the sense to collect such valuables as they could carry and hurry to take sanctuary in the mosques. Meanwhile, Prince Mustapha had had himself proclaimed Sultan.

'Do you think the majority of the people will accept him?' Roger asked.

'I fear so. You see, he will have the support of many men in high places who resent His Majesty Selim's reforms and he is the Heir Apparent.'

Roger frowned. 'I was not aware of that.'

'It is so. Unlike the European monarchies, with us the crown does not descend from father to son, but to the next eldest living Osmanli Prince, and Mustapha was born before I was. He is the son of Aimée's husband, the Sultan Abdul-Hamid by an older *Kadin*.'

'What of the Army,' Roger enquired. 'Surely a great part of it must hate the Janissaries for the idle, privileged life they lead, while other troops are fighting? There must be many regiments that would support the Sultan Selim in an attempt to regain his throne.'

It was the Pasha who answered. 'You are right, *Effendi*. But most of them are either fighting the Russians, or engaged in putting down rebellions in the Balkan provinces. I have sent messengers to such Generals as I believe to be loyal; but there is no body of troops within many weeks' march of Constantinople sufficiently strong to defeat the Janissaries.'

'For how long, Pasha, do you think you can hold out here?'

The Pasha made a wry face. 'A week perhaps, but not longer. My men are Bulgars, and can be relied on. But the castle is not provisioned for a siege. We should be starved out.'

'Then we must leave here,' Roger declared promptly. 'With an escort of your men, the Imperial party should be able to reach some more distant place where they will be safer. Still better, they could set off in disguise as a small caravan of perhaps a dozen people.'

The Kizler Aga shook his dark head. 'It is too late for that, *Effendi*. By noon Prince Mustapha had learned where my Imperial Master has taken refuge. Outside the gates of the castle there are now many hundred Janissaries, and on the water side scores more in several galleys. We are already besieged.'

'Are you expecting them to attack?'

'Not yet,' the Prince replied. 'For the moment Prince Mustapha must have his hands full in the city. He will probably come out here tomorrow and demand our surrender.'

'I'll not surrender,' growled the Pasha. 'Not unless I receive a direct order to do so from my Imperial Master.'

The Prince smiled at him. 'Good friend, you will receive no such order from the Sultan. He is in a sad state of depression, blaming himself now for having rejected my advice to take sterner measures with the Janissaries, and so bringing us all to this terrible pass. But the Sultan Validé has persuaded him to give me full authority to take all such decisions as are necessary. He will remain in his room; so at least we can die fighting.'

The evening that followed was one of the most unhappy that Roger had ever spent. It was not that he was afraid to die; as he thought he almost certainly would the next day or the day after, when the castle was attacked. He could not bear the thought of the fate that would befall the courageous and beautiful Aimée when she fell into Prince Mustapha's hands. She was only a little over forty and still infinitely more desirable than any Turkish beauty. Mustapha was, he had gathered, no fool. And no-one but a fool would kill such a pearl among women; but he would take his revenge by humiliating her. Since she had held the rank of Sultan Validé he could not possibly turn her over to his Janissaries. But he could give her in marriage as a junior wife to one of the most repulsive Pashas who had supported him.

To take his mind off Aimée Roger thought, as he often did, of his beloved Georgina. She was the great love of his life, and no other woman could ever supplant her. Time and again he had pressed her to marry him, but she had proved adamant in her refusal. She always maintained that it was only because they were separated, often for many months and sometimes even for years, by his work as a secret agent on the Continent, that the flame of their desire for each other had never flickered, and that each time they did come together for a while it was with the same wild, joyous, utterly satisfying passion that they had known in their teens.

He fell asleep still thinking of her, and she came to him in a dream. So strong was the bond between them that there had been several occasions when he had been in acute danger and her voice had come clearly to him, telling what to do to save himself.

Now he could see her bending over him. He felt her soft kiss linger on his lips. Then she said, 'Roger, dear heart. Tomorrow you will receive an invitation. Take it, and you will have no regrets.'

When he woke in the morning, he remembered his dream as clearly as though she had come to his room in the flesh. The dream puzzled him greatly, because in his present situation the last thing he expected to receive was an invitation. Then he put the matter from his mind, had breakfast, spent half an hour in the Hamam and dressed.

It was shortly before midday that a herald emerged from the camp the Janissaries had made opposite the main gate of the castle, and demanded its submission in the name of the Sultan Mustapha IV.

The Pasha replied from the battlements above the great gate that he knew no Sultan other than His Imperial Majesty Selim III; and that in his name he would defend Rumeli Hisar to the death against all comers.

The herald retired, then returned ten minutes later, to state that His Imperial Master Mustapha IV desired to preserve his subjects from unnecessary bloodshed. So would the Pasha or some responsible person come out and parley with him?

Prince Mahmoud was standing on the steps that led up to the battlements above the great gate, and he said to the Pasha, 'Tell the man that, provided none of Prince Mustapha's troops are within four hundred yards of the gate when it is opened, I will do so.'

The Pasha pleaded with him to be allowed to go himself, insisting that if the Prince went out alone, he would certainly be assassinated. But Mahmoud refused to be moved, and said, 'Your cannon are already trained upon the Janissaries' encampment. Give orders to your men that, should they see me shot down, they are to fire. Such a volley might well kill Mustapha and so save our Sultan. You know the ancient prophecy that, when the last Prince of the House of Osmanli dies, the end of the Turkish Empire will follow. If both Mustapha and I are dead, they will not dare harm His Imperial Majesty.'

'So be it then, my Prince,' the Pasha submitted. Turning, he shouted the terms to the herald, who agreed them; then he and Mahmoud descended the stone staircase together and ordered the great gate to be unbarred.

Roger and the Kizler Aga had been standing nearby on the battlements, so they had heard the whole transaction. Now they watched the Janissaries withdraw and Prince Mahmoud leave the castle. A small group of men came forward to meet him, but did not approach beyond the stipulated limit.

The gunners held their lighted matches ready to apply them to the touch-holes of the cannons should the Prince be attacked. But, after a few minutes, it seemed that the rebels, at least for the present, had no intention of harming him. At a distance of a quarter of a mile it was not possible to see the expressions of the faces of the group or guess from their gestures how their discussion was going; but it seemed to be interminable.

At least half an hour went by before Mahmoud bowed to the others, turned and started back towards the castle. Roger, the Pasha and the Kizler Aga were all so intensely anxious to hear what had passed that they went out to meet him.

He greeted them with a smile, and said, 'The lives of all of us are safe. I have made a pact with Prince Mustapha. I refused his demand that our Lord Selim should publicly abdicate; but agreed that we should become his prisoners in the Seraglio. We are to be treated with respect, and enjoy the same comforts and semi-liberty as he and his mother have been allowed during the past few years. Tomorrow morning we are to return to the Seraglio in one of the Imperial barges, with a fitting escort and the homage due to Princes of the House of Osmanli.'

Roger frowned. 'In the circumstances, the terms are generous, Prince, and I'd congratulate you were I certain that Mustapha would honour them. But dare you trust him? Once he has you all in his power, isn't it highly probable that he will murder you?'

Mahmoud shook his head. 'Nay. He swore it upon the Koran before witnesses. Did he break his word, the Mullahs would denounce him from every pulpit in Islam, and his body would be thrown to the dogs by his own household troops for having disgraced the supreme office of Caliph.'

The Pasha and *Son Altesse Noire* were also evidently of that opinion, for they were laughing and clapping one another on the back.

Selim's virtual dethronement could not be taken as cause for a celebration. Nevertheless, an atmosphere of subdued gaiety permeated the castle for the remainder of the day. The fear of imminent death had been lifted, not only from the Imperial party, but from the whole garrison.

Late in the evening, Aimée sent for Roger. To his surprise he found her alone. She greeted him with a smile. 'So it is all over. I am sure my prayers to the Holy Virgin must have helped; but it is to you we owe our lives.'

He shook his head. 'No, Madame. It is to the courage and statesmanlike handling of the situation this morning by your son.'

She smiled again. 'I am very proud of him. He will make a great Sultan.'

Roger hesitated. 'Is there . . . is there really much chance now of his ever ascending the throne?'

'Most certainly he will. Did you never hear the prophecy that was made to me when I was a young girl in Martinique? It was that I would become a Queen and that my son would rule gloriously over a mighty Empire.'

'I earnestly pray, Madame, that the second half of that prophecy may also come true. But, with regard to yourself, I am deeply distressed. The thought of your becoming a prisoner has harrowed me all day.'

'Please let it do so no longer,' she said gently. 'It means only my removal from one prison to another. The so-called "cage" in the Seraglio is a beautiful pavilion with numerous rooms and its own garden. All that we have been through was caused only by the jealousy of Prince Mustapha's mother. She envied me my position. Now that she has it, she will be content. And Mustapha is by no means ill-disposed towards me personally. I am sure he will allow me to keep all the things I treasure. I'll have my books, my needlework and my flowers.'

'Oh, *chère Madame!* You cannot imagine how relieved I am to hear this.'

'I am most touched that you should have been so concerned for me. My one regret is that our friendship cannot continue. Tomorrow morning we shall see the last of each other.' Aimée paused for a moment, then went on. 'Alas, there is little I can do to reward you for your devotion. But there is one small matter that I could arrange to give you pleasure.'

Roger threw out his hands. 'Madame, I protest. I need no reward. It has been a joy to be of service to you.'

'I am glad; but shall persist with my idea. From what Zanthé told me, you are not only a brave but very virile and amorous man. And one, too, who would not demean himself to lie with any but a beautiful and well-born girl—such, for example, as my little Fatima.'

Roger stared at her nonplussed, as she continued. 'It must have become obvious to you that she regards you as a demigod. And she is no virgin, as for a year she was a concubine to one of the young Princes who died not long ago. You have but to say the word and, given my permission, she will come running to sleep with you tonight.'

'Madame, I . . . I . . .' Roger stammered.

Aimée threw back her head, and laughed. '*Cher Chevalier*. Why be so bashful? Men of your kind do not frequent brothels, so must be starved of women when in the East. And Fatima passed her tests in the Seraglio "School of Love", so I guarantee you there is nothing she will not do to please you. But there is one condition. All must take place in complete darkness, in order to conform with Turkish observances.'

With a puzzled frown, Roger asked, 'Pray tell me, Madame, what is the reason for such a strange custom?'

'You would naturally wish to kiss your bed-fellow,' Aimeé replied. 'Therefore, she must dispense with her veil. Of course, when a couple are married, no such problem arises. But Turkish females are very different from Europeans. As I have learned from many Turkish ladies of my acquaintance when, as sometimes happens, they are left for a while alone with an attractive friend of their husband's; they will permit many liberties, but should the man lift their veil, they would take it as a deadly insult. That is why, should you wish me to send Fatima to you, I require your word of honour that you will have the shutters of the windows of your room closed, the curtains drawn, and in no circumstances endeavour to look upon her unveiled face.'

Roger was in a quandary. Face to face with Aimée as he was, Fatima meant nothing to him. Yet she was a pretty girl, with a lovely figure, and it was a considerable time since he had slept with a woman. It then occurred to him that, in any case, it would be churlish to refuse this obviously kindly-intended offer; so he bowed and said:

'Madame, I am deeply grateful to you for your thought for me as a man who for a considerable time past has not enjoyed nature's blessings. If Fatima is willing, I shall be delighted to receive her—and I feel confident I can promise to give her an enjoyable night.'

Aimée smiled. 'I am sure you will, *mon cher Chevalier*. I will not bid you good-bye now, but in the morning before I am taken away to my new prison.'

Having kissed her hand, Roger withdrew; still wondering at the breadth of this extraordinary woman's mind—that in the midst of her own troubles she should have thought about providing pleasure for a friend who had stood by her when she was in danger. Then he recalled the dream in which his beloved Georgina had appeared to him. This must be the invitation that she had urged him to accept. And he had nearly refused it, because the radiance of Aimée had made him so indifferent to Fatima's attractions. With a smile he thought, 'I've never yet questioned Georgina's advice. And, after all, Fatima is a graduate of that famous "School of Love". Maybe she can teach me something, though I doubt it. Anyhow, a night with a girl will make me feel a real man again.'

Going to his room he slowly undressed, closed the shutters, drew the curtains, then got into bed. For a while he laboured a little to read two of the stories in a Turkish edition of the

Thousand and One Nights. Rolling up the scroll, he blew out the bedside lamp.

The room was now in Stygian blackness. He could not see his hand before his face. Patiently he lay there for what seemed a very long time. At last he heard the door open, but not even a ray of light came in, as the lamps in the corridor had been put out.

The door closed. His heart began to hammer with anticipation. He caught the swish of a silk garment as it slid from his visitor's shoulders to the floor. Next moment she had pulled back the bed-clothes, and wriggled in beside him.

He drew her to him, and ran his hand lightly over her hair. It was not crinkly as he remembered, but very fine and silky. Leaning over, he kissed her on the mouth. It was not full-lipped, but very soft, and she moved it gently, touching his tongue with hers. As their kiss ended, she gave a low laugh and said:

'I've cheated you, haven't I? You've got an old woman who has fallen in love with a wonderful man.'

He had known it a moment before. It was not Fatima that he held naked in his arms, but the Veiled Crown of Turkey, who was yet to change the destiny of a great nation: the remarkable woman whom the Grand Turk had chosen to honour above all others in his vast Empire—*Naksh* the Beautiful.

II

The Road to Isfahan

On June 7th General Gardane's mission, and Roger with it, left Constantinople. The intelligence sources serving the French Embassy were good. Within a few days of the *coup d'état*, the General had learned that the new Sultan, Mustapha IV, and his mother, as a natural corollary of their opposition to Aimée who led the pro-French party, had long been in secret communication with the British and the Russians. Therefore, there was now not the least chance of Gardane's mission succeeding in Turkey.

He had, therefore, decided to take his whole party on as soon as possible to Persia. By the land route, its capital, Isfahan, was some fifteen hundred miles from Constantinople; but a good part of the journey could be done by sea, and in a vessel there was no necessity for horses to be rested while their tired riders slept in a camp or inn. Ships proceeded on their way day and night. So, although the distance to Antioch by sea was a thousand miles, and they would then still have to travel another thousand miles overland, Gardane felt that, during the summer weather, unless the winds proved unusually contrary for that season, they would save several days and themselves much exertion if they went as far as they could by ship.

For the purpose he chartered a brigantine with a hold large enough to stable their horses, and confined—but by the standard of the times, adequate—quarters for the personnel.

When in mid-morning, with the sun blazing down out of a brassy blue sky, they set sail and rounded Seraglio Point into the Sea of Marmora, Roger, leaning over the stern rail, looked back at the terraced gardens and innumerable kiosks that made up the Topkapi Palace.

For the past week he had thought of little else than Aimée. He was reassured that, apart from some quite unforeseeable happening, no harm would befall her. She had been relieved of her many duties and responsibilities, her beloved son and her dear friend, the deposed Sultan Selim, were with her and as safe from danger as she was. She would have their company, her books, embroidery and garden; but it seemed tragic that such a woman should be condemned to live the life of a nun.

Among the first words she had said to him on that night they had slept together were, 'I'm an old woman.' By Eastern standards, at forty-three, she was; but in fact she was old neither in spirit nor body. She was that rarest of beings, a beautiful European who had been taught by Oriental experts the ways in which to arouse a man's virility again and again, and to give herself each time with delirious enjoyment. Since her husband's death, conditions in the harem had made it impossible for her to take a lover, even if she had desired one of the few men who were occasionally permitted to visit her in her apartments. Now, she was fated to resume that life of chastity for good, and to remain a prisoner until she died.

That, at least, was what Roger feared would be her fate, although her unshakeable belief that her son, Prince Mahmoud, would one day rule gloriously did give a ray of hope that unforeseeable circumstances might yet restore her to the position of Sultan Validé.

Before leaving Constantinople, Roger had carried out his orders by writing a long despatch for Napoleon's private eye. In it he praised Gardane for having done everything possible to carry out the Emperor's wishes. Then he gave an account of how he, personally, had penetrated the Seraglio and gained the friendship of the Sultan Validé by representing himself to be an envoy sent by the Empress Josephine. He implied that the mission would have succeeded in its object had Aimée had her way; but the revolt of the Janissaries had brought to naught all hope of Turkey's sending additional forces against the Russians.

Having completed his report he sent Achmet out to find a sea-captain or merchant of good standing, who would shortly be sailing to Italy. After Achmet had produced three men who would be setting out from Constantinople within the next ten days, Roger settled on the third—a Venetian who was taking a cargo of coffee to Venice. To him he gave fifty gold pieces and the despatch, with the assurance that he would be well rewarded on delivering it safely. His missive was addressed to His Imperial Highness, Prince Eugene de Beauharnais, Viceroy of Italy, the Royal Palace, Milan. Inside the cover he put a note that read:

From Your Highness' old friend who had the pleasure of presenting you with your first pair of pistols. That, he knew, would identify the sender to Eugene, whom he had first met as a boy of fifteen.

In the outer cover was an inner one, enclosing the despatch, inscribed, *Urgent! To be forwarded by fast courier to Marshal Berthier, Prince de Neufchatel.* And he had little doubt that, provided the Venetian merchant was not shipwrecked, or Beauharnais' courier came to grief, his report would reach Napoleon with the minimum of delay.

The Emperor was not going to be pleased with the information it conveyed, but at least Gardane would be excused his failure and Roger maintain his reputation as active and resourceful in the Emperor's interests.

Sailing on, the brigantine passed through the Dardanelles, then clove Homer's 'wine-dark seas' that creamed on the shores of the Aegean islands. They called at Rhodes to take on fresh provisions and, while they were being loaded, visited and marvelled at the Crusaders' vast castle. It was a city in itself, enclosed in three miles of wall, which were in some places a hundred feet in height, and so broad that three coaches abreast could have been driven along its top.

The wind held fair and on June 21st they landed at Selucca Peria, the port of Antioch. In the ancient Syrian city— the first Bishopric of the Christian world, but for many centuries past under either Arab or Turkish rule—they spent two nights, while Gardane's Quartermaster made preparations for their onward journey.

They were to take the famous Silk Road, which began there and ended four thousand miles away at the city of Chang-an in China. From time immemorial it had been the tenuous link between East and West. Merchandise had certainly passed along it for over two thousand years. Cleopatra had worn silk, and for several centuries, from her day onward, the traffic had been considerable. This was due to the whole of central Asia being under the domination of four mighty, stable Empires: that of Rome in the West; adjoining it Parthia—of which Persia then formed only a small part; beyond Parthia another vast territory ruled by the Great Kushan; and finally China, under the Han dynasty.

Silk was then China's wealth. The Emperors paid for their requirements with it and rich Mandarins stored rolls of it away, just as nobles and bankers in the Roman world kept their capital in bars of gold. It was also her monopoly. Its manufacture was the most jealously-guarded of all secrets, and the Chinese succeeded in keeping it for over a thousand years. Even when it did leak out, no other people succeeded in making silk of comparable quality. In Europe it was greatly prized, and Aurelian, writing in the third century A.D., tells us that in Rome the price of one pound of silk was twelve ounces of gold.

Even so, by then there had developed a considerable commerce between East and West. China continued to send only silk, but in exchange for it received wool, myrrh, horses and Roman glass. China, too, made no attempt to enlighten the outer world with regard to the wonderful civilisation she had developed. She remained a mysterious legend, her territories only vaguely indicated on the maps. On the other hand, to her there came considerable knowledge of the peoples beyond her frontiers. Manichean, Zoroastrian and, later, Christian missionaries made their way there, and were listened to with respect. Above all, the yellow-robed priests from India and

Ceylon spread their faith so successfully that Buddhism became the religion of the greater part of the Chinese people.

With the decline and break-up of the mighty Empires, the traffic all but ceased; as the caravans had not only to face the difficulties and hardships of crossing vast deserts and ranges of great mountains, suffer gruelling heat and bitter cold, but they became a prey to bands of fierce Huns, Tartars and Tibetans. Yet great profits were the spur that continued to induce men to risk their lives and, even allowing for the heavy tolls exerted by each city through which they passed, every caravan that reached the Mediterranean made a fortune for its master.

It was estimated that goods took some two hundred and forty days to travel the four thousand miles between the Jade Gate of Chang-an and Antioch; but no caravan made the whole journey. At points along the route, merchants met others, bargained and sold their cargoes, to be sent on by other caravans. It was for this reason that very few Western traders had ever entered China, and that, even in the thirteenth century, when Marco Polo returned from his amazing journey, few people would believe him when he told them of the marvels of the East.

Conscious of the urgency of his mission, Gardane decided not to wait and accompany the next caravan, which would not be leaving Antioch for a week or more, but to set out at once with only his A.D.C., Roger and the few senior officers who had stayed at the Embassy in Constantinople. Of these, only the Colonel of Engineers, Couthon, was to be left behind in command of the junior officers and orderlies who would form part of the caravan and escort the several score of camels needed to transport the heavier baggage of the mission, the presents for the Shah and the considerable consignment of arms destined for Persia.

By far the worst part of the journey from Antioch was the last two-thirds; for, after leaving Samarkand, caravans had to cross the Pamir Mountains, then the terrible deserts of Takla and Sinkiang. So, although to reach Isfahan was one-fourth of it, Gardane reckoned that instead of sixty days his party should arrive in the Persian capital in under forty. Moreover, they would be travelling light, with only lead horses to carry their necessities and a supply of provisions against emergencies.

On June 23rd they set out. The first stage was across the Syrian desert. The midday heat was unbearable, so they travelled only from early morning until about eleven o'clock, and from the late afternoon until nightfall, between times pitching camp. Their Arab guides knew the route well, so arranged their stages in a way which enabled them to make their halts in a series of oases, where there was water and fruit to be had and shade under palm trees.

Late on the third night, they entered Palmyra. The moon being up, they were able to see the splendid Greco-Roman ruins which were all that remained of Queen Zenobia's once-splendid capital.

As ruler of the last city on the Silk Road before the caravans arrived at Antioch and the first before they moved on eastward, she had become fabulously wealthy from the tolls she imposed on the merchants trading between the Mediterranean and Parthia. Being an ambitious woman, she had used much of the money to create a quite formidable army, with the object of making her large oasis the capital of a powerful nation. Resenting this, in A.D. 273 the Romans had sent their legions against her, destroyed her city and taken her to Rome where, walking in golden chains, she had provided the principal spectacle in a Roman triumph.

Palmyra now consisted only of a few hundred mud huts and a caravanserai. Having paid a quick visit to this flea-ridden hostelry, Gardane decided that they would fare better if they stayed out of it. So they pitched their tents among the ruins of the great Temple of Baal then, early next morning, started on the considerably longer trek across Mesopotamia to the Euphrates.

It took them eight days to reach the great river at Al-Hadithah: a large town, again consisting of mud huts. Remaining there only for the night, they pushed on along a road of sorts that ran south-east. At times it followed the course of the river for some miles; then, making a great bend, the river would pass out of sight for an hour or two, later to reappear and for a stretch again run parallel with the road. On their second night out from Al-Hadithah they encamped in an oasis on the north shore of Lake Habbanizah and in the morning saw it to be such a large sheet of water that its further shore was out of sight. Early the following evening, July 7th, they entered Babylon, having accomplished over half their journey.

Well pleased with their progress so far, Gardane agreed that they should remain there for two days' rest, and to see something of the fabled city. The caravanserai to which their chief guide took them was patronised by wealthy merchants, so it was reasonably clean and comfortable. The building was oval in shape, enclosing a great central courtyard open to the sky, that had the appearance of both a warehouse and a stable. Innumerable bales, sacks and boxes were piled in the middle, for it was in such places that the merchants bartered the wares they had brought for others to take back to their own cities; and the camels of their caravans were tethered round the sites. The camel men dossed down there to protect their masters' goods from pilferage. Above, there were two tiers of rooms, all with big, arched doorways facing inward. It was in these that the richer patrons of the place both ate and slept, their own servants cooking their meals.

The worst feature of such establishments was the fleas with which they were infested and the stench of the camels. The members of the mission had found the myriads of flies, which in the desert seemed to appear from nowhere, trying enough; but the fleas were a positive pest.

The merchants regarded the strangers with friendly interest and several of them spoke Turkish. Roger learned from one of them that he had just taken over a valuable cargo of china that was consigned to the Sultan, and he undid a sacking wrapping to show Roger a plate. It was Chinese celadon, with a raised design and in a beautiful shade of green.

Another man had just acquired several chests of tea, and Roger, not having enjoyed a cup of tea for many weeks, asked if he might buy some from him. He opened a chest and, to Roger's surprise, its contents did not look at all like tea leaves; they were longer, pale and fluffy. The man explained to him that they were not the leaves, but the flowers of the tea plant, and that even in China only the very rich could afford to buy them. He added that their flavour was so delicate that to have sent them via India by sea would have spoiled it; so the comparatively rare parcels despatched to the West were always sent overland by caravan. Eager to taste such an exotic brew, Roger produced a gold coin, but the merchant refused to take it and insisted on giving him a small, muslin bag full of the precious flowers. When, later, Roger had some water boiled and made the infusion, he found its perfume marvellous and not unlike that of very fine old brandy.

Gardane hired a local guide and, mounted on asses, they went to see the remains left by half a dozen great civilisations; but found them disappointing. There were many groups of broken pillars and arches of sandstone eroded by time. Most of them were half buried, and Roger recalled how, when in Egypt, only the head of the Sphinx had been showing above the desert until Napoleon had had the sand that hid its body cleared away. Such temples as remained were hardly recognisable as such, for their once-splendid courts had become squalid slums, filled with shacks and lean-tos, between which starved-looking chickens were scratching in the dirt. The only impressive sight that remained was the great, pyramid-like Ziggurats, from the tops of which long-dead astrologers had once charted the heavens.

Early on July 10th they proceeded on their way across the fifty miles of desert that separates the Euphrates from the Tigris, where the two great rivers come closest to each other before they join and flow on into the Persian Gulf. Having been ferried over the Tigris, they took another road of sorts that ran in the same direction as the river—south-east—for a hundred and fifty miles. They then left it, but continued on for another fifty along the route of the Silk Road, which, except for a few stretches, was not actually a road at all but a half-mile-wide track of broken surface, where the sand had been churned up by the passage of countless camels, asses and horses that made up the caravans.

Still heading nearly south-east, they entered Persia, skirting the foothills of the northern half of the great Zagros mountain barrier that defends Persia's western frontier until, still in the plain, they came to the considerable city of Dezful. There they were met by officials who had been warned in advance of their approach, and taken to the Governor of the city. Through interpreters he enquired their business and, Gardane having produced papers to show that he was the head of a mission from the Emperor of the French to His Imperial Majesty the Shah, the Governor could not have been more courteous. Nevertheless, he insisted that their baggage must be examined by the Customs and that duty must be paid on all articles subject to tax when imported into Persia. Gardane protested in vain that all Ambassadorial missions were, by custom, exempt from such imposts. The following day he had to pay out a considerable sum before being allowed to proceed—a high percentage of which doubtless went to the Governor. They were soon to learn that in Persia nothing could be done without, in some way or other, greasing somebody's palm.

Some way further on, the road began to mount and wind upwards through a pass. On emerging from it they turned north of east to cover the last one hundred and twenty miles to Isfahan, and encountered the worst territory they had so far met with.

Persia is the most mountainous country in the world, and no sooner had the Silk Road crossed one chain of mountains than it approached another. For its size, the country also has the fewest rivers. Yet they never lacked for water for their horses or themselves. Every mile or so there were man-made water-holes and the *chaöushes* they had engaged in Dezful explained to them that two hundred years earlier Shah Abbas the Great had carried out one of the most marvellous irrigation works ever conceived by man. He had had underground pipe-lines laid all over the country, to bring water to every valley; so that, instead of remaining parched desert, it could become fertile and bear crops.

Shah Abbas had also faced up to the terrible problem of his country's climate. The Greek historian Zenophon had quoted the Persian Prince Cyrus as saying, 'The Kingdom of my Father is so great that there is no enduring the Cold on one side of it, nor the Heat in the other', and, in truth, up to the beginning of the seventeenth century the sufferings of travellers in Persia had, in certain seasons, been almost unbearable. But the great Shah had caused to be built many hundred caravanserai where merchants could seek relief—on winter nights from the cold of Dante's Seventh Hell, and at midday in summer the heat of Satan's Kitchen.

Although the mission travelled only during the early mornings and late afternoons, all its members were suffering from sunburn. Their faces and hands were red and their bodies baking beneath their thick uniforms. Roger suffered least as, having previously travelled for long distances in the East, he had taken the precaution, before leaving Constantinople, of buying a soothing salve to counteract the effects of the blistering sun. But he had lost nearly two stones in weight.

The scenery was magnificent. While crossing each wide plateau, upon every side of them rose jagged yellow mountain ranges, the highest peaks of which were still capped with snow, and stood out against a vivid blue sky. Below each range lay deep valleys, sheltering villages of flat-topped houses and well-cultivated fields, with abundant crops that struck a contrasting note of vivid green against the rocky precipices that protected them.

On the morning of July 25th they were only a dozen miles from Isfahan; so they had accomplished the journey in thirty-two days. It was at this point that they realised that the Governor of Dezful must have sent a courier ahead to announce that they were on their way, for half a dozen horsemen came out to greet them. One of the group was an Armenian interpreter, who said that his name was Mesrop-Li-bec, and he took charge of the party.

Half an hour later they came upon groups of houses at the

roadside and, here and there, an open market; so they imagined that they were entering the city. Actually, these were only the suburbs which seemed interminable, as they continued for several miles. It was this that first brought home to them that Isfahan was no ordinary Eastern city, but a great metropolis.

At length they came to a broad river: the Zaindeh. The Khajan bridge across it was like no bridge they had ever seen. Those of most European cities were surmounted on either side by irregular huddles of houses and shops. Those of Constantinople, the Balkans and the Near East consisted only of a number of flat-bottomed barges lashed together. This was a masterpiece of graceful architecture. On both sides of a broad roadway, it was lined by a long row of pointed arches behind each of which was an empty space overlooking the water. Mesrop-Li-bec explained that these alcoves were 'boxes', which were occupied by the Shah and his nobles when boat races and other water sports were held on the river.

On reaching the far end of the bridge, a company of richly-dressed horsemen were waiting. They were headed by the Nazir—the Grand Steward of the Shah's household. In his Imperial Master's name, he bade them welcome. It was then explained that in Isfahan the Shah owned some three hundred houses and it was customary for distinguished visitors to be accommodated in any one of these they might choose as most suitable. Gardane then said that the dozen officers and servants with him were only a small part of the mission and that when the whole of it arrived in Isfahan, including servants, it would consist of some fifty persons.

Beyond the bridge lay a broad boulevard called the Khilban. It had shops on one side only; the other was occupied by the high-domed University and, behind, a screen of tall sycamore trees, the park of Chehel Sotun—one of the Shah's palaces. The long line of shops was broken by several streets in which lay many of the largest private houses in Isfahan. The Nazir led Gardane down one of them, pointing out a commodious building and, through Mesrop, asked if the General thought it would serve to house all his people. Gardane, assuming that it had been chosen as suitable for the numbers of his party, at once agreed. He was then told that provisions to sustain the mission would shortly be brought there.

After the exchange of many bows and flourishes, the Nazir and his cavaliers then took their leave, Mesrop alone remaining to see the French into their quarters. On exploring the house they found it to be well furnished in the Eastern style, and were more than happy to see that the divans were draped in mosquito nets. Behind the building was ample stabling for the horses and a small garden in which there were orange, apricot and pomegranate trees.

An hour later a gorgeously-robed gentleman who rejoiced in the title of Mahemander Bachi—which Mesrop translated as the Guest-Keeper General—arrived. With him he brought an order on the Shah's purveyors for Gardane's party to receive at once, or at such times as they wished:

Sixty quintals of rice
Sixty quintals of flour
Sixty quintals of barley
Twelve quintals of butter
Twenty sheep
Two hundred chickens
One thousand eggs
Four hundred sacks of chopped straw for the horses.

Having expressed his gratitude, Gardane asked that a limited supply of each should be delivered as soon as possible, and said that he would ask for more when it became necessary. The Mahemander Bachi smiled his acquiescence, but appeared in no hurry to depart. Mesrop then told the General that it was customary to make this official some present in recognition of his services.

Gardane gave quick thought about what he had with him that might prove suitable; as all the gifts for the Shah and his courtiers were coming on by the caravan, which must be many days behind them. It then occurred to him that he had a musical box which, at times, they had amused themselves by playing while camping in the desert. He sent his A.D.C. for it, and a tune was played on the box before it was duly presented. The Persian was delighted and, with many expressions of gratitude, departed. As Gardane had expected to have to pay both for the rent of a large house and everything his mission consumed while in Persia, he was naturally delighted at the Shah's generosity, and considered that he had got off extremely cheaply by surrendering his musical box for many thousand francs-worth of stores. But the following morning he became somewhat disillusioned about the generosity of the Persians.

An official termed the Peskis Nuviez arrived. Mesrop came with him, and explained that his companion's function was to enquire upon what business the mission had come to Isfahan and for particulars of the presents brought by the Ambassador for His Imperial Majesty, the King of Kings.

Gardane willingly gave a résumé of the letter from the Emperor that he was charged to present. As was customary between monarchs, he had, of course, numerous presents for the Shah. To Constantinople he had brought for the Sultan a magnificent Sèvres dinner service, a miniature of Napoleon framed in diamonds, a beautiful clock and various other items. For the Shah he had similar gifts and a considerable consignment of modern weapons, to which he could now add those it had been intended he should leave in Constantinople. But he explained that all these things were in his heavy baggage and coming on with the next caravan, which could not be expected to arrive for a fortnight or more.

Recalling his own experience with the Customs at Dezful, it then occurred to him that the heavy baggage might be held up there until duty had been paid on it; so he put this question to his visitor.

The Peskis Nuviez replied that certainly would be the case. Gardane protested that in other countries the belongings of diplomatic missions were allowed in free; then he asked if it could not be arranged that at least the presents for His Majesty and the weapons should be exempted from duty.

With a bland smile the Persian said that it could, but would prove a costly matter because a special courier would have to be sent to Dezful and some compensation made to the Governor of that city for his loss of revenue.

A second supply of coffee and sweet cakes was then sent for and, in a leisurely manner, the matter was discussed. Finally, to have all the mission's baggage brought through free of duty cost Gardane eighty gold Napoleons and, to his chagrin, he felt certain that the greater part of this sum would remain in the pocket of the Peskis Nuviez.

Later that morning Gardane had still greater reason to feel exasperated at the conduct of the Persian officials. The Mahemander Bachi called upon him to say that, having learned from the Peskis Nuviez that the gifts sent by the Emperor to the Shah were not yet available, he could not, for the time being, present the General to His Imperial Majesty. Protocol ruled that presents from foreign monarchs must always be offered, examined and their worth assessed before an Ambassador could be granted an audience.

Gardane again attempted bribery, but this time without success. Evidently it was more than the Mahemander Bachi's place was worth to ignore the accepted procedure. When the official had gone, the General gave vent to his fury at being delayed in attempting to carry out the task with which the Emperor had charged him. The many additional hours of exhausting travel across deserts and over mountains endured by himself and his officers had proved wasted effort. They might just as well have come by easy stages with the camel caravan. But there was nothing he could do about it.

His wrath was somewhat mitigated that afternoon after he had received another visitor. This was the Superior of the Capuchin Fathers who had established a monastery in Isfahan many generations earlier, were well regarded by the Shah and had accumulated an exhaustive knowledge of the Persians and their customs.

The Superior assured Gardane that the two or three weeks' delay before he could be presented at Court should, in the long run, prove all to the good, as it would enable him to become acquainted with numerous Ministers and functionaries, whose goodwill was essential to the success of the mission. To gain it, he advised the General to lose no opportunity of entertaining them, making them such presents as he could and, above all, flattering them. Among the most important to be cultivated in his fashion were the Shah's twenty-four gentlemen-in-waiting, who were called Yessaouls. They were a venal crowd who openly made a fat living by obtaining concessions and favours for foreigners; but they had great influence with their master.

Of the Persians generally, the Superior said they were a kindly but intensely proud people regarding themselves, in view of their three-thousand-year-old civilisation, as superior to all others. They taught their children three things: to tell the truth, to draw a bow and to ride a horse. Even the shopkeepers went everywhere on horseback. But they were congenitally lazy, which was probably due to the climate. For a great part of the year a warm humidity, which proved most enervating, pervaded the whole country south of the great range of mountains north of Tehran. It caused bow strings to become slack and even rusted scimitars if left long in their scabbards.

In the days that followed, Gardane and his officers were treated with the greatest courtesy. As the official responsible for the well-being of guests, the Mahemander Bachi visited them frequently and arranged for them to see the sights of the city. Mesrop-Li-bec accompanied them everywhere and they learned from him that, although quite a number of higher-class Persians had a limited knowledge of either French or English and many of them understood Arabic and Turkish perfectly, it was considered beneath their dignity to converse in any foreign language. It was for this reason that Armenians were always used as interpreters.

On being conducted through the city, the French marvelled beyond all else at the Maidan Square, which had been built by Shah Abbas early in the seventeenth century. It was, Roger reckoned, about seven times the size of the largest square in Europe: the Piazza San Marco in Venice. The buildings surrounding it were uniform: each having a pointed arch in its upper storey. Centrally, on one of the longer sides, there towered up above the line of flat roofs the Shah's Ali Qipa Palace. It had a high, broad balcony, from which he and his Court could watch the polo matches played in the huge square.

Opposite the Palace stood the Lutfallah, or Ladies' Mosque, to which the *Banou*—the chief wife of the Shah—and her female companions could go unattended, by an underground passage beneath the square, to practise their devotions. Dominating the north end of the square, there rose the huge, blue dome and minarets of a still larger mosque, the Masjed el Shah, and at its opposite end lay the entrance to a covered bazaar even greater in extent than that in Constantinople.

To the surprise of the French, they were allowed to enter the mosques and were shown round them. The majority of the peoples in the Mohammedan world were *Sünies* and held that Omar, Osman and Abu Bakar were the lawful descendants of the Prophet. But the Persians were of the *Shiah* sect, the members of which maintained that Ali, Mohammed's son-in-law, had been the next in succession. The latter were much more liberal in their views and could, perhaps, be compared with Protestants as opposed to Roman Catholics, in their attitude to the practice of Christianity.

The tiles in the two mosques were superb, having a wonderful variety of patterns and rich colours. One section of tiling in the Ladies' Mosque particularly intrigued Roger. It was about six feet high by four wide and was the original design for a silk rug which Shah Abbas had sent as a present to Queen Elizabeth of England.

It was on their fourth day in Isfahan that the Mahemander Bachi suggested that, as another ten days or more must elapse before the presents for the Shah arrived, and that no business could be transacted until they did, Gardane and his officers might like to visit the ancient capital of Shiraz. With relays of horses, the two-hundred-mile journey could easily be accomplished in four days, so they could spend three nights there and be back in Isfahan before the caravan was expected.

The five officers with the General, having become fascinated with the marvels of Persia, pressed him to agree, so he consented. Early the following morning, Mesrop arrived with a dozen men leading horses, the panniers of which were loaded with tentage, food and fruit drinks packed in crushed ice. The French, accompanied by their grooms, mounted, and the cavalcade set off.

By ten o'clock they found the heat intensely trying, so Mesrop called a halt and the tents were erected. But, after they had taken an hour's rest, he persuaded them to mount again and cover another five miles until they reached a caravanserai, where they had a meal, then slept through the heat of the afternoon. Later, in the cool of the evening, they rode about twenty miles, then spent the night at another caravanserai. On these lines their journey progressed until, on August 3rd, they reached Shiraz, where they were lodged in one of the many houses owned by the Shah. It had a pleasant garden, with an avenue of orange trees; but the house itself they found quite extraordinary, as every room in it was panelled with thousands of diamond-shaped pieces of mirror.

In some ways the visitors found Shiraz even more interesting than Isfahan, and they were particularly impressed by the beautiful tombs of the famous poets Sa'adi and Hafiz. To them it seemed strange that a people should honour its poets more than they did its monarchs, statesmen and successful Generals. But that was plainly the case. The remains of both poets reposed in marble sarcophagi beneath domes supported by a circle of pillars raised up on marble platforms. Surrounding them were spacious gardens in which, despite the torrid heat, bedded-out flowers were kept in blossom by skilful irrigation and companies of gardeners who sprayed them with water every night.

On their second evening in Shiraz, Mesrop proposed that the next day he should take them out to the ruins of Persepolis, the ancient capital from which Darius, Cyrus the Great and Xerxes had ruled a vast empire. It entailed a ride of some thirty-five miles, so they set off at five o'clock in the morning, in order to arrive there and go over to the ruins before it became unbearably hot.

After leaving the suburbs of Shiraz they rode for some miles through rolling desert, eventually arriving at a broad, sandy plain which ended abruptly in a barrier of three-hundred-foot-high cliff. Immediately below the cliff, but raised about fifty feet above the level of the plain, they could discern the rows of pillars and great arches of the Palace.

As they trotted on towards it, Mesrop pointed to a group of trees that stood some way back from the track on the left-hand side and about half a mile from the great terrace covered with ruins. Among the trees could be seen the flat roof of a small building, and the Armenian said:

'Persepolis is among the half-dozen greatest monuments left to us which give some idea of the splendour of ancient civilisations; so travellers from all parts of the world who come to Persia rarely fail to visit it. Their numbers are sufficient to support a family living in that house you see. The father acts as a guide to the ruins. But he is an ignorant fellow who really knows little about history; so in that capacity, having many times conducted visitors on this expedition, I can serve you better. Nevertheless, we might rest ourselves at the house for a while, as the family provides refreshments. Wine can be had there, and excellent fruit drinks. The water from which they are made comes from an ancient spring, so you have no need to fear infection.'

Gardane shook his head. 'No. Those vast ruins must cover many acres. It will take us two hours or longer to go over them. By then the sun will be high and taking its toll of us. We'll go over the Palace first, and refresh ourselves afterwards.'

As they passed within about two hundred yards of the house, they saw not far from it several tents before which there were horses and a group of people. The group consisted of two men and two women in European clothes, and several native servants. Both the women were wearing light veils, not of the Eastern fashion, but covering the whole of their heads to protect them from the annoyance of flies and also their complexions from the sun. They were just about to mount, and one of the women was already in the saddle. She waved a friendly greeting to Gardane and his officers. They returned it, and rode on.

Two minutes later, they heard the thunder of hooves behind them. Turning, Roger saw that the other party were now all mounted and that, for some reason he could not guess, the horse of the woman who had waved to them had bolted with her. Another moment and she had raced past, vainly striving to rein in her mount.

Roger was riding with Gardane and Mesrop at the head of the French party. Instantly he set spurs to his horse and galloped after her. She was heading straight for the wall of solid rock upon which the ruins stood. Unless she could pull up her animal it would inevitably jib as soon as it saw the fifty-foot-high barrier ahead, and throw her over its head. If he failed to catch up with her and halt her, the odds were that she would be lucky to escape with only serious injuries and not have her brains bashed out.

Once before, many years ago, he had chased and caught a runaway horse. Its rider had been the beautiful Athenais de Rochambeau. The hoofbeats of his horse in pursuit had urged hers on and, not knowing that there was a hidden river in a gully ahead, he had forced her mount in that direction. His action had resulted in Athenais' being thrown and receiving a ducking. Moreover, he had followed her out riding against her wish; so all the thanks he had got was the lash of her riding switch across his face.

Recalling the episode now, he was near smiling at the eventual outcome of that affair. In due course, Athenais had come to love him as passionately as he had her. But this was no case of pressing his unwanted attentions on a spoilt and haughty girl with whom he had fallen desperately in love. He was acting simply on the instinct that would have animated any man to save a woman from disaster.

His comrades had also put their horses into a gallop. So

had the men of the woman's party. But Roger had been quicker off the mark and was a dozen lengths ahead of any of them.

Bending low over his horse's neck, he rowelled the animal savagely. With a fierce neigh, it raced on at still greater speed. When only fifty paces from the rock, he came level with the runaway. He made a grab for its rein and missed. Again he dug his spurs into the flank of his horse. Maddened, it plunged forward, carrying him half a length in front of the other horse. Suddenly the runaway saw the wall of rock ahead. Splaying its hooves, it dug them into the sand and halted rigid.

At the same instant, Roger's mount also saw the barrier. With another terrified neigh, it tensed itself to rear. As Roger felt its muscles contract beneath him, he lifted the heavy riding crop he was holding in his left hand and brought it down with all his force on the animal's head. Simultaneously his right arm shot out and encircled the waist of the woman as she was catapulted from her saddle. Exerting all his strength, he dragged her towards him.

Half-stunned, his stricken horse staggered on a few steps then, its head hanging, halted. Roger pulled the woman he had saved across his saddle bow. Her veil had been blown aside and she had fainted from terror. With her back arched over Roger's knees, her legs dangled down limply on one side and her head, with her mouth gaping open, on the other.

Dropping his riding crop, Roger raised her head into the crook of his left arm. The woman proved to be a girl who looked to be about twenty. Suddenly Roger realised that he was staring down into one of the most exquisitely beautiful faces he had ever seen in his life.

12

The Land of the Great Sophy

For the next few moments all was confusion. Gardane and the officers with him had all automatically galloped after Roger, so had the two cavaliers and the woman in the girl's party. One after another they were brought up short against the rock face. Most of them swerved in time to bring their mounts round in a semicircle, but several of the excited horses were out of control, pulled up only when they saw their own danger, and threw their riders.

Roger, streaming with sweat and gasping for breath, slid from his saddle, still holding the girl in his arms. She had Titian hair that came down in a widow's peak on to a broad forehead, below which were unusually widely-spaced eyes. Her face was heart-shaped, with high cheek-bones, a firm jaw line and a pointed, but gently rounded, chin, the mound of which was creased by Apollo's cleft. Her nose was straight and slightly freckled; her full-lipped mouth—now a little open—showed two rows of white, even teeth. To the left and a few inches above the corner of her mouth she had a natural beauty spot in the form of a small brown mole.

As Roger gazed down into this angelic face, she gave a little shudder, then her lashes lifted, revealing the colour of those widest eyes, which were the strangest he had ever seen. Their centres were a pale blue, but this merged into grey flecked with yellow, and had a curiously leonine look.

Next moment a handsome, well-dressed, middle-aged man with grey side-whiskers came up to them. He spoke swiftly in Portuguese. As Roger was fluent in Spanish, he got the sense of what the other was saying.

'May the Good Lord bless you, *senhor*. But for you, my

daughter would have been crippled for life by being thrown against this rock face, or might well be dead. Never can I repay you for saving her by your prompt action. Permit me to introduce myself. I am the Marquis de Carvalho e Mello Pombal and the Portuguese Ambassador accredited to the Shah.'

As Roger was still holding the girl in his arms he could not bow, but inclined his head and said in Spanish, 'I am more than happy to have had the good fortune to render your Excellency this service. I am Colonel de Breuc of the French mission recently sent to the Shah by my Emperor.'

The Marquis smiled. 'Naturally I have been informed of your mission's arrival, and we are—er—diplomatically on opposite sides of the fence. But that will not deter me from being of any service to you that I can while you are in Persia.'

A minute later the other woman, who was older and strongly resembled de Pombal, joined them and took the girl over from Roger, as the Marquis said, 'Monsieur le Colonel, my sister, the *Senhora* Anna de Arahna.' By then the whole company had crowded round and it was suggested that the young lady should be escorted back to the tents. But she had suffered no harm at all, and rallied surprisingly quickly after her faint. Smiling first at her aunt, then at Roger, she said:

'I fainted only from fright, and if we put off going over the ruins until later, the sun will roast us to our marrow bones. I shall be under no disability if this gallant gentleman who risked his life to save mine will give me his arm.'

Surprised and delighted, Roger returned her smile. '*Senhorita,* you overwhelm me. I could ask no greater reward than the pleasure of escorting you.'

Almost simultaneously with the Ambassador there had arrived upon the scene a tall, dark, beetle-browed man of about thirty. At the *Senhorita's* request for Roger's arm, his face had taken on a sullen look; but he swiftly hid his annoyance when the Marquis introduced him as *Senhor* Don Alfonso de Queircoz, First Secretary of the Embassy.

Roger duly presented General Gardane and the other French officers to the four Portuguese, while the grooms tethered the horses in the shade thrown by the lofty platform on which the Palace stood. Then the *Senhora* de Arahna, with her brother on one side of her and Gardane on the other, led the way along to a steep ramp, which led up to the first of many lofty flat-topped gateways.

The carvings on these gateways had been only partially blurred by time. Most of them had on one side pairs of huge, mythological beasts, and on the other pairs of human heads, with curly beards and high, conical hats that looked like those of Assyrians. About the main hall of the Palace there were still standing several sixty-foot-high pillars. In the vast sunken Treasury only the stumps of the pillars which had supported the roof remained, but there were scores of them, covering an area that in itself would have provided a large enough ground space for the Palace of any minor King. Yet the most impressive sight provided by the ruins was several very broad staircases with shallow steps. On both sides they were flanked by carved reliefs of a procession of men, each bearing some object: a jar of wine, a dish of fruit, a dead gazelle, a string of pearls and so on. They were the twenty-eight Kings bringing tribute to their overlord Darius who, from their subjugation, took his title: King of Kings.

As they walked slowly round, Roger and his breathtakingly lovely companion found that they could converse quite easily in a mixture of Spanish, Portuguese and French. He learned that her name was Lisala and that, three years earlier, her father had taken her from her convent outside Lisbon to accompany him to Persia. Apart from its extremes of climate, she liked the country and admired its people for their pride in their own civilisation and for placing such a high value on all forms of art. But she found life there monotonous owing to the social limitations.

There were many feasts and jollifications with exciting displays of juggling, horse-racing, wrestling, polo and so on; but the European population of Isfahan consisted only of a handful of merchants and occasional travellers. The Portuguese, Dutch and Russians, alone among the Western nations, had Embassies permanently established there, so she was almost entirely deprived of the pleasures that a young woman of her age and station had, she felt, a right to expect.

Ingenuously she went on to say, 'One cannot have a love affair with a Persian, a Turk or an Afghan. Alfonso de Queircoz is mad about me, of course, but I do not find him attractive. Since Prince Galitzin left the Russian Embassy six months ago, there has not been a man in the whole city whom I should be pleased to have my hand, let alone aught else. That is why this is such a happy day for me. I hope I shall see a lot of you.'

Staggered as he was by her frankness, Roger appreciated the reason for it. At the age she had left Lisbon she would normally have been about to be married off; so by now would probably be the mother of one or more babies, queening it in the highest society, with a dozen handsome beaux seeking her favours. He was fully conscious of his own good looks; but not so vain as to suppose that, in Lisala's unusual situation, she would not have regarded any personable man who came into her life as manna in the desert. He could only render his thanks to the Goddess of Fortune that it was he, and not one of the attractive junior officers of the mission, who had had the luck to save her from breaking her beautiful neck. He had been favoured by a splendid start over all those youngsters who were coming up with the caravan and, in due course, would meet Lisala, and he was determined not to lose it.

Resorting quite unscrupulously to the oldest gambit in the game of love, he pressed her arm gently and said, '*Senhorita*, our meeting today was pre-ordained. For a long time past I, too, have suffered from a terrible loneliness. My wife died in childbirth'—which was true enough, although that had happened some twelve years before—'and since then I have come upon no-one who I feel could expunge the memory of her from my mind'—which was a thumping lie. 'But the moment I looked into your lovely face, it was as though a new sun had risen on the horizon of my life.'

'Can that be true?' she murmured.

'Indeed it is,' he assured her; and as he said it he really

meant it. 'Moreover, although I am attached to this mission, I am not strictly of it. I am an *aide-de-camp* and friend of the Emperor whom I have known intimately for many years; and a Commander of the Legion d'Honneur. I tell you this not out of boastfulness, but simply to let you know that General Gardane has no power to send me off, as he might any of the others, on some special assignment. My time is my own, to do with as I will; so, when we return to Isfahan I shall count myself blessed if you will allow me to see you frequently, and place myself entirely at your service.'

By this time the party had spent an hour wandering round the ruins, marvelling that, over two thousand years ago, an Eastern Monarch should have had architects and craftsmen capable of building him a palace with loftier halls and more spacious staircases than those at Versailles. To have fully explored the whole area, with its avenues of strange beasts and innumerable scenes of Court life in the distant past carved on tall walls, would have taken half a day; but it was already well after nine o'clock, and the sun was climbing swiftly in the blue vault of the heavens. As they had yet to see the Royal Tombs, which lay some four kilometres distant, the Ambassador and the General agreed that it would be as well to set off there without further delay.

Mounting their horses, the party rode for a quarter of an hour along a track below the towering mountain barrier, until they reached the tombs. That of Cyrus the Great was in the form of a seven-step pyramid surmounted by a thirty-foot-high burial chamber; but those of Darius the Great, Xerxes and several of their relatives were man-made caves hewn out of the cliff, their entrance being fifty feet above ground level, so inaccessible. They had elaborately-carved doorways, above which were scenes from the lives of their occupants, and much lower down, other scenes: one of outstanding interest, as it portrayed Darius on a very small horse, but with an enormous head-dress, accepting the surrender of the Roman Emperor Valerian, whose legions he had defeated, kneeling before him.

By ten o'clock, both parties were back at the small house among the trees, where they had first seen one another. The encampment of tents near it had been brought from Isfahan by the Ambassador, for to have made the journey to Persepolis and back in one day would have placed too great a strain on his ladies, and they had slept there the previous night. One was a fair-sized marquee, to feed and relax in, and he invited the French officers to accept his hospitality there. Extra supplies were bought from the family that occupied the little house near by, and they all settled down to enjoy themselves.

Happily for all concerned, de Pombal had brought a dozen bottles of his own wine. It was rose colour and they all declared it to be delicious. He told them then that it was a special *cuvée* made only from grapes grown in a district near Shiraz, and had a romantic association because it was almost certainly the wine which, centuries before, the poet-astronomer, Omar Khayyám, had praised so highly.

Gardane remarked that he had been surprised to find that, although in the Koran wine was forbidden to Mohammedans, nearly all the nobles he had met in Isfahan drank it freely.

At that de Pombal laughed and replied, 'For any man who is rich, there is no difficulty about that. He has only to give his doctor a sufficiently handsome bribe to receive in exchange a certificate that drinking wine is essential to his health. All the Shahs have habitually enjoyed wine, and some of them have become confirmed drunkards.

'The Shah Safe, who reigned in the latter part of the seventeenth century, became so besotted every night while drinking in the company of his favourites that he even forced drink on others who had religious scruples. When his Grand Vizier refused to join in a debauch, he flung a cup of wine in the poor man's face, then ordered him to swallow a decoction of opium—which is not forbidden in the Qur'ân—and so reduced him to a gibbering idiot for the amusement of the assembled company.

'These Persian nobles appear to be highly civilised and are models of politeness but, believe me, they are the most treacherous schemers in the world, and cruel beyond belief. On another occasion this same Shah, on hearing that some young men had become tipsy in public and had made a nuisance of themselves, sent his police out into the city with orders that they should, on the spot, rip open the belly of every man they found drunk. Even today, should a barber's hand slip while he is shaving the head of some grandee, and he nicks the scalp, he is liable to have his hand cut off at the wrist.

'They are, too, the most inveterate liars. You may have noticed that, to impress you, they invariably take an oath upon a matter. They will swear by their soul, by their parents, by their beards—which they hold in such high regard that a man can be heavily fined for pulling out a few hairs from another's—even by the Imam Hasein; yet not a word of what they have been saying is the truth.'

Out of politeness to his guests, the Ambassador had been speaking in French, and one of the officers asked, 'Who, Your Excellency, is the Imam Hasein?'

The Marquis smiled. 'I forgot that you have come only recently to Persia. Hasein is their most venerated saint. He was the heir of Ali, the son-in-law of the Prophet and founder of the *Shiah* sect. Having married a Sassanian Princess, he was urged to contest the Caliphate and with a small band of followers advanced on Mecca. He had been promised the support of the Governor of Kufa, who commanded a much larger force; but the Governor betrayed and attacked him on the plain of Kerbela. Although cut off from water, and suffering from terrible thirst, his little band fought to the death, so he is accounted a martyr. Each year a Passion Play based on this tragedy is enacted in every town throughout Persia, and fanatics gashing themselves with knives and with horse-shoes sewn to their bare skins parade the streets wailing, "Hasein our Lord is dead." '

After they had refreshed themselves, the ladies and the two Portuguese noblemen retired to their respective tents, while the French, using their tunics for pillows, lay down in the marquee to doze through the great heat of the early afternoon. At five o'clock they all partook of another picnic meal. When they had finished it, camp was struck and the whole party set off back to Shiraz.

Lisala and her aunt rode only the first few miles, then transferred to a form of carriage common in Persia. It was actually a horse litter, having a narrow body borne on two very large wheels and had shafts both back and front, between which horses were harnessed. As the vehicle was hooded, Roger could no longer continue a delightful conversation he had been having with his newly-found divinity; so he cantered up to the front of the column and joined the Ambassador, Gardane and the black-browed Don Alfonso de Queircoz.

They were talking of the war and, after Roger had been with them for a few minutes, de Pombal remarked, 'To be honest, I had hoped that His Majesty the Czar would succeed in preventing your Emperor from becoming the master of all northern Europe; but it looks now as if his latest victory may force the Russians to sue for terms.'

Gardane gave him a quick glance. 'What victory is this of which Your Excellency speaks? I have heard of none.'

'I had news of it shortly before leaving Isfahan. Another great pitched battle took place at Friedland on June 13th, with most appalling slaughter. 'Tis reported that both armies lost some twenty-five thousand men, but the Russians had by far the worst of it. Your Emperor was advancing with the object of attacking the main Allied bastion of Königsberg. Instead of retreating on that great fortress, which would have supported his rear, General Bennigsen rashly attempted to intercept the French by throwing a large part of his army across the river Alle, with the result that, after many hours of desperate fighting, they were driven back into it. Great numbers were drowned, and by the following day such Russians as survived had become a mass of fugitives.'

For the officers of the mission this was splendid news, but knowing that Portugal's sympathies lay with the Allies, they hid their elation out of courtesy towards de Pombal, as he went on. 'One must admire your Emperor, Messieurs, as a truly great General; but I fear his ambitions bode ill for the happiness of the peoples in countries he has not yet conquered. This applies particularly to Portugal, as we still adhere to our ancient treaty with England and have refused to come into line with his Continental System by closing our ports to

British shipping. And if it emerges that he has dealt a fatal blow to the Russians, we must anticipate that he will next turn his attention to the Peninsula.'

An awkward silence followed, then Roger tactfully changed the conversation by asking, 'Am I right in supposing that Your Excellency is a descendant of Portugal's famous Prime Minister in the past century?'

'Yes, indeed,' replied the Marquis. 'I am his grandson. Sebastião José was certainly a remarkable man. Having been a diplomat up to the age of fifty-one, with no previous experience of administration it was an extraordinary feat to take over the posts of Secretary of State for both Foreign Affairs and War, and hold them successfully for twenty-seven years. He was fortunate, of course, in enjoying the complete confidence of his master, King Joseph. That enabled him to reorganise Portuguese education and finance, as well as our Army and Navy. It was his misfortune to have brought upon himself the bitter enmity of the Queen Mother and, after King Joseph's death in 1777, he was exiled from Court. But Portugal honours him today.'

On reaching Shiraz the two parties separated, with cordial expressions of goodwill and the intention of pursuing their acquaintance when they got back to Isfahan. Over supper that evening Roger was much chaffed by his companions about his obvious success with the Ambassador's beautiful daughter; but he could well afford to treat their obvious envy with amusement. He went to bed that night in an almost dreamlike state of bliss at the million-to-one chance in this distant land that had brought him into contact with an exquisite European maiden and enabled him to capture her interest immediately.

Next morning the mission set off on its return journey to Isfahan. Hoping that he might find a despatch awaiting him there, Gardane forced the pace, so they reached the capital late on the night of August 9th. A courier had arrived, bringing further details of the victory at Friedland. As usual in his bulletins, the Emperor greatly minimised the French losses and gave scant praise to his Marshals. But it was clear that

Lannes had once more displayed his brilliant leadership and tenacity, by holding forty thousand Russians at bay for the greater part of the day, with only ten thousand French, until the corps of Mortier, Ney and Victor had come up to his assistance and overwhelmed the enemy.

The despatch also contained the news that on May 20th the great Prussian stronghold of Danzig—which Napoleon, with some foolhardiness, had left in his rear still occupied by a considerable enemy army—had, at last capitulated to Lefebvre, who had been rewarded by the title of Duke of Danzig.

Roger and Gardane were much amused by this, as they guessed the reason that lay behind the honour. Lefebvre was more fitted for his earlier rank of Sergeant-Major than that of Marshal of the Empire, and totally unfitted to command an army corps. But he had been given one for this operation because Napoleon was meeting with opposition from the die-hard Republicans in the creation of his new nobility. Madame Lefebvre had been a washer-woman and, when the Emperor had been a penniless subaltern, she had laundered his small-clothes for nothing. Making her a Duchess would, he had cynically decided, cut the ground from under the feet of the old Revolutionaries who resented his giving titles to returned émigrés now forming part of his Court. But Lefebvre could not be given a Dukedom unless he at least appeared to have made a valuable contribution to the campaign. To guard against the risk of his being defeated, Napoleon had assigned to support him Lannes with his fighting devils and Oudinot with his formidable Grenadiers; but both had been given strict injunctions that they were neither to advise nor assist Lefebvre except in an emergency. As the old ex-N.C.O. had been provided with ample troops and a formidable siege train of artillery, they had done the job for him, thus enabling the Emperor to pull off his political coup aimed at the Jacobins.

The earlier distribution of these Dukedoms to the Marshals had created furious jealousies, as the majority had been Italian territorial titles, such as Mortier, Duke of Treviso; Bessières, Duke of Istria; Duroc, Duke of Friuli, and the War Minister, General Clarke, Duke of Feltre; whereas others were given titles commemorating battles in which they had played a prominent role: Lannes, Duke of Montebello; Augereau, Duke of Castiglione; Ney, Duke of Elchingen; Davoust, Duke of Auerstadt; and those not given battle honours had intensely resented the fact, so old Lefebvre was doubly lucky in having been created Duke of Danzig.

Gardane eagerly enquired of the courier whether he had seen anything of the caravan, a part of which consisted of transport bringing the presents for the Shah. Much to his relief, the man replied that he had passed it at only two days' march from Isfahan, so it could be expected very shortly.

Next afternoon, the two-thousand-strong caravan of laden camels, horses and asses arrived in the city. For over two hours that part of it destined for the French blocked the street in which the mission was housed, before the beasts were all unloaded. Colonel Couthon and the junior officers who had travelled with him had had an uneventful but dreary journey, and that evening joyfully celebrated the reunion with their comrades in agreeable surroundings.

Gardane had lost no time in despatching Mesrop to inform the Peskis Nuviez that the presents had arrived and, on the following day, that functionary came to inspect them. Having by this time had ample evidence of the avarice of the Persians, the General was now able to congratulate himself on having kept back a certain number of the presents, intended as bribes for the Sultan's Ministers should the negotiations in Constantinople not be proceeding favourably; and these he put aside as a valuable reserve to win the goodwill of the Persian courtiers.

After carefully examining the gifts originally intended for his master, the Peskis Nuviez expressed himself as well satisfied and, having graciously accepted a pair of silver-mounted pistols for himself, said that he would consult the Court Astrologer about a day when the auspices would be favourable for the presentation to be made to His Majesty.

Meanwhile, Roger had bought up all the tuberoses that he could find in the flower market, had them loaded on an ass and despatched to Lisala de Pombal. Then, late in the afternoon, he presented himself at the Portuguese Embassy. After a brief wait, he was ushered into an interior courtyard where, to his disappointment, he found, seated beside a fountain, only the *Senhora* Arahna and another elderly lady.

Seeing his face drop, Lisala's aunt laughed, as she extended her hand for him to kiss, and said, 'Do not look so unhappy, Colonel. Lisala has not been suffocated by the heady perfume of that great load of flowers you sent her. On hearing you announced, she ran upstairs to beautify herself, and she will rejoin us shortly.'

'Then, *Senhora*,' Roger smiled, 'she is wasting her time; for it is pointless to gild the lily.' He was then presented to the other lady—Dona Christina de Jahlo—who, he later learned, was Lisala's duenna.

For some ten minutes they exchanged platitudes about their visit to Shiraz and their return journeys. Then Lisala appeared. When at Persepolis she had been wearing riding clothes, and had her hair pinned up under a scarf against the dust. Now she was dressed in flowing, bright-hued Persian silks and her glorious Titian hair fell in ringlets round her shoulders. Her broad, smooth forehead, widely-spaced tawny eyes and full mouth with its enchanting smile were even more ravishing than the mental pictures Roger had been conjuring up for her.

Coffee, sweet cakes and wine were brought, and for twenty minutes Roger forced himself to devote most of the time to making himself agreeable to the two older ladies. The prescribed time for a first visit then having expired, he stood up and said to Lisala's aunt:

'*Senhora*, there are many interesting sights to be seen in Isfahan. Would you be so gracious as to allow me to offer to take the *Senhorita* Lisala to see some of them?'

After a moment's hesitation, she replied. 'To permit my niece to go into the city attended by a gentleman of your attractions would be somewhat unusual, but poor Lisala has such a dull time here that I feel I must indulge her; she will, of course, be accompanied by Dona Christina.'

It was then agreed that Roger should call for them at nine

o'clock the following morning. More intoxicated than ever by the smiling glances Lisala had bestowed upon him, and well satisfied with the progress he had made, Roger took his leave.

Next day he arrived with four sedan chairs of a form used by the Persians, the fourth being for the Armenian, Mesrop, whom he had pressed into service as their guide. Each sedan was borne by bearers in front and behind, but instead of the enclosed structure between them usual in Europe, they had a pole at the back of the seat which curved over and supported a sunshade. When the two ladies appeared, they were both heavily veiled in deference to Persian custom. Mesrop was duly introduced; then they set off.

First Mesrop took them to see the Masjid-el-Jum'a, or Friday Mosque, the oldest and largest in Persia. It dated from the tenth century, and the greater part of it had been built before the introduction of tiles. Instead, the pillars and ceilings of its many early chapels were of painted bricks, artistically laid in a variety of patterns. Unlike the majority of chapels, which could be entered through a number of archways on two or three sides, there was one specially designed for worship in very cold weather. It had only one entrance, contained a big stove and was lit through very thick slabs of glass inserted here and there in the ceiling.

Other mosques they visited impressed them with the great size of their interior courts, lofty minarets and huge domes. Many of the latter, Mesrop told them, had double ceilings with an air space of several feet between, because it had been discovered that this gave them additional strength to resist earthquakes, to which most parts of Persia were subject.

The following day Mesrop took them across the river to Julfa—a separate town, inhabited entirely by his own people. Until the sixteenth century it had been forbidden for Mohammedans even to learn European languages, let alone speak them. But Shah Abbas the Great was anxious to develop relations with the West, so he decided to use some of his Christian subjects as intermediaries. Instead of rendering a number of families miserable by carrying off the men, as most potentates of his age would have done, this truly great monarch

229

had brought to Isfahan every man, woman and child living in one Armenian town and had had built for them outside his capital a town that was a replica of the one they had left.

The architecture, shops and costumes of the people of Julfa provided a fascinating contrast with those of Isfahan, and its Greek Orthodox Cathedral was as striking as the mosques, but in an entirely different way. Every inch of the walls and ceilings was covered in magnificent frescoes in mosaic, the pillars were a blaze of gold and on one side of the centre there rose a lofty pulpit that had a bright blue, gold-starred dome surmounted by a strange, pointed roof.

One of the priests showed them round the Treasury, in which were many early, illuminated bibles and several 'top hats' worn by prelates, made of silk gaily painted with pictures of saints and angels.

For their third expedition, Roger and Mesrop arrived mounted and brought with them a Persian carriage for the ladies, as they were to visit a mosque which lay some four miles outside the city. Its special interest lay in its two min-arets. They were slender towers with wooden platforms about ten feet from their tops. Above the platforms rose roofed brick turrets, from the open arches of which the Mezzsin called the faithful to prayer, and when either of the platforms was walked on, the turret shook to such an extent that it swayed back and forth several feet out of true. That these 'shaking' minarets had never been blown down in a gale seemed positively miraculous, yet they had stood there for seven hundred years.

Half a mile or so further along the road, there rose up out of the plain a hill so large and steep that it could almost be classed as a mountain. It was crowned by a straggle of stone buildings that Mesrop told them was a Zoroastrian temple. He added that the ancient fire worship was still quite exten-sively practised in Persia, and they must not miss the oppor-tunity of visiting such an interesting place.

When they arrived at the foot of the great mound, Dona Christina at once declared that the path up it was much too steep for a woman of her years to climb; but Lisala got out of the carriage, evidently with the intention of doing so.

During the past few days Roger and Lisala had covertly exchanged many meaningful glances, but he had been unable to get her to himself for a single moment. Now, at last, he saw his opportunity. With his most charming smile, he said to the duenna:

'Remain here then, *Senhora,* and rest for a while in the shade of these trees. The *Senhorita* and I will make the climb, and I promise to take the greatest care of her.'

'No! No!' the elderly woman protested. 'The *Senhorita* is in my charge and I cannot possibly allow her out of my sight.'

To Roger's amazement, Lisala suddenly turned upon her duenna. Her leonine eyes blazing, she snapped, 'Hold your tongue, old woman! I am no longer an innocent incapable of taking care of myself. Who are you to decree what I shall or shall not do? Climb the hill and die of it if you wish. That would mean naught to me. Or remain here and snore. You are well paid for your post. Report this matter to my aunt, and I'll see to it that within the month you are dismissed and sent back to Portugal, to face the poverty you have brought upon yourself by your improvidence.'

13

The Old Sweet Game

In fascinated horror, Roger listened to this outburst, fearing that Lisala had suddenly gone out of her mind. Knowing the discipline to which young ladies of good family were normally subjected, he was afraid the duenna would exert her authority, and Lisala be punished by not being allowed to go out with him again.

On the contrary, the duenna quailed under the lash of her beautiful charge's tongue. Lying back in her carriage, Dona Christina covered her eyes with her hand and whimpered, 'Go then, you terrible child. But spare me the *Senhora* Arahna's wrath by telling her that I gave you permission.'

With a contemptuous shrug, Lisala turned away and took Roger's arm. Mesrop made as though to follow them, but Roger said to him quietly, 'Dona Christina must not be left alone. You had best remain here to take care of her.'

Several servants had accompanied them, and could quite easily have protected the duenna from unwelcome attentions; but the shrewd Armenian had long since sized up the situation. Without a muscle of his face moving, he bowed his acquiescence.

As Roger and Lisala set off up the winding track, he said, 'At last we are alone, and can talk freely. We owe that to your courage in having defied Dona Christina. You nearly scared the poor old woman out of her wits.'

'Poor old woman, forsooth!' Lisala replied, a trifle sullenly. 'She is a lazy, befuddled old curmudgeon, and has brought her present servitude upon herself by her own stupidity. My pleasures have been few enough for many months past, and I'll not tolerate her interfering with them now.'

The way was too steep for them to converse with ease, so they plodded on in silence for a while; until round the curve of the mountain, they came upon a succession of caves. Some were occupied by hermits, clad only in a garment of worn animal skin, who were seated cross-legged and gazing vacantly into space. Others were untenanted and, halting, Roger drew Lisala into one. Next moment, still breathless, but with mutual eagerness, they were clasped in each other's arms, their mouths glued together in a long, passionate kiss.

For several minutes they fervidly caressed each other; then he whispered, 'My divine Lisala, this is indeed bliss; but an interlude that must prove all too short. Another chance for us to give expression to our love may not occur for days. Is there no other way in which we could manage to be alone together?'

'Have you money?' she asked quickly.

He nodded. 'Yes, sufficient for most projects. My status as the Emperor's personal agent enables me to draw on French funds as heavily as I wish, without being questioned about the use to which I intend to put the money.'

Her wide-spaced eyes smiled up into his. 'Then you must do as did my Russian Prince last year. There is a house across a narrow alley behind the Embassy. He rented the top floor. The roofs between the two buildings are almost level and can easily be spanned by a ladder. Once you are installed there, I could cross and spend the best part of the night there with you.'

The very thought inflamed Roger to fever pitch. There could have been no clearer declaration that Lisala was not a virgin, and was longing for him to take her.

'I will, my sweet!' he exclaimed, kissing her avidly again. 'This very afternoon I'll secure that apartment, and it shall be our heaven. But what of now? It would take us at least half an hour to get up to the Temple and down again.'

'So be it,' she breathed. 'I have been too long starved of love; and, with you, near dying for want of it.'

He drew her further into the cave, where they came upon a bed of leaves left there by some past hermit. Stripping off his coat, Roger laid it on the leaves. Then, with a delighted laugh, he picked up Lisala, kissed her again and lowered her gently to their primitive couch.

Unashamedly, with shining eyes and fast-drawn breath, she undid her girdle and pulled her full skirts up to her waist, while he unloosed his breeches. Swiftly, but gently, he slid between her wide-open thighs. Gasping, she threw her arms round him and clasped him to her. A moment later she heaved beneath him and cried aloud with rapture.

Twice more within the next half-hour they repeated the act, at greater leisure and with still greater enjoyment. Temporarily satiated, but madly enamoured of each other, they reluctantly drew apart, carefully brushed off old leaves that had adhered to their hair and clothes; then, in silent, blissful communion, made their way down the hill.

Dona Christina greeted them with a worried look but, evidently fearful that she might be subjected to another outburst of Lisala's violent temper, she refrained from asking any questions. She need not have worried. The girl's lovely face showed no sign that she had ever revolted against her usual demure acceptance of her duenna's authority. Getting into the carriage, she patted the old lady's hand affectionately, and with wide-eyed innocence invented a description of the Fire Temple she had never seen. Not for the first time, Roger marvelled at the convincing duplicity displayed by women to guard their secrets, and conceded that it matched his own.

When they got back to the Portuguese Embassy, Lisala said brightly, as he formally kissed her hand on taking leave of her, 'I look forward, Colonel, to seeing you again tonight.'

For a moment he was flabbergasted, thinking that she had been imbecile enough to refer to a roof-top meeting which, in any case, he might not have the time to prepare for. To his intense relief she added, as he raised his eyes to hers. 'At the dinner to which my father has invited General Gardane, you and several other officers.'

Releasing his indrawn breath, he replied. 'As I left the

mission early this morning, the General had not informed me of it; but, naturally, I am delighted to accept.'

Having seen the ladies into the hall and thanked Mesrop for the morning's interesting expedition, he immediately hurried round to the house at the back of the Embassy. By good fortune, the owner was at home, and spoke a little Turkish; so, together with the smattering of Persian that Roger had picked up during the past three weeks, they were able to grasp one another's meaning. Fortunately, too, the last tenant of the top-floor flat had left some weeks earlier, so it was again to let. After pretending to make a thorough inspection of the apartment, which he found sparsely furnished but at least clean, Roger went up on to the roof.

There in one corner he saw, to his delight, the means used for bridging the gap across to the Embassy roof, of which Lisala had told him. It was a twelve-foot-long canvas tube containing a ladder which appeared to be comparatively light, as the sides were made of thick, bamboo poles. From them rose low hoops, supporting the canvas covering, so that anyone crawling along the ladder while crossing the gap should not see the alley below and be overcome by vertigo.

Having told the landlord that he would be occupying the apartment only to sleep in, so would be little bother to him, Roger asked the price. The man named an outrageous sum. When Roger protested, the fellow gave an impudent grin, jerked his thumb towards the ladder and said:

'I had that made a year or so ago for a Russian Prince who was having an affair with one of the young women servants in the Portuguese Embassy across the way. Since my lord is coming here only at night, I'd wager a Kashan rug against a string of onions that he means to play naughty games with the same little strumpet, or one of the companions; and a gentleman should pay for his pleasures.'

Roger stoutly denied the implication and offered half the sum asked; but was happy enough to settle for two-thirds, took the apartment for a month, gave the landlord a gold *tomaun*—equivalent to about fifteen shillings—in advance, and left with a key to the house in his pocket.

A party of sixteen sat down to dinner that evening at the Embassy: de Pombal and his ladies, de Queircoz and another secretary, two obviously rich Portuguese merchants, a Dutch couple, Gardane, Roger and four other French officers. It followed that the conversation was carried on in a jumble of languages, but all of them were at least bi-lingual and some, like Roger, could talk in several languages; so the party proved a gay one, particularly for the French officers who had been deprived of such social evenings for many months.

Lisala was seated between Roger and de Queircoz, who obviously regarded him as his rival, and made a malicious remark about gentlemen who had so little work that they could give every morning to taking ladies out sightseeing. Recalling one ravishing sight he had seen that morning, Roger could afford to ignore this offensiveness and Lisala, instead of reprimanding Alfonso for his rudeness to a guest, tactfully praised him for the valuable assistance he gave her father.

Later during the meal, Alfonso casually asked Roger if he liked shooting. When Roger replied that he did, the Portuguese said, 'Then some time you must go up to the forests on the far side of the mountains north of Tehran. There is the finest sport in the world to be had there, and I could easily arrange it for you as I speak Persian fluently and have many friends at Court.'

Before they left the table, Roger succeeded in passing into Lisala's hand a note he had written. It read:

I adore you to distraction. Tomorrow morning I cannot come for you because General Gardane told me this afternoon that we are to offer our presents to the Shah. But the apartment you told me of is now mine, and the ladder-bridge still up on the roof. I shall await you there tomorrow night with more eagerness than had I been promised a magic carpet to carry me to Paradise.

The following morning everyone at the mission was up early, preparing for the ceremony that Gardane had waited for with such impatience. To wear at the audience, the Shah had sent each officer of the mission a garment of honour, called a *calaat*, and they chaffed one another about their ap-

236

pearance when they had put on these strange, but costly, silk robes. The presentation was to take place at the Chehel Souton Palace, which was situated in the midst of spacious, well-wooded grounds. Accompanied by the Mahemander Bachi, the Peskis Nuviez and a gorgeously-clad guard of archers mounted upon curvetting chargers, they rode the half mile to the gates. There, they were told to dismount, as no one was permitted to approach the Shah on horseback.

Roger had learned from Mesrop earlier that the Chehel Souton was also called the Palace of the Forty Pillars, although in fact it had only twenty. This anomaly was made apparent as their procession advanced towards it along an avenue of sycamores and cypresses. The Palace stood at the far end of a great stone-surrounded pool, some three hundred feet long and fifty wide. The frontage consisted of a terrace raised on several steps, above which was a roof supported by thirty-foot-high pillars. There were only twenty of them, but their reflection on the mirror-like sheet of water made up the forty.

Centrally, beneath the lofty canopy, rose a graceful arch decorated with innumerable small squares of looking-glass and, in front of it, a fountain. The Shah was seated cross-legged upon a throne that blazed with jewels, and on either side of him were ranged his Viziers, his twenty-four gentlemen and many other functionaries. Mounting the steps, Gardane knelt and, as he had been informed by the Superior of the Capuchins was strictly necessary, kissed the Shah's foot. He then recited in Persian a brief speech he had been taught, calling down blessings on the King of Kings, the Centre of the Universe, and praying him to deign to give his unrivalled brain to considering the message sent him by his admiring brother sovereign, the Emperor of the French and Monarch Supreme of the Western World.

The Shah graciously inclined his head then, for half an hour, bearer after bearer laid the presents sent by Napoleon on the steps below the throne. When this had been done, the Shah said, through his chief Armenian interpreter, that he thanked his brother sovereign, of whose great prowess in war he had heard, and that his Ministers would report to him upon the communication the General had brought. Rising from his throne, he turned and, followed by his courtiers, withdrew into the interior of the Palace. The audience over, the French retired and, mounting their horses at the gate, rode back to their quarters.

That night, by ten o'clock, Roger was on the roof of the house behind the Embassy. He doubted whether Lisala would be able to join him before eleven at the earliest, but would not for worlds have chanced her keeping the assignation and not finding him there to meet her. As he paced back and forth, the time seemed to drag interminably and by midnight he began to fear that something had prevented her from keeping their tryst.

Another twenty minutes elapsed, then his heart gave a sudden lurch, as he caught sight of a shadowy figure coming towards the parapet of the opposite roof. Restraining himself for a moment, to make certain that it was Lisala, he remained still. Then in a low voice she called across to him.

Picking up the hooded ladder, he swiftly thrust it across the ten-foot gap. On the far end were large iron hooks that would secure it to the opposite parapet. Lisala disappeared into the canvas tunnel. Two minutes later, he drew her from it and clasped her in his arms.

Avidly they smothered each other with kisses, then he picked her up and carried her down to the room below. She had on only a light silk robe. Joyfully, she threw it off. For the first time, by the light of the single oil lamp he had left burning, he saw her naked. She had small, upstanding breasts, a narrow waist, big hips and, for a woman of her medium height, long, slender legs. Enraptured to find her body equalled her face in beauty, he cast aside the chamber robe he had been wearing, again took her in his arms and, murmuring endearments, gently lowered her to the broad divan.

As an expert in amorous delights, Lisala could not have rivalled Naksh; but the passion with which she gave herself was almost unsurpassed in Roger's experience. He had always heard that red-headed women were physically more inflammable than others, and Lisala became positively distraught during her erotic paroxysms. She moaned, cried aloud and once bit him so fiercely in the neck that he wrenched himself free of her with a gasp of pain.

When at length his big, turnip watch, which he had laid on a low table beside the divan, chimed the hour of four, she prepared to leave him only with the greatest reluctance; and when he began to thank her for the pleasure she had given him, she stopped his mouth with her hand, declaring that it was the woman who should thank the man capable of carrying her to such heights of ecstasy.

After seeing her safely back to the roof of the Embassy and drawing in the ladder, he was terribly tempted to flop down again on the divan and sleep. But he knew that if he did, he would probably not wake until midday; so he slowly dressed and made his way back to the quarters of the mission where he could be certain of being woken at half past seven.

At nine o'clock, he called as usual for Lisala and her duenna. Mesrop told them that, as the Shah did not live at the Chehel Souton Palace but used it only to give formal audiences, he had secured permission to take them there to see some of the royal treasures.

Except for patrolling guards here and there, the Palace was now deserted. Passing through the high, mirror-covered arch, they entered a long, lofty hall, on the walls of which were painted battle scenes. Ranged in cases about it were many precious objects, ancient Qur'âns beautifully illuminated in gold and gay coloured arabesques, fine examples of Ming china, jewel-hilted scimitars and a collection of paintings on ivory.

The majority of the latter dated from the late sixteenth and early seventeenth centuries when, under Shah Abbas, the Safavid Dynasty had reached its zenith and Persia entered on her great Renaissance. The fame of her artists, poets and architects had spread to the West and, as Roger knew, Sophy was the English corruption of Safavi. It was thus that Persia had become known as 'The Land of the Great Sophy'.

Many of the paintings were of hunting scenes; others illustrated the classic work of Ferdusi, Hafiz and Sa'adi, showing turbaned lovers with sloe-eyed maidens picnicking beneath graceful, flowering trees. The workmanship was exquisite and Roger, who had a small gift for painting himself, decided to search the Bazaar and see if he could not find a few of the same period to buy and take back with him.

That night, soon after midnight, Lisala again joined him on his roof-top. The passion with which they came together was less ferocious than it had been the previous night, but when they parted in the early hours, their delight in each other had not lessened.

Next morning there could be no expedition, because the officers of the French mission had been invited by the Shah to witness a polo match. For this they went to the Ali Qapa Palace in the huge Maidan Square. The Shah of Shahs received them on the lofty balcony which formed a perfect grandstand. The extreme formality he had observed when they had been presented to him was now considerably relaxed. Through his chief interpreter, he spoke pleasantly to the senior officers, expressing the hope that they were enjoying their visit to his capital, and telling them that if there was anything they lacked for their comfort, they must not hesitate to ask his Mahemander Bachi for it.

Before the match, a display of wrestling and javelin-throwing took place below the big balcony; then the square was cleared and the players rode out from either end of it. There were twenty a side, but there was ample space for them to gallop in. None of the French had ever seen the game before, and they found it most exciting.

For the third night running, Lisala came to Roger on his roof. By then he would have welcomed a respite of a night or two. Yet he found her so bewitching that, no sooner had she unrobed herself, than he again rose to the occasion and met her embraces with renewed fervour. Again they parted with lingering kisses, vowing that neither of them could ever meet anyone who compared with the other.

Five hours later Mesrop took them to a small mansion in which there was an exhibition of waxworks. Roger had seen that of Madame Tussaud, who had come as a refugee to London during the French Revolution; but decided that her work was of poor quality when compared with that of the Persian artists. The figures were clad in garments representative of every class, from the highest to the lowest, and there were groups wearing the traditional costume of every tribe in the King of Kings' vast dominions. But the striking thing about them was that they resembled human beings so closely that one could have expected them to speak at any moment, or walk out of their cases.

In a place of honour, at the head of a staircase, there was a figure of the great Shah Abbas, and it greatly intrigued Roger to see what this remarkable monarch had looked like. He was portrayed as on the tallish side, with powerful limbs and a handsome head of Aryan cast. His cheeks and chin were clean-shaven, but he had an enormous, handlebar moustache, the points of which stuck out well beyond his ears.

Afterwards Mesrop took them to a quarter of the city where Dervishes were wont to congregate. It was a piece of semi-waste ground, and the buildings on it were little more than heaps of tumbled ruins. The heads of the Dervishes, like those of all Persian men, were shaved; but otherwise, unlike the bulk of the male population who favoured long whiskers but only short beards, their beards were long and tangled. Most of them were wearing only a single garment of animal skin, and the majority appeared strong-limbed, well fed and healthy. The few genuine fanatics, wasted by fasting, sat alone in contemplation, obviously oblivious of their surroundings; but by far the greater number of Dervishes were sitting smoking their narghiles and talking animatedly.

Mesrop explained that, with few exceptions, protected by the cloak of religion, they were an utterly unprincipled sect of rogues. Some earned a living at snake-charming or by giving displays with dangerous beasts. Others were professional story-tellers who could recite Ferdusi by heart and knew all the tales told by Shahrazade to her Arab Caliph. But a far greater number of them battened on the superstitions of the ignorant masses. Witchcraft was rife throughout Persia. Everyone carried charms against the Evil Eye, and for many other reasons. The Dervishes made a fat living by selling bits of parchment with cryptic symbols scrawled on them, and parts of animals which, when carried on a person, were said to work wonders.

The knuckle-bones of a wolf would give courage; its gall rubbed on a woman's belly would cause her to conceive; the skin of an ape's nose was a preventive against poison; the cunning and speed of the animal could be acquired by swallowing its ashes after it had been burned; the tail of a horse placed under a child's pillow would ensure sound sleep, and horses dosed with the blood of a hare would increase their speed. However, most of the talismans concerned love. The skin of a hyena worn next to a woman's skin would keep her husband faithful, and the liver of an ape would bring back the affections of one who had become enamoured of another woman.

When, in mid-morning, Roger got back to the mission, he found the big house in a ferment. The royal astrologers had informed the Shah that it would be propitious for him to honour the French visitors by dining with them that night. Soon after Roger had left to collect Lisala and Dona Christina, the Mirzataher—as the Comptroller of the King's Household was called—had arrived with a letter from the Grand Vizier, declaring His Imperial Majesty's intention. Three sizes of wax seals were used for such communications, and this had the largest so, even before opening it, Gardane realised that it must be urgent and important.

To the General's surprise, the Mirzataher took immediate charge of the proceedings. With him he had brought carpenters, tent pitchers and carpet layers. Under his directions the whole garden was covered with canvas so that it became a great marquee. Thousands of square yards of carpet were brought in wagons to be laid in the street outside, and the floors of all the downstairs rooms were covered in precious rugs. So, too, was the garden and, at its far end, a huge, silk carpet was folded into thirty-two layers and spread with priceless shawls to form a temporary throne on which the King of Kings would sit.

At midday, a score of cooks and confectioners arrived with pots, pans and vast quantities of food, to take over the kitchen. A ton of ice was carried in to cool the wines and sherbets. Meanwhile, upholsterers had draped the whole of the front of the house with gorgeous brocade curtains. The fountains were set playing, flowers arranged in their basins and jars of perfume placed beside them, to be tipped in before the Shah entered the building.

While all this was going on, the French stood about, submitting with such grace as they could to being pushed into corners. Gardane looked on speechless and sour, for the Mirzataher had told him that people honoured by the Shah in this manner always paid the cost of the entertainment and, in due course, he would be told the sum due from him.

Early in the evening the crowd was supplemented by His Majesty's singers, and the Luti Bachi—the Shah's jester— who brought with him a score of jugglers, dwarfs and other mountebanks. The time of the King of Kings' arrival was to be after the evening prayer, and Gardane was told that he must go the Palace to precede his royal visitor in the procession. Making the best of matters, he put on his smartest uniform and sallied forth.

The people of Isfahan, having learned of what was afoot, lined the streets and roof-tops to acclaim their Sovereign during his stately progress. Heading the procession came heralds carrying weighty clubs and trumpets. They proclaimed the mightiness of their master as the Centre of the Universe and by innumerable other titles. Following them came a great body of gorgeously-clad nobles. Then came Gardane with, immediately behind him, the Shah. After them rode two Princes, the Grand Vizier, other functionaries and the royal guards.

When the Shah had duly been escorted through the house to his temporary throne, Gardane, as he had been instructed was customary, had, to his intense annoyance, to offer his royal guest one hundred gold pieces on a silver salver. The

Shah nodded acceptance of them and through his interpreter told the General that such freely-made tributes inspired confidence and would increase his condescension to his host. The courtiers made numerous speeches to their master, flattering him as the greatest, wisest and most generous monarch under heaven; then his dinner was served.

It consisted of a hundred or more dishes and basins, all of solid gold, heaped with different kinds of food. For some twenty minutes he picked a bit here and a bit there with his fingers. When he had done, the two Princes sat down and set to. Only after them were the senior hosts and the Ministers allowed to eat. The dishes were then carried to the junior members of the mission and the Court officials. Finally the still-plentiful mounds of lamb, chicken, fish, rice, fruit, nuts, cakes and sweets went in turn to the guards, jesters, musicians and servants.

An entertainment followed, the star turn of which was the recitation of new piece by a poet. It lauded the Shah to the skies so satisfactorily that His Majesty ordered the man's mouth to be filled with gold, and the French were astonished to see how many pieces he succeeded in having crammed into it without choking.

It was not until well after midnight that, with much ceremony, the Shah took his departure and his tired hosts were able to discuss the party. Gardane was in an unusually black humour which, at first, Roger attributed to the great expense to which he had been put; but soon learned that it was not for that reason only. The General had optimistically believed that the Shah's visit was to convey to him a reply to the Emperor's letter and, during the course of the conversations that had taken place, he had opened the subject with the Grand Vizier.

The Minister had expressed great surprise and had conveyed the reply, 'Surely you did not expect an important decision concerning war or peace to be decided in the course of a few days? It will be another fortnight at least before you receive a reply to your communication.'

He had then gone on to inform Gardane that meanwhile

it was His Majesty's pleasure that his guests should amuse themselves by going on a hunting expedition in the great forests north of Tehran, and that arrangements were already in train for the whole of the mission to set out, with an appropriate escort, the following morning.

Later, when discussing the matter with one of the Shah's gentlemen who spoke a little French and with whom he had become friendly, the General had received a hint that the real reason that lay behind sending the mission away from Isfahan was to deprive the French of any opportunity to bribe Ministers into favouring their designs while their Emperor's letter was under discussion.

Apart from the General and Roger, the others were delighted at the thought of the expedition. The latter was naturally alarmed, as it could deprive him for the next two weeks of further meetings with his adorable Lisala. It struck him, too, as at least a possibility that Alfonso de Queircoz, having many friends in high places at the Persian Court, might have put the idea into one of the Ministers' heads, with the object of getting Lisala's new admirer out of the way until the reply to the Emperor was ready and the mission no longer had any reason to remain in Isfahan.

He at once told Gardane that he had no desire to go hunting, so would stay on in the capital. But the General would not agree to his doing so. He said that the Grand Vizier had made it plain that the whole mission was to go, bag and baggage, and he dared not risk incurring the Shah's displeasure by leaving a French officer behind. In the circumstances, Napoleon's interests not being involved, Roger could not invoke his privileged position as an A.D.C. to the Emperor; so, seething with internal rage, he was obliged to submit.

Briefly Roger considered making his way as swiftly as possible to his roof-top. But by then it was past one in the morning. Lisala would almost certainly have heard that the mission was giving an entertainment for the Shah that night; and the odds against her still being up there waiting for him were overwhelming. Reluctantly, he abandoned the idea as futile, resigned himself to the fact that he would not even be able to say good-bye to his beloved and went up to his room to pack for the journey.

Next morning, soon after nine o'clock, the mansion the mission had occupied was almost as empty as if they had never entered it. Only two score of trunks filled with surplus clothing, plate, glass, linen that they would not require and, in the basement, a number of cases containing arms, were left behind.

It was on August 18th that, with a considerable retinue of guides, guards and professional hunters, they took the road north to Tehran. They reached the city which—until Shah Abbas had moved to Isfahan and built the marvellous mosques and palaces there—had been the capital of Persia, late on the evening of the 20th and spent the night in a big caravanserai. Their baggage train caught up with them next day and, taking what they needed from it, in the early afternoon they resumed their march towards the great mountain range that now lay ahead of them.

Although it was high summer, some of the peaks were still capped with snow. To the east, along the chain, Mount Damavand rose above the others to nearly nineteen thousand feet; the highest mountain in Asia west of the Himalayas. But their guides led them through a pass and, by nightfall, they were installed in one of the Shah's big hunting lodges.

Next day they went out equipped for the chase. The country was as unlike central and southern Persia as could possibly be imagined. Instead of precipitous, barren ridges of rock and arid, sandy waste, interspersed by fertile valleys, north of the mountains there was one vast forest, extending right up to the southern shore of the Caspian Sea.

The area was almost uninhabited, but teemed with wild life of every description. There were tigers, leopards, bears, antelopes, wild boar, buck and deer in profusion. Their kill far exceeded anything they could possibly have expected; but the French felt themselves shamed because the Persian hunters proved far better marksmen with their bows and arrows than the Europeans with their latest pattern of musket.

For another two days they rode out to kill, and Roger be-

246

came sickened at this senseless slaughter; so he was much relieved when, on the evening of the 23rd, Gardane decided that they should return to Isfahan; in the hope that, after ten days, the Shah and his Ministers would have come to a decision.

Their journey south was as uneventful as that to the north had been, and they re-entered Isfahan late on the evening of the 27th. Roger had no doubt at all that many days ago Lisala had heard the French mission had left the capital on a hunting expedition; so by going up to his roof-top that night there would not be the least chance of his finding her waiting for him.

But his absence had increased his desire for her a hundred-fold. During the journey, and even while shooting dangerous big game, his mind had wandered with great frequency to her. Again and again he had visualised her heart-shaped face; the broad, smooth forehead framed in tresses of rich, reddish hair; the widely-spaced tawny eyes; the full, smiling mouth with its rows of even, white teeth; her slim arms and hands; pouting breasts; Venus-like little stomach and long, shapely legs.

That night, thoughts of her again clasped in his arms and moaning with delight as he possessed her prevented him from sleeping. In the morning, dressed in his best uniform, as early as he decently could, he hurried to the Portuguese Embassy.

To his alarm and dismay, he found it silent and shuttered. In a panic of apprehension he hammered with his riding crop on the door. After some minutes the door was unbolted by a Persian servant. From him Roger learned, to his unutterable dismay, that His Excellency the Ambassador had received letters of recall. He had left Isfahan with his whole family and staff three days before.

14

The Call of Love

Utterly aghast, Roger gaped at the man; then turned away and, with sagging shoulders, slowly walked off down the street. Enormously as he had looked forward to renewing his liaison with Lisala, not until this moment was it fully brought home to him how much she meant to him. Susceptible as he had always been to the attractions of exceptionally beautiful women, it was not alone Lisala's physical perfection that had utterly bewitched him, nor the wild abandon with which she gave herself to his embraces. It was also the subtle fascination of her unusual personality; her strength of will, contrasting with, at times, a sweet docility; the unpredictability of her moods which could change so swiftly from hilarious laughter to violent anger; her ability to talk of serious matters with sound sense coupled with a childish innocence about many aspects of life, and an insatiable desire to learn more of the great world in which, for so long, he had played a part through his acquaintance with statesmen and monarchs. The thought that he might never see her again left him completely stricken.

It was a good ten minutes before he had recovered sufficiently to turn about and retrace his steps to the Embassy, in order to find out all he could about the sudden departure of the Portuguese mission.

His first eager question of the Persian servant left in charge of the building was: had any letter or message been left for him? But neither had. He then learned that the summons to return to Portugal must have been received by de Pombal the day after the French mission had set out for Tehran; as it was from that day that the whole Embassy had suddenly become a hive of activity. Everyone there had hurriedly set about sorting and packing the contents of the mansion. Innumerable crates and cases had been filled and corded, and arrangements made to sell off possessions of all sorts that it had been decided to abandon. The Ambassador and his staff had spent the next few days in a marathon round of visits to take leave of Persian notabilities, and on the 23rd de Pombal had had a final audience with the Shah. On the following day a caravan of over fifty hired camels had been loaded up, and that evening the whole party had taken the road to Shiraz.

From this last piece of information Roger at once concluded that de Pombal had decided, instead of making the long, overland trek to Antioch, to go down to the Portuguese trading post on the Persian Gulf, there take ship round Arabia up the Red Sea, cross the isthmus and sail again from Alexandria. In mileage, that route would nearly double the length of the journey, but given favourable winds, it should take only a few weeks longer, and be infinitely less of an ordeal.

The Persian could tell Roger nothing of the reason for de Pombal's unexpected recall. Anxious to learn anything he could about it, Roger decided that a fellow diplomat would prove the most likely source of information. Apart from the French mission, the only countries then having one in Isfahan were Russia and Holland; so he hurried round to the Netherlands Embassy and asked to pay his respects to the Ambassador, whom he had already met on several occasions.

After a short wait, the portly Dutchman received him pleasantly. Like everybody else connected with the Court in Isfahan, the Ambassador knew that Roger had been squiring the beautiful Lisala round the city; so he was not surprised by his visitor's enquiry about the sudden departure of the Portuguese.

Thoughtfully stroking his chubby chin, he replied. 'The Marquis did not actually disclose to me the reason for his recall; but from our conversation I formed the impression that, indirectly, your Emperor is responsible for it.'

'The Emperor!' Roger exclaimed. 'What possible reason could he have in concerning himself with such a matter?'

The Dutchman shrugged. 'With or without warrant, he has made the affairs of every nation in Europe his concern. And still more so since he announced his "Continental System", by which he hopes to reduce the stubborn English to poverty and impotence. During the past year he has compelled every country under his control to close their ports to British shipping, and one can hardly doubt that he will now exert pressure on the smaller countries that still retain their independence, to come into line. Of these, the most important to him is Portugal. As you may be aware, Portugal is England's oldest ally; but since the death of Pitt, Britain has waged her war against France only in a most half-hearted fashion, so whether she has either the will or the means to enable the Portuguese to defy your Emperor is open to question. However, now that he has inflicted such a crushing defeat on the Czar, it is reasonable to predict that he will next turn his attention to Portugal, with a view to plugging that serious leak in his embargo against trade with Britain.'

'Your Excellency's assumption is soundly based,' Roger agreed. 'But I still do not see why this should have brought about de Pombal's recall.'

'Do you know anything of his family history?'

'I know, of course, that the first Marquis was one of the greatest statesmen that Portugal ever produced; and that, for over a quarter of a century, King Joseph gave him a free hand to revolutionise Portugal's Army, Navy, finances, commerce and educational system. Also that, on the King's death, his widow displayed such hatred for de Pombal that he was dismissed and persecuted; but I know no more than that.'

'Then you know enough to realise that the present Marquis has the blood of a genius in his veins. I do not suggest that he is one himself; but he is highly intelligent, an able diplomat and very knowledgeable about international affairs. Perhaps even more important, he bears a name that is now rightly honoured by the Portuguese people. Does it not seem to you that, in the emergency with which his Sovereign may soon be faced, it would be a wise move to have readily available the advice and support of such a personality?'

Roger nodded. 'In that your Excellency is certainly right. But by his Sovereign I take it you mean the Don Joao, the Prince of Brazil? For many years past, old Queen Maria has been as mad as a hatter.'

'Of course. In '99, Joao was made Prince Regent, and has since performed the functions of a Sovereign. All that I have said is only speculation on my part. But I give it to you for what it is worth.'

Having thanked the Ambassador, Roger took his leave of him no less depressed, but with the feeling that this possible explanation of the sudden departure of the Portuguese was most probably correct.

For the remainder of the day and a good part of the night, he wrestled with the problem of what he should do. Since he was not acting as a British secret agent, duty did not demand that he should remain in Isfahan and, as a lodestone attracts a magnetised needle, he was drawn to rejoin the adorable Lisala at the earliest possible moment.

Should he decide to abandon the French mission and go off on his own? Gardane would protest, but he could do no more than report this desertion to the Emperor. Napoleon's displeasure might lead to a final break with him; but in the past, Roger had on several occasions produced plausible reasons for having apparently abandoned his service for lengthy periods, and he had little doubt about his ability to do so again.

By this time the Portuguese caravan was probably nearing Shiraz. If he took horse next morning and followed post haste, he could be certain of catching up with it before it reached the Persian Gulf. But what then? How could he explain his wish to join de Pombal's party and return to Europe with it? He was by no means anxious to marry again; but if he did, who, other than Georgina, could make a more desirable wife than Lisala? Her personal attractions apart, she was of high birth and, as an only child, would inherit a great fortune. He could declare that his love for her was so great that he had sacrificed his career in order to rejoin her, and ask her hand in marriage.

But how would de Pombal react to that? Roger, as an apparent deserter, would make a far from favourable impression. It was quite probable too that, in any case, the Marquis would not consider him a sufficiently good match for his daughter. Still worse, if the Dutch Ambassador's theory was correct, that the reason for de Pombal's recall was due to Portugal now being threatened by Napoleon, de Pombal might possibly jump to the conclusion that Roger's courting of Lisala was being used only as a blind; and that, in fact, Gardane had sent him to travel with the Portuguese as a spy.

'No,' Roger decided. It would not do. For one reason or another, the Marquis would reject his plea to accompany his party back to Europe.

Next morning Roger walked along to the house behind the Portuguese Embassy, to tell the landlord that he would no longer be requiring the upper apartment, so he could let it to someone else if he wished.

The man listened to his glum resignation of his tenancy, then gave an understanding nod and said with a sly look, 'I regret that affairs have turned out so badly for my lord, but a letter was left for him by a young serving woman. I will get it.'

Two minutes later, with trembling fingers, Roger was tearing open the sealed paper the man had handed to him. As he expected, it was from Lisala, and read:

My beloved one. Before receiving this you will have learned of the terrible misfortune that has overtaken us. My papa has received orders to return immediately to Portugal, with all his people.

I am desolate. My Russian taught me the joys of passion, but you alone have taught me the true meaning of love. For us to remain separated permanently is unthinkable. I beg you on my knees that you find some way to join me, in Lisbon. Given such an able brain as yours, this cannot be beyond its capacity. For you, nothing is impossible. The thought appals me that, for many weeks to come, I must live without your sweet companionship, gay laughter and those lovely, wicked caresses that send me into a heavenly frenzy. I am already half-dying with desire for you, and will know no peace until you have again become my splendid lover.

As Roger read this desperate appeal to follow her, he found his hand trembling. It was ample evidence that her longing for him equalled his for her. Somehow, he must rejoin her; but how? How? How?

Having given the landlord a gold *touman*, he walked slowly back to the headquarters of the mission and spent the rest of the day there in agonised frustration; for, badger his wits as he would, he could think of no way in which to overcome the difficulties that faced him.

By evening his state of depression was so obvious that one of the junior officers, guessing the cause, had the temerity to twit him upon it. Such was Roger's ill temper that, had the implication been made before others, the young man would have found a duel forced upon him; but, as they were alone at the time, Roger did no more than snarl at him, 'Make one more mention in my presence of the *Senhorita* de Pombal, and I will slice your ears off.'

On the following day the members of the mission were bidden by the Shah to witness an entertainment.

At nine o'clock they found some three hundred nobles at the Palace in the great Maidan Square, round the sides of which many thousand people had congregated. In front of them, to prevent them from encroaching on the square, were triple rows of the Royal Guard in resplendent uniforms.

The display opened with a parade of beautiful horses, the trappings of which were incomparably finer than any the French had ever seen. Some were a blaze of rubies, others of emeralds and others again a groundwork of diamonds patterned with precious stones of various colours; their bridles were thick ropes of silk and their hooves shod with gold. They were followed by gold and silver gem-studded carriages, driven by Indians in gold-braided coats.

A row of precious tapestries was then spread out and to each was led by a lion who lay down on it. Behind them were ranged elephants, rhinoceri, white antelopes and snorting bulls; all bedecked with splendid ornaments and kept under control by keepers clad in costumes of different colours.

A space immediately below the high balcony of the Palace was then cleared until only one lion and one bull remained on it. Roaring, the lion strained to get at the bull until, at a signal from the Shah, the lion was unleashed. In a few, swift leaps, it overtook the bull and began to tear it to pieces. In turn, each lion was presented with a bull to slay; but in two cases the bull succeeded in goring the lion, upon which the keepers rushed in with hatchets and quickly killed the bull, because, the lion being the royal insignia of Persia, its defeat could never be permitted.

Then followed displays by acrobats, jugglers, wrestlers, fencers and archers; the aim of the last being so accurate that they could shoot away the plumes from the turbans of an opposing team—except for one instance, in which an arrow pierced the turban of an opponent. As a penalty, the unfortunate marksman had his hand promptly chopped off.

The last event consisted of two bodies of horsemen, both a hundred strong. They were all young nobles, clad in chain mail and each armed only with one javelin. On receiving a hit on the body, a combatant had to retire; then, in order to throw his javelin again, the man who had scored the hit had to recover it. To do so necessitated his leaning over from his galloping mount, until his head nearly touched the ground. This extraordinary, swiftly-moving *mêlée* provided the spectators with a display of superb horsemanship.

The show ended at one o'clock, upon which the Shah retired into his palace and, after conversing for a while with some of the Persian courtiers, the officers of the French mission returned to their quarters. All of them were talking enthusiastically of the remarkable spectacle they had just witnessed, with the exception of Roger, who had sat through it with lacklustre eyes, still obsessed with the problem of how to renew his *affaire* with the beautiful Lisala.

However, he had hardly settled down in his room when he was roused from his brooding by Gardane's shouting up the fact, although its source would have remained unknown anyone seeing it would have found it difficult to inter-t, it could have proved dangerous; so, with his habitual ution, Roger had already burned it.

After much thought, just as they were about to go up to bed hat night, he tackled the General and asked to have a word with him in his office. As they entered it, he said, '*Mon Général*, I have been considering the next stage of our mission, and should like to talk to you about it.'

'Sit down, *mon ami*,' the General replied genially. 'Your observations on our business are always interesting.'

Taking a chair, Roger proceeded. 'The Emperor's instructions are that we should contact the Mahratta Princes, as they are known to be hostile to the British. Since I once crossed India from Calcutta to Bombay, he labours under the false impression that I know that vast territory from end to end, and many of its Maharajahs. But the fact is that, during my journey, I never even saw a Mahratta Prince, so I can be of no use to you in opening negotiations with any of them.'

The General nodded. 'I am aware of that. You mentioned it to me soon after we left Warsaw.'

'Since I can be of no help to you with the Mahrattas, another way in which I could make myself more useful has occurred to me. No doubt you have a map of the territory we shall have to cross in order to reach India.'

Gardane produced a map and spread it out on a divan. Roger drew his finger across the broadest part of India, and said, 'There we have the huge area, under the control of the Mahratta Confederacy. It includes in the West the great port of Bombay; so I assume it is for there you intend to make?'

'Yes. I plan to travel east through the Persian cities of Yazd, Bafq and Rapsanjan, then south to the port of Banda Abass at the entrance to the Persian Gulf; and from there take ship to Bombay.'

'That appears to be the quickest route,' Roger agreed. 'And now, you will observe that Goa, the colony of considerable extent in which the Portuguese have been established for some two hundred years, lies on the coast only two hundred and

stairs: 'Breuc! Breuc! Come down. A courier has arrived with news; extraordinary news.'

And extraordinary news it certainly proved to be. With his officers crowding about him, the General gave them particulars of the despatch he had just received from Napoleon's secretary, Meneval. After the Russian defeat at Friedland, it had been agreed that the Czar should meet the Emperor to discuss the terms of an armistice. The two monarchs had established their headquarters on opposite sides of the river Nieman at Tilsit. A huge raft, carrying a gorgeously-appointed pavilion, had then been anchored in midstream, and there, on June 25th, for the first time the two most powerful men in Europe had come face to face.

To open the conference the two Emperors met alone. During a private conversation lasting only three-quarters of an hour, a miracle had taken place. They had emerged enchanted with each other. A large area of the town had then been made a neutral zone for further conferences, attended by the principal Ministers and Marshals. On July 7th a Treaty of Alliance had been signed, which changed the whole situation in Europe.

As a young man, Alexander had held strongly liberal views and fully approved the measures of the National Assembly, which had brought Liberty to the French people. The excesses of the Revolution that followed had horrified him, and turned him against the French. Seven years later, after Napoleon, as First Consul, had shown himself to be a brilliant administrator and had brought order out of chaos, the Czar had conceived a great admiration for him, and refused to aid the Monarchist Coalition in its attempt to destroy the French Republic. But, as time went on, Alexander had gradually come to realise that Napoleon was not simply a French patriot of genius, but a man of inordinate ambition, who was set upon enslaving the people of every country. It was this that had led to his stigmatising the Emperor as a 'dangerous beast' who, at all costs, must be thwarted in his designs; and, at last joined the Allies in their most recent attempt to free from Napoleon's tyranny the countries he had conquered.

Now, in the course of one short afternoon, Alexander had changed his opinion yet again. Napoleon's magnetism and personal charm had entirely won him over. It had been agreed not only that they should sign a peace, but should divide Europe between them. The miserable King of Prussia was thrown the sop of receiving back Silesia; but ordered to forfeit all his Polish territories to Russia. His port of Danzig was to become a Free City, maintaining a French garrison. A new State called the Duchy of Warsaw was to be formed in central Poland, with Napoleon's ally, the King of Saxony, as its ruler. France was to retain military control of Oldenburg, Saxe-Coburg and Mecklenburg until peace was made between France and England.

This amazing reorientation of power and interests could not possibly have been foreseen. It would now be contrary to French interests for either Turkey or Persia to attack Russia. In fact, far from attempting to make Turkey France's ally, it was a reasonable assumption that, secretly, the Emperor and Czar had decided to overrun the Turkish Empire and divide it between them.

After the siesta, the General held a conference with his senior officers. The despatch had made it clear that the Emperor's designs on India were unchanged. Persian co-operation was essential to that. This now required a most delicate shift in policy. They had been pressing the Shah to attack Russia. Now it must tactfully be put to him and his advisers that in view of recent events this was no longer desirable, but that France still greatly desired the friendship of the Shah, and would assist in the extension of his dominions. As an earnest of this, they would leave with him all the modern weapons sent out for both Turkey and Persia, together with all the French officers nominated to train Oriental troops in their use. Since the Emperor's orders still stood that, after Persia, the mission should proceed to India, with the object of securing the Mahratta Princes as potential allies against the British, it was clear that the sooner Gardane could persuade the Persians of the Emperor's continued goodwill towards them and continue his journey to the East, the better.

Roger made little contribution to the con... mind was busy with a private letter which t... brought for him. It was in a hand he did not... signed. It read:

Our purpose has received a serious set-back; ... not despair. The gorgon has hypnotised the wolf ... door, so will now turn his attention to silencing the ... whose yapping in the back yard annoys him. But oth... that he has kept fettered in his house may seize the ... tunity to break loose while he is out in the yard. You ... only harm by taming tigers; so I trust you will find ... excuse to return and give us your valuable help in clean... the gorgon's lair.

Roger had no doubt that this missive came from Talle... rand. Their agreed purpose was to bring about the overthro... of Napoleon. The set-back was, of course, the Emperor's having turned the Czar from an enemy to a friend. The annoying little dog in the back yard could only be Portugal, and the fettered beasts Prussia, the Rhineland, northern Italy and other European countries conquered by France. The tigers were the Indian Princes, with whom Napoleon had sent Roger to treat, and the appeal to return implied that trouble was brewing for the Emperor, of which advantage might be taken to bring about his fall.

From the beginning, Roger had been averse to going to India, and determined to find some way of evading that part of the mission he had been assigned. An immediate return to Europe fitted in with his own desires; and, if Portugal was to be the next seat of trouble, he could justify his turning up there by asserting that the close association he had formed with the Portuguese while in Isfahan had led him to believe that he could better serve the Emperor by going to Lisbon, rather than to Bombay.

His problem now was to think of a means by which he could justify to Gardane his leaving the mission. If he could have shown an order from the Emperor to proceed to Portugal, all would have been plain sailing; but the cryptic missive from Talleyrand had been far from anything of that kind.

fifty miles south of Bombay. As you are aware, during our stay in Isfahan, I developed particularly good relations with the personnel of the Portuguese Embassy and as I have long been fluent in Spanish, I succeeded in becoming fairly well acquainted with Portuguese. If, therefore, I went to Goa and made capital out of my friendship with the Marquis de Pombal, I would be both well received and able to talk in their own language with the principal gentlemen in authority there.'

A slight frown crossed Gardane's brow. 'Admittedly, but I do not see in what way this could benefit our mission.'

Roger smiled. 'It could, since the Emperor has in mind the conquest of India. Obviously, if you can succeed in winning over the Mahratta Princes, the first French Expeditionary Force for their support would be landed in Bombay. Think how advantageous it would be if we landed a second force in Goa. We should then be able to initiate a pincer movement which could result in our swiftly becoming the masters of all central India.'

'As a strategic conception, I agree that it is admirable. But, as things stand, surely you do not suppose that you could induce the Portuguese in Goa to become our allies?'

'Dear me, no!' Roger shook his head. 'That is too much to hope for. But, given a month or so there as a private traveller, I could secure knowledge of all the Portuguese defences and the weak spots in them. That could ensure a French expedition's getting ashore with few casualties and seizing the colony without serious opposition, as a valuable base for future operations.'

After a moment's thought, Gardane replied, 'You are right. A French force based on Goa could be of immense advantage in the campaign. And an expert such as you, able to advise how to capture it without heavy losses, would prove a most valuable asset.'

Roger stood up and bowed. '*Mon Général*, I am happy that you should approve my idea, although it means that, for a while at least, we must terminate our pleasant association. To conclude your negotiations with the Shah and ensure the continuance of his goodwill, can hardly be done in less than a fortnight. Moreover, our routes to India will be different, as I propose to make for the Portuguese trading station at the head of the Gulf, from which it should not be difficult to secure a passage direct to Goa. There is, therefore, no point in my remaining on here, and the sooner I can get to work in Goa, the better. So I propose to make arrangements to leave Isfahan as soon as possible.'

The General agreed to that and Roger left the office well satisfied with the way in which his deception had worked. Later, of course, it would be learned by Gardane that he had never gone to Goa; but not for, perhaps, a year or at least many months. By then, if the question ever arose at all, he could easily produce a reason for the change in his plans.

During the past few days he had been unutterably depressed; now he felt his old self once more. To set out alone, except for native guides, across hundreds of miles of desert and mountain was to court many dangers. The journey would entail much hardship and privation. But at the end of it was Lisala.

15

Of Intrigues in Spain

Roger was up at dawn next morning, making his preparations. Caravans for Shiraz left Isfahan daily, and had he really meant to go down to the Gulf, that was the road he would have taken. As it was certain that his brother officers would come to see him off, in order to give credence to his intentions, as told to Gardane, he had no alternative but to take it.

However, he meant to do so for only a dozen miles, then turn back north-west, heading for the city of Najafabad. There he would strike the Silk Road and, following the same route the mission had taken on its outward journey, return to Antioch. This plan entailed an element of risk for, after leaving the caravan, he would have to cross some fifty miles of open, and mainly trackless, country. As he always carried a small compass on his travels, he had no fear of losing his way; but, outside her cities, Persia was still a lawless land, with many bands of roving brigands. It was for this reason that merchants always banded together and travelled well armed, in large caravans.

The risk of his being attacked was not a great one, as such bands did not often marauder so close to the capital; and, if he did fall in with one, he would have no merchandise that might tempt it. All the same, he felt that it would be worth the money to provide himself with an armed guard; so he sought out Mesrop and told him in confidence that he was about to set out on a secret mission, for which he needed a guide who knew the country well within fifty miles of Isfahan, a servant and six reliable, armed men who would accompany him to any place he wished to go during the next two days.

The Armenian, who had become his good friend, willingly obliged; so that very evening of August 30th, Roger, clad in the Balkan costume he had acquired in Constantinople, and accompanied by his private escort, joined the caravan for Shiraz. It started from outside the great Bazaar. Gardane and the majority of the officers who had been Roger's companions for many months, came to see him off. They were loath to part with him, and waved him away, wishing him good luck.

During the cool evening hours, the caravan covered some fifteen miles, then made camp for the night. At first light next morning, as preparations were in the making for the next stage of the journey, and the scores of camels being prodded on to their legs, Roger told the caravan leader that he had changed his plans. Then, accompanied by his bodyguard, he left.

By ten o'clock, the heat was so terrific that they had to take shelter in a mud-walled village. The stench in the hovel that the headman courteously led him to rest in was such that he was nearly sick; but he managed to doze there for some hours; then, after a meal prepared by his own men from his own stores, they set out again. Knowing something of the ways of the country, he feared it likely that, while his troop rested, the gravely-polite headman might have sent word to some brigand chief in the neighbourhood that a foreigner with only a light escort was there, and that evening would be on his way north. But this fear proved groundless. Unmolested, at ten o'clock that night, they rode into the city of Najafabad.

Early next morning he enquired of the master of the caravanserai about caravans proceeding to Dezful and learned to his annoyance that one was not due to leave until three days later. Further influenced by the knowledge that if he did go with it his progress would have to conform to that of the slow-moving camels, he decided to retain his escort and push on with them.

At the Persian border they refused to accompany him further; but he secured Mesopotamian Arabs to replace them and, later, Syrians. On one occasion when riding through a rocky gorge, they were fired upon; but, putting their horses into a gallop, succeeded in getting away, the only casualty being one of the escorts who had a bullet through the fleshy part of his left arm. On another occasion Roger woke one night in the desert, to find one of his Syrian escort in his tent, and about to make off with his musket. The attempted theft could well have been the first act in a plan by them all to mutiny and murder him, then make off with whatever money he had. He could not afford to risk that, so he swiftly cocked the pistol he always kept beside him and, as the man was crawling out of the tent, shot him in the back of the head.

After that, he met with no further troubles. There is much truth in the saying: 'He travels fastest who travels alone.' Moreover, he did not stop for two days in Babylon, as Gardane's party had done on the way out. In consequence, he made considerably better time, completing his journey in well under a month, and arriving at the port of Antioch on September 26th.

Inured to roughing it, he decided to take the first westward-bound ship available, and next morning went aboard a *felucca* that was about to sail for Cyprus. There he picked up a small but fast Greek trader bound for Crete. In Heraklion he was delayed two days, but then found better quarters on a Neapolitan brig which carried him to Catania in Sicily. Protected by the British Navy, the island was still ruled by King Ferdinand, who had fled there when the French had chased him out of Naples; so, while in Catania, Roger had to continue to wear his Balkan costume and pose, as he had done since leaving Antioch, as a Bulgarian merchant. But he was lucky in that only a day later he secured a passage to Valencia in a three-masted barque.

On the second evening out, he had cause for considerable anxiety, as the barque was sighted and chased by a Corsair from one of the ports on the Barbary coast. Armed only with six twelve-pounders, the barque could not have put up a prolonged resistance and, once boarded by a swarm of ferocious Moors, her crew would have been swiftly overwhelmed. But fortunately night was coming on, and she got away under cover of darkness, landing Roger safely at Valencia on October 25th.

The difficulties of shaving during his long journey from Isfahan to Antioch had decided him to let his beard grow and, after much thought, by the time he took ship he had formed a plan about how he should proceed when he reached Lisbon. The plan entailed a change of appearance; so he had continued to refrain from shaving, while crossing the Mediterranean, and now had a curly brown beard, moustache and side-whiskers.

Up in his room at the inn to which he had been recommended, he studied his face in the mirror, and it struck him that the whole of his lower face being covered by hair might give anyone who knew him the impression that he had deliberated attempted to disguise himself. Sending for hot water and scissors, he first cut his beard short and shaved his chin, then carefully trimmed his moustache to give it a smarter appearance. Next, as Spain was France's ally, he got out of his Eastern garments and put on the well-worn uniform that he had brought in his solitary valise.

After he had dined that evening, the heavy expenses of his long journey had reduced his funds to three gold pieces. However, for many years past he had been in the habit of always travelling with a packet of small diamonds in his moneybelt; so, next morning, he sold some of them to a jeweller for a sufficient sum to get him to Lisbon.

There remained the question as to whether he should proceed there by sea, or overland. The former would have been less fatiguing; but his recent narrow escape from being captured by Barbary pirates made him disinclined to risk taking passage in a ship that would have to sail close to the North African coast before passing through the Straits of Gibraltar. In consequence, he elected to cross the Peninsula and, knowing how bad were the roads in Spain, to take the highway to Madrid; although that entailed a detour from the direct route. Riding post, he set out from Valencia soon after midday and, four days later, on October 30th, he entered the Spanish capital.

On the following morning, he walked round to the French Embassy. Of the porter on the gate he enquired who was now Ambassador there, and was pleased to learn that it was the Marquis de Beauharnais. The Marquis was the brother-in-law of the Empress Josephine by her first marriage, so Roger had met him on many occasions, both at Court and in the more intimate family circle of the Bonapartes. He sent in his name and, a quarter of an hour later, was ushered into the Ambassador's study.

The tall, thin Marquis came out from behind his desk, gave Roger a friendly smile and said, '*Mon cher Breuc!* This is a delightful surprise; and, may I add, it is equally surprising to see one of His Majesty's *aides-de-camp* in such a travesty of his usual brilliant uniform. What brings you here, and in such a sad condition?'

Roger returned the smile. 'It is a long story, Excellency, and an even longer journey from the Emperor's headquarters in Poland via Constantinople to Persia, then from there back to Madrid. Hence the parlous condition of my garments.'

'Persia! That is indeed a far cry. Please to be seated and tell me of it.'

'Willingly, if Your Excellency has the leisure to listen. But I imagine that you must have many matters requiring your attention; so perhaps it would be better to postpone telling my story until a more suitable time. Meanwhile, I would add that my journey is not yet completed. I am on my way to Lisbon. I called only to pay my respects and, if you will be so obliging, learn from you how things now stand in Europe. For many weeks, while crossing deserts and the Mediterranean, I have been deprived of all news. Has His Majesty yet conquered England, or is he making ready to descend on India?'

The Marquis laughed. 'Neither, as yet; although, no doubt, he will do both in due course. He has, however, made yet another of his brothers a monarch. Some months ago, he consolidated a number of German Principalities into what is now known as the Kingdom of Westphalia, and gave it to Jerome. But there have been no great battles since Friedland.

'In August, Gustavus of Sweden asked for an armistice. Austria maintains her neutrality. Russia is our ally. Apart from those, His Majesty is the master of the greater part of Europe, either directly or through subservient Governments who dare not defy his wishes. England alone now remains entirely our enemy.'

'And how has the war against perfidious Albion prospered?' Roger enquired.

'Her Navy still rules the oceans; but on land there is little she can do against us. She is war-weary and, until last spring, her Government had no man of spirit in it. The Duke of Portland then became Prime Minister, with a Mr. Canning as his Foreign Secretary. Canning is a man to watch, for it was he who inspired the only serious blow against France that has been struck for the past year or more.'

'I pray you, tell me of it.'

The Ambassador took a pinch of snuff. 'It concerned Denmark. After the Treaty of Tilsit, when the Czar became our ally, the British feared that would lead to the closing of the Baltic, and that they would no longer be able to supply the Anglo-Swedish army, which was still maintaining its hold on Stralsund in Pomerania. There was, moreover, the even more important question of the Danish Fleet. The countries under the Emperor's control can send fifty-nine ships of the line to sea. The Czar could give us twenty-four and, had we been able to use the Danes' eighteen, that would have given us parity with Britain; thus giving us the prospect of reversing the decision at Trafalgar.

'France and England vied with each other in offers to induce the Danes to become their ally. The Danes wished to remain neutral and refused all overtures. Fearing that the Emperor would invade Denmark and seize her Navy, Mr. Canning initiated swift and violent action. Under Lord Cathcart, he sent the greater part of the British Navy to Copenhagen, accompanied by General Sir Wellesley with transports carrying a large body of troops. They attempted to overawe the Danes into surrendering their Fleet, by threatening to bombard the city. The Danish Prince Royal gallantly refused to submit. Wellesley landed outside the capital with his troops, and eighty-eight vessels of the British Navy proceeded to fire their cannon upon it. The end was inevitable surrender. For six weeks the British occupied the Danish fortifications, then sailed away with the captured Danish Fleet.'

Hiding his delight, Roger remarked, 'It was an unorthodox procedure to attack a neutral without provocation; but sound strategically.'

'The British paid a price for it, though,' the Marquis smiled. 'In their anxiety to overawe the Danes, they withdrew their troops and warships from the Baltic to assist in the operation. Left unsupported in Stralsund, King Gustavus was compelled to ask terms of Marshal Brune. So Sweden is now out of the war. Moreover, so incensed were the Danes by Britain's high-handed treatment of them that, no sooner had the English evacuated the strong places in the neighbourhood of Copenhagen than they declared war and are now become our valuable allies.'

'That being so,' Roger remarked, 'the only loopholes left in His Majesty's "Continental System" are the ports of Portugal.'

'Indeed yes; and long before the Emperor proclaimed his "System", he endeavoured to close them. As far back as '95 he urged the Directory to exert pressure on Spain to coerce Portugal into withdrawing from her alliance with England. In 1801 after he had become First Consul, he renewed his attempts and, ever since, when he has not been occupied with grave matters, he has again taken up the question.'

'It amazes me that over so many years he has not succeeded.'

'There have been many difficulties. The Portuguese are a stubborn people. They cannot be attacked except by an army that first crosses Spanish territory. The ruling families of both France and Spain being Bourbons, the Revolution and subsequent execution of Louis XVI provoked the greatest possible antagonism in this country, and led to Spain making war on France. Yet, even after the brief, inglorious campaign of '94, King Carlos paid only lip-service to the treaty forced on him at Basle, and refrained from exerting pressure on Portugal, because his sister is the Princess of Brazil and the wife of the Prince Regent Joao.

'In 1801, France pushed the issue to the point where Portugal actually went to war with Spain. Although the Portuguese were speedily defeated and by the Treaty of Badajoz France should have got what she wanted, Spain never enforced its terms. For a dozen years past, Portugal has alternately given way to Franco-Spanish demands, then slid back into her old alliance with England, made millions as a broker for her merchandise, and allowed her Navy to use Portuguese ports as bases.'

'It seems then that nothing short of an invasion of the Peninsula will finally solve this problem to the satisfaction of the Emperor?'

The Marquis nodded. 'That is the situation; and for its success we need Spain's full co-operation, instead of the only half-hearted support which the dictator has for so long given us.'

'You refer to Manuel Godoy, the Prince of the Peace? I met him way back in 1790 when I was here as a very young man. I thought Godoy rather charming, and by no means unintelligent.'

'Then you assessed him rightly. Most people regard him as no more than a handsome, stupid oaf with an insatiable lust for wealth, power and pretty women; who, as Queen Maria Luisa's lover, and with the absolute confidence of King Carlos, has ruled Spain for fifteen years. They are wrong. Boundlessly avaricious and lecherous he unquestionably is; but he has ideals and the cunning to defeat those who oppose them. His main objective has always been to keep Spain out of war, and in that has largely succeeded. He has also had the courage to defy the Church, and has broken its previous stranglehold on the country. Due to him there are in Spain today several Institutes which are outside the control of the Church. He put an end to the barbarous Inquisition and expelled the Jesuits. It was he who permitted the Jews to return to Spain. He is a patron of the Arts and has established a fine Botanical Garden. Villainous fellow though he is, I confess to a sneaking admiration for him. His attitude towards our master has always been most friendly; yet his reluctance to involve Spain in war has again and again thwarted French interests. And that is still the situation.'

At that moment a handsome grandfather clock in a corner of the room chimed the half-hour. Glancing in that direction, the Marquis said:

'You were right, *mon cher Colonel*. This is not the hour to indulge in a lengthy conversation, as I have much to do before leaving for Aranjuez, where the Court is now in residence. But I shall greatly look forward to hearing about your travels when I return tomorrow or the day after. Meanwhile you must, of course, be my guest. Return now to your inn and have your belongings sent here. I will tell my First Secretary, Jules Baudin, to look after you during my absence. I will, too, give you the address of a good tailor who will quickly make for you a new uniform appropriate to your rank.'

Roger gladly accepted these offers, then took his leave. As he went out into the autumn sunshine he was thinking of his previous visit to the Spanish capital. That had been seventeen years earlier. He had then been desperately in love with Isabella d'Aranda, the daughter of a former Spanish Prime Minister. He recalled their secret meetings in a garden pavilion in the grounds of her husband's house out at Aranjuez —the Versailles of Madrid—and how Manuel Godoy had aided their plan to get her husband sent to Paris, as a Special Envoy.

In those days Godoy had been only a Lieutenant of the Flemish Guard; but he was already powerful through the influence he exerted as the lover of Queen Maria Luisa. Roger had thought her the ugliest woman he had ever seen, and she had the reputation of being the most lecherous in Europe. Her husband, King Carlos IV, had then been on the throne only for two years. He was a strange individual; his only interests lay in hunting and playing the violin. He never drank wine or coffee, abhorred tobacco, had never had a mistress, and resolutely closed his eyes to his Queen's flagrant infidelities. For many years he had regarded Godoy as his closest friend, placed absolute trust in his judgment and showered him with honours. In '92 he had created him Duke of Alcudia and in '95, when Godoy had ignominiously brought to a conclusion the war with France which he had started so reluctantly, given him the title of the Prince of Peace.

As it was Roger's business to be well informed about all the Courts in Europe, he marvelled that Godoy had succeeded in maintaining his influence for so long over the nymphomaniac Queen; since she had summoned scores of other lovers to her bed, and he had been equally unfaithful to her. Quite early in their association he had openly boasted to her of his *affaire* with the beautiful Duchess of Alba; then, when she heaped furious reproaches on him, had given her a beating. He had had two children by the Queen, and taken as his wife the King's young cousin, Maria Thérèsa of Bourbon. Yet, he kept installed in their palace his principal mistress 'Pepa' Tudo. To his greed and ambition there were no limits. He collected highly-paid offices as other men collected bric-à-brac, and, greatly as he hated the thought of war, he had even suggested to Napoleon that they should dismember Portugal into three parts, one of which should be made into a kingdom for himself. Such was the man who for so many years had held the fate of the Peninsula in his hands.

After the siesta, Roger settled his bill at the inn and had his valise sent to the Embassy, where he made the acquaintance of Jules Baudin, a plump and pleasant man. He then repaired to the tailor. Having chosen the material, he was able, being something of an artist, to draw the type of uniform he wished it to be made up into. He also ordered a smart civilian suit and cloak. The man promised that his assistants should work all night, so that Roger could be fitted the next day, and receive delivery the day after that.

Roger then visited a mercer's, a haberdasher's and a hatter's, in order to replenish his sadly-depleted wardrobe and, finally, bought two stout valises in which to transport his new garments.

That evening at the Embassy he was made aware of the

power the French wielded in Madrid. It seemed that half the nobility in the city had come to pay court to de Beauharnais; as he was absent, they fawned upon Jules Baudin. Napoleon, having looted half Europe of her treasure, could well afford lavish entertainment in his Embassies, so open house was kept, and nearly forty of the callers stayed on to dinner.

Many of them spoke French and Roger had enough Spanish to converse fairly freely with others who did not. He soon found that they showed no restraint in airing their opinions. All of them hated Godoy, yet shared his reluctance to send an army to coerce the Portuguese into breaking off relations with England. They had had their lesson when Spain had last challenged the mighty sea-power. The British Navy had promptly stopped the treasure ships arriving from South America, and it was upon them that the life of Spain depended. The country had suffered acutely, and thousands of people had gone bankrupt. Should the English again take up the cudgels on behalf of Portugal, those terrible times would be repeated.

Several of them mentioned Prince Ferdinand, the Heir Apparent. His loathing for Godoy was so great that, as a means of bringing about the favourite's downfall, he had gone to the length of conspiring against his own father. Godoy had discovered the plot in time, so had saved the throne for King Carlos. The Prince had been arrested and, mean creature that he was, to save himself from permanent imprisonment, had denounced all his associates. Yet, even so, these discontented nobles would have happily accepted his rule rather than have Godoy continue in power.

The general consensus of opinion was that there would be no war; because Godoy, for all his villainy and extortions, had twice saved them from it. By one treaty he had bought non-belligerency for Spain by agreeing to furnish two million francs a month towards Napoleon's war chest. Later, in another treaty, he had agreed to raise the contribution to six million. Therefore, the nobles argued, even if it cost Spain still more, he would somehow wriggle out of sending troops into Portugal.

With few exceptions, Roger thought them a stiff-necked,

bigoted lot, so blinded by their hatred for Godoy that they had lost all sense of reality.

Three days elapsed before the Ambassador returned from Aranjuez, but Roger was not troubled by the delay. Having nearly completed his journey, he now felt that he had a good margin of time in hand before arriving in Lisbon; because de Pombal's party had gone round Arabia and up the Red Sea, so were not likely to reach the Portuguese capital much before mid-November. Meanwhile, he enjoyed strolling about Madrid, and put up with the inanities of the small-minded *hidalgos* who frequented the Embassy.

On the evening of the day that de Beauharnais did get back to Madrid, he and Roger enjoyed a long, private talk. Roger gave a skilfully-edited account of his travels, then they discussed at length the pros and cons of the threat to Portugal. To wind up, the Ambassador said:

'In spite of all this banging of drums, I think it very unlikely that it will come to war in the Peninsula. If former occasions of a similar nature are anything to go by, it certainly will not. On one such, the Emperor wrote to a predecessor of mine here: "Tell King Carlos that, unless he complies with my demands, he will be the last Bourbon to occupy a throne." But nothing came of it. Godoy bought him off by offering a greatly-increased subsidy, and the odds are that is what will happen again.'

Roger was not fully convinced. On those previous occasions Napoleon had had bigger fish to fry; so it had suited him to let Spain off the hook, at a price. But now he was not engaged in any great campaign, not a musket was being fired throughout all Europe, and he had a very powerful army at his disposal. Moreover, for the past year and more, he had been concentrating on perfecting his 'Continental System'. Now that the ports of Denmark and Sweden were closed to British shipping, those of Portugal remained the only leak. It was argued that he would think more than once about sending an army into the desolate and mountainous wastes of Spain, where it would find little to live on. But he had not hesitated to send one into the equally barren snow-covered lands of Poland. As he went to bed, Roger could only pray, for Lisala's sake that the Ambassador's appreciation of the situation was right.

Resplendent now in the brilliant new uniform the tailor had made for him, he spent another day in Madrid, intending next morning to set out on the road for Lisbon. That evening, on his note of hand as one of the Emperor's people, he drew from Baudin as large a sum in gold as he could without discomfort carry in his money-belt, and shortly afterwards went to bed.

It was an hour after midnight when de Beauharnais suddenly appeared in Roger's bedroom, clad in a chamber robe and clutching a paper in his hand. Roger was just drifting off to sleep. Rousing himself, he exclaimed:

'What is it, Excellency? What brings you here?'

'*Mon Colonel*, as you are proceeding to Lisbon, I thought you should know of this without delay,' the Ambassador replied tersely. 'I have just received a despatch by fast courier. On the 27th of last month a treaty was signed at Fontainebleau. Spain is to join France in a war against Portugal. That country is to be divided into three parts. France takes the central section, the Emperor's puppet the King of Etruria is to receive the north in exchange for his Italian lands, so that they may be merged with the greater territories already under the direct rule of France, and Godoy is to be given the southern section as a kingdom for himself. But more. The Emperor has secretly massed an army of thirty thousand men in the neighbourhood of Bayonne. General Junot is in command. He has already crossed the Pyrenees and his orders are to drive with all possible speed on Lisbon.'

16

To Be or Not to Be?

At dawn next morning Roger was to horse. Now that the die had been cast, he felt that he ought to lose no time in getting to Lisbon and finding out the situation there. He knew that Junot would move as fast as the terrain permitted. For him this was not only a matter of pleasing his master. It was a personal affair.

Andoroche Junot, now Duc d'Abrantes, had been one of Napoleon's sergeants when he had been a junior officer of Artillery at the seige of Toulon; then when promoted, Bonaparte had made him his first A.D.C. Later, when the Corsican was living on a shoe-string in Paris, Junot had frequently given him bed and board and lent him money. In view of Napoleon's well-known attribute of never forgetting, and always rewarding old friends, it had surprised everyone that, when he had announced the names of the Generals he had selected to become Marshals of the Empire, he had not included that of Junot. But, when choosing the men he had made Marshals, Napoleon had been influenced by three things. Either, like Bernadotte, they must be kept sweet because they were politically dangerous; or, like Masséna, be rewarded because they had led their troops to victory in great campaigns; or—at least like Davoust and Bessières—shown that they had the qualities needed to command an army in the field.

Poor Junot had none of these qualifications. He was just a brave but not very intelligent soldier; so he had been given the sop of being made a Duke and the Military Governor of Paris. But now, as Roger saw it, in this new campaign, where there could be no opposition from a formidable enemy army, the Emperor was giving his old friend a chance to win his Marshal's baton. That meant that Junot would drive his troops to the limit, in order to reach Lisbon at the earliest possible moment.

Three days after leaving Madrid, Roger reached Alencantares, a few miles short of the Portuguese frontier. At the inn there he again studied his face in a mirror. Side-whiskers, ending in fine 'mutton-chops' graced both cheeks, and a short moustache brushed up at each end gave him the look of a man in the latest fashion; but he was not entirely satisfied that this had sufficiently changed his appearance.

While in Madrid he had bought from an apothecary a bottle of hair dye which, had he used it indiscriminately, could have turned his hair ginger. Adding only a few drops to a basin of water, he proceeded to rinse his hair. To his satisfaction, this resulted in giving his normally brown hair, with its white wings above the ears, just sufficient tint to suggest that either his mother or father had been a red-head.

He then changed into his civilian suit, and went downstairs to eat a dinner, the main course of which was so highly flavoured with garlic that, after a few mouthfuls, he had to abandon it and make do on fruit.

At the frontier next day he presented himself as Mr. Roger Brook, an English gentleman of means travelling for pleasure; and explained his being unattended by saying that a few days earlier his servant had met with an accident, and would rejoin him as soon as he was well enough to leave hospital. At that period many wealthy English 'milor's' spent a month or more in Portugal during the winter, and were always welcome; so no difficulties were made about Roger's proceeding. On the 10th November, he reached Lisbon and took a room at the *Leão d'ouro*.

That evening, feeling certain that the Foreign Office would know if such a distinguished diplomat as the Marquis de Pombal had returned to Portugal, Roger had himself taken there in a sedan chair, and asked to see someone in the Eastern department. After a prolonged wait, he was taken upstairs and a junior official dealt with his enquiry. De Pombal had not arrived, and no news of him had been received for several months.

Momentarily Roger was shaken by the awful thought that the ship in which the beautiful Lisala was sailing might have been wrecked or captured by pirates. But he swiftly re-assured himself. After all, he had not expected that she would reach Lisbon before him, and during their long voyage her father would have had no means of communicating with the Foreign Minister.

Roger's next visit was to the British Legation. There he learned that the Minister *en poste* was Viscount Strangford. Roger had never met him, but knew him by repute. While still a young man he had made quite a name for himself in the literary world, through translating the poems of Luis de Camoens from the Portuguese. They were of a sentimental nature, well calculated to appeal to the romantic-minded young ladies of that day, so enjoyed a great vogue.

Having sent in his name, with a message to the effect that he had a communication of some interest to make, Roger was informed by a secretary that His Excellency would receive him at six o'clock the following evening.

Never before having been in the Portuguese capital, Roger spent the next day first driving round the city, then entering into casual conversation with several people in the parlour of his inn. All of them were aware that the future of their country had again become precarious; but none of them yet knew that Napoleon had already launched an army for its conquest. Having during the past six years been menaced by France and Spain on several occasions and nothing having come of it, the general opinion of the Portuguese was that the present crisis would also blow over.

Roger found them pro-British to a man. Portugal's most valuable export was the port wine from Oporto, at the mouth of the Douro, the second largest city in Portugal, and almost an English colony. In Lisbon, too, there was a whole section of the city known as Buenos Aires, in which lived hundreds of British merchants.

The British were also far more numerous and popular in

Portuguese society than the wealthy of any other nation. For many years the genial Prince Augustus, Duke of Sussex, had wintered in Portugal and many English nobles had villas there.

That evening Roger was received by Lord Strangford. The diplomat's age was then twenty-seven. He was a handsome man, whose aquiline nose, firm, thin-lipped mouth and cleft chin gave him the appearance of a born aristocrat. His hair was red, and his eyes bright blue, but set rather too close together. It was evident that he had a very high opinion of himself, and Roger was not favourably impressed by his lazy and rather pompous manner.

Having made his bow, Roger said, 'Normally, I would not have troubled Your Lordship by requesting an interview; but have only left my name as a British subject who has arrived in Lisbon. However, I have come from Madrid, and felt that it might interest you to know the present situation there.'

'Indeed,' the Minister replied a shade coldly. 'That was good of you, Mr. Brook. But I am extremely busy, and if it is only gossip that you have picked up, I doubt if it could be of much value to me.'

Roger's object in securing an interview was to find out what was going on in Portugal's highest circles; so, instead of showing resentment at this snub, he smiled and said:

'Would Your Lordship regard it as mere gossip if I stated that on October 27th a treaty was signed at Fontainebleau by which, in return for the southern part of Portugal as a kingdom, the Prince of Peace has sold out his country; and that General Junot, with an army of thirty thousand men, has already crossed the Pyrenees on his march to Lisbon?'

Strangford's bright eyes opened wide in surprise. 'How in heaven's name, did you come to learn of this in Madrid, days, nay a week ago, when I had news of it only this morning?'

Roger shrugged. 'Since I was a youth I have spent at least half my time travelling on the Continent. During those years I have made the acquaintance of Kings and Ministers. In Madrid, as in numerous other capitals, I have old friends who, at times, tell me things that they should keep secret. I also have powerful friends in England, Mr. Canning among them.'

The Minister's attitude underwent a sudden change. 'You must forgive me, Mr. Brook, for having underrated the information you may be able to give me. I should be glad to have it. Be pleased to take a chair.'

Sitting down, Roger gave an account of all that he had gathered in Madrid: the universal hatred of Godoy, the abortive conspiracy of Prince Ferdinand to usurp his father's throne, the reluctance of the Spaniards to be forced into going to war again, and numerous other matters that might influence Spanish policy.

When he had done, as he had hoped would be the case, Strangford began to talk freely of the situation with him. Heaving a sigh the Minister said:

'At the moment I find my position here one of the utmost difficulty. On account of my knowledge of Portuguese, I was sent out in 1802 as First Secretary to the Legation. In 1806, I was promoted to Minister Plenipotentiary. The Portuguese received me most kindly and have a high opinion of me. No diplomat could have occupied a more congenial post, but for one thing—his dealings with the royal family.

'As you must know, Queen Maria is completely mad. Her heir, Don Joao, Prince of Brazil, took over the reins of government from her in 1792, and formally became Prince Regent in '99. But he is nearly as mad as his mother. He is only thirty-eight, yet as timid, irresolute and as incapable of standing up to any threat as would be a palsied old man of eighty.

'For years past he has hovered and wavered under pressure from France and Britain, upon which side to come down. If only he would make a firm decision, we would know where we are, and could act accordingly. The certainty that, when less occupied with more important matters, Bonaparte would invade Portugal and push him off his throne, has led us to urge him, time and again, to retain his sovereignty by withdrawing to his Empire in the Americas.

'Bonaparte sent here as his Ambassador that uncouth firebrand, Marshal Lannes, to bully him into submission. Lannes was followed by Junot, charged with the same mission. We succeeded in thwarting them by sending a fleet under Lord Cathcart to menace Lisbon from the mouth of the Tagus if Don Joao gave way.

'Last year Lord Rosslyn, and our great Admiral Lord St. Vincent, arrived here for the special purpose of persuading him to leave for Brazil under British protection. It was even suggested that, on some pretext, he should be got down to the harbour and forcibly abducted in a boat; but they had to abandon the project.

'And now we are faced with the final crisis. Bonaparte's troops are actually on their way. In the intelligence I received this morning, there was a quotation from a recent issue of the *Moniteur*. The Corsican is reported to have declared: "The house of Braganza has ceased to rule in Europe." Within a few weeks, that may well be. If only he could be persuaded to put his trust in Britain, Don Joao could remain Emperor of Brazil. Yet this flabby-willed Prince continues to shilly-shally, and I am at my wits' end how to persuade him to continue as a Sovereign, instead of throwing away everything.'

For another half-hour they continued talking then, having become fully convinced of Roger's intimacy with many leading statesmen and wide knowlege of international affairs at the highest level the Minister invited him to dine two nights hence, and they parted in friendly fashion.

By midday next day it had leaked out that the French were sending an army to invade Portugal. Rumours of all kinds were rife and the whole city buzzed with excited apprehension.

On the evening of the 13th, Roger went again to the British Legation. He, and several other people who had been invited to dine that night, were told that the Minister was still out at Queluz with the Prince Regent, and it was not known when he would get back. The others accepted that the dinner was off, and took their departure; but Roger decided to stay on.

With grim determination he sat in an ante-room until close on midnight. At last Strangford came in. He looked harassed to distraction and evidently felt the urge to pour out his woe into a sympathetic ear; for, on seeing Roger, he said wearily, 'Come in, Mr. Brook. Come in and join me in a glass of wine. God knows I need one.'

When they were seated in his study and the wine had been poured, Strangford exclaimed, 'What a day! Oh! what a day! I argued with him for hours. No man could have done more to make the poor fool see sense. But the game is lost.'

'You mean,' asked Roger, 'that Don Joao has given way to the French?'

The Minister nodded. 'Yes. This morning he received an ultimatum from Talleyrand. It demanded that I and my staff should be given our passports, that all Portuguese ports should be closed to British shipping, that all British subjects should be expelled and that their goods should be confiscated.'

'Stap me!' Roger cried. 'To require the closing of the ports and the expulsion of our people is a legitimate war aim. But the seizure of their goods would be barefaced robbery. What did His Highness say to that?'

'The spineless creature created a terrible scene, and began to cry like a child. I told him about Bonaparte's having declared that the House of Braganza had ceased to reign; and begged him to preserve his sovereign status by letting us take him to Brazil. At that he jumped up and ran to and fro like a crazy man, yelling, "But I love it here. I have never loved Queluz so much, and you want to take me from it."

'He then ran to his mother's apartment. It being no time to observe protocol, I followed him. Falling on his knees in front of her, he implored her advice. For many years the poor old woman has been incapable of giving advice to anyone. She is convinced that when she dies she will go to hell, and thinks of nothing else. Pushing him away, she cried, "The fires! The fires of the inferno. There is no escaping them!"

'Picking himself up, he staggered to his wife's room and gasped out to her the terrible quandary in which he found himself. She at least behaved like a daughter of Spain; tore off her mantilla, threw it at him and cursed him for a miserable coward.

'The Foreign Minister, d'Aranjo, then arrived. After a

while he succeeded in quietening the Prince. They decided that the ultimatum must be accepted and an ordinance published to give it effect. But that the British should be given some days to get their goods away. Five times the Prince sat down at his desk to sign the ordinance d'Aranjo had prepared, and five times threw his pen away; but at last he did sign it, and went off in a flood of tears to don a hair shirt in the monastery. The best I could do was to persuade d'Aranjo that he would at once set about having a fleet prepared in case, at the last moment, the Prince changed his mind and decided to go to Brazil; though I think there is little likelihood of such a fleet ever crossing the Atlantic.'

There was nothing Roger could say to console the depressed Minister for this major diplomatic defeat; so, having expressed his sympathy and offered his services to help if the Legation had to be evacuated, he bade Strangford good night.

On the 14th, the ordinance was published. The Portuguese were aghast at the news that a French army actually was on its way to Lisbon, and in the English quarter pandemonium ensued. In the so-called 'Factory', where British goods were stored, there were many thousands of pounds' worth of merchandise, and to get it all away in the space of a few days was impossible. To add to the desperate plight of these long-established traders, the rates for shipping space rose within a few hours to unprecedented heights and soared still higher when it became known that the Government had commandeered a large number of ships; although the reason for this action was not disclosed.

For three days these unfortunate people fought ruin and despair with all the energy they could command. Many sold their goods to the Portuguese at great loss, all of them dismantled their houses with frantic haste, packing their most valuable possessions to take with them if they could, and arranging to store others with Portuguese friends.

Then, on the 17th, things took a new turn. A British squadron appeared on the scene and dropped anchor in the mouth of the Tagus. This caused great rejoicing among both the English and the Portuguese, as they expected a force to be

281

landed that would protect Lisbon from the French. Roger was not so sanguine; for, since the publishing of the Royal ordinance, Portugal and Britain had been, at least technically, at war. It therefore followed that, unless Don Joao was prepared to bring down on his unhappy head the wrath of Napoleon, and so reap the worst of both worlds, he would have to order his forts to open fire on any British troops that attempted to come ashore.

However, that night Roger learned to his delight that the Admiral commanding the squadron was Sir Sidney Smith, an old friend of his and a sailor of exceptional initiative. Sir Sidney had won glory aiding King Gustavus of Sweden in his war against Russia. Later, when commanding a flotilla of British small craft with orders to clear the Channel of French privateers, he had led his ships' boats into the mouth of the river Seine at night, in a daring endeavour to capture an enemy lugger. He had succeeded, but she had been caught in a flood tide and carried upstream; so in the morning, fired on from all sides by French troops, he had been compelled to surrender. He was taken to Paris and for two years had been a prisoner in the Temple. But he had managed to escape. Like Roger, he could speak many languages; and, on one occasion, to secure information about the state of things in Morocco, he had gone ashore and lived there for a time, disguised as an Arab.

When the main British Fleet was based on Naples Sir Sidney had three frigates which had been detached for duty at the eastern end of the Mediterranean. Technically, he was under Nelson, who was extremely jealous of him; but, regarding his superior as too distant to appreciate the local situation, he had ignored him. It was then that Sir Sidney had inflicted the greatest defeat on Napoleon ever achieved by the British, with the one, much later, exception of Waterloo. Napoleon's army was advancing from Egypt up the coast of Palestine, with the object of capturing Constantinople, and dared not leave the great Turkish stronghold of Acre uncaptured in its rear; so laid siege to it. Sir Sidney had sent his sailors ashore and the guns from his ships, and succeeded in holding Acre until the French army, decimated by unsuccessful assaults and wasted by disease, had been compelled to retire on Egypt. That achievement had altered the course of history.

It was during the siege of Acre that Roger had met Sir Sidney, and supplied him with most valuable information. In consequence, they were not only close friends, but the Admiral was one of the very few people who knew that Roger had a dual identity, and was a secret agent.

Next morning, Roger had himself rowed out to the flagship, H.M.S. *Hibernia*. After receiving him with surprise and delight, the Admiral took him to his stateroom, poured two glasses of Malaga wine and asked with a laugh, 'Do I drink with Mr. Roger Brook or *M. le Colonel de Breuc?*'

'I'm Mr. Brook at the moment,' Roger grinned back. 'But less than a fortnight ago I was living as the guest of the French Ambassador in Madrid.'

'Then I have hopes that you bring me news of special value.'

'Nothing of real importance, I fear; but I can inform you of the state of things in both the Spanish and Portuguese capitals.'

'Go to it then, friend. In me you have an eager listener.'

During the half-hour that followed, Roger gave the Admiral a précis of the information he had acquired, then Sir Sidney said:

'My Lord Strangford came off to see me last night. I think little of his slushy poems and still less of his ability to carry out his mission. The fellow has no guts, and what is needed here is a man who will threaten this craven Prince with death and damnation unless he does as we wish.'

Roger nodded. 'I agree. And now that you are arrived it may not be too late to force him to change his decision.'

'Since he is now at war with us, I have it in mind to bombard the city.'

'That would be hard on the Portuguese.'

'Perhaps; but it might bring him to his senses.'

The conversation got no further, because a Midshipman,

sent by the Officer of the Watch, arrived to report that a barge carrying the Minister was coming alongside.

Sir Sidney, followed by Roger, went out on to the quarter deck to receive him. On coming aboard, after exchanging courtesies with the Admiral, Strangford gave Roger a somewhat disapproving look. No doubt recalling the way in which fatigue and despondency had led him into making a confidant of Roger five nights earlier, he said:

'Good morning, Mr. Brook. Your presence indicates that, for a private citizen, you take an exceptional interest in our affairs.'

The Admiral laughed and clapped Roger on the back. 'A private citizen he may be, milord, but quite an exceptional one. He is an old friend of mine. We were together at the siege of Acre, and I know no man I'd rather have beside me at a time of crisis.'

Roger acknowledged the compliment with a bow, and Strangford replied, 'Then I'll not question the wisdom of his being present at our consultations.'

They adjourned to the stateroom. Wine was poured and, as Strangford sipped at his, he said wearily, 'I pray God that I never again have to live through such days as are just past. The Legation has been besieged by scores of our nationals, begging my help to save their properties; but there was naught I could do for them. This morning I decided that to remain longer would only embarrass my Portuguese friends; so I had the Royal Arms removed from above the door of the Legation, and am come with my most important papers to take refuge here.'

Sir Sidney bowed. 'You are welcome, milord. I'll give orders for accommodation to be prepared for you and your people. But surely the game is not yet up? For months past, there has been an understanding between the Portuguese Court and Whitehall that, should such a situation as the present arise, the Prince Regent would retire under British protection to Brazil; and we must hold him to it.'

Strangford shrugged. 'I have done my utmost; but terror

of the French has decided this miserable man to rat upon his promise.'

'Maybe we'll bring him to honour it yet,' replied the Admiral grimly. For upwards of an hour they discussed ways and means of bringing pressure on Don Joao.

Afterwards, as Roger was about to go ashore, the Admiral offered him quarters in *Hibernia*. Having thanked him, Roger said, 'Later, should events justify it, I will gladly accept your hospitality. But I have a certain private matter to settle in the city, so I shall remain there as long as possible.'

The private matter was, of course, Lisala; and he had long since arranged with an official at the docks to let him know at once should a ship come in carrying the de Pombal party.

Next day the eagerly-awaited message was brought to him by a longshoreman. Unless some evil fate had stricken Lisala during the long journey from Isfahan, she was now once again within easy reach of his arms that had for so long ached to embrace her.

Accompanying the longshoreman back to the dock, he made urgent enquiries, and learned that Lisala was with her father and aunt.

17

The Biter Bit

On receiving that assurance, Roger's heart began to pound with relief and joy. His beloved had survived the hazards of the voyage and very soon now he would gaze again on her bewitching face and form. He was greatly tempted to hurry down to the dock to see her land, but resisted it because, for her to have recognised him prematurely, could have proved extremely awkward. She and her family had known him as *M. le Chevalier de Breuc*, a member of the French mission, whereas he was now an English Admiral's son. That could be explained away only in carefully-prepared circumstances.

Instead of remaining on the dock, he had himself driven out to the de Pombal mansion. It was a fine house, standing in its own grounds on the outskirts of the city. He had already been out there several times, both to gaze with sentimental longing at Lisala's home and to reconnoitre the garden walls, with the possibility in view that a night might come when he would climb over to keep a secret rendezvous with her.

Now, he had his carriage pull up fifty yards short of the big, wrought-iron main gates. An hour went by, then another. At length his patience was rewarded. A cavalcade, consisting of two coaches followed by three wagons, appeared at the far end of the street. Evidently a messenger had been sent ahead with news that the family had landed, for the gates were opened by a gardener.

As the first coach turned in through the gates, Roger saw the Marquis clearly, then he caught just a glimpse of his divinity, and her aunt, on the back seat. Again a surge of relief and delight ran through him. His prayers that no fell disease might strike Lisala during the long voyage, had been answered.

The problem now was how to present himself. Suddenly it struck him that he had been absurdly lax in not already having thought out a way to do so during the past week. Before that, social life in Lisbon had continued normally. He had taken it for granted that when Lisala did arrive, he would find no difficulty in coming face to face with her at the Opera or at some reception to which he could get himself invited. But since the publication of the Royal ordinance, all normal activities had ceased. There were no Court functions, all places of public entertainment were closed; so, too, were many of the biggest mansions, their owners having retired to country estates from dread of the coming of the French army. That night, he racked his brains in vain for some means by which, without approaching her direct, he could appear before her.

Next day, as he again went off to the *Hibernia*, he happened to recall one of his Portuguese acquaintances mentioning that when Lord St. Vincent's fleet had been in Lisbon, the Admiral had kept open house in his flagship, and that hundreds of Portuguese gentry had been entertained in her and other vessels. He wondered for a moment if he could get Sir Sidney to give a party and include the de Pombals in his invitations. But he dismissed the thought as impossible almost as soon as it entered his head. Theoretically, at least, Portugal was now at war with Britain.

On reaching *Hibernia*, he learned that the Admiral was not aboard and might not be back for some hours, as he had only just left to carry out an inspection of one of his other ships. Strangford was in the stateroom, lazily scanning a book of Portuguese verse. After a short conversation, Roger realised that no new plan to get the better of the French was in the making, and it was obvious that His Lordship had given up. Again obsessed with his own problem, Roger had himself rowed back to the city.

That afternoon a possible way of solving it at last came to him. When in Isfahan, a Catholic chaplain had celebrated Mass every morning in the Embassy. No doubt here in Lisbon the de Pombals attended Mass daily at home in a private chapel; but on Sunday, all the odds were that they would go to church. If so, that could provide him with the sort of situation he was so eager to bring about. As it was a Friday, he would have to wait for two days before he could put his plan into execution, but at least he now had something to hope for.

He had been greatly tempted to loiter in the neighbourhood of the de Pombal mansion, on the chance of catching another glimpse of Lisala; but had resisted it because the last thing he wanted was to be recognised hanging about near the gate. On the Saturday, to keep his mind off this temptation, he again went out to the *Hibernia*. Neither Sir Sidney nor Strangford had any news for him, but the former invited him to remain on board for dinner.

It proved a somewhat gloomy meal, as Strangford was much more adept at showing his handsome person off in a mixed society, composed mainly of women, than participating in doing his share of hard drinking with men; and Roger found it difficult to keep his mind on the conversation. But he more than did justice to the Admiral's port and, when rowed ashore, was distinctly mellow.

Nevertheless, he was up by five the following morning, as there was the possibility that the de Pombals might attend early Mass. When the closed carriage which he had ordered pulled up not far from the gates of the de Pombal mansion, there were still only a few people about, and he settled down to wait with as much patience as he could. From time to time he took out his big turnip watch and the minute hand seemed positively to crawl. But at last his patience was rewarded. A large, gilded coach appeared; the Marquis and two ladies were in it. He could not see their faces, but had little doubt that Lisala was one of them. His driver already had his instructions, and they followed the coach to the Church of San Miguel.

As the de Pombal party alighted, Roger's heart gave a happy bound. One of the ladies was Lisala, the other her elderly duenna. The two footmen who had been perched on the stand at the back of the coach took *prie-dieus* for their master and the ladies from the boot, and the whole party went up the steps of the church. As soon as they had disappeared inside it, Roger paid off his coachman and entered after them.

As was usual in those days, the church had no pews, so the majority of the congregation was standing. Roger took up a strategic position in accordance with his plan, beside the holy-water stoup, which was just inside the main door. Now he was filled with impatience and could hardly wait until the service was over.

At last the genuflecting and intoning ceased and, after final bobs in the direction of the high altar, the worshippers turned about, to leave by the door. For an agonising two minutes Roger waited as the crowd flowed past, then he saw the de Pombals coming towards him. Lisala's hand was resting on her father's arm and her eyes were demurely cast down. The Marquis was exchanging politenesses with an acquaintance, so he did not notice Roger dip his fingers in the holy-water stoup and extend his hand so that Lisala could not fail to see it.

The practice of a stranger offering Holy Water to a lady after she had attended Mass was very common and nobody thought anything of it. Many years before, Roger had made use of the custom to pass notes to the beautiful Athenais de Rochambeau; but now he had no *billet-doux* palmed in his hand.

To his consternation Lisala touched his fingers, but did not look up. For a moment his heart dropped like lead. She was about to move on without even a glance at him. His ruse had failed. Then the Marquis, reacting to Lisala's brief pause, turned and looked straight into Roger's face. Halting, he exclaimed:

'It can't be! Yes, it must be, *le Chevalier de Breuc.*'

Roger bowed, shook his head, then smiled. 'No, *Senhor*. You are mistaken. But I understand the reason for your error. It has happened to me many times before. You have taken me for my French cousin. My name is Roger Brook; and I am an Englishman.'

Lisala and the *Senhora* Christina were now also staring at Roger. With a little gasp, Lisala exclaimed, 'But this is incredible! The likeness! We are recently arrived from Isfahan and . . . and came to know Colonel Breuc well there. You might be his twin.'

E.I.A.M.—K   289

'True, *Senhorita*, people have often said that.' Roger laughed. 'Our fathers were twins, and my cousin and I were born within a month of each other; he at Strasbourg and myself in England. Our fathers were so devoted that they even decided to have us christened by the same first name. But may I know whom I have the honour of addressing?'

'I am the Marquis de Pombal, and this is my daughter,' said Lisala's father.

'De Pombal,' repeated Roger with a bow. 'A famous name. I am honoured indeed. My only regret is that I should have come to Lisbon in such unhappy times. Since you are acquainted with my cousin, it may be that you will consider that sufficient introduction and permit me to call upon you. I am attached to the staff of Admiral Sir Sidney Smith, and find life with the Fleet exceeding dull.'

'Why, yes.' The Marquis smiled. 'By all means do so. I shall be happy to receive you.'

Turning, they left the church together, followed by Lisala's old duenna. Roger escorted the party to their coach and, with many bows, watched them drive off.

When they had disappeared, he drew a long breath and took stock of the situation. His ruse had worked. He felt confident that his plausible story, backed by his slightly tinted hair and now flowing side-whiskers, had fooled the Marquis and *Senhora* de Jahlo. But he was not so certain about Lisala. The great thing was that contact had been established. It was now up to him to consolidate his position.

On the following afternoon he paid his call. The Marquis was out but, after waiting some while in a pillared, marble hall, he was shown through into a spacious drawing room, with wide windows leading out on to a stone terrace, beyond which there was a lovely garden.

At one end of the room, Lisala and her aunt were seated on a sofa. Roger very nearly made the blunder of bowing first to the *Senhora* de Arahna; but realised in time that he was not supposed to know her. Lisala curtsied in response to the graceful 'leg' he made, then presented him to her aunt, who had been told of the meeting in church. She received him pleasantly and invited him to sit down.

To begin with they talked of Roger's remarkable resemblance to his French cousin. He then enquired about their journey from Isfahan. They had suffered severely from the intense heat while sailing round Arabia and up the Red Sea and, on one occasion, after passing the Straits of Gibraltar, had been terrified that their ship would go down in a violent storm. In other respects, the voyage had been monotonous, but uneventful.

Roger's first objective was to convey to Lisala that he was in fact her lover. As a means of doing so, he questioned them about Persia, then said, 'I have never been there, but have heard much about its marvels from a friend of mine who has travelled widely in the East. One of the greatest wonders that he told me of was about a mosque a few miles outside Isfahan, with minarets that shake.'

His remark could convey nothing special to the *Senhora de Arahna*; but it was immediately after visiting the mosque that he and Lisala had gone up the hill, at the top of which there was a Zoroastrian Fire Temple and, in a cave beneath it, enjoyed their first passionate embraces.

As he spoke, he was looking straight at her. She smiled and replied with a little laugh, 'Indeed, that is so. Your cousin took me to see that mosque and afterwards up a hill with many caves, some of which were inhabited by hermits.'

He felt certain then that she had received his message. But the next fence he had to take was the much stiffer one of arranging a rendezvous with her. For the purpose he had brought with him a small, three-cornered *billet-doux*, which said: *I shall come in over the garden wall tonight at midnight, and will hoot like an owl. Meet me there if you possibly can. I adore you.*

However, to get it to her was another matter. He had hoped that refreshments would be sent for, and that he might manage to pass it to her under cover while offering her a plate of cakes. But when wine and cakes were brought in they were handed round by a footman who remained in attendance; so Roger was deprived of the opportunity he had hoped for.

For a while they talked of the terrible dilemma with which the Prince Regent had been faced: either to remain in Portugal and probably be deposed by the French, or accept the protection of the English and go to Brazil. Then Roger felt that without appearing ill bred and so jeopardising his prospects of being received there again, he dared not much exceed the regulation twenty minutes for a first call. A prey to acute frustration, he stood up to take his leave. To have palmed the *billet-doux* into Lisala's hand as he kissed it could not possibly be done without her aunt seeing the manœuvre; so he did not attempt it.

A moment later, inspiration came to him. Glancing out of the tall window, he said, 'What a lovely garden you have. And that pavilion over there; how enchanting and romantic. I'd vow that if one were there at midnight, one would see the ghosts of past lovers reuniting.'

It could hardly fail to be a bullseye shot. He and Lisala were past lovers and surely Mr. Roger Brook was the ghost of *Colonel le Chevalier de Breuc*?

Seven hours later, wearing a long, dark cloak, his white cravat and the greater part of his face hidden by a silk scarf, Roger approached the garden wall. He had reconnoitred it again after leaving the mansion that afternoon and had found a place where, by climbing on to the roof of a shack, he could easily reach its top. On the opposite side there was a large nispero tree. Launching himself forward, he grasped the nearest branch, hauled himself along it and scrambled to the ground.

Cautiously he made his way forward until, from behind a screen of flowering shrubs, he could see the house. A light showed only in one upper window. Treading very carefully, he advanced to the back of the pavilion, then made his way round it to a verandah that faced the house and overlooked a lily pool. As he stepped on the verandah, a board creaked. There came the soft rustle of silk garments and a quick, light step. A figure emerged from the shadowed porch. Next moment he had Lisala in his arms.

He had come prepared to give her an immediate explanation of his change of nationality. But when, after their first long kiss, he began, 'I must tell you . . .', she whispered breathlessly, 'Later; later,' and, clutching his hand, drew him inside the pavilion.

There was only a sliver of moon, but it gave enough light for him dimly to make out that the central room was furnished with cane easy chairs and a long settee. On the latter, in preparation for his coming, she had piled all the cushions from the chairs. As they embraced again, her hands ran eagerly over him; then she threw herself down on her back on the cushions. She had on only a long, fur robe and beneath it a nightdress. Panting with desire, she threw wide the robe and pulled the nightdress up above her waist. By then Roger, no whit less eager, had undone his breeches and thrust them down. As he bent above her, she clasped her arms round his neck and drew him on to her. They came together with the same delirious, blind abandon that had overwhelmed them that first time in the cave.

When it was over, they remained locked together and lay, panting heavily, for several minutes; then Lisala pushed Roger from her, sat up, drew her robe about her and said, 'Oh God, how I have longed for you these past two months; and how happy I am that you should have followed me to Lisbon. But now tell me. Explain to me this extraordinary mystery of your having transformed yourself into an Englishman.'

Still a little breathlessly, Roger began, 'My dearest love, you are to me as a magnet to a lodestone. How could I not follow you anywhere? But to rejoin you openly I had to make use of my early life of which, while in Persia, I told you nothing. I am, in fact, an Englishman and the son of an Admiral. My father attempted to force me to make the Royal Navy my career. But I hated the thought, so in my teens I ran away to France.

'After a variety of experiences, I joined the French Army and was lucky enough to receive rapid promotion. I have served the Emperor well, but have never fought against my own countrymen. The French believe me to be a Frenchman born in Strasbourg; but I have several times been back to England and have numerous friends there. Naturally, they have no idea that I am also a Colonel in the French Army; and I account for my long absences by having led them to believe that, sometimes for several years, I am travelling in distant parts. Knowing the situation here, I felt certain that your father would regard *M. le Chevalier de Breuc* as an enemy and refuse to receive me; so, after crossing Spain, I entered Portugal as Mr. Brook and practised this deceit upon him of posing as my non-existent cousin.'

'What an extraordinary life you have led,' Lisala commented, 'and how clever of you to have thought of this way to rejoin me.'

For a while they talked of the long journeys they had made from Persia. Then they made love again, talked, laughed, and made love yet again. It was close on five o'clock in the morning before they could bring themselves to part; but with the happy prospect of renewing their bliss during the nights to come.

The following day Roger slept late then, in the afternoon, took a stroll round the docks at Belem. They had become a positive hive of activity. The British merchants were still endeavouring to get their goods away in any ship at any price, and now the Portuguese were equally active. There were eight ships of the line, four frigates, four sloops and some twenty merchantmen, all being provisioned in frantic haste, in case the Prince Regent did, after all, change his mind and decide to go to Brazil.

After dining, knowing that he had another long night of love-making before him, Roger went to bed for three hours; then, at midnight, he again scaled the garden wall and, in the pavilion, enjoyed the passionate embraces of Lisala.

Next day, the 25th, he had himself rowed out to the *Hibernia* to find out if there was any reliable news. Sir Sidney told him that Junot's advance guard was reported to have reached Alenquer only some thirty miles from Lisbon, but that the French army, with its Spanish auxiliaries, was said to be in a shocking state. Torrential rains and lack of sustenance in the country through which they had advanced had reduced their numbers by half. Hundreds of men had been drowned while fording rivers in spate, hundreds more had collapsed from illness and semi-starvation. Yet the remainder, driven by Junot who, no doubt, was being driven by Napoleon, were staggering on. In the Admiral's opinion, if Don Joao had had the guts to order his army to resist the French, even the unwarlike Portuguese troops would have been certain of victory.

Roger stigmatised Strangford as a vain, spineless popinjay; since for some days he had made no further attempt to persuade the Prince Regent to go aboard one of the warships that were being prepared for a voyage to the Americas. But that morning, under a flag of truce, the Minister had gone ashore to deliver an ultimatum from Sir Sidney, 'Either the Prince of Brazil would go to Brazil, and Portugal resume her status as Britain's ally, or the British Fleet would bombard Lisbon until it was reduced to a heap of rubble.'

Returning to the city, Roger spent an hour at his inn, then again presented himself at the de Pombal mansion. This time the Marquis was at home and he received Roger courteously; but he was in a state of considerable agitation. He had just returned from the Palace out at Queluz. Strangford and the Foreign Minister, d'Aranjo, had been closeted with Don Joao, while a host of anxious notabilities had crowded the salons and corridors. Apparently the Prince still refused to go, but at least he had agreed that the most valuable of his treasures should be loaded on to the warships, hedging with the statement that they could always be brought back to the Palace.

Roger then enquired whether, should the royal family leave, the Marquis would accompany them.

De Pombal frowned. 'How can you ask that, Mr. Brook? If Don Joao does go, it is the clear duty of every member of his Court to go with him. In fact, many more people will wish to accompany him than there is accommodation for them in the ships. When you arrived, I was just about to set out for

Belem with a view to securing in good time quarters for myself and my family.'

'A wise precaution,' Roger agreed. 'I, too, am about to go there; because in the past twenty-four hours the situation of the English here has greatly deteriorated. A number of your high officials are pro-French, or wish to curry favour with them; so they are beginning to carry out the letter of the law as proclaimed in the Royal Ordinance. A number of prominent British citizens have been arrested; so I am leaving the inn where I have been staying and returning to my quarters in the flagship.'

The Marquis at once offered Roger a seat in his coach and they set off together. That morning Roger had already decided that the time had come for him to accept Sir Sidney's invitation, and had packed a small bag with immediate necessities. On their way, he collected the bag from the *Leão d'ouro*, but left there the bulk of his belongings, either to be collected later or against his return to the inn should Don Joao finally refuse to leave for Brazil. He then drove on with de Pombal to the port, where they separated.

On board the *Hibernia* again, Roger found that Strangford had not yet returned. For a while he paced the quarter deck with the impatient Admiral, then they supped together. By ten o'clock Strangford was still not back, so Roger went ashore to keep his nightly rendezvous with Lisala.

He found her sitting in the pavilion, weeping. Putting his arms about her, he asked her what was the matter; although he had already guessed what her answer would be.

'It's terrible; too terrible,' she moaned. 'Nothing definite is settled as yet, but it seems that idiot Don Joao may yet go to Brazil. And if he does Papa has decreed that all of us must go too. This afternoon he secured cabins for us on a barque named the *Nunez*. Already all the servants have been set to work packing our most valuable pictures and other things to be sent aboard her. But I refuse to be separated from you. If we have to go, you must come with us.'

Roger shook his head and said softly, 'No, sweet. That I will not do. I sacrificed my career with Napoleon by deserting in order to rejoin you in Lisbon. But to go to Brazil is another matter. You can have no idea what that country is like. The towns are small and squalid, surrounded by jungle inhabited by every sort of poisonous reptile, and tropical diseases kill off a considerable part of the population every year. There is no culture and every form of discomfort, including appalling heat that makes life intolerable for several months each year. You and I could not possibly find happiness there.'

'But we'd be together,' she protested. 'And what possible alternative is there?'

That was a question which, during the past few days, had given Roger furiously to think. After the de Pombals had left Isfahan he had contemplated catching up with them on the pretext of asking for Lisala's hand in marriage; but had abandoned it because he thought it certain that the Marquis would refuse him as a suitor for his daughter's hand. But now the situation was very different. The Marquis would certainly think twice before dragging Lisala off to Brazil against her will when an Englishman of good birth and not inconsiderable fortune, whom she loved, wanted to marry her. He had little doubt that he could, if need be, explain away to Napoleon his having left the mission in Isfahan. But he had been within an ace of dying on the field of Eylau. Why should he expose himself to similar risks in other campaigns when, instead, he could settle down in England with the lovely Lisala as his wife? He said to her:

'My love, there is an alternative. I have a charming house at Richmond, just outside London, and enough money to provide you with every comfort. I will ask your father's permission for us to marry.'

For a moment she considered, then she shook her head. 'No, much as I should love to be your wife, I must say "no" to that. Brazil may be all you say it is at present; but with the Court there matters would soon improve and life become tolerable. To do as you suggest would mean that I should be permanently separated from my family, and I cannot think I would be happy living in England. I adore the sun, so the heat in Brazil would not trouble me. The cold and fogs in your country would depress me utterly, and to spend the rest of my life with no-one but foreigners to talk to would make me miserable.'

For over an hour Roger argued with her; but she would not be persuaded so, for the time at least, he was compelled to abandon the project. So stricken was she by the threatened upheaval in her life that, for once, she was disinclined to make love; and, after their last two hectic nights, Roger felt no desire to press her. A little before two o'clock he left her and made his way back through the dark streets to Belem, then went aboard *Hibernia* to sleep in the cabin that had been allotted him.

Next morning he joined Sir Sidney and Strangford for breakfast. The Minister was in fine form, as his mission had proved in part successful. Don Joao still refused to leave for Brazil, but at least he had been persuaded to take up his residence in the flagship of the Portuguese Fleet, and that was half the battle won. For it Strangford took all the credit to himself, although Roger felt certain that it was really due to the Admiral's threat to bombard Lisbon; and Don Joao had given in only to save thousands of his subjects from being killed and having his capital destroyed.

Roger spent a miserable day mooning about the flagship, while wrestling with his problem. After having lived for so many years actively employed in the centre of great events, the thought of going into exile and living like a cabbage in distant Brazil appalled him. Yet he was equally loath to lose Lisala. She was, he knew, entirely self-centred. Her plea that he should become a deserter in order to rejoin her in Lisbon was evidence enough of that, and now she was putting her own interests before his, without the least consideration of his future happiness. Yet she had bewitched him to such a degree that he could not bear the thought of never seeing her again. Eventually he decided that there was only one thing for it. Somehow he must kidnap her; then she would have no option but to marry him.

Late that night he went ashore and kept his usual midnight tryst with her in the garden pavilion. Again he did his utmost

298

to persuade her to let him ask her father for her hand, but she was adamant in her refusal. He then told her of his determination not to go to Brazil, upon which she gave way to one of her violent fits of temper, declaring that he could not be truly in love with her and did not deserve the great love she felt for him. There ensued a bitter quarrel, with tears and reproaches; but at length they made it up and, in a highly emotional state, relieved the tension by a passionate consummation on the settee, that left them both exhausted.

Next day, the 27th, the Prince Regent reluctantly kept his promise to go aboard the Portuguese flagship. Frightened that his people might endeavour to prevent him, he arrived at the dock in a plain carriage, hoping that he would not be recognised. But the scores of bales and cases containing objects of value which had recently, and were still being sent off to the ships, had alerted the populace to his probable intention. As he stepped from the carriage he was spotted. The crowd did not abuse him, but showed their distress that he should be abandoning them by sullen stares and a low moaning.

Strangford, Sir Sidney and Roger had gone ashore to witness the embarkation. It provided a distressing sight, for Don Joao's more resolute wife, who had wanted him to stay and fight, had to be picked up and forcibly dumped into the royal barge.

Simultaneously, scores of noble families were embarking; among them the de Pombals. From a distance Roger saw them taken off and rowed out to the *Nunez*, which was close inshore. Quickly he secured a boat and was rowed out after them. As he went aboard the *Nunez* he noted with satisfaction that the merchantman's gunwale was not too high out of the water for a person to be dropped overboard into a waiting boat, without risk of injury, provided his or her fall was broken by someone in the boat.

The de Pombals were still on deck, superintending the bringing aboard of some of their baggage. Roger bowed to the ladies, then said to the Marquis, 'My lord, I am come aboard to ask if there is anything I can procure for you in the city which might make your voyage more supportable.'

De Pombal returned his bow. 'That was good of you, Mr. Brook; but I have brought with us as many comforts as the confined space here permits finding room for. And it is not yet certain that we shall make the voyage.'

'Of that, my lord, I am aware; so I will not yet take final leave of you. Should His Highness decide to sail, my Admiral will have several hours' notice of it; ample time for me to come across and wish you fair winds and good fortune in Brazil.'

Standing nearby, Lisala had heard what he said, and gave him a sad smile. He then spent a quarter of an hour talking to them before returning to shore.

That evening he said to Sir Sidney, 'Admiral, I have been pursuing a private project while here in Lisbon. I am deeply in love with a Portuguese lady and wish to make her my wife. Would you have any objection to my bringing her aboard, then giving us both passage to England?'

The Admiral laughed. 'What a fellow you are! When we were together at Acre, I recall that you were in love with a Turkish Princess. But no matter. If you have a mind to form a more permanent association with some charming Portuguese, by all means bring her to *Hibernia*, and we'll do our best to make her voyage a pleasant one.'

In the afternoon Strangford went to see the Prince Regent in his flagship. Still, the Prince refused to give his fleet sailing orders, and insisted that he must await developments. When the Minister returned, the Admiral snapped at him:

'Bad weather is blowing up and I'll not stay to see my ships encounter it on a lee shore. Go again tomorrow and tell this cowardly oaf that, should his ships not cross the bar tomorrow, I'll blow his fleet out of the water.'

Unhappy and impatient, Roger waited next day until Strangford returned from giving this final ultimatum to Don Joao. On the Minister's return, bursting with pride in his achievement, he said, 'I used no threats, but by gentle words succeeded in persuading him to put his trust in us and honour the agreement he made with our Government many months ago. He has consented to sail tomorrow for Brazil.'

Hearing this, Roger decided that the time for action had come. That evening he asked Sir Sidney to let him have a boat to take him across to *Nunez*, and the Admiral placed a gig at his disposal.

When she was well away from *Hibernia*, Roger produced a small bag of gold. Clinking the coins in it, he said to the Petty Officer in charge, 'I go to the *Nunez* to collect a Portuguese lady. But her friends may prove reluctant to let her go, so there may be trouble. Obey my orders implicitly and this gold is yours to divide between yourself and the boat's crew.'

The Petty Officer grinned, and replied, 'Aye, aye, Sir. We'll stand by, and to hell with the Portuguese should they prove troublesome.'

On boarding the *Nunez*, Roger found a number of the gentry of both sexes strolling round the deck, taking the evening air. De Pombal was nowhere to be seen, but he soon spotted Lisala and her duenna. Directly Lisala caught sight of him, she came hurrying over with Dona Christina to the place where he was standing, beside the bulwark amidships.

Gravely Roger said, 'I am come as I promised to wish you a pleasant voyage, and to hope that in Brazil you will find happiness.'

With equal gravity she replied, 'That was kind of you; but it will do nothing to heal my broken heart. Will you not, at this eleventh hour, change your mind and accompany me?'

He shook his head. 'No, dear Lisala, my mind is set. But will you not change yours and let me make a home for you in England?'

As he spoke, he moved a little sideways, so that he would be able to seize her the more easily, heave her over the low bulwark, shout to the Petty Officer below to be ready to break her fall, then drop her down into the boat.

At that moment she, too, moved, and away from the bulwark, as she said, 'Alas, I cannot bring myself to it. But before we part, come below and we'll drink a glass of wine together, to some future love that may expunge from our minds the grief we now feel.'

For a moment Roger hesitated; then, feeling certain that she would come on deck again to see him off, agreed.

Dona Christina, hitherto knowing nothing of their passion for each other, had been staring at them with startled disapproval. As they turned away to go below, Lisala snapped at her, 'Remain here, old woman, and keep a brace upon your tongue, or I'll claw your eyes out.'

Leaving the duenna mouth agape and petrified with fear, Roger followed Lisala down the after ladder. She led him along a passage and, pointing to two adjacent doors, said, 'That is Papa's cabin and that is Aunt Anna's.' Turning into a narrower passage, she added, 'They are quite roomy and I could have had a similar one next to Papa's, but I would have had to share it with my sanctimonious old duenna; so I preferred a much smaller one along here.'

Unlocking a door, she motioned him into what was no more than a slip room, measuring about seven feet by four. It had a single bunk, beneath which Lisala's trunks were stowed. Above the bunk were cupboards. From one of them she took two china mugs half full of wine. Handing him one, she smiled.

'This was the best I could do. Knowing you intended to come aboard to bid me farewell, I purloined it from a bottle that Papa opened last night.'

Raising their mugs, they drank to each other in silence. As Roger swallowed, then lowered his mug, he asked. 'What is this wine? I don't recognise it.'

She shrugged. 'I have no idea. Papa could bring only the oldest wines from his cellar, so it is probably something very rare. But drink up. We dare not linger here for long, and I want to carry away a last memory of your loving me.'

Quickly they finished the wine and set aside the mugs. Lisala gave him a gentle shove and whispered, 'Lie down on the bunk, my love. I wish to play the man and have a glorious ride on you.' Two minutes later, they were locked together. When their first ecstasy was over, she made no move to clamber off him, but insisted that they should enjoy another. Its consummation was delayed, because Roger was feeling an unusual weakness in his limbs. When he did at length achieve it, she still did not get up, but lay, her mouth glued to his, kissing him fiercely.

Several more minutes passed before she withdrew her arms from round his neck, rolled off the bunk and quickly adjusted her lower garments.

He made to rise, but was seized with giddiness. With a sudden laugh, she slipped out of the cabin. Calling to her in a husky voice, he managed to throw his legs over the side of the bunk. Then he heard the key turn in the lock.

Staggering to his feet, he lurched towards the door, stumbled, fell against it, managed to reel back to the bunk and collapsed. Two minutes later he was out cold.

When he came to, it was pitch dark. He had a splitting headache and a frightful taste in his mouth. For some moments he could not imagine where he was. Then the motion of the ship ploughing through the waves told him that he was at sea. Memory flooded back. With bitter fury he realised that Lisala had got the better of him. He was on his way to Brazil.

18

The Ghastly Journey

On realising what had happened to him, Roger's rage knew
no bounds. That a man such as himself, who had few equals in
experience of plots and the taking of subtle measures to achieve
his secret ends, should have been tricked and kidnapped by a
girl was a terrible blow to his *amour propre*. Yet, after a while,
his resentment on that head was slightly lessened by his sense
of humour, causing him to see the funny side of it.

There remained the fact that he was being carried off to
Brazil; and that was no laughing matter. For some minutes
he wondered whether he could still evade such an unwelcome
prospect. British warships would, he felt certain, be escorting
the Portuguese flotilla for at least the first part of the voyage
and, if he could succeed in geting himself transferred to one
of them, he would escape making this most undesirable journey. But this was a Portuguese ship. She must now be well
out at sea and, the weather being roughish, it seemed very im-
probable that any boat's crew would agree to take the risk of
transferring him from the *Nunez* to a British frigate.

Jumping up from the bunk, he beat hard with his fists on
the cabin door, hoping to attract attention. But the groaning
timbers of the ship partially muffled his hammering and, apparently, no-one heard it. Hunger now added to his unhappy
state and further hours dragged by while he still sat, in in-
creasing misery, a prisoner on the edge of the bunk.

It was not until six o'clock that the door was unlocked and
Lisala stood framed in it. Looking anxiously at him, she enquired, 'Are you greatly enraged at my having carried you off?'

Roger had long since learned that there were times when it
paid to show anger, and others when it could do only harm.

In the present instance no display of the fury he was feeling would get him back on shore and, since he was now condemned to a long sea voyage, quarrelling with Lisala could make it even more uncongenial. Restraining himself, he replied with a wry grimace, 'Knowing my feelings about going to Brazil it was a scurvy trick to have kidnapped me in this way. But since it is further evidence of your love for me, how can I not forgive you?'

Smiling, she replied, 'I am much relieved. I am glad, too, not to find you still under the influence of the drug. Had I done so, I should have been terrified that I had given you too much. I took it from Papa's medicine chest, and had to guess at the dose. It now remains for us only to secure my papa's acceptance of your having smuggled yourself aboard to accompany me.'

'Smuggled myself?' Roger repeated with a frown.

'Why, yes. I'd not dare confess to having locked you in my cabin. We must say that, out of love for me and without my knowledge, you hid yourself and sailed as a stowaway.'

'And where, if you please, am I supposed to have spent the night?'

'Where I did, most uncomfortably, concealed between some bales of stores on the lower deck.' As Lisala spoke, she put a hand to her disordered hair and added, 'Just look at the state I am in. And I feel quite dreadful. Please go on deck now and show yourself, so that meanwhile I can unpack some of my things and tidy myself.'

Seeing no alternative to doing as she asked, Roger embraced and kissed her, then made his way up on deck. There were already some forty or fifty people, mostly men, standing gloomily about there. The coast of Portugal was no longer visible but, near and far, could be seen other ships ploughing through the waves on the same course as the *Nunez*. Within a few hundred yards there was a frigate flying the White Ensign. Roger looked longingly at her but, as he had feared, the sea was much too choppy for there to be any prospect of a boat taking him across to her. He had always been a bad sailor and was already beginning to feel queasy. But, for once, he resigned himself to

305

that unhappy state on the grounds that it would enable him to cut short his difficult interview with de Pombal.

Scanning the faces round about, he soon saw the Marquis standing with a group of other gentlemen just below the poop. As he advanced towards them, de Pombal caught sight of him and exclaimed in surprise, 'Mr. Brook! How do you come to be aboard the *Nunez*?'

With a bow, Roger said, 'May I have a word with Your Lordship in private?'

Inclining his head, the Marquis left his companions and walked over to a place on the windward side of the ship, where there were fewer people. When he halted, Roger bowed again and resumed:

'My lord, I have a confession to make. I am passionately enamoured of Lisala and could not support the thought that I would never see her again. This led to my forming a resolve to emigrate to Brazil. Having taken my decision hastily, I had no opportunity of securing for myself suitable accommodation for the voyage; so, yesterday afternoon I came aboard *Nunez* and stowed away. I need hardly assure you that my intentions are honourable. I am by no means without fortune, and own a pleasant property in England. I request your permission to pay my suit to your daughter.'

Greatly taken aback, de Pombal stared at Roger. After a moment he said, 'Mr. Brook, I hardly know what to say. By leaving Europe in this fashion you have clearly demonstrated your devotion to my daughter. But my choice of a husband for her is a matter requiring grave consideration. During the voyage I can do no more than allow you to make her the subject of your attentions.'

For the time being, that was all Roger required and to have gone into the matter further might have led to complications. Putting his hand quickly to his mouth, he bowed and said, 'I thank you, Sir. Now . . . now, if you will forgive me, I must leave you, as I am feeling far from well.' Then he turned and hurried away to the fo'c'sle where he knew the 'heads' lay.

During the course of the day he had good cause to resent more than ever having been forced to undertake this long voyage. He learned that over fifteen thousand people: nobles and officials with their families and servants, were accompanying the Prince Regent into exile. Every warship and merchantman in the great fleet was crowded beyond her normal capacity. Only persons of high rank enjoyed the privilege of sleeping in narrow cabins; the rest dossed down where they could on the deck or below it, in odd corners with their cloaks wrapped round them and only the valises they had brought with them for pillows.

He learned that, on the previous evening, the fleet had got away only by the skin of its teeth. Junot and his weary, bedraggled vanguard had entered Lisbon while many of the ships had still been at anchor. The French had even prevented a few ships from leaving by sending off boats packed with troops who had shot down the sailors in the rigging, then boarded the ships and captured them.

But Don Joao, in the flagship *Principe Real* and his principal Ministers, Antonio de Aranjo and the Viscount de Anadia, had got away. Other Counsellors, the Marquis de Belas, Don Rodrigo da Sousa, the Duke of Cadaval and Dr. José Carreira Pieanco, were in *Medusa* and, like de Pombal, temporarily separated from their master.

In *Nunez*, no orderly routine had yet been established. When food was produced in the main cabin at the usual dinner hour, protocol soon went by the board. Normally, the Grandees and their ladies would have been given ample time to take their pick of the most enjoyable edibles, but after a few minutes, there ensued a wild scramble and everyone piled on to his own plate spoonsful from the dishes nearest to hand.

Faced with the problem of where to sleep in the overcrowded ship, Roger went to the Captain and bartered some of his gold for permission to doss down in the flag locker. It was no more than a cubby-hole adjacent to the deck house on the poop; but at least it would not be as stifling as the crowded cabins below decks, and the flags provided a not uncomfortable couch on which to lie.

Next morning he presented himself to Lisala and her aunt. They showed no surprise, as the Marquis had already told them of Roger's presence aboard. De Pombal, who was with them, made no reference then or later to Roger's having asked Lisala's hand in marriage. Apparently, in conformity with his long career as a diplomat, he had decided to leave the matter open and await developments.

After a few days, life aboard the *Nunez* began to form a pattern. De Pombal and six other noblemen had formed a committee, the decisions of which were accepted as orders by the other passengers. A roster was drawn up, dividing them into three classes: the aristocracy, the bourgeoisie, and the servants. To prevent the unseemly jostling at meal times, three services took place at hourly intervals. The poop was reserved for the nobility, the waist of the ship for the ordinary citizens and the fo'c'sle for the menials. The stock of food was listed and strictly rationed. To minimise the appalling congestion, those who had no cabins were divided into watches which alternately spent eight hours below and eight hours on deck. Masses were said at eight o'clock in the morning and four o'clock in the afternoon, so that both watches could perform their devotions daily. Hours were set for games and competitions, the educated were formed into reading circles and held Spelling Bees; those having vocal or musical talent helped to while away the long evenings as a choral society or by giving concerts. The gentry also amused themselves with charades and playing cards.

Thus, as the flotilla ran down the coast of Africa in better weather, boredom and distress at having been uprooted from their homes was, to some extent, alleviated. But little could be done to lessen the discomfort of their quarters, the monotonous, inferior food and the claustrophobia resulting from spending all one's waking hours with hardly space to move about among the swarm of people constantly occupying the crowded decks.

Roger consoled himself as well as he could with the companionship of Lisala. As they sat side by side during the mornings and sometimes in the afternoons, he taught her to speak English. The frequent lessons enabled her to pick it up quite quickly, and soon they were able to talk together of matters that it would not have been desirable for their neighbours on the deck to hear and understand.

But for them to make love in such conditions was impossible. By night and day every corner of the ship either had someone squatting in it or it was liable to be invaded at any moment. To visit her in her cabin was equally out of the question, as at all hours people were passing up and down the passage outside, so the risk of his being seen going in or out was too great to be taken.

The fact that they were constantly together added to their frustration and, in Roger's case, it strengthened his secret determination to abandon Lisala rather than go to Brazil, if he could possibly manage to escape from the *Nunez*.

His hopes of this were pinned on the fact that all convoys bound for South America always put in at Madeira. There, stores would be replenished; fresh fruit, vegetables and live-stock would be taken on board. During that activity it seemed certain that an opportunity would occur for him to go ashore and, if British warships were still escorting the convoy, secure a passage home in one of them; or, at the worst, remain there until a ship called that would take him back to Europe.

On the evening they sighted the island he felt very heavy-hearted and talked with special tenderness to Lisala; for he was terribly distressed at the thought of parting from her. But long experience had taught him that, sooner or later, all passionate attachments, except that between him and Georgina, declined at best into no more than an affectionate relationship; and that, after a year or two he would meet with some other woman whose beauty and personality would set his brain on fire.

But his secret plans were set at naught by the elements. During the night a storm blew up. He woke in the early hours, to find the *Nunez* rolling and pitching in a heavy sea. Prone to seasickness as he was, a quarter of an hour later he was vomiting into a bucket.

When dawn came, feeling incredibly ill he staggered out on to the deck. Rain was descending in torrents, reducing visibility to less than a hundred yards. Every stitch of canvas had been taken in and, with bare masts, the *Nunez* was being driven through great, spume-flecked waves by the fury of the storm.

Roger lurched back to his cubby-hole and collapsed on the pile of flags. He was sick again and again, until there was nothing remaining inside him. Yet, with soul-searing pain, his wretched stomach automatically continued in its attempts to throw up.

Later, he was vaguely conscious that Lisala, who had proved a much better sailor than he was, had his head in her lap and was doing her best for him. But her ministrations did little to relieve his agony. For hours on end the ship continued to soar up mountainous waves, then descend like a plummet into the troughs between them. At the same time she laboured on with a ghastly corkscrew motion, causing her to shudder with every twist, and her timbers to groan from the strain put upon them. At times she rolled so heavily that it seemed certain that she must turn turtle and go down. As, unresisting, Roger rolled with her from side to side on his couch of flags, he prayed that she would. Death seemed to him preferable to continuing longer the torments he was suffering.

From time to time he lapsed into unconsciousness, only when he came to again to enter on a new bout of agonising retching that reduced him to mental and physical exhaustion.

For three days the hurricane continued. At last the ferocious waves subsided into a heavy swell. Still dazed, he crawled out of the flag locker on hands and knees and looked about him. The *Nunez* was still running with bare masts before the tail end of the storm and he saw that her foremast was missing. It had been snapped off six feet above the deck.

Round about, other passengers were lying on the deck, sprawled grotesquely in a sleep that might have been death, or squatting against the bulwarks, staring in front of them with vacant, lack-lustre eyes.

Gradually some of them pulled themselves together, levered themselves up on to the still heaving deck, and compared experiences. Roger learned that everyone aboard, with only a few exceptions among the crew, had succumbed to seasickness. A few ships in the flotilla might have succeeded in reaching

Madeira and sheltering in the bay of Funchal; but the majority had become scattered and were now out in the wastes of the Atlantic.

That afternoon, under still leaden skies, those passengers who were sufficiently recovered assembled to partake of cold food. Yet, when it came to the point, the majority of them could not face it. To the discomfort of overcrowding, which made the ship a human ant-heap, was now added the horror that it stank to high heaven with vomit and excrement.

The Portuguese officers and crew, aided by a number of the more stalwart passengers, did what they could to cleanse the decks of the sewage which had accumulated from prostrate victims of the tempest; but it was the best part of a week before the awful stench no longer caused the weaker elements of the ship's company to be again overcome by nausea.

For several days after the great storm, a heavy swell continued to make life on board far from comfortable; but at length it subsided and the daily routine established before they had sighted Madeira was resumed. Meanwhile, several other ships, including a Portuguese man-of-war, had been sighted and converged to form a small convoy. Signals were exchanged, but no news was forthcoming from any of them about the *Principe Real*, on board which were Don Joao and his family.

Every day carried them a little further southward and, to begin with, they enjoyed the warmer sunshine; but later the heat added to their miseries. Below decks, it became stifling; so the poop, the waist of the ship and the fo'c'sle were packed with a solid jam of men and women sitting or standing, all listlessly endeavouring to get a breath of air. Tempers frayed. There were angry disputes, violent quarrels over the possession of a few square feet of deck and, at times, there were fights in which knives and belaying pins were used.

Week after week the hellish voyage continued, periods of rough weather alternating with spells of calm, when the sails hung slack and the unhappy passengers suffered acutely from sunburn. Dysentery was rife, food short and water strictly rationed. Hardly a day passed without one or more deaths from various causes. During the hurricane many people had been injured and were still nursing broken bones. Others went mad from sunstroke and several, driven out of their wits by their terrible existence, committed suicide by jumping overboard. Few any longer bothered to maintain a presentable appearance. All the men let their beards grow; the hair of the women became lank or scruffy, their clothes were bedraggled and their faces peeling.

At long last, soon after midday on January 20th, they sighted land. Going down on their knees, they gave heartfelt thanks, then eagerly scanned the shore. For a while it appeared to be a solid mass of tall trees right down to the water's edge; but, as the *Nunez* came nearer in, they discerned a break in the forest, then a cluster of small, half-hidden buildings from which a score or more of boats were putting out.

As they approached, they separated, one or more making for each of the ships in the flotilla. Three came alongside *Nunez*. Two were canoes manned by Indians—small, copper-coloured men with lank black hair and painted faces. The third was a ketch, in the stern of which were three men wearing wide-brimmed hats of plaited straw, dirty cotton shirts, and leather breeches. One was a Portuguese, the other two were half-castes.

The Portuguese came aboard and announced himself as *Senhor* Pedro Sousa. He told them that the little township was Macoé, and that he ran a trading post there. When he learned that the flotilla was part of a large fleet in which the Prince Regent had sailed to take up permanent residence in Brazil, he expressed great delight; he regretfully shook his head when they expressed their eagerness to land. Macoé, he said, had no more than a dozen white inhabitants and, apart from primitive native huts, less than a score of buildings; so the accommodation there would be hopelessly inadequate to house the thousand or more people who had arrived in the convoy.

However, it transpired that Rio de Janeiro, for which the flotilla had been making, was only a hundred miles away to the south. Meanwhile, he promised to supply them with as much fresh fruit and vegetables and as many chickens and pigs as his small community could furnish; then returned to his ketch to go ashore and put this matter in hand.

An hour or so later, the canoes began to come off again to the several ships, loaded with these supplies which were received with rapture by the voyagers who, for several weeks past, had been forced to exist on a minute ration of salt pork and weevilly biscuits. With the best will in the world, Sousa could send off only enough to provide very small portions per person; but, even so, they savoured every mouthful with extraordinary pleasure.

Sousa was a guest at this meagre but greatly-appreciated evening feast. Afterwards, Roger drew him aside and said, 'Senhor, I have very urgent business in Rio which has already been too long delayed. At the moment the wind is not favourable to ships heading south; so, if you could sell me horses and a guide, I'd reach the city more swiftly by taking the coast road. How say you?'

The Portuguese hesitated. 'I could fulfil your needs; but there are certain risks. The road is rough, and you might encounter hostile Indians.'

'I'll take that risk,' Roger replied, 'so, when you go ashore, I will go with you.'

He then wrote a brief note to Lisala, which read: My love, do not be worried by my leaving the ship. I'll see you in Rio. Going below, he pushed it under her cabin door. An hour later, Sousa climbed down the rope ladder to his ketch. To the surprise of those who were seeing the Portuguese off, Roger followed him. Laughing up at them as he descended, he said:

'I've stolen a march on you. Senhor Sousa has invited me to spend the night in his house; so I will be the first to see something of our new country.' A little envious, but admiring his initiative, they waved him away.

Sousa lived in a long, low, wooden building which was also his store, where he bartered gaudy trinkets with the Indians in exchange for rare woods, alligator skins and other commodities. When they reached it, one of the half-castes was called in and, over drinking horns of maté—which Roger found similar to rather nasty tea—a bargain was struck. For two of his pieces of gold the half-caste and an Indian would convey him to Rio.

Soon after dawn the next morning they set out, the Indian riding a hundred yards ahead, to warn them of danger, and the half-caste with a lead mule loaded with a bivouac and provisions.

The road was no more than a track and, for the greater part of the way, ran through dense jungle. The trees were taller than any Roger had ever seen. Looped from their branches hung gigantic creepers; huge ferns and smaller trees bearing strange fruit grew so thickly in between that the sides of the track formed impenetrable walls of greenery. For long stretches the trees met overhead so that, in spite of the blazing sun above, the way was lit only by a mysterious twilight. The air was humid and, in spite of the shade, it soon became intensely hot.

Occasionally they forded shallow streams and after a while Roger suggested they should strip at one of them and refresh themselves with a dip. But his companion would not let him because, in addition to danger from alligators, there lived in them swarms of tiny piranha fish that would attack a man and tear every shred of flesh from his bones in a matter of minutes.

The silence, broken only now and then by the calling of a bird or rustle made by an animal in the undergrowth, was most oppressive. Once they saw a jaguar crouched on the branch of a tree; but the half-caste scared it off with a shot from his musket. From other trees twenty-foot-long pythons hung lazily, head down, and to pass them they put their horses into a gallop.

Strings of orchids dangled from roots in the forks of many of the trees; bright-plumaged macaws flapped squawking across the track; and huge butterflies flitted from bush to bush. But Roger, dripping with sweat as though he were in a Turkish bath, constantly tormented by mosquitoes and saddle-sore from moisture trickling down between his legs, was suffering far too much discomfort to enjoy these beauties of nature.

They halted to feed and bivouac on the edge of Indian villages in which the natives were semi-civilised and friendly.

Late in the afternoon of the second day, to Roger's intense relief, they rode into the outskirts of Rio. It was the 23rd January 1808, eight weeks to the day since he had, unexpectedly and most unwillingly, left Lisbon. Never in all his hazardous life had he experienced such prolonged misery. Owing to seasickness and lack of good food during the long voyage, he had lost both weight and vigour; his two-day ride had resulted in his face becoming swollen with insect bites, and he was suffering from sunburn on his hands and neck. But now, at last, he could hope for better times and a resumption of the delights that Lisala was so eager to give him.

His first impression of Rio was its staggering beauty. The broad estuary on the inner side of which it lay was so long that its discoverer, André Gonçalves, sailing up it on the first day of the year 1502, had christened it the *River* of January.

The cloudless azure sky, reflected in the waters of its many bays, made them a heavenly blue. Slopes covered with the bright green of palms and other tropical vegetation rose from them. In places spurs of high land ran right down to the sea. The spurs led up to a panorama of lofty hills, beyond which were range after range of mountains, lavender-hued as they faded into the far distance.

But as they advanced into the city itself, Roger's elation at the sight of this beautiful setting swiftly evaporated. He had expected it to resemble a second-rate town in Spain or Portugal, with straggling suburbs of poor dwellings; but, as the capital of one of the greatest colonies in the world, to have a broad main street, a spacious, tree-shaded square and a few fine buildings in the centre. It had none of these things.

The only square, which gave on to a stony beach littered with wreckage and refuse, was of bare, hard-trodden earth, with not a tree upon it. The principal street was mean and narrow. The only building of any size was the Viceroy's Palace, a low, ugly block from which the white paint was peeling and with narrow, dirty windows. Near it was the Telles Arch, an evil-smelling passageway, in which a score of scrofulous beggars were lounging. The other streets leading from it were even meaner and no more than alleyways between rows of high houses with greenish balconies and steep grey roofs. The only drainage consisted of gutters, cleansed from time to time by downpours of tropical rain; but, as the weather had been fine for the past week or so, they were now choked with garbage and excrement thrown out of the windows. The stench beggared description.

Roger's guide took him to the only inn. It was run by a Frenchman named Philippe, a robust and cheerful individual, who gave him a hearty welcome and showed him up to a passably well-furnished room. Already Roger had noted that the café on the ground floor was clean and bright, and was deeply thankful for having been brought to this little oasis of civilised living in a town of such unbelievable poverty and squalor.

Having thanked his guide and sent him and the Indian off with handsome *pourboires*, Roger ordered hot water to be brought up, so that he could have a most welcome bath, and sent for a barber to shave him. During the voyage he had grown a full beard. Now he had it shaved off, but retained his side-whiskers. It was weeks since he had looked in a mirror. On doing so it suddenly struck him that the reddish tint with which he had dyed his hair in Lisbon had grown out. But no-one aboard the *Nunez* appeared to have noticed that.

He then sought out the landlord, ordered the best bottle of wine available, and invited him to share it. Nothing loath, Philippe produced a dust-encrusted bottle of Madeira and took his guest into his own small parlour. When they had settled down, Roger asked:

'Would you like to make a large sum of money?'

'But naturally.' The Frenchman spread out his hands and grinned. 'Providing, *Senhor*, that it is within the law. Even a week in the prison here is as good as a death sentence. Each newcomer picks up from some other prisoner typhus, small-pox or cholera, and the poor devils die like flies.'

'No, it is nothing illegal. But I am in possession of a secret which could make you a rich man within a month. And I am prepared to disclose it to you if you can do me a service.'

'Tell me your requirements, *Senhor*.'

'They are quite simple. I intend to settle here, and I want

316

to lease a furnished house for not less than a year. I am aware that I cannot expect to acquire a handsome property in this miserable city. But it must be of a fair size, with, say, six or seven rooms and not in the town itself; somewhere on the outskirts with, preferably, a garden.'

'That should not be difficult if you are prepared to pay a fair price for it.'

'I am. But I want it tomorrow.'

'Tomorrow!' The Frenchman raised his eyebrows. 'That is another matter. It will take time to make enquiries. And the people here are beyond belief indolent. Any notary in Rio would take a month or more to draw up the contract.'

'No doubt. That is why I am offering you a small fortune for getting me what I want. You have the morning to work in and, by mid-afternoon, the contract must have been drawn up and signed, so that I can take immediate possession. Otherwise the deal is off.'

Philippe considered for a moment, then he asked, 'What guarantee have I that you are not making a fool of me?'

On the little finger of his left hand Roger was wearing a fine diamond ring. Drawing it off, he threw it across the table. 'There is your guarantee. Should you fail, I will trust you to return it to me.'

Picking up the ring, the innkeeper made a little bow. 'The moment I set eyes upon you, *Senhor*, I realised that you were an *hidalgo*; and there are few such in this filthy town in which fate has condemned me to make my living. Your haste in this matter puzzles me, as it will cost you much more than you would normally have to pay. But it is not for me to enquire why you are in such a hurry. You can rely on me to do my best for you.'

Roger had come from Lisbon with only the clothes he stood up in, so next morning he went out and bought a selection of poor-quality garments, which were the best he could find.

He then took a stroll round the town, and was more than ever appalled by the filth and destitution that he saw on all sides. It far exceeded the worst accounts he had had of the

317

place, by the telling of which he had endeavoured in vain to dissuade Lisala from leaving Lisbon for Brazil.

The only feature of the otherwise barren square was a rude fountain, round which was a crowd of Negro slaves, waiting their turn to fill pitchers they carried on their heads, as none of the houses had water laid on. Near the Viceregal Palace stood an ugly little church. On entering it he saw, in accordance with the dictates of religion, several corpses laid out. They were already blue and stinking, so another focus for disseminating disease; and he hurried out. He had already noted that everyone he passed was hung about with crucifixes and other sacred symbols, which indicated that the inhabitants of the place were under the thraldom of a dirty, ignorant priesthood.

At the sea end of the square there was a fish market: the stalls covered with filthy, ragged canvas which only partly kept off the myriads of flies. Further along stood the Arsenal and, anchored off it, were a number of fishing boats painted in brilliant colours; adding yet another touch to the beauty of the more distant scene. But by ten o'clock the sun was blazing down so fiercely that, his shirt sticking to him with perspiration, he went back to the inn.

At midday, Philippe returned to say he had found a house that might prove suitable, and they drove to it in a rickety carriage drawn by a starved-looking mule. The place was a rambling, two-storey building, standing in two acres of garden and woodland, on a slight eminence just outside the town. It was sparsely furnished and in bad repair; but its accommodation was ample for Roger's requirements and in front it had a long verandah, from which there was a splendid view of the lovely bay.

The owner was a childless widow who, Philippe had informed Roger on their way there, had been left badly off and was having difficulty in making both ends meet. She received them courteously and a Negress slave brought coffee for them. Evidently having seen in Philippe's approach that morning a probability that she might be able to dispose of her property for a good round sum, and settle permanently in more economical quarters, she announced that, having thought matters over, she was averse to letting the house but was prepared to sell it; and named a figure.

Roger still had a considerable sum in gold in his money-belt, but nowhere near enough to buy the property outright. Nevertheless, he was quick to realise that, when the flotilla of refugees arrived, he would be able to resell the place for ten times its present value. So he said he was agreeable to buy, provided the lady would take somewhat less, and accept payment by instalments over the next twelve months. He then excused himself to have another look at the view from the verandah, leaving Philippe, as they had previously arranged, to negotiate on his behalf.

Out on the verandah he anxiously scrutinised the bay as, should the flotilla be sighted before he had completed his arrangements, the advantage he had derived from arriving in Rio ahead of it would be lost. To his relief, only a solitary merchantman, outward-bound, was in sight.

Ten minutes later, Philippe joined him to say that he had got a third off the price. Ten per cent was to be paid down, and the remainder at monthly intervals. In spite of the grilling heat, accompanied by the widow, they piled into the carriage and drove into the town to the house of the lady's notary.

He was about to settle down for his siesta and expressed great surprise at being asked to transact any business with such urgency; but he was prevailed upon by the offer of an exceptionally large fee to draw up a letter of agreement which, pending a formal contract, would be binding upon both parties. Roger paid the ten per cent in gold and the widow duly signed, at the same time agreeing to give possession that evening, then collect her personal belongings later and several pieces of furniture which she particularly valued.

Having left the widow with her lawyer, on the way back to Philippe's inn Roger disclosed the secret he had promised the Frenchman. Don Joao was shortly to be expected in Brazil and with him were coming fifteen thousand people. The price of everything was certain to skyrocket. All Philippe had to do was to go out at once and buy every cask and bottle of wine he could lay his hands on. His profits should be enormous.

Amazed, most grateful and tremendously excited, Philippe set off immediately, to secure the supplies which would prove a bonanza for him. Roger went up to his room and, satisfied with the result of his exertions, but sweating like a pig, collapsed upon his bed.

In the comparative cool of the evening, he again went out and down to the barren square. Round the shoddy fountain he found gathered the notables of the city, as it transpired was their custom. Most of them sat lethargically in carrying chairs, fanning themselves and slowly imbibing fruit drinks laced with locally-made spirit, brought to them by Negro slaves. So enervated had they become by the climate and the dreary lives they led that the arrival of Roger as a newcomer aroused in them only a faint interest. When questioned about himself, Roger said that he was an Englishman travelling for pleasure, and the ship in which he had sailed from Europe had become so damaged in a tempest that she had been forced to drop anchor off Macoé, to carry out immediate repairs. Meanwhile he kept an eye on the entrance to the great bay, expecting that the arrival of the flotilla could not now be long delayed.

When darkness fell, there was still no sign of it, but at half past six the next morning, Philippe roused Roger with the news that it was approaching. Having dressed in haste, Roger hurried down to the square, to find half the population of the city already assembled, and the remainder flowing into it.

A fishing boat had encountered the flotilla soon after dawn and at once returned to harbour with the almost incredible news that the Prince Regent was on his way from Portugal to take up permanent residence in Brazil. That His Royal Highness was not aboard one of the ships, now only a mile away, was a disappointment but, nevertheless, the huge crowd of people was wild with excitement.

The Viceroy went off in his barge, on which the gold leaf had long since tarnished, to welcome the distinguished refugees, and brought ashore the most important ones, among whom was de Pombal. It took Roger ten minutes to fight his way through the crowd until the Marquis caught sight of him and exclaimed, rather coldly Roger thought:

'Why, Mr. Brook! You left us without explanation at Macoé and we have been wondering what had happened to you. It seems you decided to steal a march on us by making your way here overland.'

Roger gave a wry smile. 'It is as well I did, milord; for I fear you will all find Rio a far from pleasant city to live in. But at least I have secured for you reasonable accommodation.'

Another two hours elapsed before Lisala, her aunt and Dona Christina came ashore. Since the day that her charge had gone with Roger up the mountain outside Isfahan, the duenna had always regarded him with suspicious hostility; but the other two ladies were delighted to see him.

He was, however, much amused by their reactions when he took them out to see their new home. They thanked him courteously for his forethought in finding quarters for them, but by their standards it was a poor place, and they obviously found difficulty in restraining their comments on its lack of amenities.

It was not until the evening that they began to appreciate the service he had rendered them. While they rested during the hottest hours, he returned to the inn to collect an ample supply of stores that he had asked Philippe to procure for him, and the Marquis went down to the hard to superintend the bringing ashore by his servants of the most urgently-needed baggage. De Pombal got back an hour or so before Roger, and gave the ladies a first account of the amazement and distress of their companions during the voyage at finding themselves stranded in such a place as stinking, poverty-stricken and disease-ridden Rio.

The evening went in unpacking and in arranging the rooms. The latter business provided a succession of unhappy surprises for the ladies, as they found the cooking utensils scanty, dirty and worn, the beds hard; many of the sheets holed; and large, dangerous-looking spiders on the ceilings of those bedrooms that had not been occupied for a considerable time. But the

Marquis comforted them by saying that, within a few days, they would have all the household goods, furnishings and pictures that they had brought with them from Lisbon. Over an alfresco supper they became more cheerful and were at least able to enjoy the relief that their ghastly voyage was over.

The bedroom that Roger had chosen for himself was only one door away from that allotted to Lisala, her duenna's room being in between. It had been a tiring day, so they all retired to bed early. Roger restrained his impatience until midnight, then tiptoed along to Lisala's room.

It was lit by a solitary candle, and she was sitting up in bed waiting for him. In fervid whispers they exchanged greetings, then made violent love, temporarily satiating the terrible frustration to which they had both been subject for so many weeks. But both of them felt too weak and tired to repeat the act. For a long while they lay embraced and dawn was creeping through the curtains when Roger tiptoed back to his room.

Two days after the arrival of the flotilla, news came in that Don Joao and his principal Ministers had landed on January 22nd at Bahia, the old capital, eight hundred miles to the north; then that other ships of the scattered fleet had arrived at other Brazilian ports.

During the days that followed, it frequently rained in torrents, often for hours at a stretch, and the marshlands outside the city became swamps: breeding grounds for malaria-carrying mosquitoes. Meanwhile the unhappy exiles made such arrangements for themselves as they could. Quite unscrupulously the Viceroy commandeered the best houses in the town for the Portuguese nobility, and the unfortunate Brazilian owners were compelled to occupy lodgings little better than shacks. Other rich refugees who had brought large sums of money with them paid fantastic prices for houses with only three or four rooms. The majority continued to live in the ships for as long as they could, and only gradually acquired mean accommodation.

The newcomers soon began to adopt many of the customs of the Brazilians—the hours they kept, the food they ate and the clothes they wore—which had been dictated largely by the torrid climate. From Portugal the wealthy had brought only their personal servants, stewards and cooks, all of whom were white. Here in Rio mulattos occasionally filled such posts; but the great majority of servants were Negro slaves, and such exiles as could afford to do so bought one or several of them.

De Pombal purchased seven: two to do the menial tasks in the house, four to act as stablemen or carry the heavily-curtained sedan chairs used by the ladies when they went into the town, and a seventh who acted as a guard to keep the swarms of beggars from molesting them.

This last was named Baob, and he was a much superior man to the average slave. He was a magnificent specimen of the Negro and claimed to be the son of an African chief. As it was several years since he had been shipped over to Rio, he knew the city thoroughly and was unusually intelligent. In accordance with custom there, the Marquis had made for him a smart livery in the de Pombal colours. Waving his long staff threateningly as he preceded the ladies, he made a most imposing figure. When not so employed he had the free run of the house and was always on call for any small service they required.

When the people of quality had settled in, they began to visit one another at their new homes, spending hours over meagre refreshments while they aired their bitter complaints. Roger accompanied the de Pombals on these occasions, and to a reception given by the Viceroy. The so-called 'Palace' proved to be on a par with the rest of the town. Starved for many years by the Home Government of sufficient funds to maintain a state in keeping with their high office, the Viceroys had lived in penury. The rooms had not been redecorated for several generations; the furniture was conspicuous by its very scantiness; most of such chairs and sofas as there were had cotton covers to conceal the fact that in places their brocade had rotted away; and the walls were stained with mildew.

In the meantime, Roger was spending most of every night with Lisala. During the voyage being constantly in each other's company, yet unable to do more than snatch a very occasional kiss, had at times made them irritable and quarrelsome. But now that good food and leisure had restored their vigour they were enjoying the renewal of their passion with the same abandon and delight as they had experienced during the first hectic nights they had spent together in Isfahan; and, so far, they had no reason to believe that any member of the household suspected their liaison.

It was January 31st, the morning after the Viceroy's reception, that de Pombal, being alone with Roger after breakfast, said to him with a serious mien:

'Mr. Brook, for some days past I have felt that I must broach to you a matter that has been much on my mind. Either you or I—or rather, I and my family—must leave this house.'

19

A Bolt from the Blue

Roger immediately jumped to the conclusion that somehow the Marquis had found out about his nightly visits to Lisala, and that he himself was in for an extremely unpleasant quarter of an hour. To gain a little time, he frowned and said:

'My Lord, I fail to understand . . .'

'It is on account of your relationship with Lisala,' de Pombal promptly informed him.

His worst fears confirmed, Roger decided that, instead of expressing regret and bowing under the abuse he expected the outraged father to heap upon him, he would carry the war into the enemy's camp. With all the dignity he could muster, he said firmly:

'Your Lordship has long been aware of my passionate attachment to your daughter. I informed you of it the day after the *Nunez* sailed from Lisbon, and that I wished to marry her. That matters are at present as they are is entirely due to your refusal to allow us to become affianced. You have only to give your consent, and I will happily make Lisala my wife.'

With a mildness that, in the circumstances, Roger found truly amazing, the Marquis replied, 'Mr. Brook, I willingly concede that the present situation is of my own making; because, although I refused my consent to an engagement, I did give you permission to make Lisala the object of your attentions. Seeing that the two of you were about to be confined for several weeks in the close quarters of a crowded ship, I saw no alternative. But now that we are settled here in Brazil I cannot allow the association to continue. The fact that you are living under the same roof, and your constant attendance on her wherever we go, is prejudicial to my arranging for her

325

a . . . er . . . please forgive the expression but I must be plain . . . a more suitable marriage.'

Roger's surprise at de Pombal's forbearance was swiftly overtaken by relief. His last words were a clear indication that, after all, he did not know that his daughter was Roger's mistress. He was simply anxious to secure for her a husband of his own choice; and, as long as the handsome Mr. Brook continued to be her constant companion, that would prove a serious obstacle to arranging a match.

The relief Roger felt was only momentary. He had escaped the scathing reproaches of an indignant parent, but was still faced with the prospect of being again separated from his bewitching Lisala. With a frown, he asked:

'In what way, milord, do you consider me an unsuitable husband for your daughter? I possess a not inconsiderable fortune and from England I can, in due course, have funds transmitted to me here. Whereas the Portuguese nobility now in Brazil are cut off from their sources of revenue; and will remain so as long as the Emperor Napoleon continues master of the Continent. With regard to birth, I consider few of your friends my superior. I am the son of an English Admiral and, on my mother's side, have noble blood. She was the daughter of a Scottish Earl.'

De Pombal's eyes suddenly grew hard, and his voice harsh. 'So you say; but I have no guarantee that you are speaking the truth!'

'My Lord!' Roger began an indignant protest.

Angrily the Marquis cut him short. 'Can you deny that when we first met you styled yourself *M. le Colonel Chevalier de Breuc*?'

This bombshell took Roger entirely by surprise and he could not altogether conceal his dismay as the hatchet-faced Marquis went on scathingly:

'Have you recently regarded yourself in a mirror? If so, you must have seen that, since leaving Lisbon, your hair has reverted to its natural colour. There, owing to your excellent English, you practised a clever deceit upon me by pretending to be your cousin. But you could not change your mannerisms.

326

When we first met at Persopolis, you had a decided limp. Evidently you were taking great pains to rid yourself of it; for when we met again three months later, it was no longer noticeable. But while on board the *Nunez* you became too ill to control your walk so carefully. Within a week of being at sea I realised the truth.

'Had I disclosed that when we first met you were in the service of the Corsican brigand, you would have been hung from the yardarm. I refrained only because I at least gave you credit for having been inspired to this duplicity by a deep love for Lisala. It may be that you are now telling the truth, and that it is Bonaparte whom you have deceived. Be that as it may, I can regard you only as an unscrupulous adventurer; and nothing would induce me to give my daughter's hand to such a man.'

Under this torrent of acid denunciation, Roger paled, then said in a low voice, 'I thank you, milord, for your forbearance during the voyage. That I am, in fact, an Englishman, I vow upon my honour; but I do not deny that for many years past I have served the Emperor. That I should have done so does not weigh upon my conscience, and I will happily give you a full explanation.'

'I desire no explanation,' de Pombal replied coldly. 'At best it could be that you are a spy—so dishonourable a trade that it debars all those who practise it from respectable society. I had hoped that when you left the *Nunez* at Macoé I would see you no more. Then, we landed here in Rio and learned of the exertions you had gone to in order to secure for us this comfortable accommodation, I could not bring myself to repudiate you. But now I can no longer defer taking steps to safeguard Lisala's future; and our continued association stands in the way of my doing so. It remains now only for you to say if you are prepared to make the house over to me or if I must find other quarters for myself and my family.'

Ruefully Roger admitted to himself that he was completely defeated. All hope of his marrying Lisala or remaining there as her secret lover had been swept away. Standing up, he bowed and said:

'My Lord. It should be easier for me to find quarters for

·one than you for four, together with your servants; and I am anxious that the ladies should continue to enjoy such comforts as are available here. However, I paid only a deposit on this property, so no doubt you will be willing to relieve me of further liability.'

'Certainly,' the Marquis replied promptly. 'I brought with me from Portugal ample funds. Let me have particulars. I will both make myself responsible for the purchase and reimburse you for such outlays as you have already made. Moreover, I wish to make it clear that I have no vindictive feelings towards you. I shall not disclose to anyone that you have created for yourself a dual identity; and when we meet in future, as we are bound to do if you remain in Rio, it will be as acquaintances who have simply decided that we have not found it agreeable to continue living under one roof.'

Roger bowed again. 'For that I thank you, milord.' As he had been considerably worried about how he was to find the further instalments to pay for the house, its being taken over was a relief. But that had hardly crossed his mind when de Pombal delivered another blow:

'You will agree, I am sure, that a formal leavetaking would prove most painful to Lisala; so it would be best if you left here some time today, without giving any particular reason. I will then tell her that, after you and I had discussed her future, you volunteered to leave rather than continue to compromise her by your attentions.'

For Roger that meant that he would be deprived of a last night with his beloved, the opportunity to tell her the truth about what had taken place and that, her father's having identified him as *Colonel de Breuc* had wrecked all hope of their marrying. But, since he could not say that to the Marquis, he saw no option other than to agree.

He went upstairs with fury in his heart, packed his belongings into two small bags, then sat down to write a note to Lisala. In it he told her the reason for his leaving, said that he would do his utmost to devise a way by which they could meet in secret, and vowed his eternal devotion.

His next problem was to get it to her unseen. As he carried

his bags out to the stable, he ran into the giant Negro, Baob. It then occurred to him that this newcomer to the household was much more likely to prove trustworthy than one of the servants whom the Marquis had brought with him from Portugal. So he gave Baob the note, together with a *muriodor* and charged him to give the missive to Lisala when no-one was looking. With a cheerful grin the colourfully-clad black man accepted the commission.

An hour later Roger was drinking a bottle of wine with Philippe. The inn was crowded to capacity, but the Frenchman, eager to repay Roger in some measure for the fortune he was now making, at once volunteered to turn out the guest who was occupying his old room, so that he could install himself there for as long as he wished; and said that he would get for him a slave as a personal servant.

Next morning Baob arrived with a note from Lisala. It was brief but poignant. *I am utterly distraught. I could kill my father for having turned you out. You must find some way to come to me at nights. You must. You must.*

At ten o'clock that night Roger was outside the house, reconnoitring it for a possible means of getting up to Lisala's bedroom. He knew already that, like every other house in Rio, the heavy doors were securely bolted and the ground-floor windows shuttered and barred, as a protection against the innumerable thieves and half-starved, desperate men who swarmed in the city. Had Lisala's room been at the front of the house, he might have climbed to it by way of the verandah; but hers and that of the Dona Christina were at the back and on that side there was not even a creeper that might have given him a handhold to scale the wall. Her window was at least fifteen feet above the ground and, clearly, the only means of reaching it was by a ladder.

Moodily, he walked all round the house, then round the outbuildings. In a loft above the big barn the slaves slept on a thin layer of infrequently-changed straw, and no precautions were taken to prevent desperadoes entering there. The door of the barn was a little open, so he went in. The starlight was just sufficient for him to make out a long ladder against the wall;

but a glance was enough to tell him that it was far too heavy for him to lift unaided.

On recrossing the yard, he saw that Lisala's window was now dimly lit. Evidently she was expecting him; but not that he would have arrived so early. Apparently she had been listening intently, so had caught the sound of his careful footsteps, as the curtain was pulled aside and she put her head out of the window.

'Roger, Roger my love, come up to me,' she whispered.

'I cannot,' he whispered back. 'How can I without a ladder? And the one in the barn is too heavy for me to lift. You must come down and let me in.'

She shook her head. 'No. You know those bolts, bars and chains on the doors as well as I do. Undoing them would make such a clatter it's certain I'd be heard.'

At that moment there came the screech of ill-fitting wood on wood, as the Dona Christina threw up her window. Roger had just time to dive behind a wagon that was standing in the yard, then came the high-pitched voice of the old woman:

'Who's that? Who is that out there?'

Lisala had drawn in her head and swiftly snuffed her candle. Roger held his breath and remained crouching behind the wagon. Minutes passed; the silence was intense. At last the duenna decided that she had been mistaken in thinking that someone was outside, gave a raucous cough and shut her window. Before moving, Roger slowly counted up to a thousand; then he tiptoed away.

Next day Baob brought another note from Lisala. In it she implored Roger to find some way to come to her and heaped curses on her father.

Roger wrote back, saying that the only way in which he might reach her room was for her to secure somehow a rope ladder, or at least a knotted rope, which she could lower to him so that he could climb up.

The following day she replied to the effect that he must surely realise how impossible it was for her to come by a rope, or hide it if she did; so he must suggest some other means of coming to her.

330

Although he had brooded over the question for hours, he could think of none, and wrote to tell her so, ending by assuring her that he shared her distress, and of his unfailing devotion.

There, for the time being, their correspondence ended; and he endeavoured to reconcile himself to their unhappy situation. Now and then they met at the houses of mutual friends, but had no opportunity to exchange even a few words together unheard by others. On such occasions her huge tawny eyes silently reproached him, but he could do no more than acknowledge her glances by an almost imperceptible shrug, and little helpless gestures.

With February there came Lent and a fervid display of the religious fanaticism that obsessed the population of Rio. There were fasts, processions in which hundreds of people followed sacred relics of the saints, crawling on their knees along the ground, public flagellations and votive offerings, out of which the unwashed priesthood lined their coffers.

From dawn to dusk the big Candelabra Church and all the others were packed with penitents beating their breasts and wailing repentance for their sins. Out of curiosity, Roger visited a few of the churches, but left again almost at once, repelled by the stench, not only of the living but also of the dead.

For there were no cemeteries in Rio. Everyone of importance was buried either under the floor or in cavities in the walls of the churches. Owing to the high rate of mortality, there had been recent interments in all of them and, quite often, the stones had not been securely replaced, with the result that the horrible emanations from rotting corpses pervaded these places of worship.

Slaves and the destitute who died in the gutters were not buried at all. Their bodies were roughly bundled up in straw, thrown into carts, then dumped on the waste ground outside the city. Great flights of vultures descended upon them and, within a few hours, picked the bones clean.

One day Roger rode out to see the slave market at Vallonga. It was situated in a long, narrow valley between two wooded hills, one of which ended in a high cliff dropping sheer to the sparkling sea. On it stood a small, whitewashed Chapel to the

331

Virgin and the big warehouses into which the human cargoes from Africa were herded, after the tax upon them had been paid to the Crown.

Their sufferings during the long crossing were so terrible that it was a miracle that any of them survived. Three hundred and more were packed into the holds of small ships, where they lay for weeks head to foot like sardines, manacled and bound. To weaken them and so decrease the possibility of mutineering, they were deliberately half-starved. Even so, at times they were seized by a suicidal despair. Groups of them staggered to their feet; then, weeping and cursing, beat with their handcuffs on the iron gratings that confined them. The frenzy spread until the hold became a seething mass of screaming men and women. But their hopes of deliverance were invariably crushed. A dozen of the crew would descend with muskets and pour volley after volley of buckshot into the demented swarm of Negroes, killing some, wounding others so that they soon died from untended wounds, and cowing the remainder into submission.

When the survivors were flogged ashore, their bodies were those of living skeletons, scarcely able to walk, their ribs sticking out under the taut skin of their chests. Still manacled, they were kept in the long warehouses for several weeks while being fattened up for sale. Their stomachs shrunken from many weeks of semi-starvation, they were unable to keep down the quantities of corn mush with which they were forcibly fed, and spewed it up. Lying in their vomit and excrement, they gradually put on weight until they were thought sufficiently saleable to be auctioned.

Roger knew, too, that their last days would be scarcely less terrible. In the Southern States of America, it was the custom that, when the cotton-picking slaves became too old to work any longer in the fields, they were allowed to sit idle in the sun and given enough food to support them. But that was not so here in Brazil. When slaves, through illness or old age, became a charge upon their master, they were turned out to fend for themselves. For a year or two they might continue a miserable existence begging their bread in the streets then, incapable from weakness or disease of doing so any longer, they died like pariah dogs; and the sanctimonious frequenters of the so-called Christian churches did not even spare a glance for the wasted bodies of such human offal.

Utterly appalled by this spectacle of ruthless inhumanity, had Roger been a less rational man he would have gone into the Chapel of the Virgin and overthrown her image for permitting such atrocities. As it was, having long since rejected the belief that, if a Christian God did exist, he had any power whatever to protect his votaries, he rode back into Rio sick with rage and disgust.

At the end of the month, news arrived that caused the merchant community of Rio to become delirious with joy. For three centuries Brazil, as a colony of Portugal, had been restricted to selling her products only to the mother country; and Portugal could absorb only a limited quantity of the valuable merchandise that Brazil could supply. Under the liberal influence of José da Silva Lisboa, Viconde de Cairu, the Prince Regent had issued an Ordinance opening Brazilian ports to the ships of all nations. A still further cause for rejoicing was that Don Joao had left Bahia and was on his way to Rio, which he intended to make his permanent capital.

Lenten tribulations were swept aside and the Carnival that normally followed it was anticipated by several days. The city became a Bedlam. The wealthy retired into their houses. The narrow streets became solid rivers of dancing, laughing people. Silk and satin garments, which slaves were normally forbidden to wear, were donned by the Fiesta Kings and Queens elected by them. Carried high upon swaying palanquins, they made their way slowly through the throng, preceded by drummers, trumpeters and rattle-wielders.

All order vanished. The Viceroy's dragoons were powerless to stop even the worst excesses. Reeling with drink, the Negroes defied their masters, broke into the shops and copulated joyfully with their women in the gutters.

This saturnalia continued for several days; then it eased a little, only to be renewed when on March 7th Don Joao and his Court, accompanied by several thousand other exiles, arrived. The Prince was received with unbounded enthusiasm. Every window in the city remained alight all night. The following morning, a thousand dead-drunks lay snoring where they had fallen in the alleys adjacent to the Viceroy's Palace. The great horde of diseased, crippled and destitute descended on them like flights of vultures, to rob them of the few coins or trinkets they possessed.

From the beginning Roger had decided that Rio was an impossible place for a civilised man to make his permanent home in. For the week he had been living under the same roof as Lisala he had put all thoughts of the future from him, except the possibility that, in time, her father would consent to their marriage. All hope of that had been shattered, and even his ingenuity had failed to devise a means by which he might continue to be her lover.

Several weeks had now passed since they had slept together and the feeling had been growing upon him that there was little likelihood of their ever doing so again. The unsavoury city, with the din of church bells calling its religion-obsessed population to some service every hour of the day, and the disgusting orgies that had been taking place during the past fortnight had, at length, decided him to endeavour to forget Lisala and make his way back to Europe as soon as an opportunity offered.

It came on March 20th, with the arrival of the British frigate, *Phantom*. Roger gave her Captain time to go ashore and make his number with the Portuguese authorities; then, the following morning, had himself rowed out to her. Her Commander was a Captain Jackson and it chanced that, in the eighties, he had served in the Caribbean as a Midshipman under Roger's father. Over a bottle of Canary Sack, they talked of the Admiral and other matters.

Captain Jackson had brought out a despatch from Mr. Canning to Don Joao's Foreign Minster and, when a reply was ready, would return to England. He willingly agreed to take Roger with him.

The *Phantom* had left Portsmouth on February 10th, and up till then there had been little difference in the situation on the Continent. Junot had swiftly subdued Portugal, and Napoleon was continuing to perfect his 'Continental System'. The Kingdom of Etruria, in northern Italy, had, in 1802, been created by him as a puppet State for the daughter of Carlos VI of Spain. That winter he had arbitrarily taken it over, and incorporated the Kingdom in that of Italy, which was governed for him by his stepson, Eugene de Beauharnais. Then, in January, when the Pope had insisted on maintaining his neutrality and refused to close his ports to Brittish shipping, the Emperor had sent an army to occupy Rome.

Knowing the dilatoriness of the Portuguese, it was not to be expected that a reply to Mr. Canning's despatch would be forthcoming for at least a week; so Captain Jackson said he would let Roger know when it came to hand, which would still give Roger several hours' notice before *Phantom* was ready to sail.

Towards the end of the week Roger began to wonder what course he should pursue with regard to Lisala. If there had been any possibility of securing a private meeting with her, he certainly would have done so; but if he made a formal call on the de Pombals, nothing was to be gained by that, and the unexpectal announcement of his coming departure might quite possibly lead to a most undesirable scene in the presence of her family. Eventually he decided to write a letter and get Baob to deliver it to her.

Next morning, up in his room, he set about it, giving as his reasons for leaving Rio: the hopelessness of their again being even temporarily united and—which was true enough—the fact that, having all his life lived at the centre of great events, he could not bring himself to remain any longer in exile in such uncongenial surroundings. He was just about to add how much her love had meant to him and how he would always treasure the memory of it, when Mobo, the slave whom Philippe had procured to act as Roger's servant, came up to say that Baob was below asking to see him.

Putting aside his letter, Roger told Mobo to go down and bring Baob up. On entering the room the huge, gaily-clad

335

Negro bowed profoundly and, as Roger had felt almost certain would be the case, handed him a letter from Lisala.

Breaking the seal, he opened and read it. To his consternation she had written to tell him that she was *enceinte*, and to implore his help. She had done everything she could think of to terminate her pregnancy, but had failed. In due course, Dona Christina, or her Aunt Anna, could not fail to realise her condition, and would tell her father. The fate of girls of good family in such circumstances was ordained by custom. Her baby would be taken from her and she would be forced to take the veil. The thought of spending the rest of her life in a convent was more than she could bear. She would rather commit suicide. Her only hope was in him. Somehow he must get her out of the house and take her to some distant place where she could have his child and they would afterwards live happily together.

Roger's brain began to race. For a moment he visualised the sort of existence Lisala would be compelled to lead in a convent: fasts, penances, perpetual discomfort in rough clothes or on board-hard beds, periods of enforced silence, having to kneel on the cold stones of a chapel several times a day. He could not possibly abandon her to such a fate. And she was carrying his child. From long experience he had always been most careful about taking every possible precaution. But obviously they must have slipped up on one of those first nights in Rio, when weariness after their hideous voyage had made them careless.

How to get her away from her family presented a problem that seemed to defy solution. At least he could thank his gods that a British ship lay in the harbour and, if only he could get Lisala on board, he felt sure that Captain Jackson would give her passage with him to England. But how could that be done?

If the de Pombal ladies had made frequent excursions into the town, he could have hired a band of desperadoes to help him kidnap Lisala; but, as far as he knew, since the beginning of the horrible Fiesta, except on one occasion to pay homage to Don Joao, they had never left the house. And they might not do so again for another week or more. In the meantime, the odds were that the *Phantom* would have sailed. To make sure of her sailing with them he must have Lisala in his keeping within forty-eight hours.

There was only one thing for it. He must abduct her from the house. Already he had racked his brain in vain for a way to get up to her room. That could only be done by raising the heavy ladder, and he could not do that without help. His first thought was to take Mobo with him; but he promptly dismissed it. The Negro was barely capable of brushing his clothes and running small errands. As a companion in a dangerous undertaking he would prove a liability rather than an asset. The penalties for slaves who broke the law were so terrible that they did so only when driven by dire necessity. When Mobo's dull brain grasped the fact that he was being used in an illegal act, he would first take the opportunity to do a bolt, and chance his luck in coming upon one of the numerous encampments of runaway slaves who were scraping a living in the depths of the jungle.

Looking up, Roger's glance settled on Baob, who was standing silently in the doorway, waiting to know whether he was to take back an answer to Lisala's letter.

Baob was a very different type of man from Mobo. He was intelligent, self-confident, and was well acquainted with the layout of the de Pombal property. Moreover, he was already accepting money to act as the carrier of a secret correspondence between Roger and Lisala.

After a moment's thought, Roger asked him, 'Would you like to earn enough money to buy your freedom?'

The ivory teeth of the big black flashed again, and he replied in bastard Portuguese, 'Yes, lord. To do that I's your man.'

Roger nodded. 'Then tell the *Senhorita* Lisala to have no more fears. I will do as she has asked. Later today—say between seven and eight o'clock—return to the town and meet me on the foreshore below the square.'

Salaaming deeply, the Negro said, 'Will do, lord.' Then he turned and went down the stairs.

337

Thinking matters over, Roger could not decide whether this unexpected development was a good thing for him or not. The thought of again enjoying Lisala, after not having done so for so many weeks, held an allure that, as he contemplated it, made his heart beat faster. But he was nearly twice her age, and she was extremely highly sexed. In fact she was nearer than any woman he had ever known to being a nymphomaniac. Uneasily, he wondered whether he would prove capable over a prolonged period of satisfying her cravings. Again, enchanting though she was as a companion, he knew her to be utterly selfish, that on occasion she displayed a most evil temper, and that in her character there was a vicious streak.

But she was now carrying his child; and in him lay her only hope of any happiness in the future. So fate had clearly ordained that, for better or for worse, a link existed between them which he could not ignore.

During the siesta hours he thought out in detail what had to be done to succeed in carrying off Lisala. Then he had himself rowed out to the *Phantom*. To Captain Jackson he gave a version of his situation which was very near the truth. He said that he was in love with a Portuguese lady who returned his love; but her father would not consent to their marrying. He had, therefore, determined to abduct her. He then asked the Captain if he would consent to receiving the lady on board and conveying her with him back to England.

After a short hesitation, Jackson replied, 'I should like to oblige you in this, Mr. Brook, and in these troubled times it occurs not infrequently that ladies must be accepted as passengers in British men-of-war. But I am averse to letting myself in for trouble with the Portuguese. If you can bring her aboard without their knowledge, well and good. But should they come after her and her father demand her return, I'll have no alternative but to let him have her.'

This was as much as Roger could expect. Having thanked the Captain, he raised the question of money. Although he had been repaid by de Pombal for his original outlay on the house, his nine weeks in Brazil had made heavy inroads into the sum he had brought with him. He had also had an unpleasant surprise when he had endeavoured to dispose of a few of his stock of small diamonds. Only then had he discovered that Brazil was one of the few countries in the world that produced considerable quantities of diamonds, and the sum he had been offered was so paltry that he had rejected it. Now he produced the bag of stones, emptied it out on the cabin table and said to Jackson:

'I have another favour to ask. To carry through the enterprise I intend to undertake I need gold to bribe a man to give me his assistance. In England that little lot would fetch at least three hundred guineas. Would you oblige me by taking them as security for a loan of a hundred?'

The Captain prodded the stones with his finger and replied, 'I do not doubt your word, Mr. Brook; but I know nothing of the value of precious gems. However, I will do as you wish if you are willing to back the transaction with your note of hand.'

'By all means,' Roger agreed; upon which Jackson produced for him pen, ink, paper and a sand-horn, then unlocked an iron-bound chest. Ten minutes later, having told the Captain that he expected to bring the *Senhorita* aboard at about one a.m. the following morning, Roger was being rowed ashore, with the gold in his breeches pockets.

On the stony, wreck-strewn beach he found Baob waiting for him. He had decided that it could only prove dangerous to mislead the big Negro about his intention; so he told him that he needed his assistance not only to get up to Lisala's room, but that he meant to carry her off. He then outlined his plan. It was to arrive the following night at midnight on horseback, and with a led horse for Lisala. Having tethered the horses at the back of the big barn, he would go round to its entrance. Together they would raise the heavy ladder to Lisala's window. While Baob kept watch in case any of the slaves in the loft were aroused and possibly came out to see what was happening, he would go up and bring Lisala down. Baob was to tell Lisala what was planned, so that she would be fully dressed in travelling clothes and have a single valise ready packed with only a change of attire, fresh underclothes and her most precious possessions.

The African showed no surprise at Roger's revelation that he had in mind much more than a secret meeting with Lisala, and displayed his intelligence by asking several shrewd questions. Roger than produced a handful of guineas from his pocket and said:

'Fifty of these are for you if you are willing to do all that I require of you: twenty-five before we leave, if I can get safely away with the *Senhorita*.'

For a slave the sum offered was a fortune. As Baob stared down at the gold, his eyes opened wide, their whites contrasting sharply with the black skin of his face. Roger picked five of the guineas from the top of the pile in his palm and offered them to the Negro as an earnest of good faith. Eagerly Baob accepted them, bowed to the ground and swore on St. Balthasar, the patron saint of the slaves, to follow Roger's instructions to the letter.

The next day Roger could settle to nothing. The hours seemed to drag interminably. At last dusk fell. He supped, as usual, in the coffee room. Another two hours crept by, while the other inmates of the place went to bed. The inn fell silent. Having left in an envelope enough money to settle his score, he crept down the back stairs and let himself out into the yard.

After supper he had ordered Mobo to saddle his horse, and another that he had hired from Philippe that afternoon, then take them out and walk them quietly up and down at the far end of the big, barren square. Slaves normally never asked questions, and were used to exercising infinite patience; so he was confident that, even if Mobo were left walking the horses for four or five hours, he would continue to do so until his master appeared. Actually he had been out there for only a little over two hours when Roger joined him, took over the horses and told him to remain near the fountain until he returned.

At an easy pace he rode out to the house. There was a quarter moon, which gave more light than he could have wished for;

but it was not yet high in the sky, so the trees threw big patches of shadow, of which he took advantage wherever it was possible. In the outskirts of the city nothing was moving, and the silence was broken only by the croaking of the tree frogs. Without incident, he reached the back of the big barn, tied the reins of his horses to a nearby tree and, going round to the front of the barn, found Baob waiting there for him.

Together, making as little noise as possible, they got out the big ladder, carried it across the yard and set it up under Lisala's window. Roger took from his pocket a small bag containing the guineas he had promised the big Negro as the first instalment of his bribe. Baob murmured his thanks, kissed Roger's hand and took the money.

Roger then mounted the ladder. Lisala's window, like all the others in the house, was in darkness; but it was open. Immediately he tapped on the upper pane, the curtains parted and she threw her arms round his neck. After a prolonged kiss he whispered, 'Give me your valise and I'll take it down; then I'll come back for you.'

As he spoke, he felt the ladder suddenly shift beneath him. Another moment and it was wrenched away to fall sideways with a crash in the yard. Wildly Roger clutched at the window-sill. Dangling there, he heard Baob shout:

'Thieves! Thieves! A man is breaking into the *Senhorita*'s room!'

20

The Betrayal

At that awful moment, as Roger clung to the sill of Lisala's window, the question that flashed through his mind was: Why should Baob have betrayed him? By doing so, the herculean Negro had nothing to gain. On the contrary, he was throwing away twenty-five pieces of gold—more than he could have earned, had he been a free man, by a year's hard work.

But this was no time for idle speculation. Tensing his muscles, Roger heaved himself up, threw his body across the window-sill, then clambered, breathless, into the room. Baob was still shouting, 'Thieves! Thieves!' and, by now, his shouts had roused the household. From the next room there came the sound of a creaking bed, then the opening and slamming of a door.

Lisala, staring wide-eyed at Roger, gasped, 'Holy Virgin! What are we to do?'

Roger drew his sword. His blue eyes were blazing with anger and his lips were drawn back, showing his teeth in a snarl. 'Fight our way out. 'Tis our only chance. Otherwise this means death for me and a living death in a convent for you. Can I but get at that treacherous slave, I'll cut his testicles off and ram them down his throat.'

He was still speaking when the door was flung open and Dona Christina burst into the room. Her hair was in curlers and her flabby cheeks unrouged. Without corsets, her breasts sagged beneath her hastily-donned dressing gown, giving her, with her broad bottom, a grotesque pear-shaped appearance. The moonlight was just sufficient for her to recognise Roger. At the sight of him her mouth fell open and her eyes bulged.

Lisala was standing several feet nearer the door than Roger.

With the ferocity of a tigress, she flung herself on the old woman, clawing at her face. Screaming, the duenna backed away, tripped and fell. In one spring, Lisala went down on top of her and pounded at her face, yelling:

'I hate you! I hate you! You sanctimonious old cow! For spying on me all these years, take that . . . and that . . . and that!'

Stooping, Roger seized Lisala and dragged her off, crying, 'Enough! Enough! Quick. Never mind your valise. We've got to get away. It may already be too late.' Grabbing her wrist, he pulled her after him out into the passage.

The light there was dim, but sufficient for Roger to see the Marquis, sword in hand, hurrying towards him. Halting, he cried, 'My Lord, I beg you to put up your sword and parley with me.'

'So it is you, Mr. Brook!' de Pombal rapped back. 'Nay, I'll not parley with an unscrupulous adventurer.'

At that instant another door further down the passage opened and the *Senhora* de Arahna appeared. Turning his head for a moment, the Marquis snapped, 'Anna, return to your room and lock the door. You can be of no help to me in dealing with this villain.'

Recognising Roger with Lisala behind him, and realising that this was an attempted elopement, Dona Anna wailed, 'Lisala, what are you about? Dear child, think of your future. To leave your father's roof with a man to whom you are not married would be a terrible thing to do.'

'He wished to marry me,' Lisala retorted angrily. 'But Papa would not have it. 'Tis he who has driven us to this present pass.'

The *Senhora* turned on her brother. 'Joaquim! Our reputation can yet be saved. Mr. Brook is of good birth and some fortune. Far better let them marry than have the name of de Pombal dragged in the mud by such an appalling scandal.'

'Nay, Anna,' the Marquis cried furiously, 'that I will never do. Have you not realised that this Mr. Brook is no other than *Colonel de Breuc*, whom we met in Isfahan? For years, on his own admission, he has played a double game, either as a spy for Bonaparte or the English. I know not which, but it is unthinkable that I should give my daughter to such an unprincipled rogue.'

It was Lisala who caused the already boiling pot to run over. With equal fury she shouted back, 'The choice is not yours. He has long been my lover, and I am now carrying his child.'

The *Senhora* gave a gasp, 'Dear God! What have we done to deserve this tribulation!' Putting her hand to her head, she slid to the floor in a dead faint.

De Pombal gave a sudden hiss. Seething with rage, he raised his sword and came at Roger, rasping, 'I'll kill you for this! I'll kill you!'

Roger threw himself on guard, parried the Marquis' first thrust and cried, 'My Lord, I implore you to desist. I am accounted one of the finest swordsmen in the Emperor's army; and I am twenty years your junior. To have to wound you would distress me greatly, but if you continue to lunge at me, I'll have no alternative.'

Ignoring Roger's warning, de Pombal continued like a maniac to thrust and cut at him. Such wild strokes could be dangerous; but from years of sword-play, Roger found no great difficulty in warding off the attack. For a good minute their blades clashed, slithered and threw out sparks. Suddenly, Roger felt his right ankle grasped, there came a sharp pull upon it which sent him off balance. He lurched, made a wild effort to recover his stance, failed and crashed to the floor face down.

It was Dona Christina. Bleeding and battered she had crawled out from Lisala's room unnoticed, while the terrific altercation was taking place. Thrusting an arm past Lisala's feet, she had grabbed Roger's ankle and jerked it towards her with all the strength of which she was capable.

Catching sight of her duenna's outstretched arm, Lisala stooped, seized the old woman by the hair and banged her head viciously against the wall, until she became unconscious.

As Roger hit the floor, his breath was driven from his body, and his sword jerked from his hand. He needed no telling that he was now in peril of his life. Still fighting to get air back into his lungs, he managed to swivel round his head and look up. The Marquis towered over him, his eyes gleaming with intense hatred. He had drawn back his sword, so that it now pointed downward, and was about to thrust it with all his force through Roger's body, pinning him to the floor.

Only just in time, Roger jerked himself aside. The point of the weapon passed within an inch of his side, pierced the woven matting along the passageway, penetrated an inch deep into the floorboards, and remained quivering there.

Frustrated but undefeated, de Pombal flung himself down on Roger's prostrate body, grasped him with both hands by the throat and strove to throttle him.

Roger seized his wrists and endeavoured to tear them apart. For what seemed an age, the awful struggle continued. Although getting on for sixty, the Marquis had kept himself in good condition. His tall, slim figure was almost entirely bone and muscle. With the strength of a madman he clung on to Roger's neck, forcing his nails into the flesh until blood began to seep from the wounds.

Squirming, kicking and striking at his attacker's face, Roger, half strangled, fought desperately to wrench himself free. Suddenly the Marquis gave a long, agonised groan. His grip relaxed and he collapsed inert on Roger's prostrate body.

It was the best part of a minute before Roger got his breath back sufficiently to pull de Pombal's now limp fingers away from his throat and push his unresisting form aside. He could only suppose that this unexpected ending of the conflict was due to his adversary's having had either a heart attack or a haemorrhage of the brain. Still panting, he sat up, then wriggled round on to his knees. As he did so, his glance fell on the Marquis's back. The light was dim, yet sufficient for him to see that a narrow object about five inches long was sticking up from it. Next moment, petrified with horror, he realised what it was.

The roads being dangerous, it was not unusual for ladies in southern Europe, when going on a journey, to wear a stiletto under their skirts, strapped to their leg. Lisala evidently followed this custom. She must have whipped out the weapon and driven the long, thin blade up to the hilt through her father's back straight down into his heart.

Staggering to his feet, Roger stared at her. With her eyes half closed, her lips drawn back, she returned his stare, and whispered in a hoarse voice, 'I . . . I had to do it.' Then, with a sudden change of manner, she burst out defiantly, 'He would have forced me to take the veil. I'd kill a dozen men rather than live buried alive as a nun.'

Roger swallowed hard, picked up his sword and muttered, 'What's done is done. Come! We are not yet out of the wood.' Lisala's aunt still lay where she had fallen, in the doorway of her room. She had not come out of her faint, but showed signs of doing so. Stepping over her legs, he led the way downstairs.

Normally he would not have been afraid of the slaves, as for one of them to give a white man even a surly look could lead to a terrible thrashing, and to lay a hand on one meant certain death. But Baob was of a different kidney and, having betrayed him, would have good reason to fear retribution if Roger got away. It was an unpleasant possibility that, on the excuse that Roger was carrying off the Marquis' daughter against her will, Baob might induce the others to attack him.

There were, too, the Portuguese servants de Pombal had brought with him: a valet, a cook and the *Senhora* de Arahna's personal maid. Their quarters were in a separate wing of the house, on the far side of the staircase. As Roger came down the hall, he found them crouching there together, apprehensively. The valet, Miguel, was holding a pistol; but his hand was trembling.

Roger now displayed the resource which had so often saved him when in a tight corner. In a harsh voice, he cried:

'Get you upstairs. Tragedy has stricken this house. I came here late tonight to transact secret business with your master. Above us we heard a commotion. Going up, we found that Baob had put a ladder up to the *Senhorita*'s window. He was in her room, and about to assault her. We fell upon him, but he fought savagely. As *M. le Marquis* bent above his fainting daughter, Baob seized on the dagger she keeps at her bedside, and stabbed him in the back. I then succeeded in driving Baob

346

from the room, out of the window and down the ladder. It may be that to save himself he is now persuading the other slaves to mutiny. Go up to your master and do what you can for him. My first duty is to convey the *Senhorita* to a place of safety.'

His story was thin. Dona Christina and Dona Anna had both seen him, sword in hand, quarrelling violently with de Pombal; but neither had actually witnessed the murder of the Marquis. It was Baob's shouts that had aroused the household; but he might have done so in an attempt to cover up the fact that his own act had triggered off the whole awful business.

In any case, Roger's rapid explanation of his presence there was readily accepted by the Portuguese servants, and he had implicated Baob in the investigation which was certain to ensue.

The Marquis alone knew the whole truth about what had taken place, and he was dead. It could be argued that Dona Christina and Dona Anna suddenly awakened, had not grasped the full significance of what was happening, and both had become hysterical. Lisala could be counted on to swear that when attacking her duenna, she had, in the dark, believed that she was fighting off Baob. In Rio, there was one law for the white and one for the black. Whatever view a Court might take of the affair, even the suggestion that the big Negro had attempted to assault his master's daughter was enough to ensure him a very painful death.

Without another glance at the trembling servants, Roger walked to the front door, pushed back the bolts, turned the key in the lock and swung over the thick, swivel bar. Opening the door, he peered out. The moon had risen, and its light enabled him to see for some distance. There was no sign of movement. Turning, he beckoned to Lisala. With a calm and resolution that filled him with admiration, she followed him out.

Frowning, he murmured, 'Having told these people that I drove Baob out of your window, what they will make of my saying that I am taking you for your safety from the house, God alone knows. But, at least, for the moment I have muddied the waters. When the story of this awful night's work

347

becomes common property, no-one will know what to believe. Now we have to get hold of the horses and, as Baob was to have had them ready for me, that may be far from easy.'

Together they walked very quietly round to the back of the house. Screened by a clump of bamboos, they could see both its windows and the yard. The windows were now lit, and the sound of wailing came from them. In the yard the Negro slaves were squatting, talking in low voices and, now and then, looking up to the lighted windows. Baob was not among them.

Taking Lisala by the hand, Roger drew her away and round to the back of the barn. To his relief, the two horses were still tethered there. Roger sheathed his sword and extended the palm of his hand. Lisala put her left foot in it and vaulted into the saddle of the nearer horse. He freed the animal's reins and gave them to her. Standing alongside the other horse, he was about to put his foot in the stirrup when there came a sudden rustle in the nearby undergrowth.

Baob leapt from it, holding on high a murderous machete, with a razor-sharp blade of which the slaves on the plantations hacked through the thick stalks of the sugar-canes. Swinging round, Roger bent double, at the same moment whipping out his sword. Agility had always been his best card when fighting duels. Now, with the swiftness of a cat, he leapt aside and, in one clean thrust, drove the sword straight through the big Negro's stomach.

With an awful groan, Baob collapsed, falling on his back. Roger put his foot hard on the Negro's groin, then drew out his blade. As he did so, he said:

'Why you should have betrayed me, I cannot think. Now you have received your just deserts. Owing to your treachery, the master who was good to you has been killed. Had it not been for that, I would have driven my sword through your heart, and you would have had a quick death. As it is, you will be dead by morning, but will first writhe in agony for several hours. May your own strange gods have mercy on your black soul.'

Bending down over the prostrate, gasping giant Roger rifled through his garments until he found the twenty-five guineas he had given him. Putting the coins in his pocket, he mounted his horse and said to Lisala:

'It is as well for us that he was lying in wait here to kill me. By killing him I have eliminated another witness to this night's events. When a Court is held, it will be more mystified than ever as to how your father met his death.'

As they rode side by side down towards the harbour, Roger badgered his wits for a plausible account of what had occurred, to give Captain Jackson.

No-one, other than Lisala, had actually seen her father and Baob killed. Only the two *Senhoras* could testify that Roger had been in Lisala's room and that she had declared herself to be eloping with him because her father had refused to consent to their marriage. As against that, the Portuguese servants believed that Roger had come to the house to transact some secret business with their master, and that it was Baob who had broken into Lisala's room.

After furious thinking, Roger reconstructed a version of what might have taken place. He and de Pombal had been downstairs discussing business. They had heard sounds above and had gone up. Baob, alarmed by the sound of their approach, had slipped out of Lisala's room, and crept to the head of the stairs. Dona Christina had emerged from her room, failed to notice Baob behind her, and gone into Lisala's. Rendered hysterical by Baob's attempted assault, Lisala, in the semi-darkness, had believed the duenna to be the Negro renewing his assault, and so attacked her. Roger and the Marquis, the latter leading, had then come up the stairs. Baob had sprung out from the dark corner of the landing and, evidently gone berserk, stabbed de Pombal in the back. Roger, whipping out his sword had then driven it through Baob's stomach. In spite of the wound, Baob's great strength had enabled him to reach the window and get away down his ladder. Roger had not realised that the wound he had inflicted was mortal, so feared that Baob, knowing his life to be already forfeit, might induce the other slaves to mutiny. He could not have defended all three ladies from an attack by the slaves, so had decided that his first duty was to get Lisala away to safety.

Parts of this story, contradicted by the two *Senhoras*, might be suspect; but in the main it would be difficult to refute. Roger gave it to Lisala and made her repeat it so that she should have clearly in her mind what to say if she was questioned. During their ride she had remained silent; owing, Roger supposed, to shock and remorse at her awful deed. But now she replied to him quite calmly, so he told her that, when they went aboard the ship, she must show great distress. A quarter of an hour later they reached the shore.

Mobo, squatting on his haunches, was dozing near the fountain. Roger gave him a small packet he had prepared, containing money enough to keep him for a couple of months, then told him to take the horses back to the inn.

As soon as the slave had disappeared, Roger walked with Lisala along the shore in the direction of the Arsenal. Tied up there were scores of boats of varying sizes. Selecting a dinghy, Roger helped Lisala down into it, cast off and rowed out to the *Phantom*. On the way, she dipped her handkerchief into the sea, so that the wet rag would give the impression that she had been crying into it.

The terrible affray that had followed Baob's betrayal had occupied no more than a few minutes and, although it seemed difficult to believe that so much had happened in a single hour, it was only a little after one o'clock. The officer of the watch had been warned to expect them at about that time, and took them aft to Captain Jackson's state-room.

The Captain received them most politely, complimenting Roger on his lady's exceptional beauty. Roger wondered grimly what the gallant sailor would have said had he been aware that the sylph-like young creature who was dabbing her wonderful eyes as she curtsied to him had, some fifty-five minutes earlier, murdered her father. He could only thank his gods that he had been the sole witness to that awful crime.

Anticipating that his guests might be hungry after their midnight elopement, the Captain had had a cold collation prepared for them. As they were about to sit down to it, Lisala groaned and, lurching against Roger's shoulder, pretended to faint. Jackson exclaimed:

350

'Poor lady! It is most understandable that, having arbitrarily left her parent, she should be overcome with emotion.'

'She has far greater cause than that, Sir, to have become distraught, as I must tell you,' Roger replied quickly. 'But before I speak of it, could we not get her to a cabin?'

'Indeed, yes. One has been made ready for her.' Together, they supported Lisala out of the state-room along to a single-berth cabin. There, knowing there would be no women on board to assist her, she appeared to recover sufficiently to assure them that she could look after herself.

Only too well Roger realised that he now had to take one of the stiffest fences he had ever encountered. Unless he could persuade Jackson that he and Lisala were entirely innocent, the Captain would put them ashore, and they would have lost their chance of getting back to Europe.

When they returned to the state-room, he gave Jackson an edited version of the night's events, upon which the Captain became extremely worried.

Roger asserted firmly that, although his real reason for having been in the house had been to carry off Lisala, no-one could prove that he had not gone there on business at the invitation of the Marquis; that his arrival and Baob's attempted assault on Lisala had been only a most unfortunate coincidence, and that no charge could be brought against him other than having driven his sword through, and probably killed, a slave who had, a few minutes earlier, slain his own master.

' 'Tis a terrible business,' Jackson said glumly. 'A full inquiry is certain to be held and you will be called on to give evidence.'

'That I will do,' Roger agreed, 'but only here in this ship to a magistrate sent aboard by the Portuguese authorities. Should I go ashore to attend a Court, 'tis certain they'll detain me for further questioning. That would mean my losing this chance to return to England, and that I will not do. As a British subject against whom no serious charge can be brought, I claim the right of sanctuary in this ship.'

Jackson scowled at him. 'You can be charged with having abducted the *Senhorita*. I want no trouble with the Portuguese. If they insist on your appearing before a Court, I must hand you over.'

Roger banged the table with his fist. 'Sir! You will do so at your peril. I have a second identity. I am also *Colonel le Chevalier de Breuc, aide-de-camp* to the Emperor Napoleon. For many years Mr. Pitt accounted me his most valuable secret agent. Mr. Canning and others in the present Ministry are old friends of mine. God forbid that I should have to take such a step against one of my father's former officers; but do you abandon me to the Portuguese, I vow I'll have you broken.'

The Captain cast down his eyes, avoiding the harsh stare in Roger's blue ones; but remained silent. He had only his pay, and a family at home to support. Instinctively he had the feeling that Roger was not lying and, for him, the threat was a terrible one.

After a moment, Roger resumed. 'I apologise. I have gone too far, and put you in an impossible position. You must do what your conscience dictates, and I'll think no worse of you, nor do you harm. I'll say only that when one Englishman is in difficulties, he should be able to count on the help of another.'

He had given Jackson the loophole to escape without dishonour. After a moment the Captain nodded. 'So be it, Mr. Brook. I will refuse to surrender you, and carry you back to England. But what of the *Senhorita*? Had she simply eloped with you as planned, and her relations learned that you had brought her aboard my ship, then sought to regain her, I could have maintained that, as she was of marriageable age and had come willingly, it was a purely private matter in which I had no intention of intervening. But these two killings put a very different complexion on the affair. Her aunt may assert that you abducted her by force and call on the authorities to claim her. Should such a demand be made on me, how can I refuse to hand her over?'

Roger sighed. 'That certainly is a problem. For you to give me, as a British subject, sanctuary is one thing; but to give sanctuary to her is quite another. Yet I am most loath to aban-

don her. It would mean her being forced to take the veil and,
enduring the living death of life as a nun.'

For some while they sat silent, then Jackson said, 'There
is one way in which you could save her. As Captain of this
ship I am empowered to marry any couple aboard it. Make
her your wife tomorrow, and she will become a British subject.'

During the past months Roger had frequently contemplated
making Lisala his wife. But that night she had finally revealed
herself. Not only was she obsessed by sex and abnormally
selfish. Behind the face of a Madonna, lay an unscrupulous
and vicious mind. To gain her ends she had gone to the length
of murdering her own father. Her beauty was only skin deep.
She was Evil in a Mask.

21

A Very Ticklish Situation

It was one of the worst nights that Roger had ever spent. It had begun with betrayal, involved him in violence and murder, necessitated his blackmailing an honest sea-captain, and ended in hours of terrible indecision.

Why Baob should have betrayed him still remained a mystery. The result of that betrayal had shocked him profoundly. About his ability to force Captain Jackson into doing as he wished he had had no serious doubts. He had in the past defied and got his way with Pitt, Napoleon and half a dozen other powerful personalities on the European stage; so experience had taught him that, by a mixture of charm, subtle argument and brutal determination, he could bend most men to his will. But now he was faced with an issue that only he could resolve. Should he, or should he not, marry Lisala?

It could be argued that it was to save him that she had murdered her father. But Roger had grown to know her well enough to feel certain that that had not been her prime purpose. The deed had been inspired by her determination, whatever the cost, not to be forced into spending the rest of her life as a nun. Her beauty was staggering, and her sexual attraction such that a hermit vowed to celibacy would have thrown over his chances of heaven for the opportunity to possess her. Yet, concealed by that flawless loveliness lay a mind that was abnormal. She had not even shown remorse for her crime, and had faked tears only to impress Captain Jackson. The only indications of her abnormality were that her magnificent eyes were a trifle too widely spaced, the violence of her temper and the voluptuousness of her movements.

Recalling the eagerness with which she had abandoned herself to him that first time in the cave up on the mountain, and the frenzy of passion she had since displayed during those brief spells when they had been able to consummate their love in Isfahan, Lisbon and Rio, he had grave doubts about his ability to satisfy her abnormal sexual craving over a prolonged period. Yet, to take her to Europe, then abandon her seemed too heartless to contemplate. And, above all, she was carrying his child. Dawn found him mentally exhausted and heavy-eyed, but he had decided that he must go through with it.

At seven o'clock he went to her cabin, to find her sleeping as soundly as a virgin in a convent, with no more on her conscience than the necessity to make confession that the sin of gluttony had led her to steal a piece of chocolate cake. Rousing her, he explained the situation to her, adding that if the Captain married them, it would have to be in accordance with the Church of England ceremony. He told her this, with half a hope that, as she was a Catholic and he a Protestant, she might refuse marriage if not celebrated with the rites of her own Church.

During the many years Roger had spent in France, it would have proved a serious handicap to admit that he was not a Roman Catholic; so he had attended such services as he could not avoid, although, like many officers who had inherited atheism from the Revolution, he had never gone to confession. He had adopted the same policy while crossing the Atlantic in the *Nunez* and later in Rio. Moreover, both in Isfahan and Lisbon he had given de Pombal the impression that he was a Catholic; so his admission that he was not caused Lisala considerable surprise.

Nevertheless, she remained quite unperturbed and said to him, 'The time people waste on their knees and the veneration they give to reliquaries filled with old bones has always been a mystery to me. And that women should deny themselves the enjoyment of their natural desires in hope of some vague future happiness seems to me a great stupidity. I have, too, always resented having to tell lies once a week, as so many people do, to some smelly old priest in a confessional. I give

355

not a hoot how we are married, provided it be legal and your child born in wedlock.'

This last possible postponement of the issue having been brushed aside, Roger repaired to Captain Jackson and reported his decision. At nine o'clock, the Captain had all hands piped on deck and, with Roger and Lisala on either side of him on the poop, read the service out of the prayer book, duly uniting them. Roger then asked that the ship's company should be given a double issue of rum at his expense, which provoked hearty cheers from the British tars. The health of the newly-weds was enthusiastically drunk, and they descended to the state-room to partake of a glass of wine with the Captain and his officers.

Their Commander had informed them before the ceremony that his reason for not having ordered a wedding breakfast was on account of Lisala's having lost her father the previous night; so he felt that such a jollification would be out of place. In consequence, even this small reception was embarrassing to its participants and, Roger reflected grimly, a poor augury for the future. Fortunately it was cut short by a Portuguese officer coming aboard to request the presence of Captain Jackson at the Palace at noon.

Already dressed in his best uniform, with a long face, the Captain duly went ashore, expecting to have to resist a demand for the surrender of Roger and his bride. He had every intention of keeping the promise he had made in the early hours of that morning; but was greatly troubled by the fact that three Portuguese men-of-war lay anchored in the estuary, so he was hopelessly outgunned and, if the Portuguese turned nasty, he would find himself in a most unpleasant situation.

Roger, too, was aware of that and knew that if a threat was made to open fire on the *Phantom*, he would have no alternative but to throw in his hand. He could only endeavour to comfort himself with the thought that, if the worst happened, luck and his skilful planning had combined to eliminate any evidence that either Lisala or he had had any hand in the murder of her father. Nevertheless, he could not escape the charge of having abducted her; so, if they were arrested and taken ashore, things would go hard with both of them.

For three extremely anxious hours they strolled up and down, or sat about, under the awning over the poop. At last Captain Jackson returned. As he came alongside in his gig, they saw that his thick uniform was stained with sweat, and he was mopping the perspiration from his face with a bandanna handkerchief.

When he had been piped aboard and they had followed him into the state-room, he said gruffly:

'The city is in a ferment concerning the Marquis' death. While I was at the Palace, there was talk of nothing else. People are much mystified, as the accounts of the affair differ greatly. For a slave to have assaulted his master's daughter is a thing unheard of. The only explanation offered is that he must have gone mad; but he is dead, so has escaped torture, and no-one will ever now know the truth of the matter. You, Mr. Brook, are greatly blamed for having abandoned the injured duenna and the *Senhorita*'s aunt. Apparently there was no question whatever of the other slaves mutinying, and you had already driven your sword through the one who might have incited them to do so, as he scrambled out of the window. It is said, too, by the *Senhora* de Arahna that, sword in hand, you had a violent quarrel with the Marquis before carrying off the *Senhorita*. The duenna is still too ill to make a statement. But, when she is sufficiently recovered to give an account of what occurred, more light should be thrown on this terrible affair.'

Roger paled. It was Dona Christina who had pulled his leg from under him when he had actually been crossing swords with de Pombal. The testimony she would give could be refuted only by asserting that she had temporarily gone out of her mind and had imagined the whole scene. Would that be believed? And the story that Baob had come up through the window, with the intention of raping Lisala? That rested solely on the word of Lisala and himself; and it was with her stiletto that the Marquis had been stabbed through the back.

With narrowed eyes and his heart beating fast, Roger said, 'Maybe, in the excitement of the moment, I was foolish to

357

adhere to my original plan to abduct the *Senhorita*. All would have gone smoothly but for the unforeseen aberration of that accursed Negro. What attitude are the authorities taking in the matter?'

The Captain shrugged. 'Naturally they are anxious to question you; so they have issued an order for your arrest.'

'I'll not leave this ship unless the Portuguese threaten to fire upon her,' Roger declared firmly.

'You will not need to. No-one ashore is aware that you are aboard her.'

'Thank God for that! And I am greatly your debtor, Sir, for not having divulged that . . . that my wife and I are your guests here.'

Jackson's leathery face broke into a smile. 'I was not even questioned about you, Mr. Brook. I think now I have sufficiently paid you out for the way in which you spoke to me in the early hours of this morning. The rowing boat in which you came out to *Phantom* was cast adrift and washed ashore on the incoming tide. In it was found a high, tortoiseshell comb that had evidently fallen from your wife's dishevelled hair, and has been identified as hers by her aunt. It is assumed that you went out to a Portuguese barque which sailed on the dawn tide, and paid her Captain well to take you up to Recife.'

Out of habit, Lisala crossed herself and exclaimed, 'Holy Virgin be praised!'

Roger gave a wry smile and admitted, 'I deserved the fear you inflicted on me these past few minutes. But, relieved as I am now, I fail to understand why you were sent for from the Palace if it was not to be asked if we had taken refuge aboard *Phantom*.'

Jackson returned his smile and drew from the big, flapped pocket of his coat a large envelope with heavy seals. 'It was to receive this. 'Tis the reply to the despatch that I delivered eight days ago.'

'Then, your mission accomplished, you are free to sail,' Roger exclaimed joyfully. 'We'll not have to remain here dreading that someone ashore may yet get wind of it that we are aboard.'

'Yes, Mr. Brook. I deplore having become involved in this whole unsavoury business. But I admire your resolution, and it is clear that the gods have favoured you. *Phantom* is fully watered and provisioned. On the evening tide we sail for England.'

In their role as 'the eyes of the Fleet', frigates were one of the fastest types of ship afloat, and rarely reefed sail, except when meeting exceptionally bad weather. In consequence, she made the crossing in six weeks. But it was a far from comfortable one, and the last form of honeymoon Roger would have taken from choice. As was always the case, rough seas made him wretchedly seasick. However, that at least provided him with an excuse for keeping within bounds the amorous demands that Lisala made upon him.

On May 9th, *Phantom* docked at Portsmouth. Being the bearer of a despatch, as soon as Captain Jackson had cleared his papers he hired a coach to take him to London, and with him he took Roger and Lisala.

As was Roger's custom when returning from long absences abroad, he went straight to Amesbury House in Arlington Street. It was the town mansion of the Earl of Amesbury, the father of Roger's best friend, Lord Edward Fitz-Devérel, who had permanent apartments there, and was always happy to put him up.

They arrived shortly after eleven o'clock, and Roger sent up his name, together with the information that he had brought with him from Brazil a lady whom he had recently made his wife. The footman returned to say that His Lordship had just finished breakfast and, if they would forgive his still being in *déshabille*, he would be delighted to receive them at once.

Lord Edward was an unusual character. Owing to short-sightedness, he had a permanent stoop, which had caused his friends to nickname him 'Droopy' Ned. He abhorred blood sports and spent much of his time collecting old jewellery, studying ancient religions and experimenting on himself with Eastern drugs. But he was very well-informed, extremely shrewd and had often given Roger sound advice.

He received them in a flowered silk chamber robe and wearing a Turkish turban. After kissing Lisala's hand, he peered at her with his short-sighted eyes, then smiled and said:

'M'dear, much as I'd like to congratulate Roger, I can hardly find it in me to do so. Now that you are come to London, and the season is in full swing, within a week there will be a score of beaux besieging so lovely a creature as yourself, and he'll not get a wink of sleep from having to drive them off.'

Roger laughed. 'You're right, Ned, that Lisala will prove the toast of the season. But we have spent the night driving up from Portsmouth, so her present need is a good sleep.'

Droopy had already ordered wine and ratafias for their refreshment. When the footman brought them, he told him to find the housekeeper and have her prepare a double bed-room for Mr. and Mrs. Brook as speedily as possible. For a quarter of an hour the new arrivals described their journey and the state of things in Brazil when they had left it. The housekeeper then arrived and, after Lisala had thanked their host in her pretty, broken English, led her away. Roger's first question, as he poured himself another glass of Bordeaux, was, 'How fares it with my beloved Georgina?'

Raising his eyebrows, Droopy replied, 'She married again, over a year ago. Did you not know? Since then she has lived abroad with her new husband, the Baron von Haugwitz, a Prussian ex-diplomat who has a castle on the Rhine.'

Roger frowned. Georgina remained the great love of his life. Between his long absences abroad, they had again and again ignored other ties to spend happy, laughing days and nights together. To learn that, on this occasion, he was to be denied yet another glorious secret reunion with her was a heavy blow.

At length he said, 'I think I once met the Baron in Paris towards the end of '99. Just before Talleyrand sent me as Envoy Extraordinary to Mr. Pitt in an abortive attempt to agree a peace. If I remember, he was a tall, handsome man of about forty; a cousin of the King of Prussia's First Minister, and had for a while been Ambassador here in London.'

'That is the man,' Droopy agreed. 'When he was here as Ambassador, he was mightily taken with Georgina, but at that time married. On his wife's death, he returned to England and pressed his suit successfully with our vivacious Countess.'

'Dost know what she has done about the children?' asked Roger.

'Her little Earl she took with her; your daughter, Susan, remains at Stillwaters in the good care of her great-aunt Marsham. Not knowing when, if ever, you would return, I have been down on several occasions to see them.'

'That was good of you, Ned. How fares the child?'

'Well enough physically, and she bids fair to become a beauty. But she is sad at heart. How could it be otherwise when, for eleven years she shared nursery and playroom with Georgina's boy; then, by this new marriage, they were reft apart?'

'Eleven years!' Roger gave a heavy sigh. 'She must then now be rising thirteen; and I have spent little more than that number of weeks with her in her whole life.'

'Take that not too much to heart, dear friend; for it was duty that kept you abroad, and few men can have served their country better.'

'Aye, Ned, I've pulled a trick or two on Britain's enemies. But, all the same, I've proved a sorry parent, and I am by way of becoming one again.'

Droopy raised his eyebrows. 'M'seems you've lost no time, since you tell me you married this Brazilian belle only in March.'

Roger had no secrets from his old friend, so he gave him an account of his year-long affair with Lisala, suppressing only the fact that she had slain her father.

When he had finished, Droopy commented, 'All's well that ends well, then. With such a wife you'll be the envy of the town. That Madonna face crowning the body of a Venus; rarely, if ever, have I beheld a female with attractions so calculated to bewitch a man.'

'Bewitch a man! You've said it, Ned. She has indeed put a spell on me, and I still cannot make up my mind whether I am glad or sorry that fate should have thrown me in her path. When I am apart from her for a while, I see her as she really is—a beautiful mask, behind which lies a mind that lacks all humane qualities. She is utterly selfish and would go to any lengths to gain her ends. At times she displays the temper of a virago; and I have become convinced that for her love means one thing only—the satisfaction of sexual craving. Yet when we are together and her eyes light up, her lips part and she gives me that dazzling smile, I count myself the luckiest man in Christendom.'

Nodding his narrow, bird-like head, with its great beak of a nose, Droopy said, 'What you have told me does not bode well for a happy marriage. But I am inclined to think that you have been too long divorced from civilised society so, from lack of other interests, brooded overmuch on certain episodes which have revealed to you your wife's shortcomings. Maybe they are not so ineradicable as you have come to suppose. Furthermore, when she has her child, that may make a different woman of her. 'Tis often so.'

He then stood up and added, 'But you have been up all night. Now I am sending you to bed. By this time, doubtless, Madame is sound asleep; so you had best occupy the bed in the dressing room. We'll meet again this evening. My cousins Lady Caroline and Judith Stanley are both here on one of their periodic visits. I'll tell them about Mrs. Brook, and you may be sure they will do everything in their power to make her stay with us a pleasure.'

Lisala had only the sadly-worn clothes she stood up in; but the ladies of the family lent her garments that fitted her well enough for her to be presentable at dinner. The Earl was still in the country, but relatives, friends and hangers-on usually numbered from twelve to twenty at every meal. All of them proved most eager to hear about the royal family's flight from Portugal, and about Brazil; so Roger and Lisala were the centre of attention. But, pleading the fatigue they still felt from their journey, they escaped early to bed.

The following morning Roger went alone to Droopy's apartment, to breakfast with him. Over their mutton chops, washed down with good bordeaux, they discussed the future. Roger's intention was, as soon as practical, to take his bride to the

'Grace and Favour' residence, Thatched House Lodge, in Richmond Park, of which Mr. Pitt had given him the tenure for life. But first Lisala had to be provided with an entire new wardrobe, and he wished to spend a couple of nights at Georgina's lovely old home, Stillwaters, in order to see his daughter.

Droopy assured him that Caroline and Judith would be delighted to take Lisala to the best mercers, modistes and milliners and would also introduce her to many of their friends, so she would have plenty to occupy her while Roger was out of London. Roger then said:

'Tell me now, what has been happening in Europe? During my long absence I had little reliable news.'

Heavily buttering a muffin, his friend replied, 'The war goes on, of course, but oh! how drearily. Since Billy Pitt's death, England seems to have lost all power of initiative. The so-called "Ministry of All the Talents" failed lamentably, both in its attempts to agree a peace and to prosecute the war. Since His Grace of Portland became Prime Minister, with Mr. Canning as his Foreign Secretary, we have had hopes that matters would improve. But, so far, the only notable success—of which you must have heard—was the seizing of the Danish Fleet at Copenhagen. The expedition to Egypt proved a fiasco. We took Alexandria but were defeated at Rosetta and, in September, had to evacuate our forces. Admiral Collingwood has, alas, become a tired old man. Although he had a fleet of some eighty ships in the Mediterranean, he failed to prevent the French from entering the Adriatic, revictualling Corfu and returning unmolested to Toulon. That apart, we continued to be mistress of the seas. Two sizable squadrons despatched by Bonaparte into the Atlantic to disrupt British commerce did us little damage, and have since become dispersed and impotent.

'But Bonaparte now rules the roost unchallenged on the Continent, from the Baltic to the Mediterranean. His alliance with the Czar leaves him nothing to fear in the North. They treat their third partner, Prussia, with contempt and have despoiled her of half her territories. 'Tis said, too, that they plan to divide the Empire of the Great Turk between them. Meanwhile, Alexander's army has overrun Sweden's Finnish

363

lands and Napoleon bullies the states in the south into accepting his "Continental System".

'Portugal, Spain, Etruria and the States of the Church are now all occupied by his troops, and in January he even succeeded in coercing neutral Austria into closing her ports on the Adriatic to British shipping. His policy is inflicting the gravest hardship upon both his own people and all others who have submitted to his will. Our industrial revolution gave us a virtual monopoly in manufactured goods. Europe had become dependent on Lancashire cottons, and Yorkshire woollens. They are, too, starved of the many exotic goods brought by our merchant fleets from the Indies and the East. Sugar is now almost unobtainable on the Continent, and coffee is worth its weight in gold.'

'It surprises me that supplies are as short as that,' Roger put in. 'Although British bottoms carried to the Continent far more than those of any other nation, there remain the neutrals, particularly the United States. The merchants there must be making fortunes out of such a situation. Surely, too, neutral ships could be used to take in our manufactured goods?'

Droopy shook his head. 'On the contrary. The Government is carrying out a counter-blockade. Our merchants are much opposed to it, because by using neutral ships they could continue to export their goods. But that has been forbidden, bringing trade almost to a standstill and threatening many merchants with bankruptcy. Neutral ships sailing from their own countries are also barred from entering Continental ports. You can well imagine the resentment that such a high-handed action by us has caused. We are already at war with half the world, and the other half would now like to see us speedily defeated.'

'Then things are come to a sorry pass,' Roger commented, 'and no-one seems the gainer. Smugglers excepted, of course. They must be reaping a golden harvest.'

'They are indeed, for they no longer have to fear the Excise men on the other side, at least as far as Bonaparte's allies are concerned. In secret they defy his ordinances and welcome cargoes of illicit goods. Even the French themselves are prone to do so on occasion. Would you believe it, not long since Bourrienne, who was once the Emperor's *Chef de Cabinet*, and is now his agent at Hamburg, was ordered to supply fifty thousand uniforms for the French troops up in Poland. At his wits' end where to find them, and not daring to disobey his master, he had the cloth for them smuggled over from England.'

Roger laughed. 'Poor Bourrienne. I knew him well. He was a charming man and of the very highest intelligence. His only fault was that, having made a bad speculation, he recouped himself from the Public Funds. Although a thousand others were doing the same, Napoleon dismissed him for it; and, after years of invaluable service. Never did a master more surely cut off his nose to spite his face. But what of Spain? While waiting at an inn for the coach that brought us up from Portsmouth I heard two officers say that the French are having trouble there.'

'So I heard in White's some days ago. The course events will take in Spain has been the main subject of speculation for the past two months. I think it as good as certain that Bonaparte intends to take the whole country over, just as he has Portugal. In mid-March Murat, or the "Grand Duke of Berg" as he is now styled, arrived in Madrid as Napoleon's Lieutenant-General. With him he brought a considerable body of French troops. The pretext for doing so was that they are to assist the Spaniards in resisting a British invasion. But obviously their presence was to enable Murat to coerce King Carlos into doing as Bonaparte wishes; so he might as well have named him Viceroy.'

'Then, after all these years, the Prince of Peace has been forced into second place?'

'Oh, Godoy! That wretched man now has no place at all. Within a day or two of Murat's arrival, the mob rose, sacked the Prince's palace and half-killed him. It was Ferdinand who brought about his downfall. For plotting against his father, the Heir Apparent had been under house arrest for some while. 'Tis said he learned that his parents contemplated following the Portuguese pattern of sailing for their territories in the Americas, and tipped off the French. To stop them,

Napoleon sent a fleet to blockade Cadiz, and gave Ferdinand his head. Having got Godoy out of the way, he forced his father to abdicate and had himself proclaimed King. Although the people acclaimed him with delight, Murat refused to acknowledge him; and, ten days later, King Carlos repudiated his abdication as having been forced upon him under duress. So now there are two Kings of Spain, but neither has the power to lift a finger without Murat's sanction. Realising this, the populace is showing intense resentment, and on May 2nd the Madrileños rose in revolt against him. He quelled the riot with much bloodshed. More than that is not yet known here.'

'The Spaniards are a proud people,' Roger said thoughtfully; 'and, if they get the bit between their teeth, Murat's position may become very difficult. I doubt, though, whether that could greatly influence the general situation.'

'Nor I,' Droopy agreed. 'Meanwhile the war drags on. Our people here are utterly weary of it and, short of surrender, would give anything for peace. But I see no hope of it.'

Three days later, early in the morning, Roger rode down to Richmond. At Thatched House Lodge he found the faithful Dan, who welcomed him with a shout of joy. His now ageing henchman had, as ever, proved a most conscientious steward. With the aid of a cleaning woman and a gardener, he had kept the place in excellent order. Roger told him of his marriage and, to the old ex-smuggler's delight, that having at last come home, he intended to take up permanent residence there.

Dan happened to know of a good woman, now seeking a place, who would prove an excellent cook-housekeeper and promised to engage within a week such other staff as would be required. Roger then spent an hour wandering round the house and garden. For him they held nostalgic memories of Amanda and the happy year they had spent there before sailing for the West Indies, where she had died giving birth to his daughter Susan. He then remounted his horse and rode on to Ripley.

The sight of Georgina's splendid home, looking out on its placid lake, from which the house had taken its name, Still-

waters, evoked still more poignant memories of past joys. Yet
he had no sooner entered the spacious hall than they were
replaced by bleak depression. Nothing there had been altered:
the same marble busts of long-dead Caesars still gazed sightless
from their pedestals, the broad, grand staircase with its gilded
iron balustrade rose gracefully to the floor above. But the
place seemed eerily to have become peopled with unseen ghosts
and had lost its soul.

Mrs. Marsham greeted him with pleasure, but said that
Colonel Thursby, Georgina's father, who lived there for a good
part of the year, was away in the North; which was a big disappointment to Roger. Susan then came in from the garden
where she had been picking flowers. Shyly she accepted his
kiss, then impulsively thrust the flowers at him. A little awkwardly, he accepted the gift, then gave her the big parcel of
presents he had brought for her. Eagerly she undid the package
and was soon exclaiming with delight at the lovely silks, costly
knick-knacks and a string of small pearls suitable for a girl
considerably older than herself.

As he watched her, he marvelled at the way in which she
had grown. In spite of her puppy fat, she was already a young
lady. She had her mother's auburn hair, and his bright blue
eyes. Unquestionably, in a few years, she would be a beauty.
He felt a surge of pride in the fact that she was his daughter.

Over the evening meal, for which, as a treat, she was allowed
to stay up, he endeavoured to entertain her and her great-aunt
with accounts of Turkey, Persia and Brazil; but it soon became clear to him that these distant places meant no more to
them than voyages to the Moon. When she had gone to bed,
Roger told Mrs. Marsham of his new marriage, and said that
he had not brought his wife down because he had feared that
to produce her without warning might upset Susan; but he
would break the news to her the following morning.

Mrs. Marsham told him that she did not think it would
make much impression on the girl, because she saw him so
rarely. But she was troubled about the child, on account of a
depression she had manifested since Georgina's departure.
There could be no doubt that she was pining for her long-

time playmate, the young Earl, and bitterly resented having been parted from him.

Of Georgina Mrs. Marsham had little news. Owing to the blockade, communications with the Continent were very difficult. Only two letters had got through. In them Georgina had described the castle on the Rhine in which she now lived, and said that she found the very limited society there somewhat boring but, apart from that, she gave the impression of being contented and happy.

Next morning, Roger told Susan that he had married a lovely Portuguese lady whom he would shortly bring down to see her. The girl took this news with indifference, merely remarking dutifully that she hoped they would be happy.

Roger had intended to stay two nights, but felt that he could not bear the dead atmosphere of the house for so long. He had known it filled with the cream of the fashionable world: statesmen, Ambassadors, beautiful and witty women. They had dined, gambled, flirted, conversed with knowledge on the problems of the day and, above all, there had been those many glorious nights of play and laughter in Georgina's great bed. At midday he said that urgent business required his presence in London and, heavy-hearted, rode away.

By then Lisala was beginning really to enjoy herself. With Roger's guineas and the aid of Caroline and Judith, she had purchased a fine array of furbelows. From new acquaintances, invitations were coming in to routs, balls and parties at Ranelagh and Vauxhall Gardens. The London season was at its height. Wherever she went, tribute was paid to her beauty. Very soon she became known as *La Belle Brasilienne*, and the most desirable men jostled one another to secure a dance with her.

After twelve days in London, Roger said to her one morning, 'My beloved, I feel that we have accepted Lord Edward's hospitality for long enough. By now my house out at Richmond should be ready for us to occupy it. Within a day or two we'll go there and settle in.'

To his amazement, she shook her head and replied, 'No. We cannot do that. We must return to Portugal.'

'In God's name, why?' he demanded. 'Are you not happy here?'

'Yes. I find London far more agreeable than I had expected it to be.'

'Then why this urge to leave it? From Richmond it is no long drive to the metropolis. We can continue to accept the invitations with which we are being showered and, at the same time, enjoy a home of our own.'

'Maybe. But by the time we can get to Lisbon, news of my father's death will have reached there. As his heir, I must claim my inheritance.'

Roger was momentarily shocked by her callousness. Then he said, 'That is unnecessary. I have money enough to support us both.'

She shrugged. 'A few thousand guineas perhaps. But no great fortune. Unfortunately, Papa took with him to Brazil the family jewels. So those are lost to me, at least for some time to come. I have a craving for rubies, emeralds, diamond and pearl necklaces to adorn my person; and those you cannot afford to buy. So to Portugal we must go, in order to claim my inheritance before those filthy French get their hands on the de Pombal properties, declaring that they have gone by default.'

In vain Roger argued with her, urging that it was far from easy now to get to Portugal. But she swept aside his protests, asserting that there were smugglers who would run them over, and that if he did not love her enough to go with her, she would go alone.

During the day Roger gave the matter much thought. To allow Lisala to make such a voyage unaccompanied was out of the question; so his problem was how most speedily and safely he could convey her there.

Eventually he decided to seek an interview with Mr. Canning. As a pretext, he could say he had recently returned from Brazil, so could furnish an account of the state of things in that country. Accordingly, he wrote to the Foreign Secretary.

Two days later, Canning welcomed him as an old friend, recalling the evenings when they had shared the exhilarating company of Billy Pitt and thanked him for his communication from Vienna. For some ten minutes Roger spoke of the hideous voyage endured by the exiles, the miserable conditions in Rio, and the potential natural wealth of Brazil. Then he mentioned that, before leaving Lisbon, he had spent a week in Madrid.

Immediately the Minister displayed greater interest, and asked his impressions of the leading men there. Roger gave him such information as he could, then Canning said:

'Spain has now become our principal preoccupation. Having in the past been our most successful secret agent and attached to Bonaparte's staff, you will doubtless know that he has long had designs on the Peninsula and postponed them only while having to deal with Prussia and Russia.

'His pact with the Czar at Tilsit freed him to turn his gaze south; and he has played his cards there with his usual unscrupulous cunning. By tempting Godoy with a Kingdom in southern Portugal, he induced him to use Spanish troops to help subdue that country. As France's ally, he then requested King Carlos to send a considerable contingent of Spaniards to assist in garrisoning Hanover; and that moron of a King did as he was asked.

'Thus Spain was denuded of her best regiments and, theoretically, vulnerable to invasion by us. On that pretext, Bonaparte infiltrated many thousands of his own troops into the Peninsula and by guile, or forged documents, they have since gained possession of all the principal fortresses, including Pamplona, San Sebastian, Figueras and Barcelona. With these in his hands, twenty thousand troops in Portugal, forty thousand in northern Spain and another twelve thousand in Catalonia, he has Spain by the throat.

'When that dawned on the slow-witted King, he decided to seek safety in his American dominions. But by then it was too late. His son, that unsavoury young Prince Ferdinand, prevented his departure and forced him to abdicate. Bonaparte played with Ferdinand for a while, persuading him that he intended to support his claim to the throne, then sent General Savory to lure him to Bayonne. There he was confronted by his parents and Godoy who, after being half-killed by the mob and spending a month in prison, had been released at the order of the French. My intelligence sources report that most terrible scenes ensued. But, of course, Bonaparte had the last word. With Godoy, he drew up a Convention by which King Carlos and Prince Ferdinand surrendered their claims to the Spanish throne.'

Roger nodded. 'So there is now no King of Spain; but Godoy gets his Kingdom of the Algarve after all.'

'By no means. He, too, becomes a permanent exile, and Bonaparte has come out in his true colours. He does not intend to partition Portugal, but keep it for himself.'

Canning took a pinch of snuff, then went on, 'But Spain has now become our major concern. The Spanish people took great umbrage some while since at a proposal by Bonaparte that Spain should be deprived of the Balearic Isles, so that he could give them in exchange for Sicily. His treatment of the Spanish royal family has further incensed them and to such a degree that on May 2nd there were bloody riots in Madrid. Now, I gather, the whole country is seething with hatred of the French. Having told you all this, I should like to have your opinion. Do you think there is any chance at all of the people rising *en masse* and driving the French out of Spain?'

' 'Tis hard to say, Sir,' Roger replied. 'I took a poor view of the nobility that I met when in Madrid; but the people are tough, courageous and deeply religious. If their priests inflamed them further against their oppressors, they might succeed in forcing the French to retire into their fortresses. But Napoleon would still hold Spain, unless . . . yes, unless we could send an expeditionary force with ample artillery to support the insurgents.'

'Ah!' exclaimed Canning. 'That is the very thing I have in mind. But we dare not take such a risk unless we have sound reason to believe that the Spanish people will fully commit themselves. And now a thought has come to me. I am, of course, aware that, since the death of our dear friend, Billy, disgusted with the Government that succeeded him you refused to accept further missions abroad. Would you consider re-entering the Service as my special agent? Having been a member of Bonaparte's staff, you are in a unique position to find out how the French view their chances of holding down a widespread rebellion. Such knowledge would be invaluable to me. Will you go to Spain on my behalf?'

22

Back into the Battle

After hesitating for a moment, Roger smiled and said, 'It so happens that I came here today to ask if you would aid me to get to Lisbon. I recently married the daughter of the late Marquis de Pombal. She has inherited a great property there, and is anxious to go to Lisbon so that she can claim it. Knowing that British ships of war are constantly patrolling the coast of Portugal, it occurred to me that you might be good enough to secure for my wife and me a passage in one, and enable us to be put ashore on a dark night in some secluded bay.'

'My congratulations, Mr. Brook. I shall be happy to arrange matters as you wish. May I take it you will then go on for me to Madrid?'

'I thank you, Sir. But to proceed to Madrid may not be necessary. Do you know who now commands in Lisbon?'

'Yes, General Junot. At least, he did so up until a week ago; and, as he has occupied that post ever since the Braganzas fled, there is little likelihood of his having been superseded.'

'Excellent!' Roger smiled again. 'He is one of my oldest friends, and it is certain that he will be well informed about how matters are shaping in Spain. If the frigate that lands us can return after a week or so, and send in a boat, I'd be able to transmit to you by her a sound appreciation of the situation.'

'An admirable idea. That could save us weeks in learning what our prospects are should we send an army into the Peninsula.'

They parted most cordially, Canning having promised to let Roger know when a frigate was sailing to relieve another in the fleet that was blockading Portugal.

Two days elapsed; then, late at night on May 25th, a note arrived for Roger from Canning, to let him know that *Gadfly*, a sloop-of-war which was lying off Greenwich, would be sailing the following noon with despatches for the Admiral commanding the British squadron blockading Lisbon; and that her Captain had been given orders respecting Mr. and Mrs. Brook.

Next morning Lisala threw one of her fits of temper when Roger told her that she must leave behind all the pretty clothes she had bought, because they were to make a secret landing, so could take only what they could carry. To his insistence she had to give way and, when they went downstairs, her face had its usual angelic expression.

Droopy conveyed them down to Greenwich in his coach; Caroline and Judith came too, to see them off. The ladies exchanged tearful farewells and the Brooks went aboard *Gadfly*, to be received by a young Lieutenant named Higgins. He apologised for the narrowness of the quarters in the sloop, but gallantly gave up his own cabin to them. It was a sunny afternoon when they dropped down the Thames and the weather proved clement for the remainder of their voyage. On the night of May 30th, he put them ashore in a small cove some ten miles north of Lisbon.

Roger would have preferred to face the long walk to the city, rather than risk giving themselves away by seeking transport; but Lisala would not hear of it, and showed at her best in dealing with the situation. She knocked up the people at the nearest farmhouse, boldly told them who she was and, without giving any explanation of their presence in such a lonely spot in the middle of the night, demanded to be driven into Lisbon.

The Portuguese peasants being accustomed to obeying orders from the nobility without question, the farmer harnessed two mules to his wagon, put some bundles of straw in it for them to sit on, and they set off.

As they entered the city, the early summer dawn was breaking. Already they had planned what they intended to do. Having been twice to the de Pombal mansion as an Englishman,

374

Roger feared that, if a pro-French servant recognised him, that might cause him considerable inconvenience. So Lisala was to leave him near the *Leão d'ouro*, and proceed to her home on her own. Then, later in the day, he would get in touch with her.

At the inn the servants were just starting the daily round. Roger sent one of them to rouse the landlord, who came downstairs in a chamber robe and night-cap. On seeing Roger, he exclaimed:

'*Senhor* Brook! Where have you been all this time? You disappeared without giving me a word of notice. But no matter. By returning to Lisbon you have run your head into a hornets' nest. If the accursed French learn of your presence here, it will be the worse for you.'

Roger laughed. 'Don't worry. I can take care of myself. But what of my baggage? Is it still here, or have you disposed of it as payment for what I owe you?'

'No, *Senhor*. Expecting you would return in a week or so, I had your things put up in the attic. Then, to tell the truth, I forgot all about them.'

'Praise be for that! Please give me a room, have them brought down to it, and hot water sent up so that I may bathe myself.'

An hour later, Roger came downstairs. He had shaved off his side-whiskers and was dressed in the resplendent uniform of a French Staff Colonel, that he had had made for him in Madrid.

At the sight of this metamorphosis the landlord's eyes opened wide. Roger quickly put a finger to his lips and said in a low voice, 'I had this uniform made secretly when I was here last November, intending to don it when the French arrived and to pass myself off as one of them. Most unfortunately, I was aboard a ship when the tempest arose and was carried off to Brazil. I am only just returned but, I trust, not too late to be of service to my country in this guise.'

The landlord began to laugh until his big paunch wobbled. Bending towards Roger, he whispered huskily, 'Be easy, *Sen-*

hor. No one here will say a word of this. And may God prosper your activities against the accursed French.'

After giving the man several pieces of gold to settle what he owed, Roger sat down to a hearty breakfast; then returned to his room and slept for a few hours.

At four o'clock he ordered a carriage and now, as a high-ranking officer of the occupying Power with nothing to fear, he had himself driven out to the de Pombal mansion.

While discussing with Lisala his reappearance in Lisbon they had been faced with the fact that, on seeing him again, most of the de Pombal servants would recognise him as Mr. Brook; but there were others who had accompanied the Marquis to Persia, so if Roger arrived clean shaven and wearing French uniform, they would tell their companions that he was the *Chevalier de Breuc* who had paid court to Lisala in Isfahan.

He therefore presented himself in this role and said to the footman who opened the door to him: 'There is a rumour in the city that the *Senhorita* de Pombal has returned home. If that is so, I should much like to pay my respects to her, as I made her acquaintance while she was in Persia.'

A major-domo showed Roger up to the big salon and left him there for a short while, then returned to usher in Lisala. With apparent surprise and evident delight, she greeted Roger, exclaiming how pleased she was to see him again after many months.

No sooner had the servant left the room than they burst into laughter and embraced. Then Roger said, 'All has gone well, my love. The landlord at the *Leão d'ouro* now believes me to be an English spy, and can be relied on to keep his mouth shut. Now that we are established in the eyes of your servants as old friends, they will feel no surprise if I visit you here frequently. In the meantime, you must see your attorney and urge him speedily to make good your title to your inheritance. I will see General Junot and, if any difficulties arise, seek his influence to brush them aside. And, now, fatigued by your night's adventure, you must to bed, lest the roses in your lovely cheeks become faded.'

Roger marched out of the house as he had entered it—a master in yet another land which had become subject to his all-powerful Emperor. That evening he went to the Palace which Junot had taken over, and sent up his name. The Duc d'Abrantes had him brought up, flung his arms round him, kissed him on both cheeks and cried:

'*Mon vieux! Mon vieux! Mon cher Breuc!* Where have you been? What have you been doing all this time, and what brings you to this God-forsaken country?'

Roger returned the hug and kisses. '*Mon cher* Androché, it is a long story. The Emperor sent me with General Gardane's mission to Turkey and Persia. Later my travels were extended further than he intended. I was here when the Braganzas left and aboard one of their ships. A storm rose, and I could not get ashore. To my fury I was carried off with them to Brazil. From there I have only just returned. I fear the Emperor will be exceeding angry with me, owing to my long absence. As you know, he is capable of venting his displeasure in no mean manner on those who have failed to carry out his wishes.'

'Do I not?' Junot angrily slapped his thigh. 'Regard my own case. You were there at the siege of Toulon when, as an officer of little significance, he promoted me to be his first A.D.C. When he was still poor, I housed him and lent him money. I have accompanied him on all his campaigns and many times been wounded in his service. Who, if not I, when he distributed his batons, deserved to be a Marshal of the Empire? Yet he ignored me, and fobbed me off with a dukedom, which means nothing to a soldier.

'Last autumn, he promised to promote me to Marshal, did I succeed in preventing the royal family from leaving Portugal. 'Tis true that he gave me thirty thousand men and a corps of Spanish auxiliaries. But he could have had no idea of the territory I had to cross. The rain descended in torrents, the rivers became near-unfordable, the peasants preferred death to yielding up to us the food they had hoarded for the winter. Believe me, it was a nightmare march. Two-thirds of the Spaniards perished and thousands of my own men fell by the wayside. I reached Lisbon with no more than fifteen hundred, and

I was only one day too late. Yet, despite all my efforts, the Emperor turned on me and rent me because I had failed to prevent the departure of the Braganzas.'

'He'll make you a Marshal yet.' Roger gave his old friend a consoling pat on the shoulder. 'Meanwhile, you could be worse off than as the uncrowned King of Portugal.'

'True. When I was here previously, as Ambassador, the Portuguese were so pro-English that they were frequently discourteous to Laure and myself. But now matters are very different. They shower us with presents and fight to kiss our hands.'

'You were lucky to be sent here, instead of to Madrid.'

'Indeed I was. Poor Murat was given a most unpleasant task. Our master refused to reveal to him his true intentions, telling him to keep both sides sweet; so he knew not which to back when Ferdinand forced his old father at gun point to abdicate, and whether to protect Godoy or allow the mob to hang him.'

'I gather that scamp was very lucky to get away with his life.'

'Yes. While the mob sacked his palace, he managed to hide; but, after twenty-four hours, became so plagued by thirst that he had to come out and, on asking a gendarme for a glass of water, was recognised. The mob gave him a most terrible beating and, before he could be saved by arrest, battered in his face. He would have been executed next day had not that lecherous old cow, Queen Maria, gone down on her knees and begged his life of her son. Ferdinand granted it, but is a veritable swine and kept him in prison for a month without even allowing him a doctor. The Emperor then ordered that he should be conveyed to Bayonne, and it was he who drew up the treaty that has put an end to Bourbon rule in Spain.'

'What terms did the Emperor force these awful people to accept?'

'Carlos handed over the Crowns of Spain and the Americas for an income of seven and a half million francs a year, with the estates of Compiègne and Chambord. Ferdinand signed away his rights for a castle and a pension.'

'And now they are gone, who is to occupy the throne?'

Junot laughed. 'That question has been quite a comedy. As the Emperor had made his brothers Joseph, Lucien and Jerome Kings, Murat considered that, as brother-in-law, he had a good claim to the next vacant throne. Think, too, of the enjoyment he would have derived from designing for himself new costumes as King Achille I. But our master had other plans. He has been far from pleased at the way in which Louis has ignored many of his orders regarding Holland. 'Tis said he wrote to him, saying that the air of the Low Countries was not good for his health, so he should have the Crown of Spain instead. Can you believe it, Louis refused it on the grounds that the Dutch people needed him and that he owed having become their King, not to his big brother, but to a call of God.'

'Was there ever such a family as the Bonapartes?' Roger raised his eyes to heaven. 'But I'm not surprised. Louis has always been a neurotic and has now become a monomaniac. Who, then, is to have the throne of Spain?'

'Joseph. And, in his case, without even being asked if he would like it. The Emperor simply ordered him to leave Naples and join him in Madrid, where he is at present. Murat is to replace Joseph as King of Naples; so, after all, our handsome swashbuckler has not come off too badly.'

Roger nodded. 'The eldest brother is by far the best of the hatch. But I don't envy him his new Crown, from all I hear of the situation in Madrid.'

'*Mon Dieu*, no! Spain is about to blow up about our ears.'

'Do you really think that?' Roger raised a sceptical eyebrow.

'I'd wager my chances of yet getting a Marshal's baton on it. The *émeurt* in Madrid on May 2nd sparked the trouble off. The news of it ran round Spain like wild-fire. The Spanish notables had been summoned by the Emperor to Bayonne, and accepted the Constitution he thrust at them; but the people rejected it with angry contempt. By the middle of the month the hardy mountaineers of the north began to arm themselves, on the 24th, their little province of Asturias actually declared war on France. A few days later, Galicia and Léon followed

379

suit. My latest intelligence is that the south, too, is in a ferment. Andalusia, Mercia and Valencia may join the rebellion any day. Within a month there will be fighting throughout the whole Peninsula.'

Roger shrugged. 'What can such rabble do against our well-armed and well-disciplined troops?'

'They can render the country near-untenable by raids and ambushes. No small body of French troops will be safe outside the cities, and in them they'll no longer dare to go abroad at night, for fear of assassination. The odds are that we'll be compelled to withdraw into the fortresses.'

'But with them in his hands, the Emperor will still hold Spain. They, at least, are impregnable, except from assault by a regular army with cannon.'

'Of course. But what if the English take advantage of our difficulties to seize one of the ports? Given a base, they could supply the rebels with arms and ammunition, and land an army of their own. To provision our garrisons across a hostile countryside would, in any case, be far from easy. Supported by English regulars, the Spaniards could reduce them one by one.'

Feigning anxiety and distress, Roger exclaimed, 'Do you really fear then that we may be driven out of Spain?'

'Not without a long and ghastly struggle. But if the English do land an army, it may well come to that.'

Roger had his answer for Mr. Canning, and much more quickly than he had expected. His only regret now was that he had told the young Captain of the sloop not to return to the bay for a week.

Over a bottle of wine, he told Junot about the awful voyage to Brazil, and of the state of squalor they had found in Rio; then of his marriage to Lisala and her inheritance. Having congratulated him, Junot asked, 'But how did you succeed in getting back here?'

With a laugh Roger replied, 'How do you think? In a British ship, of course. As you know, I am bi-lingual. Before you reached Lisbon I was here on the Emperor's business, posing as an Englishman. The Portuguese believed me to be one when

I was carried off to Brazil and I succeeded in maintaining the fiction there until I could arrange with the Captain of a British frigate to give my wife and myself passage to England. After a short spell there I persuaded another British Captain to take us across to Algeciras. From thence we came overland.'

Junot nodded. 'Tell me now about your wife.'

'Willingly. I had intended to. She is a most lovely creature but our present situation is a difficult one, and I would be grateful for your help.

'Her father died recently, so she is heir to a great inheritance and has returned to Lisbon to claim it. Naturally I have accompanied her, but now that Portugal is subject to France I could not come here as the Englishman her people supposed me to be when I married her in Brazil. For the moment we are keeping our marriage a secret and have been compelled temporarily to separate. She has returned to her family mansion; I have secured quarters at the *Leão d'ouro*. There is naught to prevent my calling on her frequently as her servants are aware that I was previously acquainted with, and enamoured, of her when she was in Persia and I was there as a member of Gardane's mission. We shall go about together and shortly let it be known that we intend to marry.'

'What an amusing farce! But the sooner your situation is regularised the better. Bring her to dine with us tomorrow. I will tell no-one but Laure your secret. She will be delighted to see you again, and both of us will look forward to meeting the lovely heiress you have captured.'

Roger happily accepted. For a while the two old friends talked on together then, having satisfactorily established his position in Lisbon, Roger took his departure.

He had known the vivacious Laure Junot, Duchesse d'Abrantés, when she had been Mademoiselle Permon. She received him with a radiant smile and made much of Lisala. Some thirty people sat down to the meal, most of them soldiers with whom Roger had served in past campaigns, and it proved a gay occasion. When he condoled with the Duchesse on the Emperor's not having made Junot a Marshal, she exclaimed:

'The ingratitude of the man! Of course, he is now "Sire" to everybody; but time was when to his face I used to call him "Puss-in-Boots". I am now writing my memoirs, though, so I'll pay him out with posterity.'

During the days that followed, all went well. Roger paid frequent visits to Lisala and, in front of her servants, she welcomed him more warmly on each occasion. It was soon clear to the de Pombal household that their mistress was having a hectic *affaire* with the handsome *Colonel de Breuc*; but while they might privately disapprove of this fraternisation with one of their conquerors, they were too well trained to show it.

Meanwhile, Lisala had summoned her steward and the family lawyers to a series of conferences. They had recently learned of the Marquis' death, but had heard only garbled accounts of it. All reports agreed that he had met his death in a fracas caused by an Englishman's attempt to abduct Lisala. Some said he had died as a result of a heart attack, others that he had been murdered by a mad slave, and others again that it was the Englishman who had killed him. But a two-month-old Brazilian news-sheet that had recently reached Lisbon gave an account of his funeral service in the Candelabra Church, so there could be no doubt that he was dead.

Fortunately for Lisala, practically the whole of the Portuguese Court had accompanied Don Joao to Brazil, so there remained in Lisbon no relatives or elderly, close friends of the family, who might have questioned her; and no-one suspected for a moment that *M. le Colonel Chevalier de Breuc* could be the Englishman mixed up in the affair.

Roger spent a lot of his time with his old comrades-in-arms, and had several more long conversations with Junot. The curly-haired Pro-Consul was confident that he could hold down the Portuguese, at least for the time being; but news kept coming in of further uprisings in Spain.

A week after Roger had landed, he wrote a long appreciation for Mr. Canning. In it he gave as much reliable information as he could gather about the areas in rebellion, and strongly advised the sending of representatives to the rebel leaders with a view to their arranging for the arrival of a British Expeditionary Force.

That night he rode out with his despatch to the deserted cove ten miles north of the city. Unfortunately, there was a high wind, and it was raining hard, so visibility was too poor for him to make out whether the sloop was lying offshore or if her Captain had decided that the weather made it too dangerous to keep the rendezvous. After waiting for three hours, he gave up and, soaked to the skin, returned to his inn.

All next day he was greatly worried, as it was possible that the sloop's failure to send a boat ashore might be due to her having been sunk or captured. If so, his only line of swift communication with England was cut, and it might be many weeks before he would be able to get to the Foreign Minister information, the use of which could give a new turn to the war in Britain's favour.

At night he again rode out to the bay. To his relief, he could discern *Gadfly* half a mile out and, presently, she sent a boat in to the beach. Lieutenant Higgins had come himself. Roger handed him the despatch and impressed upon him the importance of delivering it in London as a matter of the utmost urgency.

He was now free to give his attention solely to Lisala's affairs. Like men of the law the world over, the Portuguese attorneys were habitually dilatory. Normally, while their fees piled up, they would have taken many months to secure for Lisala an order of the Court that she was at liberty to deal with her father's estate.

To expedite matters, Roger sought Junot's help. Following the example of their Emperor, his representatives had become accustomed to taking swift decisions and asserting their authority to have them quickly carried out. Junot sent for the Chief Justice, told him curtly that he would be very displeased if Lisala's affairs were not settled within the next ten days, and that, should the Court rule against her, he would have those responsible clapped into prison.

It was an arbitrary pronouncement that ignored any pretence of maintaining justice. But in the lands the French had conquered they rode roughshod over every law. Feeling slightly guilty, but also a shade contemptuous, Roger watched the old Chief Justice submissively walk with bowed head from the palatial salon in which the resplendent Junot gave audience.

On June 20th, the Court met and, cowed by fear, gave the decision required of them. As Lisala's petition could hardly be challenged, they would almost certainly have done so in any case; but her right to dispose of her father's estate as she wished had been granted to her many months sooner than it otherwise would have been.

After the case had been heard, Roger accompanied Lisala back to the de Pombal mansion. Over a dinner *à deux* that evening, he said to her, 'Now, my love, that your business has been formally settled, I suggest that during the next few days you give detailed instructions to your steward about how you desire your property and revenues to be handled. Then I will devise a means by which we can return to England.'

'No,' she replied sharply. 'Why should we? I now see the Duchess almost every day, and she has been sweet to me. I find, too, that the French officers are much more amusing than your stodgy friends in London. We have ample money; the ground has now been made ready for us to announce our engagement, we will then go through another marriage ceremony and you can move in here and live with me, instead of our putting up any longer with making love at odd hours and infrequent intervals.'

An argument ensued. Having accomplished his mission, Roger was most averse to remaining in Portugal. More than ever he was anxious to settle down in the comfortable home that for so long he had been unable to occupy.

For three days they continued to bicker over the question. Then, on the morning of June 24th, an officer arrived at Roger's inn with a message that His Excellency the General-Duke desired to see him upon an urgent matter.

Going to the palace, Roger found his not very intelligent but normally cheerful friend looking far from happy. Having greeted him awkwardly, Junot said:

'*Mon vieux*, I am greatly distressed because I fear that, unwittingly, I have brought misfortune upon you. In a recent letter to the Emperor, I happened to mention that you had recently returned from Brazil, where you had captured a beautiful young heiress, and were here in Lisbon. From him, only a few hours since, I received a despatch. He has ordered me to send you to him in Madrid under close arrest.'

23

Caught in the Web

Since his return to Lisbon at the beginning of the month, Roger had not given a thought to Napoleon. His mind had been occupied by, in turn, the importance of getting his intelligence on the situation in Spain to Canning, Lisala's affairs, and his desire to persuade her to return to England.

For several years past, his mind had seesawed between the desire to be done for good with courts and camps, and settle down to a safe, pleasant life at home; then, after a period, the restless urge to play again a part in great affairs. Sickened by the terrible crossing of the Atlantic, which had been forced upon him, and the dreary discomfort of existence in Rio, the fortnight he had recently spent in England had made residing there permanently seem more than ever attractive. Only Lisala's insistence on claiming her fortune had persuaded him to contemplate returning to Portugal and Canning's appeal to his patriotsm finally decided him to do so. But he had had no intention of remaining there a day longer than was necessary, much less of re-entering the service of the Emperor. Now, once more, he had become involved, and most dangerously, with Napoleon.

Giving a resigned shrug, he said to Junot, 'Since our master has ordered you to send me to Madrid, I must obviously submit. But why he should require my presence there—and under arrest—I cannot think.'

Junot shrugged. 'Surely the explanation is not far to seek. Having learned that you are once more in Europe, he resents the fact that you should have dallied here in Lisbon, instead of reporting at once to him. I can only say again how sorry I am that I should inadvertently have brought this about, by a mention that, at a reception I gave not long since, you and your beautiful wife were among the guests.'

'That was understandable enough. But what of her? Can she accompany me on the journey, and will you give me a day or so in order that she may have time to prepare herself for it?'

'I would I could; but I dare not. She can follow you, of course. But the order is marked "immediate". And you know our master well enough to be sure that he will tolerate no delay. While I send to your inn for your belongings, you can write her a note explaining your sudden departure; but you must set off within the hour.'

Putting as good a face as he could on the matter, Roger sat down and penned a letter to Lisala.

They had never spoken of her having murdered her father and he had, as far as possible, put it out of his mind. Recognising that, when thwarted, rage could temporarily rob her of all control, he told himself that she had not intended to kill the Marquis, but struck out in blind fury, concerned at that moment only with saving him, her lover.

Since leaving Brazil, apart from occasional outbursts brought on by her determination to get her own way, they had been happy together. Her beauty had continued to have a mesmerising effect upon him and, owing to their circumstances during the past three months, her demands that he should make love to her had been no greater than he had been happy to meet.

In consequence, his letter expressed genuine distress at being parted from her and an assurance, about which he was very far from confident, that they would soon be re-united. However, thinking it wiser to await the outcome of his interview with the Emperor, he did not suggest that she should at once follow him to Madrid. Instead, he told her that, should any trouble arise, she could rely on the friendship of Junot and his Duchess, as the General had already promised that they would take every care of her.

Shortly before midday, the Captain of Hussars who had brought Roger Junot's message that morning, came in to report that a coach was now loaded with baggage and provisions and ready to set out. Junot said that the Captain was to act as escort; so Roger formally surrendered his sword to him and took leave of his old friend. Ten minutes later, the coach was jolting over the cobbles, on its way to Madrid.

The Captain was a pleasant young man and, knowing Roger's high reputation with the Army, did all he could to make the journey agreeable. But for Roger it entailed four days of gnawing anxiety. He had always previously succeeded in producing to Napoleon plausible reasons for his long absence from headquarters. But the present case was going to be exceptionally difficult to explain away.

He thought it certain that General Gardane would have reported his departure from Isfahan on a project of his own invention—that he would proceed to Goa, the Portuguese settlement in India, and there assess its vulnerability to a surprise attack by the French. But he had never been to Goa and, if he had, he could not possibly have reached Lisbon until several weeks after Don Joao's fleet had sailed for Brazil. How, then, was he going to account for having been in one of the ships and carried off in her, owing to a storm?

Napoleon was extraordinarily indulgent to old friends and, even when his Secret Police reported that one of his early comrades-in-arms was conspiring against him, would do no more than transfer the offender to some distant command, where he was deprived of any opportunity to make mischief. But in matters of discipline he was adamant. Those who disobeyed his orders did so at their dire peril. He had reduced at least one General to the ranks, and other victims of his displeasure had found their prospects of advancement blighted for good after interviews during which he had vented his wrath upon them.

Roger was no longer concerned for his career in the French Army; but, the nearer they came to Madrid, the more he feared that, for having deliberately ignored the Emperor's instructions, he might shortly find himself serving a sentence in a fortress.

On June 29th, they drove into the Spanish capital. At the

Royal Palace, the young Captain handed Roger over to the Provost Marshal, and obtained a receipt for him. The Provost asked him for his parole. Knowing that an attempt to escape would be to admit guilt, he gave it willingly. He was then taken to a not unpleasant room on the third floor and left there.

Presently, in deference to his rank, a soldier servant was sent to bring up his meals and attend to his other requirements. During the three days that followed, no-one else entered his room, and he was left to brood in considerable apprehension on what the future held in store for him.

It was early in the evening of the fourth day that two officers arrived, to escort him to the Presence. As he tidied himself up, his heart began to beat a little faster, from the frightening knowledge that, within the next half-hour he would, unless he played his cards supremely well, find himself stripped of his uniform and being taken off to a cell.

Placing himself between his escorts, he was marched downstairs, to the lofty main floor of the building. The guards at a pair of tall double doors came smartly to attention. An equerry rapped sharply on the doors with a silver-headed wand, waited a moment, then threw them open.

They gave on to a huge, white and gold salon, at the far end of which Napoleon was pacing slowly up and down. Abruptly coming to a halt, he turned and with a gruff word, dismissed Roger's escort. As the two officers fell back, Roger continued to advance, his eyes fixed on the Emperor.

He was, as usual, dressed in the white breeches and green tunic of the Guides. Since Roger had last seen him, he had put on weight and now had a small, but definite, paunch. His face was very pale, and his smooth forehead seemed to bulge more than ever under dark hair which had thinned a little and was brushed sideways. The two most striking things about him were the breadth of his head, with its powerful, forward-thrusting jaw, and his fine eyes, which were now glowering with anger. The expression of those eyes showed that he was in one of his blackest moods.

Within a few feet of a broad, satinwood desk littered with

papers and maps, Roger halted and bowed three times. Napoleon snarled at him:

'What have you to say for yourself?'

'A great deal, Sire,' Roger replied quietly, 'having, as ever, been most diligent in your service.'

'You lie! Instead of carrying out my orders, you have been gallivanting across half the world, pursuing some woman.'

Roger knew that, if he allowed himself to be bullied, within a matter of minutes he would be dismissed and finished. Permitting himself a slight smile, he said, 'Do not we all at times? That is, men who are men, like Your Majesty and me. I trust the Countess Walewska is in good health; or has she . . . er, been replaced by . . .'

'Silence! I have not had you brought here to talk of bedfellows, but to demand an explanation of your flagrant disobedience.'

'Then talk of bedfellows we must, Sire. What goes on in the beds you frequent is known only to Fouché, but . . .'

'That rogue!'

'Why, yes.' Roger proceeded to develop the red herring. ' 'Tis common knowledge that it is reported to him every time you use a chamber pot.'

'Who in hell's name told you that?'

'Oh, er . . . a charming lady who later pleasured me with her embraces.'

'Her name? Who was this spying whore?'

Roger shook his head. 'How can you ask such a thing? Your Majesty and I are men of honour. We do not kiss and tell. Suffice it that she took me only because she was overwrought with distress at having been abandoned by you, Sire.'

Slightly mollified, the Emperor snapped, 'That Fouché should spy upon my private life is intolerable.'

'You are unfair, Sire. He does so only for your protection, and no monarch could have a more competent Chief of Police.'

'He is as cunning a rascal as ever drew breath, and useful in such matters as dealing with these eternally rebellious Chouans. But I long since took the Ministry of Police from him and gave it to General Savary.'

'Of that I was aware; but Fouché still concerns himself for Your Majesty's safety. Savary, I am told, showed great ability in luring Prince Ferdinand across the border to you in Bayonne.'

'He did indeed; and it was no easy task. That great block-head, Murat, got on his high horse and declared that, as a soldier, it was beneath him to soil his hands with such a business; and the Spanish people did their utmost to prevent the Prince from leaving Madrid. But Savary beguiled him with a promise that we would let him have the throne and, on the last stage of the journey, when he endeavoured to break away, virtually kidnapped him.'

For a moment Napoleon paused, then he went on reminiscently. 'What scenes took place when I did have them all at Bayonne. That imbecile old King, his ugly, lecherous Queen, poor Godoy with his handsome face a mass of scars, and that cowardly young swine of a Prince. They near tore one another to pieces. But I made them all dance to my tune, then packed them off to Talleyrand at his château of Valençay.'

As Roger listened, his spirits rose. It was like old times for the Emperor to be talking to him in such a familiar strain. But he was counting his chickens before they were hatched. With a sudden change of mood, Napoleon glowered at him and said:

'But we are not here to talk of such matters. Enough of police and women.'

'Forgive me, Sire,' Roger put in quickly, 'but a woman is the cause of your displeasure with me. I was about to say that you take women to bed only as a relaxation; whereas I have frequently gone to bed with one in order to learn secrets that are of value to you.'

'And what have you learned in this case?'

'Alas, Sire; nothing of any importance. But, had fortune favoured me, I might have done, and I may yet.'

Napoleon scowled. 'You have the effrontery to tell me that on this slender chance you ignored my commands and absented yourself from duty for many months?'

'That is not so. I did my utmost for you both in Turkey and Persia, then . . .'

'Then, instead of accompanying Gardane's Mission to India, you told him some cock-and-bull story about going off on your own to Goa.'

'It was as good an excuse as I could think of to leave his Mission.'

'Excuse to chase this woman who had besotted you back to Europe, instead of obeying my instructions regarding the Mahratta Princes.'

'I told you, Sire, before leaving Poland that, although I had once crossed India, I knew little of that vast country, and I considered that I could serve you better . . .'

The Emperor's eyes blazed and his face was becoming purple, as he bellowed, 'So you set yourself up to be a better judge of my interests than I am.'

'Sire!' Roger held up a warning hand. 'I beg you to have a care. Last time we had a . . . a slight difference of opinion, you . . .'

'Slight, *mon Dieu*! You had seduced my sister Pauline, and had the infernal impudence to ask my consent to your marrying her.'

Roger managed to force a laugh. 'Oh, come, Sire. 'Twas she who seduced me; and you know her amorous inclinations well enough to believe that. I was about to say, though, that our interview ended by Your Majesty's having an epileptic fit.'

Turning away, Napoleon began to walk up and down, his hands clasped behind his back, as he fought to regain control of himself; then he muttered, 'Yes . . . yes. That is true. But no-one must know of these . . . these occasional attacks. You have not mentioned it?'

'Is that likely? I am Your Majesty's most loyal servant.'

'Fiddlesticks! Were that so you would not have disobeyed me.'

'It was in your interests. The lady concerned is the daughter of the Marquis de Pombal. He was the Portuguese Ambassador in Isfahan.'

'I know it.'

'Very well then. He was recalled to Lisbon. As one of the most trusted advisers of Don Joao he would have been privy to all the Prince Regent's secrets, and I would have learned them through his daughter. Knowing from long past Your Majesty's designs on Portugal, I decided . . .'

'So that is your story. You are as plausible as ever. But I do not believe it. Fathers do not divulge State secrets to their daughters. And how, pray, did you think to serve me by going off to Brazil?'

'It was not my intention. I was aboard a ship endeavouring to influence de Pombal into persuading Don Joao to postpone the sailing of the fleet, in order to give Junot time to arrive and capture it. A storm blew up, I could not get back to shore, and was carried off to Brazil against my will.'

'Junot! That bungler! What a mess he made of things.'

'You are unfair, Sire. Junot performed a miracle by reaching Lisbon at all. He led his troops through storm, flood and a land naked of provisions. His army of thirty thousand literally fell to pieces. When he did arrive, he had left only fifteen hundred starving men.'

'But he failed, he failed! And I accept no excuses for failure.'

Roger decided that the time had come to take the offensive, and he burst out with simulated anger:

'I know it! And you should be ashamed of yourself for having denied poor Junot his Marshal's baton. He, I and scores of your other old friends go through fire for you and suffer incredible hardships. Yet, if fate thwarts our efforts, what do we get from you? Only kicks and curses. Why any of us should continue to serve such a master, I cannot think.'

Halting in his stride, the Emperor bellowed, 'How dare you talk to me like this? How dare you? In all my Army, no other officer has the impertinence to address me in such a manner.'

'They are professional soldiers, trained to unquestioning obedience,' Roger snapped back. 'I am not; and I speak my mind to you for your own good. Time was when you would listen to reason. But that is so no longer. You rate yourself the new Charlemagne, with all Europe as your footstool. You have made your incompetent brothers puppet Kings, and looted a dozen countries of their riches. But you are not a Habsburg nor a Romanoff. Your Empire was created only yesterday, and is built on sand. It is maintained by terror, oppression and the loyalty of your old friends. If you continue to treat them so ungenerously and reject the advice of such men as Talleyrand . . .'

'Talleyrand! That venal scoundrel?'

'Yes, Talleyrand.' Roger sprang to his friend's defence. 'The greatest statesman France has produced since the Cardinal-Duke de Richelieu. Do you ignore his counsel and that of others who see clearly the best interests of France, your Empire will come crashing about your ears.'

'Not while I live! Not while I live!'

'It will. You have come to believe yourself infallible. But you are not. You are bleeding France to death, and by keeping your head above the clouds, will bring about her utter ruin.'

'*Sacré nom!* You must have taken leave of your senses. I'll not tolerate such insolence for another moment. You shall rue the day you had the effrontery to question the wisdom of my policies.'

Roger saw that he had gone too far, but now there could be no drawing back. He might as well be hanged for a sheep as a lamb. Inflamed by genuine anger, he cried contemptuously:

'Your policies! And where have they led us? Talleyrand endeavoured to persuade you to give reasonable terms to Prussia. Instead you robbed her of half her lands and she is longing for the chance to stab you in the back. He begged you to make Austria your friend. Instead you filched from her vast territories which she has ruled for centuries. While she licks her wounds she is recruiting new armies to have at you again as soon as she is strong enough.'

'Stop, I say! Stop!' roared the Emperor.

'I'll not stop,' Roger flung back. 'Talleyrand did his utmost to dissuade you from going into Spain; but you ignored his advice. And look at the result. Your maltreatment of their

394

royal family has raised such indignation among the people of Spain that the whole country has risen in arms against you, and . . .'

'A rabble! I'll soon drive those mangy curs back into their kennels.'

'On the contrary, it is they who will drive your troops into the fortresses and besiege them there. Again and again Talleyrand has advised you to make peace with England. Instead you are endeavouring to bring her to her knees by your "Continental System". And at what a price. Discontent throughout your whole Empire through depriving millions of people of . . .'

'Peace with England!' The Emperor banged his fist violently on his desk. 'Never! Commerce has always been their strength. They are a nation of shopkeepers; and by my measures I'll break them yet.'

With equal violence, Roger thrust out an accusing finger. 'You are no longer the great First Consul who restored law and prosperity to France. The lust for power has unbalanced your mind. If you do not cease to play the part of God without his wisdom, you will become known as the "mad Emperor".'

Napoleon was again going purple in the face. 'I'll hear no more!' he screamed. 'What you have said is *lèse majesté*. I could have you shot for it.'

Roger had known from the beginning that he had little chance of walking out of the room a free man. Now indignation had led him to burn his boats entirely. His eyes blazing, he shouted back:

'Shoot me then. I give not a damn. I'll be no more than another of the million men who, for your selfish ends, you have caused to die on battlefields.'

For a full minute the Emperor remained silent, breathing heavily. Then, as often happened after being shaken by one of his terrible rages, his anger drained away, and he said quietly:

'Nay, I will not do that. You saved my life that night when we were together on an island outside Venice. I now give you yours. I will go further. I'll not hold against you what you have just said of me. It was due only to your mind not being large enough to appreciate that my acts, of which you disapprove, were necessary in carrying out my great designs.'

Suddenly his voice became harsh as he went on, 'But in my service I have no place for deserters. That you neglected my interests to pursue this woman, I am convinced. I hereby deprive you of your rank, of your status as a Commander of the *Legion d'Honneur*, and sentence you to five years' imprisonment in a fortress.'

Roger paled. He had expected no more than a sentence of six months, or a year at the worst. There was nothing more he could say or do. He had hopelessly overplayed his hand and lost.

Then, as the Emperor put out his hand to the bell which would summon the escort, a side door in the big salon was thrown open and Josephine came running in.

In her hand the Empress held several sheets of parchment, covered with close writing. 'Napoleon!' she cried. 'I have news! The most wonderful news.' Then she threw her arms round her husband and kissed him.

Frowning at being disturbed, he half drew back and asked testily, 'News? What news?'

Josephine was about to reply when she caught sight of Roger. Turning, she ran towards him, with both hands outstretched, as she exclaimed, 'Why, here is the hero of it all! Our paladin! Our Sir Galahad! The most valiant gentleman in all France. How right they were to name you *le brave Breuc*.'

Roger took her hands and kissed them. He had been a close friend of Josephine's for many years. Over those years he had often given her sound advice. By saving her reputation he had enabled her marriage to Napoleon to take place. Later, when Napoleon had threatened divorce on account of her infidelities, Roger had again saved the situation. There had been an occasion when she had saved his life. Her present outburst left him entirely at a loss. Wildly his mind clutched at the thought that she might save him now.

Napoleon, equally puzzled, exclaimed, 'Come! What is all this about?'

Gaily she waved the long letter. 'This should have reached me ten days ago, had it not had to be sent on from Paris. It is from Turkey; from my beloved cousin Aimée Dubucq. All is changed. There has been another revolution there. When Baraiktar, the Pasha of Rustchuk, learned how Mustapha and his evil mother had dethroned the Sultan Selim, he marched his army from distant Bulgaria to Constantinople, surprised those devilish Janissaries and defeated them. Poor Selim is dead. He gave his life while the Seraglio was being stormed, to defend his young cousin, Mahmoud. Mustapha is now a prisoner and Mahmoud proclaimed Sultan. The prophecy of our youth, that Aimée and I would wear crowns, came true, and now the last part of it will follow. Dear Aimée's son, the enlightened friend of France, will reign gloriously.'*

'This is indeed good news,' agreed the Emperor. 'But what has all this to do with Breuc?'

'Had it not been for him, Aimée, Selim and Mahmoud would all have been murdered on the night that the Janissaries revolted.' Josephine again waved the letter. 'It is all here. He was in the Seraglio that night, dining with them *en famille*. When they heard the screams of the eunuchs who were being slaughtered, and the Janissaries began breaking down the doors of the apartment, Selim resigned himself to death. But *le brave Breuc* took command. He got them all up a chimney on to the roof, then, at great peril, out of the Seraglio to a boat in which they rowed up the Bosphorus to a castle with a loyal garrison. It was that which enabled them to parley and so save their lives.'

The Emperor stared at Roger. 'Gardane told me nothing of this.'

* *Historical note.* The prophecy did come true. For thirty-one years Mahmoud ruled the Turkish Empire. During his reign he revolutionised Turkey by introducing many reforms and Western customs. But this normally mild man never forgave the Janissaries. Aimée died, venerated by all, in 1817. Nine years after her death, Mahmoud, having slowly created a new body of Household troops loyal to him, decided to deal with the Janissaries, who were again giving serious trouble. He had five thousand of them slain in a single night and abolished the corps for ever.

Roger bowed. 'Why should he, Sire? It was, like my last, a private venture; and differs only in that it did not fail. As a result of it I am happy to think that I preserved not only the Empress' dear friend, but a Sultan whose pro-French leaning should prove of value to Your Majesty.'

'You must decorate him!' Josephine cried. 'Make him a Count, or at least a Baron.'

Frowning, Napoleon said curtly, 'On the contrary, Madame, I have sentenced him to five years in prison.'

'Prison! No; it is unthinkable. What can he possibly have done to incur so great a measure of your displeasure?'

'He is a deserter. Instead of obeying my orders to go to India, he came to Lisbon and has since absented himself from my service for many months.'

Josephine's big dark eyes flashed angrily. 'Is that so great a crime when, for many years, he has served you faithfully? And I doubt not he had a good reason for absenting himself.'

'He did so to pursue a woman.'

The anger in Josephine's eyes swiftly disappeared. Throwing back her head, she laughed, for once showing her only bad feature—uneven, discoloured teeth. 'Now I am truly amazed,' she said to her husband. 'Even my great Eagle does not give all his life to waging war and affairs of State. How can he expect lesser men not at times to give way to the most natural of temptations?'

Roger knew what that laugh had cost her. During the early years of her marriage, Josephine had been flagrantly unfaithful to Napoleon. But time had wrought a change in her. Not only had she become devoted to him, but his infidelities to her pained her greatly. She had made light of a man neglecting his duty for a woman only to strike a spark of sympathy in Napoleon's mind for the frailty of which Roger was accused.

A cynical smile twisted Napoleon's lips for a second. 'In one sense you are right, my dear. Certain impulses must be satisfied unless a man's work is to suffer from their repression. But Breuc has overstepped the mark by indulging his own inclinations for far too long.'

'Sire,' Roger protested swiftly, 'I erred only in going to

Lisbon, as I thought in your best interests, instead of to India. To Brazil I was carried off against my will.'

'Do you swear that?'

'I do, Sire; upon my honour.'

Coming round from behind the desk, Napoleon stretched out his plump, beautifully-modelled hand, seized the lobe of Roger's left ear and tweaked it painfully. While making this curious gesture of approbation, he said, 'Very well, then, you amorous scoundrel. You are reprieved. For that you must thank the Empress.'

Hardly daring to believe that he had heard aright, Roger went down on one knee and kissed the hand Josephine extended to him. Quickly she raised him and cried, 'You owe me nothing. I felt sure that all the time the Emperor was only trying to frighten you. He has far too big a heart to behave harshly to an old friend.'

Roger admired her tact, but had the gravest doubts about her statement as applying to himself before she had come upon the scene. Meanwhile, she was going on, 'You must join us for supper and it will be quite like old times. Afterwards I will read you Aimée's letter, and you must tell us all about your recent adventures.'

Napoleon nodded, and said, 'You were right about the state of Spain. It is causing me considerable concern. Tomorrow you can go into the matter with Berthier. He will find plenty of ways in which we can make good use of you.'

Bowing his acquiescence, Roger suppressed a sigh. Although he had had a miraculous escape, gone was all prospect of a speedy return to England. Once more he had been caught in that tangled web, on the unravelling of which depended the future of Europe.

Josephine proved right, in that supper was very reminiscent of the informal meals that Roger had enjoyed in the old days at Malmaison, with only a few intimate friends present. As a raconteur he was at his best and, rallying himself after the ordeal through which he had just passed, he held the interest of the small company with an account of the trials and tribulations he had suffered both voyaging to and in Brazil.

Then he told them about his marriage. Everyone congratulated him, and Josephine cried, 'Now I can reward you myself for saving dear Aimeé. You must send for your wife, and I will make her one of my ladies.'

But Napoleon habitually ate fast, so the meal was soon over, and they adjourned to a small drawing room. After such suppers at Malmaison, they had often played charades or the First Consul had had all the candles but one put out and frightened the ladies by telling ghost stories. Those days were gone and, having listened with slight signs of impatience while Josephine read Amée's letter, he began to fire questions at Roger about Syria, Mesopotamia and Persia. Roger's replies were always swift and to the point; and, by the end of the evening, he was confident that he had again established himself in the Emperor's good graces.

Next morning he reported to Berthier. The dome-headed little Chief of Staff spread out a map on which were marked the places in Spain where there had been outbreaks of rebellion and the estimated numbers of the insurgents. The picture was even more formidable than Roger had been led to believe. Moreover, Berthier told him that a Convention had been formed by leading representatives of all the groups to co-ordinate measures against the French; but where it held its meetings was unfortunately unknown.

That evening, Roger wrote to Lisala, telling her that he would be remaining with the Emperor, of the honour the Empress proposed to do her, and that she should set out for Madrid as soon as possible. He also wrote to Junot asking, in view of the unsettled state of the country, to provide an escort for her.

During the ten days that followed, alarming reports of the state of the country continued to pour in. The news of the revolts that had broken out spontaneously in half a dozen places had acted like dynamite on the whole people. With incredible speed, the long-suffering Spaniards in every city, town and village had loosed their hatred of the French. With fanatical zeal they had taken up arms to destroy their oppressors. Blood-lusting mobs had seized Mayors and other authorities who were puppets of the French administration and hanged them in the squares. Many considerable towns were now in the hands of the insurgents. They gave no quarter, and small bodies of French troops were continually ambushed and murdered.

Then the news arrived that, on July 4th, Canning had entered into an alliance with the Convention representing the people of Spain. Grimly Napoleon had to accept the fact that Spain, for so long his unwilling ally, had gone over to the enemy and was now, officially, at war with France.

With his usual dynamic energy, he issued innumerable orders, concentrating his troops in vital areas. The road from Bayonne via Burgos to Madrid was to be kept open at all costs. Bessières, with eighty thousand men, would hold the north; Dupont, with another army, would suppress the revolts in the south. But on July 20th the most staggering news came in. After early successes, General Dupont, his troops weighed down with plunder, had been forced to retire into Beylen. On the previous day he had surrendered and his twenty thousand men had laid down their arms.

Napoleon's fury knew no bounds. He was escorted to his apartment, screaming curses. When he had been somewhat calmed down, he sobbed, 'Could I have expected that from Dupont, a man whom I loved and was rearing to become a Marshal? They say he had no other way to save the lives of his soldiers. Better, far better to have died with arms in their hands. Their death would have been glorious; we should have avenged them. You can always supply the place of soldiers. Honour alone, when once lost, can never be regained.'

It was a terrible blow, for it shattered the Grand Army's belief in its invincibility, and the surrender of one of its corps to a rabble of peasants armed with ancient shotguns, scythes and pitchforks was the last ignominy.

On the 22nd, Lisala arrived. She had delayed to collect as much money as she could. With her she also brought her old nurse, Josefa Bilboa. She had a nerve-racking journey as, in spite of the escort of Chasseurs supplied by Junot, her convoy had been fired upon three times. One of the men had been killed and several wounded; but she had escaped unharmed.

Although Lisala was now six months pregnant, her condition was still not obvious at first glance and, when Roger presented her to Josephine, her striking beauty made a great impression on those present. The Empress received her with the greatest kindness and told her at once that only very light duties would be expected of her, as she must rest a lot and take care of her health.

As a married couple, the de Breucs were given a comfortable suite, and Lisala soon made friends with several of Josephine's ladies. But she was greatly disappointed by the Court. She had heard so much of the magnificent balls and fêtes given by the Emperor whenever his headquarters were in a city, and had expected life in Madrid to be a round of pleasure. Instead, the inmates of the Palace now lived much as they would have done had they been in a well-provisioned fortress.

Since the revolt, all social activities had ceased. The ladies were forbidden to leave the Palace and had to while away the time as best they could with needlework and music. The brilliantly uniformed Staff Officers could give no time to entertaining them. Roger and his companions spent many hours each day writing despatches, sifting intelligence and routeing convoys of food and ammunition to isolated garrisons. They could snatch only hasty meals, and often did not get to bed until the early hours of the morning. Sweating and dust-covered, an unending succession of couriers clattered in and out of the courtyard. The Emperor, stern and gloomy, was rarely to be seen.

In spite of the continued success of the insurgents, Napoleon still refused to recognise the magnitude of the struggle with which he was faced. He stubbornly maintained that, given good leadership, twenty-five thousand French troops could quell the rebellion. Then, early in August, he suddenly decided to return to Paris. Overnight everyone began hastily to pack, scores of coaches and wagons were mustered, and the mile-long cavalcade took the road to France.

It was a far from pleasant journey. The broiling sun on the roofs of the coaches made the interiors like ovens; and, in many places, owing to lack of habitable accommodation, their stifled occupants had to sleep in them. Daily couriers overtook them, with news of further French reverses. The surrender at Baylen had injected into the Spaniards a positive conviction that only courage was needed to drive the French out of Spain.

In the north-east the hardy Catalans had risen and, by sheer audacity, forced the French to retire into the fortresses at Barcelona and Figueras. In Aragon, Saragossa had become the scene of appalling slaughter, with ferocious street fighting, in which the French garrison was driven from house to house.

Joseph, now King of Spain, had arrived in his new capital a few days after Napoleon's departure. He remained there only a week. Fearing that a great body of insurgents which was marching on Madrid would capture it, he had fled with the army of which he was the titular Commander, north to the far side of the river Ebro. Savary had given up the line of the Upper Douro, and was fighting a rearguard action in an attempt to join up with Bessières. Finally, to crown this tale of woe, when they reached Paris they learned that a British army under the command of Sir Arthur Wellesley, had landed in Portugal and was advancing on Lisbon.

As soon as the Court had settled into its quarters in the Palace of St. Cloud, Roger went to call on Talleyrand. The elegant Prince de Benevento had just finished entertaining some friends to an epicurean breakfast. When they had taken their leave, leaning on Roger's arm he led him into a small library, and the two old friends settled down to talk.

They had no secrets from each other. After Roger had given an abbreviated account of his doings in Turkey, Persia, Brazil and, finally, of his narrow escape from spending five years in a fortress, the great statesman laughed and said:

'That so resourceful a man as yourself should have been outwitted and kidnapped by your charmer I find most amusing; but your escape from the Emperor's wrath shows that your lucky star is still in the ascendant. You are lucky, too, to be out of Spain. From the reports I receive, I gather all hell has been let loose there.'

'It has, indeed, although our little man refuses to recognise it.'

'He has become the victim of *folie de grandeur*, and will no longer listen to anyone. By his treatment of the Spanish royal family at Bayonne, he signed away Spain. That was the match that lit the bonfire. They are, admittedly, the most miserable people; incompetent and cowardly to the last degree. But that does not alter the fact that they are venerated by the Spanish masses.'

'I am told that you had them for a while at your château of Valençay.'

'Yes, although Napoleon has lost his judgment he retains his cunning. He sent them to me in order to implicate me in his treatment of them; although, from the beginning, I have made it plain to him how strongly I disapprove of his intentions regarding Spain.'

'What of the rest of Europe?'

Talleyrand shrugged. 'He has sown the wind and will reap the whirlwind. Austria is again arming against us. The Archduke Charles and Prince Metternich are counselling caution; but others, who have the Emperor Francis' ear, are impatient for revenge. Prussia is seething with hatred for the humiliations we have put upon her; King Frederick William is a broken reed; his Consort, Queen Louisa, a most gallant lady, but her influence is not strong enough to make her husband defy Napoleon. In Prussia, as in Spain, resistance will not come from the top, but from the people. Stein is busy modernising their Army; student bodies and the intellectuals are already openly urging the people to revolt. To all appearances our little man is now at the summit of his power; but it is only a matter of time before his ruthless ambition brings about his downfall.'

'How stand our relations with Russia?' Roger asked.

'That is difficult to answer. Outwardly there have been no signs of their deterioration since the pact made at Tilsit. But I have a feeling that, underneath, all is not well. Napoleon senses that, too, and is anxious to consolidate his relations with the Czar by another meeting. That was his reason for returning from Spain. Endeavours are being made to arrange one; but Alexander is averse to coming to Paris, and Napoleon will not go to Moscow. No doubt some neutral city will be chosen for a Conference. There Napoleon will produce his great plan for the aggrandisement of both Empires. It is that they should join forces, attack Turkey and divide the vast territories of the Sultan between them. The Czar is to have the Danubian lands, Bulgaria and all Turkey in Europe; while France takes Egypt and Turkey's dominions in Asia as a springboard to India.'

Roger smiled. 'I must congratulate Your Excellency upon your private intelligence service. It keeps you remarkably well informed about matters up to the latest moment.'

'No, no!' Talleyrand took a pinch of snuff. 'Napoleon sent for me last night, and himself told me his intentions.'

'Indeed!' Roger raised an eyebrow. 'But when on my travels, I heard it said that you were no longer Foreign Minister.'

'True, dear friend; quite true. After Tilsit I decided to resign. I had become weary of giving advice that was not accepted, and drawing up treaties of which I strongly disapproved —treaties which, in my view, must ultimately lead to the ruin of France. Napoleon was much annoyed, but could scarce ignore the many services I have rendered. As you must be aware, there were a very limited number of High Dignitaries created when our little man crowned himself Emperor. Joseph was made Grand Elector, and Louis High Constable. On my retirement, I was made Vice-Grand Elector, with equal status to the others, and an additional half-million francs a year revenue; so I did not do too badly. Our old enemy, Fouché, put about a rather delightful *mot* concerning my elevation. He said, "It is the only Vice that Talleyrand had not got".'

Roger roared with laughter. Then he said, 'Although you no longer hold the Foreign Office portfolio, apparently Napoleon continues to consult you.'

'Yes. He gave the portfolio to Caulaincourt, a pleasant and quite able man. Yet, hate me though Napoleon now does, it seems that I have a strange fascination for him. He takes no step of importance without informing me of it, and asking my opinion, even though he frequently rejects it.'

'You will, then, be attending this forthcoming conference?'

'Almost certainly.' After a moment Talleyrand gave a cynical smile and added, 'There I may find an opportunity to send Alexander away more dissatisfied than ever at having entered into an alliance with us. As long as Napoleon can count on Russia to menace Austria, his position remains comparatively strong; but, should the Czar break with him, that could bring about his fall. And you and I agreed at Warsaw that that has become necessary as the only means of restoring peace and prosperity to Europe.'

Roger nodded. 'Somehow it must be done. But I have not yet congratulated your Exalted Highness on having been made Vice-Grand Elector. I do so on two counts. Firstly, in that this honour places you on an equal footing with the Bonaparte Princes. Secondly, on having resigned your office when you did. Now, when the Empire does collapse, and others scuttle from the sinking ship, no-one will be able to accuse you of having waited to leave it with the rats.'

Early in September still worse news came in from the Peninsula, which was now the focus of all eyes. Wellesley had driven the French vanguard from Rolica; then, on the 24th August, he had met Junot's main force at Vimiero and inflicted a crushing defeat upon it. Junot's whole army would have been cut off from Torres Vedras, but for the fact that an officer senior to Wellesley, General Sir Harry Burrard, arrived just at that moment, took over command and, most idiotically, called off the pursuit.

Shortly afterwards the hopeless idiocy of Britain's old-fashioned senior Generals was further manifested. Burrard was superseded by Sir Hew Dalrymple. Instead of demanding the surrender of Junot's defeated army, he entered into a pact with Junot at Cintra. By it Junot and all his troops were to be sent back to France in British ships.

Napoleon, angry as he was at Junot's defeat, got back many thousands of troops who would otherwise have remained prisoners in Portugal. With a sour laugh he declared, 'How fortunate I am in having British generals fighting my wars for me.'

The unfortunate Dupont and his principal commanders had also been released by the Spaniards and returned to France. Upon them, for their surrender at Baylen, the Emperor vented his wrath, consigning all of them to prison.

Meanwhile, it had been agreed that Alexander and Napoleon should meet at Erfurt, a town in Thuringia some sixty-five miles south-west of Leipzig.

By mid-September, when the Court was about to set out, Lisala was expecting her baby in from six to eight weeks. For some time past, Roger had been treating her with the utmost tenderness; and waiting anxiously for her delivery, hoping that she would bear him a son. As Erfurt meant a journey of three hundred and sixty miles, he was most averse to her undertaking it. But she had been greatly enjoying herself in Paris, and was most loath both to being left alone while the Court was in Germany, and missing the many splendid entertainments which would take place at the conference. It was unlikely that the conference would last more than a fortnight; so she argued that they should be back in Paris at the latest within five weeks. In consequence, Roger reluctantly agreed to her setting out with the Empress and the Court officials who were to make the journey in moderately easy stages.

Several days later, Napoleon, who always travelled at great speed, followed, accompanied by his staff. To salvoes of cannon they entered Erfurt on September 26th. The Empress had arrived there that morning. From the Quartermaster, who had taken over the Town Hall, Roger learned that he and Lisala had been billeted not far from the centre of the town, at the house of a notary named Gunther. Eager to see Lisala, he went there at once.

No sooner had he made himself known to the notary's wife than she exclaimed, 'Colonel, we are in a great taking here. The long journey had most unfortunate results on your lady. When she arrived this morning, she was already in labour. I understand that her accouchement was not due for some weeks yet. But an hour ago she gave premature birth to your child.'

'My wife?' he asked swiftly. 'Is she all right?'

'Yes, yes!' the woman assured him. 'We called our doctor. A good man. Her delivery was quite normal.'

Brushing past her, Roger ran up the stairs three at a time. Behind a slightly-opened door on the landing he heard a faint mewling. Thrusting the door wide open, he strode into the room.

Lisala's nurse, old Josefa Bilboa, was sitting there in an easy chair, gently rocking a bundle on her lap. As she saw Roger, her dark eyes widened with fear.

'Is it a boy?' Roger asked eagerly.

The old woman nodded. 'Yes, *Senhor*, but . . .'

Advancing on her, Roger smiled and said, 'Let me see him. Let me see my son.'

Josefa shrank back, pressing the bundle to her flaccid bosom as she whispered, '*Senhor*, be merciful. This . . . this will be a shock to you.'

Roger frowned. 'Do you mean that the child is malformed?'

'No, *Senhor*, no! But . . . but . . .'

Stretching out a hand, Roger pulled the swaddling clothes aside and gazed, horror-struck, at the infant.

It had curly red hair; its nose was flattened and its lips were thick; its skin was brown; beyond all doubt, it was the child of a Negro.

24

Surprise at Erfurt

Utterly aghast, Roger stared down at the small, dark, wizened creature. Never before in his life had his mind been so paralysed by shock. Momentarily his numbed brain suggested to him that he was the victim of a nightmare. He was brought back to awful reality by the sound of footsteps behind him. Swinging round, he saw that Frau Gunther had followed him into the room.

Wildly he sought some explanation that he could give of this scandalous event, which could not be concealed and must soon become the talk of the town, bringing disgrace upon Lisala and making him the laughing stock of everyone he knew. His normally swift reaction to unexpected situations suddenly returned to him. White-faced, he confronted the woman and said:

'*Meine Frau*, I beg your indulgence in that my wife's delivery should have occurred in your house, causing you much inconvenience. Aware of the terrible experience that befell her before she left Brazil, I had intended to take her to some secluded house, where she could have her unwanted child. But her giving birth prematurely has defeated my intentions. While in Rio de Janeiro, my wife was raped by a Negro slave.'

The portly Frau Gunther nodded sympathetically. 'I felt sure, *Herr Oberst*, that there must be some such explanation. It makes me shudder to think of what the poor lady must have suffered. But please be assured that my husband and I will do everything possible for her comfort and yours.' Pointing to a door behind him, she added, 'Would you now like to go in and see your wife?'

Feeling that he must have time to think before deciding

what to do about Lisala, Roger replied, 'No. Her delivery having been so recent, it is essential that she should remain undisturbed. I feel, too, that for some nights at least it would be detrimental to my wife if I shared her bed; and my servant will shortly arrive with my baggage. Could you provide me with another room?'

'I can if the *Herr Oberst* would not mind a small one on the top floor of the house.'

Roger raised a smile. 'As a soldier, I consider myself lucky when I have a roof over my head. You will forgive me if I leave you now. I have urgent work to do at headquarters.'

With a bow to Frau Gunther, he stepped past her and stumped down the stairs. Turning into a high-walled alley that ran alongside the house, he paced up and down for half an hour, thinking furiously. He did not believe for one moment that Lisala had been raped; but his story that she had would at least protect him from the degradation of being secretly mocked as a cuckold, and should gain sympathy for her rather than opprobrium.

Deciding that it was better that he should himself announce the awful event, rather than let it reach the Court by way of gossip spread by the Gunther household and the doctor who had delivered Lisala, he went to the mansion which had been taken over for Napoleon, and requested an audience with the Empress.

Half an hour later she was condoling with him on his misfortune. When a girl in Martinique, she had heard of occasional cases in which Negro slaves had gone mad and raped white women, so she accepted Roger's story without question. He said that Lisala would, of course, resign her appointment and, as soon as she was sufficiently recovered, he intended to send her back to Paris. Josephine, who was the most kindhearted of women, replied:

'If that is her wish, I will not oppose it; but it would be said that I had dismissed her, so imply that she is guilty of a crime and lead to her being ostracised by society. It would be most cruel to inflict further suffering on her after the terrible experience she has been through. By showing special warmth towards her when she reappears at Court, I can ensure that no malicious person dare cause her embarrassment.'

Having thanked Josephine for her generous attitude, Roger went out to prowl the streets, but found that, to walk unimpeded through the narrow ways overhung by the upper storeys of the old, timbered houses, was next to impossible. French and Russian officers, Hussars, Chasseurs, Cossacks and Artillerymen jostled the gaping town-folk, while coaches and carriages, occupied by notables, frequently blocked the way. The inns were equally crowded, and there seemed no place in which he could think out quietly what he should do about Lisala. In desperation, he returned to his billet.

There Herr and Frau Gunther asked him to honour them by supping with them. Feeling churlish but quite incapable of making polite conversation, he refused, sent his servant out for a couple of bottles of wine, and went up to his room. During the next two hours he drank the wine, but it did not make him even mildly drunk and, when he went to bed, he had formed only one decision. He must rid himself of Lisala as soon as possible.

Next morning he left the house early and, somehow, got through his duties. Then, unwilling to talk with his brother officers, he ate a meal at an inn, but found difficulty in swallowing. Feeling that he could no longer put off the interview from which his whole being shrank, he went to his billet. No-one was about, so he walked straight upstairs to the room in which he had seen the infant. A cradle had been procured, and old Josefa sat there, rocking it. Without giving her a glance, he crossed the room and pushed open the far door.

Lisala was sitting up in bed. As is so often the case with women soon after their delivery, she had never looked lovelier. Her cheeks were a little pale, her splendid, wide-spaced eyes glowing with health, and her milk-filled breasts showed clearly through a nightdress of gossamer-thin muslin. As he entered the room, her lips parted, showing her perfect teeth, in a smiling greeting.

Grim-faced, he stood at the end of her bed and demanded harshly, 'Well, Madame; what have you to say?'

She shrugged. 'Only that I regret that the child is not yours. I could not be certain, and hoped up to the last moment that it would be.'

'Who is its father?'

'Why, Baob, of course.'

'I suspected as much. And that this was no case of rape, otherwise you would have told me of it. You admit then, that you willingly gave yourself to a Negro?'

'He was an African Prince.'

'Prince, be damned! He was a Negro slave.'

Lisala's eyes flashed. 'He proved a better lover than you.'

'Maybe. I am not accustomed to competing with black giants. But how could you possibly have brought yourself to submit to this abomination?'

'I did not submit. He would never have dared lay a finger on me had I not encouraged him by allowing him one hot afternoon to see me naked, then lain down on my bed and beckoned to him.'

Roger gave a gasp. 'My God! Such conduct is utterly iniquitous.'

'It is not when one feels a great urge to be made love to, and a stalwart man is readily available.'

'Lisala, we all feel such urges from time to time. But ordinary decency demands control. For a woman of your birth to give herself to the first man who comes along is positively outrageous.'

She sighed. 'It may be so for some people, but is not in my case. You have never understood me. From the age of thirteen I craved for such sensations. Knowing nothing of men at that time I satisfied these sensations every night myself. Then in Tehran my Russian Prince came along and taught me the full joy of being possessed. For a few months after he left I was driven nearly crazy with desire. You arrived and, you will recall, at the first opportunity I positively flung myself at you. In you I found something more than physical satisfaction. You are handsome, courageous and fascinating to talk to. But such attributes weigh only when I am with you. On the long voyage we made from the Persian Gulf and up the Red Sea, I took the First Officer of the ship as my lover. While crossing the Mediterranean, a young super-cargo fulfilled my needs. Then came that ghastly crossing of the Atlantic, when we were daily together, yet could never be alone. During that time I nearly died of frustration. In Rio we again enjoyed a brief intimacy. Alas, my father put an end to that. When he had forced you from the house, what was I to do? To meet you in secret or, in that rigid society, secure one of my father's friends as my lover, proved impossible. What does a black skin matter, provided the man be vigorous? Baob meant nothing to me. When you killed him I felt not a qualm; but those afternoons when he ferociously enjoyed me gave me peaceful sleep at nights.'

Appalled, Roger stared at her, then he asked bitterly, 'And after I left you in Portugal, during the time I was in Madrid, whom did you pick on to satisfy your insatiable lust?'

She smiled serenely. 'Junot. He is something of a blockhead, but passable to go to bed with.'

For a minute Roger remained silent, considering the situation. Lisala's admission that she had had an *affaire* with Junot touched him in a very soft spot. He was well aware that Napoleon's Generals and their wives were an immoral crew. When away in distant commands, the men invariably took mistresses, and their wives, left as grass widows in Paris for many months, frequently took handsome young officers as their lovers. But he was not prepared to have it said that, during his absences, his wife was easy game for any man who wanted to jump into bed with her.

If he accepted Josephine's generous gesture, and Lisala remained one of her ladies, that would inevitably happen. Better to cut the knot now, whatever people might think or say. In the circumstances, her retirement could be put down to reluctance to continue at Court, with everyone aware of her misfortune. Within a few weeks the whole matter would be forgotten. So he said:

'I have heard of other cases in which women's bodies rule their minds to the exclusion of all decency. But I am not the man to continue with a wife who will become known as the

Court whore. When you are well enough, Madame, you will seek an audience with the Empress, tell her that your misfortune causes you such embarrassment that you cannot any longer bring yourself to remain in her service. I'll then send you back to Paris and later, if conditions permit, to Portugal.'

With a complacent shrug, Lisala replied, 'Oh no, my dear husband, you will not do that.' As she spoke, she picked up a letter from her bedside table, and went on, 'This morning I received this from the Empress. She assumes that I was raped, condoles with me upon my terrible experience, and assures me that she will show her extreme displeasure to anyone who assails my reputation on account of my having given birth to a black baby. I have never enjoyed myself more than while being a member of the Court, and I receive special prestige as the wife of *le brave Breuc*; so disabuse yourself of any idea of sending me away. Here I intend to remain.'

'In that you are mistaken, Madame,' Roger said firmly. 'You will render thanks to the Empress for her kindness, then go. Even the Emperor cannot intervene between husband and wife. A husband's decision is law, and I intend to send you away.'

Lisala's smile was seraphic as she replied, 'I do not think you will—Mr. Brook.'

Roger's heart missed a beat. He had temporarily forgotten that she was aware of his true identity. If she denounced him, it would be only her word against his. But some people might believe her, and that could seriously weaken his position. How big a hold she had on him he did not realise until she went on:

'When you were first in Lisbon, you lived there under your true colours—hobnobbing with Lord Strangford at the British Embassy, and going off to consult with Admiral Sir Smith in his ship. In Brazil, too, you were known to scores of the nobility there as an Englishman. Above all, there were those weeks we spent in England. I can give chapter and verse about your house at Richmond, your friends, your club and your meeting with Mr. Canning. It may take time for the French to check the information I give them; but they have their spies as well. And, once they know you definitely to have been working with their enemies, they will have you shot.'

Forcing a casual indifference, Roger said, 'You overrate your powers, Madame. The French have long believed me to be a Frenchman with English connections, which enables me to pass as one and spy for them. It would take more than a few trumped-up charges by a disgruntled wife to make them believe otherwise.'

Yet, even as he spoke, he knew that he could not afford to have such well-supported suspicion cast on him. To court that was too dangerous. He dared not risk it. So he resumed icily:

'Your excessive lust may be due to causes beyond your control. But to threaten with such perfidy one whom you have professed to love is inexcusable. Making such accusations as you suggest could, I admit, be used by my enemies and put me to considerable inconvenience to refute. Therefore, for the present, I agree to continue to regard you publicly as my wife. Apart from that, everything is over between us. Now, what of the child?'

Lisala shrugged. 'Do with it as you will. I was shown it shortly after it was born, and never wish to see it again. That is why I sent Josefa out with it to the ante-room. I'll not have it in here, far less suckle it.'

'It is in keeping with your character as recently revealed that you should lack all maternal feeling,' he said acidly. 'But, in the circumstances, I welcome your decision. The sooner I can get it away from here, the less talk there will be about it.' With a curt bow, he turned and strode from the room.

Going downstairs, he sought the help of Herr and Frau Gunther. They were a pleasant, elderly couple, and tactfully conveyed to him that, immediately after the birth of the infant, they had realised that it was not a matter to be bruited abroad. They had, therefore, enjoined silence on their servants, and told Roger that the discretion of their doctor, who had delivered Lisala, could also be relied on.

He thanked them warmly, then asked Frau Gunther if she could find a wet-nurse for the child—preferably some farm labourer's wife who lived outside the town. She said that some might object to suckling a coloured baby, but when he told her that money was no object, she agreed to do her best. Meanwhile Josefa would continue to feed the baby with spoonfuls of fresh cow's milk.

By the following day the conference had got into full swing. On the surface all was amity. The two Emperors rode out together, exchanging smiles and compliments. French and Russian Marshals and Generals entertained one another with great cordiality. Bands played daily in the park. Minor Kings, Grand Dukes and Princes, with their retinues, patiently waited their turn to pay scrupulously equal homage to the Emperor and the Czar. The ladies from Paris and St. Petersburg competed in the splendour of their toilettes and displays of fabulous jewels. Beside them the poor German women looked frumpish and their principal royalty, Frederick William of Prussia, although a third party to the alliance, was barely acknowledged by the Caesars of the North and West. The days were given to meetings; private conversations between the two Emperors in the mornings and discussion round a great table by Ministers and Marshals in the afternoons.

In the evenings all was gaiety. From Paris Napoleon had brought the actors of the Comédie Française to perform Voltaire's plays. On other nights they enjoyed favourite operas, or attended brilliant receptions, followed by balls. In addition to statesmen and soldiers, many distinguished scientists and literary men were present, Goethe among them, who smilingly received the *Legion d'Honneur* from Napoleon's hands.

But, beneath it all, those in the know were aware that the enthusiasm for the alliance achieved at Tilsit was lacking. Then it had been agreed that Alexander should withdraw his troops from the Danubian provinces and Napoleon evacuate Silesia; but neither had done so. The Czar, too, was chagrined that Napoleon demanded from Prussia an indemnity which it was impossible for her to pay, and as a surtax, still retained garrisons in the fortresses of Stettin, Glogau and Küstrin, which menaced Russia's frontier.

The revolt in Spain had great weakened Napoleon's hand. Portugal was now occupied by a British army and, although

Junot's troops were being repatriated, a considerable force had been lost to France. Earlier, when King Carlos had cringed before Napoleon, in addition to paying a huge subsidy, he had agreed to send fifteen thousand of Spain's finest troops to assist in garrisoning Hanover. Inflamed by the news of the rebellion in their own country, they had become anxious to return to it. Their Commanders had succeeded in getting secretly in touch with Canning, who had sent a squadron to the Baltic, taken the Spanish Corps aboard and repatriated them, thus greatly strengthening the insurgents.

The escape of this contingent was a severe blow to Napoleon's hold on North Germany, and the success of the rebellion by the Spanish people had enormously encouraged those Germans who were secretly planning to throw off the yoke of the French.

In the previous year Frederick of Prussia had given his Minister Heinrich Stein virtually the powers of a civil dictator. Stein had then revolutionised his country's political system, by bringing in most drastic reforms. He had abolished serfdom, admitted all classes to the ownership of land, and imbued municipal Governments with new vitality. This had resulted in the masses now feeling that they had a real stake in their country's future. Meanwhile, his colleague Scharnhorst, at the Ministry of War, had conceived the new idea that in peace time all able-bodied men should serve for a period in the Army, then become available as reserves. Foreseeing danger to himself in this, Napoleon had forced Frederick William to sign a treaty agreeing that the Prussian Army should never exceed forty-two thousand men; but this failed to invalidate the fact that Prussia was steadily building up a great reserve of men trained to arms.

Napoleon, continuing to discount the war in the Peninsula and the ominous rumblings now coming from Germany, was still obsessed with his dreams of conquering the East and sought to woo Alexander by a glamorous prospect of adding Turkey's European dominions to the Imperial Russian Crown; but they failed to agree on the thorny subject of Constantinople.

The Czar desired to turn the Black Sea into a Russian lake,

with an exit through the Dardanelles to the Mediterranean. The Emperor could not bring himself to allow another Great Power to occupy the Porte and Narrows, lest later it might menace his operations in Asia.

Meanwhile, Frau Gunther had secured a wet-nurse for the Negro infant, and Josefa had gone with it to live in a farmstead outside the town. In answer to the enquiries of his friends about his wife's accouchement, Roger gave this information while, naturally, refraining from mentioning the baby's colour. Somewhat to his surprise and much to his relief, the discretion shown by the Gunthers appeared to have proved effective. Two people casually mentioned to him that a lady in the town was said to have given birth to the child of a Negro, but it was obvious that neither connected this scandal with Lisala. It therefore seemed that, after all, he need not have disclosed the affair to Josephine; but he was not to know at the time that gossip would not swiftly inform her of it, and he had always held that it was better to be safe than sorry.

Being young and healthy, Lisala made a speedy recovery and, greatly annoyed at having already missed several splendid entertainments, on the fifth night she insisted on attending a ball given by the Czar. When they were presented, Roger felt certain that Alexander would recognise him, so having bowed low, he said:

'I am happy, Sire, to have this opportunity of again thanking Your Imperial Majesty for arranging my exchange last year.'

Alexander smiled and replied, 'On two occasions while you were a prisoner, Colonel, I found your conversation most interesting. We must talk again. At a convenient time I will send one of my officers to request your attendance on me.'

As they entered the ballroom, Roger began to point out to Lisala numerous people of interest, among them Count Haugwitz. He was the pro-French statesman whom Napoleon had forced King Frederick to make his Prime Minister, after the defeat of Prussia, instead of the pro-English Count Hardenberg. Talking to him were a slightly taller man and a dark-haired woman with a voluptuous figure. The couple had their backs to Roger but, as though impelled by an impulse, the woman suddenly turned right round. At the same moment Roger took a quick step towards her. Their eyes met, and both gave a cry of delight. She was his beloved Georgina.

Introductions followed. Georgina had not heard that Roger had remarried. After a swift appraisement of Lisala, she smilingly congratulated him on the peerless beauty of his new wife. Roger had met the Prussian Prime Minister's cousin, Baron Haugwitz, once before, at the Tuileries toward the end of '99. The Baron had then just been transferred from Ambassador to the Court of St. James to that of Napoleon who was at that time still First Consul. It was Haugwitz who had told Roger that when he had left London, Georgina had been reported desperately ill and so led to Roger's returning to England in record time. But neither had been aware that the other was in love with her.

Soon afterwards Haugwitz presented Lisala and Roger to Louisa, the beautiful and courageous Queen of Prussia who, while her craven husband sullenly submitted to Napoleon's bullying, was fighting the Emperor tooth and nail, in an endeavour to make him reduce the taxation which was ruining her people, and give up the important fortress of Magdeburg.

Later, Georgina and Roger twice waltzed together. Dances were too brief for them to exchange detailed confidences; but the bond between them which had existed since their teens, was as strong as ever. They had not taken three turns in their first waltz before both said simultaneously, 'You are not happy.'

They laughed at this evidence of their life-long rapport. Then Georgina went on, 'She is so superb a creature that I do not wonder you fell in love with her. But those splendid eyes of hers are too far apart for a normal mind to lie behind them, and about her I sensed an aura of evil.'

Roger had many times had evidence of the psychic perception which Georgina had inherited from her gipsy mother, so her statement did not surprise him. 'You are right,' he agreed. 'And what of your Baron? He's a devilish handsome fellow, and has both charm and intellect. In what way do you find him unsatisfactory?'

'He was charming enough when in England,' she replied. 'But, like all Germans, he is harsh and dictatorial at home. Still, he is no more tiresome to live with than was my first husband Humphrey Etheredge.'

'How is young Charles?' Roger asked.

She hesitated a moment. 'I could not have a more loving son, and he is growing into a fine youth. But he does not like living in Germany, and he misses the companionship of your little Susan terribly, as indeed do I.'

During their second dance, he twitted her. 'You always vowed that you would be a Duchess before your hair turned grey. But now you have taken a step down, from Countess of St. Ermins to be a German Baroness.'

She winked a naughty eye and whispered, 'For your ear alone, dear heart, I at least recently achieved an Archduke as a lover.' Throwing back their heads, they both laughed uproariously.

Before the dance finished, she said earnestly, ''Tis all too long since we have seen anything of each other. And I am confronted with a problem that I need to talk to you about. As soon as the conference ends, please bring your wife to stay at my new home, Schloss Langenstien, near Bingen. This is important to me, my love, very important. So you must come. You must.'

'Of course I will come,' he assured her immediately. 'And I would that I could come alone. But that is not possible. As things are I'd be grateful if you would give Lisala and me separate rooms.'

She made a little grimace. 'So things are already come to such a sorry pass with you. 'Tis so also with myself. Ulrich and I now sleep apart.'

Giving her a wicked grin, Roger murmured, 'That being so, most beloved of beloveds, perhaps . . .'

Georgina made a movement of her full red lips, as though blowing him a kiss, and whispered, 'The vintage will be over, but for you I shall ever be as a ripe grape ready to fall.'

The ball went on until three o'clock in the morning. Captains and Kings, Russian Grand Duchesses and beautiful prostitutes who had become the wives of the gallant warriors of the French Empire, Germans, Poles and Danes, mingled together, laughed, flirted outrageously and quaffed glass after glass of champagne. At length, many of them far from steady on their feet, they began to drift away. Lisala had naturally refrained from dancing; but had enjoyed herself enormously, having spent the evening surrounded with a succession of handsome officers eager to talk to her. And Josephine had beckoned her over, and had spoken to her with great kindness.

When Roger escorted her home, he felt a new man. His depression and gloom about the future had been banished as by the wave of a fairy's wand. His brief encounter with the love of his life had restored him, as nothing else could have done, to his old optimistic, confident self.

A few days later he went out to see Josefa. He told her that he had arranged for her to travel back to Paris at the end of the month with one of the last convoys conveying the Gobelin tapestries and other rich embellishments the Emperor had sent to add lustre to his presence at the conference. He then gave her gold and a letter to his old and trusted friend Maître Blanchard at *La Belle Etoile*, in the Rue St. Honoré, telling her that the innkeeper and his wife would take good care of her and the infant until she received further instructions from him.

The conference continued for a further ten days. During this time the two couples met again nearly every evening, either at receptions, the theatre or at balls; but it was only at the latter that Roger was able to hold brief private conversations with Georgina. Ulrich von Haugwitz did not attempt to conceal the fact that he found Lisala most attractive, and he had heartily endorsed Georgina's invitation that the de Breucs should spend some days at Schloss Langenstein when the conference was over. But there was one aspect of the visit which had given Roger cause for thought, and during a dance he raised it with Georgina.

'I have been thinking,' he said, 'about young Charles. Your husband and everyone here believe me to be a Frenchman; but the boy can have no suspicion of the double life I lead. When I arrive at the Schloss, all the odds are that he will rush

421

to embrace me, and that would put the fat in the fire with a vengeance.'

Georgina thought for a moment, then said, 'You are right, so you must not travel with us, but arrive a day or two later, so that I shall have time to warn him. He is now twelve, a sensible lad and entirely to be trusted. It could be said, too, that while you were in England on your mission for Napoleon in '99, I invited you, as I often did foreign Ambassadors, down to stay at Stillwaters. Then, should Charles make some slip, that would explain away your knowing the house and his having as a child seen you there.'

It was on the last day of the conference that the Czar sent for Roger. He was seated at ease in a small room with his friend and adviser, Prince Adam Czartoryski. When the equerry who had presented Roger had withdrawn, Alexander smiled and said:

'*Monsieur le Colonel* . . . or should I say Mr. Brook, when last we met Russia was at war with France, and it was understood that, if I arranged your exchange, you would do your utmost to supply me with useful information.'

Roger bowed. 'I was eager to do so, Sire; but was deprived of the opportunity.'

'So I have been informed. You were sent with General Gardane's mission to Turkey and Persia, were you not? So I do not hold against you your failure to keep your word. However, I should like to hear your views on the present situation.'

For some five minutes Roger held forth on the war being waged in the Peninsula and the unrest in Germany. Finally, he said:

'The Emperor is still wielding immense power and resources. Does he turn his will to it, I believe him capable of subduing Spain and throwing the English out of Portugal. In Germany, as long as he holds the principal fortresses, little can be done against him. But of his eventual fall I am convinced. It will be brought about by the leading men among his own people. They have come to realise that his wars are no longer in defence of France, but to satisfy his own insane ambitions. He is bleeding France to death, and at the first favourable op-

422

portunity, to save their country, many of those whom he has raised up will turn upon him.'

The Czar and Prince Adam exchanged a smile, then the latter said:

'This we have learned, and from a very high authority. One such said to His Imperial Majesty only the other day, "Sire, what are you coming here for? It is for you to save Europe, and you will only succeed in that by resisting Napoleon. The French are civilised, their sovereign is not. The Sovereign of Russia is civilised, her people are not. Therefore the Sovereign of Russia must be the ally of the French people."'

Roger smiled. 'I would stake my life that I could name the man who said that. It was the Prince de Benevento.'

'Why should you suppose so?' Alexander asked coldly.

'Because, Sire, every word has the ring of Talleyrand. He has been my close friend for over twenty years. He knows as you do that I am, in fact, an Englishman. We have worked together ceaselessly, although so far without avail, to bring about peace between our two countries, so that this bloodshed may end and the nations of Europe again enjoy security and prosperity.'

Alexander raised his eyebrows. 'Then, Mr. Brook, you are an even more remarkable man than I had supposed, and can be of great service to us. Policy dictates that we should renew our treaty with the Emperor, but we shall not pay more than lip service to it. Talleyrand has seen to that, and Napoleon must indeed have become insane to have put him in charge of negotiations here, instead of relying on his Foreign Minister.'

'I was not aware that he had, Sire,' Roger admitted, 'as I have had no private conversation with the Prince since we arrived in Erfurt. But 'tis said, "those whom the gods seek to destroy they first make mad", and that is the case with Napoleon.'

Rising to terminate the interview, the Czar extended his hand for Roger to kiss and said, 'Mr. Brook, we know you to be our friend, and any service you can render us will not go unrewarded.'

Next day, October 12th, the new treaty was signed. An

423

hour later, Roger sought an interview with the Emperor and asked for leave.

Before he could say more, Napoleon rounded on him and snapped, 'What! And after you have been back in my service for no more than three months? I suppose on account of your weak chest you wish again to idle the winter away in sunshine at that little château of yours in the South of France? But I will provide you with ample sunshine. I intend to go to Spain and teach those Spanish curs a lesson they will not soon forget. You speak many languages, have travelled far, and possess a knowledge of affairs greatly exceeding that of the majority of my *beaux sabreurs*. I can find many uses for you, so I mean to take you to Spain with me.'

Roger smiled. 'Sire, you flatter me; but you did not hear me out. I meant only to ask permission to spend a few days with Baron von Haugwitz and his wife at their castle on the Rhine.'

'Ah! That is another matter. Go then; but rejoin me in Paris before the end of the month.'

Next day the conference began to break up, with more salvoes of cannon and fanfares of trumpets. Roger was present when Queen Louisa went out to her coach. At a private dinner with her husband, Josephine and Napoleon, she had pleaded eloquently with the latter to return Magdeburg to Prussia. Having made her an evasive answer, he had taken a rose from a vase on the table and handed it to her. Those who knew him realised that the gesture had been inspired only by his invariable gentleness towards women; but she had taken it as a deliberate indication that he did not regard women as qualified to discuss affairs of State.

Immersed as ever in his own urgent business he did not pay her the courtesy of coming to see her off. It was Talleyrand who limped forward and offered her his arm, condoled with her for a while on her failure to help her country, then handed her into her coach. Afterwards she recorded:

'I was astonished beyond belief that this renegade priest, whom I had always thought of as the most evil, depraved and treacherous man of his time, should have been the only one to show me sympathy and understanding during the conference at Erfurt.'

The Haugwitzes left on the same day. Having noticed that Gunther's study had only a small bookcase and that several score of law books were in piles on the floor, Roger went out and bought for him the finest bookcase he could find in the town, and expensive presents for Frau Gunther and the doctor who had delivered Lisala. These simple, kindly Germans received them with surprise and gratitude; but he assured them that he could not sufficiently repay the care they had given to his wife. Next morning he and Lisala set out for Schloss Langenstein.

The journey was something under two hundred miles, so could be done comfortably by coach in four days. Lisala took with her in the coach a young girl named Gretchen, whom Frau Gunther had procured for her as a maid, after Josefa had moved out to the farm with the Negro baby. Roger rode beside the coach, and his soldier-servant, François, behind him.

During the conference, husband and wife had exchanged barely a word, except during the evenings when they were with other people. But now that they were alone, he had to make up his mind how he should treat her. Although he was determined to reject any overtures she might make towards resuming their former intimacy, he decided that it would cause great awkwardness at the inns if they did not at least appear to be on good terms; so, when they halted at the wayside for their first picnic lunch, he said:

'Lisala, what has happened cannot be undone. During the times we spent together in Isfahan, Lisbon, Rio and Madrid, I was many times perturbed by the violence of your temper and your extreme selfishness; but my passion for you was such that I made allowances for the unattractive side of your mind, believing it to be beyond the power of your will to control.

'But the day after we reached Erfurt you revealed to me your true nature, even glorying in the fact that you are governed entirely by your baser instincts. That destroyed my love and any latent affection I might feel for you. However, since we are to remain together, it would only be a continual

425

harassment to us both did we do so in a state of enmity. There-fore, I propose henceforth to treat you as I would a sister or cousin, with whom circumstances had made it necessary for me to share a home.'

She shrugged her fine shoulders. 'That suits me well enough. It was your personality that made you more attractive to me than other men, and I greatly enjoyed our early intimacy. But since you returned to the service of the Emperor, your work has absorbed you to a degree that makes you a poor hus-band. My only interest now is to retain the status that being your wife gives me, and my position as one of the Empress' ladies. I have only to lift my finger, and I could secure more lovers than I would have the time to pleasure.'

'That I do not doubt,' he retorted tartly. 'And, your nature being what it is, I am not fool enough to expect you to remain chaste. But I now give you fair warning. Not only must you be discreet about your *affaires*, you must also impress the necessity of discretion upon any lover you may take. Should one of them be rash enough to boast that he has had you, I'll call him out and kill him. I will then kill you.'

He knew he would never carry out the last part of his threat, but it had its effect. She paled, cast down her eyes and mur-mured, 'It has not escaped me that you, too, have a ruthless streak, and are an ill man to cross. So be it then. I will take great care not to provoke a scandal.'

Neither of them had ever lacked subjects of interest to talk about; so, at the inns where they took their evening meals, any casual observer would have put them down as a long-married couple upon good terms with each other. But Roger always asked for a separate room, on the pretext that he suf-fered from insomnia, spent half the night reading, and was loath to keep his wife awake. On the afternoon of Wednesday, October 20th, they reached Schloss Langenstein.

It dated from medieval times: a rambling, irregular pile, surmounted by a tall tower and perched upon a rocky emin-ence overlooking a bend in the broad river. The coach had been sighted while slowly climbing the zigzag road that led up to it, so the von Haugwitzes were at the great wooden, iron-studded door to welcome their visitors. Young Charles, now a handsome, well-grown lad, with his mother's dark, curly hair and his father's blue eyes, stood beside them.

Roger felt a momentary alarm as the boy's eyes lit up at the sight of him; but he was reassured when Charles looked away as though indifferent about the new arrivals, and began to pat the head of a wolfhound standing nearby. When the elders had exchanged greetings, Georgina said to him:

'Charles, you remember *Monsieur de Breuc*, who came to stay with us for a few nights at Stillwaters, years ago when he was on a mission to London?'

'Yes, Mama,' the boy replied in French. Smiling, he held out his hand to Roger, and added, 'But not very well, for I was then very young.'

The visitors were shown to their rooms, and Roger noted with satisfaction that his was in a different wing from Lisala's; for, in spite of their conversation four days earlier, he had thought it just possible that, if she felt the urge, she might pay him a midnight visit and try her wiles upon him.

Ulrich von Haugwitz proved an excellent host, and Georgina had done many small things to dispel the grim atmosphere of the old castle, so that the rooms had at least something of the atmosphere of an English country house.

The evening meal was admirable: freshly-caught Rhine trout, roebuck, and sweet, white grapes which had been kept on ice since the recent vintage. The wines were superb, ending with a Hock of twenty years from the Baron's *Kabinett* reserve, grown on his own estate.

Charles had been allowed to stay up for the meal, but was sent off to bed as soon as it was over. Roger saw with pleasure that the Baron showed a great affection for the boy, rumpling his hair and kissing him on both cheeks, as though he were actually his father.

Afterwards they spent an hour or so talking about the conference; then, as the visitors had had a long day travelling, they went to bed. Roger felt no inclination to sleep, as he was hoping that when the Castle was wrapped in slumber, Georgina would come to him; so by candlelight he re-read Voltaire's *Candide*, which was among the books beside his bed.

Soon after midnight, his hopes were realised. The door opened quietly, and Georgina slipped into the room. He greeted her with a smile, but she ignored it, threw off the chamber robe she was wearing, blew out the candles and, without a word, slid into bed beside him.

Clasping her warm body to him with a joyous laugh, so that her fine breasts flattened against his broad chest, he sought her mouth for their first kiss. But, to his astonishment, she turned her face away, then burst into tears.

Her arms round his neck, she clutched him with sudden fierceness, and sobbed, 'Roger! Thank God you are come. I need your help. I need it most desperately.'

25

Roger to the Rescue

Several minutes passed before Roger succeeded in quietening Georgina's wild outburst of distress. Having sought to soothe her, he at length took her by the shoulders and shook her, as he said tersely:

'Georgina! Cease behaving like an hysterical girl. Whatever trouble you are in, I'll get you out of it. You must know that. We have been like father, mother, brother and sister to each other, as well as lovers, ever since we were children. I would give my life for you any day. For God's sake, tell me what causes you such grief, so that I may provide a remedy for it.'

Her sobs lessened, and she moaned, 'It is Ulrich. His behaviour revolts and horrifies me.'

'Why? Is he a sadist and brutal to you?'

'No; he has always treated me with consideration, and is proud to have me for his wife.'

'What then?'

'He is heterosexual. He enjoys women, but also boys. He orders the stable lads to his bed. Such practices have always revolted me. It was when I first found that out that I refused ever again to sleep with him, and demanded a room of my own.'

Roger considered for a moment, then he said, 'It is known that the Greek vice has now become a German one. Your revulsion I understand, but why the terrible distress? Does it stem from the fact that you love him, so are jealous of his complaisant sodomites, and yearn to have him back to make love only to you?'

'No, no,' Georgina whimpered. ' 'Tis not that. Such attraction as he had for me soon faded after he had brought me here. He is handsome, intelligent and bold; but underneath cold and cynical. As I can get no money from England until peace comes, I cannot leave him; but I've no wish even to keep a hold on his affections.'

'Why, then, this extreme perturbation? Many women who no longer love their husbands readily ignore their vices and console themselves by having *affaires* with other men. You did so yourself when married to Humphrey Etheredge.'

'I know; I know. But this is different. I am afraid for Charles.'

'Charles!' Roger repeated, aghast. 'You do not mean . . . ?'

'I do. Did you not see the way in which Ulrich fondled the boy before he retired after our *arbeitsessen*?'

'I did,' Roger agreed, 'but thought him to be showing only paternal affection.'

'You were wrong. He has set his evil heart upon seducing my son. Oh, Roger! What can I do? What can I do?'

Again Roger was silent for a minute, then he asked, 'What of Charles? Do you think him inclined to lend himself to your husband's designs upon him?'

'No, I am certain he would not. Ulrich flatters him and loads him with presents; but Charles instinctively shies away from his caresses. My awful fear is that, should he continue to fail to respond to him, Ulrich will lose patience, enter his room one night, and force him.'

'Then,' Roger said firmly, 'our only course is speedily to remove the boy from here.'

'You are right,' Georgina murmured. 'But how can we? How could this possibly be done?'

'I know not,' Roger replied. 'I must have time to think upon it. But take heart, my love. You may be sure that I'll not leave you in so dire a strait. You know well that I have ever loved your son as though he were my own. And my love for you knoweth no bounds of time, distance or any other loves that may temporarily engage us. Such passions of the body are naught but episodes. Our spiritual link has remained unbroken all these years. We are as one, and nothing in this world is worth an iota compared to our going on together in life and death until eternity.'

'Oh, Roger, bless you! I never doubted for an instant that I would call upon you in vain. I know that you will think of something. My mind is already at rest, and I am relaxed. Now make love to me as you have so often done. Nibble my ear, then enter me so that my soul can shudder with yours in delirious delight.'

Twenty minutes later, Roger gently persuaded Georgina to return to her room. Their passionate embrace had restored her calm, but her heart-rending outburst earlier had taken a lot out of her and, as he was to stay five more nights at Schloss Langenstein, he felt it best that she should, that night, get an uninterrupted sleep.

Next day, Roger saw Georgina in her old role of a most accomplished hostess, for the Baron had invited a number of his neighbours to dinner. In Germany the old custom of dining early was still maintained, and the ten guests sat down at one o'clock to a gigantic meal, helping one another from a dozen dishes of fish, game, poultry and veal, which were set on the table simultaneously.

It was close on three o'clock when the ladies left the men to indulge in a bout of heavy drinking, and talk of sport or politics. As was to be expected, the conference at Erfurt was uppermost in all their minds. Only the Baron and Roger had been present there, and the former gave his friends an account of it, although it transpired that one of his guests was far better informed about what had actually taken place there.

This was Prince Claus von Metternich, who was paying a brief visit to Johannisberg, his estate a few miles down the river, which was famous for producing the finest white wine in the world.

Roger had never previously met the Prince, but he had heard a lot about him. The son of a distinguished diplomat, he had imbibed a knowledge of international politics from his youth. While a student at the University of Strasbourg during the French Revolution, he had witnessed the murderous ferocity of the mob, and this had led to his becoming a life-long enemy of 'Government by the People'. After leaving Strasbourg, he had made a long stay in England, then went to Vienna where, in 1795, he had married a grand-daughter of the Austrian Chancellor, von Kaunitz. In his case, nepotism had proved justified, for his appointment as Ambassador to Berlin had proved a great success. So pleasant had he made himself to the French Ambassador there that Napoleon had asked for him to be transferred to Paris. In the French capital he had proved extraordinarily popular, making many close friends, including Napoleon's sister, Caroline Murat. It was said that she had become his mistress. His handsome presence, charming manners and ready wit made him a great favourite among the ladies. Now, at thirty-eight, he had become one of the most important personalities on the European stage.

Roger realised that, since everyone there believed him to be a Frenchman, the opinions expressed were on the cautious side, for to criticise Napoleon in his presence could have proved dangerous. But Metternich went as far as to say:

'From Austria's point of view, the conference ended very satisfactorily. The Emperor endeavoured to persuade the Czar to threaten my country with hostilities unless we ceased re-arming; but the Czar refused. That was largely due to the admirable exertions of Baron Vincent, whom I sent as our observer, and perhaps even more to the influence of Talleyrand.'

'I judge Your Highness right,' Roger remarked. 'It is no secret that the Prince de Benevento has always cherished the hope of restoring the old Franco-Austrian alliance which existed for so long under the Kings of France. The Emperor is well aware of that. One day, while at Erfurt, I heard him snap at the Prince, "You are always an Austrian." Talleyrand replied, "A little, Sire; but I think it would be more exact to say that I am never Russian, and always French".'

Metternich laughed. 'How typical of his finesse. While I was Ambassador in Paris, I had numerous conversations with him, and we see eye to eye on many matters. For us, his resignation as Minister of Foreign Affairs was a sad blow; but he was right to follow the dictates of his own conscience.'

'Despite his resignation, the Emperor cannot bear to be without him on all important occasions. Witness how, at Erfurt, he made him chief negotiator, over the heads of both Caulaincourt and Champagny.'

'Yes; Baron Vincent realised that, although Talleyrand had no official status; and I have a feeling that he may yet play a decisive part in the affairs of France.'

They talked on until past five o'clock; then several of them, unsteady on their legs after the quantities of rich wine they had drunk, collected their ladies and departed in their coaches.

That night, when Georgina came to Roger's room, he said, 'I have given much thought, my love, to the matter of dear Charles. For me to make off with him is out of the question. In no time Ulrich would set the forces of law in motion and we would be caught long before we could cross the frontier. In fact, it is essential that there should be no suspicion that I have anything to do with his disappearance. Therefore, he must leave a day, or better still, two days before Lisala and I do.'

'But a boy of twelve could not possibly cross half a continent on his own, however much money we gave him,' Georgina protested.

'My love, I do not suggest it. What I have in mind is that he should appear to have run away, but actually lie hidden somewhere nearby for a couple of days. Then I would pick him up and take him with me to Paris.'

Georgina nodded. 'That seems a good plan; but after Paris? What then? The Emperor never remains in Paris for long, and you will have to accompany him when he next sets out for Italy, Spain or Berlin. You could not take Charles with you. And I would be loath to have him left in Lisala's hands.'

'I agree. And there lies our worst difficulty. Obviously we must endeavour, in some way, to get him back to England, so that Stillwaters again becomes his home. But how? In the old days I had many ties with smugglers and might have got him across. That is not so now. Alone, if hard put to it, I doubt not I could find a way. Accompanied by a lad who might be called on to answer awkward questions, it would be a desperately dangerous undertaking for us both.'

They remained silent, thinking hard, for more than a minute, then Georgina exclaimed, 'I have it! My Archduke.'

'I have been meaning to ask you about him; but last night
was no time for that.'

'He is John, the youngest of the Emperor Francis' brothers.
Last August, he was making a tour of the Rhine, incognito.
Through some mismanagement by her Captain, the yacht in
which he was voyaging struck a rock in the shallows a mile
or so away, and so badly damaged her rudder that another
had to be sent for from Mayence. To pass the time, he and
his gentleman-in-waiting came ashore, trudged up to the
Schloss and asked permission to see the view from the tower.

'Ulrich was then away from home, in Berlin; so it was I who
received them. He introduced himself as Count Stulich; only
later he told me that he was an Imperial Highness. On learning
of their plight, I naturally invited them to remain and dine
with me. Within the first half-hour the subtle spark passed between us. He is charming, intelligent and most courteous;
everything a true gentleman should be. It seems that he found
in me all the qualities to be admired in a woman. No sooner
had we finished our meal than he packed his gentleman off
down to the yacht to bring up some sketches he had made of
castles on the Rhine. Then . . .'

'Then he proceeded to make love to you,' Roger broke in
with a laugh.

'Indeed he did. But, thank God, I kept my head. Otherwise
the affair might have ended with a tumble on the sofa. Having
repulsed him vigorously, I let things bide a while. Then I said,
quite casually, "If you have to wait some days for your new
rudder, I feel sure I could find for you and your friend more
comfortable quarters here than you have in your yacht".

'Oh, Roger, darling! You should have seen his eyes light
up. For the next three days and the best part of three nights
he never left my side. He parted from me with the greatest reluctance and vowed that, had we both not been married he
would have risked his brother's, the Emperor's, displeasure,
to marry me.'

'What a delightful romance, and what a clever witch you

434

are.' Turning over in bed, Roger added, 'Does Ulrich know of this?'

'I could not conceal the fact that two gentlemen had stayed here in his absence. But I had already found out about his disgusting practices; so, had he asked me, I would have told him the truth. No doubt it was to avoid the possibility of a futile scene that he refrained from doing so.'

'Tell me, though, how can the Archduke help us in the matter of your Charles?'

Georgina propped herself up on one elbow. 'Why, do you not see? Austria is not under the yoke of Napoleon. As an independent Power, Napoleon cannot prevent her maintaining diplomatic relations with England. Couriers must come and go between Vienna and London. Can you but get Charles to Vienna, I am confident that John will see to it that he is conveyed safely home.'

Pulling her down again, Roger kissed her. 'Dear heart, you have solved the worst part of our problem. Now, this is what must be done. Tomorrow you must tell Charles that, greatly as it grieves you, for his sake you are sending him home, and that it must be made to appear that he has run away. He should leave a letter for you, saying that he is homesick and can bear life here no longer; then ask your forgiveness for having taken money and some of your less valuable trinkets to pay for his journey. The latter you will give him; I will provide him with money. The next day, Saturday, he must vanish; but remain concealed somewhere in the neighbourhood where I can pick him up when we leave on Monday morning.'

Georgina pondered for a time, then she said, 'Your plan is sound, but where to hide him for two days I cannot think. There is a hut some half a mile away, down on the shore, where we keep our fishing tackle. When you leave here, your coach will pass within a hundred yards of it. But, once Charles is missed, and I produce his letter, there will be a most ghastly rumpus. The whole district will be searched for him, and it's as good as certain that someone will look in the hut.'

'Let him go there, then; but not until first thing on Monday

435

morning. Meanwhile, surely there is some place in the Castle where you can hide him?'

'They will search it from cellar to attic, on the off chance that, at the last moment, he lacked the courage to make off, and has hidden from fear of punishment.'

'I cannot believe that there is no place in this great pile where they would not look.'

'Wait!' Georgina sat up again and said excitedly, 'I have it. The *Weinstube* at the back of the Castle. The vintage is over; the pressing room will remain closed until next year. Charles could lie concealed inside one of the big presses. Then, even if someone looked into the room, he could not be seen, and on the Saturday and Sunday nights I could take him food.'

'To remain in such confined quarters for two nights and a day would be a considerable ordeal,' Roger commented dubiously. 'Think you the boy could endure it?'

'For that I'll vouch,' Georgina replied with conviction. 'Young as he is, he prides himself upon being an English nobleman, and a direct descendant of Charles II. He knows backwards the story of the King's forty-three days and nights escaping from his enemies after Worcester fight. He will think of himself as hiding in Boscobel Oak.'

'Ah, now you reassure me! That, then, is the plan we will adopt. One thing more. Before Saturday night I want you to get for me something of his. A penknife, or an odd sheet of work that he has done for his tutor, would do. Anything which would enable me to lay a false trail, that will be found after his disappearance.'

On the Friday, the Baron took Roger and a party of other gentlemen to shoot buck in his forests inland, beyond the vineyards. That night, Georgina told Roger that, greatly as Charles was distressed at the thought of leaving her, he had agreed that it was for the best; as he realised what was behind his stepfather's attentions, and loathed and was frightened by them.

Roger then told her the full truth about Lisala. When he had done, she sighed, 'How terrible that such evil should lurk in so beautiful a person. And your lot, my love, is worse than mine. Apart from being a pervert, Ulrich is not a bad man. He would never delight in flinging his depravity in my face, much less murder one of his parents.'

Saturday they went to dine at a neighbouring castle, but Roger was careful to drink sparingly of the rich wine, as he had work to do during the coming night. At one o'clock in the morning, he and Georgina took Charles down to the *Wein-stube*. There were three large, circular presses there, about six feet in height; with, protruding from each, four great capstan bars which, when pushed round by the vintagers, wound a stout lid down an enormous screw, and so crushed the grapes.

When they had lined the bottom of the press with a layer of cushions, and lowered into it a supply of food and drink, the boy took a tearful leave of his mother, shook Roger by the hand, and bravely climbed into the press. Then Roger assisted the weeping Georgina back to her own room, where he spent half an hour doing his best to console her.

Reluctantly leaving her, he again went downstairs, let himself out of a side door, and walked down the steep, curving road to the big boathouse on the shore. To get in, he had to force the lock but that suited his plan. In the long shed there were seven boats of various sizes. Clambering into one of the smaller rowing boats, he tethered the smallest of all to her stern, then unlatched the water gate and rowed out into the river.

To cross it entailed a quarter of an hour of hard pulling and the strong, swift current swept him nearly a mile downstream before he reached the far bank. Having beached the boat he was in, and untied the rope by which he had towed over the smaller one, he drew it right up on to the shore. With him he had brought a small book belonging to Charles, which Georgina had got for him. It was in English, and a history of King Charles' escape after Worcester, so was a perfect clue to the identity of its owner. He left the book in the prow of the boat, as though it had fallen unnoticed from Charles' pocket as he jumped ashore.

Although he recrossed the river as directly as the current would permit, and made the greater part of his way back close in to the shore, it took him over an hour of strenuous effort before he reached the boathouse. Tethering the boat where he had found it, he wearily ascended the winding mountain road, eventually to reach his room stumbling with fatigue.

On Sunday mornings, it was customary for everyone at the Schloss to attend chapel. The inmates were about to take their places, when Charles' tutor arrived hotfoot, to report that the boy had not slept in his bed, and he could not be found. The service was abandoned, everyone exclaiming in dismay; Georgina went to her boudoir, then produced the letter Charles had left, saying that she had just found it lying on her work basket.

The Baron was furious, and declared that the boy must be caught and brought back at all costs. A party that had been arranged for later in the day, to taste the *must* of the new vintage, was promptly cancelled. Georgina, in tears that needed no forcing, went to her bedroom, but soon after emerged to say that several of her rings were missing, and some sixty *thalers* that she kept in a drawer against emergencies. Lisala, ignorant of the secret manœuvres that had taken place, endeavoured to console her for the loss of her son. Roger expressed his deepest sympathy for his host, and offered his aid in the search for the missing Charles.

To Roger's amazement, von Haugwitz burst into tears and exclaimed, 'I loved the boy. I loved him.' Ostensibly, that could be taken as a strong expression of the affection a man had developed for his stepson. But to Roger it was evidence of the strength of his host's illicit passion. Swiftly recovering, the Baron summoned the bodyguard which tradition allowed him to retain, and who were now employed in the Castle as servants, gamekeepers and vine-dressers. As Georgina had foreseen, a number of them were set to search the Castle, in case Charles' courage had failed him at the last moment, and he had hidden himself somewhere in it. Others were despatched to east and west along the shore of the river, and others again to scour the wooded hinterland.

Shortly before midday, it was discovered that a small rowing boat was missing from the boathouse. By two o'clock it was found, and Charles' book brought to the Baron. He gave way to a passion of rage and tears, for the land on the west bank of the Rhine had, for many years past, been a part of France, and he could not send his men across, because he had no authority there. Now despairing, he called the search off and, in a state of misery, shut himself up in his room.

In the small hours of the morning, having taken fresh food to her boy, Georgina was able to tell Roger that Charles was bearing up well. But she was unutterably distressed at having finally parted from him. All had, so far, gone well with their plans, and it was their last night together, but a far from happy one. Roger held his love tightly in his arms, while she sobbed on his shoulder. When, at length, she was about to leave him, she said bitterly:

'We have both made fools of ourselves by our recent marriages. But I am the more to blame. They would never have come about had I only listened to your pleading last time we were together in England. Oh, how happy we could be as husband and wife at Stillwaters. But perhaps some day . . .' Then, like a wraith, she vanished, and the door closed silently behind her.

Next morning, after many expressions of gratitude and renewed protestations of distress at Charles' having run away, Roger and Lisala took their departure. Instead of mounting his charger, Roger had his man lead it, and entered the coach with Lisala.

As soon as the cumbersome vehicle began, with its brakes on, to slither down the steep descent, Lisala remarked lightly:

'Well, I trust your old love came up to your expectations in bed.'

Roger turned to stare at her, as she went on. 'Maybe you have forgotten that, when we were so passionately enamoured of each other in Isfahan, you told me of your boy and girl *affaire* in Hampshire before you went to France; and that, although you have since seen the lady only at long intervals you had become life-long friends. The moment I saw your great Georgina at Erfurt, I realised that it was she who, on and off, for years has been your mistress.'

'Believe that if you wish,' Roger shrugged. ' 'Tis all one to me.'

'Oh, I make no complaint.' Lisala smiled sweetly. 'I found the Baron excellent company. He came to my room the second night and played a man's part vigorously; and again on Friday. Saturday he was so upset that he failed me. But I now understand the reason for that. Last night he came to me again and persuaded me to play the part of a boy. It was a new experience for me, and one I did not greatly care for. But with practice it might have possibilities.'

'For Christ's sake, be silent!' Roger stormed. 'You utterly disgust me! But you are right about the Baron being a pederast and that is the true reason for young Charles' disappearance. Georgina and I stage-managed it, and shortly we shall pick him up.'

Lisala's great eyes opened wide. 'So Georgina's weeping was all a sham?'

'Certainly not. If you had any maternal feelings, you would realise her acute distress at having had to send him away.'

By that time the coach had reached the road that wound along the river bank. When it came level with the hut where the fishing tackle was kept, Roger called to his coachman to pull up. Getting out, he glanced back up at the Castle. Trees hid it, except for its topmost tower. Reassured that no-one there was likely to be overlooking them, he ran towards the hut. At that moment, Charles emerged. He was pale and looked very woe-begone, but Roger took him by the arm, laughed and said:

'Well done, my son. The endurance you have displayed does you great credit. Your mama and I are very proud of you. And be of good heart. Within a few weeks, you will be back at Stillwaters.'

Pushing the boy into the coach, he said to Lisala, 'Here is someone new to exercise your charm upon, but I pray you refrain from questioning him.' Then he mounted his horse and the coach moved on.

Eight days later they reached Vienna, and put up at the

440

Double Eagle. Next morning, Roger went to the Hofberg and enquired for the Archduke John.

To his relief, the Archduke was in residence and, a quarter of an hour later, received him in his apartment. With due respect, Roger presented a letter Georgina had given him.

While the Archduke was reading it, Roger studied him with an appraising eye. He was of medium height, stalwart and handsome, apart from the thick Habsburg lip. He had spoken crisply and had the bearing people always hoped to see in a man of his high rank. Roger decided that, this time, Georgina had had ample reason to succumb to a lover's personality.

Looking up from the letter, the Archduke said, 'It is sad that the Baroness should find it necessary to part with her son. But I understand her feeling that a noble youth of English birth should be educated at Eton. Bring him to me, *Monsieur le Colonel*, and you may rely upon it that I will arrange for him to be sent safely back to England.'

He then asked eagerly after Georgina. Without going into particulars, Roger disclosed that he had known her for many years. For half an hour they talked in most friendly fashion of her charm, then the Archduke invited Roger to dine the following night. But Roger begged to be excused, because duty required him to rejoin Napoleon with a minimum of delay.

That evening he handed Charles over. The boy displayed great reluctance to be parted from him; but the Archduke showed him such kindness, saying that he must call him Uncle John, that Charles' fears at being left dependent on a stranger ebbed away and, when Roger bade him farewell, he accepted his situation quite cheerfully.

Lisala was most loath to leave Vienna after no more than having been driven round it. She was well aware that, through the French Embassy, Roger could have obtained numerous introductions which would have led to a fortnight or more of gaiety in the Austrian capital. But Roger proved adamant, because the long detour to Vienna had already caused him to overstay the leave Napoleon had given him. So, on the 4th November, they left for Paris, arriving there on the 13th.

As members of the Court, they went straight to the Palace

of St. Cloud. Roger learned that Napoleon had left for Spain on October 29th; so he enquired for his old friend, Duroc, Duc de Fruili, Grand Marshal of the Palace.

Duroc was, for his time, an unusually puritanical man. He had great integrity, and was utterly devoted to his Emperor. Having served with him in Egypt and other places, Roger knew him well and had a considerable admiration for him. Duroc at once assigned to Roger suitable accommodation in the Palace for himself and his wife. Then he said, 'Among the instructions the Emperor left with me was one that, immediately you arrived you should follow him to Spain.'

Roger smiled. 'In this case, I must regard "immediate" as a somewhat elastic term; since I need a few days in Paris to arrange my affairs.' Actually he was in two minds whether to go to Spain or rid himself of Lisala by breaking for good with Napoleon and making his way to England.

'Bien, mon ami,' Duroc replied. 'But attend to them speedily, or you will find yourself in trouble.'

Owing to the unsettled state of Spain, Napoleon had not taken Josephine with him; so Lisala at once resumed duty as one of the Empress' ladies. Next day Roger rode into Paris. At La Belle Étoile, his old friends, the Blanchards, greeted him with open arms.

He had known the good Norman couple since he had first come to Paris when still in his teens. He had lodged with them while an impecunious young gallant, but one received by Marie Antoinette at Versailles; they had sheltered him while he lived disguised as a sans culottes during the darkest days of the Terror; they had seen him rise to become the friend of Napoleon and le brave Breuc of the Grande Armée. They still kept for him in their attic a chest containing clothes of several kinds, into which he could change in an emergency; but they had never enquired into his business, because they loved and trusted him.

On his enquiring for Josefa, they directed him to an upstairs room, where he found her and the baby, both in excellent health.

Although Josefa had been Lisala's nurse, she was not over

442

fifty, having only the appearance of being older which is common among women who, during their early years, have lived the hard life of peasants. Assuming that she was capable of fending for herself and looking after the child, Roger suggested that he should rent for her a cottage outside Paris, until arrangements could be made for her to return to Portugal. She readily agreed to that, saying she would much prefer it to continuing to live in the city.

Later, as he had so often done in the past, Roger enjoyed an excellent dinner with the Blanchards in their private parlour, listening to all the gossip of the Faubourgs. Madame had cooked for him one of his favourite omelettes, followed by a duck, Normandy style, and they washed it down with one of the best bottles of Burgundy from the Maître's cellar, finishing up with old Calvados.

Over the meal Roger asked them to find a cottage for Josefa, and said that he would make arrangements for money to be sent them every month for the rent and her keep. They promised to do so, and said they would keep a friendly eye on her.

Well dined and wined, he set off back to St. Cloud. As he rode along at an easy pace, he wondered if this was the last time he would have enjoyed the company of those loyal, unpretentious friends. More and more he inclined to the idea of cutting loose from Lisala, even though the price must be retirement from participation in great events. He had only to pretend to leave for Spain, taking with him civilian clothes, change into them by night, then ride to the coast. A few discreet enquiries and, for a handful of gold, some smuggler would put him across to England. It could be a month or more before anybody even wondered where he had gone.

He was still debating the matter with himself when he reached the Palace. Up in their suite, Lisala was reclining on a *chaise longue*, reading. As she laid her book down, he noticed the title. It was *La Philosophe dans le Boudoir*, by the Marquis de Sade. Looking up, she said:

'I have a message for you. The Empress desires you to wait upon her.'

Having spent a few minutes tidying himself, Roger went

down to the Imperial apartments. One of Josephine's ladies announced him at once. The Empress received him with her usual graciousness, dismissed the woman and, when they were alone, went to a bureau, from which she took a heavily-sealed letter. Turning to Roger, she said:

'Chevalier, this is for the Emperor. It deals with matters which could be highly dangerous to me were it to fall into wrong hands, so I am afraid to trust it to an ordinary courier. But I am told that you are leaving for Spain almost immediately. Would you do me the kindness to deliver it personally into the Emperor's own hand?'

Roger bowed, wondering how he could possibly excuse himself. But an immediate reply had to be made and he saw no alternative to making that which was expected of him. 'With pleasure, Your Majesty. I am as ever entirely at your disposal.'

When he had taken the letter, they talked for a few minutes, then he returned to his apartment.

Josephine was an old and dear friend. Simply to disappear with the letter, which was clearly of great importance to her, or to pass it on to someone else who might lose or tamper with it, was unthinkable. Next morning, with great reluctance, he set out for Spain.

26

The Great Conspiracy

Now that the die was cast and Roger fated to rejoin the Emperor, as he had overstayed his leave he rode all out, requisitioning fresh horses at every garrison town through which he passed. Six long days of hard riding enabled him to arrive at Grand Headquarters on November 21st. He excused his tardiness in reporting by saying he had been laid up for a week with fish-poisoning. Napoleon was in a good mood, spoke to him kindly, thanked him for having brought Josephine's letter, then sent him to Berthier to be given particulars of the situation.

Immediately after Napoleon had left Madrid, on August 1st, such serious revolts had broken out that King Joseph had fled from his capital and, covered by Marshal Moncey's corps, sought safety across the Ebro. Bessières, who was holding the road through Burgos, inflicted a defeat on the insurgents; but that same month Wellesley had defeated Junot, and occupied Lisbon. The Convention of Cintra, by which Junot and his twenty-five thousand troops had been evacuated back to France and allowed to take all their loot with them, had so outraged the Government and people of Britain that all three Generals: Wellesley, Burrard and Dalrymple, had been recalled and court-martialled. General Sir John Moore had succeeded to the Command and another, smaller, British force, under General Baird, was said to have landed at Corunna; but the whereabouts of these two armies were at present unknown.

Meanwhile the French had been in serious straits, holding only a triangle based on the Pyrenees, pointing in the direction of Madrid. Several of the garrisons outside the triangle were isolated. General Ducherme, commanding in Catalonia, was cut off and boxed up in the fortress of Barcelona. In Saragossa, led by the patriot leader, Palafox, the insurgents had inflicted heavy losses on General Verdier's troops by many days of terrible house-to-house fighting: a form of warfare to which the French were not accustomed.

The French were at a further disadvantage in that the majority of Bessières' and Moncey's men were Swiss or German levies, with little heart in the battle, and such French troops as they had were largely raw conscripts. In the autumn a well-concerted effort by the Spaniards, now stiffened by the nine thousand regular soldiers whom the Marquis La Romana had brought back from Hanover, could have driven the French back across the Pyrenees. But their failure to press on to victory was due to disunity. The 'Central Junta' of thirty-five delegates which had been formed, wasted its time debating the terms of a new Constitution for Spain, and could not even be brought to appoint a Commander-in-Chief for the whole of the Spanish forces. The result was that half-a-dozen Generals, appointed by their own local Juntas, could not agree a common strategy, refused out of jealousy to support one another, and quarrelled bitterly among themselves about the division of money and arms that were being sent to them from Britain.

Although still refusing to regard the Spanish rebellion as a serious threat to his suzerainty of Europe, Napoleon had determined to crush it once and for all; so he had ordered south from Germany the hard-bitten corps of Soult, Ney, Mortier, Lannes, Victor and Lefebvre. With his usual ability in directing great armies, the Emperor had waited until this force of two hundred thousand veterans had concentrated in Navarre. Divided counsels had led the Spaniards to dispose the majority of their troops on the two flanks of the French-held triangle, leaving their centre weak. Napoleon had sent orders launching his massed legions on October 29th against this weak spot, smashed through, then directed his Marshals against the numerous Spanish forces to east and west, overwhelming them one by one.

Roger arrived at Headquarters while this devastating tide of victory was in full spate. Within ten days, organised Spanish resistance to the French advance had been quelled and Napoleon was approaching Madrid. The city had no walls; but, in a frenzy of hatred, the population endeavoured to defend it by throwing up barricades. Their resistance lasted only a day. On December 3rd, the Emperor had again installed himself in the Royal Palace.

While resting his troops for a fortnight, Napoleon planned the subjugation of the remainder of Spain. Lannes had already been ordered to b siege Saragossa and put an end to Palafox. Soult was directed to invade Léon. The next move would be to march on Lisbon, where Sir John Moore's army was assumed to be.

Then, on the morning of the 19th, intelligence came in that Moore was not there at all. He was much further north, had entered Spain and was advancing on Valladolid. Soult was in that neighbourhood, but had only twenty thousand men. The numbers of the British force were unknown, but might be considerably greater and, if Moore defeated Soult, Napoleon's communications with France would be cut.

The Emperor immediately dictated a despatch to Soult, warning him of his danger and ordering him to stand on the defensive until he, Napoleon, could bring up from the neighbourhood of Madrid the main French army, by-pass Moore and cut off his retreat into Portugal. They would then crush the British between them.

This magnificent chance to destroy an entire British army filled the Emperor with elation. No sooner had the despatch been sealed than he gave it to Roger, as the A.D.C. on duty, and told him to ride hell-for-leather with it to Soult.

Roger's mind had been made up instantly. He could not possibly stand by while thousands of his countrymen were killed or captured. Even if it cost him his own life he must warn Moore of the trap into which he was walking. As a precaution against emergencies, he always travelled with a small valise containing civilian clothes. Collecting it from his room, and wrapping himself in his fur cloak against the bitter cold, he ran down to the stables. Normally, he would have been accompanied by his orderly; but he told the officer-in-charge of the stable that his business was too urgent for him to wait for the man to be found.

Taking the road to Valladolid, he covered the one hundred miles to the road junction at Tondesillas, twenty miles south-west of the city, in eleven hours, arriving there a little after ten o'clock that evening. As was the case with all the towns and villages on the road north, it was guarded by a French detachment. Snow was falling, and in the Officers' Mess he found the inmates huddled round a glowing fire. After snatching a hasty meal and changing his horse for the fourth time, he again took the road; but, instead of taking that to Valladolid, he proceeded due west, along the road leading to Zamora and the Portuguese frontier.

A mile outside the town he dismounted, changed, shivering, into civilian clothes behind a haystack, and stuffed his uniform into the valise. The moon had now risen and gave him enough light to see some distance ahead. After riding another twelve miles he saw, upon a slight rise, an encampment of bivouacs. A hundred yards further on, he was challenged by a sentry.

He asked to be taken at once to the man's officer. As it was now well on in the night, the sentry at first demurred; but Roger's air of authority overcame his scruples. The troops proved to be a vedette of Hussars, commanded by a Captain. Roger told him that he had intelligence of the first importance for Sir John Moore, and requested a guide to his Headquarters. As he had no credentials he could show, the Captain thought it possible that he might be a spy and said he would send him on only if he agreed to be blindfolded. Roger readily consented. Then he said:

'I have ridden close on a hundred and twenty miles today, and am near exhausted. Could you, perchance, send me on in a trap or some other conveyance? But it must be fast-moving, as every moment is precious.'

Roger's state of fatigue was obvious, so the Captain said he could go in the mess cart and, while a good horse was harnessed to it, made him take a long drink from a flask of port wine.

448

Ten minutes later, Roger was again on his way, now blind-folded, but lying on a straw-filled palliasse, and covered with a pile of blankets against the intense cold of the winter night. In spite of the jolting, he soon fell asleep. For how long he slept he did not know; but, to his great relief when the driver woke him, he saw that it was still dark; so there was a chance that he might reach Valladolid without too great a delay to explain away when he delivered his despatch to Soult.

On getting out of the cart, he saw that he was in the middle of a great camp, and that the vehicle had pulled up before a marquee. Outside, a soldier of a Highland regiment stood on guard, and he called his Sergeant. The Sergeant evidently suspected that this stranger, arriving in the middle of the night, might have been sent to harm his General. But Roger's mother had been Scottish, and in his youth he had imbibed something of her accent. Using it again now, he allayed the Sergeant's suspicions, and the man took Roger into the marquee, where an A.D.C. was dozing. Again there occurred an infuriating delay while Roger stressed the extreme urgency of his business. At length the A.D.C. consented to rouse his General; and, a few minutes later, Sir John emerged from an inner division of the marquee.

To him Roger said quickly, 'Sir, you will not recall me, but we met once before. It was while Mr. Pitt was out of office and commanding two battalions of Fencibles at Walmer. You came over from Hythe to give a talk on the new tactics you have invented, by which infantry should advance in open or-der, each man trained to fight independently, instead of offer-ing a good target to enemy guns by going forward in massed formation.'

The General nodded. 'I remember the occasion and vaguely recall your face. What brings you here?'

Roger produced the despatch for Soult. 'Time does not now permit, Sir, for me to give you particulars of how it is that I am one of the Emperor's *aides-de-camp*. But I was charged to deliver this despatch with all speed. It instructs Marshal Soult to stand on the defensive should you attack him. Meanwhile the Emperor will already be giving orders for his main army to advance into the country to your south, and so encircle you.'

'That is bad news, indeed!' Sir John exclaimed. 'I have been delayed by a fool of a Spanish General telling me that the mountain roads were impassable for my artillery, which proved quite untrue when I crossed them with my main body; but I had already sent the guns round by a long detour. They reached me only a few days ago, and it was not until then that I was able to make contact with General Baird. But now, with twenty-seven thousand men, I had good hopes of routing Soult and cutting Napoleon's communications with France.'

'Alas, Sir,' Roger shook his head, 'that is now out of the question. Within a week, the Emperor will have at the least one hundred thousand troops massed against you.'

'I must retreat at once then, and by forced marches escape the trap. Given good fortune, I may yet get my army back to Corunna in time to embark them in our ships and take them off to fight another day. Entrust me, please, with your name, Sir, that I may report confidentially to Mr. Canning or Lord Castlereagh this great service you have rendered me.'

'I am known to both, and am the son of the late Admiral Sir Christopher Brook. But I pray you, let that knowledge go no further.'

'Ah! Now I recall meeting you at Walmer. But, Mr. Brook, you look sadly worn. You must have refreshment and rest. I'll see to it.'

'Nay, I thank you, Sir.' Roger shook his head. 'Do I delay overmuch in getting this despatch to Soult, I'll be finished with Napoleon. I must return at once to Tondesillas with all possible speed.'

Sir John had a gig which he used on occasions. By the time Roger had drunk a glass of wine and munched a hastily-made sandwich, it was brought round. Having wrung his hand, the General saw him off. An hour later, he reached the vedette. The Captain of Hussars had had Roger's horse watered and fed. It was quickly saddled up, and Roger was off again.

By the time he reached the outskirts of Tondesillas, the late winter dawn was breaking. Behind a barn he changed back into his uniform. Skirting the town by byways, he came out on the road to Valladolid. The last twenty miles were agony. He was half-frozen, saddle-sore and incredibly tired. Half a mile outside the city, he turned into a bridle path, dismounted, removed his valise from the back of the saddle and gave his mount a sharp cut on the rump with his riding switch, causing the animal to bolt. Rallying his last reserves of strength, Roger walked into the town, to arrive at Marshal Soult's headquarters just before ten o'clock.

The grey-haired Marshal, whom Roger had met on many occasions, received him immediately he was announced. Roger had worked it out that, even had he ridden with less speed from Madrid, he should still have reached Valladolid in the early hours of the morning; so he had several hours to account for. Leaning heavily on a chairback, he told Soult that, after passing through Tondesillas, he had been shot at from behind a hedge; his horse had thrown him and bolted, and he was lucky to have escaped with his life, as he had rolled into a ditch where, in the darkness, his assailants had failed to find and murder him. He had not dared to leave the ditch for a considerable time, then had had to walk the rest of the way to Valladolid.

Such occurrences had become so frequent in Spain that the Marshal did not even think of questioning his statement; but ripped open the despatch, read it, shouted for his staff to give them urgent orders, then sent Roger off to bed.

Dead to the world, he slept through the day, roused in the evening, only to take a glass of wine and eat a wing of chicken which a friend of his on Soult's staff brought up to him, then slept again. On the 21st, he set off back to Madrid, but his thighs were still sore so he took the journey in leisurely fashion, not arriving until the 24th.

To his surprise, he learned that the Emperor had left Madrid for Paris in great haste on the evening of the previous day, so he must have passed along the road through Valladolid while Roger was sleeping. Between the 19th and the 23rd, Napoleon had placed Ney in command of the army despatched to outflank Sir John Moore, and for the past four days had been constantly sending couriers after him to insist that he press on in spite of a blizzard which was rendering the mountains of Galicia almost impassable. In view of the frenzied excitement the Emperor had displayed at this chance to destroy the British, his sudden departure was more than ever a mystery. But Roger learned the reason from Lavelette, one of his fellow A.D.C.s.

Undoubtedly, after the Emperor, Talleyrand and Fouché were the two most powerful men in France. Both had made immense fortunes, but their backgrounds and personalities were as different as it was possible for them to be.

The two men loathed and had constantly opposed each other. Napoleon had always secretly feared the intellect and influence of both; so it suited him admirably that his two principal lieutenants in directing the affairs of France should be irreconcilable.

It now emerged that the Emperor had learned that these erstwhile enemies, who never attended the same function if they could avoid each other, had been seen arm-in-arm at a reception given by Madame de Remusat. Still more formidable, Napoleon's stepson, Eugene de Beauharnais, Viceroy of Italy, had intercepted a letter from Talleyrand to Murat, informing the King of Naples that relays of horses were being stationed across France to bring him to Paris with the utmost speed in case of a certain eventuality.

Roger instantly saw the implications. He already knew that Talleyrand was secretly working to bring about the Emperor's downfall. Evidently Fouché now also realised that Napoleon's ceaseless wars were bleeding France to death, so his rule must be ended. They had decided to stage a *coup d'état* while the Emperor had his hands full in Spain.

But why put Murat on the throne? Because, even if Joseph had been prepared to accept it, the French people would not have him, or any of the other Bonaparte brothers, as their Emperor. On the other hand, Murat, the handsome, dashing Cavalry leader, hero of a score of battles, was immensely popular and, pushed on by his boundlessly ambitious wife, Caroline, would not scruple to supplant his brother-in-law. Moreover, such a vain and stupid blockhead was just the sort of figure-head who would give no trouble, so enable Talleyrand and Fouché between them to rule France.

As they discussed the matter, Roger found that Lavalette had reached the same conclusion. He had been left behind to see to certain matters which Napoleon had had no time to settle, but had now completed them. So, on the following morning the two A.D.C.s left Madrid together, speculating on whether, when they reached Paris, they would find that the two great conspirators had been arrested, or that Napoleon was deposed and the capital in a turmoil.

They arrived at the Palace of St. Cloud on January 7th. Everything there was proceeding as smoothly as usual in this new year of 1809, and discreet enquiries soon informed them that both Talleyrand and Fouché were still at liberty. After reporting to the Emperor, Roger went to his wife's apartment.

Lisala was lying on a day-bed, reading. Throwing her book aside, she jumped to her feet and cried, 'So there you are! I thought the Emperor might have left you in Spain for good. I am delighted to see you.'

Roger had been absent for some six weeks, but during that time his sentiments towards Lisala had not changed in the least. He had no desire at all to resume relations with her, and was surprised that she should apparently wish him to; so he said quietly:

'It is polite of you, Madame, to welcome me back; but I have no intention of again succumbing to your blandishments.'

She laughed. 'You poor fool. Months ago I accepted the fact that we no longer had any use for one another physically. But you are still my husband, and I have been hoping that you would return to fulfil your obligations. The money I brought from Portugal ran out some time ago; and, while the war continues, it is impossible for me to secure more from that source. It is a husband's duty to support his wife, and I need money.'

Turning, she opened the drawer of a bureau, produced a sheaf of bills and handed them to him.

Glancing through them, he saw that she owed milliners and

modistes some eleven thousand francs. During the years he had amassed a considerable fortune, but that lay in England. While on the Continent, he was dependent on his pay as an A.D.C., and honorarium as a Commander of the Legion of Honour. These were handsome; moreover, he lived mainly at the Emperor's expense and, while on campaigns, spent little. Even so, he could not afford to allow her to spend at such a rate. Abruptly he told her that he would settle her debts, but in future she must limit herself to one thousand francs a month, otherwise he would be unable to meet their liabilities.

This new imposition of having to pay for expensive clothes, in order that she could enhance her attraction for other men, was another thorn in his flesh. As he left her, he wondered whether, when he had been with Sir John Moore, he had been foolish not to remain with the British army and so return to England.

Against the sickness he felt at being saddled with Lisala could be set the present intriguing situation. Having for so long been on the inside of the events that had led to the Revolution, the fall of Robespierre, the *Directoire* and the rise to supreme power of Napoleon, he could not bear the thought of not participating in the moves which might result in the Emperor's downfall, now that such powerful influences were scheming to bring it about.

For close on three weeks, no event of importance occurred, although in Court circles rumours were rife. It was said that the slippery Fouché had cleared himself of participation in a conspiracy. There was no evidence whatever against him, except that, during the Emperor's absence, he had openly become friends with Talleyrand. 'Why not?' he was reported to have argued glibly. 'Although our ideas and tastes differ in many ways, we both have Your Imperial Majesty's interests at heart. Surely it is for the benefit of your administration that we should have buried the hatchet and endeavoured to reconcile our points of view?'

To refute that Napoleon could find no argument, so Fouché remained Minister of the Interior, working from dawn to dusk and long into the night, directing his countless army of spies who permeated every country on the Continent.

During these days, apart from a few loyal personal friends, Talleyrand remained isolated. Few of the throngs that had formerly graced his salons were prepared to take the risk, should the Emperor's wrath suddenly descend upon him, of having appeared to be his associates. Roger was shrewd enough to realise that, as they already understood each other, only harm could be done by their publicly displaying their friendship at this juncture; so he simply sent a note to the effect that, if Talleyrand wished to see him, he would be happy to meet him at any time or place.

Meanwhile, Napoleon was obviously hesitating to grasp the nettle. Any lesser man he could have dealt with summarily; but not the Prince de Benevento. He had made the Prince a High Dignitary of the Empire, so that he was equal in status with his own brothers. To strike at him was to strike at one of the props of his own throne. But, on the 28th January, he decided to postpone the issue no longer.

A Council was called at the Tuileries, at which numerous Dignitaries and Ministers were present, Talleyrand among them. After routine business had been discussed, Napoleon detained him, Cambacérès, Lebrun, Decrés and Fouché, but dismissed the others. The Emperor walked up and down, his hands clasped behind his back, gradually working himself up into a fury.

He accused Talleyrand of constantly working against his interests; of having advised him to have executed the Duc d'Enghien; of having persuaded him to go into Spain; of circulating rumours designed to destroy public confidence; of influencing wealthy speculators to depress the funds. Then he charged him with the implications in the letter to Murat.

Talleyrand, who was leaning against the mantelpiece for support, merely raised his eyebrows and shrugged:

'But, Sire, you were at the war. Your courage is well known. You expose yourself most recklessly. Any day you might be killed. France cannot be allowed to fall into anarchy. We must be prepared for eventualities. None of us would wish to see a

Bourbon again on the throne. The situation could be controlled only by a man popular with the people whom Your Imperial Majesty has raised in his shadow and would continue to pursue his policies. Who more suitable than your sister's husband, whom you have made King of Naples? But only, I repeat, in the terrible eventuality of Your Majesty's being suddenly taken from us.'

The Emperor stared at him, stony-eyed, then burst out, 'I do not believe a word of it. You are a thief! You are a coward! All your life you have deceived and betrayed everyone.' For over twenty minutes Napoleon continued to rave at the Prince, finally winding up:

'You would sell your own father. You deserve to be broken like a glass. I have the power to do it, but I despise you too much. You are shit in a silk stocking.'

Talleyrand's face was white, his eyes half-closed, and his lips compressed. He displayed no dejection, but an icy disdain.

Angered beyond endurance by his attitude of apparent indifference, Napoleon sought to shatter his aristocratic calm by shouting at him:

'Why did you not tell me that the Duke of San Carlos was your wife's lover?'

Still imperturbable, Talleyrand replied, 'Indeed, Sire, I did not think that this news was to the increase of Your Majesty's glory, nor mine.'

Defeated, Napoleon strode towards the door. Casting a menacing look over his shoulder, which included Fouché, he snarled, 'Know that if a revolution does suddenly come about, both of you will be the first to be crushed by it.' Then he slammed the door.

The eyes of all the others remained fixed on Talleyrand. Leaving the mantelpiece, he limped towards the door. Pausing there, he turned and said:

'What a pity, Messieurs, that such a great man should have been so badly brought up.'

Those who had witnessed this amazing scene did not long keep it to themselves. Within a quarter of an hour Roger had an account of it; and, while it appeared that Talleyrand had exonerated himself, he waited anxiously to see what the next move would be.

The following morning, the Emperor, yet again half cowed, half fascinated by the unbreakable spirit of the great aristocrat, did no more than deprive him of the office of Grand Chamberlain. That evening, to everyone's amazement, Talleyrand ignored the fact that he was in disgrace and appeared, as imperturbable as ever, at a Court reception.

On the 30th, Roger received a note from Talleyrand, asking him as a matter of urgency to meet him out at his house at Passey a little before midnight. The summons brought Roger many recollections. The charming *petite maison* on the outskirts of Paris had been Talleyrand's home before the Revolution. There he had entertained the foremost Liberals of the French nobility who were striving to bring in long-overdue reforms. It was there that Roger had first met men who afterwards made history. Later, during the Terror, when Talleyrand had had to escape from France, Roger, as a member of the dread Paris Commune, had commandeered the house and so saved it and its contents for its owner. During those terrible days he had at times lived there, once with his wife Amanda, and at another time with the beautiful Athenais de Rochambeau.

Dressed in civilian clothes, he drove out there in a hired coach. It was a bitter winter night and raining. Muffled in his cloak, he walked up the garden path, and hammered with the knocker on the front door. It was opened almost immediately by Antoine Velot. He and his wife, Marie, as butler and cook-housekeeper, had been the only permanent staff there for many years. During the long period of Talleyrand's exile, Roger had paid their wages and, in return, when he made brief visits to the house, they had given him most faithful service.

Antoine was now well advanced in years; but, having received Roger with delight, he declared that *le bon Dieu* had blessed himself and his wife by keeping them both hale and hearty. He then showed Roger into the small library. Talleyrand was there, lounging on a sofa, with Fouché seated opposite him; while old Marie was putting the finishing touches to a cold collation on a side table. After greeting the two men, Roger put his hands on Marie's shoulders as she curtsied to him, raised her up and kissed her withered cheek. It was one of those gestures that made him loved by humble folk. The others looked at him in surprise, but he smiled and said:

'In the days when Paris ran with blood, this was my refuge. Marie was like a mother to me, and Antoine could not have showed more devotion to a son.'

When Marie had left the room, Talleyrand said, 'Doubtless you have heard about the scene that took place at the Tuileries the day before yesterday?'

Roger nodded. 'The little man has become impossible. I wonder that you did not strike him with your cane, and so be done with him once and for all.'

Talleyrand shrugged. 'That evening I dined with the Countess de Laval and I told her of it. She said I should have used the poker. I replied that I was too lazy. But that is not quite the truth. I submitted to his insults because I am determined not to break with him until I have broken him.'

'I admire Your Highness' tenacity,' Fouché remarked, 'and between us we will yet save France from being totally destroyed by him.' Then he gave a loud sniff. He suffered from a perpetual cold, and his face was as cadaverous as ever. His long, grey coat was ill fitting and his waistcoat stained with snuff.

Continuing to address Roger, Talleyrand went on, 'We asked you to join us, *cher ami*, because much depends on our being informed of the true state of affairs in Spain and, having but recently returned, you should be able to tell us if there is more or less percentage of the usual lies in the bulletins issued by the Emperor. But first let us refresh ourselves.'

Fouché helped himself to a meagre portion of boned chicken stuffed with sausage meat and truffles. Roger went for the Duck Montmorency, one breast of which had been removed and replaced with foie gras, and the whole decorated with red cherries. Their host chose the lobster patties crowned with oysters. There were Château Latour, Corton Clos du Roi,

Montrachet and Anjou to hand to wash these good things down. It was only an alfresco supper, but typical of the table kept by the Prince de Benevento.

While they ate, they talked of minor matters; then, putting his plate aside, Roger said, 'The Emperor would have the people believe that he has quelled the rebellion; and that, with Joseph re-established in Madrid, the whole trouble is over. But that is far from being the case. The insurgents still hold four-fifths of the country and the whole of Portugal. With British troops to stiffen them . . .'

'No, no,' Fouché interrupted. 'The English have been driven out. Reports from my people have been coming in for some days. To begin with, they were vague, but today quite definite. General Sir Moore was too precipitate in his retreat. 'Tis said that he force-marched his men seventeen miles a day to escape the trap set for him. As a result he lost several thousand from exhaustion, on the way to the coast. The English fought more determined rearguard actions. In one, their Hussars cut the Chasseurs of the Imperial Guard to pieces. That enabled General Sir Moore to get his main body to Corunna without it being defeated. But there he was forced to turn at bay. Again the English and Scottish fought with great bravery and the majority of them succeeded in getting away in their ships; but Sir Moore was killed during the battle.'

This was sad news for Roger, as Sir John was considered to be Britain's finest General; but he could comfort himself with the thought that his timely warning had probably saved the army from complete annihilation. After a moment he said:

'As soon as the Emperor learned of Moore's whereabouts and launched his greatly superior force against the British, it was clear that they would either suffer a disastrous defeat, or have to take to their ships. What I meant was that, with the Peninsular in its present state, you can count it certain that they will return. They would be mad to neglect such a God given opportunity to establish themselves at last on the Continent. And they still hold Lisbon.'

'Yes, with some nine thousand troops. But for how long

will such a comparatively small body of men succeed in maintaining themselves there?'

'With luck, until they are reinforced by much greater numbers.'

'But that cannot happen for a month or more at least,' Talleyrand put in. 'Meanwhile, Ney's corps, and others, will be on their way to the Portuguese capital and should easily overwhelm so small a garrison.'

'I disagree,' Roger replied. 'Sir John Moore's Number Two, General Baird, could sail down the coast in a matter of days, with the men taken off from Corunna and throw them into Lisbon. That is the obvious strategy. At a fair estimate it could raise the garrison to some twenty thousand men. And, should they hold the lines of Torres Vedras, Ney will find it no easy business to dislodge them.'

'What of Spain?' Fouché asked, sniffling again. 'We have some two hundred thousand men there: Soult, Bessières, Victor and other well-tried Marshals. Surely within a few months they will prove capable of overcoming all resistance?'

Roger shook his head. 'I do not think so. The Spaniards are gone mad, and their priests, regarding the French as atheists, are leading them into battle. Every peasant and townsman in the country has armed himself with some weapon. At least a million of them are out to spill French blood. Two-thirds of the cities are still in their hands, many French garrisons are now locked up in fortresses, half-starving; and there is hardly a road along which a convoy of supplies to relieve them can be sent without its being ambushed.'

Talleyrand refilled their glasses, and said, 'Then you are convinced that this rebellion is no flash in the pan, and cannot soon be crushed, as Napoleon maintains it will be?'

'I am. Had he remained in Spain to direct operations himself, his genius is such that he might have succeeded in coping with this hydra-headed monster. But few of his Marshals have the ability to do so. Soult is a good General but not, I think, good enough. Davoust has the brains to deal with the situation, and Masséna probably; but they are both in Germany. Even were either of them given the task, in my opinion it would take at least a year to reduce these fanatical Spaniards to even partial submission.'

Glancing at Fouché Talleyrand asked, '*Monsieur le Ministre*, are you of the opinion that we should now proceed?'

Fouché never looked anyone directly in the face. His eyes were downcast, but his voice firm, as he replied, 'Yes, Your Highness. There can hardly occur a better opportunity to bring him down.'

Talleyrand turned his heavily-lidded eyes on Roger, and said, 'For some time past I have been in secret communication with Prince Metternich. Although still comparatively young, he has the makings of a diplomat of the highest order. As you must know, for many months past Austria has been re-arming with a view to taking revenge on the Emperor for the humiliations he has put upon her. The Archduke Charles is urging restraint and is averse to his country again challenging Napoleon until the early summer. But the Prime Minister, Count Stadion, and Prince Metternich favour prompt action, to take advantage of the Emperor's involvement in Spain. Should that be only temporary, Austria would be better advised to wait until her new levies are fully trained. If, on the other hand, the Emperor is compelled to retain a great army in the Peninsula for many months to come, Austria has no need to fear the reappearance of those legions on her frontier; so the sooner she acts, the better.'

'There is also the situation in Prussia,' Fouché put in. 'The impassioned discourses of Fichte and others have led to the formation of a patriotic association, known as the *Tugenbund*, pledged to throw off French domination. Then there is the matter of Stein. Early in December, while in Madrid, the Emperor sent King Frederick William what amounted to an order. It read, "The man Stein is a troublemaker. I require you to dismiss him from your service and confiscate his lands." The craven King did as he was bade. This persecution of a leading patriot has inflamed the nation to fever-pitch. My agents report from all quarters there that the people are declaring that Prussia should follow the example of Spain, rise in its wrath and destroy the French garrisons. If Austria acts promptly, there is a good chance that this present wave of hatred may cause the Prussians to take up arms. But if Austria delays for several months, it will die down.'

Finishing his wine, Talleyrand set down his glass. 'With the prospect that the Spanish will continue to occupy a great French army in the Peninsula, and the possibility that the Prussians will rise, thereby detaining further large French forces in the north, the army that the Emperor could bring against Austria would be outnumbered. Given a victorious campaign by the Austrians, Napoleon's power will be shattered. I feel that there could be no better time to strike. What is your view, *Messieurs*?'

Both Fouché and Roger nodded their agreement.

Smiling, Talleyrand said, 'The die is cast then. I will communicate with Metternich tomorrow, and tell him to urge upon the Emperor Francis that the time has come to liberate Europe from the thraldom it has suffered all too long.'

27

The Gathering Clouds

Later, Roger learned from various sources of the decisions taken in Vienna as a result of Talleyrand's communication to Metternich, coupled with the Austrian's own assessment of the anti-French feeling now greatly on the increase throughout Europe.

On February 8th war was decided upon, although no open declaration of war was to be made. Obviously, Austria's chances of victory would be greatly strengthened if she could form a Fourth Coalition.

Strenuous efforts were made to induce Prussia to avenge herself on Napoleon. Her Ambassador in Vienna, von der Goltz, put forward the proposal that his country should contribute eighty thousand men to an Allied army. Scharnhorst, Gneisenau, and other members of the war party persuaded Frederick William to agree; but later, from fear of Russia, the spineless King went back on his promise.

Count Starhemberg was despatched to London, but found the British about to commit their best troops to the Peninsula. Canning could do no more than send a subsidy of two hundred and fifty thousand pounds in silver bars to Trieste and promise that, as soon as more troops became available, he would use them to create a diversion in the Low Countries.

Austria would, therefore, have to fight alone. However, she had one consolation. At Erfurt, Alexander had promised Napoleon that, should Austria start hostilities while he was occupied in Spain, Russia would intervene. But the Czar was still fully occupied with wresting Finland from Sweden; and, now that he had cooled towards the French, that provided a good excuse for not going to their aid. He had indicated to

Count Schwarzenberg that, should he have to keep his word, only a token force would be sent.

The French army was believed to number eight hundred thousand men. But three hundred thousand of them were now in Spain, two hundred thousand in France and sixty thousand in Italy. It was estimated that not more than two hundred and thirty thousand were in Germany and Poland, whereas Austria could put into the field two hundred and eighty-three thousand regulars and a further three hundred and ten thousand partially-trained militia. Moreover, Napoleon's army was very far from being the magnificent Grand Army that had threatened England with invasion in 1805. More than half of it now consisted of Rhinelanders, Dutch, Danes and Poles; while the French units contained a very high proportion of young conscripts called up a year, and even two years, before they would normally have been liable to serve.

On February 25th, Austria began her strategic concentrations. The Archduke Charles, unquestionably their best General, was to command the main army and endeavour to defeat the French army in Germany, which was commanded by Marshal Davoust. A second army, under the command of the Archduke John, was to strike down into Italy with the object of regaining the Tyrolese and Venetian lands, which had been reft from Austria after her last defeat. A third army, under the Archduke Ferdinand, was to invade the Grand Duchy of Warsaw.

Unfortunately for the Austrians, in spite of the reforms introduced by the Archduke Charles, their military machinery was still slow and cumbersome. It was not until early April that they were ready to strike, and the Archduke issued his proclamation:

'The freedom of Europe has sought refuge beneath our banners. Soldiers, your victories will break her chains. Your German brothers, who are now in the ranks of the enemy, wait for their deliverance.'

This eloquent appeal met with an enthusiastic response. Between them, Stadion and the Archduke had abolished a good part of the hidebound bureaucracy, and ousted the inefficient

Generals who had previously held commands only owing to their noble lineage, or through Court favour. Now, the troops had been given similar opportunities to those Napoleon had held out to the French, when he had declared, 'Every private carries in his knapsack a Marshal's baton.'

Moreover, as in the case of Spain, Catholic Austria was indignant at Napoleon's treatment of the Pope, in having the previous year annexed a large part of His Holiness' States of the Church.

Towards the end of March, Austria's concentrations were complete and the war opened well for her. On April 9th, the Archduke John invaded Italy and on the 16th defeated a Franco-Italian army under Eugene de Beauharnais. Meanwhile, he had despatched General Chastler with ten thousand men into the Tyrol, against the Bavarians who, as Napoleon's allies, had received that territory as part of the spoils of victory by the Peace of Pressburg.

The deeply religious Tyrolese were eager both to avenge the insults to the Pope and again to become Austrian subjects. In their villages these hardy mountaineers rose almost to a man, armed themselves and began to attack the Bavarian garrisons. In four days, the Bavarians had been driven out of all northern Tyrol, and the Austrian flag again flew over Innsbruck.

The Archduke Ferdinand was equally successful. Advancing rapidly into Poland, on April 19th he defeated the Franco-Polish army under Prince Poniatowski and, on the 22nd, occupied Warsaw.

However, the Archduke Charles was not so fortunate. He had assembled six corps in Bohemia and two corps in upper Austria, with the object of invading Bavaria. Davoust was in difficulties, because his troops were scattered far and wide over Germany. But the French Marshals knew far better how to use time than did their enemies. While the Austrians, owing to bad supply organisation, were advancing only by half-day marches, Davoust succeeded in concentrating the major part of his forces on the line Munich-Ratisbon-Würzberg. Yet, with only eighty-nine thousand men, he was far inferior to the army the Archduke could bring against him. His situation was then rendered more desperate by an order issued from Strasbourg by Berthier, whom the Emperor had placed in command of the operations in Germany. It was that Davoust should concentrate round Ratisbon.

Roger's relations with Lisala had been deteriorating from day to day, so it was a considerable relief to him when, on April 13th, he left with Napoleon for the front. On arriving at Donauworth, the Emperor swiftly corrected the errors that Berthier had made and, at a risk that he did not at the time appreciate, ordered Davoust to march his four divisions across the enemy's front. At Haussen, on the 19th, the Marshal was fiercely attacked but, by magnificent generalship, fought his way through. There ensued two days of violent conflict between widely separated forces. Then, on the 22nd, at Eckmühl, Napoleon inflicted a major defeat on the Archduke.

The Austrian centre was shattered. The left, under General Hiller, was driven south-east, towards the river Isar. The main body, under the Archduke, retreated north and, on the 23rd, succeeded in getting across to the left bank of the Danube. But in the five days of fighting in the neighbourhood of Ratisbon, the Austrians had lost forty thousand men in killed, wounded and prisoners.

One of Napoleon's great strengths as a commander of armies was the way in which he succeeded in driving troops, already exhausted by battle, to follow up a defeated enemy. With ruthless determination, he pursued Hiller towards Vienna. On May 13th, the Emperor again rode into the Imperial city as a conqueror.

Nevertheless, the Archduke's army had escaped destruction. Having succeeded in getting across the Danube to the left bank, it was joined by the surviving regiments of Hiller's force and the garrison that had been driven from Vienna. Again a formidable army, it occupied the *Marchfeld*, some five miles south-east of the capital. It was on this historic field that Rudolph of Habsburg had defeated the famous Bohemian warrior-King Ottakar II in 1276, and so founded the Austrian Empire.

The position not only raised the morale of the troops by its historic association, but was an extremely difficult one to attack; as the river there was from two to four and a half miles wide. Between the banks lay a dozen or more islands, much the largest of which was Lobau. Napoleon decided to cross and occupied the villages of Aspern and Essling, but he was not aware that the Austrians were so close at hand. On May 21st, Bessières had barely taken up his position with only seventeen thousand infantry, when they were fallen upon by eighty thousand infantry and fifteen thousand horse. Nevertheless, Lannes succeeded in holding Essling, and it was not until dusk that the Austrians had driven Masséna from the centre of Aspern. The Emperor's attempt to break through the enemy's centre by a great cavalry charge failed and, by nightfall, the French positions were almost surrounded.

In the small hours, Masséna reopened the battle and drove the Austrians out of Aspern. Meanwhile, the Imperial Guard and Oudinot's Grenadiers had crossed the river. Desperate fighting ensued all through the 22nd. Under one determined onslaught some Austrian battalions began to waver, but the Archduke seized the banner of the Zach regiment and flung himself into the fray. His example rallied his troops, and the French were driven back. In a magnificent charge the French cavalry routed the Austrian cavalry, but were robbed of the fruits of their achievement by themselves being driven back by Austrian Grenadiers.

During the morning, Napoleon received the alarming news that the largest of the bridges which he had built across the Danube had been set on fire, and that others were being swept away by trees and barges sent down the flooded river. This meant annihilation for the French should they fail to hold their own. They were now fighting for survival. Essling was lost, but regained. Aspern finally fell to the Austrians. By then both armies were utterly exhausted. By superhuman efforts the French engineers had repaired a number of bridges. That night the Emperor withdrew the remains of his army into the island of Lobau.

The slaughter had been appalling, approaching that of Eylau. Austria lost twenty-five thousand and France twenty thousand men, among them the irreplaceable Marshal Lannes. The finest assault leader in the army, he had a hundred times led his men up scaling ladders and through breaches made by cannon in the walls of fortresses. He had been wounded more than twenty times, and it was said that bullets only bent, never shattered, his bones; but, at last, he had received a wound that was mortal. Napoleon tenderly embraced the dying Marshal, but Lannes' last words were to reproach him for his boundless ambition which was causing such a terrible loss of French lives. Like many others, for a long time past his heart had not been in the Emperor's wars, and he had continued to serve only out of a sense of duty. A staunch Republican and convinced atheist, he had often openly criticised Napoleon for creating a new aristocracy, and for his rapprochement with the Church.

In this last matter, having paid lip-service to religion in order to gain the support of a large part of the French people, the Emperor had now become so convinced of his absolute supremacy that he could afford to humble the Pope. In Vienna only a week before, on May 17th, he had issued a decree depriving His Holiness of all temporal power, and annexed that part of the States of the Church that he had spared the previous year. Asserting himself to be the 'successor of Charlemagne', he relegated the Pope to merely Bishop of Rome, with a stipend of two million francs. When Pius VII protested and excommunicated him, he retaliated by having him arrested and taken as a prisoner from Rome to Florence.

The battle of Aspern-Essling had a great effect on public opinion throughout the whole of Europe. Eylau had in fact been a stalemate, but Napoleon had been able to claim it as a victory because, on the night following the battle, the Russians had withdrawn. Aspern-Essling was also a stalemate, but in that case it was the French who had withdrawn, leaving the Austrians in possession of the battlefield. The belief that Napoleon, when commanding in person, could not be defeated had at last been deflated.

Had the Archduke Charles been in a position to attack the

island of Lobau next day, it could have brought Napoleon's Empire crashing about his ears; for, not only had the majority of the French no more fight left in them, but they were without food and had run out of ammunition. But the Austrians, too, were utterly exhausted; so, under flags of truce, while the battlefield was being cleared of its mounds of corpses, a seven-week Armistice was agreed upon.

While the French army remained on Lobau, the Emperor installed himself in the Palace of Schönbrunn, just outside Vienna, and sent for his Court. During June, by feats of brilliant organisation, he brought from all quarters large reinforcements and huge quantities of stores and ammunition.

Meanwhile, from both south and north bad news for the French kept coming in.

Of the three British Generals court martialled for the Convention of Cintra, Sir Arthur Wellesley alone was acquitted. Lord Castlereagh had a great belief in his abilities and induced the Cabinet to send the future Duke of Wellington back to the Peninsula as Commander-in-Chief of a considerable army.

Napoleon had laid down the strategy to be followed by his Marshals. Gouvion St. Cyr was to clean up Catalonia, Victor was to destroy the Spanish army in Andalusia, Ney was to hold down Galicia while Soult advanced from there to take Oporto, then Lisbon. In mid-March Victor crossed the Tagus and defeated the Spanish regulars, but was so weakened that, without reinforcements, which King Joseph in Madrid could not send him, decided that he dare advance no further. Towards the end of the month Soult arrived in front of Oporto. Led by the Bishop, thirty thousand insurgents put up a most heroic resistance; but, lacking even a semblance of organisation, were massacred by the thousand. Having captured the city, but still surrounded on all sides by hordes of enemies, Soult, too, felt he dared advance no further.

Such was the situation when, on April 22nd, Wellesley landed in Lisbon. With twenty-five thousand British troops and sixteen thousand Portuguese, he decided that he was strong enough to defeat first Soult, then Victor. Marching northwards, he carried out a most daring crossing of the Douro

where the cliffs were so steep that Soult had left the river un-
guarded. Taken by surprise, the French Marshal was chased
out of Oporto, then found himself cut off by dispositions Wellesley had made. In despair, he burned his baggage, sacrificed
his plunder and abandoned his artillery. The remnants of his
shattered corps, reduced to a starving rabble, made their way
as best they could by goat tracks over the mountains back to
Galicia.

No such major disaster as the destruction of an entire French
Army Corps took place in northern Europe; but there were
portents of trouble to come. Sickened by the pusillanimity of
his King, Frederick von Schill, who commanded a regiment
of Prussian Hussars, left Berlin with them on April 28th. He
endeavoured to surprise the French and take from them the
great fortress of Magdeburg. In that he failed, but in other
actions he met with considerable success, including the capture
of Stralsund. But there he was overwhelmed by Napoleon's
Danish and Dutch troops and mortally wounded.

Schill's gallant exploits raised the patriotic fervour of his
countrymen to fever-pitch and incited the young Duke of
Brunswick to follow his example. He had formed a corps of
volunteers in Bohemia. With them he invaded Saxony and,
on June 11th, captured Dresden. After several times defeating the troops of Napoleon's brother, King Jerome, in Westphalia, the Duke decided to fight his way right across Germany. After many perilous encounters, he succeeded, and with
his men was taken off by British ships to England. His little
troop became the nucleus of the 'King's German Legion', that
later fought with great gallantry under Wellington in Spain.

During the battle of Aspern-Essling, while carrying a message from the Emperor to Masséna, a bullet had knocked
Roger's hat from his head and ploughed through his scalp.
It was not a serious wound, but resulted in his being sent, after
a few days on Lobau, with one of the batches of casualties,
into Vienna for treatment by a civilian doctor.

There, he found that Duroc was already allocating accommodation in the Schönbrunn Palace, in anticipation of the
arrival of the Court. Since the Palace would also be used as

Great Headquarters, it was certain that it would be crowded and very noisy. As additional accommodation, Duroc had commandeered a number of small private houses just outside the Park. Roger suffered from severe headaches as a result of his wound, so he was anxious to secure quarters where he would be as quiet as possible, and he asked Duroc if he might occupy one of the houses. His old friend readily granted his request.

It was a pleasant little, double-fronted villa, with a wing consisting of stables and coach house at ground level and servants' quarters above. To the right of the front door, a drawing room ran the whole depth of the house, with a similar room as best bedroom on the first floor. To the left, there was a small dining room and kitchen, with two more bedrooms over. Opposite the top of the stairs, between the big bedroom and the other, smaller room at the back, was a slip room which could be entered from either. It could have been used as a dressing room, but Roger saw that it had been fitted up as a clothes closet.

At the back of the house there was a verandah, and along the first floor a broad, covered balcony looking out on a half an acre of pleasant garden. Roger decided that he would leave the big bedroom to Lisala, and himself occupy the smaller one further along the balcony. There, with his soldier servant and groom to serve him, he rested for some days, getting up only for meals and strolls round the garden, until his scalp had healed and his headaches ceased.

By that time, Napoleon was living in the Palace and Roger reported back for duty. A week later the Court arrived and, as one of the Empress' ladies, Lisala. She was, Roger had to admit to himself, as beautiful as ever; but she stirred no trace of desire in him. Treating her with the same politeness he had shown her in Paris, he took her to the little house. She was enchanted with it, and declared that she wished she could laze away the summer days in the garden instead of having to attend on Josephine. However, hardly had she settled in than, to his intense annoyance, she produced another sheaf of bills that considerably exceeded the one thousand francs a month he had agreed to allow her.

There followed a violent quarrel. She maintained that, in her position, it was essential always to appear in the latest mode. He argued that other ladies-in-waiting did not always do so and were far less extravagant. She had found out from someone what his pay and allowances amounted to, and declared that he could well afford to indulge her tastes. He admitted that he could, but only within reason, and he would soon be beggared if she continued to run up bills at this pace. She remarked with a smile that spies who had given themselves away should not grumble at having to pay for their continued immunity. Seething with anger, he agreed to settle her bills, then stamped out of the house.

For the hundredth time he contemplated the terrible fix into which he had got himself, and felt that to go on like this indefinitely was impossible. Yet only two alternatives offered themselves. One was to kill her, the other was to throw in his hand, quietly slip away from Vienna, then make his way to England.

During his time, Roger had caused many men to die violent deaths, but to murder a woman in cold blood was a very different matter and, although he had come to hate Lisala, he knew he could not kill her. He was almost equally reluctant to free himself from her by absconding, because he felt that Europe was now hovering on the brink of the greatest crisis that had arisen for many years. It needed only one major defeat of Napoleon by the Archduke Charles to bring about the Emperor's fall. In adversity, every hand would be against him. In Paris, Talleyrand and Fouché, backed by many of the Marshals, would seize power. Both of them knew the truth about Roger, so he would then have nothing to fear. He could divorce Lisala and send her packing.

While continuing with her, he had only one consolation. So far no rumour had reached him that she had taken a lover. Her nature being as it was, he had little doubt that, after he left Paris, she had had one or more, and that she would shortly select one here in Vienna. But at least she was exercising discretion in her amours. Perhaps because she had taken seriously his threat that, should she fail to do so, he would kill her. In any case, she had not as yet brought public ridicule upon him.

During the last half of June Schönbrunn became nightly the scene of balls, operas, plays and brilliant receptions. The Emperor appeared at them all, attended by his subject Kings and Princes, and giving the impression that he considered the war with Austria as good as over. But, during the days and far into the nights, he was in his Cabinet, working with frantic energy to build up the army that still occupied the island of Lobau.

By early July, Napoleon had succeeded in massing over one hundred and seventy thousand troops on the island, and now had a superiority in numbers; for the Archuke had not been so able or so fortunate in bringing up reserves.

After the Archduke Ferdinand's first success in taking Warsaw, the tide had turned against him. Early in May, Prince Poniatowski took the offensive and prevented him from crossing the Vistula. Meanwhile, the Czar, feeling that he must at least make a show of honouring his promise to Napoleon should Austria attack France, despatched a corps towards Lemberg. Now threatened from both sides, Ferdinand had to evacuate Warsaw and, by mid-June, had withdrawn to Opatoff. There followed a number of minor engagements, in which the fortunes of both sides varied; but the Austrian army of thirty thousand continued to be tied up in distant Poland, so could not be brought to the assistance of the Archduke Charles.

Fortune had also deserted the Archduke John. After defeating de Beauharnais and freeing the Tyrol, a large detachment he had sent into Dalmatia had been thoroughly defeated by the able Marshal Marmont. By then, de Beauharnais had called up considerable reinforcements and, after a series of conflicts, driven John out of Carinthia; from where he withdrew into Hungary. De Beauharnais had followed him up and, on June 14th, forced him, after a pitched battle outside the fortress of Rueb, to retire again. While retreating in the direction of Pressburg, the Archduke received an urgent summons from his brother Charles, to join him outside Vienna before the seven-week armistice with the French expired. John's original force of fifty-three thousand men had by then been reduced to twenty thousand effectives, and he was a considerable distance from the capital; but he altered his line of march, hoping to arrive in time to participate in the great battle that was about to take place in the neighbourhood of Lobau.

In consequence, the Archduke Charles could dispose of only one hundred and thirty-five thousand men, as opposed to Napoleon's one hundred and seventy thousand. On the other hand, the French had to cross the arm of the Danube separating the island from the mainland, then advance through Aspern-Essling and four miles of open country before they could attack the Austrians' major concentration, which occupied a ridge of hills where there stood the village of Wagram.

For some time past, with great labour, the Austrians had been throwing up very strong defences opposite the north shore of Lobau, as it was there, the river being at its narrowest, the French were expected to make their attempt to cross. But Napoleon had prepared a most effective deception plan.

On the night of July 4th, the French opened a terrific cannonade directed at the Austrian trenches north of Lobau. Meanwhile, sufficient boats to form six bridges that had been kept under camouflage, were swiftly hooked together and swung into position from the east end of the island, across the much broader channel to the mainland.

When the battle opened, a violent storm was raging. Forked lightning streaked down, and the crashes of thunder could not be distinguished from the roar of the bombardment. In torrents of rain the divisions of Oudinot and Masséna streamed over the bridges. The Austrian earthworks were outflanked and rapidly evacuated, their defenders swiftly retiring to the ridge of hills. Dawn saw the whole French army deployed for battle on the mainland.

At midday, the French marched steadily forward and, in the afternoon, launched an attack in close columns on the heights held by the Austrians. But, by seven o'clock, they had been beaten back from Wagram with heavy losses. The battle was then broken off, to be renewed on the morning of the 6th.

The Archduke took the offensive, launching his right with such force that he drove Masséna back on to Aspern. The Austrian centre then advanced, and several hours of most bloody conflict ensued, as the White-Coats gradually gained ground from the French. Realising the danger in which his army now stood of being driven into the river, the Emperor massed one hundred cannon, afterwards known as the 'Grand Battery', and, under its devastating fire, the Austrians' advance was checked. He then launched a solid column consisting of thirty thousand infantry and six thousand horse, under General Macdonald, against the enemy's centre. It gave, but did not break, and the Archduke might yet have emerged victorious, because his left wing was almost intact.

It was the brilliant Davoust who really saved the day. His corps had been allotted the task of preventing the Archduke John's army from arriving on the scene. On learning that battle had been joined, Davoust left only a light screen of troops to mislead the Archduke into believing that his way to Vienna was still barred, then hastened with the bulk of his corps to Napoleon's assistance. He arrived late in the afternoon, but in time to drive the Austrians from the village of Neusiedel, and so threw their left into confusion. At length the whole of the Archduke Charles' army was forced back from the heights of Wagram, although it retired in good order, and covered by a murderous artillery fire.

The Emperor naturally claimed Wagram as a great victory, but it was far from that. The Austrians had fought with splendid heroism against much superior odds and, although they had lost twenty-four thousand men, they had accounted for eighteen thousand French. Moreover, they had fallen back as a still orderly and unbroken army. For two days, the French followed them up, but only feebly. Napoleon's army, now largely composed of teen-aged recruits, had sadly deteriorated. They had neither the stamina nor the *élan* of the hard-bitten troops who had fought at Marengo and Austerlitz. The Austrians had proved better soldiers and had covered themselves with glory. At Zneym, on the 12th, another armistice was agreed.

Roger had been lucky in the battle as, after the first great clash had occurred on the 5th and the French had been driven back, Napoleon had sent him post-haste to Vienna, to raise every small detachment he could from the scant garrison left there and bring them to the battlefield. He had worked all through the night, despatching cooks, clerks and storekeepers, who were of little value, out to Lobau, and himself had not returned until the terrible carnage on the 6th was nearly over.

To give greater credence to his proclamation of victory, Napoleon distributed a number of honours and awards. For the part Macdonald had played in leading the decisive charge, the Emperor gave him on the field his baton as a Marshal. A few days later, when the list was published, Roger learned that, for special services, he had been elevated to the Napoleonic peerage, and was now *Colonel Baron de Breuc.*

That evening, as he did now and again for appearances' sake, he dined at his little house with Lisala. They had reached a state where they now hardly bothered to talk to each other. But he told her that he had been made a Baron.

Looking up from her plate, she fixed her huge eyes on his and asked, 'Will that mean an increase in your income?'

'Yes,' he told her. 'The Emperor always grants a life pension to those he ennobles, in order that they may support the dignity to his credit.' With a cynical smile, he added, 'However, it will not amount to a fortune, so you need not suppose that you will be able to increase greatly the blackmail you are already levying upon me.'

She shrugged. 'About such paltry sums I have now become indifferent. As well as clothes I desire jewels which I know that you are in no position to pay for. But I have recently been offered a means by which I can make a mint of money. I intend to run a brothel.'

28

Mission to Paris

Roger dropped his fork. 'Lisala! You cannot mean that!'

'Indeed I do. 'Tis, I am told, a most profitable occupation.'

'But . . . but . . . all else apart, you are one of the Empress' ladies.'

Lisala made a derisive gesture. 'Oh, Josephine! I am much wearied of dancing attendance on her. And, in any case, she is finished.'

'What mean you?'

'Surely you must have heard that the Emperor intends to put her from him?'

Roger had heard. Everyone had known for a long time past that Napoleon's dearest wish was to found a dynasty. Although Josephine had had two children by her earlier marriage, she had failed to give him one. He had, therefore, come to believe himself to be incapable of becoming a father. This belief had been invalidated when one of his many temporary mistresses, Elénora Denuelle, had borne him a son, about the identity of whose father there could be no possible shadow of doubt. It was this that, dearly as he had come to love Josephine, had first put into his mind the idea of divorcing her.

But if he was to take a new wife, nothing less could now satisfy him as a consort than a lady having the royal blood of one of the great hereditary ruling families. It was, therefore, not until the conference at Erfurt that he had disclosed his secret intention to anyone. There, as Roger and a few of Talleyrand's other intimates knew, Napoleon had contemplated asking the Czar for the hand of his sister. Talleyrand, being strenuously opposed to a Russian alliance, had warned the Czar that the proposal was likely to be put forward; so, when Napoleon had broached the matter, Alexander had been ready to evade committing himself, by replying that the selection of a husband for his sister was entirely in the hands of her mother.

This feeler and polite rebuff had been whispered about only among a very limited circle; but recently there had been much more widely-spread rumours that, when Napoleon had conquered Austria, he intended to ask, as part of the peace terms, to be given a Hapsburg Princess as a bride.

As one of Josephine's oldest and staunchest friends, Roger deplored the possibility that, for reasons of State, she might be deprived of the husband that she had come to love so deeply. But, knowing Talleyrand's pro-Austrian leanings, he saw the great statesman's hand in this. Abused and insulted by the Emperor as he had been six months earlier, he had regained considerable influence with him. And it could not be denied that a Franco-Austrian alliance fortified by an Imperial marriage would materially strengthen both countries.

Staring hard-eyed at Lisala, Roger said, 'Naturally, I am aware that certain people would like to see the Empress replaced by a Hapsburg Princess; but Austria is far from having been conquered yet.'

Lisala shrugged. 'Whether Josephine stays or goes is all one to me. I intend to submit my resignation to her, and employ myself in more profitable activities.'

'But a brothel!' Roger cried. 'You seek only to shock and horrify me for your amusement. You cannot possibly really mean that you intend to run a brothel.'

'I do, and out of doing so I'll get even more amusement than seeing your face as it is at this moment. In brothels, as you must know . . .'

'I do not know,' he cut in harshly. 'I entered one only once, when I was in my teens, then fled from it in disgust.'

'Then I'll inform you. There are peepholes in the walls of all the rooms. Through them one can witness the peculiar games in which couples at times indulge. That will provide me with much entertainment. And, when I witness some gallant who performs with unusual vigour, I'll give him an assignation to come another day and have me "on the house".'

'You . . . you vile creature!' Roger burst out. 'Undertake

this foul enterprise, and I vow I'll burn the place down with you in it.'

'For that you will have no opportunity, as it will be neither here in Vienna nor in Paris.'

'Where then?'

'That is my affair.'

'Wherever it may be, I'll run you to earth. Yes, whatever it may cost me, I'll not submit to the ghastly humiliation of it becoming known that my wife is running a whorehouse. And it will become known. Satan has endowed you with too great a beauty for your identity not be bruited abroad in any city.'

'In that you are mistaken. I am as anxious as yourself to keep this matter secret. I intend, from time to time, to return and inflict my company on you. Now that I am a Baroness, I shall find Court functions more enjoyable than ever.'

'What you propose is impossible. From having been a member of the Court for above a year, your face is known to hundreds—nay, thousands of people. Inevitably some officer: French, German, Dutch, Italian, will visit your brothel, recognise you and tell others of your infamy.'

'Again you are wrong.' Lisala smiled and shook her head. 'While exercising my profession I mean to wear a black velvet mask with a long fringe. My body is beautiful enough to tempt any man I desire, without his seeing my face. In fact, a mask will prove an added seduction for such encounters. And, should a lover of the moment be so imprudent as to tear it off, I'll drive my stiletto between his ribs.'

Roger could find no more to say. Short of killing her, there was no way in which he could prevent her carrying out her plan; and that he could not bring himself to do. Rising, he flung his glass of wine in her face, then left the room and the house.

That night, the little sleep he got was at an inn, and next morning he sent a message to Berthier that he was ill after having eaten bad fish. For three days he did not go out, and ceaselessly pondered the problem of what he could do about having been cursed with such a wife. To that he could find no answer. Even making off to England was no longer a fully satisfactory solution, as he could not bear the thought that if Lisala was found out, the fine name he had made for himself in the French Army would for ever be besmirched. He could only endeavour to comfort himself with the possibility that Lisala would succeed in remaining incognito while pandering to her insatiable lust for sexual excitement.

When he forced himself to return to Court, several people condoled with him on his wife's illness. Then Josephine spoke to him most kindly, regretting that Lisala had had to leave her on account of having been ordered by a doctor to take the waters at Baden-Baden. A good actor, as he had always been, Roger produced the reactions expected of him. That evening he returned to the little house, to find that most of Lisala's clothes were still there, but she had gone; so he settled in again.

The armistice continued, but negotiations for a peace got no further, as the terms proposed by Napoleon were unacceptable to the Emperor Francis.

Early in August, it was learned that the British had landed a strong force on the large island of Walcheren at the mouth of the Scheldt. Roger deplored this strategy both for timing and place. Had the landing been made six weeks earlier it could have enormously encouraged the Austrians to still greater efforts, and had it been made at Stralsund it could have incited the Prussian patriots to force their King into joining Austria in her war against France. As things were now, it seemed to be a grievous waste of effort, for he felt sure the Dutch would not rise against the Emperor, and knew the malarial swamps in the estuary of the Scheldt to be one of the most unsuitable places possible to form a bridgehead for an invasion of the Continent.

News then came in from Spain. The remnant of Soult's army had straggled back, without guns or baggage, into Galicia. There Ney's men had derided them as cowards and tempers flown so high that the two Marshals had been with difficulty prevented from fighting a duel. Meanwhile, Wellesley had turned speedily upon Victor. Realising his peril, the Marshal had swiftly retreated towards Madrid; but, on July 27th,

Wellesley, supported by a Spanish army, had brought him to bay at Talavera and inflicted a severe defeat upon him.

In the middle of August, Lisala returned to Vienna for a few days. Roger refused to speak to her, and took his meals out. She made no attempt to be received again at the Palace and, having collected a few more of her clothes, disappeared again.

On the 25th, the Emperor called Roger into his Cabinet and said, 'Breuc, I am much disturbed about what is happening in France. I have received intelligence that, in my absence, Fouché has assumed the powers of a dictator. Proceed to Paris at once, return as soon as possible, and report to me what is going on there.'

Taking to horse with a minimum of delay, Roger set out and reached Paris in nine days. After refreshing himself at *La Belle Etoile*, he went straight to the Ministry of the Interior, where the Minister received him within ten minutes of his having sent in his name.

When Roger had explained the object of his mission, Fouché, sniffling as usual, began, '*Mon cher Baron*, let me . . .'

'So you know that I have been elevated to the nobility?' Roger cut in with a smile.

Fouché's corpse-like face twisted into what for him was the semblance of a grin. 'I knew weeks ago. Very little that goes on in Europe escapes my agents. I even have a flotilla of boats patrolling the sea from the Pyrenees to the Baltic; so that I am informed of most of the smuggling operations permitted by our administrators in order to line their own pockets. But my congratulations. And, now, as I was about to say:

'On July 29th, forty British ships of the line, thirty frigates, eighty sloops and four to five hundred transports appeared off the mouth of the Scheldt. They landed forty thousand men and one hundred and fifty cannon on the island of Walcheron. It was evident that their intention was to incite a rebellion in brother Louis' Kingdom of Holland. About that I was little worried, as my people had long since dealt with all subversive elements there. The English succeeded in swiftly subduing Middleburg and, by August 15th, the defences of Flushing. One could then deduce that their next step would be to attack our important base of Antwerp, as the English have always regarded it as a pistol pointed against their heads.

'That did concern us somewhat here in Paris, because many of the people in those parts still feel a loyalty to Austria, to which, up till recent times, the Belgian Netherlands belonged. Moreover, the majority of them are Catholics. A revolution in those parts, similar to that which has taken place in Spain, could have proved most embarrassing, particularly as our regular forces there were almost non-existent.

'A Grand Council was called to debate the situation. Cambacéres, as the nominal head of the Government during the Emperor's absence, took the chair. No-one had any suggestions to offer except Decrès, who proposed that we should call up the citizen militia, as we did in the old days of the Revolution.

'The others quailed at the idea of taking such an unorthodox step without the Emperor's sanction. But I felt that a certain use might be made of it. Next day, my Ministerial colleagues learned to their horror that I had overridden their authority and called up the National Guard in fifteen Departments. I went further. I circulated a letter to the Prefects and Mayors, which ran:

' "Show Europe that even if Napoleon's genius may lend splendour to France, yet his presence is not indispensable to repulse her enemies." '

Roger gave a sigh of admiration. 'The devil you did! That was a bold stroke indeed. But the Emperor may well call you to account for it.'

'He may.' Fouché gave a little snigger. 'But I doubt it. He has always been a trifle frightened of me; yet has found me too valuable to dispense with. In any case, I have sent out my message to the people of France. Should their Emperor fall by the wayside, they can rely upon me to take the reins of Government firmly into my hands.'

'*Monsieur le Ministre*, you have my utmost admiration,' Roger declared with a smile. 'I will return and report to His

Imperial Majesty that, when others feared to act, you took steps to defend France which you believe he would have taken himself had he been in Paris.'

They parted most cordially, and late on the evening of September 13th, Roger arrived back at Schönbrunn. Two hours later, the Emperor received him, and he made his report.

When he had done, Napoleon grunted, then remarked, 'I know that you have always disliked Fouché; so are not attempting to excuse his faults. But he has acted in a most arbitrary fashion.'

''Tis true, Sire, that I have a personal antipathy to the man,' Roger replied promptly, 'but that does not detract from my admiration of the manner in which he has served Your Majesty. He has uncovered several conspiracies that might have cost you your life; succeeded in subduing those troublesome Breton Chouans, who for years all the Generals you sent failed to quell; and now, by taking it on himself to contain the English in their bridgehead, he has spared Your Majesty the necessity of sending considerable bodies of your regular troops to Flanders.'

'True; true! He is a slippery devil, but no-one can question his efficiency. And, in many matters he has served me admirably. Now I know how matters stand, I'll let them rest. Here we make no progress; the Emperor Francis is proving as stubborn as a mule.'

'Since things are at a standstill, Sir,' Roger hazarded, 'may I crave a few days' rest? I rode monstrous hard to Paris and back, and I am desperately fatigued.'

The Emperor stopped his pacing up and down, smiled at Roger and twisted his ear. 'You may, Breuc. Few of my couriers can match the speed with which you travel, and there is now little to do. Take a week or two if you wish.'

Roger had already handed over his mount at the Palace stable to be at once rubbed down, watered and fed; so he walked the short distance across the Park to his little house. When he reached it, he saw with some surprise chinks of light coming from between the curtains of the window of the largest bedroom. Evidently Lisala had returned on another visit.

483

Tired as he was, the last thing he wanted was another acrimonious discussion with her. That could well occur if he roused the house and, as it was close on midnight, he knew that the front door would be bolted.

It then occurred to him that as he had duties which often kept him late at the Palace, he had given his man instructions that, as he hated stuffiness, the window of his bedroom was always to be left a little open. Going round to the back of the house, he quietly climbed up the iron trellis work to the balcony, tiptoed along it and got through the window into his room.

Lighting the candles, he wearily undressed. Then he noticed that, since he had not been expected, his man had not laid out a nightshirt for him. His underclothes were kept on shelves in the clothes closet. Still anxious to get to bed without Lisala's coming in to talk to him, he opened the door very quietly. A streak of light two inches wide at the far side of the closet showed that Lisala had left her door to it ajar. As he stretched out his hand to pick up a nightshirt, he caught the sound of voices. Lisala evidently had someone in bed with her.

29

Death on the Rhine

Roger was more thankful than ever now that he had not made his return known. Had he done so, and Lisala's lover failed to dress and get away by the verandah in time, he would have been under the unpleasant necessity of calling him out; and it would have annoyed him greatly to have to fight a duel over a woman whom he now detested.

However, curiosity to know if he could identify his wife's latest lover by his voice led him to take a step nearer the door of her room. Breathing very lightly, he listened to their conversation.

It was at once obvious that they were not making love. On the contrary, they were quarrelling. The first words of Lisala's which he caught were:

'How can you expect wealthy men to frequent such a place? As I told you after I first saw it, I was greatly disappointed. You must at least do up the salon where visitors are received and take their refreshments.'

The man replied, 'The place was doing good business when I took it over; and, at the moment, I cannot afford to pay for expensive decorations.'

Roger recognised the voice, but could not place its owner. Lisala resumed fretfully, 'And the girls! Fat, frumpy German *mädchen*. What man of taste would wish to go to bed with such cattle?'

'They are at least good strong animal material, and could satisfy a dozen men a night if called on to do so.'

'That is not the point. They have no *finesse*. They have never been trained to pander to unusual tastes. What we need are some pretty young French girls.'

It was obvious to Roger that they were discussing Lisala's brothel, and that the man who was with her had put up the capital for it. In a surly voice, he retorted, 'In cities like Mayence, it is impossible to procure the really attractive type of whore that you have in mind; and I am being ruined by the taxes, so have not the money to import them from abroad.'

'Money,' Lisala sighed. 'If only this cursed war would end. My estates in Portugal are worth a great fortune. If I could but get even a small part of my revenues, I would renounce my status as a great lady and we'd run a bordello in Paris that would be the finest in the world.'

'I am in much the same situation,' the man replied. 'Given peace I could bring over from England enough money to buy even the services of certain ladies of the Court known for their licentiousness; provided they were allowed, as you do, to disport themselves masked.'

'How so?' Lisala asked. 'Methought all the money went to the young Earl, and he would see you in hell before providing you with a centime.'

Roger drew in a sharp breath. The man with Lisala could only be Ulrich von Haugwitz. He, in turn, was speaking now. 'No. Charles has a fine estate, White Knights Park, in Worcestershire, and also a mansion in Berkeley Square. But Georgina is very wealthy in her own right. She owns a great house named Stillwaters, near Ripley, and her old father is exceedingly rich. As she is an only child, when he dies his fortune, too, will come to her.'

'Since you have no love for each other, are you not afraid that, at any time, she may leave you? She might escape to England and so deprive you of getting your hands on her money.'

'She'll not do that,' von Haugwitz replied with conviction. 'She pines for Charles, so would join him if she could. But, secretly, I have set a guard upon her. My steward, Big Karl, and his men, have orders to watch her closely and, should she attempt to escape from Langenstein, bring her back.'

For a moment Lisala was silent, then she said, 'Do you really believe that, when the war is over, she will go to England with you and tamely hand over her fortune? If so, you are more of a fool than I took you for.'

'She may prove difficult, I agree. But by law she is my chattel, and all that she owns belongs to me.'

'In law, yes. But I gathered that in England she has many powerful friends. They will not stand by and see you rob her of her wealth. To make certain of obtaining it, only one course is open to you.'

'What is that?'

'She might meet with an accident. Once she is dead, you will hold all the cards. She will not be there to dispute her fortune with you, and call on her friends to aid her. You would only have to go over and collect it.'

Again there was a moment's silence, then the Baron said, 'That is indeed a thought. But it poses one great danger. As you have told me, it was that devil of a husband of yours who cheated me of Charles. He has been in love with Georgina since their childhood, and he is aware that there is no love lost between Georgina and me. Should he learn that she has met with a sudden death, there is a strong possibility that he will arrive at Langenstein and insist on being given full details of her end. He has a clever, subtle brain. To make away with a woman and leave no trace of how she died is by no means easy. Should he find me out, he would stop at nothing to avenge her death, and might well kill me.'

'That is a danger, I agree,' said Lisala thoughtfully. 'And it must be guarded against. But when he returns from the mission he is on, could you not get him to visit Langenstein again, then arrange an accident which would put an end to both of them? As I've told you, he has threatened to kill me should it get out that I have taken a lover, and I believe he meant it; so I'd be glad to be rid of him once and for all. If both of us were free, we could marry and when the war ends, enjoy an enormous fortune between us.'

The Baron laughed. 'Such a thought is enchanting, and we'd make a perfect match. We have similar tastes and neither of us feels bound by the absurd conventions. Providing I can have you now and then, I have not the least objection to your taking other lovers; while you, I know, are of the opinion that a man who has numerous women becomes ever more expert in the art of love; and you think no worse of me because occasionally I prefer to caress a smooth-cheeked boy. I am at a loss, though, to think how, at one stroke, we can both regain our freedom.'

'In that I cannot help you. Should you force a quarrel on de Breuc, he might kill you before you could kill him. And, in any case, your wife would remain immune. Poison I judge too dangerous. Doctors these days are far more knowledge-able than of old, and one would have to be called in. He might see symptoms in the bodies that would arouse his suspicions. No, I must leave it to you to devise some way in which we can rid ourselves of them.'

There came another long pause in the conversation, then von Haugwitz exclaimed, 'I think I have it! The stones of the battlements at the top of the tall tower have become loose from age. We could get them both up there. One good push from behind by me, the stones would give and de Breuc would go hurtling downwards. We'd throw her after him. Our story, that they had been leaning side by side on the battlement and it had given way, would not be questioned.'

'Is it not possible that someone below would see us push them over?'

'Only a stranger to the district, someone perhaps in a pass-. ing river boat, would stare up at the tower top. And if one did, he would be too far off to see clearly anything that hap-pened there.'

'What if one of them was not killed outright, and perhaps recovered, then sought to be avenged on us?'

'Impossible. It is a sheer drop of nearly three hundred feet to the road below. People whose bodies have been smashed to pulp can tell no tales.'

For some minutes there was silence, then Lisala yawned and said, 'I am tired now, dear Ulrich; so let us sleep on it. But wake me and make love to me again before you leave in the morning.'

Before they could put out their candles and the light from Roger's room percolate into theirs through the partly-open door of the closet, he slipped out of it and closed his door behind him.

His mind was in a whirl. As he thought of the peril that now threatened his beloved Georgina, he saw that his hands were trembling. Lisala he knew to be utterly unscrupulous, and that von Haugwitz should not be averse to killing him in revenge for his having deprived him of Charles was understandable. But that the Baron should calmly have agreed, at Lisala's first suggestion, to murder his wife in order to make certain of getting hold of her fortune, filled Roger with rage and horror.

On a sudden impulse, he took two steps towards his sword, with the intention of bursting into the next room and, by slaying von Haugwitz there and then, put it forever out of his power to harm Georgina. With his hand already extended he pulled up. If he killed the Baron he would have to kill Lisala too, otherwise she would remain an eye-witness to the deed. Now he would have had no qualms about putting an end to her. She was the embodied evil responsible for this vile plot; the Baron was no more than an unprincipled lecher in whom she had found a willing accomplice.

But there was no way of concealing that he had returned to Vienna that night. If he killed one or both of them, it would undoubtedly be assumed that he had found them in bed together and allowed his rage to get the better of him. He would have to be well away from Vienna before dawn; by midday he would be a hunted man and, if caught, pay for their deaths with his own life.

Roger's next thought was to set out at once and snatch Georgina from the Castle now destined to be her grave. His tiredness had fallen from him. In three days of hard riding, he could reach Langenstein. But what then? He well remembered Big Karl, the steward who was also chief of the small bodyguard that feudal privilege allowed the Baron to maintain—the twenty or more servants, grooms and gamekeepers who had been sent in pursuit of young Charles. Von Haugwitz had left orders that Georgina was to be prevented from leaving the Schloss. They would never allow Roger to take her away, and there were far too many of them for him to attempt to do so by force.

But wait! The plotters intended to lure him there, so that they could stage the 'fatal accident' that would account for Georgina and himself at the same time. That would give him the chance to use his wits and, only in the last event, his sword. Georgina would be safe until they had him there with her. He must wait for the invitation, accept it; then, when inside the Schloss, plan with her some way in which they could escape together.

He had forgotten to collect his nightshirt from the closet, so slipped naked into bed, and blew out the candles. Fatigue again engulfed him. In spite of the new peril of which he had just learned he would soon have to face, he fell asleep almost instantly.

Next morning he slept late, but was downstairs before Lisala. When she appeared, he expressed mild surprise at seeing her, then spoke to her more pleasantly than he had for some months past. She reciprocated, asking where he had been. He told her of his journey to Paris, and that, arriving back late the previous night, he had not wished to get the servants out of bed so had got into his room by the window.

After a while, she remarked casually, 'An old friend of ours is now in Vienna, Ulrich von Haugwitz. I met him in the *Kertnerstrasse* yesterday and invited him to dine with me here this evening.'

Roger raised a laugh. 'Dine and sleep, you mean, eh? But I have given up worrying about how you amuse yourself, provided you keep your amours from the servants.'

Smiling back at him, she said, 'I am glad you are become more reasonable. And you know that you can count on my discretion. I had intended to have him take his leave at a fairly early hour; then, after the servants had gone to bed, for him to return and I'd let him in. But with you and I both in so small a house as this, an awkward situation might arise, so tonight I fear the poor man must put up with a disappointment.'

When von Haugwitz arrived that evening, he looked slightly embarrassed on seeing Roger; but quickly expressed his pleasure at finding him there. To Roger's enquiry about Georgina the Baron replied that she was in excellent health, and that he had left her at Langenstein only because the vintage had just started. It was essential that one of them should supervise it, and he had had to come to Vienna on a matter of urgent business.

Half-way through the meal, Roger deliberately played into the hands of the plotters by remarking, 'I have most pleasant memories of our stay at Langenstein, and hope that one day you will invite us to repeat it.'

Von Haugwitz smiled. 'My dear fellow, at any time you can get leave you would be most welcome; and a visit from you, would, I know, delight Georgina.'

'It so happens that, having just completed a very tiring mission for the Emperor, I am on leave at the moment,' Roger hazarded. 'But the business for which you are here no doubt requires your continued presence in Vienna; so we must postpone this pleasure.'

'On the contrary,' the Baron declared. 'My business here is completed. I leave for home tomorrow. Why should you and Lisala not accompany me?'

Roger looked across at Lisala. She readily smiled her acquiescence, so the matter was settled.

Early next morning Roger went into the city, where he called at an apothecary's and bought a bottle containing a powerful concoction with a base of opium. It was guaranteed either to put anyone into a deep sleep or reduce to semi-consciousness soldiers when they were being operated upon for serious wounds. He had no definite plan for using the mixture, but felt that it would prove a valuable asset should circumstances arise in which drugging a person or animal could ensure his giving no trouble.

By mid-morning the party was on its way, Lisala in the coach that Roger had hired for her when she had first arrived in Vienna, and the two men riding on either side of it. On the evening of the 20th they reached Schloss Langenstein. Georgina, overjoyed at this unexpected visit by Roger, did not seek

491

to disguise how delighted she was; and, hiding her intense dislike of Lisala, she welcomed her warmly.

Tired after their journey, they went early to bed, after an enjoyable supper. Roger felt certain that, as soon as all was quiet, Georgina would come to him; and a little before eleven o'clock, she slipped into his room.

Their first fond embraces over, he told her of the abominable plot that was afoot to kill them both. After a moment she said:

' 'Tis truly horrifying that Ulrich should contemplate so evil a deed. But I am not altogether surprised now that he has fallen under the influence of Lisala. He is desperate short of money, owing to the brutal taxes the French have imposed on his estates in Prussia. They are eating into his fortune to such an extent that, unless the war ends soon, he will be reduced to living on a shoe-string.'

'You mean unless it ends by the defeat of Napoleon and a general pacification, which would relieve Prussia of her burden. That is possible. It needs only one major victory by Austria to bring Prussia in. And, with the war in Spain also going against him, the Emperor would be finished. But until there is peace with England, Ulrich stands no chance of laying his hands on your money, whether you are alive or dead.'

'True. He must know, too, that when peace does come, I shall at once return home and proceed to divorce him; so Lisala was right when she pointed out that his only chance of securing my fortune is to kill me, and so become the legal owner of it, while France and England are still at war.'

'That is the nub of it,' Roger agreed. 'And he must do it soon. Otherwise, should Austria renew the war and bring about Napoleon's fall, Ulrich would find that he has left it too late. As for myself, Lisala is eager to be rid of me, and she told Ulrich that it was I who got young Charles away from him. That was so severe a blow that he would derive great pleasure from pushing me over the battlements.'

Georgina sighed, 'Oh, my dear love. What are we to do?'

'For us to attempt to leave openly is out of the question; and it is quite possible that Ulrich posts guards at night to prevent any attempt by you to slip away. Our best card is that they have no suspicion that we are aware of their intentions. The odds are that tomorrow we shall be invited to go up to the top of the tower to enjoy the view again. In no circumstances will we do so; but you can leave that to me. I shall propose that on Monday we all drive in to Frankfurt, on the plea that I have never seen that city, and would like to do so. That will be a lie. Actually I was there in '95, in the time of the Directory, to borrow from the House of Rothschild, on behalf of the British Government, a huge sum with which to bribe the Republican General Pichegru to refrain from overwhelming the much smaller Austrian army.* But that is beside the point.'

'Frankfurt is quite a distance from Langenstein,' Georgina remarked, 'a good forty miles.'

'No matter. Mayence is much nearer, but on the French side of the river. For that reason it is possible—as they know that we love each other and hate both of them—that Ulrich just might suspect that we have suddenly decided to run away together, and refuse to agree to my proposed expedition. On the other hand, Frankfurt is well inside German territory. If we leave early, we should be there by midday. We shall dine there at an inn. Afterwards you and I will refuse to re-enter the coach for the return to Langenstein. In the midst of a crowded city, Ulrich could not force us to, and would not dare attack us. His only course would be to apply for a warrant to prevent you from leaving the country. Long before he could secure it, we should be safely across the frontier.'

'Oh, Roger!' Georgina turned over and threw her arms round his neck. 'You are a most wondrous man, and I shall forever be grateful that all through my life, whenever I have been in danger, by some mysterious means you have been sent to protect me.'

Next morning they all went out to see the gathering of the grapes. Although it was Sunday, once the vintage had started, not an hour of good weather could be lost in getting in the golden harvest. Scores of women, including those who were servants at the Castle, plucked the fruit, while men of every

* *The Dark Secret of Josephine.*

station humped the big panniers on their backs as soon as they were full, and tipped the contents into the waiting, large-wheeled carts.

On their return, the Baron and his party passed through the *Weinstube*. The great hall was deserted, but at one end of it was a huge pile of grapes, weighing many tons; for the quantity that was picked each day always exceeded that which could be pressed at night. As they walked towards the door leading into the Schloss, Georgina and Roger glanced at each other, then at the now empty press in which Charles had lain hidden for close on two days.

After the midday meal, von Haugwitz suggested that they should all ascend the tower to see the splendid view.

Georgina felt herself going pale, and swiftly averted her eyes from her husband's, lest he should see the fear in them. But Roger only laughed and shook his head.

'No thank you, Herr Baron; you must excuse me. I am prone to vertigo; and last time I went up there I felt a terrible temptation to throw myself over. I've no mind to subject myself again to that type of mental agony.'

Von Haugwitz hid his annoyance by simulating humour, and began to twit Roger, coming near to calling him a coward; but Roger was not to be drawn and stuck firmly to his refusal to make the ascent. He then suggested that next day they should all drive into Frankfurt.

Pleading the vintage, the Baron strongly opposed the idea; so Roger said, 'I saw enough of picking grapes today, so perhaps you would not mind if I drove in with Georgina, to be taken by her round the city. Lisala could come with us or, if she prefers, remain here to keep you company.'

For a long moment von Haugwitz did not reply, while Roger, idling with a toothpick, wondered anxiously if his suspicions had been aroused. Then the Baron suddenly became the genial host again and said, 'Since you are set on it, we will all go. I will order coaches for eight o'clock.'

That night Georgina came again to Roger. As she scrambled into bed with him, she drew a sharp breath annd sighed, 'Dear heart, we are undone. Ulrich has outwitted us, and laid a trap in which we may be killed tomorrow.'

'How so?' Roger asked quickly.

'My personal maid, Ilse, who loves me dearly, told me of it when she was seeing me to bed tonight. In spite of the new laws, the peasants hereabouts still look upon themselves as serfs. Ulrich's word is law to them and they would never dream of questioning his actions. This evening he sent Big Karl to give them their orders. Tomorrow the keepers and foresters are to dress themselves in their oldest rags, so that they will appear to be a band of brigands. At a lonely spot, soon after we take the road for Frankfurt, they are to fire their muskets, pretending to aim at the coach, and so waylay it.'

'What then? Surely this normally law-abiding people would not go so far as to kill us?'

'Not deliberately. They are being told that it is only a practical joke, to scare you and Lisala. But when Ilse learned this from her fiancé, Adolf, Ulrich's valet, she became frightened for me. She looks on you, rightly, as the type of man who, if he thought himself attacked, would fire back. That could result in further shooting. Ilse fears that, during such a scrimmage, I might be hit. So she felt she must warn me, and begged me not to go with you.'

Roger nodded. 'This is bad. And you are right. Ulrich does not intend that we should come out of this affair alive. I can picture the sort of thing that is likely to happen. He will say to me, "Come, we must drive these villains off"; then, when pretending to aim at one of them, shoot me. As you get out of the coach to come to my aid, one of his men to whom he has paid a heavy bribe, will then pretend to aim at him, and instead shoot you. Afterwards, he will gloss the whole business over as a tragic series of accidents; and, whatever the rest of his people may suspect, none of them will dare air his suspicions except among themselves.'

'Oh, Roger! What are we to do? We dare not go on this expedition to Frankfurt now. The best way out would be for me to sham illness. For them to stage two fatal accidents in succession would be to court inquiry, and so too great a risk.

495

If I don't go, they will await another opportunity to murder us together.'

'That's so, my love; and for that very reason we must not give them that opportunity. Because next time the odds are against our receiving warning of their plan. Our only chance is to take the offensive and deal with the situation tonight. I wish to God that we could take to horse and make off together within the hour. But as the grooms sleep above the stable, we'd never succeed in securing mounts and saddling up without rousing them. What we must do is to render Ulrich and Lisala *hors de combat*, then leave without them in the morning. Luckily, I brought with me a powerful drug. Now is the time to use it.'

'But how could you possibly administer it to them?'

Kissing her, he said, 'Leave that to me, dearest. Go now and return here in two hours' time with a dark lantern and a dozen strips of linen suitable to tie their hands and ankles. And . . . yes, a large carving knife.'

While Georgina was gone, Roger dressed, buckled on his sword, primed his pistols and put the little bottle of drug in his pocket. He had told her not to come back for two hours because, by then, there would be a better chance of Ulrich and Lisala being asleep. But he found the suspense of awaiting her return almost unbearable.

At last the door opened and she came noiselessly in, carrying the things he had asked her to bring. 'Now,' he said, 'we will go first to Lisala's room. If they are both there, it will be much more difficult to overcome them. You must threaten her with your knife, while I tackle him. And, take this; it is the bottle of drug. I assume that, as here, in both their rooms there is a carafe of water and a glass beside the bed?'

Taking the bottle, she nodded, and led the way out into the corridor. Sufficient moonlight was coming through the diamond-paned windows for them to see their way. Very quietly they walked side by side, along several passages, up a flight of stairs and into another wing of the Castle, where Lisala's room was situated. At her door they paused for a moment to still their breathing. Roger took a firm grip of the door

496

handle, turned it slowly, then pushed gently with his knee until the door opened just sufficiently for him to see that it was dark inside.

Gently releasing the door handle, he took the dark lantern from Georgina with his left hand, and moved its slide back half an inch, so that it threw a narrow beam of light. Directing the beam towards the floor, he gave the door a harder push and tiptoed into the room. No sound came in response to his movements. For a moment he thought the room must be unoccupied, and Lisala with the Baron. Then, as he raised the lantern and swept its beam across the room, he saw that Lisala was in bed, sound asleep. Over his shoulder he whispered to Georgina:

'Wake her gently, then hold the knife to her throat.'

Stepping aside so that Georgina could pass him, Roger glided to the foot of the bed, fully unmasked the dark lantern, then drew a loaded pistol from his sash. By then Georgina had her hand on Lisala's shoulder, and was giving it a slight shake. As Lisala roused, Roger shone the beam full in her face and, raising his pistol, held her covered. In a sharp voice, he said:

'One murmur, Madame, and I will shoot you through the head. Sit up and do as you are told.'

Muzzy with sleep, Lisala struggled into a sitting position, while Georgina held the knife to her throat. Roger then said to Georgina, 'You can now lay your knife aside. If she utters a sound, I will shoot her. Pour into her bedside glass a quarter of the drug, add water and hold the glass to her lips.'

As Georgina poured the drug, Lisala gasped, 'No! You mean to poison me. I won't drink it! I won't!'

'You will,' Roger snarled. 'And I vow to you that it is not poison, only a sleeping draught. Either you drink it, or a bullet will come smashing between your eyes; so that, beautiful as you have been in life, you will look horrible when dead.'

Her great eyes distended with terror, Lisala swallowed the potion in little, choking gulps. As Georgina withdrew the empty glass, Roger said to her, 'Now take one of your strips

497

of linen. Force it between her teeth, then tie it tightly behind her head.'

When Lisala had been gagged, Roger put up his pistol, took from Georgina two more strips of linen, tied one to each of Lisala's wrists and the other ends to the headposts of the canopied bed. She could now neither cry out nor escape.

With a sigh of satisfaction, Roger murmured to Georgina, 'Well, we have dealt satisfactorily with one of them. I pray God we may prove as fortunate with the other.'

Together they left the room and made their way stealthily down the corridor to its far end. Outside von Haugwitz's room they paused again, then Roger went through the same procedure of easing the door open a little until they could see that the room was in darkness. A moment later, like two ghosts, they slipped inside. The narrow beam from Roger's nearly-closed lantern was directed on to the floor. Taking two steps forward, he raised the lantern and swept it round until the beam fell upon the bed. The Baron was lying there, apparently asleep. But immediately the light passed over his face he suddenly sat up and cried:

'Who's that?'

'De Breuc,' Roger replied instantly, again pulling out his pistol. 'I have you covered. Raise your voice and you are a dead man.'

'What the devil is the meaning of this?' von Haugwitz demanded.

'That your wife and I know your intentions towards us, so we mean to steal a march on you and are come to bid you good-bye.' As he spoke, Roger unmasked the lantern fully, so that the Baron could see the pistol.

Von Haugwitz gave a gasp. 'What! You . . . you mean to murder me?'

'No; only put you into a sound sleep, so that you cannot rouse your varlets to prevent our leaving.' Keeping his eyes fixed on the Baron, Roger went on, 'Georgina, prepare the potion. The same proportions as before; then give it to him. But have a care that he does not seize you. Should he attempt to, stick your knife in his eye.'

Roger knew that, in spite of the threat, to get von Haugwitz to swallow the drug was going to be a very tricky business. If he chanced a stab and pulled Georgina over him, she would become a shield that would protect him from a bullet. In order to have a hand free, he set the dark lantern down on an occasional table, so that its light continued to shine on the Baron. Transferring the pistol from his right hand to his left, he advanced to within two feet of the side of the bed.

Meanwhile, Georgina had laid aside her knife and, keeping well away from her husband, secured his bedside glass and water carafe. When she had mixed the potion, she picked up her knife again and held the glass out to him.

Shaking his head, he refused to take it.

Roger said, 'Either you drink, or I'll shoot you through the heart.'

'No,' he rasped. 'No! I'll vow 'tis poison in that glass. So I'll not drink, and you'll not shoot me. The noise of the shot would rouse the house. You'd never get away then; and my people would tear you both to pieces.'

'Maybe they would,' Roger replied. 'But you would be dead, so derive no benefit from it. Georgina, hold your knife ready and put the glass to his lips.'

Although conscious of the risk she was running, Georgina did not hesitate to do as she was bade. Roger, too, realised the risk; but it had to be taken. With her knife in her left hand and she glass in her right, Georgina bent over her husband to administer the drug.

Suddenly he struck out with both arms simultaneously. His right sent Georgina reeling back. With his left, he dashed the glass from her hand, so that it rolled across the floor, spilling its contents on the carpet. Flinging himself sideways, he wrenched open a drawer in his bedside table. In it there lay a pistol.

But Roger was too quick for him. Before he could grab it, Roger's right fist caught him a terrific blow on the side of his stomach, just below his ribs. He gasped, and rolled over on his back. Roger's fist came down again, this time full on his solar plexus, driving the breath out of his body. Next moment Roger had sprung upon him and was holding him down. But he needed little holding. His limbs had gone limp, his eyes were bulging from his head, and he was making horrible retching sounds.

'Quick, Georgina,' Roger cried. 'Pour another measure of the potion, and bring it to me.'

Picking up the glass, she tipped half what remained of the drug into it, added water and brought it to Roger.

By then von Haugwitz's breath was coming back in choking sobs, but he still had not the strength to struggle. Instead of taking the glass from Georgina, Roger said to her, 'Pinch his nose tight with one hand, and pour the stuff down his throat with the other. But slowly, a little at a time, or he will sick it up.'

Georgina took her time. Her husband, pinned down by Roger, lay glaring helplessly at her, while the potion trickled down his throat. When the last drop was gone, Roger said, 'Now gag him. Then tie a strip of linen to each of his wrists, and their other ends to the bedposts, just as we did with Lisala.'

Five minutes later, they had von Haugwitz firmly secured, and left him. Enormously elated by the success of their desperate undertaking, hand in hand, but still a little breathless, they made their way in silence back to Roger's room. When they reached it, Georgina asked in a husky voice:

'What do we do now?'

Seating himself on the side of the bed, he drew her down beside him. 'We have to wait until the drug has had time to take effect. We'll then be faced with our worst problem. Where to hide them, so that in the morning the servants will believe that they both got up early and went out.'

'Why not in the wine press where we hid Charles?' Georgina suggested at once. 'No-one is ever in the *Weinstube* during the early part of the day. Pressing does not start until late in the afternoon.'

'Bless you!' Roger exclaimed. 'It will be no easy business to get them down there. But we'll manage somehow.'

Half an hour later they went to Lisala's room. She was in a deep sleep, and when shaken violently showed no reaction.

Having removed her gag, freed her wrists and pocketed the strips of linen, Roger proceeded to remove her nightdress, as he said, 'We must leave this here, so that the maid will find it and assume that she got up early and dressed herself.'

For a moment he gazed down on the superbly beautiful body from which, many months ago, he had derived such delirious pleasure; but it meant no more to him now than a hunk of dead meat. Hoisting Lisala's naked body over his shoulder, he made towards the door. Georgina preceded him, carrying the dark lantern. They moved cautiously through long passages and down winding flights of stairs, fearful that von Haugwitz might have posted a night watchman to make sure that no-one left the Castle without his permission. But, apparently, he had relied on nobody being able to secure horses without rousing his grooms, and that anyone who made off clandestinely on foot could be pursued and brought back within a few hours. Twenty minutes proved enough for Roger to get Lisala to the *Weinstube* and lower her gently into the wine press.

Returning upstairs, they went to Ulrich's room. He, too, was in a deep slumber, snoring loudly. With him they followed the same procedure; but he was a heavy man and to get him down proved much more difficult. Several times Roger had to rest. At others, Georgina took her husband's feet while Roger supported his head and shoulders. But, at length, they carried him into the *Weinstube*, hoisted his naked body up and let it fall into the press beside that of Lisala.

Spent by their exertions, Roger and Georgina went to the dining room and fortified themselves with glasses of Muscatel wine. By then it was three o'clock in the morning. After they had rested a while, Roger said:

'It was arranged that we should start for Frankfurt at eight o'clock in the morning. You will have your breakfast brought to you in bed as usual. I shall have mine downstairs. We must be ready to set off promptly. The drug should keep them asleep until at least midday. That will give us four hours' start. But, with luck, they will sleep on well into the afternoon, which will give us longer before Ulrich can send his men in pursuit of us.'

Georgina laughed. 'Whenever they wake, it is going to be mightily embarrassing for them to find themselves naked, and have to make their way back to their rooms in the nude. At least one of the servants is certain to see them. But it would be even more amusing if they are still in the press when the vintagers arrive to start pressing. They would then become the laughing stock of the country for miles round.'

Roger laughed too, then yawned. 'I'm desperate sleepy. Let us snatch two or three hours' rest before we play the final act and make our bid for freedom.' Lovingly they kissed; then, again hand in hand, went upstairs to their rooms.

At seven, the footman who was looking after Roger woke him from a deep sleep. At seven-thirty he went down to breakfast. As usual, Big Karl stood near the door of the dining room, superintending the service. Roger had never suffered from nerves, and said to him quite casually:

'The *Herr Baron* came to my room a while ago. He has decided not, after all, to go in to Frankfurt, and has already gone out to supervise the vintaging. The *Gnädigefrau Baronin* will come with me, to show me the city. But my wife intends to remain behind, and keep the *Herr Baron* company.'

Big Karl bowed stiffly and accepted this information with a stolid face. Servants in great houses miss little of what goes on among their betters. Karl and his underlings, male and female, knew well enough that their master was sleeping with Roger's wife, and that Roger was sleeping with their mistress. Roger had, in fact, counted on it that they would put their own interpretation on the wish of von Haugwitz and himself to spend a day alone with each other's wives, and so not suspect that he intended to make off for good with Georgina.

Shortly before eight o'clock, Georgina appeared. Ilse was behind her, carrying two heavy valises. For a moment Roger feared that the sight of them might arouse suspicion that she was about to run away with him. But she promptly stilled his fears by saying, loudly enough for Big Karl to hear, 'These are the things that Ulrich wished to have valued by the silver-smith in Frankfurt.'

A coach stood ready at the door. It was, as Roger had expected, one of the Baron's, which meant that he would have to leave his own behind; but that could not be helped. A groom stood nearby with Roger's charger. As Georgina got into the coach, she gave Ilse a long, grateful look. Roger mounted and they set off down the curving mountain road.

When they reached the main road which ran alongside the broad river, the coachman reined his horses to the left, in the direction of Mayence and Frankfurt. Relieved that they had succeeded in getting away from the Castle without a hitch, Roger had allowed his thoughts to wander. They had traversed a good half-mile when, with a sudden, awful shock, it struck him that von Haugwitz's arrangements for the coach to be held up must still stand.

The Baron's men would obey his order to fire from their ambush in the direction of the coach; and, when it was brought to a halt, surround it. But what then? They would expect him to be with it, to give them further orders and call off the joke. If he was not, what course would they adopt? The most probable answer seemed that they would feel called on to continue to play their role as bandits, capture the occupants of the coach, carry them off to some nearby hiding place, and send to the Castle for instructions.

When the Baron could not be found, Big Karl would take charge of the affair and, no doubt, decree that the prisoners should be held until his master reappeared. By afternoon the infuriated von Haugwitz should again be in a position to give orders. One way or another he would contrive that they spelt death for Roger and Georgina.

Spurring his horse forward, Roger called to the coachman to pull up. With a look of surprise, the man obeyed. Roger then said, 'Now turn about.'

Instead of doing so, the coachman replied, 'We are going to Frankfurt, *mein Herr*.'

'No. I have changed my mind. We are going to Coblenz.'

The man scowled at him and protested sharply. 'I am driving this coach to Frankfurt. Those are the *Herr Baron*'s orders.'

Roger felt certain then that the coachman was in the plot, and knew about the hold-up that was to take place further along the road; perhaps even only a few hundred yards ahead. He gave a quick glance in that direction, but could see no movement among the trees and bushes which covered the slope up from the roadside. Pulling a pistol from his holster, he pointed it at the coachman, and cried:

'Do as I say. Turn the coach about, or I'll put a bullet into you, then drive it myself.'

Muttering an oath, the man turned the vehicle round. As he did so, a young footman who had been perched on the boot, jumped down and ran off into the bushes.

Cursing his own negligence in having forgotten both the ambush and that, according to custom, a footman would ride on the back of the coach, Roger roared at the coachman, 'Now put your horses into a gallop, or I'll blow your head off.'

Cowed by the threat, the man whipped up his horses, and the coach rattled along the stony road at full speed. But now Roger was really worried. The footman would report to Big Karl what had happened. They would search for the Baron in vain. It was quite possible that the steward was fully aware of his master's intentions. In any case, he knew that it had been planned to ambush the coach; so the odds were that he would take it on himself to send mounted men after it.

Inside the coach, poor Georgina was bounced from side to side. She had caught only Roger's last shouted order to the coachman. Clutching the window-frame, she thrust her head out and called to him, 'What has happened? Whither are we going, and why at such a pace?'

'To Coblenz,' he shouted back. 'This rogue on the box would have driven us into the ambush had I not thought to make him turn about in time. But Coblenz is thirty miles or more downstream. I fear we'll be pursued, and there alone lies safety, so we must make all possible speed.'

As the coach passed below the Schloss, the horses were still going at a gallop; but after a mile, their pace began to slacken. Few men knew more about the staying power of horses than

Roger; and he grimly admitted to himself that, if they were to complete the journey, the most that could be expected of them was a fast trot, eased every mile or two by dropping into a walk.

Having ordered the coachman to slow down, Roger began to assess their chances of getting away. For the footman who had bolted to get back to the height on which the Schloss stood, then trudge up the road to it should take a good three-quarters of an hour. Another half-hour might be spent in unavailingly searching for von Haugwitz in the vineyards, then a final quarter of an hour for Big Karl to decide to act on his own and have his men saddle up.

That meant that the coach would have at least an hour and a half's start. But it could not travel at much more than ten miles an hour, whereas mounted men could do twenty. By the time they started, the coach should be about half-way to Coblenz, but after that the gap would swiftly close. If the pursuers rode hard, they might overtake the coach at any spot on the last ten miles to Coblenz.

'What then?' wondered Roger. As the Confederation of the Rhine was a part of Napoleon's empire, he had gone to Langenstein in uniform. Once in Coblenz, where there was a French garrison, no-one would dare lay a hand on him; although, now that he had ditched Lisala, it was certain that she would betray him, so he must disappear before he could be caught and hauled back to face a firing squad at the order of the Emperor. It followed that his chances of getting away would be better if no-one in Coblenz could report that he had passed through that city.

But speculation about the future was, for the moment, beyond the point; since the odds were that von Haugwitz's men would overtake the coach before it reached Coblenz. Would they dare detain a French Colonel? Since they owed allegiance only to the Baron, he feared they would; for it was he, not they who would have to account for the act. And von Haugwitz could justify it by the fact that Roger was making off with his wife.

The slow descent from the Schloss, their setting out towards

Frankfurt and turning the coach round had delayed their taking the road to Coblenz by a good half-hour; but they had covered fifteen miles by ten o'clock—roughly the hour that Roger judged Big Karl might send his men in pursuit of them. With the horses trotting and walking alternately, they progressed another five miles. Then disaster overtook them.

For the first hour, Roger had ridden alongside the coachman, keeping a sharp eye on him. Then, assuming that the man had become resigned to driving them in to Coblenz, he had, now and then, dropped a little behind, to talk to Georgina. He was doing so and the coach was moving at a smart trot, when it suddenly swerved and hit with its near forewheel a large boulder at the side of the road. As a result of the impact, the front axle snapped and, tilting sideways, the vehicle came to an abrupt halt.

Convinced that the coachman had caused the accident deliberately Roger, swearing like a trooper, rode up alongside him, lifted his riding switch and slashed the man with it again and again across the head, shoulders and face. Screaming with pain the man fell into the road from the far side of the box. But this ferocious chastisement could not mend the axle.

A village could be seen in the distance; and, for a moment, Roger thought of galloping into it to fetch a wheelwright. Then he dismissed the idea as useless, for it would have taken several hours' work to repair the damage to the coach. Another possibility was to mount Georgina behind him, ride into the village and take the ferry across the river to the far bank. But to do so would be to court great danger. In theory, the other side of the river was French territory, but French writ did not run there. Napoleon's garrisons were stationed only in towns many miles apart. Between the rivers Rhine and Moselle lay the Hunsruck mountains. Bands of deserters of all nations roamed their forest heights; robbing, looting, murdering at will. He could not possibly take Georgina across the many miles of almost trackless territory inhabited by outlaws.

Georgina had scrambled from the lurching coach. With a courage that had all Roger's admiration, she said quietly, 'This is most unfortunate. What would be best for us to do now?'

By then, Roger had come to a decision, and replied, 'There's only one thing for it, m'dear. We'll take the horses from the coach, and you must ride.'

Kicking the recumbent coachman in the ribs, he said, 'Get up, you filth. Help me unharness the horses. You're lucky that I have not thrown you in the river to drown. And I will yet if you give me the least trouble.'

Mopping his bleeding face, the man staggered to his feet and, with trembling fingers, set about unbuckling the harness. Handing the reins of his charger to Georgina, Roger adjusted the stirrups and mounted her upon it. Then, as soon as one of the coach horses had been freed, he strapped on its back the coach rug, folded into a thick pad to serve as a makeshift saddle for himself. The other horse he intended to use as a lead horse, and lashed to its back the two valises containing Georgina's most precious possessions. Finally, he turned to the coachman and snapped:

'Take off your coat. I want it.'

For a moment the man stared at him in surprise; then, feeling that it was a cheap price to pay for escaping with his life from this terrible Frenchman, he wriggled out of the garment and handed it over. He was a tall man; the coat a long one, coming down nearly to his ankles, and it had a wide, triple collar. It had occurred to Roger that it would completely cover his uniform, and thus enable him to pass any French troops they might encounter in Coblenz, without being saluted and, possibly, remembered. Picking up the coachman's hat for good measure, he hauled himself up on to his makeshift saddle and, with Georgina beside him, rode away from the wrecked coach.

But now it was more than ever uncertain if they would reach Coblenz without being caught. The breakdown of the coach had cost them a good twenty minutes, and it was close on eleven o'clock. If mounted men had been sent after them by this time they could not be far behind; and there was still a third of the way to go. Yet, as sometimes happens, good comes out of seeming ill-fortune; since, without the heavy coach to pull, the horses were capable of greater speed.

With Roger now and then glancing apprehensively over his

507

shoulder, they passed through two more villages and made another five miles. Then, as they were coming to the end of a long, straight stretch of road, he looked back and saw that five horsemen had just entered the stretch at a fast trot.

'They are after us,' he called to Georgina. 'But their horses must be near as tired as ours. Get all the speed you can out of yours.'

Spurring their mounts, they rounded the bend at a canter, with Georgina, who had always been a splendid horsewoman, leading. A quarter of a mile further on, Roger shouted to her to ease up. He had seen, as he had hoped he might, a track leading off the road up through the vineyards. Turning into it, they rode on for a couple of hundred yards, then dismounted and led the horses in among the vines. Unlike the low-growing vines in most countries, those on the Rhine and Moselle are trained up six-foot-tall poles; so anyone hiding among them could not be seen from the road.

Ten minutes later, they caught the sound of hoofbeats. Roger went on tiptoe to steal a glance through the vine tops at their pursuers. Then he began to laugh. The horsemen were not von Haugwitz's people, but a little troop of Hessian Hussars.

For a few minutes they stood there, then Roger suddenly had an idea. 'Quick!' he exclaimed. 'We must mount again and go after them.'

Puzzled, but without questioning him, Georgina swung herself into the saddle and followed him down the track. Their horses having had a breather, were capable of cantering again, so they were soon only fifty yards behind the Hussars. Hearing them come up, the leader of the troop, a Corporal, turned in his saddle. Roger had not yet put on the coachman's coat and hat, but had them tied to the lead horse. Seeing his resplendent uniform, the Corporal called his men to attention, and saluted. Roger returned the salute, and gave him a friendly greeting. Then he said in a low voice to Georgina:

'Ease your pace. I don't want to have to talk to them, only remain near enough to them for it to appear that we are with them.'

Two miles further on, the spires of Coblenz were in sight.

But a minute later hoofbeats sounded on the road behind. They had just rounded another bend of the river, and Roger turned to see four horsemen flogging their steeds into a gallop. Their leader was Big Karl.

As they approached, Roger said to Georgina, 'Ride on, and leave this to me.' Then he reined in his horse, and turned it to face von Haugwitz's men. When Big Karl pulled up in front of him, Roger asked with a smile :

'Where are you off to in such a hurry?'

Karl's eyes glinted angrily, as he replied, 'We have come to take you and my master's wife back to Schloss Langenstein.'

'Have you indeed?' Roger said quietly. 'Then I fear you will have had your ride for nothing. You will observe that the *Gnädigefrau Baronin* and I have an escort. Dare to lay a hand on us and, as a French Colonel, I will call on those soldiers of a country allied to France to seize you; then, in Coblenz, I'll charge you and your men with attempting to carry us off with intent to rob us.'

With a contemptuous smile, he turned his horse about, and cantered off to join Georgina. For a few minutes Big Karl and his men remained where they were, arguing heatedly. Then they too turned their horses about, and rode slowly away.

A mile further on, they entered the last village before Coblenz. Checking Georgina, Roger said a word of farewell to the Hussars who, quite unconsciously, had served them so well; then turned off down a side street. Beyond the last house there were again vineyards. Dismounting among the vines, he donned the coachman's coat and hat. Then they rode back to the main road and into the city. The bells of the churches were chiming midday as they walked their tired horses over the bridge of boats to the safety of French territory.

They had been up for most of the previous night, and the strain endured during their thirty-mile journey had been severe; so, at an inn on the outskirts of the city, they pulled up to rest themselves and their horses. After spending an hour drinking a bottle of wine and eating a platter of *brödchen,* they rode on again, as Roger was anxious to get away from

Coblenz where, despite his thin disguise, he might be recognised by an officer of the garrison.

Their way now lay along the beautiful, winding valley of the Moselle. On one bank there were lush green meadows with cattle grazing in them, and orchards of apple, cherry and plum; on the other steep gradients clothed with tall vines. Soon after they left the city, Roger took off the coachman's coat and hat as, wherever they stayed the night, he would have to reveal his uniform; but he removed his decorations and the insignia that showed him to be a Staff Colonel.

Some eight miles from Coblenz, they came to the village of Winningen. The inn there, with its vine-covered terrace, looked a pleasant place; so, deciding they had gone far enough, Roger took a room for them there in the name of Captain and Madame Bonthon.

Now, very, very tired, but marvellously content to be alone together, they ate an early supper, then went to bed and slept the clock round.

Next day they spent lounging on the terrace in the September sunshine. They spoke little, but smiled at each other frequently. It was not until the evening that Roger said:

'My love, we have to make a plan. When Lisala gets back to Vienna, she will cook my goose with Napoleon once and for all. She knows too much of the truth about me not to be believed. My career as *M. le Colonel Baron de Breuc* is finished.'

Georgina stretched out a hand, grasped his, pressed it and said softly, 'And you have sacrificed it in order to save me.'

He smiled. 'Dear heart, I am happy to have done so. It could well have ended on a battlefield, and that could have done no-one any good. In due course, I will make my way back to England; but the trouble is that did I attempt to go now it would be exceeding difficult to take you with me.'

'Then let us remain in these parts,' she suggested. 'I brought my jewels with me in one of the valises. Their value far exceeds the sum needed to purchase a small property. We could give out that we are refugees from some part of the country

510

that has been devastated, and fade into a rustic background until the war is over.'

Sadly he shook his head. 'No. There is nothing I would love more; but it is not practical. If one has to hide, it is easier to do so in a city than in the country. Villagers are inveterate gossips. The arrival of two well-born strangers such as you and me would incite their curiosity to the utmost. Our elopement from Schloss Langenstein and my having turned out to be a British spy will be talked of far and wide. Sooner or later, someone will recognise a description of one of us and our bliss would end in tragedy. I would be hauled up to be shot and you would be left without anyone to protect you. And, as an Englishwoman among your country's enemies, a protector you must have.'

'Roger, you know well that there is no-one whom I can rely on as a protector, except you.'

'Yes, my love; there is . . . the Archduke John.'

'Oh, John. Yes, but . . .'

With a wave of his hand, he cut her short. 'All today I have been thinking of this matter. Having your best interests at heart, I feel that the right thing to do is to take you to Pressburg, or wherever his headquarters may now be, and hand you over to him. He will, I am sure, see to it that no trouble befalls you; and, as soon as it is possible, he will be able to send you back to England under diplomatic protection.'

After a moment's thought, she said, 'Much as I was taken with John, I have never lived openly as any man's mistress, and am not prepared to do so, even for an Archduke. But you are right, that he could get me back to England. And I do wish that. I long to be with Charles during his teenage years that can do so much to form the character of a man. But what of you?'

He laughed. 'Don't worry your sweet head about me. Old campaigners never die. I'll procure civilian clothes and go into hiding for a while. But, sooner or later, I'll turn up on your doorstep at Stillwaters.'

So it was agreed that next day they should start to make their way to Upper Austria.

When morning came, they went down to breakfast in the little coffee room. The waiter handed Roger a news-sheet printed in Coblenz the previous afternoon. For a moment he glanced indifferently at the headlines. Then he exclaimed:

'God alive! Georgina, listen to this.'

'MOST MYSTERIOUS TRAGEDY OF THE CENTURY.

'*It is reported that the Herr Baron Ulrich von Haugwitz, and a French lady, the Baronne de Breuc, were found dead yesterday in the most extraordinary circumstances. The questioning of the servants at the Herr Baron's Schloss Langenstein leads to the belief that the two were lovers. For some utterly inexplicable reason, they elected to consummate their passion for each other in a wine press. Presumably they fell asleep there, and failed to wake when, in the late afternoon, vintagers tipped hods of grapes into the press upon them. Or it may be that they were swiftly suffocated.*

'*Their presence at the bottom of the vat remained undiscovered until the must running from the press took on an unusual pinkish colour. The Kellermeister ordered the press to be emptied. Only then, when a ton of crushed grapes had been removed, there was revealed, to the amazement and horror of those present, the naked, flattened corpses of the Herr Baron and the French Baronne.*'

Falling silent, Roger stared across at Georgina.

After a moment she murmured, 'How terrible, darling. But now Lisala can never denounce you to the Emperor; and both of us are free. Really free.'

If you would like a complete list of **Arrow** books
please send a postcard to
P.O. Box 29, Douglas, Isle of Man, **Great Britain.**